Books by Herman Wouk

NOVELS
Aurora Dawn
City Boy
The Caine Mutiny
Marjorie Morningstar
Youngblood Hawke
Don't Stop the Carnival
The Winds of War
War and Remembrance
Inside, Outside
The Hope

PLAYS
The Traitor
The Caine Mutiny Court-Martial
Nature's Way

NONFICTION
This Is My God

THE HOPE

HERMAN WOUK

THE HOPE

A NOVEL

LITTLE, BROWN AND COMPANY
BOSTON   NEW YORK   TORONTO   LONDON

The Hope is a work of fiction set in a background of history. Israeli and other public personages both living and dead appear in the story under their right names. Their portraits are offered as essentially truthful, though scenes and dialogue involving them with fictitious characters are of course invented. Any other usage of real people's names is coincidental. Any resemblance of the imaginary characters to actual persons living or dead is unintended and fortuitous. The simplified map, of a region much subject to clouded boundary disputes, is intended only to illustrate the narrative. Further clarification of certain distinctions between fact and fancy appears in the Historical Notes at the end of this volume.

First Edition

Library of Congress Cataloging-in-Publication Data

Wouk, Herman
    The hope : a novel / Herman Wouk. — 1st ed.
      p. cm.
    ISBN 0-316-95519-1
    ISBN 0-316-95521-3 (deluxe edition)
    1. Israel — History, Military — Fiction. 2. Jewish families —
Israel — Fiction. I. Title.
    PS3545.O98H66   1993
    813'.54 — dc20   93-4427

10 9 8 7 6 5 4 3 2 1

MV-NY

Published simultaneously in Canada by Little, Brown & Company
(Canada) Limited

Printed in the United States of America

To

צה״ל

The Israel Defense Force

Above all to those who fell

And to those who survived, to those who now stand guard, and to those who will stand guard until by God's grace Israel dwells in peace with all her neighbors

This tale of Hope is dedicated

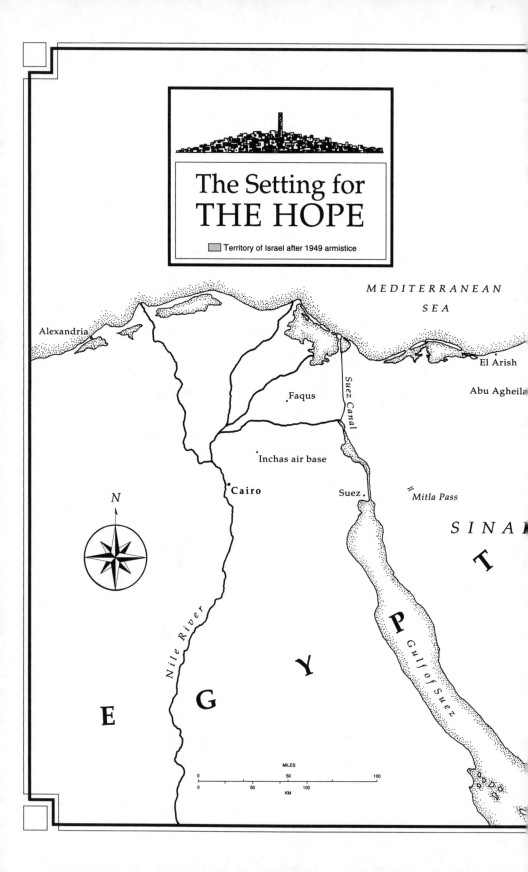

The Setting for
THE HOPE

Territory of Israel after 1949 armistice

MEDITERRANEAN
SEA

Alexandria

El Arish

Abu Agheila

Faqus

Suez Canal

Inchas air base

Cairo

Suez

Mitla Pass

N

SINA

T

E   G   Y   P

Nile River

Gulf of Suez

MILES
0   50   100
0   50   100
KM

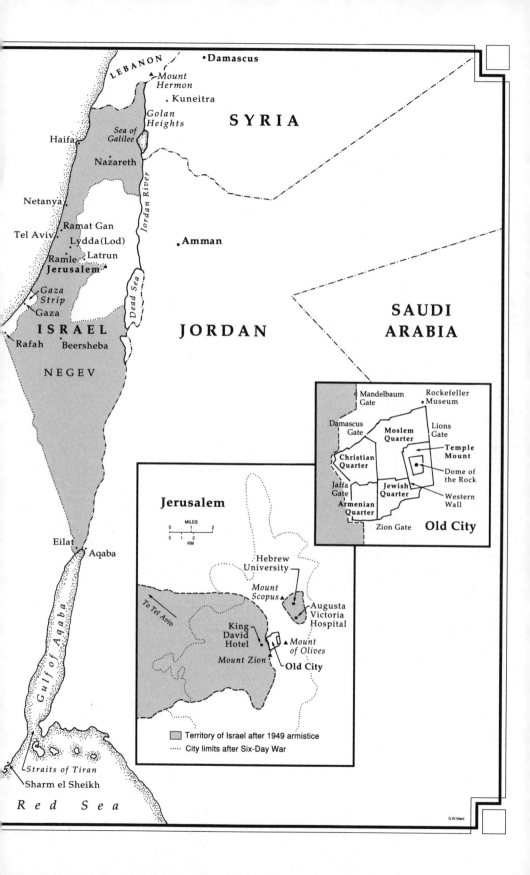

LEBANON

•**Damascus**

▲*Mount Hermon*

• Kuneitra

Golan Heights

S Y R I A

Haifa•

Sea of Galilee

Nazareth•

Netanya•

Jordan River

Tel Aviv•
Ramat Gan•
Lydda(Lod)•
Ramle• •Latrun
Jerusalem•

•**Amman**

Gaza Strip

Gaza•

I S R A E L

Dead Sea

J O R D A N

S A U D I ARABIA

Rafah• •Beersheba

N E G E V

Eilat•
•Aqaba

Gulf of Aqaba

•Mandelbaum Gate

Rockefeller •Museum

Damascus Gate

Moslem Quarter

Lions Gate

Christian Quarter

Temple Mount

Dome of the Rock

Jaffa Gate

Jewish Quarter

Western Wall

Armenian Quarter

Zion Gate

Old City

Jerusalem

MILES
0   2
0   1   2
KM

•Hebrew University

Mount Scopus▲

•Augusta Victoria Hospital

King David Hotel•

▲*Mount of Olives*

Mount Zion

Old City

To Tel Aviv

☐ Territory of Israel after 1949 armistice

···· City limits after Six-Day War

 ∫*Straits of Tiran*

 ∿Sharm el Sheikh

R e d   S e a

G.W.Ward

THE HOPE

Prologue

The Outpost

"Ha'm'faked!"
No response.
"Ha'm'faked! Ha'm'faked!" ("Commander! Commander!")
The watch sergeant roughly shakes the company commander's shoulder. Haganah captain Zev Barak, born Wolfgang Berkowitz, rolls over and half opens heavy eyes. "What now?"
"Sir, they're coming again."
Barak sits up and glances at his watch. *L'Azazel!* Asleep a mere ten minutes, how can he have dreamed such a long crazy dream, himself and his Moroccan wife Nakhama in the Vienna of his boyhood, rowing on a lake, riding a Ferris wheel, eating pastry in a Ringstrasse café? Around him on the ground the militiamen sprawl asleep. Beyond the sandbags and the earthworks rifle-toting lookouts pace the hilltop, peering down at the narrow moonlit highway from Tel Aviv to Jerusalem, which here goes snaking through the mountain pass.
Wearily, Zev Barak gets to his feet in a cold night wind. Unshaven, grimy, in a shabby uniform with no insignia of rank, the captain at twenty-four looks barely older than his troops. He follows the sergeant to an outcropping of rock amid scrubby trees, where the sentry, a scrawny boy in a Palmakh wool cap, points

down at the road. Barak edges out on the rocks and looks through binoculars at the moving shadows. "All right," he says, sick at heart, to the sergeant. "Go ahead and wake the men."

Within minutes they stand in a semicircle around him, some thirty tousle-headed youths, many of them bearded, yawning and rubbing their eyes. "It's a pretty big gang this time, maybe a hundred or so," he says in a matter-of-fact voice, though he feels that in this fight against odds, after months of close calls, he may really be about to die. He has been hearing that anxious inner voice more than once lately. Here he is still alive, just very worn out and scared, and he must keep up the spirits of these weary hard-pressed youngsters. "But we have plenty of ammunition, and we've beaten them off before. This hill is the key to Kastel, so let's hold our ground, no matter what! Understood? Then prepare for action."

In minutes, Barak's troops, armed and helmeted, surround him once more. No more yawns now; grim youthful faces under variegated headgear, from World War I tin hats to British and German steel casques, and also some ragged wool caps.

"Soldiers, you're a fine unit. You've proven yourselves. Fight the way you did before, and you'll repulse them again. Remember, the Russians had a motto, *If you have to go, take ten Germans with you.*' So if any of us have to go, let's each take twenty of them with us! We've got the high ground, and we're fighting for our lives, our homes, and the future of the Jewish people."

The captain's bristly round face, pallid in the moonlight, takes on an angry glare.

"Now, I'm forced to say one more thing. When we lost this position yesterday and had to retreat down the hill, a couple of fakers claimed that mere grazes, just bloody scratches, were real wounds. They even let able-bodied boys carry them down." Captain Barak's voice rises and hardens. "So now I'm warning you, if any man falls down crying he's been hit, I'll look at his wound right away, and if I find he's shamming I'll shoot him. Do you hear me?" A silence. "I said *I'll shoot him!*"

By the appalled boyish glances as they disperse to their battle stations, Barak surmises that they believe him. In the North African desert, when he was serving with the British army in the volunteer

Jewish Brigade, a hard-nosed lieutenant from Glasgow once made that threat. It ended the shamming, and the lieutenant did not have to shoot anybody. In his foreboding mood Barak feels quite capable of shooting a faker. For months he has been carrying casualties away from skirmishes, and he himself may all too soon be dead or wounded, and need to be carried off. Dim in the moonlight, the sentry on the rock outcrop signals, *Not coming up yet.* This is a grim part, waiting for the blow; too much time to think of the disagreeable possibilities.

But since the United Nations vote that recommended partitioning Palestine, and the brief rejoicing that ensued in the Yishuv — the network of Jewish settlements — there have been few agreeable possibilities. Division into a Jewish State and an Arab State; a bitter drastic shrinking of the Zionist dream, but all right, Barak has figured, let it be so, and let the bloodshed at least cease! The Jews have accepted the resolution, but the Arabs have scorned it, and for five months now hostilities have sputtered between the local Arabs and the Haganah, the Jewish armed underground.

Yet worse is soon to come. For in three weeks — on May 15, 1948, a long-fixed official date — the British Mandate will end, the British government and army will pull out of Palestine in toto, and a showdown is bound to explode. Five neighboring Arab countries are pledged to march their armies into Palestine on that selfsame day, to wipe out the Zionist entity in a week or two. The British Balfour Declaration, which encouraged Zionism, the Arabs have always considered a monstrous illegality, and this is their chance to reverse it. Can the scattered Yishuv really hold out for long, Barak wonders, against all those mechanized armed forces?

But the Haganah captain has long since learned to live one day at a time, and one fight at a time. The Arabs have closed the highway below. The Jews in the Holy City are besieged. The hilltop outpost he defends has been taken, lost, and retaken by the Haganah in a desperate effort to reopen the road. Since Roman times, this mountain pass has been the chief access from the seacoast to Jerusalem, Barak's hometown. From the fortress of Latrun, where the gorge begins, he has been traversing the ten-mile ascent to Kastel and Jerusalem all his life; but now, once relief convoys enter the defile at Latrun, they are being decimated or destroyed. So the Haganah has launched an operation to lift the siege, with a code name Barak thinks all too apt: NACHSHON, after the prince of Judah who first leaped into the Red Sea, when Moses commanded the waters to part. The Jews badly need another miracle like that to give them hope, but —

Sudden signal from the sentry: *Here they come!* Barak shouts his final orders, and his heart races and pounds as his troops go on the alert, bracing for the assault. The Arabs ascend in a swarm, blasting machine guns at the sandbags and hurling grenades that throw up flames and showers of earth. Some attackers fall and roll back down the slope. The rest keep climbing. Standing on a high point slightly back of the breastworks, Barak commands the fight, holding some of his best fighters in reserve. Once the action starts he is calm. When the first Arabs overrun the barriers, he sends small squads forward, calling out, *"Chaim, go and back up Roni . . . Arthur, look sharp, they're coming around Avi's position, hit them hard . . . Moshe, plug that hole in the center, quick!"* It becomes a head-to-head melee of crisscrossing blazing fusillades, frantic shouts in Hebrew and Arabic, screams of the wounded. Barak's battle anger swells as he sees his own boys fall, yelling in agony. No faking this time, of that he is sure! A brief confused deafening gunfight by moonlight, the flashing of knives, and all at once the enemy is running back down the hill. "After them!" Barak shouts, plunging through his troops down the slope, firing as he goes, and he feels a searing crunching pain in his left arm.

PART ONE

Independence

1

Don Kishote

That smashed elbow was still in a crooked cast after a month of repeated surgery, when Zev Barak emerged from a dingy reddish building on the Tel Aviv waterfront, into blinding noontime sunlight and a blistering hot breeze. By then the war with five invading Arab armies had been raging for ten days, and on top of everything else that was going wrong, *hamsin*, the heat wave from the desert! Bad, bad news for that ragtag new Seventh Brigade, patched up of immigrants and motley Haganah units, on the move toward the Latrun fortress since before dawn. Less than two weeks into this war for survival, the despatches from the other fronts were worrisome enough, but that silence at Latrun was truly ominous; the worst-conceived operation yet, that attack was, and entirely the Old Man's doing. *"Latrun will be taken AT ALL COST!"*

Now what to do in this brief breath of burning air? Try again to call Nakhama? But the telephone system was in chaos, like the mail and the electric power. No doubt the British had planned it this way. No silver-platter transfer of essential services; if the Jews wanted a state so much, let them sweat for it.

He strode down a side street to Ben Yehuda Boulevard, wrinkling his nose at the stink of the trash and garbage tumbled everywhere. Anxious-faced civilians were hurrying about their business, though the Egyptians were now twenty miles south of Tel Aviv, units of Transjordan's Arab Legion were in the city's eastern outskirts at Lydda and Ramle, and the Syrians were driving down on the northern settlements. No matter what, life went on! Inside the war room of the Red House the battle picture was even more grim than these civilians knew, for near Netanya, halfway up the coast to Haifa, the Iraqis had rolled within ten miles of the sea, threatening to cut the entire Yishuv in two; while Jewish-held parts of Jerusalem were shuddering day and night under the Arab Legion's artillery barrages, and the city's hundred thousand Jews were drinking rationed water, and were close to running out of food.

How long could it go on this way? In the scrawny Hebrew newspapers stories of victories and heroism abounded, some true enough; but there were plenty of rotten stories, too — cowardice, desertion, profiteering — that could never be told about this frightening time. Zev Barak tried to see things as they were, a habit of thought learned on the battlefield; and he feared that this tenuous new "Jewish State" might not last out the month of May in which it had been declared. Still, since Ben Gurion had bulled ahead into history and run up the flag, there was nothing to do now except hang on and fight. *En brera!* (No choice!)

The cast was a nuisance that now and then drove him mad with itching, but the elbow was healing and he could shoot a gun. For better or worse, the fateful battle to open the Jerusalem road was already on at Latrun. That was where he should be right now, with his battalion. But the Old Man had assigned him as liaison officer between the old Red House war room and the new unfinished army HQ in Ramat Gan. In plain fact he was now just a jobnik, running secret orders and messages in a jeep for the Prime Minister, safe duty away from any front. Being the son of Ben Gurion's boyhood friend had its plusses and minuses!

When Ben Gurion had summoned him from the hospital on May 15, the very day the Arab armies invaded, he had not been told why he was being sent for. The Old Man wanted him in his Ramat Gan office, and that was that, so he awkwardly got out of bed and into uniform and went there. When he arrived Ben Gurion simply waved him to a chair, ignoring the heavy cast on his arm, and went on talking to his chief operations officer, Colonel Yadin.

"I tell you it's an order, Yigal! You will form a new brigade, and with it you will reopen the road to Jerusalem once for all! And to begin with, you will take Latrun."

The last British troops, except for a small rear guard, were departing from Haifa. The day before, Ben Gurion had solemnly declared that the little patchwork Yishuv was now a state called "Israel." Yesterday an aging pugnacious Zionist politician under the Mandate, today David Ben Gurion was already the Jewish Churchill, giving ringing orders to his army chief. Trouble was, the army itself was just the same old militia, nine diminished and utterly worn down brigades, deployed on five fronts or shuttling between them to face the advancing Arab army invasions. Unlike Ben Gurion, the armed forces had not been transformed overnight; nor in fact did he himself look much changed, in his faded open-collar khaki shirt.

"Form a new brigade? Take *Latrun*?" The chief operations officer peered at Ben Gurion, gave Barak a side-glance, and wiped his bald brow. By training an archaeologist, Colonel Yigal Yadin at twenty-nine was a seasoned underground planner and fighter. "That fortress? With what? With whom?"

"It will be done! *B'khal m'khir* [at all cost], I say! Or will we let Jerusalem starve and surrender?"

"Ben Gurion, the recruit camp is empty. And where do we get more armored cars, field guns —"

"Empty? Why empty?" The paunchy old man looked to Barak and jutted out his chin in the way that Barak knew meant trouble, heavy eyebrows a-bristle, wings of white hair floating out from his tanned pate. "Wolfgang, weren't you in charge of training the refugees in the internment camps on Cyprus?"

"Sir, I did lead the training in some camps, but —"

"Good, I thought so. And aren't those same Jews now pouring into Haifa by the boatloads? Hah, Yigal? What will they do in the middle of a war — pick oranges? Form a brigade with them."

"With those immigrants? Their drilling in Cyprus was nothing, Ben Gurion, they marched around with broomsticks —"

"What broomsticks? Nonsense." The Old Man turned on Barak. "See here, Wolfgang, when you came back from Cyprus you gave me very good reports on them. Did they drill with broomsticks? Is that true?"

"Well, wooden guns, sir," said Barak. "That's all the British allowed. We managed clandestine drill with small arms, but —"

Colonel Yadin broke in. "Ben Gurion, they've never shot a rifle, those refugees! They've had no combat training, not even target practice, and —"

"So give them training for a week or so, Yigal. Issue them rifles and show them how to shoot! They'll surprise you. They've got something to fight for now, their own country."

"You're telling me," Yadin persisted, "to march a new brigade of immigrant recruits against the Latrun fortifications? I won't do it."

"Who's telling you to do that? Am I crazy? Of course not. Find an army battalion here, a company there, a few reserve platoons, mix some experienced soldiers in with them, and you'll see, they'll take Latrun."

Colonel Yadin hesitated, pulling at his mustache and glancing at Barak, who kept a blank face. Then he got up and walked out.

The Prime Minister's scowl relaxed, and he gestured to a chair. "Sit down, Wolfgang. No, it's Zev now, isn't it? Zev Barak. That's very nice." Politician's memory, thought Barak, always surprising. "You know, I talked to your father last night. The connection to that motel in Long Island was terrible, but I mentioned that you were better. Zev, he says the UN is all agog over the instant recognition of Israel by President Truman, and they expect the Russians to follow suit tomorrow. It's a new time! A new world! So, what happened to your arm?"

Barak baldly told him, and the Prime Minister sighed. "Yes, and now we've lost Kastel and that whole string of strongpoints. *En brera*, all our boys are needed at the fronts. But never mind, we'll recapture those outposts after we take Latrun, and we'll reopen that road once for all. So what will you do now?"

"Return to my company."

"With that arm?"

"Sir, I can use a rifle, I've practiced." Barak wiggled his free fingers. "I'm due for battalion command."

Making a skeptical face, Ben Gurion pushed toward him a stack of mimeographs on his desk. "Have a look at these. You had experience with the British army. I want your opinion. And I'll tell you what, Zev. For now you'll report to the Red House once the doctors let you go, and you'll help out in the old war room. They're going crazy there."

"Prime Minister" — the title sounded strange to Barak on his own lips — "I have my orders back to my battalion, and my medical clearance will come any day."

The telephone rang. With a shrewd glance and a nod of dismissal Ben Gurion picked it up. "That'll be all right. I have something important in mind for you."

Going out, Barak riffled through the mimeographs, army manuals drafted by one Colonel Stone. This would be Ben Gurion's American military adviser, Barak guessed, a West Point graduate, and according to army rumor, a Jew from Brooklyn who couldn't speak Hebrew and knew *bopkess* (goat shit) about fighting Arabs.

That had been the start of it, and ten days later Barak still had no inkling of what the "something important" might be.

At the street counter of a tiny eating place off Ben Yehuda Boulevard, Barak's father-in-law, an aproned portly Moroccan Jew with bristling jowls and a huge beaked nose, was sweatily dishing out food to the breakfast crowd, mainly soldiers on brief leave. "Wolfgang!" He hailed Barak with a wave of a fork. "Miriam, coffee for Wolfgang!" Nakhama's mother, a kerchief on her head, took a simmering pot from the smoky grill, and with a tired smile poured coffee. She was a small shapeless drudging woman, but her mouth and her smile were like Nakhama's, lovely and heartwarming. He sat down at the little table under his wedding picture, displayed here for four years and getting too sooty to make out: himself in snappy British uniform, grinning with a bridegroom's pride, Nakhama in the plain dress of their hasty wedding, looking stunned.

He had been twenty then, Nakhama seventeen; they had known each other only a week or so, he was about to ship out to North Italy, and their blood was on fire. So Wolfgang Berkowitz, son of eminent Zionist socialists, had plunged on passionate impulse and married the daughter of Moroccan immigrants who ran a Ben Yehuda eating place. Four years and one child into the rushed match he had no regrets whatever, despite his parents' lingering displeasure; but he wished his in-laws would drop the European "Wolfgang," which they considered high-class. He had been Zev Barak for a while now, conforming to Ben Gurion's preference for Hebraized names.

"Have you heard from Nakhama?" He raised his voice over the street noise and the chatter of customers. His wife and son had left Jerusalem in a crawling steel-shielded bus, in the last convoy to get out; and he had ensconced them in his parents' home in the fancy section of Herzliyya.

His mother-in-law gave him an odd, guarded look. "You haven't talked to her?"

"You know what the phones are like. I keep trying, but —"

"Can't you find time to drive to Herzliyya? Twenty minutes?"

"Why, is something the matter?"

"Well, she's all right."

"And Noah? What about him?"

"He was sent home from the kindergarten for fighting." Another peculiar side-glance. "You'd better go and see Nakhama, Wolfgang."

A jeep pulled up at the curb and a yellow-haired girl in army fatigues leaped out, waving at him over soldiers clustered at the counter, and calling, "Zev! Zev!" This was Yael Luria, a Red House runner. More trouble.

"Now what the devil? Look," he said to his mother-in-law, "if you talk to Nakhama tell her I was here and I've been trying to phone. My elbow's better, I'm going day and night, and I'll come to Herzliyya when I can."

The response was a shrug over frying eggs and meat, and a muttered, "*B'seder* [Okay], Wolfgang," as he went out.

"Yigal wants you to go to Latrun," Yael Luria said, meaning

Colonel Yadin. The underground custom of using first names for senior officers had not changed.

"What's happening out there?"

"That's just what Ben Gurion wants to know. He told Yigal to send you. At once."

"I don't have my gun, and I told my driver to get some sleep."

"I'll drive you, and I brought your gun."

"Let's go, then."

He jumped into the jeep after the runner, whose lithe figure and long tossing hair were causing grins and nudges among the watching soldiers. Now here was a fetching creature of pedigree, he thought, whom his parents would have rejoiced to see him marry; Yael Luria of the Nahalal moshav, related to the Dayans. Perfect! Barak was keeping his distance from Yael, a charged-up eighteen-year-old whose firm jaw signalled her nature. He thought she might well get into trouble one of these days with a married officer, if not with him; but no doubt she could handle trouble. At any rate, she was a fast good driver, and she was handy with that Mauser in her lap. His own Czech pistol had been empty, but she had loaded it, and locked the tricky safety catch.

As the jeep sped out on the Jerusalem road, through orange-laden groves and empty shuttered Arab streets, the battle problem of the war starkly confronted Zev Barak: a strategic nightmare, this Israel, a lumpy strip of coastline with one forlorn finger of land stretching eastward up into the mountains to Jerusalem, some forty miles from the sea. In the distance beyond green farmlands, smoke was billowing up into the hazy sky. The far-off heavy thumps could only be the Arab Legion's British guns. The Haganah had no such artillery.

How were those immigrant recruits reacting to the thunder of cannon? And to the heat, the *heat?* In the open jeep, the air was rushing past as though blown from a furnace. Even for the experienced fighters out there, slogging under a cruel white sun through the fields and the flies must be like North Africa at its worst; so what was it like for those bewildered refugees, on a battlefield for the first time in their lives, carrying heavy bayoneted rifles of half a dozen different makes? Only yesterday there had been a big sudden flap about water bottles, not nearly enough to go around. Raw recruits were out there with glass jars of water tied to their belts, going up against a strong fortification atop a steep hill!

They were paying for two generations of Zionist shortsightedness, Barak bitterly reflected, in leaving the hills and ridges in Arab hands. War meant communications, roads! Command of high ground over the roads! The Arabs had settled in the hills because of the malaria down on the lowlands, which the Zionist pioneers had drained and made healthy and fruitful. Well and good, but the founding fathers had failed to think ahead. However harebrained this attack plan might be, Ben Gurion was right about one thing: if Jerusalem was to be part of the Jewish State — and how could it be otherwise? — Latrun had to fall.

Twenty miles along the highway the police fort and monastery of Latrun were in plain view, with clouds of artillery smoke puffing up and rolling over the brown walls. Outside the trees of the Hulda kibbutz, rows of dilapidated Tel Aviv busses stood empty, military transport for the Seventh Brigade. Jewish warmaking! Yael drove off the highway into the standing wheat, bumping and swerving toward the tent of the field headquarters, where they came on Sam Pasternak, a stocky captain in a sweated-through undershirt, shouting into a telephone, surrounded by arguing soldiers who poured perspiration, all in a swarm of loud-buzzing black flies.

"Zev, thank God!" Pasternak exclaimed, handing the phone to a fat female soldier whose hair hung down in sweat-soaked strings. "Keep trying, Dina." He gave Barak a quick dank hug. They had been high school classmates in Tel Aviv, and had served together in a Gadna paramilitary youth unit. "Tel Aviv doesn't answer, Zev, Jerusalem doesn't answer, and Latrun is throwing down a shit rain of fire! It's a total failure of intelligence! The whole Arab Legion must be up there! When did they sneak in? Why weren't we told?"

Barak was staggered. He himself had routed to the Seventh Brigade, *highest urgency,* the intelligence that the Legion was back in Latrun in force. What kind of breakdown was this? He feigned a calm tone. "What's happening?"

"Utter and complete *balagan*!* That's what's happening! Shlomo's doing his best, but we're in heavy, heavy trouble."

He gestured toward the brigade commander, a lean trim figure in khaki a hundred yards away on a high knoll, intently watching the battle through binoculars and issuing orders on a walkie-talkie. Barak had served with Shlomo Shamir in the British army; an able colonel who had accepted this command at Ben Gurion's urging, and had agreed to the attack plan, which he considered premature, with considerable reluctance. Pasternak was his deputy.

"Where's the armor, Sam?" By armor Barak meant a few trucks and vans shielded with "sandwiches," wooden panels between steel sheets.

"Pinned down at the intersection. They can't advance. Half the vehicles are knocked out, and they've got a lot of wounded and some dead."

A bearded soldier in a torn bloody undershirt came running up, babbling wildly about water. Another officer led him away.

"What about that infantry battalion?" Barak persisted. "Those Cyprus immigrants?"

"Zev, we *don't know*! They marched off singing in Yiddish, but we've been trying for half an hour now to raise them. Field communications are rotten, rotten!"

The flies were horrendous here. They were at Barak's eyes, and each time he opened his mouth they were on his tongue, in his throat. "Listen, Sam, Yigal Yadin sent me to get a battle report at first hand."

Pasternak jabbed a thumb toward Colonel Shamir. "There's your man. Ask him."

Not far from the colonel's knoll was a "Napoleonchik," a small old French artillery piece, standing silent with its crew sitting or lying around it, swatting at the flies. Barak stopped to ask the gun captain why he wasn't fighting.

"No shells. They ordered me to start firing at dawn, so I did. I woke up the Arabs, and finished. It was insane."

---

* BALAGAN. In modern Hebrew, mess, foulup, snafu, fiasco. A loan word from the Russian, used in Israel with extraordinary frequency.

Barak borrowed his binoculars and saw red tracer bullets streaking down from Latrun. The answering fire from the field was scattered and feeble. Dimly through the dust he could see vehicles in flames, and men stumbling through the high wheat toward the rising ground. He hastened on to Colonel Shamir, who was peering through binoculars as his walkie-talkie squawked static. Shamir greeted him eagerly. "Zev! Any good news? Any reenforcements? I've been trying and trying to get through to Yigal for help! Doesn't he realize what shape I'm in here?"

Reluctantly Barak told him that communications were not functioning, and that he had come for a report. The colonel gave Barak a curt workmanlike reading of the entire battlefield. The fight was not going well at all, he summed up, and the most obscure element was the status of the immigrant recruits; they were somewhere out there in the smoke and dust, but answering no signals. "Tell Yigal Yadin, for God's sake, what I've just told you, Zev. I await orders and I'll fight on while I can, but things are looking very bad."

Back at the operations tent Zev Barak found Pasternak and the others staring at a lanky bespectacled dust-covered boy of sixteen or so, wearing a rusty British tin hat and mounted bareback on a muddy white mule. The animal was swishing its tail, shaking its ears, and stamping its hooves in a loud buzzing of flies, and the boy was flailing at the flies with a broom handle.

"Who is this idiot?" Barak asked Pasternak.

"Don Kishote, I guess," said Pasternak. (He was pronouncing Quixote the Hebrew way, *Key-shoat*.) "He just now wandered in. Reenforcement!"

Gloomy as things were, Barak smiled. In a way the boy did indeed look a bit like the crazy old knight. "What do you want here, Don Kishote?" he snapped.

The Hebrew answer came in a decided Polish accent. "My father sent me from Haifa to find out how my brother was. They told me at the training camp that he went to Hulda. I didn't know there was a battle."

Pasternak said, "So, are you volunteering?"

"Why not? I'm eighteen. Give me a gun."

Amid all the heat, loudspeaker static, and swarming flies, this comic relief was making the soldiers laugh. "And you came here from Haifa on a mule?" asked Barak, trying to sound stern.

"I got the mule on the road" — a gesture over his shoulder — "back there."

Colonel Shamir's voice, loud and clear on the receiver: "Sam! Sam! Shlomo here."

Pasternak seized the mike. "Sam here."

"Sam, I've got that infantry commander at last. He says those recruits off the boats speak only Yiddish, his translator has fallen with heat stroke, and they don't understand Hebrew orders. Shells are starting to drop among them, and they're just milling round and round, and yelling, or advancing any old way, firing their rifles. It's a total balagan!"

A soldier with a bloodily bandaged head spoke up. "Sam, it was just like that when we jumped off. They just kept bawling at each other, *'Voss, voss, voss? Voss shreit err vi a meshugener? Voss tute men yetzt?'*" ("What, what, what? Why is the officer screaming like a maniac? What do we do now?")

"I speak Yiddish," the boy on the mule said.

"Sam, come here." Barak put his arm through Pasternak's elbow and drew him away from the others. In a low voice he said, "Shlomo should call off this attack."

"Call it off?" Haggard and pouring sweat, Sam Pasternak rubbed his chin with a pudgy hand. "Then how does he face Ben Gurion?"

"Listen, the brigade's giving a good account of itself, so is Shlomo, but things have gone very wrong here, and —"

"God knows that's true! I can't begin to tell you, Zev. Half the ammunition never arrived, also —"

"Sam, this isn't your day. Call it off. Save the brigade to fight again."

A pause. Pasternak said, "Come with me."

"Okay, I will."

Shamir listened with a somber mien to the two young officers, sadly nodding. "Shall I try again to get through to Yadin, or Ben Gurion?"

Barak looked to Pasternak, who said at once, "Sir, you're the man in the field. Just do it."

"Very well." Shamir spoke with abrupt decision. "First things first, Sam. Get those immigrants out of there."

"Right. Let's go, Zev."

They hurried back to the tent, where Pasternak got on the field telephone and ordered the infantry commander to break off the attack, swing south to a hill outside the field of fire, regroup, and fall back on Hulda. He repeated the order several times, his voice rising in exasperation, as Barak stood beside him with binoculars and told him that the recruits were still advancing.

"It's the same damned thing," Pasternak exclaimed to Barak. "The commander doesn't know Yiddish, and they don't know anything else. He can't make them understand, no matter what —"

Barak suddenly shouted, "Hey! Don Kishote! Come back here! Where the devil are you going?"

But rider and mule were already beyond earshot, on the trot toward the dust clouds of the battlefield, the broom handle flogging the beast along. "That kid is stark mad," exclaimed Pasternak.

Barak thought he must be. The chances of a mule surviving on a battlefield were zero, even assuming he could goad the beast into the zone of fire. What was the matter with this freakish Don Kishote?

Nothing was really the matter with Don Kishote, whose name was Joseph Blumenthal. The smoke, the sound of guns, the sight of battle attracted him, and he wanted to help out with his Yiddish, and perhaps find his brother. He passed soldiers lying moaning and bloody on crushed wheat stalks, and others gasping and wailing for water, and he rode on unperturbed. The strange mingled smells of gun smoke and ripening wheat were exciting, and to him the anguished men bleeding on the ground were almost like figures in a war movie. Of real war he knew little. He had seen warplanes overhead in Europe, he had suffered privation and brutality in refugee camps, but he had been through no bombardments. His father had moved the family from Poland to Rumania, then to Hungary and Italy, in flight from the ever-advancing Germans. Now here he was at a real battle. Wow!

Bizarre things can happen on battlefields, maddened areas of noise, confusion, and odd turns of luck, as well as sanguinary harm and death. This stripling on his mule (that is, a mule he had recently stolen) actually got through the high wheat to the rabble of Yiddish-shouting rifle-waving recruits and their battalion commander, who was bellowing into a bullhorn on a rise of ground, and gesturing toward a hill behind him. Bullets whizzed and whined in the air, shells were throwing up dirt with earsplitting explosions, some of the recruits were firing impotently at the fortress, and all was frantic disorder. Many men lay here and there on broken wheat stalks in clouds of flies, some bleeding, some trying to get up, most of them crying, *"Vasser! Vasser! In Gott's nommen, VASSER!"*

"What? You speak Yiddish?" The officer was too beset to be amazed at this bespectacled apparition on a mule. "Good, good, tell these lunatics to stop advancing and get up that hill! Double time! Spread the word!"

But the youngster's remarkable luck ran out as he rode around bawling this simple order in Yiddish. A deafening shell-burst showered him and his mount with earth and splintered wheat stalks, the mule threw him off and ran, and he landed on a groaning soldier. Rolling off, he became streaked with the other's blood, which welled from a wound on his leg.

"Pick me up, I want to get out of here," said the soldier in crisp Hebrew, such as Don Kishote had admired in the Haganah instructors on Cyprus. "If I lean on you, I think I can walk."

Much shorter than the youngster and very broad-shouldered, the soldier limped along holding on to him for about a hundred yards, through the clamoring jostling recruits. "Wait, I'd better stop the blood if I can." He tried to tighten a handkerchief around his leg, and toppled over. "Maybe you can do it," he groaned.

"I think I can." The youngster tied a crude tourniquet. "How's that?"

"Better. Let's keep going. What are you, one of these Cyprus guys?"

"Right, I'm a Cyprus guy."

"You're pretty young for that. What's your name?"

"Joseph."

"Here you're Yossi, then." They stumbled along for a while. "It's the heat, I guess," the soldier said in a weakening voice. "I feel terrible, Yossi." His legs were giving way.

"Then let's try this." Don Kishote bent down and lifted him on his back. "Can you hang on?"

"Hey, I'm too heavy for you," muttered the soldier, wrapping hard-muscled arms and legs around him. The youngster carried him through the trampled field dotted with fallen, groaning, pleading men toward the stretcher bearers, continuously shaking his head to get rid of the flies, sometimes so blinded by them and by perspiration that he almost fell, laboring and gasping more from the heat and flies than from the burden. The soldier on his back hoarsely called, "Stretcher here!" A bearer came on the run. Kishote, or Yossi, took one end of the stretcher, and so they brought the soldier to the field hospital, an open space near Shamir's headquarters where wounded lay on the ground in bloody moaning rows.

Zev Barak was leaving the scene in the jeep. "Look, Yael, there's that fool kid who was on the mule. Stop and pick him up."

She braked alongside Don Kishote and exclaimed, staring at the stretcher he was putting down, "L'Azazel, that's my brother!" She jumped down and leaned over him. "Benny! Benny, how are you?"

The soldier said in faint annoyed tones, "Yael? What the devil are you doing out here?"

Barak came to the stretcher. "So, Benny, you caught it." Yael's brother had once been in a youth unit he had led. "How bad is it?"

"There's shrapnel in my leg, Zev, but mostly the heat's got me. I gave all my water to those recruits. They were fainting and crying all around me. Elohim, what a balagan."

"Let's put him in the jeep, Kishote. Yael, you sit with Benny and hold him up."

"Me? Then who drives?"

"I do. Kishote, let's go." Together they lifted Benny Luria and placed him in back, with his sister beside him. Barak awkwardly took the wheel, and drove one-handed across the field. "Can you handle a pistol?" he asked the immigrant.

"On Cyprus I practiced."

"Give him yours," Barak said over his shoulder to Yael. "And what happened to your helmet, Kishote? It was very becoming."

"The strap broke and I lost it."

"Wherever did you get it?"

"A nice old lady in Hulda made me take it. I stopped there for water. She said it was her husband's, long ago, and I was crazy to go to the battlefield, but if I was going, to wear it."

"This kid carried me off the field," Benny said faintly. "His name's Yossi. He's b'seder." Barak was giving them a rough ride through the standing wheat. "Easy, Zev," Benny moaned.

"We'll be on the road in a minute." Barak glanced at Kishote. "You carried him?"

"Till we found a stretcher. I fell on him when the mule threw me off. I'm all covered with his blood."

"Don't complain, it's not your blood," Benny said, his voice fading away.

"Keep quiet," said Yael.

As they raced back toward Tel Aviv, Barak questioned Don Kishote about his family and its journeyings. He had one brother, he said, out there somewhere on the Latrun battleground. His mother had died of pneumonia in a refugee camp in Italy. His father had been a dentist in Poland, and was hoping to do dentistry here, but he couldn't speak Hebrew and would have to learn.

"Where'd you get your Hebrew, Yossi?" Yael spoke up from the back.

"My mother was a religious Zionist. Papa was more of a socialist. Mama sent us to Hebrew-speaking religious schools."

"Are you really religious?" inquired Yael.

"A lot more than my brother Leopold. Leo says God died in Poland."

After a silence Yael said, "I think Benny's passed out."

The jeep rocked and jolted, and Benny hoarsely exclaimed, "I haven't passed out, Yael, you idiot, I just closed my eyes. The leg hurts."

"Nothing to do, anyhow," said Barak, speeding up, "but get him to the hospital." He glanced back at them, and Benny gestured at him to go on, go on!

Seen side by side, Yael and Benny Luria might almost be twins, Barak thought; same strong jaw and squarish countenance, though Yael's softer face was girlishly seductive. In fact they were but a year apart, and in force of character not too different, except that she was all wiles and whims, and Benny was straight, no tricks, very earnest. Once at the youth unit's campfire, when the talk turned to what the boys wanted to become, Benny Luria had said, "Chief of Staff of the Jewish army." The others had laughed, but not Benny.

They deposited him at an army hospital, and Yael drove Barak to the new Ramat Gan headquarters. He inquired as he got out, "So, Kishote, do you want to go back to Haifa now?"

"My father isn't expecting me back. I told him I'd try to get into Leopold's unit."

With a wink at Yael, Barak said, "And you're eighteen."

"Going on eighteen."

"Take him to the recruiting office," Barak said to Yael, "and get him a uniform. That is, if they can fit him," he added, looking the long bony figure up and down.

"Then what?" asked Yael.

"Then bring him to the Red House. We can use another runner."

Yael said sarcastically as they drove on, "Eighteen! How old *are* you, Yossi?"

"How old are *you?*" returned Kishote, pushing his glasses up on his nose with a forefinger, and giving her an impudent adolescent glad eye. Yael shrugged and let it pass. A Polish dentist's son, maybe sixteen, not worth even a brush-off. If Zev Barak wanted this kid as a runner, fine! He had helped her brother under fire. He was b'seder.

2

"Colonel Stone"

The air in Colonel Yadin's little office was grayish with pipe smoke. He broke into Barak's report when he had hardly begun. "Zev, what are you saying? *We* knew the Arab Legion had reenforced Latrun. Why didn't Shlomo?"

"That I have to track down! He says he never got our signal. Yigal, the balagan was unbelievable. A frontal attack in broad daylight in a hamsin —"

"Broad daylight? *Mah pitom?* They were supposed to jump off in the dark, and storm the fortress at dawn. That was the whole concept!"

"Everything went wrong. I don't know where to begin. Raw recruits trying to advance uphill into the sun, I tell you, across open fields, against heavy artillery —"

"What about those recruits? Did they run away?"

"They went marching right into the fire."

"They did?" A wan smile made the chief operations officer fleetingly look his twenty-nine years, instead of a harried forty or more.

"I saw it myself. They didn't know any better. They'd have tried to climb the heights if Shlomo hadn't called off the attack. That was the right thing to do. The only thing."

"I concur!" Yadin vigorously nodded, relighting his pipe with flaring puffs. "So! Ben Gurion was right about those immigrants, at least."

"They were splendid. We failed them, Yigal. There'll be far more casualties from thirst and sunstroke than from enemy action. It was a disgrace. We're not an army yet. Communications were disastrous . . ."

As Barak went on, Colonel Yadin smoked in grim sad silence, sinking lower in his chair. "I argued against this operation, as you well know," he remarked at last. "It was unrealistic, suicidal, and I said so, but Ben Gurion ordered Latrun taken, *at all cost*. Well, we're paying the cost, and we haven't got Latrun." He glanced at his watch. "You'll have to repeat all that at the staff conference. Tell it straight, and make it short. You've met Mickey Marcus?"

"Would that be 'Colonel Stone'?"

"That's him."

"Not yet."

"You will now. Come along."

"Why the code name?"

"The British might make trouble with the Americans about a West Pointer advising our Prime Minister."

In the long low war room, much larger than the one in the old Red House, dishevelled officers sat or stood about the conference table, and large fans whirled the humid air. A muscular balding man in khaki shorts and a short-sleeved shirt was lecturing in English, rapping with a pointer at a large military map on the wall and pausing as a young officer translated. Ben Gurion, coughing and looking feverish, slumped at the head of the table. Seeing Barak, he called, "One moment, Mickey." The speaker paused. "Nu, Zev, let's hear what's happening at Latrun, and talk English for Colonel Stone."

At Barak's report of the fiasco, the Prime Minister's lips tightened in the old stubborn scowl. Marcus leaned against the map with thick brown arms folded, his aspect calm and intent. The staff officers who understood English took in the story with glum faces. The others doodled or yawned.

"Very well, we will attack again. At once!" Thus Ben Gurion, slamming a heavy fist down on the table. "And this time we will *take* Latrun." Silence. Gray tobacco smoke rolling in layers, circulated by the whirring fans. "Mickey, go on with your analysis."

Marcus took up the pointer, and again faced the array of hard-bitten Israeli veterans about half his age. In those weary faces Barak saw a cynical challenge: *What the hell do you know about our situation, you fat old American civilian?* Marcus had acquired a heavy desert tan, and some credit in the army, by taking part in Negev raids against the Egyptian lines; his doctrine manuals, however, had been received with snickering. He had come from America to share the Yishuv's dangers, and that was in his favor, but these men all knew that after graduating from West Point he had gone to law school, and thereafter had served only briefly as a reserve officer in World War II.

"Yes, sir. Tactically, then, Israel is a beachhead like the Normandy landing," Marcus resumed, "and the Arabs have blundered as the Germans did against Eisenhower. Once the British pulled out, the enemy had you at an overwhelming disadvantage — half-disarmed by the Mandate, attacked from all sides, your supplies interdicted except by sea. That was the key to the war. The enemy should have cut you in half by now at Netanya. The Iraqis had less than ten miles to go when they halted, God knows why. Then they could have rolled up your two ports, Haifa and Jaffa, and strangled you."

Restlessness was mounting around the table: drumming fingers, shifts in the chairs, skeptical glances among the officers.

"It should have been over in a week, as most foreign military experts were predicting. You've proved them wrong. By pulling off a classic perimeter defense on interior lines, you've survived. You've had hard going, but you've held your ports. Supplies are coming in. Your beachhead is confirmed."

Such big-power military talk obviously captivated Ben Gurion, who was listening with bright hectic eyes. But to these officers, Barak realized, particularly the Palmakhniks, who had been battling Arab marauders for years in night fighting amid rocks and sand dunes, it could only be a lot of hot air. Also, calling Israel a beachhead implied that Zionism was an invasion of Arab soil, not a return to the Promised Land. A total American Jew, this guy, however well-meaning.

There was a bright side even to today's setback at Latrun, Marcus went on. The attack had drawn away much strength of King Abdullah's Arab Legion from the siege of Jerusalem, and perhaps prevented the Legion from helping the Iraqis drive to the sea. Battles that looked like defeats could bring ultimate victory. "In the next battle for Latrun," his voice cheerily rose, "you'll take it, and you'll lift the siege of Jerusalem!" With this he laid aside the pointer and sat down.

Ben Gurion harshly coughed, blew his nose, wiped his eyes. "Exactly so. Thank you, Mickey." He switched to rapid Hebrew. "Gentlemen, an imposed cease-fire is in the air at the UN. When it comes, Jerusalem must not be cut off. The road to Jerusalem must be open, and our convoys must be moving freely. *Otherwise the UN will award Jerusalem to King Abdullah of Transjordan by right of conquest.* That whole preposterous scheme for 'internationalizing' Jerusalem will be dropped, forgotten." He paused and glared around the room. "Absolutely inevitable, and that is King Abdullah's whole war aim. He knows, as I know, that without Jerusalem the Jewish State will have no heart, and won't live."

No comment from the somber faces around the table. After a pause, Zev Barak summoned up nerve and raised a hand. "Prime Minister, has Shmulik reported to you about the bypass road?"

"You mean, about the three soldiers who sneaked through the woods past Latrun? Yes, he has. What about them?"

"Sir, they got from Jerusalem all the way to Hulda via a route in the wilds, hidden from Latrun by a high ridge."

"Yes, yes, but what kind of route?" Ben Gurion snorted. "A cowpath? A footpath?"

"They went by jeep, Prime Minister."

"So what? So would the Arabs stand by and let us grade and pave a new Jerusalem road bypassing Latrun? Maybe lend us some bulldozers and steamrollers? Hah? Don't talk out of turn, Wolfgang, and don't talk nonsense."

Marcus asked what this abrasive exchange was about. As Barak translated, Ben Gurion drooped in his seat, said he was feeling very ill, and turned the chair over to Colonel Yadin. "When the meeting adjourns," he added to Barak, a shade more cordially, "come and see me, Wolfgang. I'm going home."

"Yes, Prime Minister."

"But first, I have an announcement. Colonel Stone will be especially interested." Ben Gurion sat up and coughed hard, looking around sternly at the staff. "The Jerusalem front, gentlemen, needs an urgent consolidation of all forces. No more discussion. No more arguments. A new united command, a new commander. The Provisional Government has decided that this will be Colonel Stone, and he will have the new rank of *aluf*." He turned to Marcus, faintly smiling. "That is Hebrew for a duke or a general, Mickey. You'll be the first general of a Jewish army since Bar Kochba! You will of course receive a written appointment."

Marcus responded with brisk dignity. "Prime Minister, I accept. I shall serve to the best of my ability." Clearly he had been primed for this all along. "Gentlemen, at 2000 hours we will meet again here, to confer on my plan for the next Latrun attack."

Ben Gurion rose, whereupon all got to their feet, and he went out with Marcus, leaving the general staff looking at each other thunderstruck.

When the staff meeting ended, Barak came out and told his waiting driver, "We go to Tel Aviv, Ben Gurion's apartment."

"Yes, sir."

Tel Aviv was having a sunny steamy afternoon. War or no war, people sat under café awnings in the torrid heat, drinking tea, eating ice cream, and arguing. Sweaty shoppers bustled in and out of stores, and vendors sold cigarettes and newspapers to customers lined up in the glaring sun. How would Tel Aviv handle the news when it came out, Barak wondered, that the first general of a Jewish army since Roman times was an American lawyer?

He was still digesting the surprise. The style was pure Ben Gurion; sudden sharp blow of an axe at a tangled political knot. In Jerusalem, even under the deluge of Arab shelling, the armed commands of several Zionist parties were squandering lives and ammunition at cross-purposes. The two major commands were the army itself, formerly the Haganah, based on Ben Gurion's labor socialists, and its old antagonist, the Irgun force of the Revisionists; besides these there were the elite Palmakh striking force of the radical kibbutzim, and the nationalist splinter, Lehi. If this complete outsider Marcus could merge the squabblers into one fighting force, marvellous! Barak had his doubts, but he could understand why the Old Man was doing it. None of these factions would accept an overall commander from among themselves, and appointing "Colonel Stone" at least finessed all the rifts.

Ben Gurion had gotten into bed and was thumbing through despatches, resting on large pillows. His wife, in a faded housedress, was feeling his flushed forehead. Colonel Marcus sat in a rocking chair by the bed, looking through papers and scrawling in a pocket notebook. Spread higgledy-piggledy on the coverlet were maps, file folders, and mimeographed reports.

"You have to eat something," Paula Ben Gurion was insisting. Her dark hair was pulled back in a severe bun, she was short and squat like her husband, and her rugged face was as determined as his.

"All right. Let it be eggs. Zev, what news from Deganya, and what about those French heavy guns? Have they been unloaded?" The Old Man was very hoarse.

"How do you want your eggs?" inquired Paula.

"It doesn't matter. Fried. Those guns must go straight to the Seventh Brigade."

"Fried won't be good for you. I'll boil you some eggs." Paula went out.

Barak handed the Prime Minister a sheaf of the late despatches. He read and initialled them, making terse comments, and had Barak translate some for the American. Marcus shook his head as he listened. "Right away, the logistics need reorganizing, Prime Minister. Also the fronts must be stabilized. The way things are going —"

"Fronts? What fronts? The whole country is the front," said Ben Gurion peevishly.

Paula Ben Gurion looked into the room. "We're out of eggs."

"It doesn't matter," said Ben Gurion. "I'll just have tea with jam. Zev, I want to see that manifest on the Messerschmitts —"

"You need some food. Zevi, be a good boy, run over to Green-boim's store and get me four eggs."

"Paula, we're having a top staff meeting," Ben Gurion said irritably.

"How long will it take him? Two minutes?"

Barak stood up. "No problem," he said. "I'll go for the eggs." She tended to treat him familiarly, and indeed as a child he had sometimes called her Aunt Paula.

"Stay where you are!" Ben Gurion thrust out his jaw at Barak, then turned on his wife. "Give me anything. A bowl of soup, all right?"

"Never mind, Zevi. I'll get the eggs," said Paula, departing.

"Show him your plan," Ben Gurion said to Marcus.

The American passed to Barak an operational map of the La-trun area. Fresh red and green arrows sketched a second attack, mainly a variant of the first, with a new Palmakh diversion from the southeast. Marcus described his plan, and said he would order all newly arrived armaments moved to Shamir's brigade at the Latrun position.

"Well, Zev?" Ben Gurion prodded the silent Barak.

"Shoot," said Marcus, "if you have any criticisms."

Barak pencilled circles around two hilltop villages. "First of all, the Arabs must have moved back in there. Laskov's armor took heavy fire from that flank this morning. I'd say recapture those villages before the next attack goes."

Marcus slowly nodded. "Sound thought."

Paula reappeared. "Greenboim is out of eggs, too."

"We're discussing an important matter," snapped Ben Gurion. "For God's sake, forget the eggs."

"He may have some later. You said soup? There's that nice canned American soup Yitzhak brought back."

"Good. I'll have that."

"It's peppery, though. It'll bother your throat. I'll make you some soup." She put her hand to his bright pink face. "You're cooler already."

Scrawling notes on the battle map, Marcus gave Barak an appraising glance. "Now, Zev, this bypass idea you brought up. Anything to it?"

"If you capture Latrun, Mickey," Ben Gurion interjected, "why a bypass road? I don't want the troops hearing about a bypass road. They have to *attack*."

"It's very rough terrain, sir," said Barak. He summed up different reports he had heard. Some called the bypass notion preposterous, others favored trying it.

"Soup," said Paula Ben Gurion, entering with a tray.

"Thank you, Paula."

"Taste it. Hot enough?"

"Burns my tongue," said Ben Gurion, taking a spoonful of the greenish soup.

"Good. I made it in a hurry. I thought it might be cold." She went out.

"It's cold," Ben Gurion said.

Marcus persisted. "Come on, Zev, what's your opinion? Is it a pipe dream or not?"

"It's a *bobbeh-myseh*, Mickey," Ben Gurion snapped at Marcus. "Know what that means?"

Marcus smiled at the Yiddish byword. "Sure, a grandma story, but why?"

"Never mind! You just concentrate on Latrun." He picked up a despatch from the coverlet. "These French armored personnel carriers, Mickey, due to arrive tomorrow — Shamir's brigade should get them straight from the boat."

"Can you handle that?" Marcus asked Barak.

"If those are my orders." Barak knew that, in the wild confusion at Haifa port, the chances of the vehicles arriving at all, let alone being unloaded in time for the attack, were very slim. He saw no point in saying so. Ben Gurion was fretful enough.

"French matériel. That's good," said Marcus. "Don't rely too much on Czechoslovakia. Stalin can shut off that faucet overnight."

"Yes, a Zionist Stalin isn't," said the Prime Minister. "He lets the Czechs sell to us, so as to kick the British out of the Middle East. We know that. That's why his bloc votes our way in the UN, too.

Meantime we pay good dollars to the Czechs, and they also sell to the Arabs, you realize. Communists don't know from embargoes."

Marcus pointed at a yellow cable form on the bed. "Now, what about this new British cease-fire move at the UN? Is that on the level?"

The Prime Minister waved both hands in dismissal. "A bluff, a bluff. By now, an old trick." He fell into Talmudic singsong with thumb gestures. "The UN calls a cease-fire. We obey it. The Arabs ignore it and grab some territory. The war starts up again, we regain the lost territory." He shook his head at Marcus. "But no more! When they stop fighting, we stop. Not before, and they're not ready to stop."

The Prime Minister lay back on the pillows listening politely to Marcus's next comment, but his face and bald pate kept getting redder. If a cease-fire wasn't imminent, Marcus argued, the attack on Latrun should be delayed. The new Seventh Brigade still needed some hard drill. The heavy guns and personnel carriers could go to other fronts meantime to gain ground. For when a real cease-fire took effect, those lines might become Israel's permanent boundaries.

"Mickey, do me a favor, keep one thing in mind." Ben Gurion raised his voice, and a stubby forefinger. "Your responsibility is Jerusalem. *Jerusalem!* And that means one thing. Latrun! *Latrun!* No delay, Jerusalem is starving! Cease-fire lines are not your problem, not now!"

Paula Ben Gurion came striding in. "Now what? Why the screaming? Do you have to burst a blood vessel? Greenboim just sent up some eggs, after all. Do you want them boiled or fried?"

"Boiled," said the Prime Minister, in a drop of tone to complete calm.

"You're red as a beet. Behave yourself." She felt his forehead, nodded, and turned to Marcus and Barak. "Maybe you can let him get some sleep? He was awake all night, sweating and tossing."

Marcus stood up as she left. "She takes good care of you, Prime Minister. Like my gal does."

Ben Gurion gestured at Barak. "What about Zev?"

"Ah, yes. Zev, since I'm to take command of the whole Jerusalem front, I'm bound to need an English-speaking aide. Interested?"

Nonplussed, Barak did not respond.

"You got some objection, Zev?" inquired the Prime Minister. "This is what I've had in mind for you. Extremely important."

Paula appeared in the doorway. "Suppose I scramble them with onions? We have nice green onions."

"Now you're talking," said Ben Gurion, with a trace of appetite.

"Is there a bar around here?" Marcus inquired, shading his eyes from the low sun as they came outside.

"A bar?" Barak glanced around at the bleak concrete apartment houses, their balconies draped with washing. "I'm not sure."

"I could use a drink."

"We can pick up a bottle of cognac at Greenboim's."

"Good enough."

In Greenboim's *makolet,* a small general store piled with pots, pans, fresh vegetables, canned goods, magazines, bread loaves, laundry soap, toilet articles, hats, underwear, sieves, washboards, Bibles, and folding chairs, an apparent infinity of such items receded toward the shadowy rear, but no liquor. Up front sat Greenboim by an open counter, where cheesecloth covered defunct fish and chickens, and flies covered the cheesecloth.

"Cognac? The best," said Greenboim, a potbellied bearded man in a bloody apron, and he produced a very dusty bottle of Palestine brandy out of a bin full of potatoes sprouting eyes.

"Outstanding," said Marcus, as Barak paid. "Now, where do we drink it?"

"Mrs. Fefferman's bakery next door has a table and chairs."

"Fine."

At a rickety table by the display of pastries, the gray-haired Mrs. Fefferman provided water glasses for the brandy, and slices of crumb cake. Marcus poured his glass half full and drank it straight down. Barak had seen such quaffing in the British army, but it jarred him. He cautiously sipped the raw brandy and ate cake.

Marcus poured more for himself and murmured, glancing at the yawning proprietor, "Can we talk?"

"Mrs. Fefferman doesn't know English."

"Okay. Will my plan for Latrun work?" Barak only blinked at the American. "If you have doubts, Zev, state them. I don't want to issue a bum operation order, first time out."

"Well, it's a night attack, sir. That's good. Giving the brigade more training first is excellent. Mandatory." He hesitated. "As to that Palmakh battalion you've got attacking from the southeast —"

"What about it?"

"Colonel, they've been fighting the Egyptians since the war began. They're badly cut up."

"Yadin told me they're what's available. The Palmakh's dead set against assaulting Latrun. Why?"

"There are a lot of opinions in Palmakh." The brandy was burning Barak's throat and stomach. He drank very seldom, and never by day.

Marcus looked him in the eye. "Zev, you talked straight to Ben Gurion. Talk straight to me. Not everybody does here."

In rapid dry sentences, Barak ran through the strategic disagreement that had been plaguing the war: Ben Gurion's obsession with Jerusalem, and his hankering for textbook military operations, derived from hasty reading of authorities like Liddell Hart and Fuller, versus the Palmakh concept of knocking out the Arab forces by proven tactics suited to Palestine, and to the volatile nature of the enemy. Marcus kept drinking as he listened.

"Well, Zev, there's only one commander-in-chief here," Marcus commented, "and that's Ben Gurion. Look at George Washington. You know our Revolutionary War, don't you? Washington made fearful mistakes. Took terrible defeats. But he was commander-in-chief, he was a leader, and he won."

"Sir, Washington was a soldier. Ben Gurion's a great man, but what he knows is politics."

"You have to go with the leader you've got. He's your George Washington."

"And you're our Lafayette," said Barak, putting his glass to his lips and surprised to find it empty. Marcus laughed and poured him more, though Barak tried to wave away the bottle.

"Lafayette brought over a trained army," Marcus said, "and got the French fleet to fight on the American side. That's really how old George beat the redcoats. I bring you bopkess. If you know that military expression."

"Napoleonic term, I believe," said Barak, "for moral support."

"Exactly." Marcus grinned. "You'll have to win this war all by yourselves. And you will. Know why? Two reasons. One, your soldiers *want* to fight."

"Well, they have to, sir. No choice."

"Okay, whatever the motivation, they're as good as the best damn soldiers I've ever seen. The other is your secret weapon." Marcus gulped brandy. "The Arab High Command. Zev, what the hell's the matter with them? Why didn't they overrun you two weeks ago?"

Barak said after a moment, "Sir, they're not very experienced armies, you know."

"So what? They had plenty of British training, didn't they? And they had you surrounded, outgunned, and outnumbered."

"Sir, in the manual they gave us in the British army in North Africa, three words were printed in big black type, *define the mission,* and —"

"It's in all military manuals," Marcus interrupted. "It's in the doctrine I dictated for your army."

"I saw that, sir. Well, the Arab mission in this war was to wipe out the Yishuv. Wasn't it? No more of this little excrescence calling itself Israel! Three simple words: *define the mission.* But instead they've been tearing apart the land the UN awarded to the Palestine Arabs — Egypt grabbing Gaza and the Hebron area, Syria snatching at the north, Abdullah swallowing the West Bank and trying to swallow Jerusalem. They distrust each other. They lie to each other. They won't admit defeats. They keep announcing victories that didn't happen. In short, unclear on their mission, sir."

"Do you really want to be my aide?" Marcus asked. "Nobody's forcing you."

"Colonel Stone, I'm honored."

"Well, then, you're hired."

"Good. I request a few hours off duty, starting now."

"You do? There's a soldier. What for?"

"To see my wife. She's not far, in Herzliyya. It's been a while."

"How long have you been married?"

"Four years."

"Kids?"

"One son."

Marcus sighed. "Emma and I have missed out on kids. Israeli lady?"

"Yes."

"Army?"

"No."

"How'd you meet?"

"At a party, when I was on leave from North Africa. A guy from the Brigade told me he was bringing the most beautiful girl in Tel Aviv. He wasn't just talking. A week later I married her."

"Outstanding. Three hours off duty granted. Then meet me in Ramat Gan. Let me have that bottle. We'll work out the logistics tonight for Latrun. You people have things to learn about logistics."

"About everything. We're still guerrillas, and pretty amateurish."

Marcus struck his shoulder. "You said it, I didn't, young feller. In the Negev kids were fighting without helmets and barefoot, in flimsy uniforms, on freezing nights." As they walked out of Mrs. Fefferman's, Marcus went on. "No doubt your wife's been raking you over the coals, like my own darling. It's been goddamn hard on Emma." Marcus heaved a deep sigh, almost a groan. "Well, I've got me a general's star, something I never made in the U.S. Army. Maybe that'll please her." He fell silent as they walked, then said slowly, "And my first combat assignment is to defend *Jerusalem*, the Holy City! How about that? You know something, Zev? Emma said, night before I left, 'Why you? It's not your fight.' I asked her, 'After what happened in Europe, don't you think a Jewish State should exist?' "

"What did she say, Colonel?"

Marcus took a moment to reply. "She said, 'If my husband has to go over there to fight for it, maybe it shouldn't exist.' "

"Is she Jewish?"

"Yes." A short laugh. "Not Orthodox, you know. Neither am I."

They came to the small gray Vauxhall the army had given Marcus. The driver was asleep at the wheel. Marcus startled him awake with a heavy rap on the hood.

"Go and see your wife, Zev."

"Thank you, Colonel."

"That's Mickey. Now, about that bypass idea B.G. called a bobbeh-myseh. Anything to it, really?"

"Sir, I can reconnoiter the area tomorrow and let you know."

"You mean yourself? Kind of risky out there, isn't it, snipers and such?"

"No problem. I'd take an armed patrol."

"Well, we'll see. We'll discuss it in the war room tonight."

Driving to Herzliyya, Barak found himself cheering up. Why? The war situation was as threatening as ever. Prospect of seeing Nakhama and his boy? Reason enough, maybe, but there was more to his lift of spirits than that. It was Marcus. Barak knew all the commanders in Jerusalem, and he had observed their brabbling at first hand. Marcus was a likable and forceful presence, but as a front commander in Jerusalem, lacking Hebrew and without a savvy interpreter, he would be a tongue-tied outlander. Barak was sure he could help the man in the defense and relief of Jerusalem, and it was an important job, about that the Old Man was correct. If there were plusses and minuses in being too close to David Ben Gurion, this sudden temporary reassignment was a plus. And right away there was also the plus of putting his good arm around Nakhama's exquisite soft slim waist.

The house was very quiet, and still redolent of his father's Schimmelpfennig cigars, though Meyer Berkowitz had been in America for months at the UN, where he headed the Israeli delegation. Barak called, "Anybody home?"

Trampling on the stairs. Nakhama's voice, alive with joy: "You! Finally, *you!*"

She came dancing into the book-lined living room in a dingy housedress, flinging arms and legs this way and that like a child. "Mama phoned me that she talked to you, but she didn't think you'd come today! How's your elbow?"

He encircled her waist with the good arm, and drew her to him with the heavy crooked cast. "See, it works!"

Laughter, a light kiss or two, then a close embrace and passionate kissing. "Oo-ah, darling," she exclaimed, bending away from him. "What is this? You're stinking drunk! In the daytime, on duty? You?"

"It's part of my new job."

"A new job? What new job? Guzzling like a goy is part of a job? Can I make you something to eat?"

"How's the boy?"

"Fine, having a nap, but listen —"

"I'm not hungry. You listen!"

He drew her down on the red plush couch his parents had brought from Vienna, presciently departing with all their possessions before Hitler marched in. The house was furnished with that stuff, and the books had never quite lost the mildewy aroma acquired on the long slow sea voyage. Barak told her of his assignment as aide to Marcus. Nakhama had heard gossip of an American adviser to Ben Gurion, but all she wanted to know was whether this meant she would see more of him.

"Well, I think so. He won't be running me around night and day like Ben Gurion."

"But — Jerusalem Command? How on earth will you get to Jerusalem? And if you do, won't you be stuck there?"

"You look beautiful, you know?"

"Stop that" — she deflected his good arm — "and explain!"

Barak described how Piper Cubs still flew in and out of the capital, maintaining military communication.

"Oh! Then you'll see our apartment. Maybe if it's not bombed out, you can use it."

"I intend to."

"Zev, I still feel rotten about running away. If not for Noah I wouldn't have left."

"He's why I got you out."

"But tell the truth, darling, are we really better off here? What about the Egyptians, the Iraqis? Two weeks ago we danced in the streets, and now it's such a nightmare!"

"I didn't dance, Nakhama, I knew all this was coming. So did the Old Man. I saw his face when he read the Declaration. Let's go up and have a look at Noah."

The boy, a skinny three-year-old naked but for shorts, lay perspiring on the bed. Nakhama put an arm around her husband. "He misses his friends," she whispered, "but he's been very good."

"I heard he got into trouble in kindergarten."

"Not so. He's a new kid, so they torment him. He won't tolerate it, he fights back. His father's son. Now what? Where are you taking me?" He was leading her by the hand to their bedroom across the hall, his old room. "What is this, Zevi? No, no, not on your life! In broad daylight?" She dug in her heels.

"What's the matter?"

"Your mother —"

"Why, where is she?"

"She's in Ramat Gan, she won't be back till dinner, but all the same —" Reluctantly she let herself be pulled into the bedroom, where a suitcase lay open on his bed, packed with her things. He stared at her and she stared back, half-guilty, half-defiant. "All right, I was going to tell you. I'm moving with Noah to my parents' flat."

"The devil you are! Why? They have no room for you there."

"My mother always has room for me."

"Nakhama, your brother sleeps on the sofa, and there's no place else."

"So I'll sleep on the floor with Noah. Mama has mattresses. At least I'll feel at home. Your mother can't stand having me under her roof."

Oh, God, thought Barak, that again. "Now what? You had an argument?"

"Your mother never argues, you know that. She doesn't have

to, I'm beneath her. Just the servant girl with your name and your son."

This had been going on since the day they married. *"Wolf-gang, she's wrong for you! I know she's beautiful, I know you're in love, but she has no culture, no background, you'll live to regret it!"* And in truth all the books and classical records in this house meant nothing to his wife, except to make her self-conscious. But words would not help on that topic. Nakhama had war nerves, nothing more. Barak closed the suitcase and slung it off the bed. She said, "Wait, wait, what's the big idea?"

"Look, *motek* [sweet], the colonel's no slave driver like B.G. I'll try to come back and spend tonight here, how's that?"

She widened glad brown eyes. "Truly? You will?"

"I will. I'll try."

"Then, if you're really coming back tonight, why are you pulling down the shades?"

"Didn't you object to broad daylight?"

"Oo-ah! So, it's *z'beng v'gamarnu* [bang and finish], hah? Right this minute, hah? The army wife's love life, hah?" Nakhama closed the bedroom door. "Zev, Zev, careful with that arm now! Easy, easy, darling!"

3

The Alamo

Two days later several jeeps, one with a mounted machine gun, went bouncing through brush and boulders on the dirt track hidden from Latrun by a wooded ridge. Dead ahead a dazzling white sun was rising. The vehicles halted at the brink of a broad ravine, and Sam Pasternak and Zev Barak got out. The descent to the rock-strewn bottom, which lay in deep shadow, was an almost sheer drop of broken stones and thick brush, with a footpath zigzagging down the slope. "When the Arabs first mined the main road," said Pasternak, "their villagers used that trail for a while on donkeys or on foot. Not in recent months. So the Hulda kibbutzniks told me."

Several soldiers from the jeeps began hurling stones out over the wadi, including Kishote in extremely ill fitting khakis, and Yael Luria, whose uniform fitted her a shade too well. Kishote pitched the farthest, with wide sweeps of a bony arm, but Yael made surprisingly strong throws.

"Well, what do you think, Sam?"

"I think we'd better take Latrun," Pasternak said drily. The Seventh Brigade had already begun heavy drilling for the next assault.

"I'm supposed to report to Colonel Stone," said Barak, "whether a bypass is feasible at all."

"Well look, the road work could probably be done, Zev, though it's a gigantic job. But is it practical? The Legion would sortie in short order and slaughter the road crews, wouldn't they?"

Barak was peering down into the chasm. "Would they? Suppose we'd work only at night, Sam? Minimum illumination, minimum noise, no blasting? We're a couple of miles from Latrun, deep in the wilds."

"You mean build a paved road *secretly*? Hmm." Pasternak's eyes half closed, in a shifty expression familiar to Barak. Covert action was Sam's specialty. "But you've got a four-hundred-foot drop right here, Zev. Lot of engineering! Three or four miles of rough country beyond. Hardly realistic." He rubbed his chin, and added with a foxy little smile, "I tell you what, though! Think about mules, and maybe it gets interesting. What's more, if the truce doesn't come too soon —"

Shading his eyes from the brilliant sun, Barak stared out at the dry wash, crisscrossed with deep gullies and dotted with boulders, as Pasternak talked. "Look, Sam," he said abruptly, "in the African desert my battalion crossed steeper drops than this in trucks and jeeps. If not for this elbow, I'd try going down right now."

"I'll take you down, Zev." Yael Luria had quit the rock-throwing contest to edge up and listen.

"This girl sure will, if you let her, Zev," Pasternak said. "Whether you'll survive — that's something else."

"Come on," said Barak, getting into the jeep. As Yael took the wheel Don Kishote leaped into the back. "Out, Yossi!" Barak jerked a thumb. "Out!"

"Suppose you roll over?" Kishote inquired. "Then I could help."

"Good thought," said Barak.

"But if you do reach the bottom alive, Zev, how do you get back up?" Pasternak inquired. "Thought of that?"

"One thought at a time," said Barak. "Let's go, Yael."

The jeep crawled in low gear along the brink, then turned and crashed downward on the zigzag path. It struck a rock hidden by brush and nearly tumbled over, but Yael fought the wheel and righted it. Twisting this way and that to avoid stone outcroppings, she drove down and down, lost the path, and plunged the jeep straight for the wadi floor. Kishote clung to the side whooping wildly, evidently having the time of his life. Barak hugged his elbow and hoped for the best. After a very rough ride they levelled off and stopped. He cupped his hands to yell, "Not that bad, Sam!"

"What now?" Pasternak called, his voice echoing *"now . . . now,"* in the hills.

"Send that kid down, and I'll phone Colonel Stone from Jerusalem. I'm going on." "That kid" was one of the soldiers who had bypassed Latrun in a jeep. "And you," Barak said to Yael, pointing a thumb upward, "back to headquarters."

"What? No! Why? Who'll drive?"

"On your way."

"Oh, please do let me come." Yael's big blue eyes turned gentle and lustrous as she rounded them at Barak. "I have family in Jerusalem, you know, a sick aunt, and my mother's so worried about her —"

"Yael, you heard me. *Zuz* [Move]!"

When Yael Luria jutted her jaw and scowled, the look on her face was no girlish pout. "Zev, you're being ridiculous."

"Sergeant Luria, get your behind up that slope."

With a glare at him and then at Kishote, who blinked innocently through his glasses, Yael went climbing up, using her hands as well as long shapely brown legs.

Working the wheel one-handed, Barak drove slowly along the wash. The soldier sat with his rifle across his knees, yawning; a swarthy youth with a heavy drooping mustache, and a small skullcap clipped to his thick black hair. He said he was from Tunis. Kishote had never before encountered a Jew who so much resembled an Arab. But then, everything on this journey was novel — the rifle in his lap, the jolting ride in a rocky roadless ravine, where behind a boulder or a clump of brush an enemy might be taking aim at him; above all, the exalting surprise that he was on his way to Jerusalem! Too dry and stony for Arab pasturing, far out of sight of Latrun, the wadi was a trackless no-man's-land. Barak bore eastward, watching the sun, avoiding the biggest boulders, sometimes halting abruptly at a gully's edge. In some places he was able to follow jeep tracks in the sand. They bumped and pounded uphill for a couple of miles, and came at last on a rutted dirt road wide enough for one vehicle and piled with animal droppings. "This has to be the Hartuv road," Barak said to the soldier.

"Yes, sir, it is, and we got shot at here by snipers."

"No doubt. The highway's not far. Sharp lookout, both of you!"

Barak turned and followed the rutted road through rolling stony pastures and untended weed-choked farms where goats and sheep grazed. Of Arabs, no sign. When the jeep emerged on the empty two-lane blacktop it seemed to glide like a boat. From the melting asphalt, where grass sprouted in cracks, a tarry smell rose, and burned-out trucks and "sandwich" vehicles lay tumbled on the roadside. They continued uphill and trucks began to snort by, spewing dirty fumes: one carrying bleating sheep, another piled with hay, a third full of unshaven bored soldiers. On a long hill the jeep got stuck behind a groaning tank truck.

"Gasoline?" Kishote inquired.

"Water," said Barak. "Drinking water for Jerusalem from the local cisterns."

The tank truck went over the top and down the hill, and Barak pointed at a crest far ahead.

"Jerusalem, Kishote."

"Really?" It was a decided disappointment, just a line of low buildings on a ridge. Still, he put a hand on his hatless head. "Then I have to make a blessing. *Blessed art Thou, Lord our God, Ruler of the world, who has kept us alive, sustained us, and brought us to this time.*"

"Amen," said the pious Tunis youth and the agnostic Barak.

As the jeep came rolling into Jerusalem, Barak was sickened at the way the city had deteriorated. All the gardens and parks were overgrown. Main thoroughfares were filthy, barricaded, shell-pocked, wire-tangled. Buildings had been shelled to rubble. Again and again he had to detour around raw concrete barriers and streets closed off with barbed wire. Most shops were shuttered, and long queues stood outside the few that sold rationed food. At water trucks women were lined up around the block holding pails, jugs, or tin cans, many of them gripping little children by the hand or carrying babies.

But Don Kishote hardly noticed these things. Years in wartime Europe and refugee camps had accustomed him to barricades, barbed wire, roadblocks, bombed-out houses, long queues, and patrolling soldiers. This first glimpse inside the Holy City enchanted him. Now *here* was the Jerusalem of his visions! Wherever he looked he saw beauty, different and radiant; a stone city hewed of some lovely light-colored rock, not quite tan or rosy, but something of each. In all the pictures he had seen, this glow of Jerusalem stone had been missing. The translucent air, deep blue sky, and mighty sunlight, so different from Tel Aviv's haze, brought out the glow. Everywhere flowers bloomed amid palm trees, blossoming trees, and tall old shade trees; Eden on earth, the City of God.

Yerushalayim!

With his first lisped parroted prayers he had prayed to return to "Yerushalayim." Even after eating a cookie, there had been a long rote grace to say: *We thank Thee for the produce of the field, and for the broad and pleasant land you gave our fathers. . . . Rebuild Yerushalayim the Holy City speedily in our days, and let us go up in its midst and rejoice in its rebuilding. . . .* For just one bite of cake, he had had to recite all that. In the *heder,* the primary school, he had learned that Yerushalayim was the gateway of Heaven, where prayers went upward straight to God. Later in the Zionist scout troop there had been Yerushalayim songs, slides, and movies. And now here he was in the Holy City, in Zion, in Yerushalayim! The words of a psalm ran in his mind. *"When God returned us to Zion, we were as dreamers . . ."*

But they turned into Ben Yehuda Street, and Kishote was shocked out of the dream. Stopping them was an enormous crater ringed by smashed buildings, and blocked off with police fences and high coils of barbed wire. "My God, what happened here, sir?" he asked Barak.

"Big car bomb, months ago. British army deserters did it, paid by the Arabs."

Slow-moving workmen were picking at the ruins, but from this old disaster the stink of broken buildings and torn-up sewer mains still rose, almost as on the day of the colossal explosion. Barak parked in a side street near the crater. The Tunis youth jumped out with his rifle and trotted off. "Wait here, Kishote," Barak said. He went into a concrete building and groped up five dark flights; elevator not working, stairway unlit.

"Zev! You're in Jerusalem? Since when?" The once jolly plump secretary of Hermann Loeb looked gaunt and nervous, as after a wasting illness.

"Is he in, Rivka?"

"He's on the phone."

"Then the phone's working. Good."

"His phone will work to the last." A sad bitter laugh. "He's in charge of food, you know."

"Can you get through to Tel Aviv?"

"Sometimes. I can try."

"Is this Zev I hear?" A lean small man in a black suit and tie bustled out of his office, and threw an arm around Barak. "What happened to your elbow? What are you doing here? How is Nakhama?"

"Hermann, I must speak to Tel Aviv."

"Give Rivka the number, and come inside."

By Jerusalem standards the office of Hermann Loeb was luxurious: heavy German furniture, abstract paintings, glass cases of Canaanite artifacts. He was an amateur archaeologist, and in peacetime a prosperous dealer in farm products; a Yekke, a Swiss-German Jew, never seen without a coat and tie, except possibly by his wife at bedtime. The telephone rang as he motioned Barak to a couch in his office.

"Loeb! Ja?" His expression hardened, and he barked in German, "Break the locks! Clear out the warehouse! Every last bag of flour. . . . What authority? On *my* authority." Pause. "Why? Because it's abandoned property, that's why. . . . It's abandoned because *I say* it's abandoned! Tell him to sue the municipality after the war, if he's still alive!" Crash of receiver. "Damned profiteer," Loeb said to Barak, "biggest baker in Jerusalem, claimed he ran out of flour. Hoarding it and getting black-market prices, the swine. We knew where he had his flour. Is that elbow serious?"

The telephone rang again and Loeb got into a shouting match about sugar. Barak broke in. "My call is highest army urgency, Hermann."

Loeb hung up and told the secretary to hold all calls and keep trying Tel Aviv.

"Hermann, what is the fuel situation for trucks here?"

"For trucks? Tolerable, since the convoys stopped coming and refueling. Why?"

"What about fuel for power? And where do you stand on food?"

Hermann Loeb responded with brisk figures. Jerusalem's hundred thousand Jews, most of them in the New City, consumed about two hundred tons a day, he said, of fuel, food, ammunition, medical supplies, and such. Rations had been cut, and cut again. Electric power had been cut to a couple of hours a day. Shortages were becoming serious. Flour was the worst. Flour for "the daily loaf" for every inhabitant was down to an eleven-day supply. Thereafter the Jews of Jerusalem would begin to starve. They were being heroic, ten thousand shells had fallen on them and they were uncowed, but starvation could prove the finish of Jewish Jerusalem.

Barak knew this man well, for Loeb was Pasternak's father-in-law. The marriage of Ruth Loeb to Sam Pasternak, the son of Mishmar Ha'emek pioneers, had been a big Jerusalem social event, but now Ruth lived in London with her two kids, the marriage a bust. So much for suitable matches! Hermann Loeb had come to Palestine in the twenties, lived in Jerusalem and loved it, but spent most of his time travelling on business. Now, like all Jerusalemites, he and his family were trapped, and he was wielding an iron hand as food czar.

The man was absolutely honest and reliable, and he could keep his mouth shut, so Barak said, "Hermann, listen carefully. An alternate route bypassing Latrun is possible. I've just traversed it by jeep." At Loeb's excited exclamation, he held up a hand. "Not for convoys. There's a long stretch that won't take trucks. But the trucks could come from Tel Aviv to a point past Hulda and off-load onto mules. The mules could carry the stuff to the Hartuv road, where your trucks could meet them. I doubt that mules can transport two hundred tons a day on that trail, but it might help —"

Loeb nodded excitedly. "It would, it would! A big help, a godsend! Can we start this at once?" He picked up the ringing phone. "Here's your call to Tel Aviv."

Marcus's buoyant American accents gave Barak an instant lift. "Hi, Zev! So you're in Jerusalem, hey? That bypass really works?"

"Well, it's no bobbeh-myseh. I hope we take Latrun, but we should start surveying and building the road, top priority." He rattled off Pasternak's interim plan for mule transport.

"Outstanding. Will do," said Marcus. "All of it. I'll talk to Ben Gurion when I hang up, and I'll get the mule trains going tonight. That's a splendid idea. Now listen, Zev. I'm goddamned glad you're in Jerusalem. B.G. is in a frenzy. We've just got word that the Jewish Quarter in the Old City is considering surrender. Have you heard anything about that?"

"I just got here. I'm in the office of a municipal leader. Hold on."

"I'm holding."

Barak shot the question at Loeb, who mournfully nodded, pointing to a map of the Old City on the wall, a diamond shape with the small Jewish Quarter at the bottom colored in blue. Red hatching showed the Arab Legion holding all the rest, and streaks of red penetrated the blue area as well.

"It's a siege within a siege, the Jewish Quarter," said Loeb. "If we only had some real leadership, Zev, we could win back the whole Old City, we've got the troops! But four commands keep pulling four different ways. They've made joint attempts to break in and relieve the Quarter. Always aborted."

Barak repeated this to Marcus, whose voice took on urgency. The Jewish Quarter, he said, was militarily valueless; he had seen it before the siege, a warren of ancient houses and synagogues, with only a few hundred ultraorthodox families. But a small force of Haganah and Irgun troops were in there defending it from the Legion. Ben Gurion wanted it held at all cost, because Jews had lived there for over two thousand years, and its fall would be a political catastrophe. King Abdullah might even call for a truce after such a triumph, while Jerusalem was still cut off.

"Ben Gurion's the commander-in-chief," Marcus went on. "I have my orders, so I'm going to relieve the Quarter. We attack tomorrow night, the twenty-eighth. I'll fly there at dawn with my plan and assume overall command of the forces there. You'll be my operations officer. Call a conference of the combined Jerusalem Command staff for 0730 hours."

"Yes, sir."

"Now, Zev, there's this young Haganah leader inside the Quarter — Motti something —"

"I know him. Motti Pinkus, a good boy."

"You do? Great! Jerusalem Command is having some kind of trouble with the guy. He has to be informed of my intent to attack, and promise he'll hang on till tomorrow night."

"I'll convey that word to him. Motti will believe me."

"Outstanding. I'll start working on this bypass thing."

Barak asked Loeb how he could get inside the beleaguered Quarter. The food czar pulled a very long face. "Well, maybe at night, at great risk — but what could you accomplish? It's a hopeless position. Those old Yerushalmis are quaint and charming, salt of the earth, but they live in the seventeenth century." Loeb sadly shook his head. "They think Zionism is blasphemy, because it aspires to replace the Messiah. They've lived with the Arabs for hundreds of years. They don't understand this whole war, and they want no part of it. They're the ones talking surrender, and it's just a matter of time."

"I have to get in there, Hermann."

Loeb peered out of the window. "I tell you what. There's an old fellow you might talk to, right across the street down there. The tailor shop, with green blinds."

Kishote had just gone into the dark little shop. In his heaving and straining at the jeep when it bogged down in a gully, he had split the seat of his badly fitting uniform. A graybeard in a skullcap and a four-corner *talit katan* with long fringes looked up grumpily from a sewing table. "I'm very busy," he said in Hebrew. "Can't take on more work."

"Little father," Kishote ventured in Yiddish, "have pity on a Jewish boy." He turned around and showed the tailor his predicament, whereupon a loud peal of silvery giggles startled him. A little black-haired girl, eleven or twelve, stood in an open doorway at the back of the shop, doubled over with laughter.

"Shayna, shame on you," exclaimed the old man, but he was laughing, too.

"I'm sorry, Grandpa," she gasped, and vanished.

The old man closed his door and went to work on the pants. Kishote stood in his underwear, glancing nervously at the back door. "Shayna won't come out, don't worry," said the tailor. "She's a truly modest girl. Where are you from?"

"We just came over from Cyprus. Originally, from Katowice."

"Katowice?" The tailor's stern face softened. "We had family in Katowice. All murdered, peace to their souls. And what is your name? What does your father do?"

They were still talking about Katowice, and Kishote was trying on the trousers, when Barak entered the gloomy shop. "So, Kishote, here you are." Squinting at the tailor he exclaimed, "By my life, is this Reb Shmuel?"

The tailor blinked and replied, "And is this the dancing soldier?"

Zev Barak had retained very little religion from his schooling, but on merry days like Purim and the Rejoicing of the Law he liked dancing in the Quarter, where the pious men took him into their dignified gambols, no questions asked. They knew him only as "the dancing soldier," and he knew this tailor only as Reb Shmuel, an imposing straight-backed patriarch with a huge nose, in a silken caftan and fur hat. The hunched-over old man in an undershirt, suspenders, and talit katan was obviously the same person in workaday guise, but he seemed the less real of the two Reb Shmuels.

"Yossi, wait for me in the jeep." Kishote went out. Barak took a confidential tone. "Reb Shmuel, I'm told you keep some kind of contact with the Old City. That even the military governor comes to you for information."

"Nu, nu." The tailor shrugged, his face blank.

"My job now, Reb Shmuel, is aide to the new army commander of Jerusalem. He's an American officer, a colonel."

"An *American?*" The tailor's entire aspect changed and brightened. "Jerusalem's getting an *American* commander? Truly? Thank God for a miracle! How can I help you?"

Presently Barak emerged from the shop, and drove the jeep through the middle of town, detouring around closed-off streets to a block of apartment houses. "Here's where I live, Yossi." He jumped out. "I won't be long." When he returned, he was carrying a big black flashlight. "We'll get something to eat now at the army mess. It may be a long night. Hungry?"

"I'm starved," said Kishote. "I just didn't want to bother you."

Barely visible, the ledge along the vaulted cistern wall looked to Barak no more than three inches wide. Far below, black water faintly reflected the flashlight beam. Using his good arm and hand to clutch the dank rough wall, holding the light awkwardly in his left hand, he sidled after the girl, who was scurrying along the ledge like a rat. Behind him Don Kishote came sidewise, step by cautious step. "Slower, Shayna!" Barak's voice boomed and reechoed between the arch and the water, which, the girl had mentioned, was very deep and very cold.

"B'seder," she piped.

Barak did not remember ever coming on this huge cistern in his scout troop's explorations of these labyrinthine tunnels. Conceivably it could date back to Hasmonean times, he thought, or even to the era of David, for the earth under the Old City was a honeycomb of ancient history and war. But the water was probably fresh, since in advance of the siege the city's water engineers had filled every cistern in Jerusalem, some of them unused for generations. Teetering along the ledge, he gasped with relief as he stepped off onto a stone tunnel floor. "That was fun," remarked Kishote behind him.

The girl led them through low-arching passages smelling of earth, of graves, of musty decay. Barak ripped his blouse, crawling after her through a hole in a half-collapsed wall. A heavy wooden barrier encrusted with mold and spiderwebs almost stopped them. The girl and Kishote slipped through a narrow opening, but Barak had to wriggle hard to get by. At last they climbed broken rubble-strewn stairs and emerged into a cool smoky night; around them wreckage, rubbish, the rattle of small arms, and the glare of fires. They followed Shayna through crooked streets to a chilly basement of bare sooty cement, where an unshaven youngster in a torn sweater sat, marking up a map by the light of a kerosene lamp. "I have no idea where Motti is," he said, peering at Barak with black-ringed haunted eyes. "Maybe at the hospital. Ask next door."

In the adjoining candlelit cellar room, teenagers sat in a circle on the cement floor, stuffing yellow plastic into tin cans. Barak had produced his share of these homemade grenades, and the sour gelignite smell woke boyhood memories . . .

. . . of teenagers working in the summertime by candlelight to make grenades, "pomegranates," in the hay-piled barn at Mishmar Ha'emek, Sam Pasternak's kibbutz, while outside a girl paced the fence on the lookout for British soldiers. Scary, exciting time! Sam cracking irrepressible morbid jokes about getting blown up, until the humorless Young Guardian supervisor lost his temper and bawled him out: "There's nothing funny about these pomegranates, Pasternak, they're meant to kill Arabs, and that's serious business!" A sort of loner in the kibbutz, Sam was, a Czech boy among mostly Polish kids, disliked by the supervisor because he attended a "bourgeois" school in Tel Aviv; probably why he had brought Barak to the kibbutz that summer, when they had become really close friends . . .

"Shoshana, Shoshana, Shoshana!" The girl singing outside very loud, and the popular waltz triggering a scramble to hide all the stuff in the hay, so that the soldiers found the kids around a campfire outside the barn, some eating, some singing, some dancing to a concertina . . .

Barak asked the stripling with a scraggly goatee who seemed in charge of the grenade squad, "Where's Motti?"

"Last I heard he went to Hurva."

Outside Shayna and Kishote were watching shells streak and shriek across the smoke-fogged sky. "Hurva? B'seder," said Shayna, and she led them through eye-stinging smoke to the majestic main synagogue, where crowds of the pious poor were huddled inside. Mothers were trying to soothe crying infants, bearded men with earlocks sat crouched over books, and a circle of men were reciting psalms in the old singsong by candlelight. White faces everywhere in the gloom wore looks of terror or apathy. As Barak came in, leaving Shayna and Kishote outside, a nearby explosion made the massive building shudder, and wails arose in the gloom.

A boyish soldier at the door told Barak that Motti was in a council meeting in the *beit medrash,* the study hall.

"What are all these people doing here?"

"Oh, they jam in when the shelling starts. It's crazy. One solid hit on the roof can kill them all. They'd be safer back in their own cellars. But no, they run in here."

Several elderly civilians were coming out of the study hall as Barak went in. Alone in the room lined with tall Talmud volumes, his head in his hands at a long table, Motti Pinkus sat. He glanced up, and the dulled despairing look on his bristly face changed to lively surprise. "Zev Barak! Elohim, is it a breakthrough? Where are the troops?"

Barak told the grimy leader how he had come, and why. Pinkus seized on the news about Marcus. "Honestly, an American? A West Point colonel? There's a hell of a change! I only hope to God it's not too late."

"Motti, you haven't been answering urgent signals from Jerusalem Command. Why not?"

"Don't talk to me about those dogs! Those swine!" Pinkus pounded the table, grinding his teeth. "Liars! Cowards! Phony promises, and nothing happens!" He flung an arm toward the wall. "A few hundred yards from here, Zev — right outside the Zion Gate — the Palmakh is sitting on its ass! Safe and sound on Mount Zion! They broke in, brought some lousy supplies, and pulled out again! We're in here fighting to prevent a massacre, and out of a hundred thousand Jews, the Jerusalem Command can't even send in a platoon to reenforce us! The hospital is piled up with our kids, the doctors are putting the overflow into a synagogue next door, it's horrible! Zev, in these narrow streets twenty-five fresh guys would be like a battalion, but if reenforcements don't come we're done for!"

"Why, how many fighters do you have left?"

"I'm not sure anymore. I've lost track. The wounded keep going back to their posts. Effective fighters, Haganah and Irgun together, maybe sixty. Includes girls. All exhausted, but still —"

Barak knew the defenders were sparse, but this astounded him. "*Sixty?* Against the Arab Legion?"

"Look, Zev, these Arabs, once they occupy a street — even the Legionnaires — they fall apart. They start looting and burning, dancing and screaming. No discipline. We regroup, set up new machine gun positions. Sometimes we can even counterattack. They pay plenty for every street they take."

"Can you hold out till tomorrow night?"

Pinkus threw up his hands. "Who knows? Food and water, okay. Ammo, some left. It's the artillery, Zev, the shelling. It crazes these poor civilians. They run around in panic, making trouble, bribing, hoarding, pleading for favors —"

"Any serious talk of surrender?"

"Any talk? You saw that council going out? They're ready to organize a white-flag approach to the Red Cross! They voted to do it! But I vetoed that, and I had to get damned tough. I don't like to shoot Jews, but I may have to, if I'm supposed to hold out much longer. Some of these *haredim* [pious folk] have been okay and given us a lot of help, but those others —" Pinkus stood up with a groan, shaking his head. "Did you know Kobi Katz? We grew up together. The best of the best, and he just got killed."

"I knew him, Motti. I'm sorry."

"I've got to" — Pinkus's voice cracked — "go to his post. Come along."

Barak sent Shayna back to the command cellar, and he and Kishote followed Pinkus to an alley where about a dozen young fighters in ragtag uniforms crouched behind a barricade of furniture and rubble. Beyond the barricade Barak recognized the little synagogue where he had danced with Reb Shmuel on holidays. "We know where the sniper is who killed Kobi," said a youth in cast-off British fatigues, hunkered down by a heap of the tin-can grenades. "We tried to advance through here, we could have secured this whole sector if we'd gotten through. But Kobi went first as always, and that bastard up there blasted him. We had to carry him back out." He pointed to the synagogue roof. "Too far to throw the grenades. We've been trying. It's the way the alley curves —"

Pinkus and Barak were both peering up at the synagogue roof when two cans flew over their heads. One fell in the street, the other struck a wall, both exploding in fire and roars.

"What the devil!" exclaimed Barak, turning in time to see Kishote snatch a third can and heave it. The can tumbled end over end, starkly visible high in the fiery air, and landed with a blast on the synagogue roof. A machine gun came tumbling down, and crashed in the street. "Got him! Got him!" yelled the youngsters.

The soldier in fatigues stared at Kishote. "Who are you? What's your name?"

"Yossi."

The soldier slapped his back and turned to the others, calling, "After me!" He went sliding along the wall. The unit followed him, while a disheveled girl piled the grenades into a sack. "I'll take that," said Kishote to her, picking up the sack.

"Just don't drop it, then," she said. "You'll make a big noise."

"Kishote, where are you going? Come back here!" shouted Barak.

With a wave and a grin, Don Kishote slipped down the alley after the girl, and faded off in gloom and drifting smoke.

Pinkus said, "What is that kid, your runner? You want him back?"

"Well, it seems he wants to fight." Barak shrugged and shook his head. "So let him!"

"Okay. I'm returning to the hole."

"Motti, I'm leaving. I have to report to the American colonel tonight. Listen, *don't despair*! This time tomorrow night, the Legion will have their hands full. They won't know what hit them!"

Pinkus eyed him with a look of bitter skepticism. "Maybe!

Anyhow, you've seen how our kids are fighting. It's the civilians, Zev. I'll try my best to keep them in line."

"One more day, Motti." Barak threw his good arm around Pinkus's shoulders, and hugged hard. "Twenty-four hours."

"I can't promise anything. I'm doing what I can."

In the dark outside the command cellar Shayna asked him, "Where is that big skinny fool with eyeglasses?"

"He went off with some soldiers to fight."

The girl said, "A bigger fool than I thought." She scampered off, Barak hurrying after her.

When dawn showed at the glassless window of his bedroom, Barak got up, still in uniform. Nakhama would have a fit, he thought, at the state of the flat. Shattered glass and blown-in rubbish were strewn all over the floor under layers of plaster dust. No electricity, no running water, no gas; appalling, yet they had been lucky. Across the street, a whole wall had blown off the building, and smashed furniture lay on the sidewalk or half hung out of wrecked rooms.

He had hardly slept. Visions of the embattled burning Quarter and concern about that crazy Don Kishote had haunted him, and the din of shelling had roused him whenever he dozed off. Had Kishote lived through the night? Such combat spirit in a fugitive Polish kid! Ben Gurion had been dead right about the Cyprus immigrants, setting foot on the soil of the Land did something to them.

Rapid hard knocks at the door broke into his reverie. He opened the door, and the first general of the Jews in two thousand years strode in bareheaded, still wearing his wrinkled khaki shirt and shorts, a rolled-up map under his arm. "Hi. Meeting laid on?"

"Yes, sir, 0730. Haganah headquarters."

"Excellent. Beautiful flight up here, in a two-seater, just a flea hop!" Marcus unrolled the map on a dusty table, pushing off shards of glass. "I see you've had some bomb blast. All Jerusalem's taking one hell of a beating, Zev. Breaks your heart to see it from the air. And say, Yadin commends your reconnoiter into the Quarter. So do I. Well done! Now look here, and speak your mind."

Studying the map as Marcus talked, Barak had immediate

strong doubts about the plan, a textbook encirclement of the entire Old City, requiring large forces and risking heavy casualties. He would have opted instead for a straight smash through the Zion Gate, only a hundred yards or so from the Quarter.

"Any comment?"

"No, sir." Speaking his mind at this late stage could not improve the plan, much less reverse it.

"Good. I've turned B.G. around on the bypass, Zev, he's going for it. The Seventh Brigade retook those two hilltop villages you pinpointed, and it's shaping up for the next Latrun attack. Things are really moving."

When they came out on the street Marcus paused at a sunlit board fence, where fresh placards were crudely slapped over older bills. "I barely remember the Hebrew from my bar mitzvah," he said. "It's damned frustrating. Tell me what those posters say."

Barak started with the black-bordered list of Haganah soldiers fallen during the past week. In the placard beside it, the military governor announced reduced food and water rations; and in big scare letters, with many exclamation marks, he threatened stiff penalties for hoarding and profiteering. The rest were political placards, parties denouncing one another for cowardice and suicidal policy, and also a notice of a chamber music concert by the "Municipal Emergency Council for Culture."

Marcus wryly laughed at the last one. "That's refreshing. Culture, no matter what, hey? The whole goulash is very Israeli, isn't it? Mainly politics, with lots of hot pepper."

"In our politics, we can't taste anything else."

They got into a muddy command car parked behind Barak's jeep, the only vehicles on the desolate street. Marcus said, "Let's go to the King David Hotel first, see if we can scare up some brandy there."

"The King David? It's closed, sir. It was the British HQ."

"I know, but there's a skeleton staff now. Refueling stop. I was up all night."

The hotel lobby was empty, the furniture sheeted. Barak managed to find a waiter in shirt sleeves, who with raised eyebrows brought Marcus a glassful of brandy, and a cup of tepid ersatz coffee for Barak. They drank out on the terrace. Smoke was rising above the walls of the Old City, and the rattle of small-arms fire echoed across the ravine.

"God, Jerusalem is so beautiful," Marcus said. "And such a goddamned setup for a siege."

"Since time immemorial," said Barak. "Since Sennacherib. And I'll never live anywhere else."

"That Quarter in there" — Marcus pointed at the smoke with the hand holding his brandy glass — "is the Jewish Alamo. You've heard of the Alamo?"

"Texas," said Barak. "The outpost that got massacred to the last man."

"Right. At West Point we used to argue whether that stand was heroism or folly. The Alamo was militarily indefensible. So's the Quarter. The boss man wants us to hang on for reasons of state, so that's that. Let's go."

Staff officers of the various forces crowded the war room of Jerusalem Command. Marcus's attack plan, as Barak translated it line by line at the map, brought glances among them, and coughs, and shufflings. One officer with a touch of gray in his hair remarked in careful English that the Haganah had long advocated exactly such an operation, but the other commands had dragged their feet. A Palmakh brigade leader protested in rapid Hebrew, an Irgun officer raised his voice to denounce the Haganah, and the meeting was spinning out of control when a woman soldier burst in with a scrawled despatch, and handed it to the Haganah commander. He read the Hebrew aloud in a choking voice. Total quiet. Drawn faces. Marcus looked to Barak for translation. "The Quarter is surrendering," Barak said.

"Who has signed that despatch," Marcus coolly inquired, "and what else does it say?"

Barak took the despatch and translated word for word. Motti Pinkus was reporting that a civilian delegation, with his reluctant permission, had asked the Red Cross this morning for the Arabs' terms. Jerusalem Command's failure to send help had gone on too long. A last-minute offer to parachute ammunition in was futile. *"There is nobody left to use the ammunition."* A delegation would leave the Jewish Quarter under a white flag at 9:30 A.M. to meet Red Cross and Arabs at the Zion Gate.

Marcus glanced at his watch. "That's in fifteen minutes." An abrupt gesture at his map. "The relief of the Quarter is cancelled."

"My post is on Mount Zion, Colonel," said a stocky Palmakh officer. "You can watch this happen, if you want to."

"I do," said Marcus.

From the roof of a monastery, a grim group of officers and civilians watched the delegation, under a dirty white sheet borne on two poles, walk out of the Jewish Quarter toward the Zion Gate. Hermann Loeb was there at Barak's elbow. "I stood on a hill, watching the people of Etzion getting slaughtered," he murmured. "Now I watch this."

Arab soldiers emerged from the shadows of Zion Gate, and led the delegation out of sight. The roof crowd dispersed like people at a funeral, with no smiles and few words. Marcus said to Barak as they descended deeply grooved stone steps, "Well, that's it. This means we're now probably racing a cease-fire. So *both* Latrun and the road are life-or-death urgencies, Zev. I'm flying back to Tel Aviv. You'll remain here as my liaison with Jerusalem Command. Ride with me to the airstrip."

On the way Barak could scarcely concentrate on Marcus's rapid instructions about defending Jerusalem. The Jewish Quarter gone! Motti Pinkus and all those worn-out young fighters in the night, marching off to captivity, if the Arabs weren't already mowing them down, cutting their throats, as they had done after the white-flag surrender at Etzion. And that poor madcap Don Kishote, among them because he, Barak, had brought him in and left him there. That did not bear dwelling on.

When the command car returned him to his house and stopped behind his jeep, Zev Barak was as nearly sunk in despair as he had been since the State had been declared. Some of the wisest Zionist leaders had been against the Declaration. The American Secretary of State, General Marshall, had gravely warned Ben Gurion not to take the fateful plunge. Had Ben Gurion led the Jewish people, already decimated by the Nazi massacre, into its final suicidal mistake?

A soldier had crawled into the back seat of the jeep, and was curled up asleep. Nothing unusual about that, but when Barak went to wake him up, he was stupefied. Smeared with dirt, his face scratched and bloody, a small flashlight protruding from a pocket, there lay Don Kishote.

4

Flour for Jerusalem

Whether Don Kishote had ever really driven a garbage truck on Cyprus or not — and Barak knew he was given to offhand romancing — he was handling the jeep well enough as they rolled down the highway. In the past couple of days, ever since the rough crawl through the tunnels to the Old City, Barak's wound had been flaring up inside the cast, and the aching and itching were maddening, so Kishote was at the wheel, and Barak was cradling the elbow in his other arm and trying not to think about it.

"Where are we going, sir?" Kishote inquired.

"Just watch what you're doing," Barak said irritably, squinting in the afternoon sun. "I'll direct you."

"Yes, sir."

Except for army trucks there was very little traffic, and Kishote's passing was risky but tolerable. Marcus had summoned Barak to join him at Hulda, for the second attack on Latrun; and instead of leaving Jerusalem in a Piper Cub, Barak had decided to go via the bypass and see what was happening there. The mule trains were already going, he knew, but no vehicles as yet.

"*Kishote,* for God's sake!"

"Sorry, sir." Kishote whipped the jeep back in line ahead of a tank truck, barely in time to let a lorry full of soldiers grind past the other way.

"No more of that. There's no hurry. Understood?"

"Understood, sir." An unabashed grin.

This youngster was an original, Barak thought. Certainly he did not lack brass or ingenuity. To lift a flashlight from a hospital under siege was not a saintly act (Kishote claimed he had "found it on the floor"), but it argued ruthless presence of mind; and he had clearly taken sharp note of Shayna's route via the cistern that night, and had groped his way back. Barak thought he would make Kishote a squad leader in any company he led, and would move him up to platoon leader fast. If he did not get himself killed he might amount to something.

The sun had gone down when they halted in a pileup of parked trucks on the Hartuv road, at the start of the bypass. Here in the fading twilight stomping braying mules were being unloaded and their burdens stacked on the trucks, amid coarse yells and curses by drivers and loaders, and a considerable stink of mule droppings. "It's not bad duty," remarked a burly bewhiskered army driver to Barak. "These mule guys bring you cigarettes, sometimes a drop to drink —"

"Food for the kids," said another. "Sardines, cheese —"

A third put in, "Yes, down in Tel Aviv they're living the life, all right, while we're starving and getting shelled. And where's Ben Gurion? Not in Jerusalem!"

As long as any light was left in the sky Kishote followed the downhill track of the bypass trodden by the mules, then switched on the low parking lights. The jeep careened and banged along, painfully jolting Barak's elbow. They began to pass astonishing masses of clanking and snorting road machinery, strung out for a mile or more in clouds of dust under scarcely visible kerosene lamps. Heavily laden mules were plodding up the trail, also bellowing droves of cattle, kicking up dust so thick that Kishote sometimes had to stop, or wander off into the trackless wadi, bouncing over stones and crevices.

It was a long tortuous nasty trip, and Barak had plenty of time to reflect on all this, and to worry that the prodigious road-building effort might well prove a pitiable aborted waste. Whatever Ben Gurion's military failings, his political instincts were keen. King Abdullah of Transjordan had already announced he was interested in a truce! And why not? With the Old City in his hands and Jerusalem ringed by his Arab Legion, he was now the one clear winner in the war. The superpowers had long been pressing for a truce; and while the other Arab governments were so far making conflicting noises about it, plainly little time remained to save Jerusalem.

Off beyond the ridge that hid Latrun came intermittent cannon thumps, and when the dust thinned, the flash of explosions; artillery barrages before the attack. The Seventh Brigade did have some heavy guns now, also more armored vehicles, as well as flame-throwers and mortars. The immigrant recruits had been blooded in battle and had drilled hard for almost a week. So maybe this time it would work! But Marcus's plan remained in essence a replay of the first failed operation, except for a diversionary attack at the rear of Latrun by a combat-worn Givati battalion pulled from the Egyptian front. Barak was going into this with less hope than foreboding. The command to attack *"again, at once,"* was a political decision, to be executed with whatever military means could be mustered.

At last the steep ascent at the other end loomed straight ahead, a sheer black cliff. A figure with a lamp approached through the swirling dust and growling bulldozers. "Is this Zev?"

"I'm Zev."

"Okay, I'll take the wheel." The figure eased the jeep a few yards to the right, and stopped.

"Now what?" inquired Barak.

"*Rega.*" ("One moment.") He vanished into very thick dust. Barak and Kishote sat and waited, coughing. Three dark figures approached. Two began banging at the front of the jeep. "You'll be winched up," said the one with the lamp. "No problem, just hang on. The main thing is — ah, there you go."

With a jerk the jeep lunged forward, tilting sharply upward

until the wheels barely touched ground. Overhead a cable screeched and scraped and a windlass whined, as they went up the rocky slope in bumpy joggles. Above the dust clouds there came in view a double line of moonlit men bending under large sacks, going down the serpentine turns of the trail. Some of them also carried guns, others dim lamps. The winch pulled the jeep to level ground, and shut off with a groan. Sam Pasternak stood by the cable drum, dust-caked and grinning. "How about that road, Zev? Progress, eh?"

"Amazing. The attack is on schedule?"

"Absolutely. Shin-hour is midnight. No change." He gestured at the line of stooped figures. "I'm just checking on these fellows."

"Flour?"

"Fifty-pound sacks. My idea. Two hundred men, two trips per man, ten tons of flour into Jerusalem per night, it's something."

"It's great, Sam. Army or civilians?"

"Mostly civilians. Volunteers."

"Kishote," said Barak, "get on this line and carry flour. At sunrise go back to my flat and wait."

"B'seder, sir." The tone was woeful. "I volunteer." Kishote climbed out of the jeep and trudged off to a queue at a truck, where flour sacks were being handed out.

"Could you see much of the road work down there?" Pasternak asked.

"Actually, what with the dark and the dust, not too much."

"Well, it's unbelievable! Five hundred road workers and stone-cutters are hard at it, Zev, and every bulldozer and steamroller operator in the country! We've posted plenty of patrols, too, to keep out Arab snoopers. By my life, I'm convinced the Legion doesn't yet suspect what's going on."

"How long before it's ready for truck convoys?"

"Maybe a week. Possibly less."

"Where's Colonel Stone?"

"At Hulda, expecting you. Let's go. I'll drive." Pasternak weaved through a clutter of trucks to a communications jeep where Yael Luria sat at the transmitter-receiver. She took her earphones off, and Pasternak shouted at her, "Follow us."

She nodded and called to Barak, "Where's your favorite idiot, Kishote?"

"Carrying flour to Jerusalem."

She burst out laughing.

"Zev, what's happening in the Quarter since it fell?" Pasternak inquired as he drove on. "We can't get any dope here."

"Well, in some ways that picture's better than we hoped. They're looting the houses, of course, and blowing up the synagogues. I was watching from Mount Zion, Sam, when the Hurva Synagogue went sky-high. By God, they used enough dynamite to blow up a pyramid! The ground shook under my feet like an earthquake, and —"

"Then in what way is it better, for God's sake?"

"Let me finish! Just before I left I met with the Red Cross woman. Nice gray-haired lady, Belgian. Her report was heartening, I tell you."

There had been no massacre, Barak emphasized. The British officers of the Legion had seen to it that the civilians were evacuated unharmed to a nearby village, and that the surviving fighters were being treated strictly according to the Geneva Convention. The Legion commander was astounded, the woman said, at how few, how young, and how ill-armed the defenders were. She quoted him: *"If we'd known, we'd have charged them with sticks and stones."*

"They'd better treat those kids well," Pasternak growled. "We've got prisoners, too. A hell of a lot more than they have."

"What's Yael Luria doing here, Sam?"

"My signal sergeant got sick. I coopted Yael," Pasternak said with a side-glance. "Smart kid. Quick on the uptake."

"Too smart."

"Did you see my father-in-law, by chance?"

"Yes, first thing. He's running food supply up there like a true Yekke. Discipline! *Befehl!*"

"Hermann's all right. Ruthie was the problem," Pasternak said wryly. "Yekke wife." Off in the Latrun direction came brilliant flashes, and after seconds the rolling crumps. "Zev, our new artillery teams are good. We've got a chance this time."

*

So as not to lose his way in the choking fog of dust, Don Kishote kept his eye on the bobbing sack in front of him. His sack was loosely fastened, the shifting straps galled his shoulders, but the strain, the pouring sweat, the slow rhythmic plod, felt pretty good, at that. After all, he was carrying bread to besieged Jerusalem, behind a short stout grayhead, and how could he do less than such an old man? The road workers whom they passed cheered them on with rough jokes. At a water cart along the way he drank big tin cupfuls, all he wanted. Never, not even in the worst transit camp, had water tasted so sweet.

On foot he could see much more than he had from the jeep. A week ago all this had been scrubby wasteland, and now there was a real road; narrow, winding, broken by stony outcroppings, but still a discernible dirt road. Stonecutters were attacking the obstructions by lamplight, and bulldozers were shoving aside the debris. The road was being built like a tunnel from both ends, for the work was much further along near the descent than in the middle; and toward the end the track once again widened and levelled out, with steam-rollers growling between heaps of stones along the sides. To reach the trucks the flour bearers had to pass through a herd of lowing cattle, and Kishote had stepped in so much mule and cow dung that he was resigned to each new slippery squish. His care was only not to fall down in it, as the man behind him did, with loud curses at the natural fact of shit.

After the long slow trudge of nearly two miles, the return march felt almost like dancing on air, so light and easy was progress without fifty pounds on his back. In no time at all, it seemed, he was frisking back up the trail at the other end. After eating and drinking their fill at an army field kitchen the bearers took on flour sacks again, and Kishote realized that his shoulders were rubbed raw, probably bloody, inside his uniform. But no complaints! Artillery was continuously thundering behind the black ridge, and the night sky was blazing yellow and red, so the second Latrun battle was on. He was enduring nothing compared to those fellows out there on the slopes of Latrun.

Early the next morning, so dirty and bedraggled as to be hardly recognizable, he was shambling along a Jerusalem street in the slant sunlight, utterly played out. Shayna almost dropped her brimming pail when she saw him. Was this really the bespectacled beanpole with the long serious face, who had stayed behind in the Quarter? "You! You're alive! You're not a prisoner!"

A tired prankish grin broke out on his face, where dust was streaked to mud by sweat. "Little Shayna," he croaked. "What's new?"

"Why are you so filthy? When did you get out of the Quarter, and how? I thought you were done for. Would you like a drink of water?"

"Definitely."

She handed him the pail, and he lifted it to his lips.

"Phew!" she said. "Were you sleeping in a stable?"

"I guess I don't smell so good." He hoisted up the pail, lifted his face, and dumped the water all over himself, exclaiming, "Ahh! Good." It was a blessed relief to his bloody shoulders.

"Eeek! Don't do that! *Stop! DON'T!* You're crazy! You're a criminal! That was for my family!"

"I'll get you more water."

"Where? How? The water cart is gone! It won't be back until the evening! You lunatic, that was for washing, for cooking, for everything!"

"Go on home. Tell Grandpa that the boy from Katowice is bringing the water." He stood there dripping, grinning, muddy, holding the empty pail, and she was inclined to pound him with her fists, but what good would that do? "Shayna, if I don't bring you water," he reassured the dumbstruck girl, "may I drop dead."

"Amen!" She ran off.

Her grandfather and mother were amazed by her story. "That boy Yossi is crazy," said the mother, a gaunt woman in her forties, wearing the prescribed pious wig, and the prescribed pious kerchief over the wig. "You'll never see him again, and you've lost our pail."

Reb Shmuel sat by the table, reviewing the Torah portion as he did every morning. "If he's so crazy, how did he get out of the Old City without Shayna? Is he an angel? He flies?"

"He didn't smell like an angel," said Shayna.

"You don't know how an angel smells," rapped her annoyed mother.

"I know an angel doesn't smell like a mule's . . . *that*," said Shayna. The Yiddish euphemism brought frowns on both faces.

"Well, there's no water to make tea or breakfast," said the mother, "so say your prayers, do your lessons, and watch your mouth."

Before long, there came a knock at the door of the closed tailor shop. Shayna rushed to open it and there stood Don Kishote, still damp all over, with two dripping pails of water.

"You again?" The girl tried to cover her relief with a sharp tone. "Well, come on in then."

Kishote was ready with a white lie about where he had gotten the water and the second pail — actually from the secret truck depot, where there was a special supply for the drivers and loaders — but Reb Shmuel invited him to breakfast with a smile and no questions. Shayna served them tea and coarse potato cake, then joined her mother in doing washing.

Kishote made a hit with the old tailor in three simple ways. He knew what the Torah portion of the week was, he put on his ragged army cap to make a blessing, and he spoke the correct benediction for a cake made of potatoes, not grain flour. The old man rewarded him by expounding subtly on the Torah text, and he listened with serious attention, nodding from time to time. It was a while before Reb Shmuel noticed that he had stopped nodding, and that his heedful look was fixed and glassy. Kishote was in fact fast asleep, sitting up with a rigid smile, his eyes wide open.

Long before daybreak, Barak knew that the second Latrun assault had also failed. He was with Marcus, observing the battle from a hill close to the fire zone — too close, he thought — and for a while victory seemed to be within grasp. The armored battalion succeeded in storming the fortress, and the flaming combat inside Latrun was lighting up the sky. Mickey Marcus, in high excitement over the gallant advance of the armor, was swigging brandy from a canteen as he paced, offering drinks to the other officers, and hanging on every new word from the battlefield. But then two of the busses bringing the infantry into the battle caught fire, whether from mines or artillery hits, and all the busses turned back; and not long after came the decisive blow. Barak talked to Colonel Shamir by field telephone, and had to relay the bad news to Marcus.

"Sir, Shlomo Shamir has finally raised the commander of the Givati battalion."

"Yes, yes, well? How's that attack in the rear going?"

"They ran into heavy resistance. They were taking unacceptable losses and couldn't advance. They're withdrawing."

Marcus said nothing for long moments, while nearby the guns inside Latrun volleyed and flared. He spoke in a changed voice. "What now, Haim?" Lieutenant Colonel Haim Laskov, the commander of armor, was conducting his battle from this vantage point.

"It'll be daylight in an hour, sir," said Haim. "Without infantry support I've got to pull my armor out of Latrun, or I'll lose it. I must ask Colonel Shamir to give that order. The attack hasn't succeeded. You agree, sir?"

Marcus looked to Barak, who nodded. Haim Laskov was perhaps the best professional officer in the army, and there was no countermanding him. After a pause, with a strange sarcastic smile, the American also nodded, and dropped down on the grass. *"For God's sake, let us sit upon the ground,"* he said, *"and tell sad stories of the death of kings . . ."* Barak had heard Marcus quote scraps of poetry before, mostly martial or comic verses. The lugubrious words and tone were new.

"I'll have that drink now, thank you, sir," said Lieutenant Colonel Laskov. He tilted the canteen to his mouth, took a good pull, and passed it back to Marcus.

Hulda kibbutzniks were eating breakfast that morning as usual in the dining hall, with much clatter of tin plates and cutlery. Most of the maps and signal gear of Marcus's improvised headquarters had been cleared away. In a corner by a wall map Marcus paced, dictating to Barak, phrase by bitter phrase, a battle summary. Colonel Shamir and Haim Laskov sat drinking coffee, glancing at each other as the account of the defeat took shape. Marcus was getting the facts right but the blame wrong, Barak thought. The battle had unfolded more or less as he had feared. A steep risk with inadequate forces had not paid off and that was that. Any blame lay with the political decision to attack.

"Conclusion!" Marcus barked. His eyes were bloodshot, his voice hoarse. He had long since emptied the canteen, but was quite sober. "I was there, start to finish. Observed the battle. Can sum up simply. Plan — good! Artillery — good! Armor — excellent! Infantry —" he paused, then growled, "disgraceful!"

"That's too strong," said Laskov.

"I don't think so. I think it's charitable."

"We don't have all the facts, sir," said Shamir. "An inquiry is certainly called for, but —"

"Damned right, and there *will* be an inquiry, starting today. We have plenty of facts already. The reserves turned back because a few busses caught fire. Givati turned back because they had *two killed*. The battalion commander reported this himself! Two!"

"In both cases, sir, companies mostly of green recruits," put in Barak, "trying to storm heights under heavy fire. Not an outstanding performance, true, but —"

"That's my report," said Marcus. "Now let's all get some sleep. Then we figure out how we try again. The Old Man wants Latrun, and I'll deliver Latrun to him, but next time it will be a new plan, and *my own plan,* A to Z!"

Later in the week, in the dead of night, Marcus was walking with Barak in a swirl of stone dust to inspect a bottleneck of the bypass. Here mules and porters were laboring down and up the slopes of a wide rift, for the road engineers had ruled that trucks could not traverse the dip, and had ordered a straight cut through a granite outcropping. Dozens of stonecutters, all that could be found in Israel, were hammering and clanking away. Blasting was forbidden, so this and other stretches of the mountain bypass were being hewed by hand, as in ancient times. Beyond the ridge gunfire once again arched, boomed, and flared, for the early probes of the third Latrun attack were on.

"By God, tell these guys I'm proud of them!" exclaimed Marcus. "I want to shake hands with every man."

Marcus went among the stonecutters, shaking hands, slapping backs, examining the tools, sparking excited talk in several languages — Hebrew, Yiddish, Italian, Polish, German, Russian, Arabic, and some babble quite alien to Barak. Marcus spoke English, letting Barak translate, and the very sound of it seemed to exhilarate these Jews from all over. Here was the fabled friend, the Jewish general who had left safe America to risk his neck, create the wonderful road, and free Jerusalem! Marcus's good cheer was invigorating workmen all along the road.

But riding back to Tel Aviv, Marcus sank into silent gloom, which Barak could well understand. There was no heart in the general staff for still another thrust at Latrun. The demoralized and broken Seventh Brigade was now merely guarding the bypass and carrying flour; and a veteran brigade had been pulled out of the northern front to try yet again to take the fortress. Only Ben Gurion could have forced the staff to risk leaving the north unguarded against Syrian assault, and even that brigade was attenuated and battered, its muster filled up with raw recruits as the Givati battalion had been; and Givati had failed in the second attack because its best fighters had fallen battling the Egyptians, and the new troops had panicked. In plain truth the army was nearing the end of its rope.

"I'm in a bind, Zev," Marcus spoke up. "On the basis of what we've seen of the bypass, I can't tell the Old Man to call off this next attack. Those road men are working their hearts out, but the road just won't do the job, it can't take truck convoys."

"Not yet. It will soon."

"Irrelevant. As of now it's still a mule track, and the assault has to go in the next forty-eight hours, if at all. That's the bind. I'm not thrilled at sending more Jewish boys to storm Latrun, but I'm a soldier and I'm going to do it."

The walls of Marcus's inner office were covered with war maps, except for pictures of Herzl and Ben Gurion. He sat down at his desk under Herzl, handed Barak the operation order for the third attack, and glanced through piled despatches and letters. The hollows under his eyes, accentuated by the harsh fluorescent light, were deep and black. Never a spic-and-span sort, he needed a shave, and though his fringe of hair was brownish the three-day growth on his face was all gray. He drooped lower in his chair as he skimmed papers, shaking his head, tightening his lips, and yawning. Neither man had yet slept that night.

Barak's arm and shoulder ached, and he hung the crooked cast over the chair back while he read Marcus's operation order. Here was work of a staff man par excellence, like the manuals Marcus had written for the army at Ben Gurion's request. The mimeographed papers brought back British army days. Here were detailed maps of each sector, annexes for logistics, transport, and intelligence, a meticulous order of battle. L'Azazel, what an effort! Only, the document was a fantasy. The array of forces, formidable on paper, was in fact a list of eroded and broken units, some so far below complement as to be little more than memories. Available supplies would fall far short of the logistics annex. The attack plan — a frontal assault yet again, but this time a deception, while the main surprise punch came from the brigades around Jerusalem — was professionally conceived, but the fresh manpower to bring it off was not there. So Barak gloomily estimated.

"Not much cheer in this stuff." Marcus passed him despatches from several units assigned to the operation, reporting difficulties, delays, breakdowns, and shortages. One commander recommended postponement; another, a different plan to relieve Jerusalem, using the forces now in place. "No stomach for the fight, Zev, that's what they're all really telling me. As though Latrun is my idea," said Marcus, with a frustrated gesture. He pulled open a desk drawer, produced a bottle and two glasses, and grinned. "Firewater?"

"Why not?"

"How are you on World War I poetry, Zev?"

> *If I should die, think only this of me:*
> *That there's some corner of a foreign field*
> *That is forever England.*

"Rupert Brooke — heard that one often enough in North Africa," said Barak moodily, "over fresh graves."

Marcus poured himself a full glass, drank deep, and recited the poem to the last word in a tired voice, moisture glistening in his eyes. " '. . . *In hearts at peace, under an English heaven.*' "

"It's beautiful," said Barak.

"There's another poem that's been running through my mind for days."

> *I have a rendezvous with Death*
> *At some disputed barricade.* . . .

He was looking straight into Barak's eyes, his expression somber and drawn. "Ever heard it?"

Barak reluctantly sipped brandy, feeling something like pity for the first Jewish general in two thousand years. How to lift the spirits of this beset outsider, this well-meaning fish out of water, burdened by David Ben Gurion with a thankless command and a hopeless mission?

"Sir, may I say something?"

"Go ahead." Marcus refilled his own glass and drank.

"These Latrun attacks have thrown the Legion way off balance. Otherwise they'd surely have sallied out to kill the road workers and blow up the bypass."

"Well, that's probably true."

"It's a fact, sir. You've prevented that. By now they must know what we're up to. They've even planted mines to try to stop us, but they haven't been able to. What's more, the Legion hasn't moved to capture Jerusalem. Their golden chance is running out unused, because they're split between Jerusalem and Latrun."

Wanly smiling, Marcus took a long drink. "Okay, Zev, you're trying to cheer me up. It's appreciated. I could just get on an airplane and go home, you know. My wife thinks this isn't my fight. I told you that. I'm sending more and more kids to get killed at Latrun for one reason. I think the Old Man is a wise tough old bastard, probably a great man, and I'm a Jew, so I'm carrying out his orders." He resumed reciting.

> *When spring comes back with rustling shade,*
> *And apple blossoms fill the air.*

I have a rendezvous with Death
When spring brings back blue days and fair . . .

The sadness in his tone and face hurt and scared Barak. He set his glass on the desk, intending to ask permission to leave. Marcus was smiling in the strange sarcastic way he had smiled on the embankment, realizing that the first battle he had launched as commander was a fiasco. He spoke the entire poem, and at the last words,

And I to my pledged word am true,
I shall not fail that rendezvous . . .

he lifted his glass to Barak, to Herzl's picture, and to Ben Gurion's picture, and he drained it. "Zev, you're not drinking your firewater."

"Thanks, Colonel, I've had plenty."

"Probably not a great poem," said Marcus, "I'm no judge of poetry. But by God, it says what a soldier thinks when he's low. Now, what about my op order?"

"First of its kind in this army," said Barak.

Marcus nodded, pleased. "You guys will have to learn. You've got a country now, and by God you'll have to fight for it. Your kids, too. Maybe your grandchildren. After 1776 came 1812, you know. Civil War, World War I, World War II —" He glanced at the gray windows. "Christ, it's morning, me lad. Let's get about our business."

5

The Road Is Ours

Yael Luria came off twelve straight hours of runner duty, fagged out and soaked in sweat, for the June nights in Tel Aviv were becoming very humid and hot. In the bathroom of the women's barracks, covered with soap from head to foot, she was eking out a shower in the weak warm trickle from failing plumbing when a shout echoed at her, "Yael, telephone. Red House."

"To all the devils!"

A quick incomplete rinse, a dash to the wall telephone. "Can you be here in fifteen minutes?" inquired Zev Barak.

"What? I just got off duty. I thought you were in Jerusalem."

"Put on a fresh uniform and look your best."

"What is this?"

"It's an order."

Yael took a bit longer than fifteen minutes, but when she arrived at the Red House she was prettied up as though for a fund-raising poster, and soldiers lounging outside Barak's office whistled. Zev was on the telephone, amid rough-looking civilians crowded around his desk. Yigal Yadin sat beside him, smoking his pipe. "The truck convoy is ready, Colonel Stone," Barak was saying. "I've got most of the drivers here with me. It can go anytime. Small trucks, twenty-five or so, about seventy tons of supplies."

A pause. Yael knew that "Colonel Stone" was in headquarters outside Jerusalem, preparing to conduct another Latrun attack, but what had this to do with her?

"Yes, sir, of course there's a risk. But if the world press announces tomorrow that there's a road and the siege has been lifted, we'll have created a tremendous fact."

A long pause. Barak shook his head at Colonel Yadin. "I'll tell him, sir." He covered the phone. "He's dubious. If anything happens to those correspondents, he says — a mine, a sniper, an accident, whatever — we've blown the secret, created a catastrophe, and probably lost the road."

"I'll talk to him. . . . Mickey? Yigal. Shlomo Shamir's brigade is out in force, patrolling the bypass. He reports it's clear. The truce doesn't take effect for another thirty-six hours, so — no, I'm right, sir, ten A.M. on the eleventh. After the truce the Arabs are bound to assert that it's not a passable road. The UN truce commission will back them up, of course — that goes without saying — and award the city of Jerusalem to King Abdullah. But we can preempt all that with headlines about a truck convoy that breaks the siege and enters Jerusalem the day before the truce begins. Sir, I recommend that we take this risk."

A long pause, indistinct telephone sounds. Yadin hung up. "Green light," he said, and went out.

"It's on," Barak said to the drivers, glancing at a wall clock that showed half-past midnight. "Round up the rest of the guys and finish the loading. We go at 0200." They hurried out, all talking at once. Barak looked Yael up and down. "Had anything to do with foreign correspondents?"

"No."

"Come along, and be very sweet. Try, anyhow."

"At your orders, Major." With the honeyed tones went a burlesque batting of huge eyes.

"Excellent."

They went outside, and there was Don Kishote sitting at the

wheel of Barak's jeep. He pushed his glasses up on his nose with a forefinger, grinning at her. "Oo-ah! Rita Hayworth!"

She worked the eyes and the sexy voice at him. "Don't exaggerate, Kishote."

"How's your brother Benny?"

"All better. Back on duty."

"Great."

As they drove through blacked-out empty streets Barak told Yael that she would act as army liaison with two foreign correspondents, in the first truck convoy to Jerusalem in many weeks. Kishote would be her dogsbody. They would all ride in Shlomo Shamir's command car, Yael supplying feminine charm to keep the journalists amused. "I don't know about this Reuters fellow, St. John Robley," said Barak. "Robley's one of these tall Englishmen with grayish hair and pink jowls. Reuters has been giving us rather hostile coverage. Naturally, it's a British service. But it's worldwide, and very important. The *Los Angeles Times* man is Saul Schreiber. Little redheaded guy. Jewish, talks Yiddish. Not a heavyweight like Robley, but smart."

They found Schreiber and Robley waiting as agreed in a dim corner of the lobby of the hotel where the press stayed. Schreiber had with him photographic equipment and an overnight bag. Robley had only a cigar, which he lit and smoked as Barak told them what was up.

"You mention hazards. What hazards?" asked the Englishman, with a skeptical squint at this odd-looking threesome purporting to bring him a major scoop — a young officer with one arm in a sooty cast, a painted-up pretty girl soldier in a bandbox uniform, and a skinny bespectacled youth in very shabby khakis and a Palmakh wool cap.

"Well, sir, there will be a battle in progress in the area. We'll be travelling safely clear of the firing zone, but that's one hazard. The road is new, and still being worked on. The convoy will drive without lights. It's the dark of the moon."

Robley grunted. Schreiber scratched his head.

"Besides, though the road's a well-guarded secret — and

strongly patrolled — the convoy will be breaking a long siege, and the enemy's still out there."

"Major, what do you call a convoy?" Schreiber asked.

"Some thirty trucks," said Barak, shading the figures in his press relations capacity, "carrying about a hundred tons of supplies."

Robley raised bushy eyebrows. "A hundred tons? Going to Jerusalem *tonight*?"

"Leaving in an hour. Arriving in Jerusalem about sunrise."

"Your government is prepared, then, to give away the secret of this road?"

"Why not? The way to Jerusalem is open now, and will stay open."

Another grunt, and a long puff on the cigar. In her most charming British Mandate accent, Yael said to Robley, lightly touching his arm, "Sir, Yossi here can help you with your luggage."

Unsmiling, but his eyes somewhat friendlier, he said to her, "Luggage? What for? If I go, and if there's a story, I'll want to get right back here to cable it."

"We've arranged cable facilities in Jerusalem," said Barak. "A Jerusalem dateline might be interesting."

"What about the military censor?" Schreiber asked.

"Available in Jerusalem, too." Barak added to Robley, "Of course, we can also return you at once to Tel Aviv, by the road or by Piper Cub. But we think the relief of Jerusalem is quite a story, and you may care to remain overnight, or even for a day or two. If so, a suite in the King David Hotel will be at your disposal. It's closed, but special service will be available for you."

"I'm ready to go," said Schreiber.

Robley crushed out the cigar, stood up, and said to Kishote, "Come along, young fellow."

The shadowy column of parked trucks southeast of Tel Aviv stretched far ahead into the starlit Jerusalem highway. As Barak's jeep drove to the front of the convoy, the renewed combat at Latrun threw brilliant flares like summer lightning on the sky ahead.

"You truly believe," Robley asked Barak, "that the Arabs won't try to stop this convoy? There are Arab towns all along the way! Surely the word will travel fast —"

"We've been using the bypass quite a while now, sir, for lighter traffic. That's how Jerusalem's held out until now, and the enemy hasn't interfered. Anyway, our Seventh Brigade is on road guard. I don't expect to be stopped." He peered over his shoulder at the back seat, where Yael sat pressed between the journalists. "But frankly, this won't be a drive through Kew Gardens in lilac time, if you want to change your mind."

Silence in the back seat. A grunt, and then a high-pitched laugh from Robley. "Actually, Major, in lilac time one walks through Kew Gardens, and talking about hazards, one can get trampled by the crowds."

Engines started with roars all along the line, and the convoy rolled out on the highway, winding without lights through the Ayalon valley, a vague long shadow creeping in the night, except when gunfire flashes lit the trucks with brief lurid glare. At the Hulda kibbutz Barak's party joined Shlomo Shamir and his driver in Shamir's shielded command car, all but Kishote, who followed with the jeep, now filled by soldiers with tommy guns. The two correspondents kept scrawling notes by flashlight as they passed huge earth-moving machinery, herds of cattle, and porters and mules loading up from massive trucks. This approach part of the bypass was now wide, level, and well graded. Artillery pounded and thundered beyond the high ridge, and the sky in moments turned to fiery day. The ingenuity of the bypass was self-evident here, and Schreiber said as much with open admiration. Not a word out of the Englishman.

The one patch of the bypass that was really worrying Barak was the first plunge at the steep descent. "Hey! Roller coaster!" exclaimed Schreiber, watching the armored vehicles ahead of the command car vanish one by one over the edge.

"Exactly, shoot-the-chutes, hang on and enjoy the ride," said Zev Barak with shaky jollity. At Hulda, headquarters' early reports about the third attack had not been good. All might well depend now on the road.

The command car went over the edge and dived down groaning in low gear, rocking and bumping, the steel netting squealing beneath the car. Barak's advice to hang on was no joke; the hood seemed to be plunging straight down into blackness, though he knew the angle was within a calculated safety limit. They all clung to some projection. Schreiber kept saying, "Ee-yow! Ee-yow!" Yael merrily laughed, clinging to both journalists in mock terror, and Robley yielded a grunt or two. As they dove they could see porters and mules scuffling dust up and down the long hairpin turns of the trail. The engineers had been unable to make that trail ready for trucks, and had cut instead a very short steep temporary roadway which they had covered with steel netting. Barak had made it up and down the netting several times in the jeep, although once he had needed rescue by the winch. This part was touch and go, especially on the climb. He was gambling that the two correspondents would go back to Tel Aviv by plane, or maybe via Latrun after the cease-fire. Finally, the command car bounded out on the wadi bottom, where the armored cars waited. "Hell of a ride," said Schreiber, somewhat breathless.

Robley inquired, "Trucks can manage that drop?"

"Of course."

"Shall we stand by and watch a few?"

"Why not?" said Barak, forcibly reminded that some Englishmen tended to be too damned astute.

One after another, trucks poked their hoods over the brink and came screeching and grinding down. Each truck traversed the steel netting alone, with another waiting at the top to follow, and each descent was a suspenseful show. One top-heavy truck going too fast tilted on two wheels and teetered for scary seconds before righting itself and plunging to level ground.

"Well," said Robley after half a dozen such hairbreadth displays with happy endings, "I suppose we should proceed."

"Done," said Barak, and the command car with its escort ran bumpily to the head of the convoy.

"And all this, I gather," remarked Robley as they drove on in choking dust from the armored cars, "is the doing of that American general."

A long awkward silence. "American general?" Barak said with blank wonderment.

"Yes, one hears that a West Point general, a Jew, under an assumed name, has secretly taken charge of your war, which is why it's going better."

"It's going better," snapped Colonel Shlomo Shamir, from the front seat — he had been silent until now — "because our soldiers are whipping their soldiers. The enemy's been outfought, though we were invaded on five fronts, and far outmatched in numbers and weaponry."

"I've read your despatches, sir," said Barak more genially to Robley. "You've reported that generalship has little to do with this diffuse war, and you're probably right. It's being fought on the platoon and company level. If we're doing better, and that remains to be seen, it's because we're fighting for our homes, our farms, and our families, with our backs to the sea. Not too unlike your country in 1940 facing Hitler."

"No truth at all then" — cool persistence — "to this report of an American general?"

"Oh, it's true," Yael spoke up, "so why not admit it? An American general is running the whole war."

"What!" Schreiber exclaimed, while Barak turned to stare at her.

"Yes, David Ben Gurion is really an American general. He's fooled everybody for years." This went with a silly little girlish giggle, and a nudge of an elbow in the Englishman's ribs.

St. John Robley grunted, the others laughed, and Barak made a mental note to commend Yael. Just right for this job. No more was said about the American general.

As the slow ride dragged on, conversation lagged and died. There was almost nothing to see in the darkness and the all-encompassing dust. Yael Luria's excitement gave way to accumulated fatigue and, joggled and shaken though she was, she dozed off. The car windows were no longer black but violet when she opened her eyes, and found a head resting on her shoulder, the *Los Angeles Times* man dead asleep. St. John Robley was sitting up straight, smoking a cigar that glowed scarlet when he puffed.

"What happened?" she yawned. "We're riding so smoothly."

"We're on the highway to Jerusalem," Robley said.

"On the highway? We *are*?"

Saul Schreiber woke at these words. "The *highway*? No kidding!"

"We left the bypass a while ago," said Zev Barak. "I hope you feel rested."

"By my life," Yael said, looking back, "this is a sight!"

The procession of trucks in the dawn stretched down the curving two-lane paved road, up a rise and out of view. "I swear to God," Saul Schreiber said, peering through the rear window, "you people have pulled it off. Absolutely fantastic!"

"Mmph," said St. John Robley.

It was bright day when the command car rolled into Jerusalem. Barak had no idea how the people had learned the convoy was coming. Such news, he supposed, could not be suppressed. They lined the sidewalks waving at the passing trucks and fluttering Star of David flags; young and old, civilians and army, women with water pails and babes in arms, children gambolling alongside the convoy like dolphins by a ship. The soldiers in the armored cars and Kishote's jeep perked up and began to sing. Waving back at the people, Yael made subdued weeping sounds.

"What the devil are you snivelling about?" exclaimed Robley, looking unmoved and a touch disdainful at the happy shabby Jerusalem Jews.

"Who's snivelling? You journalists are expected at the King David Hotel, sir, by the Jerusalem Command. Breakfast will be ready when you get there."

"I'll have coffee and go to my suite," said Schreiber, "to bat off my story. Afterwards maybe, breakfast."

Robley nodded agreement. "One understood," he said, glancing up at the facade of the King David when they pulled into the driveway, "that you Jews blew up this hotel and killed a lot of Englishmen. You've patched the place up, I see."

"We Jews regarded that as a disaster," said Barak, "and condemned the perpetrators."

"Price of empire," said St. John Robley. He shrugged and got out of the car. "Nothing like India, you know. Hindus and Moslems butchering each other by the thousands right now, and British Tommies caught between them."

Kishote's jeep stopped behind the command car, and he came up to Barak and Yael with another soldier. "Guess what? This is my brother Leopold," he said. "He's been at Hulda, doing road patrol. His squad was assigned to the convoy."

Leopold Blumenthal looked a few years older than Kishote, and he was much shorter. His thick hair was well groomed, his uniform fitted, and he had an alert shrewd air about him. No glasses, sharp greenish eyes, features like Yossi's but handsomer; a man of the world at twenty or so. Refugee kids matured fast, Barak thought, and he said to Yossi, gesturing at the luggage, "Maybe your brother can help you. These press fellows are in a hurry."

"Who are they?" put in Leopold.

Yael told him.

"Okay," he said, switching to Polish-accented English and addressing Schreiber with smiling deference. "Which is your stuff, mister?" Leopold's English was much better than his brother's. Picking up Schreiber's bags and photo equipment, he followed the correspondent up a staircase and into an exceedingly musty room with closed slatted blinds. "You're really from Los Angeles, mister? That's where I intend to go."

Schreiber wrestled in vain with the clumsy antique blinds. Leopold could not budge them, either. Yael came in, inquiring, "Everything all right? Oh, let me." With no trouble she pulled the blinds rattling up, and caught her first sight in months of the lost Old City, the sunlit ancient golden walls under the blue sky of morning, and the no-man's-land in the ravine below, full of barbed wire, shell craters, broken structures, sandbags, and other detritus of war. "Poor Jerusalem," she said after a silence, and went out touching a handkerchief to her eyes.

Schreiber snatched a camera from a leather bag, exclaiming, "What a knockout of a view!"

"Mister, we had a real chance to go to America," Leopold said, as Schreiber shot picture after picture, "when we were in the DP camp in Italy. But no, my father wanted only Palestine, Palestine, so we landed on Cyprus. And here we are."

Schreiber set aside his camera, opened his portable typewriter and set it on a table. "And you'd rather be in Los Angeles than here? You're not a Zionist?"

"Plenty of Zionists in America, mister, no?"

"Well, Los Angeles is a tough town. Don't let the movies fool you."

"Can I come and see you there at your newspaper?"

Schreiber turned on the tap in a sink. Nothing happened, so he sloshed his face with water from a basin and jar. As he dried with a faded towel, and the chummy youth showed no sign of going, he said, "Look, soldier, I have work to do."

"I'm not really a soldier," said Leopold. The correspondent sat down and started typing rapidly, and Leopold left.

Accustomed to urgent deadlines, Schreiber had his story written in half an hour. He sealed it in a large envelope and delivered it to Zev Barak, who was waiting in the lobby on one of the sheeted couches. "Breakfast in there," Barak said, indicating the dining room, "if you're interested."

"Hell, yes. You'll take that copy on to the censor?"

"Yes sir, soon as Mr. Robley gives me his material."

"Right. Let me know if there's a problem."

Barak sat drumming his fingers on the envelope, tapping his feet, his eyes on the staircase and the elevator. From the dining room, where the Los Angeles man joined the Jerusalem Command staff, bursts of male laughter betokened a good mood, but Barak thought the jollity must be forced. The reports from Latrun were sounding worse and worse. The Arabs had certainly held their ground again, that was already clear, though he did not yet know what exactly had gone wrong with Marcus's plan.

The flannel-clad legs of St. John Robley came down the stairs, then the tweed jacket, the wool tie, the ruddy face and gray hair. Barak strode to meet him, and was handed a folder of clipped papers. "There's my article. If the censor passes it, please file it at the cable facility, highest priority. Otherwise bring it back, and I'll fight your fellow after I've had my breakfast. The Tel Aviv chap can be a nuisance, but he and I have been muddling along." This was as lengthy a statement as Barak had ever heard from him. "By the bye, if you want to read it, you may."

"I appreciate that."

"Oh, I daresay you would anyhow." More laughter from the dining room drew his glance. "Is there anything decent to eat?"

"Kippers and eggs, for one thing."

"Kippers! Mmph."

Barak darted into the men's room to scan the story. At the first paragraph a sense of relief flooded him. He wanted to cheer. He saluted himself in the mirror, ran out to the jeep, and ordered Kishote to speed to headquarters. Kishote's brother was asleep in the back seat.

"You look happy, Major," said Kishote, "how come? I hear we lost the battle."

"Who told you that?"

A thumb jerked to the back seat.

"What the hell does your brother know, and how?"

"Well, he's wrong sometimes."

The censor was a long-nosed Haganah major named Podotzur. Barak knew him well, a mediocre platoon leader, then a disastrous company commander. Sidetracked from combat, he felt ill-used and was a crabby censor. Podotzur slowly scanned the stories, grumbling all manner of objections, until Barak picked up the censor's army telephone. "Operator, this is Major Zev Barak. Do you have Colonel Stone's personal command number in Abu Ghosh? Good, get him right away."

"Wait, wait, Zev," said Podotzur. "What's all this?"

"Clearing those stories as written is a national urgency, Podotzur. I have to report that you won't release them."

Podotzur knew, as everyone in the army now knew, that Zev Barak was close to the Old Man and to Colonel Stone, the oddball American liked by some, resented by many, but undisputed boss of Jerusalem Command. "Hang up. Will you put that in writing?"

"Put what?"

"That national urgency statement. And sign it as Colonel Stone's deputy?"

Barak seized a pad and a pen and scrawled a chit. Clipping it to a long mimeographed form, Podotzur began methodically to fill in the blanks.

"Look Podotzur, I must talk to Colonel Stone on a secret matter. Will you step outside? I'll report your cooperation and commend you." Podotzur gathered up the forms with a defeated shrug and went out.

Marcus sounded spent and old, his voice almost a croak. "It's very bad, Zev, much worse than last time. Great plan, but terrible foul-ups in communication, not enough manpower —"

"Sir, the convoy made it safely and sailed into Jerusalem, people were out in the streets cheering —"

"Yes, yes, so we've heard. But the intelligence is that the Arabs will counterattack tonight, south of Latrun. If they reach Hulda the road's kaput. We'll be ready for them, but —"

"Colonel, I've got the press accounts of the convoy here. Podotzur's just cleared them. Please listen to Reuters. Just the lead. It's very dramatic —"

"Well, go ahead."

" *In a remarkable show of their ability to improvise, the Israelis have opened a new and secret road bypassing Latrun to link Jerusalem to the Tel Aviv front. This development transforms the truce picture, and could prove the turning point of the war . . .'*"

"Zev, that's Reuters?"

"Reuters, sir. Good old anti-Israel Reuters! The *Los Angeles Times* is even better."

"Christ, go on with Reuters, Zev."

" *This correspondent travelled in a command car at the head of a convoy which last night trucked a hundred tons into Jerusalem, decisively breaking the siege. There was no enemy interference . . .'*"

"By God, I don't *believe* this! Read on, it's adrenaline!"

" *It was a rough ride, bucking and bouncing in a fresh-cut road which climbs, dips, and winds through the rugged wild Judean hills.*

Gunfire around Latrun lit up the sky, but on the road soldiers prodded along cattle and loaded mules, human chains of porters trudged peacefully in both directions . . .' "

As Barak read off the three pages, Marcus kept interjecting, "Marvellous! . . . Wonderful! . . . Outstanding!"

"Listen to how he winds up, sir. *'Whatever one's views of Israel's politics, the construction of this miniature "Burma Road" in the shadow of defeat is a stunning military coup. Together with their demonstrated competence in the field, it confirms the Jews as a force to be reckoned with hereafter in the Middle East.' "*

"That's it? That's the end? It sounds almost like an editorial."

"That's it. He's got a big scoop, and he's making the most of it. Reuters! Front page tomorrow in every capital in the world! Want to hear the *L.A. Times?*"

"Never mind. 'The Burma Road'!" Marcus laughed like a boy. "Terrific! Hold everything, Zev, I have to tell this to Colonel Allon."

Barak could hear the deep voice of Allon, a kibbutz farmer in his twenties, a hardened Palmakh commander, in animated converse with Marcus, who soon came back on the line. "Allon's tremendously moved, Zev, and you know what? We're going to defy the Old Man! He's been after us to attack Latrun yet *again*! Tonight! Fourth time! He's crazed! Yitzhak Rabin is down in Tel Aviv arguing with him right now. It's been going on for hours. Now I can tell him, *forget it,* and I will! Jerusalem is saved, and not another Jewish boy is going to die at Latrun!"

"You've done it, Colonel. You pushed the road through."

"Well, there's plenty of credit to go around. Meantime there's that Arab attack tonight, but Allon assures me we'll crush them! Look, come to my Abu Ghosh headquarters, Zev, and we'll talk."

"I've got those press guys on my hands, sir. Got to baby them."

"Agreed. Just come when you can."

"Yes, sir. So we have a rendezvous at Abu Ghosh."

Marcus guffawed. "Good memory, me boy, and a mighty different rendezvous, hey? Rendezvous with life! A whole new ball game, Zev! You people are wonderful, you've pulled off a miracle, you've held on to the beachhead by your fingernails." Marcus's spirit was soaring, it rang in his voice. "By God, maybe I was born to save Jerusalem, but if that's so, it's done! Now everything starts!"

The Blumenthal brothers wandered into the King David dining room as Yael was checking over the bill with the headwaiter, and Barak was talking to the hotel manager. The officers and journalists were gone, and plenty of food was left in platters on the table: fish, cheese, meat, and cakes. "Leopold wants to ask you something," Kishote said to Yael. She ignored them and went on arguing about the price of items, while Leopold helped himself heartily to the food until an old waiter in a stained apron came up and snarled, causing him to desist with a last fast filch of a cheese wedge.

"*Mah ha'inyan?* [What's up?]" Yael inquired of Leopold, as she signed the bill.

"How do I get out of the army?"

She gave him a chilly stare, up and down. "You don't."

"Why not? I didn't volunteer, I was put into uniform the day we landed in Haifa. I have to get a job to support our father, he isn't well. There's a truce tomorrow. If there's another war, well, I'll join up."

"Don't bother me. Talk to your platoon commander."

"That shithead? I don't think he can read or write."

Yael decided to be offended. He had some of his brother's peculiar buoyancy, but he was too fresh by half. She hitched a shoulder and walked out.

"*Ayzeh hatikha!* [What a piece!]" exclaimed Leopold devilishly to Kishote, in recently acquired slang.

Upon returning Barak to his flat, Kishote got permission to use the jeep, and drove to the tailor shop. "Wait," he said to his brother, and he carried two large paper sacks inside. "Reb Shmuel, some food from Tel Aviv."

"So! You came with the convoy!" The old man gestured at the back door, smiling. "Shayna and her mother are in the kitchen."

Kishote had been in the dark little apartment only once before. Passing through the gloomy hallway, he opened what he thought was the kitchen door. Shayna stood in a tin tub, her back to him, luxuriantly squeezing a large sponge over her head, a pink slim Eve pretty as a flower. *"AI!"* She saw him in a looking glass and flung the sponge over her shoulder, a mirror shot that got him square in the face. He backed out, slamming the door.

"Fool, give me back my sponge!" It was rolling on the floor, but with his glasses gone and his eyes drenched he was blind.

"First you give me back my glasses!"

"They're not here, fool. Oh, yes, here they are." A dripping white hand and arm reached out. "Take them, fool."

Shayna's mother appeared in the hallway. "What's going on? Hello, Yossele." She picked up the wet sponge, and exclaimed at the door, "Shayna, what nonsense is this?"

"Oh, Mama, go away," cried the girl in a singularly mature tone, and the naked arm snatched the sponge.

Soon the two brothers were greedily downing bread and soup at the kitchen table. "So tell me, Leopold," the mother inquired, "what do you think of Jerusalem, now that you've seen it?"

"Lots of damage."

"Yes, but that we'll repair."

"It's nice. Just a small town, though, not like Tel Aviv."

Shayna entered, drying her long black hair with a towel. "God in heaven," she blurted to her mother, "is that idiot still here?"

"Meet my brother Leopold," said Kishote, unoffended. "He's no idiot."

"Faugh!" The girl stamped out.

"The war has upset Shayna," her mother said. "Pay no attention."

Leopold thanked the mother and left to find his unit. She smiled approval as Yossi said an after-meal grace. "How is it that you're religious and not your brother? He ate without a blessing, no hat, no grace."

"The war has upset Leopold."

*

Barak took the two correspondents to Mount Zion that afternoon, so they could see the dynamited synagogues in the Old City, and the great ancient cemetery on the Mount of Olives being used as a quarry, the gravestones trucked away openly for construction or paving. The Palmakh commander there, David Elazar, was short but imposing, a charming Yugoslavian Jew who knew almost no English, and so could not be questioned too closely. Elazar led Barak and the correspondents to a high point on the Mount. "This was as far as we could advance," he said, Barak translating. "We did push patrols into the Jewish Quarter, but there wasn't the manpower to keep the lines open, and we had to pull out. So the Quarter fell."

"Then you've lost the Old City for good," said Schreiber, "if this truce leads to peace."

"We have a saying — 'If my grandmother had wheels, she'd be a carriage.' "

St. John Robley inquired sharply, "You don't believe the truce will hold?"

Elazar took his time about replying. The soldiers of his unit were gathered around, their eyes alight with regard for their commander. "Well, I think we'll get the Old City back," David Elazar drawled, "though I admit I don't know when or how."

Until darkness fell, Barak drove the correspondents here and there to the many battle sites of besieged Jerusalem, where they talked with the commanders still on guard. By the time they headed back to the King David, shells were sailing from the Old City over Jerusalem in arches of red fire, with loud explosions and many blazes springing up. The correspondents seemed to enjoy the fireworks. "The Arabs are finishing up with a bang before the truce, aren't they?" said Schreiber.

"Putting up quite a show," said Robley. "To little avail."

In the shuttered hotel they found an excellent dinner laid on, considering the austerities of a siege; and the staff officers who joined them were in high spirits over word that the Arab counterattack was being bloodily repulsed. The dinner became a sort of unbuttoned wine-fueled review of the whole war, the correspondents prodding the officers with questions and scribbling notes, the euphoric Israelis vying to tell their personal tales of combat. It went on for hours, with some minor security lapses, but Barak perceived that the journalists seemed engrossed, so he made no attempt to interfere. It was very late before the talk broke up and he could escape and drive to Abu Ghosh.

"*Haderekh shelanu* [The road is ours]," he replied to a sentry's challenge from the dark gateway of the headquarters, an abandoned monastery. That was the password for the night. As he walked into the vaulted stone hall, three officers saw him and broke off conversation, looking peculiarly embarrassed.

"Zev, you here? Mah ha'inyan?" a former battalion commander of his inquired.

"Colonel Stone asked me to come and meet with him here, but I was delayed. If he's having a nap, don't disturb him."

The battalion commander took his arm. "You won't disturb Colonel Stone." He led Barak into a small room where a candlelit body lay on the floor wrapped in a white blanket. He lifted an edge of the blanket. The face was Mickey Marcus's. The eyes were shut, the expression coldly peaceful. Shocked speechless, Barak shuddered.

"He went walking outside the camp perimeter, evidently wrapped in that blanket. Nobody knows why, or exactly when." The battalion commander's voice trembled. "Somebody heard a shot about half an hour ago, and went out to check. He was lying on the ground in the blanket, shot through the chest."

"How? By whom? A sniper, way out here?"

"What else?" The commander spread his hands in an unhappy gesture. "He's gone."

Another officer looked in. "The ambulance is here. The doctor is waiting down in Abu Ghosh."

"Too late for doctors," said the commander.

Barak followed the stretcher to the ambulance, and watched till the vehicle disappeared down the dirt road. The stars were paling in the indigo sky when he walked aimlessly out into the camp.

"*Mi sham?!*" The challenge was boyish and nervous, the armed figure tense in the twilight.

"Haderekh shelanu," said Barak, fighting back dry sobs, and under his breath he added, "Ah, God, Mickey, Mickey, the road is ours."

* * *

A few hours later the cease-fire took effect. A truce of a month was on. Before it ended the Holy Land trembled on the edge of another civil war, this time between Jews and Jews.

6

Diamond Cut Diamond

Ten warm June days into the truce, Barak's apartment was shaping up. Clad only in sneakers and faded shorts, his arm out of the cast and usable though stiff and crooked, he was cementing glass into a window sash, happy with such relaxing mindless chores. Nakhama was out shopping, Noah was back at his old kindergarten, and all was quiet in the household. In a week of hard work he and Nakhama had restored it to its former neat look, and there might never have been a war, except that the telephone remained dead, the water supply was chancy, and gas for the stove had not been restored until that morning. Electricity still came on only two hours a day, but candles and kerosene lamps diffused a romantic glow at night, suited to a sort of second honeymoon in their own flat, their own bed.

A knock came at the door and a soldier delivered a despatch which made Barak groan aloud. When he came out of the shower in a bathrobe, there lay on his desk a slaughtered duck, its feathers all bloody, and off in the kitchen Nakhama was clattering pots and singing an Arabic song of her childhood, a signal of great good cheer. "Where to all the devils did you get this?" he asked her, flourishing the carcass by the legs.

"Never mind! Fresh-killed! Tonight we celebrate, motek."

"Celebrate what?"

"Having gas in the stove, that's what."

Barak put down the duck and showed her the despatch. She cried, "*Ai!* But he *promised*! He promised you two weeks!"

"I know, and he's a man of his word. I'll have to find out what's up, though."

"*L'Azazel!*" She clanged a pot down in the sink. "Why did I have it slaughtered? A live duck doesn't spoil. Noah could have played with it till its time came."

"But then he wouldn't have let you kill it. He'd have named it Joshua or Itzhak, and fought you off."

"Hah! No doubt. Well, so it goes in the Bluestein refrigerator." The lady next door was the envy of all tenants, for American cousins had once brought her a Kelvinator. "But don't let him cheat us of our two weeks, you hear? You come back home!"

Instead of having to fly a dogleg to avoid antiaircraft fire, the Piper Cub went buzzing straight over the Latrun fortress, and the young pilot pointed down at half-dressed Legionnaires strolling about. "Very glad not to be fighting, what?" he shouted over the engine noise. "Same as us!" In the beautiful green Ayalon fields, on both sides of the invisible partition line, Arab and Jewish farmers bent to their work and tractors peacefully crawled. The small plane bucked and teetered, coming down in the sea winds north of Tel Aviv. Outside the terminal shed a short barrel-chested man in coat, tie, and a fedora hat, eating a thick sandwich from a paper bag, said as Barak walked past him, "What's the matter, big shot, you don't talk to civilians?"

"Sam! Emigrating, are you? Very sensible!" Pasternak only laughed and bit his sandwich. "Come on, Sam, where to now, of all times?"

Pasternak lowered his voice and replied, chewing. "Prague. Detached duty. The Czech arms market is breaking wide open, Zev. Surplus Messerschmitts, tanks, cannons, machine guns, rifles, ammo! Anything we can pay for and carry away, we can have now."

Since the Pasternak family were Czech Jews, and Sam had

done gunrunning in the underground, his mission was no surprise. "But the embargo, Sam? The truce terms? We can't bring that stuff in."

With a mirthless smile, Pasternak said, "No, of course we can't. The Arabs are hauling weaponry in by the ton, because the UN observers can't monitor all their borders and coastlines, but those UN snoops are all over *us* like fleas, aren't they?" The old foxy look creased his big-jawed face. "Still, a Jew can find a way sometimes, hah? And you? I thought you were on leave."

"I am. B.G. summoned me here by plane, God knows why."

"I know why."

"Then tell me!"

Pasternak put an arm through his crooked elbow and drew him aside. "He didn't mention Begin?"

"Begin! Not a word."

Ben Gurion's fire-eating rightist political opponent, Menachem Begin, led the *Irgun Zvae Leumi,* United National Force, the rightist faction of Zionism.

"Well, Begin's people bought an old surplus LST, one of those big landing ships, in America, and filled it chockablock in Marseilles with French munitions. It's off our coast right now, about to unload. But who's to get the weapons? The army, or the Irgun? *That's* what's up, Zevi, and it's a ticking bomb, I warn you. Good luck!"

The Old Man was hunched over tea and cake at his desk, his white wings of hair blown by a noisy fan. "We've finally heard from the Americans about Marcus," he said without ado. "The story is out, it's getting a big play in their newspapers, and they plan a funeral with full military honors. Burial at West Point, a very grand occasion. No more than he deserves. A true hero. Moshe Dayan will accompany the body, but I'm still trying to hire a transport plane in Europe. So expensive! And the insurance! Terrible!" Ben Gurion heaved a deep sigh, sipped tea, and went on with the sly side-glance of an insider. "Well, it's all very sad. You know what really happened?"

"Yes, a sniper bullet."

Ben Gurion slowly shook his head. "Bobbeh-myseh! If Mickey had known any Hebrew, poor chap, he'd still be alive." He paused to relish Barak's puzzlement. "Those Palmakhniks at Abu Ghosh threw him a big party late at night. Celebrating the road, the truce, lifting the siege, and so on. You know, he liked his drop, and I guess he drank plenty! He must have wandered out in that white blanket to relieve himself. Anyway, a sentry challenged him, a new recruit who didn't know English. When poor Mickey couldn't say *'Haderekh shelanu,'* or just tell him who he was, the young fool shot and killed him. Thought he was an Arab infiltrator, all wrapped in white like that. And then when the kid found out what he'd done, he tried to commit suicide."

"No!" Barak felt dizzied and sick. "Killed by a sentry!"

"Yes. Of course, that's a great secret. The sniper is the story. Now, Dayan's English is not so good, therefore you'll go with him to West Point once we line up a plane. It'll be a while."

So this was why he had been summoned, Barak thought, and for once the all-knowing Pasternak was wrong. The duck dinner might still be on, and that was a relief.

But next Ben Gurion pushed aside the tea tray, clasped his hands on the desk, and in one of his sudden shifts of mood, his face took on formidable fury. "Now then, Zev, do you know that we face civil war, and that it could break out in hours?"

Barak was used to the Old Man's melodramatic style, yet even though forewarned, he was shocked. "What's happening, Prime Minister, and where?" *(Score one for Pasternak!)*

Holding up a stubby hand, Ben Gurion said, "You'll soon hear, I'm forming a crisis team. You'll keep the minutes."

"Prime Minister, forgive me. You said two weeks, and Nakhama —"

The Old Man snapped, "I know, I know what I said. This is an emergency."

When Ben Gurion told the half-dozen officers of the crisis team about the LST, they were visibly astonished and concerned. The first to break a heavy silence was the Palmakh chief, Yigal Allon. Almost thirty, he looked younger than Barak, with his thick curly hair growing straight up like a boy's from a rugged sunburned farmer's face. "Prime Minister, how long has the government known about this LST?"

"I've been negotiating with the Irgun about it for several days. Ever since the great Mr. Begin disclosed the thing to me." Ben Gurion took a testy tone. Allon was no great favorite of his, for the tough elite Palmakh came mainly from kibbutzim far to the left of his socialist party. "I've had to keep it top secret because it's a gross violation of the truce. I thought we might try a surreptitious unloading, but they're impossible! Terms always being changed, no way to make a deal —"

Colonel Yadin came in puffing at his pipe, his high bald forehead all wrinkled. "All right. I have the picture from army intelligence officers at the scene."

His report was dismaying. Anchored in a cove near Netanya, the LST was already discharging great heaps of cargo, and the Irgunists who were manning the *Altalena* — that was what they had dubbed the landing ship — or who had come to help unload the weapons, were defying all orders by the army or the government. "But I assure you the army has sealed off the waterfront, Prime Minister. We've set up roadblocks, and no arms will leave that beach for now, that's flat." Ben Gurion nodded grim approval. Colonel Yadin went on. "However, sir, I must add that army units loyal to the Irgun have been deserting their assigned posts and heading for that beach."

The officers looked at each other, and Palmakh chief Allon spoke up with brisk calm. "This thing has to be defused. What does the Irgun really want, Prime Minister, what are your minimum terms, and how can the gap be closed?"

Ben Gurion grated, "The ship and its cargo must be surrendered to the army, or confiscated by force. Nothing else."

By contrast to Allon, Colonel Yadin spoke in a voice slow and grave. "And if the Irgun tries to force its way off the beach, Prime Minister?"

"Then I order you to answer fire with fire!" Ben Gurion's fist came down hard on the desk. "*There can be only one armed force in a country, and the government must control that armed force.* On those two points I can't compromise. The Irgun signed an agreement to integrate its units with the army, didn't it? Those Irgunists leaving their posts are deserters!"

"Prime Minister," said Barak, "the army troops on the beach may not obey orders to fire on other Jewish boys. The Irgun might well be counting on that."

"Zev is right," said the Palmakh chief. "That's a possibility, a serious one."

Ben Gurion screwed up his face angrily at Barak, then looked around with slitted eyes. "Are all you gentlemen telling me," he growled, "that this government has no power to deal with a potential armed uprising? With civil war? That there are no soldiers in the Israel Defense Force who will obey me?"

Colonel Yadin took a leisurely pull at his pipe. "Prime Minister," he said as he exhaled a gray cloud, "let us send Moshe Dayan to that beach."

Moshe Dayan commanded the light battalion in the new armored brigade based outside Tel Aviv. It was in fact an armor battalion in name only, a raggle-taggle outfit of jeeps and half-tracks sheeted with steel plates, capable at most of hit-and-run raids, since its firepower was limited to mortars and mounted machine guns. Still, *armor* was a prestige word, and soldiers had vied to volunteer for "Dayan's commandos." Moshe Dayan had readily accepted Benny Luria, a boy from his own moshav, and in the hasty informal recruiting of the truce time, Benny had brought along Don Kishote. Benny was already a platoon leader due to his aptitude, or Dayan's favoritism, or a bit of both.

"Guess what?" he said, returning from an orders group to their low hot tent, where Don Kishote was cleaning his rifle. "Full battle alert, preparing to move out tomorrow."

"Why? Where are we going?"

"Vitkin Village."

"Where's that?"

"It's a seaside moshav north of Netanya."

"Seaside? Why the seaside? Are they expecting a surprise landing by the Arabs?"

"That's all I know."

"You don't know much."

"I know what I'm told. That's all I or you have to know."

Next day the battalion went rattling past the moshav and halted at the steep drop to the sea. "Why look, that's an LST," said Don Kishote, squinting out at an enormous anchored vessel painted in camouflage colors. "I saw a hundred of those in Naples harbor. What the devil is an LST doing here?"

Their half-track overlooked the entire scene below, where a semicircle of army troops closed off the beach near the *Altalena*. Within that perimeter scores of nearly naked men were carrying large crates away from the LST on a wobbly pontoon bridge, while others waded ashore with the contraband on their heads. Munitions heaped on the beach were being loaded into trucks, and guarding these were Irgunists who looked no different from the army troops, but were facing them with guns at the ready.

In Benny's walkie-talkie, recognizable crisp Dayan tones: "Battalion, advance as previously directed."

"Here we go," said Benny. The armored machines went winding down the escarpment. People on the beach stopped moving about, arguers fell silent, unloaders ceased their work, and all stood staring at the approaching army vehicles. "Okay, Yossi, now when we reach the beach we take station between the army and the Irgun guys, got it?"

"What are we doing, Benny, protecting our own soldiers?"

"They're from the local brigade, the Alexandroni. We're reenforcements."

"But what have we got against the Irgun, anyway? Those Irgun fighters in the Jewish Quarter were good guys, I'll tell you that."

"Oh, it's all politics. Very complicated."

An open car was coming along the hard sand at the water's edge. Benny exclaimed, "Oo-ah, now it's getting interesting! There's the mayor of Netanya, and look, see that small fellow in the white shirt and glasses, getting out of the car? That's Menachem Begin."

"That little guy? He looks like a teacher, or something."

"Well, he's a wild orator and fighter. Begin *is* the Irgun. Now the fun starts."

The little bespectacled man in the white shirt trotted out on the pontoon bridge to board the vessel, then after a long while came back ashore for vehement arguing with the mayor and a cluster of army officers. This happened over and over. The hours dragged. On both sides the soldiers fell into relaxed postures. The sun was going down, and Kishote began to get drowsy. "This is all nonsense," he said. "Talk, talk, talk. We're not about to fight our own guys, Benny. You know that."

"Look, you know Dayan. If he orders us to shoot, we shoot."

Kishote yawned, yawned, hunkered down, and fell asleep, his head on his knees. Gunfire woke him. He came alert like a cat, grabbed his rifle, and flung himself prone beside Benny Luria, who was flat on the ground, his eye to the gunsight of a tripod machine gun. It was almost dark. "Benny, what's going on?"

"Can't you hear? I don't know who started it or how, but look sharp, it's serious!"

Dayan's commandos were firing as they had been drilled, from prone positions or from the armored cars. The gunfire from the beach was sporadic, but bullets were whining and whistling overhead. Walking along a slight rise, Moshe Dayan came on Kishote, standing erect with his rifle, shooting back. "Get down, you!" The black eye patch and the voice were unmistakable in the smoky gloom.

"Sir, I don't see too well lying down," Kishote shouted over the gunfire.

Dayan struck his shoulder. "Down, babyface!" He walked on.

Kishote dropped beside Benny Luria, who was reloading his tripod machine gun. "Say," he bawled, "isn't this a pretty funny way to run a country?"

"Yeah, sidesplitting," yelled Benny.

When the engagement petered out and they ventured to sit up, they saw the LST shadowily on the move, and they could hear the heavy rattling of the anchor chain coming up.

Still at the Ramat Gan headquarters, Zev Barak got little sleep trying to track and record the crisis. All night long an army corvette pursued the *Altalena* down the coast with the two captains arguing on shortwave — in English, for both were American naval reserve officers — and Barak did his best to keep notes of their dispute, a jumble of threats and defiance in legalistic nautical jargon. Just before sunrise the *Altalena* headed into the Tel Aviv waterfront, only to run aground not far out from the Dan, a beach hotel, while reports began piling up of Irgun units streaming toward Tel Aviv.

Early in the morning, at a meeting of the bleary crisis team, Ben Gurion opened by castigating the chief of naval operations, a red-bearded youngster in a turtleneck sweater, for the failure of the corvette to intercept and seize the LST. Rounding on the other officers, he demanded an immediate plan for neutralizing or destroying the ship if it would not surrender.

"Prime Minister," observed Yigal Allon, in his Palmakh tone of dry menace, "one three-inch howitzer shot will finish that LST now. It's an eggshell, sitting out there at point-blank range, helpless."

"An eggshell full of munitions," Colonel Yadin said. "One shell hit can blow it sky-high and kill everybody aboard."

Moderating his manner and voice, Ben Gurion said, "Nobody's discussing that yet. What's the balance of troops in Tel Aviv?"

"Highly unfavorable," said Yadin. "It's an Irgun town, sir, as you know, and our army units need more time to get there."

"Zev, you'll have to handle the foreign press." Ben Gurion turned to Barak. "The whole world will be watching this debacle. The whole wide world! Draw up a government statement — careful, discreet, but *forceful*. Say the Israeli government won't tolerate this flagrant breach of the truce. The ship is manned by dissidents and terrorists. It will be seized, the arms will be turned over to the UN, and so on — Now, gentlemen, what are your ideas?"

Barak went to a quiet cubicle and worked hard over the statement. When he brought it to Ben Gurion, the Old Man was in his small inner office, discussing the style of new army uniforms with the chief of supply and two civilians in the clothing business. Sample blouses and trousers were draped on chairs and on his desk. "None of the lapels are right," he said, peering through his glasses at the garments. "Where is the military dash? Ah, Zev. You have the statement?"

He glanced through Barak's scrawl, striking out some words and inserting others. "Fine, fine. Take it to the press office, get it distributed, and keep me informed.

"I don't like the buttons, either. How much more would metal buttons cost?"

An early riser, St. John Robley of Reuters noticed from his window in the Dan Hotel the strange sight of an LST entering the harbor, tailed by a corvette. He hastily dressed, snatched his binoculars, and went down to the balcony restaurant facing the sea. There he ordered coffee and watched the LST halt offshore, instead of beaching and dropping the ramp. Through the glasses he could see the crew signalling to Irgun soldiers massed on the shore that the vessel had struck an obstacle and run aground.

Before long Zev Barak appeared, carrying a portfolio. "Ah, good morning, sir."

"Well, well, good morning, Major. What's that landing ship doing out there?"

Zev had posted Yael Luria in the lobby, with a sheaf of mimeographed statements for the correspondents; but it was like this keen Englishman to be on watch up here with binoculars. "Actually, sir," Barak pulled a copy of the release from the portfolio, "this tells the story."

Robley rapidly scanned the two pages. "Government handout, Major. Soft stuff. Why *Altalena*? What does that mean?"

"Pen name of Jabotinsky, sir, first leader of Revisionist Zionism, founder and idol of the Irgun."

"These Irgun chaps are a peppery bunch, what?"

"They're patriots, sir. It'll all work out."

The Dan restaurant crowded up with journalists, curious Israelis, and UN observers sporting blue armbands. On the stranded ship there was frantic action, while along the beach more Irgunists kept arriving, and on the embankment above them army units were building up too.

"Major Barak, you know what?" said St. John Robley, pointing out at the armed standoff. "It's 70 A.D. again in the Holy Land. You Jews were at each other's throats, you know, when Titus captured Jerusalem."

A shout in several languages, *"There they come!"* A loaded landing craft was casting off from the LST. With its heavy cargo of crates and machine guns, and its crowd of crouching armed men, the boat's approach was sluggish. Talk died in the restaurant. Tension shot up.

"There's no doubt you Jews have become soldiers, Barak," Robley went on, binoculars fixed on the incom.. ˮ launch, "and that is remarkable. I wonder, though, whether you really can be trusted with guns."

Barak was only half listening, staring out at the launch. "I'm not sure what you mean."

"I mean guns are for war. They shouldn't become a louder form of Talmudic dispute."

"May I borrow your binoculars?" Barak took a long hard look at the oncoming boat. "Thank you, sir." He handed them back and hurried from the balcony, down the hotel stairs into the locker area leading to the beach, for commanding that launch was an old friend from scouting days, Zulu Levy.

Very dark-complected, Levy had once played a cannibal with a bone in his nose in a school skit, and ever since he had been "Zulu." Now a hotel manager, Levy was a red-hot Irgunist, close to Menachem Begin; so here was a slim chance, Barak figured, to put out this fire by trying to talk sense to Zulu, and through him to his difficult leader. It meant crossing the no-man's-land stretch of beach between the guns of the army and the Irgun. No reason for anybody to fire on him, but there was always the trigger-happy fool. As he went slogging out of the hotel over the empty sands, he was thinking ruefully of Mickey Marcus's fate and shouting through cupped palms, "Zulu! Zulu! It's me, Barak! *Ma nishma?*" ("What's new?")

Levy looked around at him, smiled and waved to him to approach. "Zev! Are you coming from Ben Gurion?"

"In a way, yes."

"Then where's your white flag?" Raucous laughter from the men unloading the boat. His eyes wildly agleam, Levy gave Barak a rough hug. "Glad to see you! Zev, you can tell your boss there are four more shiploads of this iron waiting for us in Marseilles. Four more! The Irgun's bringing in more and better arms than he's been able to provide for his whole Yiddisheh-mammeh army!"

"Listen, Zulu, it won't work. It can't. If you peaceably surrender, this crazy mess can still be salvaged. Yigal Allon has been put in charge of this waterfront crisis, and he's moving up a cannon."

"Ha, ha!" Zulu's laugh was uncertain. "A bluff."

"Zulu, do you know Yigal Allon?"

Levy burst out, "In God's name, Zev, who raised the money in America for this ship? Who negotiated for those mountains of French arms? That bully Ben Gurion is demanding the impossible, he's refused all compromises, and now —"

Words in English suddenly thundering across the water: *"This is the captain of the* Altalena *speaking. Menachem Begin will shortly address the people of Tel Aviv and all Israel from the deck of this historic vessel . . ."*

"There we go," said Zulu, striking Barak lightly on the shoulder. "Listen, and then inform your fathead Prime Minister that he's been outwitted and licked!"

"The cabinet meets in ten minutes." Ben Gurion was alone in his inner office with Barak. "Give me your impressions. How bad is it down there?"

"Not good, sir. When I left, Begin was on a loudspeaker, urging everyone in Tel Aviv to help unload the arms, and more and more guns were being set up on deck."

"Have they brought any more stuff ashore?"

"Not since that first boatload, but they were lowering several loaded launches."

"All this, with UN observers and the press corps looking on!"

"Yes, hotel balconies jammed with UN, photographers, and newsreel cameras —"

Ben Gurion slumped deeper in his chair, resting clenched fists on the desk. "This is a mutiny, politically inspired and led. If it is not put down, it will destroy the state." He rose. "Wait here, Zev."

Left alone in the small bleak office, Barak stared over the paper-strewn desk at the wall, and Theodor Herzl, the Viennese father of Zionism, stared back at him — black squared wavy beard, commanding dark eyes, silent perpetual challenge, *If you will it, it is no dream.* Beside the portrait hung the dream, willed into fact: an inked outline of Israel on a map of Mandate Palestine, all defaced by the graffiti of war and politics; red-and-blue battle diagrams, thick green cease-fire lines of the different fronts. Weary despair forced Barak's head down on the desk, resting on his crooked arm. Never an optimist about the precarious new Jewish State he lived in and loved, he now felt it quaking under him.

The former Wolfgang Berkowitz's trouble as the Israeli Zev Barak — such was his self-analysis — was that he remained enough of a Middle European to see more than one point of view. Begin was not wholly wrong, and Ben Gurion was far from wholly right. They were a pair of East European ghetto politicians contending for a tiny imperilled new country. After nineteen centuries of dispersion the Jews were back home. The Jewish State, Herzl's dream, had existed for only five weeks, and with the enemy at the gates, Jews had Jews in their gunsights! It was too much for him. Let Ben Gurion handle it, as he handled everything down to army uniform buttons.

A buzzer on the desk sounded. He went to the cabinet room door and knocked. "Come in!" The Prime Minister sat at a table with eight middle-aged or elderly Zionists, all in open-collar shirts except for one rabbi in a black suit and tie. Barak knew them all. Some nodded to him unsmiling. Weighty silence in the room. Sadness, foreboding, fear on the drawn pale faces around the table, all except Ben Gurion's. "Our good Mr. Begin has gone stark mad," he rasped, his color good, his mien pugnacious. "The issue on the table here is whether Allon is to use his howitzer if the situation continues to deteriorate. In that case, Zev, you will handle the press without further reference to me. Understood? You know the picture."

"Yes, Prime Minister."

He heard Ben Gurion say, before he closed the door going out, "Let's be clear that *taking action* means killing Jews. If that's the decision of the Provisional Government, very well, but I want a vote, and I want it now —"

Driving back to the waterfront, he had to maneuver the jeep through honking cars and a horde of pedestrians hurrying the other way. A policeman told Barak that the neighborhoods near the beach were being evacuated. Barak could see numbers of soldiers shouldering against the mob toward the beach; Irgun deserters from the army, coming to fight for that damned gunrunning LST.

When the pandemonium of gunshots erupted all over the harbor without warning, balcony onlookers came scrambling inside the restaurant. Waiters and diners dived for the floor. Saul Schreiber, the *Los Angeles Times* reporter, had joined St. John Robley at his table, and they both kept their seats, watching the heavily loaded second launch zigzag through a thick spray of bullet splashes. They saw it lurch onto the shallows off the water's edge and stop; saw the men in it returning fire, saw the wounded being dragged to the beach by people who waded out to help.

"This is as fantastic a spectacle," remarked the Englishman, "as I have seen in my life, and I have covered a lot of war."

"Brother against brother," said Schreiber sadly. "Sheer lunacy."

The barrages slackened. The people on the floor in the restaurant sheepishly got up and dusted themselves. The arms remained in the abandoned half-sunken launch. On the waterfront, an oppressive protracted calm ensued. The sun was declining, casting a long glitter on the sea, when an army lieutenant came in and announced, "Gentlemen, a press representative of the government is on the way." Journalists and UN people crowded in from the balcony.

"Well, Major Barak should have some hard news for us," Schreiber said to Robley, but Yael Luria appeared instead, in a form-fitting uniform and fresh makeup. She threw them a bright smile of recognition, so Schreiber shouldered to her through the crowd and helped her up on a chair. Stammering at first but steadying as she went, Yael read from a sheet:

"The Israel Defense Force announces that the ship Altalena *has asked for and been granted a cease-fire, so as to evacuate the wounded. A peaceful end to the crisis is being urgently negotiated. Under no circumstances will the illegal arms be landed in Israel, in defiance of the truce and the government's orders."*

Questions shot at her from all sides, but with a helpless gesture she shouted, "That's all I have. There will be a detailed briefing very soon by Major Zev Barak."

Schreiber darted after the departing Yael. Canny of Major Barak to stall the press with that blond eyeful; but she must know a lot more than that, and a Jewish reporter might get it out of her. But she was not in the lobby, nor in the quiet avenue outside. Gone. Damn!

Never had Yael seen Tel Aviv streets so deserted, and — despite sporadic rattle of guns — so quiet. At a new crude roadblock of oil drums near the Red House, armed Irgunists in street clothes stopped her, and one who looked like her brother Benny brusquely asked to see her papers. Yael produced them at gunpoint, feeling exceedingly strange. These fellows were joking among themselves in her own Hebrew army slang, but she was being treated like an Arab. The Irgunist gave back her papers with a friendly smile that she did not return. Hurrying back to the Red House, she came on a platoon of disarmed soldiers outside a school building, guarded by others with submachine guns. One prisoner waved at her. "Hi there, Yael," he called in English. "I'm under arrest. We all are."

After a moment she recognized Don Kishote's brother, Leopold, who seemed in surprisingly good spirits, unlike the rest of his hangdog platoon. "Hello there!" she called. "What's happened to you?" An armed guard, puzzled and irritated by the English talk, growled at her. She ignored him. "What did you do wrong?"

"We refused to shoot! I was the first one to say I wouldn't. I threw down my gun, then the whole platoon did. I said I didn't come to Palestine to kill Jews, I saw enough Jews killed in Poland."

"Asur l'daber! [No talking!]" snarled the guard.

A scared-looking woman opened the school door. The guards began to march the prisoners inside.

"Tell Yossi," Leopold called.

"I will."

He shouted, as he went through the door, "See you in Los Angeles!"

Volleys of gunfire once more broke the silence, this time followed by the booming of a cannon. Sliding against the sides of buildings, Yael edged her way to the waterfront. Peeping out at the harbor, she was struck sick with horror. The LST was on fire. Men were throwing rafts over the side, jumping overboard, or climbing down ropes and nets. A ragged white flag waved on the mast, hardly visible through the smoke and the leaping flames.

"Oh God." The words broke from her. "We're finished! Israel is finished, Zionism is finished. It's all over."

It was the best duck dinner he had had in his life, Barak thought, and Nakhama had been at pains to look beautiful. Or was that an effect of the candlelight? Noah downed two helpings like a tiger cub, then fell asleep at the table. Nakhama carried him off to bed, and Barak sighed with pleasure. What a treat! Perfect dinner, lovely wife, great kid, warm home, wonderful refuge from the melancholy *Altalena* disaster and its all-day aftershocks. Crisis blown over as fast as it had boiled up; shut it out! The worst had been averted today, there would be no civil war. Question: tell Nakhama or not about his impending trip to America? Disclosure now might cause trouble and chill the night's promised delights. Then again, whenever he did have to leave the barbed query would come. "So! Why didn't you tell me sooner?"

"Time for the news," said Nakhama, marching in and snapping on the battery radio. First item, Begin had instructed and exhorted his troops to return to their posts and obey army orders. Direct quotes from his talk on an Irgun command network: *"We will not engage in fratricidal warfare, our enemy is not the Israeli army, but the Arabs. . . ."* Nakhama nodded approval. Like most Moroccans, who knew the Arabs well, she was a tacit Irgunist. At that moment Zev decided against telling her now. Why spoil the magic of the duck dinner? She was smiling as she cleared the dishes, and the candle flames were sparkling in her eyes. "You've had a hard time, Zevi. Early to bed."

"Definitely, motek," he said.

From the final paragraph in St. John Robley's featured analysis for Reuters on "the *Altalena* affair":

> . . . Of course the Ben Gurion government had the firepower and won out, but Mr. Begin created a martyrology and a legend. He was last off the burning vessel, and he had to be dragged off. Then he rose to the moment by ordering the Irgun units to go back to their posts and obey the orders of Ben Gurion's army. He thus averted a civil war, and he was the only man in Israel who could have done it. If the victory was David Ben Gurion's, the laurel was Menachem Begin's. It was diamond cut diamond.

7

America

"Statue of Liberty," shouted the pilot over the engine roar, pointing down at the little green figure with upraised arm, on an island in the sparkling harbor where many ships crawled.

"I see it," said Barak. What a vision ahead, those tall, tall Manhattan towers between two shining rivers, and what rivers! The Jordan was a trickle, even the Danube just a stream, compared to those rivers. *America!*

Grating voice on the cockpit loudspeaker: *"One-six-five Jig Baker, cleared for landing. Immigration and customs officials on hand with all clearance papers. Notify General Dayan. Out."*

In the plane's malodorous cargo area, Moshe Dayan still slept on a mattress beside the flag-draped coffin, secured to deck rings which were there to restrain racehorses. In the cockpit too one breathed stable smells. No other plane had been obtainable, and this one only at exorbitant charter and insurance fees. Zev Barak could only hope that Israel's escorts of the fallen American would not arrive diffusing too rich an aroma of horse manure.

"Moshe, we're coming down." Barak touched Dayan's shoulder. The good eye opened, bright and alert. "Entry documents are all set."

"Excellent." Dayan nodded, yawned, and glanced at his watch. "Long ride."

The plane landed and rolled to a stop. Through an opened side port, sunshine flooded the fuselage as three young officers in beribboned army uniforms, bristle-headed and stiff-backed, leaped in and saluted the Israelis. Reverently they removed the flag from the coffin. Two of them draped over the box an enormous Stars and Stripes, while the third folded the Star of David flag and handed it to Barak. He could see on the tarmac, under large American and Israeli flags flapping in the brisk wind, a long line of black limousines. An honor guard of policemen in dress blues — at least a hundred, Barak estimated — snapped salutes as the coffin was handed out of the plane, for Mickey Marcus had once been New York's commissioner of correction. Dayan and Barak also received a mass salute, emerging in the gaudy dress uniforms dreamed up overnight by Tel Aviv tailors at B.G.'s orders, much to Dayan's amused disgust: dark green jackets with epaulettes and gold buttons, ornamented black berets, and gleaming Sam Browne belts. Behind them an officer carried their bags.

A gray-haired army colonel approached, saluted, and shook hands. "Mrs. Marcus would like Colonel Marcus's aide to ride with her. It will be an honor, General," he added to Dayan, "if you will share my car."

From the back seat of the leading limousine a strong-faced pretty woman in her forties, in a black suit and a large black straw hat, held out her hand to Barak. "You're Zev," she said drily as he got in. "My husband wrote to me about you." Her glance at the flag was so frigid that he laid it aside without a word.

The cortege formed up, headlights burning, and wound through Brooklyn streets lined with onlookers to an immense crowded temple. After a brief memorial service there by a blue-robed rabbi and a white-robed choir, the procession rolled across the famous Brooklyn Bridge, which Barak recognized from movies and picture books, and past a reviewing stand at City Hall; where rows of dignitaries stood with hats over their hearts, more huge flags fluttered, more policemen saluted, and ranks of soldiers and sailors saluted too. All that time the widow was silent and dry-eyed.

Barak's ears still buzzed from the plane noise, and he was awed and numbed by the magnitude of it all: the temple, the vast bridges, the river, the canyons of skyscrapers. The widow's silence chilled him. The grandiose pomp astounded him. It was like newsreels of President Roosevelt's funeral. All this, for poor Colonel Stone!

Along the wide Hudson's cliff-lined waters, the sixty limousines rolled to West Point. Mrs. Marcus did not speak, staring white-faced out at the river. Despite the newness of all this, and the rich green beauty of the Hudson valley, Barak had to fight off a tendency to doze, for he had slept little since leaving Israel and had traversed several time zones. The Academy superintendent, a resplendent three-star general, waited at the door of an imposing chapel, flanked by two civilians, the tall gloomy former Secretary of the Treasury, Henry Morgenthau, and the short perky Governor Dewey of New York; Mrs. Marcus spoke up to tell Barak who they were, and said no more. Ten pallbearers from Marcus's West Point class, all colonels or generals in full-dress uniform with medals, carried the coffin to the grave site. Hard put to it to keep his voice steady, Barak read aloud the Israeli army citation and Ben Gurion's cable of sympathy to the widow. Dayan, standing beside him, then delivered a brief tribute in Hebrew, which he translated for the somber gathering.

And so farewell, Mickey Marcus, gone because he went out in the night at Abu Ghosh to piss and couldn't talk Hebrew; how wise of the Old Man to suppress the truth! The Americans wanted to honor a hero of war, not to pity a victim of Israeli balagan. And who was to say, Barak thought as the coffin sank into the earth to the piercing bugle notes of taps and the echoing thunder of a twelve-gun salute, that — balagan or no balagan — this hero's farewell was not the real thing? Yes, it was smart politics for that governor to be here; he was running against President Truman, and New York had a big Jewish vote. Truman was no fool either, sending here Roosevelt's famous Jewish cabinet member. All that took nothing away from Colonel Stone. He had died in the field, an American volunteer in the Jewish fight for Palestine. Death was death, however it came.

Mrs. Marcus sat staring straight ahead, clasping the folded

American flag in her lap, as the cortege headed back south along the Hudson. "Look Zev," she said abruptly, "you can help me if you will."

"Anything you say, Mrs. Marcus."

"Thank you. The wife of one of Mickey's best friends is the New York chairman of Hadassah. They have a big-givers' parlor meeting today, to raise emergency funds for the hospital in Jerusalem. I agreed to attend as guest of honor before —" She paused and bit her lip. "— Well, I can't go. They realize that. But they couldn't call it off, it's too late. Will you go there, and read that message from Ben Gurion and the citation? Maybe say just a few words too?"

Big givers . . . Zev Barak, performing beggar . . .

"Of course I'll do it, Mrs. Marcus."

"Emma." She touched an icy hand on his. "You're kind. It'll be a hen party, not another man in sight. Sure you're up to it?"

"Well, in our army we get these tough assignments off and on."

She managed a wintry smile. "Mickey was fond of you. I see why."

Barak took a plunge. "Can I say something, Emma?"

She turned glittery eyes at him and nodded.

"Colonel Marcus once quoted Rupert Brooke to me — '. . . *There is a corner of some foreign field that is forever England.*' "

"Mickey was always quoting poetry." The eyes slightly softened. "He loved that one, yes."

"Emma, there's a corner of West Point that is forever Israel."

She tightened her mouth and did not cry, but pointed to the blue-and-white flag on the seat and held out her hand. He gave the flag to her. When she left him off at a tall apartment building on Central Park West, she was holding both flags close to her.

From his Vienna boyhood onward, Barak had eaten and relished all manner of cream pastries, but the elephantine layer cakes at the parlor meeting were a novelty. In Israel two would have fed a large wedding party, but here there were ten cakes for about twenty women, all dressed to the nines, all in big modish hats. Slim or stout, they consumed the cakes ravenously, chatting in low tones, with shy glances at the handsome Israeli officer who stood aside at a window, devouring his thick slice and looking out in wonder at the grand rectangle of green park and its spiky borders of skyscrapers. One of the older women, plump but comely, with gray-streaked hair under a plumed hat like a hussar's, kept smiling at him. Uncertainly he smiled back, whereupon she came to him, almost at a trot. "So you do recognize me! You've only seen pictures."

"Well — is this Aunt Lydia?"

"Lydia Barkowe. That's me, Wolfgang! I mean Zev, of course." She laughed, seized his hand and pecked his cheek. "What a surprise when Emma phoned you were coming in her place! Your father's staying with us, you know. I'll take you home to dinner."

"I didn't know my father was with you, Aunt Lydia, I thought the mission rented a place near the UN."

"Yes, but he's visiting us to get away from Lake Success, for a breather. He's fine. Your uncle will be thrilled to see you. My kids too, they're all home. Kids, listen to me! One a father, the others twenty-one and seventeen!" Her eyes gleamed at him. "You look so *dashing,* you know?"

The women sat down in folding chairs to hear him. Their chairman, a buxom lady in a tailored suit, introduced him with a few brisk excited words, clearly delighted, as were all these shiny-eyed matrons, at his transforming a lugubrious fund-raiser with his dazzling martial presence. His aunt in the front row was beaming at him, and it was a long time since he had felt so boyish, so self-conscious, and so phony.

But as he read the tributes and saw the women's eyes cloud with sadness, those feelings faded. He was moved to say something about Marcus and the Jerusalem front, and how the Burma Road had broken the siege. He said whatever came to mind. He found himself talking about the whole war, the truce, the hazardous geography of Israel, and the bravery of the soldiers in victory and defeat. He heard gasps as he described the march of the untrained immigrants from Cyprus into the fire at Latrun. When he figured he had gone on too long he broke off lamely and randomly, and was astounded when they jumped to their feet applauding.

"I'm to take you away now," his Aunt Lydia said, coming up to him and hugging him. "Magnificent. The chairman will start twisting arms when you've gone. She won't have to twist hard."

He put his bag into the back seat of a tan Cadillac as long as one of the funeral limousines. She said, edging it casually into the heavy Central Park West traffic, "Of course I phoned your father as soon as I heard from Emma Marcus. He wants you to meet him at the UN, so I'll drop you off and go on ahead. It's only twenty minutes to our house, and he'll bring you to us. It's the cook's night out and we were going to eat Chinese, but none of that. We'll fix something."

"Listen, Aunt Lydia, Chinese is fine. Don't fuss, I can't stay long, anyway."

"Chinese? A guest like you? *Zev Barak?*" She said it with a proprietary smile, and made it sound like a stage name. "We can always barbecue lamb chops. I keep tons of them around, my boys are roaring meat-eaters. You like lamb? Isn't that what they eat in the Middle East, lamb?"

"Yes, Aunt, we eat lamb."

"Nissim v'niflaot! [Miracles and marvels!]" Barak's father exclaimed, leading him through the wide semicircles of vacant seats in the General Assembly Hall at Lake Success. Meyer Berkowitz was almost as short as Ben Gurion and had much the same paunchy figure; also the wild white hair, a socialist trademark. "Miracles and marvels! This is exactly where I was sitting — on this chair, Zev — when Venezuela voted yes and made the two-thirds vote. Sit down in that chair! Then you can tell your grandchildren you did."

Barak had not seen his flamboyant father for many months, and was slightly ashamed at his lack of feeling for him. Irreversible things had happened in the family besides his marrying Nakhama. He compliantly sat down, feeling no thrill, hearing no grand chord of history. It was just a chair in an empty hall. But his father supplied the grand chord, his voice booming and echoing. "Yes, the Jewish State reborn after two thousand years! In my time! And I sat right here, a representative of that State! *Even though I am not worthy or qualified . . .'*" He was quoting the Yom Kippur liturgy in the old-time Yiddish accent. Barak's father was all contradictions: a well-to-do fur trader and a doctrinaire socialist, an unbeliever who observed the holidays and ate no pork products, a Hebraist who loved Yiddish and wouldn't Hebraize his name, an egalitarian who disapproved of his son's marrying a poor Moroccan girl. This inconsistency was taken for granted in the family, except in occasional lacerating arguments.

"*Ai,* were the British wrong!" said his father, leading him out to the foyer. "Miracles and marvels! How could the damned Jews ever win a two-thirds vote for partition, they calculated, with the Soviet and Arab blocs both voting no? Only Stalin, may his memory be blessed and his name wiped out, laid them six feet in the ground by ordering his whole gang to vote yes! Miracles and marvels!"

"Look, Papa, what miracles and marvels? Stalin just wants to shove the British out of the Middle East for good. That's why he did that, and that's why we're getting Soviet arms from Czechoslovakia."

"Yes, yes, maybe he *thinks* that's why he did it," his father boomed, "but the hand of God was upon him — in a manner of speaking, of course. So, Aunt Lydia's waiting. I warn you, I don't drive a Cadillac, Zev."

As they left Lake Success in a creaking Ford, Barak told his father that the army leaders were preparing for an immediate new offensive once the truce ended; assuming that Israel would accept the truce extension which the Americans and British were pushing, and that the Arabs would turn it down. It would be a chance to seize the initiative before the enemy moved, and win rational borders within which Israel could hang on for a few years and draw breath. His father shook his head vehemently. "Ben Gurion will be making a terrible mistake. More bloodshed, more deaths! Half a million Jews can't conquer seventy million Arabs. If they attack again we should defend ourselves, of course, until they come to terms."

"Their terms are simple, Papa. We die, or we leave."

" *'Grasp a lot, and you haven't grasped,'* " the father quoted the Talmud. " *'Grasp a little, and you've grasped.'* That's what Begin forgot in that awful *Altalena* balagan."

"Did the papers make much of that here?"

"We were lucky. The Russians crowded it out with their Berlin blockade."

Houses and grounds were looking bigger and fancier as they approached Great Neck. The Ford bumped across a railroad track into the suburb, and Barak began exclaiming at the clustering mansions. "What palaces! Do many Jews live here?"

"These are shacks," said his father. "Sheds. Slums. Harry lives in Kings Point. You'll see."

They passed into a wooded area much like a park, where through leafy boughs large edifices could be glimpsed. "This is Kings Point," said Berkowitz. The Ford drove up a gravel driveway to a white house with an immense pillared porch. Five shiny cars — three small convertibles and two Cadillac sedans — left little room for the Ford, but he slipped it between Aunt Lydia's tan Cadillac and a high flowering hedge. Out of the house rolled Aunt Lydia with Barak's Uncle Harry, who much resembled Meyer except for a short haircut, and behind them came two sons and a daughter. Greetings, embraces, laughter and joking all around, and soon they were seated on a screened porch that faced a wide lawn, watching Leon, the older son, barbecue lamb chops with the daughter helping, while they drank powerful brown concoctions full of fruit, called old-fashioneds.

The unaccustomed alcohol lifted Barak's mood, but he was really wrung out by now. Though the sun shone through the trees he was perishing for sleep. Great Neck was as hot and steamy as Tel Aviv. The heavy uniform irked him. There was something altogether disorienting about Uncle Harry's Kings Point house, with its *Gone With the Wind* pillars and the five automobiles. Barak felt no trace of envy, but he wished those delicious-smelling chops would get served up, so that he could leave and lie down somewhere.

Aunt Lydia was bubbling about his performance at the fundraiser. "Sensational! Marcie Cohen phoned me. Ninety-three thousand dollars, Wolfgang! I mean Zev, of course. Do you realize that's three times what Golda Meyerson raised from that same group?"

The younger son asked Barak, "Have you seen much action? I just missed our war. I was in army boot camp, all set to get shipped to the Pacific, when we dropped the bomb."

"Well, Arthur, it's different in Israel. We're all strung out along the coast, and altogether our country's no bigger than New Jersey, so you get in an army truck or jeep for a short ride from home, and there you are in the war. I saw a little action, yes."

"Tell me something, do girls really *fight*?" inquired Aunt Lydia. "I've seen the pictures of them in uniform. Suppose Arabs captured them? Wouldn't that be too *horrible*?"

"They're usually not where they can be captured, Aunt. Many are in signalling."

"What are they saying in Israel about the Berlin airlift?" Uncle Harry inquired. "Do they think the Russians will back down?"

"That's a real mess," Meyer Berkowitz interjected. "At the UN they're talking about World War III."

"Foolishness," said Uncle Harry.

"Harry, Berlin needs twenty-five hundred tons of supplies a day," retorted Meyer. "The Americans can't airlift that much, and the word now is that Truman is planning to send an armed convoy through the Russian roadblocks. *Then* we'll see who backs down!"

"Why, it's just like Jerusalem and the Burma Road," exclaimed Aunt Lydia. "That was so fascinating, Wolfgang, the way you explained it. You've got to tell my children all about it."

"That's probably Betty for me," said the younger son, darting at a ringing phone. "Hello . . . Dad, it's a Mr. Perlman calling from Los Angeles."

"Dave Perlman," said Uncle Harry in an aside to Zev, as he took the phone, "major film producer. Old friend. . . . Hello, Dave! . . . Yes? Yes, Dave. We're all fine. If I can do anything, why not? Yes . . ." A long pause. Uncle Harry glanced at Barak. "Well, as it happens, my nephew's sitting right here now. He's having dinner with us. Hang on." Putting his hand over the mouthpiece, Harry said, "Wolfgang, do you know an Israeli named Pasternak? Sam Pasternak?"

"Pasternak? Sure, I know him."

"He wants to talk to you."

"From Los Angeles?" This was even more disorienting. *Pasternak,* not in Prague?

Uncle Harry handed him the telephone, and on came the gruff voice. "Zev! You're living the good life in Kings Point, hah?" Gravelly cement-mixer tones, the jocular Pasternak.

"What's up, Sam?"

"Have you ever been to California?"

"No, why?"

"It's nice here. Come on out."

"Yes, sure. What else?"

"Look, I'm serious. Get on a plane and come here. I'll meet you at the Los Angeles airport. Let me know what flight."

"Are you crazy? I'm with Dayan, and we're going back in the same Dutch charter plane we came in. I'm due for a battalion command. We're just waiting for a shipment of bank notes, the new Israeli currency, to be loaded on the plane tomorrow."

"Zev, I've already talked to Dayan. It's okay. There's a girl, Bonnie, at the mission office in Lake Success. She'll arrange your air ticket. Here's her phone number, and here's mine."

Barak noted the numbers to avoid arguing. "What's up?"

"Your uncle will tell you." The voice hardened momentarily in a switch to Hebrew. "There's more I can't get into on the phone, but I need you here." Then in English: "How did the funeral go?"

"Very moving."

"Ai, that poor bastard Marcus. Well, have a good flight."

They sat down to shrimp cocktails, around a long wicker table on the porch. It was Friday night, but Aunt Lydia didn't bother with candles; nor did Barak expect her to, although in his home Nakhama remained punctilious about that.

Dave Perlman was an immigrant from Minsk, Uncle Harry said, and they had become friends on the Polish ship coming over. Perlman had drifted from job to job in New York, and at last had gone on to California. After some years, during which Harry had done well in the old family fur trade and then switched to real estate, Perlman had written him to ask for a loan to make a movie.

"I always believed in Dave," said Harry. "I didn't ask to see the script, I sent the money. Thirty thousand. In those days, a bundle. He made a small movie you never heard of, a western. It did all right. He made more movies. Eventually he sent me back the thirty, with interest. Now he's a power out there. I've never asked Dave for anything until now. I asked him to give this fellow Pasternak ten thousand dollars, no questions asked. He did it, like *that*." Harry snapped his fingers.

The lamb chops were thicker than any Barak had ever eaten, three bones to a chop. The meat was luscious, the red wine excellent, and he was reviving. "Uncle, do you know Sam Pasternak?"

"Never heard of him before. We have this group, a few of us, we try to help out on Israel's purchase problems. You know, what with the arms embargo and all. The chairman called me and said this Israeli in L.A. needed the ten, so I called Dave."

"You want to be careful, Dad," said the married son, a real estate attorney about Barak's age, "about the embargo law. Don't go sailing too close to the wind."

"We're careful, Leon."

Barak asked his uncle, "Why does Pasternak — or Perlman — want me in Los Angeles? Do you know?"

Uncle Harry grinned at Aunt Lydia. "Well, Zev, it seems Dave's wife's having a Hadassah parlor meeting Sunday. Betty Grable's coming, just to pull them in. Pasternak was supposed to talk, but Marcie Cohen's been spreading the word about your hit today with her women. She even called Selma Perlman in L.A. to brag, they're old fund-raising competitors. So Dave went and asked Pasternak to get you out there. He mentioned that you should wear your uniform."

"It's a yummy uniform," said the daughter. "Arthur, can I have your car for a few hours? My brakes have gone out."

"Sorry, I need it."

"I thought you'd be working on your thesis."

"I have a date with Betty."

Leon said, "Don't ask for mine, I'm picking up my wife and son at eight-thirty."

A complex discussion of automobile usage ensued. Uncle

Harry grew testy about too frequent borrowing of his Cadillac, causing an awkward silence. The talk turned to the new best-sellers and Broadway plays, and Barak thought, as he listened, how well-informed, well-mannered, and self-assured these three young Barkowes were. In Israel they would all be in uniform, the married one too, ground down with fatigue, not concerned about their cars, since they would have none, much rougher in speech and narrower in outlook, and lucky if they were all alive and unscathed. Their schooling would have been arrested. They would have few or no opinions about world politics. Barak could find no fault in them, but their lack of interest in Israel puzzled him. The younger son had asked him the question about seeing action, and that had been the end of it.

"They're good kids," Meyer Berkowitz said as they drove back to Lake Success. "Hard workers, fine scholastic records. Leon will be a big lawyer one day. He looks a lot like you, did you notice? Peggy writes short stories, they've been printed in magazines. That boy Arthur is a math wizard, he just won a scholarship."

"They don't give a damn about Israel, do they?" Barak said without rancor.

"Well, they've got their own interests."

"Yet Harry and Lydia are involved."

Meyer Berkowitz shrugged. "Different generation."

In a tiny office of the Israel mission piled with books and reports, and smelling strongly of mimeograph ink, they found Bonnie, a woman of thirty or so from Haifa with frizzy hair, darting movements, and slangy Hebrew. "Hi, Moshe Dayan left a message for you." She picked up a scrap of paper and read, " *We don't go back for three days. Problem with the currency printing. Regards to Sam. Watch out for those Hollywood starlets.*' Do you need a ride to the airport?" She handed Barak a round-trip ticket to Los Angeles.

"I'll drive him," said his father.

"Thank God," said Bonnie. "There's no one around here but me."

Most of the way to La Guardia airport they drove without talking, not because there was nothing more between father and son to say but because there was too much. The diplomatic and military situation of Israel did not lend itself to automobile chatter. Their family problems and disagreements were stabilized, and best handled with silence.

Berkowitz and his son had long since agreed that his mother's obsessive snobbism, her unending push to move among Israel's small elite — the native-born socialists of Second Aliya parentage, the old Jerusalem families, the foreign diplomats — was folly, yet enough of it had rubbed off on Meyer, the son thought, so that he could not talk comfortably about Nakhama, her parents, or even about Noah. The topic of Zev's younger brother, Michael, who had unaccountably turned religious, was another touchy one. Touchiest was an affair paunchy little Meyer had had a few years ago with a secretary in his Histadrut office, which had left a shadow on the whole family and nearly broken it up. Barak had sided with his mother in that mess. His father, he thought, had just seen too many Schnitzler plays in his Vienna years, for the woman was dumpy and stupid.

"I suppose," said Meyer, abruptly breaking the silence as the flashing beams of the airport came in view, "that if I'd gone to America like your uncle, I'd have done well enough. Maybe we'd be living in Kings Point, and you could be driving a Cadillac convertible." He wryly laughed. "When we were boys in Plonsk, Dovid Gruen was my friend, not Harry's. Now he's David Ben Gurion, and I'm in the UN, not Kings Point."

"I like it as it is, Papa," said the exhausted Barak, with a strong mental flash, almost like a dream, of the stony hillside near Kastel, and the hot stinging shock of being hit in the elbow. "I wouldn't change a thing."

At the plane gate Meyer Berkowitz had to reach up to give his son a hard hug. "Well, you'll see your mother before I will. Tell her I love her. Best to Nakhama and my grandson. Happy landings, and if it's war again, be careful."

8

Sam Pasternak

Storms churned the air all the way to Chicago, where the plane circled for an hour in turbulent black rain before landing. After that the journey seemed only to begin, and to go on and on and on. Zev Barak had spent long nights in his life — lying in ambush for infiltrators on the Syrian border, pacing a hospital corridor through Nakhama's labor, agonizing in an army infirmary bed with his smashed elbow — but this seemed the longest. How could one country be so gigantic? He did not recall falling asleep, yet all at once a stewardess was touching him to offer coffee, and the plane was drumming over sunlit rocky peaks capped with snow.

"Is this California?" he asked her, taking the coffee.

She smiled. "Those are the Rockies, sir. California in about two hours."

"Do we fly over Pasadena, by chance?"

"Pasadena?" She peered out the window. "On this flight I'm not sure. Why?"

"Just wondering."

Zev Barak's forlorn dreams of peace included graduate work in chemistry one day at the California Institute of Technology. He still had a year to finish at Hebrew University, and who could say when that would be possible? But his favorite professor had studied at Cal Tech, and had talked so much about it that Barak had come to envision the school as something like Plato's Academy, in a flowery Athens called Pasadena.

"Where the hell did you get that uniform?" Sam Pasternak said at the plane gate with a bear hug. "You look like the doorman at the Ritz."

"I'm here," said Barak. "Now what?"

"Now we take you to a hotel, and you have a shower. You'd like a shower?"

"I would turn Christian for a shower. I haven't been out of this stupid getup for two days."

"Interesting you should mention Christian. He's quite a guy."

"Christian? Christian who?"

"Cunningham. You must meet him. Counterintelligence guy in OSS, big wheel now in this new Central Intelligence Agency —"

"Look, Sam," Barak broke in, "what are you doing here? What happened in Prague? Why'd you drag me out here, really? What have I got to do with intelligence?"

"Later. Chris Cunningham is important, believe me. I'll be out front in Perlman's white Lincoln." Pasternak grinned, crinkling his Tartar eyes. "There may be other white Lincolns. There's a lady in this one. A nice lady, in a red dress. You don't mind?"

"I like red dresses. Nakhama wears them a lot."

"Ah, Nakhama! How is she?"

"All right."

"You think I forgive you for stealing Nakhama?" Pasternak shook a thick finger at him. "I'll be revenged yet." Pasternak half winked one eye and walked off.

As Barak waited at the baggage chute, remembrance flared of his first encounter with Nakhama. Just back from North Africa on leave, he had run into Sam Pasternak in a sidewalk café, and with that same one-eyed half-wink Sam had told him about "the most beautiful girl in Tel Aviv," a waitress in an *amami* eating place; he was taking her to the birthday party of a classmate of theirs from the Herzl School, and he persuaded Wolfgang to drop in on the party.

One look at the waitress, and Barak forgot about driving to Tiberias to join his girlfriend Tamar there.

He was not the only one struck by Nakhama at that fateful party. Without trying, the seventeen-year-old girl caused a commotion in her plain red dress, simply moving here and there and smiling. She had the looks, the voltage, and the unaffected presence to make the fellows stare and the girls narrow their eyes, though they were mostly a university crowd, and this dark daughter of Moroccan immigrants was hardly their sort. When Barak walked next day into the place where she worked she seemed a lot less fetching in her apron and kerchief, rushing here and there to serve the food her parents cooked or to remove dirty plates. But he was past noticing the difference, and when she threw him a casual but heated welcoming smile, that was that. In the few minutes they had talked at the party, she too had been snared.

. . . First kiss, walking on the Tel Aviv beach at midnight, Nakhama gasping, "Oh, no! Me and my weakness for British uniforms! No more!" But there were many more. Proposal, one week to go in his leave, very late at night at a table in the empty eating place; her parents cleaning up and pretending not to take notice, but careful not to interfere. "So Nakhama, when do we get married?" The first mention of marriage by either of them. The words burst from him; from Wolfgang Berkowitz, level-headed British lieutenant, serious promising chemist, betting his life on one cast of passion's dice.

"Did you say when, Wolfgang? *When?* That's all? I must be too easy. Tomorrow?"

The miserable wedding in a Moroccan rabbi's apartment, the two sets of parents hardly looking at each other, his mother's dreadful last-minute sobbing . . . and from her viewpoint, why not? Tamar Rubenfeld, clever pretty daughter of the rector of Hebrew University, a former professor in Berlin; discarded for this — this *waitress?*

And then, the incandescent honeymoon by the sea in Ashkelon . . .

Down tumbled his valise in a pile of bags, and Barak seized it.

*

As Pasternak's consolers went, the woman in the red dress at the wheel of the creamy Lincoln was by no means notable. Whatever that squat ugly fellow lacked in life it was not for pretty women. He was estranged from his wife, who had gone to London with their two children when the Arab riots broke out after the partition vote; but attractive ladies abounded to cheer him. This one was in her mid-thirties, dyed blond, elegantly groomed, scrawny from dieting rather than naturally slim, with bright starved eyes. "This is Mrs. Shugar," said Pasternak. "Ellen, this is Zev. Ellen is coordinating the Perlmans' parlor meeting."

"Lot of excitement among the girls about you, Zev," said Mrs. Shugar, with a hungry glint over her shoulder at Barak in the back seat. "The word is that you're electrifying."

"Oy, vay," said Barak, as she started the car, "electrifying? If I don't get some sleep, I'll go into that meeting with dead batteries."

"It's not till tomorrow afternoon," said Mrs. Shugar. "You'll be marvellous."

All the way to the hotel she chattered brightly about the parlor meeting. Betty Grable was a big draw, but the word of mouth about the handsome Israeli officer, Mickey Marcus's aide, was really crowding up the guest list, even though the minimum pledge was a thousand dollars. As the Lincoln wound through Beverly Hills, Barak was distracted from her trickle of talk by the eye-filling mansions arrayed cheek by jowl along the palm-lined streets; ranch house, Tudor house, French chateau, Swiss chalet, all enormous, all with barbered lawns and sculptured trees, no two alike in architecture, and none with any breathing room on either side. Uncle Harry's Kings Point plantation house would be dwarfed here, he thought, but at least Uncle Harry would not be trespassing if he yawned and stretched.

"Is that all right, Zev?" asked Mrs. Shugar anxiously over her shoulder.

At a venture, Barak replied, "Absolutely."

"Oh, super! She'll be so pleased." Leaving them off at a rambling pink stucco hotel, Mrs. Shugar twiddled her fingers at them. "Take it easy, boys."

"Who's paying for all this?" Barak exclaimed, as they entered a cottage set amid lushly growing palms and flowering trees, and then passed into a broad living room with a fireplace, a bar, a grand piano, and masses of fresh flowers.

"Dave Perlman's firm leases this villa by the year for visiting big shots — movie stars, directors, and such. It happens to be free now. So? Go take your shower."

"Immediately." Barak went into the bathroom and came out holding a lacy red negligee. "This was hanging on the shower head."

"That Ellen!" Pasternak shrugged and laughed. "Nice lady, but a rattlebrain. I'll get it to her."

Barak dropped in a chair by a dining table, took a huge yellow pear from a crystal bowl of fresh fruit, and bit into it. "Such fruit! California! Sam, be straight with me, what's going on here? What was that ten thousand dollars for?"

"Oh, you know about that? Well, I'll explain, but if you're dining with Betty Grable you'd better get some sleep."

"Dining with Betty Grable? Me?"

"Weren't you listening to Ellen? You agreed to go. Small dinner party."

"Both of us?"

"Just you. The *Los Angeles Times* had a big write-up on Marcus's funeral. You were mentioned. Right now you're hot stuff."

"Why aren't you in Czechoslovakia?"

"Airlift problem." Pasternak sat down beside him and ate grapes from a purple cluster, crunching and swallowing the seeds. "Now that we can buy in quantity, B.G.'s ordered our lift capacity expanded. Our guys over here lined up six army surplus Constellations. For a new Panamanian airline, their story was. These Connies are giants, Zev, they can lift ten tons at a crack. Ten tons! But the State Department got wise and the ceiling fell in. Civil Aviation Administration, the FBI, the CIA, customs — equipment unsafe, embargo violated, papers confiscated, planes impounded — they gave us the works! Still, our guys did manage to fly one Connie out to Panama before the shutdown. I'm here to get it to Czechoslovakia, and that's where Christian Cunningham comes in. The money I got from Perlman is for grease in Panama. I had to have it in hand — you're falling asleep on me."

Barak was in fact nodding over the half-eaten pear. "I'll shower later. Betty Grable . . . wake me when it's time."

"B'seder, and I'll get your lovely uniform pressed. It's all wrinkled."

Yawning and standing up, Barak said, "Sam, tell me something. How did you know about the *Altalena,* when Yadin and Allon didn't?"

Pasternak replied with a half-wink as he peeled a banana.

Edward G. Robinson greeted Barak on Betty Grable's grandiose flagstone patio, overlooking the spangled spread of Los Angeles under the moon. "Hi. *Ani ohaive Yisroel.*" ("I love Israel.") He was smoking a long cigar, and even in black tie he looked just like the film gangsters he played. The Hebrew words, growled in an American accent, took Barak aback. Robinson went on, *"Ani no-sane har-bay kesef."* ("I give much money.")

"That's very nice," Barak said.

Robinson lapsed into English to tell Barak about his Hebrew schooling, and then about his art collection. He talked at some length, the dinner being delayed because the main course had been ham, and Betty Grable had switched to roast beef upon receiving the thrilling last-minute news that the Israeli major was coming. "I hope that's all right," she said, resplendent in a strapless clinging evening dress and batting big blue eyes at Barak. "That's a magnificent uniform. We can't wait to hear about Mickey Marcus and the Burma Road."

She sat him at her right hand. He gathered from the small talk around the table that most of the men were film producers or agents. The women were all very pretty, though none rivalled the hostess, and their clothes and hairdos tended to the grotesque, which Barak supposed was California high fashion. It was a while before the conversation turned to him. He answered a few questions about Marcus, then found himself being consulted on the prospects of the Berlin airlift, the impact of television on the movie industry, the preference in Israel for Truman or Dewey, the probable outcome of the massacres in India, and the comparative roles of America and the Soviet Union in winning World War II.

"You can settle a bet here," said a tall man called Shorty, who was Betty Grable's agent. "Is Palestine north of Syria, or south of Syria?"

"South of Syria."

"You owe me a yard," Robinson growled. Shorty gave him a hundred-dollar bill from a money clip, saying he would win it back that same night at gin rummy.

"*A-ni no-sane zeh l'Yisroel* [I'm giving this to Israel]," Robinson said to Barak.

"That's very nice," said Barak.

Next day Barak, in slacks and a short-sleeved shirt, sat with Mrs. Perlman in a two-story wood-panelled library which she called "Dave's den." The balconied room was lined with leather-bound sets of standard authors, shelves of large art volumes, and mint-condition best-sellers; also festooned with inscribed photographs of movie stars and various plaques and scrolls praising Perlman's philanthropies. There were framed letters from Franklin Roosevelt and Henry Morgenthau, thanking him for his war bonds efforts. Two Oscar figurines under glass flanked a special case of Winston Churchill first editions bound in red morocco. Mrs. Perlman showed Barak these things with frank pride, before settling down to talk over coffee about the parlor meeting. A gray-haired motherly woman in a light orange sundress, she reminded him of his Aunt Lydia.

"*I get so fucking mad!*" Into the den burst a man in a black suit and black homburg, which he flung across the room. "If there's anything I hate, it's rabbis. I get so fucking mad!"

"Dave, dear," said his wife hastily, "this is Major Barak. You know, of the Israeli army."

Barak stood up to shake hands. David Perlman's manner changed to pleasant cheeriness. "Oh, yes, you're the fellow who's going to give the speech. Glad to meet you." His aspect reverted to angry gloom. A tanned fleshy man with slick grizzled hair, Perlman produced extravagant musical films. "I get so fucking mad," he said to his wife. "I need a drink."

"Was the temple crowded?" She poured whiskey from a crystal decanter at a wheeled bar.

"Standing room only. Sid was forty-two years old, Selma. Did you know that? The rabbi said so. A kid! He was bald and fat, so it was hard to tell, but that's all he was! He had three films in production. Probably what killed him. Christ, he was *somebody* in this town. And poof! That goddamned rabbi, spouting all this crap about how Sidney didn't die, he lives on in his movies, blah blah, and old Sid lying *right there* in the open coffin, a frightening dummy in a tuxedo and pancake makeup, with his eyes closed. Selma, I played gin with Sid at Hillcrest *last Saturday!*" Dave Perlman was gnawing at his nails. His wife handed him the drink. "Thanks. I get so fucking mad!"

"Pardon me, Mrs. Perlman." A maid in a starchy costume looked in. "Mrs. Shugar is on your private line."

Perlman was lighting a large cigar. "Dear," his wife said as she got up and started out, "not so early in the day."

"The hell with it. I'm damned upset." He took a deep swallow of whiskey. "Major, Sid Feller was never sick a day in his life. A real talent. Poof. Well!" He brightly smiled at Barak. "Quite a story in the *L.A. Times* about your boss Marcus. Real hero, eh? Have some more coffee? Or a drink?"

"Thanks, no. This is a splendid house. Very nice of you and Mrs. Perlman to give a parlor meeting here."

Perlman waved his cigar in deprecation. "To be honest, I'm no Zionist. Selma fools around with that stuff. I'm interested in Jewish hospitals and such. There's an old folks home in Yonkers named after my father, I paid a bundle for that. He's still alive, and it gave him a big kick. Your Uncle Harry is the Zionist. Terrific guy, he gave me my start, and I don't forget such things. Maybe I'll hang around for your talk."

"Well, I hope you do."

"I guess the Jews should have a country, why not? I've never given it much thought. That Burma Road story could damn near make a movie. With Marcus and all. Except that nobody in the audience knows where Jerusalem actually is, or gives a shit about it or about the Jews. That's really the problem. Bible movies are different, of course."

Mrs. Perlman came in looking perturbed. "Betty Grable isn't coming to the meeting."

Perlman slammed down the glass he was putting to his lips so that whiskey splashed. "What? Who told you that?"

"Shorty Goldfarb called. Betty has a stomach flu, he says. Anyway, she's out."

Perlman jumped up. "I'll talk to Shorty."

"Dave, dear —"

"God if that isn't the END! I ask you!" Perlman turned to Barak. "We deliver *you* to Grable, because the French ambassador pulled out on *her,* and now she pulls out on *us!* If that isn't this fucking town for you! Well, Shorty Goldfarb's balls are going into the meat grinder right now!"

"Honey, don't take on, *please!*" The death of Sidney Feller appeared to be much on Mrs. Perlman's mind. "We'll do fine without her. We've got Major Barak. Betty isn't even Jewish."

But Perlman was through the french doors, shouting, "You're not having a flop meeting in this house!" His wife followed him into another room, where his voice could be heard, shouting on the phone and sounding fucking mad. At this point Sam Pasternak walked in unshaven and yawning. "Zev, I just got a call from Dayan. I thought I'd better come right over here."

"What now?"

"The printer delivered that truckload of currency a day early. Dayan's leaving."

"*Leaving?* Leaving when?"

"Clearances will take a few hours. Sometime tonight. The Arabs are rejecting the extension of the truce, and Ben Gurion sent him a cable to rush back and take over Jerusalem Command."

Convulsively Barak extricated himself from a deep blue leather armchair. *Bye-bye, the thought of visiting Cal Tech!* "I've got to get back to New York. I'll check the flights."

"Hold on." Pasternak put a restraining hand on his arm. "I already checked all connections. You can't make it."

"Well then, I'll call Dayan and tell him to hold the plane."

"Hold the plane? When he has B.G.'s orders to take off?"

"Sam, I've got a battalion command waiting."

"You're committed to talk here today, and Zev, we *owe* this guy Perlman. I'll get you back to your battalion, maybe even ahead of Dayan's plane, that old Dutch clunker."

"You? How?"

"On the Constellation out of Panama. Those Connies travel like bullets."

"Hello there, Sam." Perlman picked up his glass as he came in, poured more whiskey, and said to Barak, "Goldfarb swears Grable has a temperature of a hundred and five. Maybe she does, maybe she doesn't. I know this, if it was an Academy Award dinner, she'd show up if she was *dead*. And do a tap dance if she won." He gulped his drink. "Well, it's no skin off our nose. We've got *you*. You're a million times better than Grable. You're for *real*. Just wear that uniform, I hear it gives all the ladies a temperature of a hundred and five." He laughed hoarsely and coughed hard.

Making the Marcus speech again, Zev Barak felt like a dancing bear doing his tricks for carrots. Afterward the women swarmed around him. Ellen Shugar held on to his arm with self-important possessiveness, explaining that the major had to fly to Washington at once on an urgent secret mission, and so the ordeal was cut short. Dave Perlman walked them out to the white Lincoln, where Pasternak already sat. "I tell you what," he said. "I'm going to put a couple of writers on that Marcus story. It's a toughie, but you got me interested. Gentile writers. Jews might get subjective."

At the TWA departure entrance Ellen Shugar stopped the white Lincoln, rolled a self-conscious glance at Barak in the back seat, then hugged and kissed Pasternak. "Sammy, take care of yourself." Barak saw tears roll down the tanned starved cheek.

"Nice lady. Sort of sad," said Pasternak as they went inside. "She has two no-good kids. The girl bums around on motorcycles, and the boy dropped out of school and surfs. Her husband is a contractor, earth moving. They were religious till they moved from Long Island to California. I'll check us in, and see you at the plane gate."

As Barak slipped through the terminal crowd with his suitcase, he heard a loud call: "Adon Barak, shalom!" On a nearby airport bench, in an ill-fitting gray suit and stringy tie, there sat Don Kishote! But on a second look no, not Kishote, but his brother. The last Barak had heard of this fellow, he had been in an army prison. "Blumenthal, what the devil are you doing here?"

"Right now," Leopold replied in saucy English, "waiting for my boss."

"Who is that?"

"Sheva Leavis."

Barak had vaguely heard of a nimble Tel Aviv fixer by that name. "How did you get here?"

Leopold explained that in the prison compound he had met Leavis, whose nephew had been in his mutinous platoon. Leavis was an Iraqi Jew who dealt in war surplus munitions, paid spot cash for them, and arranged to evade embargoes and ship the stuff to Israel. "He was surprised how much I knew about currencies. He took a liking to me," said Leopold. "I was trading foreign currencies under the nose of the Germans when I was fifteen. My father brought us out of Katowice by bribing the SS, with Swiss francs that I scrounged. Well, Leavis got his nephew released, and me too, and now here I am."

"What about travel papers? Passport, visas, and so on?"

Leopold crookedly grinned. "Sheva."

"And the army let you go?"

"Well, I just went." With a flourish, Leopold offered a pack of Camels.

"No thanks. You're a deserter, then."

Leopold put a flaming Zippo lighter to his cigarette. "If you say so."

"Come back, Blumenthal. I'll buy your air ticket for you. Right now! Deserting is bad business."

An obstinate pout hardened Leopold's face. "I'm flying with Sheva to the Philippines. American tanks are rusting out there by the hundreds. The Filipinos can't take dollars, dollar transactions are all traced. It's complicated, lots of currency switching."

The airport loudspeaker was scratchily announcing Barak's flight to Washington. "You'll have a hell of a problem when you come home."

"This is home."

"America? You can't stay here. Immigration won't let you."

With a knowing, condescending grin, Leopold blew a smoke ring. "Yossi likes Israel? *Kol ha'kavod* [all honor] to him."

"Not that it matters" — Barak picked up his suitcase — "but you might not be alive, and you undoubtedly wouldn't be here, if our people hadn't smuggled you out of Italy and then —"

"I didn't volunteer to come to Israel, Adon Barak, or to join your army," Leopold broke in. "I was shipped around like a horse, and in Haifa I was drafted like a horse. I'm still a Zionist, I'll contribute more over here. You'll see."

Barak shrugged and walked off.

"Regards to Yossi," he called at Barak's departing back, "and to Yael Luria."

Pasternak was waiting at the plane gate. "Come, come, they're boarding. We're in luck, our flight's on a Constellation."

"What do you know about a guy named Sheva Leavis?" Barak asked, when they were settled in the roomy second-class seats of the vast aircraft.

"Sheva? Why?" Barak described his encounter with Blumenthal. Pasternak nodded. "That's Sheva, all right."

"Does he accomplish anything?"

"For Sheva, yes. For Israel, well, I won't say he's done nothing. He plays his own little game and skims some cream. It all helps, I guess."

The roar of the swift steep takeoff broke the thread of their talk. After that Sam Pasternak spoke in low rapid Hebrew about the clandestine Constellation deal and others like it. A few American and Canadian Jews who had started life as immigrant junk peddlers were now in the scrap metal business, he explained. As the War Assets Administration sold off incalculable masses of unwanted munitions and arms-making machinery, the detritus of a finished world war, these dealers knew where the stuff was and how to obtain it at preposterously low cost.

But they also knew about the embargo. Resale for combat use was lawbreaking, said Pasternak, and that was the real catch. These men might sympathize, but they could not risk their livelihoods and perhaps jail. So it was up to the Yishuv Jews somehow to obtain the warmaking scrap — tanks, trucks, bulk TNT, lathes for turning out rifle barrels, communication electronics, old bombers, fighters, and Constellations — without bringing down the law on the effort. Stories of recruiting aviators, communication engineers, gun designers, cryptologists, then a long lunatic account of buying an aircraft carrier and reconditioning it for sea, all in vain — Pasternak went on for hours. Through his anecdotes of dashing success and calamitous failure, ran two threads, scarlet and gold, of derring-do and money; too much scarlet, not enough gold. Uncle Harry's ill-defined "few fellows who were helping out" Pasternak described as a small circle of businessmen committed to finding the money for almost any grotesque scheme that might put arms in Jewish hands in the Holy Land; and they were so drained at this point that Barak's Uncle Harry had had to ask Dave Perlman to come up with ten thousand dollars.

"While you and I were fighting the battle of the roads," Pasternak said, "the wildest business was going on overseas. Ben Gurion knew there would be war once the State was declared. He wanted weaponry procured and piled up outside, so that the minute the British pulled out the stuff would pour in. He hoped he'd get some of it, at least, in time to fight off the invaders."

"And so he did," said Barak.

"Well, barely. Now we've got the airlift from Czechoslovakia, a more solid basis for supplies. That's why" — he rapped his knuckles against the fuselage — "we need a Constellation! And we'll get it."

"When?"

"That depends on Christian Cunningham. Doesn't this thing ride smoothly? Like a dream, hah? Ten tons at a crack, Zev, ten tons!"

9

The Terrible Tiger

Pasternak sat in his underwear, smoking a cigarette by an open window which offered a fine view of Pennsylvania Avenue clear down to the Capitol dome, gleaming white in the afternoon sun. The wheezing air conditioner in another window was not perceptibly cooling the narrow bedroom in the Willard Hotel. Enter Barak, in a seersucker suit, straw hat, white shirt, and red tie, carrying a box.

"Look at you! Yankee Doodle!"

"I wasn't going to wear this foolish masquerade" — Barak brandished the box — "to your friend Cunningham's house. If it wasn't government property I'd burn it. When do we go?"

"I'll get dressed." Pasternak walked around him. "Not a bad fit. Tight in the shoulders."

"Best I could find to walk out of the shop in. Very cheap."

"America is cheap. They've got everything, and no war damage."

The rented car was approaching the Memorial Bridge when Barak said, "Let's stop here." Pasternak halted and parked. Barak climbed the steps of the memorial, contemplated the giant seated Lincoln for several minutes, and returned. "To be an American," he said somberly, "must be something wonderful."

"Most of them don't know it." Pasternak started the car.

Barak shook his head. "They know. Maybe they don't talk about it."

On the other bank of the Potomac they drove for a while through leafy roads and lanes, then down a narrow winding dirt road to a gravelled circular driveway before a brick house with a small white wooden porch. Pasternak rang a chiming doorbell. From inside a cupola overhead a startling voice hollowly asked, "Who's there?"

"Sam Pasternak and friend."

"Who is Sam Pasternak? And how do I know you're him?" Faint mischief in the cracking tones.

"We ate octopus together in Genoa, Chris, and you got sick as a dog."

A sepulchral chuckle. The door buzzed and opened. A pretty black maidservant said, "Good evening. This way, please."

A lean angular man rose to greet them in a long room facing the river, where a large rosewood grand piano dominated old-fashioned furniture. He had thick graying hair, heavy horn-rimmed glasses, and prominent bony jaws, and despite the heat he wore a gray three-piece suit, with a gold watch chain across the vest. "Drat that octopus, Sam, it darn near finished me." Like the voice from the cupola, he spoke in deep tones that faintly cracked.

"Chris, this is Zev Barak."

"Hello there." Strong handshake with a cold dry hand. "The sun's over the yardarm, gentlemen, what do you say to mint juleps? The lady of the house doesn't drink, so come along."

On a curving brick terrace that offered a broad vista of the Potomac and a distant glimpse of the Washington Monument and the Capitol, they settled down in wrought-iron chairs at a glass-top table. The maid brought frosted pewter mugs rimmed with green mint leaves, and set out bowls of pretzels and peanuts. "Watch out, Zev," Pasternak said. "If you've never had a mint julep, it can put you under."

"You Israeli fellows have no head for strong drink," said Cunningham, sipping. "American Jews, now, drink even with a man, by and large. It's interesting." He peered at Barak. "Zev Barak. What's your real name?" Barak blinked at him. With a thin smile Cunningham persisted. "Does that question offend you?"

"No, but that's my name. I was born Wolfgang Berkowitz, if that's what you mean."

"What does Zev Barak mean in Hebrew? I know you people tend to take on Hebrew names in Palestine."

Barak replied with good humor, "Zev means wolf." Pasternak had warned him that Christian Cunningham was an odd man with odd manners. "Short for Wolfgang, you might say."

"I see," Cunningham nodded. "And Barak, short for Berkowitz."

"Well, yes, but it's a common name in Israel. It means lightning."

"Lightning Wolf. Not bad! Could be almost American Indian." He turned to Pasternak. "Is your friend a lightning wolf?"

"Zev is okay." Pasternak was drinking his julep. After one taste of the powerful stuff, Barak was only pretending.

"It's interesting," said Cunningham. "In America Jews change their names to seem less Jewish. You people tend to Hebraize your names and make yourself more Jewish. Now why is that?"

"Getting away from Europe, I suppose," said Pasternak, "in one direction or the other."

"Aha!" For the first time Cunningham smiled widely, showing cigarette-stained even teeth. "Well said. Not the whole answer, but interesting. And here's the lady of the house."

A thin girl of twelve or so in a tennis dress ran lightly onto the patio. "I beat him, father. He's fifteen, and a blowhard, and I won two sets." She stopped on seeing the Israelis. With a touch of shyness yet cheerily she said, "Hello, I'm Emily."

"Dinner at seven-thirty, Emily, with Mr. Pasternak and Mr. Barak."

She smiled at them and was gone. Cunningham's whole manner changed. His eyes drooped half-shut, he hooked thumbs in the gold watch chain, and he sank in his chair. The voice sharpened. "Sam, I think the Constellation thing will be all right from our embassy end. After dinner we'll have to see a chap who lives nearby, for half an hour or so."

"Okay, Chris."

"As for the Panama people we can help you somewhat, but that'll be mostly up to you."

"We're prepared for that."

Straightening in his seat, Cunningham reverted to his acerb social vein. "While we're gone the lady of the house will have to entertain Mr. Wolf Lightning."

"An agreeable prospect," Barak said.

"You'll find her articulate, if a little silly. Her mother's in England, you see, visiting our son at Oxford. If I were a Jew," Cunningham turned to Pasternak, after a long sip of his julep, "I'd certainly want to remove myself as far from Europe as possible. Especially from Russia. *'From the north will the evil come,'*" he quoted Jeremiah. "Russia has been your misfortune. Hitler is your bugbear, but he went to school in Russia, you know."

Pasternak nodded. Barak said, "I'm not sure I understand that."

With evident relish for a fresh audience, Cunningham thrust a long bony finger at him. "From the pales and the pogroms of the czars, Mr. Wolf Lightning, Adolf Hitler learned that western liberalism was all bosh. That he could treat the Jews as subhuman without any international trouble, just some futile squeaks and finger-pointing. From Lenin he learned the use of concentration camps and totalitarian terror. From Stalin he learned that vast massacres could be covered up and baldly denied, and the world wouldn't give a tinker's damn."

Cunningham paused to empty his pewter mug with a toss. "Hitler's only innovation was to import all those horrors from the depths of Slav darkness into the light of Middle Europe. That Hitler turned on his teachers is a great irony of history. A still greater irony is that we saved Russia from Hitler with Lend-Lease — Russia, the one mortal menace on the planet to our country. Will you gentlemen join me in another julep?" The Israelis eyed each other, and both declined. Cunningham refilled his glass from a tinkling jug and went on about the iniquity and the menace of the Soviet Union.

Pasternak had warned Barak, too, of Cunningham's obsession with the evil nature of the Russians. As sunset reddened the river, the intelligence man held forth to Barak on this theme. Christianity had come too late to Russia, he said, a full thousand years after Christ, and then only in a corrupted form via Byzantium. It had never quite reached the Tartar heart of the Slavs, but had left them a dangerous schizophrenic mass, half savage conquerors, half milksop idealists, the savage side inexorably emerging and dominating their society and their politics.

"That national split personality emerges equally in Tolstoy and in Dostoyevsky. It's the only way to understand such far-apart tortured geniuses, Major Barak, only way to relate them, nationally and rationally, to each other. That split is in their music. In their architecture. In their art. Ever see Repin's painting of Ivan the Terrible with his eldest son dying at his feet, after Ivan smashed in his skull with a gold-headed cane? Ivan's face, the son's face? There's your whole story, in one gory image."

"Dinner is served," said the maid at the french doors.

The girl, dressed in plain gray, was on her dignity in her mother's chair at the foot of the table, saying little, ringing for the maid to give her sotto voce orders, and quietly urging on the guests second helpings of the vichyssoise, broiled chicken, and sherbet. Barak and Pasternak ate in silence and exchanged glances as Cunningham frankly laid out the prevailing American intelligence estimate of Israel. The Jewish military successes were being sized up, he cautioned them, as a surprising and on the whole negative development. The Arabs would never accept the Zionists in their midst, not for generations. If defeated again and again, they would vent their frustration on the western powers by turning to the Russians for support. That could upset the entire power balance in the Middle East. Hostile Arab governments could nationalize western oil assets, and even close out British and American strategic bases in the region. As for the Israelis, said Cunningham, his colleagues tended to think of them as an unyielding aggressive lot, hungry for expansion. Worst of all, from the standpoint of American national interest, they were said to be mostly socialist or downright Marxist.

Full of Russian Jews, Israel was being armed by Czechoslovakia with Soviet-controlled munitions. A pro-Soviet political stand in Israel was entirely possible.

"That's moonshine," said Pasternak. "We know the Russians. Our founders fled from Russia to create Israel."

"Of course, but it's the task of intelligence to put the worst case. I lose patience, I must say, with the short sight of my colleagues. When I worked in the FBI years ago, before the war, I played some part in exposing the Soviet Union's spy rings. Yet from 1941 to 1945, we poured Lend-Lease to that bone-deep enemy of ours. Now mind you" — Cunningham waved his sherbet spoon at them for emphasis — "Lend-Lease was *sound*. Hitler had to be smashed. But the total switchover to loving the Russians, Hollywoodizing them, we will live to regret for a hundred years. It was a colossal four-year security disaster. My view is that Israel can develop into our strategic bastion in the Middle East. At the OSS I had superiors who listened to me, however skeptically, and some of them are now in the CIA."

"Well, that's reassuring," blurted Barak.

"Not necessarily. Much depends on your Mr. Ben Gurion. One is told that you have his ear, Major Barak, so let me be blunt." Cunningham talked straight at him, and Barak began to understand why Sam Pasternak had brought him here, and why Cunningham had received him. "Your Prime Minister is a formidable personality, but his real test is now at hand. He has to change fast from revolutionary to statesman. All those years of Zionist political infighting have made him rough, hard, small-minded, and obstinate. His rhetoric shows his Russian origins, the hammer and sickle are all over it. Does Ben Gurion believe in God?"

This sudden shot, with a piercing direct look, gravelled Barak. Pasternak was watching him with a tart smile, and the quiet girl too stared at him. "Well, the religious faction in our country gives him a big pain, that I know."

"That isn't what I asked." Cunningham sank lower in his chair. "The return of the Jews to the Holy Land is an anomaly of history. In the long view Ben Gurion's either an instrument of Providence at the start of a vast new beginning in world affairs, or he's a trivial person, an insignificant passing accident of time and chance. In that case so is your country, probably."

Barak said, "He isn't religious in the least. He'll eat anything, and he doesn't observe the holidays, none of that."

"Again, that's not what I asked."

Barak shrugged, and after a moment Cunningham went on, "Are you religious?"

"You're a grand host, Mr. Cunningham, and I've been fascinated listening to you, but that's really none of your business."

Christian Cunningham straightened in his chair and burst out laughing. "Everything is the business of an intelligence man. Sam, we have to go. Emily, give some more coffee to Mr. Wolf Lightning, and try not to bore him."

The girl said when they had gone, "Would you like more coffee?"

"Please."

"Brandy?"

"No, thanks."

"In Israel, do you have fireflies?"

"Fireflies? I've never seen fireflies. We have glowworms."

She touched the bell. "Estelle, please bring us coffee on the terrace. . . . Come." Barak followed her through the french doors to the patio and down a curving brick stairway, where she took his hand in a cool small clasp. "The darn lights are kaput out here. Don't stumble over the potted plants. . . . Here we are." She released him on the flagstone terrace, and they sat down; he on a padded lounge chair, she in a cushioned swing. "Just to make me a liar, the fireflies probably won't show. . . . Oh, there's one. And another."

The moving green flashes in fact were all over a lawn that sloped down to dark trees, beyond which the river gleamed in the moonlight. "You certainly tickled my father, he loves to be talked up to. If you've got a point, that is."

"That beautiful smell here — what is it?"

"Gardenias. They line this terrace. My mother's favorite flower. What's the matter with your arm?"

Her directness nonplussed Barak as Cunningham's had. He

thought he was using his arm normally. "What makes you ask?"

"The way you move it." In the light diffusing from the patio above, he could see her swing her whole arm, slightly bent, in an emphatic gesture. "Were you wounded?"

"Yes, but it's all better."

The maid arrived with the coffee. Emily poured two cups. "Have you ever read Emily Dickinson's poetry? I'm named after her. My mother grew up in Amherst, her birthplace."

"Isn't that in New England? Your father talks like a Southerner."

"Oh yes. He's from Georgia. They met on a boat. Romantic. I write poetry, but not like Emily Dickinson. She had constipated emotions."

The self-conscious show-off remark left Barak with no immediate reply. Pause. "Well, those fireflies are very nice. You should write a poem about them."

"I have. Tell me about your wound."

"Do you want to write a poem about it?"

"I've never talked to a warrior before. I'm just interested."

"Well, all right." As he described the midnight skirmish with the daughter's gaze fixed on him, he began to relive it, recounting with vivid detail the Arab assault and retreat, and the way he had been shot.

"You're sure it was an accident? Was there a soldier in your company angry at you?"

Smart girl, he thought. On being hit from behind, he himself had at first suspected that a lazy malcontent or coward in his company might have done it. "No, the poor guy is a *shlemiehl* — a clumsy fool — but he loves me. He ran up at once as I lay there bleeding, and told me it was his doing. He was devastated."

They watched the fireflies. Emily's swing creaked. A river breeze stirred a scent of green leaves and gardenias. "And I'm not a warrior, you know. We all have to fight because the Arabs don't want us there. I was studying chemistry. That's what I hope to be one day, a chemist."

"How utterly boring. Makes me think of drugstores."

"Excuse me, Emily, but that's very childish. Chemistry is the foundation of everything. You and I, for instance, are two small chemical machines making noises at each other. Those fireflies work by chemistry. So do the stars."

Emily dropped her eyes and twisted her fingers in her lap. "Sorry. Actually, when we girls talk about chemistry among ourselves, it means whether we like a boy or not."

"I have a younger brother," said Barak, "who's studying physics. One day he may be a great physicist. Physics and chemistry are what the world's all about, Emily. Including war."

"No, war is about men," she said, "and you know that. I'm glad your wound healed. Do you know *Othello?*"

"Well, I've read the play."

" '*She loved me for the dangers I had passed,*' " Emily intoned, in a high strained little voice, " '*and I loved her that she did pity them.*' "

Barak said awkwardly, "At your age, do you think much about love?"

"Juliet was twelve and a half." Silence, creaking of the swing. "I could tell you about my own wounds, but I think I hear my father returning. Most of my poetry is about that."

"Then it's sad stuff."

"No, some of it is very merry. Even funny." As they stood up and went toward the dark staircase, she clasped his hand again. "This way. . . . Incidentally, it's all about another girl. Did you like the fireflies?"

"They're magical."

Cunningham said as they came in from the patio, "Well, did she bore you to death? Or get too inquisitive?"

"She's as pleasant a hostess as you are a host."

"Oh? Dubious compliment!"

"Good night," the girl said to Barak and Pasternak. "Nice meeting you." Looking at her in the light, Barak noted that she was flat-chested, a child. "Good night, father." She kissed Cunningham and almost ran out.

"We have to go, Zev," said Pasternak. "We have a plane to catch in New York."

Cunningham held out a hand to Barak. "Hope you didn't mind my little jokes about Wolf Lightning, or my disquisitions. It's just my way."

"I enjoyed it all. Also your daughter's company."

"That's nice." Cunningham's thin lips widened in a cold smile. "If you remember anything I said, you're free to mention it to Mr. Ben Gurion."

Driving to the airport, Pasternak opened up about Christian Cunningham more than he had before.

"Now that you've met him, let me give you some background. He's one of a kind. He was serving in the OSS in Italy in 1945, and I was in the underground there, getting Jews out in boats bound for Palestine. That was when we ate octopus. We'd worked with each other before, in France, but we both got really involved in a deal between the OSS and some German generals in northern Italy who wanted to surrender separately to the Anglo-Americans. It came to nothing, but he and I got to know each other well. He helped me obtain a boat in Genoa, in fact, that made two successful runs through the British blockade, loaded with DPs. I passed him some underground intelligence on German troop movements, ammunition dumps, and so on. By luck our people in Provence also got hold of a Wehrmacht coding machine, and I gave it to him. That was late in the war. I don't know that it did any good, but he appreciated it. I imagine it earned him points with his bosses . . . Say, why are you so restless? What's the matter?"

"Nothing's the matter. This is a damn strange way to get back to Israel, that's all," said Barak irritably, "via New York, Panama, Brazil, and Czechoslovakia."

"Relax, Wolf Lightning."

At the wheel of a parked jeep, sweating in the humid evening, Yael watched the racehorse plane approach over Tel Aviv, circle to the east through distant AA tracer fire and black puffs, and bounce hard as it returned and landed. Dayan came striding across the tarmac in a strangely gaudy uniform. *"Dode Moshe!"* Yael called. Since her childhood in Nahalal he had been *Dode,* Uncle, to her.

He came through the gate, glancing here and there. "Hello, Yael."

"Isn't Zev Barak with you?"

"No."

"I was ordered to meet him."

"So, you've met me." He jumped into the jeep. "I don't see my driver. Take me to Tel Hashomer."

The two pilots of the plane walked by, looking shaken. "Those poor Dutchmen had to come in over the Arabs," he said, "because there was no wind. Well, they're collecting double pay."

"How was your trip?"

"Rough. Storms all the way." Dayan yawned, put both arms behind his head, and settled in the seat. "I'll be glad to get to camp and into bed." He fell fast asleep in a moment. Yael drove to the armor base, detouring where roads passed within enemy gun range. The full moon was well up in the sky when she turned toward the Tel Hashomer gate. Here scout cars, jeeps, and half-tracks were grinding out in low gear, manned by helmeted soldiers in full battle dress. Dayan woke with a start. "What's all this? That's my battalion!" He leaped out and snapped an order to an officer in a half-track, who repeated it on his walkie-talkie. The vehicles clanked to a stop as Dayan hurried off to the head of the column. From the wheel of a gun-mounted jeep close by, the driver saluted Yael, and pushed his glasses up on his nose.

"Kishote! Where's Benny?"

"Three cars behind us." He pointed, and Yael saw her brother standing up in a half-track by the gun. She trotted to him. "Benny, how are you?"

"Me? I'm fine. What brings *you* here?"

"I drove Dode Moshe in from the airport."

"Dode Moshe? Then he's back! *Shiga'on!* [Crazy, marvellous!] We thought we'd have to fight the war without him."

"Where are you heading?"

"Jumping-off point. As soon as the truce ends, we go."

"Good luck and success, Benny!"

The night was stifling, and she was wiping her face with a

handkerchief when she returned to her jeep. Don Kishote was perched on its hood. "Ah, you're back," he said. "Good, give me something of yours. Give me that handkerchief."

"What are you talking about?"

"I'm going into battle. It's an old custom. Didn't you ever read Walter Scott? I'm supposed to carry a favor from a lady."

"Only from a lady you love, idiot."

"B'seder, I love you. You know you're the prettiest lady alive." Grinning, he held out his hand. "A handkerchief is fine."

Yael hesitated and giggled. "You're kidding me."

"I'm serious. Give it here."

The declaration of love, even if playful, rather got to Yael Luria. She ate up homage, however gross, and she was not wholly indifferent to Don Kishote. Ever since he had carried Benny off the Latrun battlefield, her brother had certainly taken to him, and the sometimes uncivilized glint behind the youngster's glasses tickled Yael's own wild streak.

"Okay, okay." She gave him the handkerchief. "It's wringing wet, but there you are. Good luck!"

"Do I get a kiss, too?"

"Oh, go fight the war, child."

He tucked it into his helmet and ran to his armored jeep, for the column was starting to move with great shouts and clanging.

"You'll be firing the cannon," Benny Luria told Kishote next day. They were peering into the cramped dark interior of a captured Arab Legion armored car, which stank like a broken toilet. Half-naked soldiers perspiring in the broiling sun were frantically wiring up a new radio, welding patches on shell holes, and oiling and fueling the vehicle. It was still attached by a tow cable to the half-track with which Dayan himself had salvaged it under enemy fire. Benny Luria had volunteered to go with him to attach the cable, and that had earned him command of the car.

"Me? What do I know about cannons?"

"Who does? A gunnery guy is coming out from Tel Aviv."

Amid fragrant crushed stacks of millet the commandos were

changing shot-up tires, plugging bullet holes in leaking radiators, replacing broken caterpillar tracks and the like, and medics were bandaging the wounded; for the light battalion, slicing into the salient threatening Tel Aviv, had already surprised and subdued two little villages by dashing in without a mortar barrage, all guns firing and Dayan leading the charge. The surprised villages had fallen quickly, if at some cost.

"Who can read this stuff, anyway?" Kishote gestured at the blurry instructions in Arabic stencilled all over the interior. "How will you run the thing?"

"A car's a car, a gun's a gun," said Luria. "We'll run it. Dayan says this one cannon doubles our battalion's firepower."

The artillery expert showed up, a burly sabra hoarse from yelling at recruits. He dinned elementary gunnery into Don Kishote, making him swivel the turret, train and elevate the weapon, and aim at targets far and near. Kishote was cramped into a tiny space, the smells of gasoline and piss choked him, and the instructor's guttural barks bewildered him, the more so as the banging and screeching and sawing at the car went on without cease. After a while Moshe Dayan showed up. "Well, well, can he shoot?"

"Give him an order," said Luria.

Dayan pointed to a tall tree far down the field. "Take off that bottom branch."

Don Kishote let fly with a roar and a puff of flame. The branch leaped off the tree.

"That's that," said Dayan. "So now we are invincible. We go into Lydda."

The battalion blasted westward into the well-fortified airport town past antitank ditches, thick cactus hedges, and heavy fire from gun emplacements, risking hitting minefields but luckily avoiding them. The trouble began when the column reached the town center. Dayan's attack plan was clear. Half the column would turn north led by the armored car, now dubbed the Terrible Tiger, and he himself would lead the other half south. After shooting up the town in both directions to spread havoc and fear, they would rejoin and dash out by the road they had come in; the mission, to soften up the objective for an assault by an advancing mechanized brigade. Dayan was not acting on orders, but improvising this raid on the basis of some confused communications, and he well knew that his battalion lacked the firepower to secure the town.

The Tiger went charging toward the north end of Lydda as ordered. The inhabitants were indeed shocked by the apparition of an Arab Legion armored vehicle running amuck and blazing away in their streets, but all too soon they recovered and began to make it very hot for the Tiger with grenades and rifle fire. It was a while before Benny Luria, directing the vehicle from the turret and shooting the machine gun, fully realized why the townspeople were being so bold. From the garbled shouts by Dayan in his headphones he understood at last that everything was going as wrong as possible, and he halted the Tiger in an open square.

Kishote, peering around through a forward slit at the milling Arabs, yelled over the engine noise, "Say, Benny, where are the rest of our guys?"

"They all went south with Dayan, through Lydda and on down to Ramle."

"What, all of them? All the way to Ramle? How come?"

"Balagan, that's how come!"

Rattle of bullets on the armor, roar of exploding grenades, car rocking violently.

"You don't mean we're here in Lydda by *ourselves*?" shouted Kishote. The driver, a blond young kibbutznik who had volunteered, turned round eyes at Luria, all the whites showing.

"That's exactly right! By ourselves. So shut up and fire at that roof to the left! See the smoke? Machine gun nest! Fire!"

Kishote fired. The recoils were making his chest sore, blood was staining his shirt, the shell fumes were choking him, but the exhilaration of battle was on him and he didn't care. "Don't stop, no more stopping," Luria called to the driver, "we move and we fire, we move and we fire, and when I order you, we head back and join the others!"

A welcome sight the Terrible Tiger must have been to Dode Moshe, as he led his beat-up battalion back through Ramle and

Lydda, taking heavy punishment all the way; and Benny Luria was decidedly glad to see Dayan returning. The Tiger was cannonading and machine-gunning a fortresslike police station which was erupting fire and barring the way out of Lydda.

"Well, there they come!" Luria shouted. "We'll cover them till they get past the station, then we run for it and bring up the rear!"

Kishote jumped to the slit to look at the commandos. After the protracted harmless hail of bullets on the armor he felt snugly safe, but he wasn't. A sudden burning blow on his temple dizzied him. Putting a hand to the place he brought it away sticky with warm bright red blood.

"Rotten luck!" exclaimed Luria. "Hurt bad?"

"No, no, I'm all right. Just grazed."

"Good, keep firing! Hey, there's Dode Moshe going by! Elohim, those guys have taken a battering! Lot of wounded lying in those cars, Kishote, God knows how many may be dead . . ."

Kishote shot round after round into the fort. The Tiger's shells were nearly gone when the enemy fire at last slackened. The rear battalion vehicles were going by, half-tracks pushing scout cars, scout cars pushing jeeps, radiators boiling, tires flat, a sorry array. Luria ordered the driver to turn and follow the last jeep, and Kishote pulled Yael's handkerchief from his helmet to stanch the blood running down his cheek.

"Your sister's handkerchief did it," he said. "It brought me luck. It made that bullet miss. Walter Scott is a real authority."

"You want to believe that? Kol ha'kavod," said Luria. "Only in that case, how did that bullet get through the slit? Why didn't it bounce off like a thousand others? That's a pretty inefficient handkerchief."

All this was shouted through a lot of engine racket and rumbling of wheels over broken ground. They were heading out of danger, alive and feeling exalted.

"Your trouble is you're superstitious," yelled Kishote. "Suppose I walked out there naked with her handkerchief? Are all the bullets supposed to miss me? Foolishness. You better read Walter Scott again. My question is, did we win the battle?"

"Maybe Dode Moshe knows," said Benny Luria. "I sure don't."

"One thing I know," said Kishote. "From now on I want armor, the thicker the better."

"Not me. Me for the air force, if I can qualify. Get above all this dust and noise."

10

The Constellation

Until the Constellation actually soared off the runway in Panama, Barak wasn't sure that he was not stuck indefinitely in Central America, at a small sweltering airport bordered by banana plantations. His passport was gone, collected by an official wearing a uniform even gaudier than the fantasy of the Tel Aviv tailors. A gasoline truck drawn up before the nose of the giant plane blocked it from moving an inch. Still the pilots and the crew, a diverse gang of Israelis, volunteer Americans, and Canadians, went on pottering with the awesome engines and the interior instruments. They did not disturb the passenger cabin, handsomely furnished with long rows of new beige seats for the "Panama airline," and decorated in grays and browns with modernistic panels of Panama scenes, including the Canal locks.

Sam Pasternak appeared unworried. "No use just hanging around," he said to Barak, who sat sweating and fretting in the plane, drinking Coca-Cola. "Why don't you do some sightseeing? The Canal's worth a look."

"But what's happening? When do we leave?"

"Pretty soon. Have no fear, we won't go without you."

"Sam, the truce is over. The war may be on already."

"Impossible. They'll hold the war for you."

A cabdriver took Barak to view the immense locks, and he had the good luck to observe an American aircraft carrier being towed into a lock, then slowly starting to sink as the water was let out. On his return late in the afternoon, the Constellation's engines were roaring, the wheels straining at the blocks, but the truck still barred it from moving. Sam Pasternak greeted him by handing him his passport. "B'seder, glad you're back. It won't be long now."

"What about that gasoline truck?"

"Yes, that's the problem. We're just testing the engines."

They were standing in the open door of the plane, at the top of the ramp. "What problem? You're cleared to go, aren't you?"

"Well, yes and no. It's a strange place with strange regulations. Ah, there we are." A stout man in overalls was approaching the gasoline truck. "Quick, come inside."

Pasternak slammed the door shut and twisted the air lock. The plane began to move. Looking out a window, Barak saw the truck driving off the field. Amid much English and Hebrew shouting in the open cockpit, mingled with garbled high-pitched radio transmissions in Spanish and English, the plane gathered speed, whirled onto a main runway, and went to full throttle. A police car raced onto the tarmac, its siren screaming over the noise of the engines. It drew almost alongside the accelerating aircraft, and through an open car window a uniformed man was brandishing a rifle, but in seconds the Constellation left the car behind and leaped into the air.

"Well, that's that." Pasternak was at Barak's shoulder, peering out the window as the plane climbed and banked over a lush green plantation. "Next stop is in Brazil to refuel, then Dakar. *Parlez-vous français?*" He gestured at the rows of vacant seats. "The boys will have to rip up all this camouflage before we get to Czechoslovakia. Pity! It cost us a fortune to install. When we land in Zatec, it must be ready to dump, so we can load up with airlift cargo, refuel, and go home."

"What did that driver of the gasoline truck cost you?"

"Actually, the police car cost more." Pasternak crinkled his eyes in a grin. "But I have plenty of that ten thousand left. Good thing, too. No telling what we'll run into in Natal and Dakar." He dropped into the soft seat beside Barak, and tilted back. "A shame to get rid of this classy interior, isn't it? Best quality. The fact that the U.S. Embassy didn't have the plane impounded — also the return of our passports an hour ago — we owe to Christian Cunningham."

"Sam, is all Czech cooking this abominable?" Barak inquired, wrinkling up his face over smelly boiled fish and watery potatoes served on chipped old plates.

"This isn't Czech cooking, this is Marxist cooking, and like everything else about that system, it stinks," Pasternak replied, and went on joshing the stocky, heavily painted waitress in fluent Czech.

The plates were marked Hotel Masaryk, though the new sign outside read Hotel Stalin. Clearly this fusty hostelry near the Zatec air force base had been shut down for years, and reopened just to isolate the personnel of the Israeli airlift. All the airlift activity was quarantined in one corner of the base, well removed from the Czech air force hangars. Though the world press had long ago written up the "secret" operation, it still did not officially exist for the Czech government.

The waitress was decidedly flirtatious, delivering the dreary victuals in a clumsy inexperienced way. "Listen, Zev, she has a friend," Pasternak said, "and she's very interested in having some fun this evening. She volunteered that she likes Israelis, we're cute. Her apartment isn't far from here."

"Sam, I'm not interested in Czech whores," said Barak.

"Now, that isn't nice. Why whores? They're just spies. Don't talk politics or airlift with them, that's all."

"Enjoy yourself, Sam."

In the crowded smoky dining room the language was generally English, with a scattering of Hebrew. After dinner Barak joined some aviators in the lobby to drink imitation coffee and bad brandy. Like Pasternak's stories, their reminiscences were eye-openers. All Barak's recent fighting had been within the Yishuv, where battle plans and movements were measured in tens of miles. This airlift spanned the earth, he gathered, its reach if not its tonnage exceeding even the colossal Berlin airlift that was making all the headlines.

Vaguely he had known of the operation, but here were the

men who were doing it, World War II fliers from all over the globe. Mostly American, but not all, mostly Jewish, but far from all, mostly volunteers — Frenchmen, Canadians, South Africans, Australians — the gentile volunteers in it because they sympathized with the Jewish struggle to survive, or for the adventure, or, like the hard-bitten Americans who flew the largest chartered transports, as frank mercenaries. By this motley band the whole planet was being ransacked for arms in any quantity, for no government would openly help the Jews.

"I tell you you're in luck, mate, with that Constellation," a gangly Australian said to Barak. "You can hop straight to Oklahoma, and skip the bloody refueling at Jockstrap. That's the hell of a nuisance."

"Oklahoma? Jockstrap?"

"Jockstrap is Corsica," put in an American with a bristly gray haircut, quaffing beer from a big stein. "Only goddamn place in the Med that'll refuel a plane going to Israel. Oklahoma, that is."

Barak sat up late listening to their tales of the adventurous time before the State had been declared; of crashes and near-crashes, of airplanes taking off without clearance or without navigational equipment into cloudbursts and black fog, flown by pilots who had never been in the machines before, and so on. This sort of thing had gone on in the early days, they said; now the airlift was routinized, tame, and relatively efficient. Barak stumbled off to bed past two, much enlightened and encouraged. Pasternak had not yet returned, and whether he ever got any sleep Barak could not tell, for when he woke Sam was shaving, fully dressed and singing a plaintive Czech song.

A wheezy taxi dropped them at the air base as dawn was streaking the sky. Beside the towering Constellation the fancy passenger furnishings lay piled helter-skelter halfway as high as the wings. A tank truck was rhythmically pumping in fuel, and lined-up working parties were passing crates aboard from open trucks. "Machine guns," said Pasternak blithely, seeming none the worse for his night out. "Solid machine guns and ammo, this shipment. Good stuff, number-one priority."

Noisy workmen some distance away were trying to shove an

aircraft fuselage inside another, larger plane. "Messerschmitt fighters," Pasternak said, pointing to a line of the spindly machines nearby. "We have to take off the wings and ship them separately. The Czechs made these Me-109s for the Germans, and they're not very good planes, our guys tell us. Very tricky to fly. And on price the Czechs are skinning us alive. Still, we buy what we can get."

During the loading Barak walked around the airlift buildings, code-named Zebra, noting for his report to Ben Gurion the vast mounds of crated weaponry, stencilled in Russian, Czech, and French, the busy traffic of trucks and cranes, the variegated aircraft, and the feverish work of mechanics and loaders. Pleasant fields of ripening grain bordered the airfield, where almost a mile away the Czech air force planes were all in their hangars, a dead scene but for a few pacing sentries. When at last he and Sam went aboard the Constellation, it was so crammed with lashed crates that for takeoff they had to stand stooped in the cockpit. The pilots were the same Americans who had flown the plane from Panama, but the radioman-navigator was now an Israeli. The lumbering takeoff required a run to the very end of the field before the plane lifted into the air, barely above telephone wires.

"Tell Zev about Dayan," said the navigator to Pasternak, as the Constellation went soaring toward the rising sun over checkered green farmlands and a meandering silvery river.

"Dayan!" Barak exclaimed. "He's back home then?"

"Back home?" Pasternak grinned. "He's turned the whole war around."

"What are you talking about?"

"Dayan pulled off a terrific raid on Lydda and Ramle. I don't know details, but we've got those towns now, and Lydda airport, too! The UN is all screams and twitters, like a ladies' room when a guy barges in. A week ago the Arabs refused to extend the truce. Now the British are howling for a new truce, which means of course that the Arabs want it. So it's bound to come soon."

"Sam, where did you get all this?" Barak was glad but incredulous.

"I telephoned our guys in London while you were having your stroll, to tell them we're loading up and going. The papers there are full of the dashing one-eyed Jew commander. Same thing in America, they say." Pasternak tapped the navigator's arm. "Look, do we stand like this all the way to Tel Aviv? We'll be round-shouldered for life."

The navigator showed them a blocked-off space in the crates behind the cockpit, where there were mattresses and water jugs. Barak said as they lay down, "And you were going to get me home ahead of Dayan!"

"It was the delay at Dakar. Who could figure our fixer there would go off to Tangier with some dame? Frenchmen! Don't worry, Zev, there'll be plenty of war left."

"So, this time you did show up," Yael said sassily to Zev Barak, ignoring Pasternak as they got into her jeep. "What a huge airplane! Shiga'on! Is it ours now?"

"Not your business, Yael. Drop Sam off at his flat, then take me to Jerusalem."

"Pardon, sir, I have orders to bring you both straight to Ben Gurion."

"Oh? So do it."

Pasternak, sitting beside Yael, smiled and squinted at her as she started the engine. "You know, Yael, it's been years since I've been to Nahalal. How is your family?"

"All fine, sir. I don't remember ever seeing you there."

"But I was. I remember you well as Nahum Luria's fat little daughter."

"Truly? Well, I've lost weight." With a toss of her head and a swish of thick blond hair, Yael sent the jeep leaping forward.

"Yes and no," said Pasternak. His appraising look at her brought to Barak's mind both Mrs. Shugar and the Hotel Stalin waitress. He thought, however, that if any girl could handle Sam Pasternak, Yael Luria was that girl. As St. John Robley had put it in another context, it was diamond cut diamond.

Yael delivered them to Ben Gurion's Ramat Gan office and parked outside. She was primping at a hand mirror when a command car drove up and Moshe Dayan stepped out. She jumped to plant a kiss on his cheek. "Dode Moshe! The hero of Israel! The hero of the world!"

"*Al tagzimi!*" ("Don't exaggerate!") With a pleased crooked smile, Dayan patted her shoulder and went inside. Only then did Yael notice who his driver was.

"So, what happened to *you*?"

"Hello, there." Kishote showed her the handkerchief, stiff with black blood. His temple was thickly bandaged.

"Ugh! How did it happen? Tell me!"

He had spoken only a few sentences when she broke in. "You? *You* were in that Tiger? The story is all over the papers!"

"Yael, your brother commanded the Tiger. He made me the gunner."

"Benny actually *commanded* it? Is he all right?"

"Not a scratch. Benny was cool and tough and great."

She listened with wide shiny eyes to his story, then held out her hand. "All right, give me that silly handkerchief."

"By your life, no."

"Fool, I'll only wash it for you."

"No. It saved me, and I'm keeping it."

"You're a genuine madman. Is that wound serious?"

He imitated her, going into falsetto. "Why, I'm driving the hero of Israel! Of the world! How serious can it be?"

She made a face at him. "I'm glad you weren't badly hurt, but don't give the credit to my handkerchief."

"Only the handkerchief."

Yael hitched her shoulders, looked to the sky in despair, and went back to the jeep.

"Ten tons of machine guns!" Ben Gurion's disordered white hair, blowing in the breeze from an open window, gave him a look as excited as his tone. "In one plane, in one hop from Czechoslovakia! Now *that's* an airplane. And for fifteen thousand dollars! Pasternak, it's a sin about those other Constellations. No way to get them over here?"

Pasternak and Barak were sitting across the desk from him.

Pasternak spread his hands, palms up. "Prime Minister, do you have a friend in the American State Department? State has to release for sale abroad any plane that weighs over thirty-five thousand pounds. We got this one out with a trick that won't work twice."

"A friend in the State Department?" Ben Gurion's mouth curled. "General Marshall, maybe?" The telephone on his desk rang and as he picked it up Moshe Dayan walked in with Yigal Yadin, whose bald brow was corrugated, his pipe clenched in his teeth. "*Ken* [Yes] . . . *ken,* Yadin just came in with Dayan." He threw peculiar cold looks at Dayan. "I see. Well, better talk to him." He passed the telephone to his chief of operations. "For you. Trouble in Lydda. Uprising. Arabs attacking our soldiers."

He got up heavily from his chair and paced, while Yadin talked in low tones. "There you have it," he said to the others. "The people in Lydda surrendered. Mula Cohen gave them the most generous terms. No expulsion, no roundup of able-bodied men, just turning in their arms. They claimed they had done it, too. Now they're roaring out into the streets with rifles, knives, grenades, mobbing our boys. It's touch and go right now."

"No it isn't." Yadin was hanging up wearily. "Mula's got it under control. What happened was, a Legion tank patrol showed up on a hill nearby, so out the townspeople came looking for blood. The patrol retreated, and now they're surrendering again. The terms this time will be tougher."

Ben Gurion turned on Dayan. "You see? What you did wasn't warmaking. You took no objective, you destroyed no enemy forces. For a while you scared them, that's all. It wasn't a conquest, it was a prank."

"Prime Minister, pardon me," said Colonel Yadin, "Moshe's raid was the most daring action of this war, and the most successful."

"A prank, I say." Ben Gurion jutted his jaw at Dayan. "When you take over Jerusalem Command, I expect you to be more serious. Meantime your commandos are needed in the south. Before a cease-fire comes we must open up a secure corridor through the Egyptian lines. Those Negev settlements can't be sealed off again.

Can your battalion still fight, or did you destroy its combat readiness?"

"My men are splendid. Tremendous morale," Dayan briskly shot back. "They believe they won a great victory. Our vehicles, however, are all shot up."

"You'll be provided with vehicles," said Yadin.

"Then I await orders." Dayan's taut look relaxed in a smile at Barak. "Zev, I hear you made a big hit with the California ladies." He turned to Yadin. "My deputy was badly wounded. Can Zev come south with me and replace him? Then when I go to Jerusalem, he can take over the battalion."

Yadin glanced at Ben Gurion, who said a shade grumpily, "No objection."

"I accept," said Barak at once.

"That's settled. Pasternak, you're going back to Prague?"

"He's not, with your permission, sir," put in Dayan. "I've requested him for my deputy in the Jerusalem Command."

"That's confirmed," said Yadin.

Ben Gurion looked hard at Dayan. "A good choice. And I didn't say that what you did wasn't brave or inspiring. I said it wasn't warmaking. We aren't partisans anymore."

"With all respect, Prime Minister, you're a great politician, and you know a lot about Arabs. What I know is how to fight them. That's what I've been doing, except for farming, since I was a boy."

Ben Gurion held out his hand, and after a slight pause Dayan shook it. "You'll do a job in the Negev, I have no doubt."

"I'll try my best."

Coming outside, Barak and Pasternak found the bandaged Kishote sitting on the hood of Yael's jeep and chatting with her. "Kishote!" said Barak. "You caught it, did you?"

"Nothing. I'm okay."

"I saw your brother in Los Angeles."

Yael's eyes opened wide, and Kishote hopped off the jeep. "Leopold? You did? He really made it there?"

"Yes, and he says he's going to stay there."

"Then he probably will. Leo does what he wants."

"And maybe you'll join him, eh?"

"Why should I? This is home." He touched his bandage. "Look, I've already paid taxes."

"Next time you're in Nahalal," Pasternak said to Yael, "give your father, and also my Uncle Avram, regards from Sam Pasternak."

"I'll try to remember, but I'm seldom there."

"Tell you what, Zev," Pasternak said. "You're off to the Negev with the commando battalion." He gestured at Yael. "I'll want a driver in Jerusalem Command. All right with you?"

"Highly recommended," said Barak.

Pasternak smiled at her. "Like the assignment?"

Yael gave him a slow calm blink. "Why not?"

In her bathrobe, Nakhama was sleepily frying up eggs and potatoes at 3 A.M. while Barak showered. He came into the kitchen in a fresh uniform, saying, "So, do I look like an armored battalion commander?"

She flashed him an appreciative glance, and gestured with a fork. "Coffee's hot. You'd have had a battalion command long ago if not for your wound, and then all the running around for B.G., and flying to America and whatnot —"

"Not an *armor* command, motek. I happened to be there in the room when Dayan and the Old Man were talking, and Dayan's eye fell on me. So it's all turning out for the best, even the running around." He drank coffee at the table. "It's a big chance. Armor's the future, and this mission is crucial."

"Can you talk about it?" She put the food before him.

"Why not? It's no secret." He talked as he ate. "The Egyptians are sitting on truce lines which almost seal off the Negev. We must shoot open a wide enough corridor so that the Negev remains linked to Israel, and there's no way to build a Burma Road, it's mostly all flat open sand."

"So, another long hard battle?" she said with affected casualness.

"Hard, possibly. Long, no. We fight at the end of a dog leash, and —"

"A dog leash?" Nakhama sat down with a cup of coffee. "What are you talking about, a dog leash?"

"I mean as long as the Arabs advance, the Security Council adjourns or dawdles. The minute we turn the tide and start to win — YANK, a cease-fire resolution! Ever since Dayan panicked Lydda and Ramle, the British have been calling for another cease-fire. The Americans tend to go along with them, so it'll pass any day. We have to do the job before the yank on the leash comes."

Nakhama shook her head. "Such a bitter way to look at it!"

"The bitter truth, motek."

"Abba, why you dress?" Noah appeared in pajamas, rubbing an eye. His baby talk was becoming clearer by the week. "No go away."

"I have to, son."

"Why?"

"I have to make sure that you won't have to fight when you grow up."

"I strong," said Noah. "I fight Arabs."

The parents looked at each other over his head. They had never talked to him about Arabs or war. Nakhama said in her rusty French, "It's the kindergarten."

Barak shrugged. "It's in the air."

She took the boy inside, and returned to dish up the rest of Zev's breakfast. "So, tell me something about America, at least. What about California? Is it really so beautiful? And you were in Hollywood! Exciting, was it?"

"I liked Washington," Zev said.

11

A Gentile Trade

In the so-called Ten-Day War between the two truces, the Jews made notable gains. The enemy was more or less cleared out of the north, the front with Jordan was quieted; and they won some connective central territory, which made the narrow jigsaw country more viable. On the other hand, two more attacks on Latrun failed, and in the south the cease-fire left large Egyptian forces inside Israel, at one point still only twenty miles from Tel Aviv. A corridor into the Negev was open, but barely. The Egyptian command refused to discuss a genuine armistice, content to sit on the cease-fire lines for long dreary months of stalemate, with sporadic clashes and casualties far more costly to the small Yishuv than to populous Egypt.

But late in December the forces of General Yigal Allon, now commanding the southern front, stunned the world by thrusting westward deep into Sinai, then wheeling north toward the Mediterranean, to compel an armistice by cutting off the whole Egyptian army still camped inside what had been Mandate Palestine. Once threatened themselves with being pushed into the sea, the Jews had turned the tables and were now thundering toward the sea, the invaded becoming invaders! Result, a frantic UN demand for their instant withdrawal from Egyptian soil, and a menacing British ultimatum to back it up, conveyed by the American ambassador in Tel Aviv. As Allon neared the outskirts of El Arish, the seacoast capital of the Sinai and the key to the enemy's withdrawal route, the Egyptian government and army were — so experts were saying — on the verge of collapse; and at that point Ben Gurion yielded to the British warning and ordered Allon to pull back.

General Allon flew to meet with the Prime Minister, and pleaded in vain to get the order reversed. Trying to preserve his victory meantime, he sent forces to seize the main junction of Rafah, farther up the coast, on the Palestine-Sinai border. The UN's withdrawal demand did not apply there, he argued, and the Egyptian forces might still be bagged by this cutoff and compelled to surrender. But under Allon's threat to Rafah, the Egyptians all at once gave in and for the first time offered a genuine armistice. With the original aim of Allon's attack thus achieved, Ben Gurion accepted the offer forthwith.

Raging, despairing, Yigal Allon decided to send an emissary to Ben Gurion to plead yet again for one more swift blow at Rafah, to end the war in a way that would force a lasting peace.

*   *   *

"I told him!" said Allon as he stood with Zev Barak at a Sinai map hung in his headquarters tent and a sandstorm rattled on the canvas. "I *told* him that this withdrawal from El Arish would be a disaster for unborn generations to mourn! He wouldn't listen. Zev, for God's sake convince him that if we don't take Rafah and bottle up their whole army, we condemn ourselves and our sons to twenty more years of war. If we do it, Egypt may sit down and talk real peace. Not otherwise!"

"I'll do what I can," said Barak. He had lost his fight against going, but was still most dubious about leaving his battered battalion to try to change the Old Man's mind. He agreed with Allon's strategy but saw the problem. The dog leash was yanking hard.

"I'm counting on you. You're a favorite of his. I'm not, God knows. Why, now the bastard has gone and dissolved my Palmakh!

We'll thrash all *that* out after the armistice, but meantime there's a war to win. We've got it won, Zev, if he won't throw it away!"

The sand was still lightly hissing on the windshield and roof of the command car as Don Kishote drove Barak through a brownish fog to the nearest airstrip. Barak's mood was low. Of all things, he did not want to be entrapped again, by an encounter with the Old Man, in some kind of distracting staff or political assignment. He loved his commandos, the light armor battalion, he loved the clear air, pure blue sky, and pristine expanses of the Sinai; in a way he even loved the bleak hard-driving General Allon. Wolfgang Berkowitz, he sometimes thought, was finding himself at last as Zev Barak in this protracted stretch of long desert boredom and brief desert fighting. Harried and busy with maintenance, patrolling, and training, as well as the intermittent action, he felt good to the bone.

One experience above all, in the days just before the great thrust into Sinai, had crystallized for him this growing sense of identity and purpose. Allon's attack plan called for the commandos to capture at the outset a key Egyptian position on the Sinai border. The road that twisted south toward the border had been fortified with enemy strongpoints, and Barak's light vehicles could not by-pass these with an end run on the desert sands, so the mission looked like a hard bloody slog all the way.

But the archaeologist-soldier Yigal Yadin advised General Allon of an ancient Roman road out there under the shifting Negev sands, which might lead straight and fast from Beersheba to Barak's objective if it was usable. Ordered by Allon to reconnoiter the area, Barak spent an entire day with army engineers inspecting what was left of the road. The surprising decision emerged that with the worst potholes bridged by stout planks, he could actually advance his battalion on this long-forgotten track of uneven antique cobblestones; another sort of "Burma Road," in fact, built by men dead two thousand years, some of them perhaps Jewish slaves of the Romans.

When a few days later the lightly armored column went rolling out on that rough road in a cold desert dawn, with Barak bouncing along in the lead over Roman-laid stones in an American-made command car, to spearhead the thrust to drive the Egyptians from the Holy Land; when the stars faded, and an edge of white sun rose glittering up over the Sinai crags, Zev Barak was overwhelmed by a rush of mystic elation, a sense of riding a majestic tide of history which only a Jew could know, and only a Jew in the new Jewish army sprung out of the sacred earth. That exaltation lasted all during the grand rumbling rush to El Arish. And when Allon had to halt just as victory seemed sure, and the chance to win a lasting peace — as Allon asserted and Barak truly believed — was going glimmering, his own mind cleared, once for all.

Farewell, Cal Tech! He was an officer of *Zahal*, the Israel Defense Force. He would give the career his best years, and he would rise as far as he could, wearing the uniform and protecting the Land.

Ben Gurion received Barak cordially in his office, and listened in silence to his vehement argument, urged with a Sinai map spread on the desk. "Prime Minister, we can always pull out of Rafah, but meantime let's take it and hold it!" Barak concluded with a pleading gesture of both arms. "Your bargaining position at the peace table will be that much stronger, sir. Yigal is absolutely right about that."

"Yes, yes, Zev, that was his argument about El Arish, too." Stooped over, sad-faced, barely past a serious illness, the Prime Minister stared at him with drooping eyes. "He's young, he's a brilliant fighter, but he doesn't yet grasp that what he can do militarily, maybe I can't do politically." A slow shake of the head. "The British aren't bluffing, I assure you, about entering the war. They never thought we'd win, Zev. They thought there would be chaos and the UN would send them back into Palestine. We can't give them the slightest pretext to intervene now." He gave Barak a haunted look, such as Zev had never seen on the Old Man's face before. "It's the one way we can lose everything, don't you see? At the last minute, after all our sacrifices, all our dead, we can lose the State!"

"But the Egyptians aren't observing the armistice, Prime Minister. We're tracking troop movements, we're taking artillery fire . . . why should we stop?"

"You know why. Because we are the Jews." With a sigh that was almost a groan, Ben Gurion went on in slow heavy words.

"And that's why I won't order recapture of the Old City, though now I believe we have the strength. We've beaten them all, Zev. North, south, east, we've driven them out. We've won the war. Our State is established. Everywhere I go I face people who have lost a son, a brother, a husband. It's terrible. Six thousand dead in our little Yishuv! Enough blood for now. Enough dying."

"Prime Minister, I say this under four eyes," Zev persisted in a lowered tense tone. "Unless the commander besieging Rafah hears from me by midnight, '*No go*,' he'll attack and capture that junction 'by mistake.' Then once we've secured the position, Allon will reprimand him for misunderstanding orders. Meantime we'll be there."

Ben Gurion removed his glasses, rubbed his eyes hard, and stared at the ceiling, the lips of his broad mouth tightened to a line. Barak knew that look well. A spark of interest! "So, how long would it take him?"

"He'll have it by morning."

"Where will you be an hour from now?"

"The Parks Hotel. I phoned Nakhama to meet me there."

A tired wave of a pudgy hand dismissed him. "So go meet Nakhama."

A dozen or so soldiers wearing caps tilted at absurd angles came tramping into the quiet bar lounge at the Parks Hotel in Tel Aviv, singing and waving beer bottles. They swarmed to the bar demanding cognac, slapping each other on the back, laughing, singing, shouting, making swooping hand gestures of aerial combat. One jumped to the small upright piano and banged out an accompaniment as they bawled

> *Roll me over in the clover,*
> *Roll me over, lay me down, and do it again!*

"Our air force," said Barak to Nakhama. He sat drinking Coca-Cola with her in a booth, and she was laughing at their boisterous antics.

"But they're speaking English," she said. "And what's that song?"

"Never mind, it's not nice. Sure, English, they're mostly volunteers from outside. Our own pilots trained abroad, too." He waved at a big officer with a toothbrush mustache. "Ezer, hello! That's Ezer Weizman, the tall one. You've heard of him, Chaim Weizmann's nephew. He won his wings in the RAF."

"Zev! You here?" Weizman approached with a sizable snifter of brandy. "Not in Sinai? And who's the raving beauty?"

"Meet my wife Nakhama, Ezer, and never mind the raving beauty stuff."

"Hello, Nakhama, you're thrown away on this desert rat." A charming grin, and she smiled back. "Can I borrow him for a moment?"

In a dark corner of the bar Weizman took a deep swallow and said, "Now Zev, listen to me, and listen carefully. Today our squadron got into a battle with British Spitfires, and *we shot down five of them*." The aviator's eyes gleamed savagely. "Five RAF fighters! We saw them crash! All confirmed! And we all came back, every last one of us. Unbelievable? It's true!" He was gripping Barak's arm. "It's historic, isn't it? Isn't it sensational?"

"God, yes. Where did this happen? When?"

"Midday. Over Nirim. They were intruding in our airspace, not a doubt of it, and so we shot 'em down!"

"They must have been Egyptians."

"RAF, I tell you! Four of us served with them in the war, don't you think we know the markings? . . . Ha ha, Zev, will you look at that crazy guy! Go to it, Scotty!" Weizman clapped in time to the music. "That's Scotty Hubbard, born in Glasgow, his family moved to Rhodesia. Great guy, born flier, he got one of the Spitfires!"

The swarthy little aviator was doing a lively Highland fling on the small dance floor, to a Scottish tune thumped on the piano. All at once Nakhama jumped up and joined him, her cloth coat flying but not interfering with the graceful jigging of her pretty limbs. It was a complete surprise to Barak that his Moroccan wife could do a Highland fling. The aviators gathered around the cavorting pair, laughing and clapping, and Weizman hugged him. "Come on, Zev, let's make a night of it! Nakhama's a sweetie! What the hell, we've got plenty to celebrate! The armistice is on. Let's have some fun!"

The bartender came to them. "Major Barak, a call for you."

It was the Prime Minister's military aide. Ben Gurion had gone home, feeling very ill. There was no other word.

Silence gave consent. The "mistaken" Rafah capture was on.

With Don Kishote at the wheel, the jeep sped to Jerusalem under a starless sky, on a narrow new tarred road. There was no way for Barak to return to the Sinai in time for the Rafah attack; it would be over before he could get there. He was seeing Nakhama for the first time in a long while, and he was eager to snatch a night with her and to see his boy. Holding her hand tightly he said, "So, Nakhama, this is the new Highway of Heroes, eh? When was it finished?"

"Some time ago, *ahoovi* [my love], but the first time I've been on it was in the bus today."

"Is the Burma Road still being used?"

"For mule traffic, maybe. Anyway, it served its purpose, didn't it, Zevi? It saved Israel."

"That's newspaper talk, darling."

"Newspaper talk? Why?"

"Well, the road was a great feat, but our soldiers in the field reversed the war, not the road builders. We were fighting heavy battles all that time. If even one of the fronts had broken the Arabs might have overrun and finished us, *chick-chack,* and the Burma Road would have made no difference."

"You say that, sir," Kishote spoke up over his shoulder, "because you didn't walk knee-deep in mule shit, carrying fifty pounds of flour six kilometers, two and three times in one night. Saving Jerusalem saved Israel."

"Nobody asked you," said Barak. "Watch the road."

As they drove into dark Jerusalem, Kishote asked for permission to stop at Reb Shmuel's flat, so Barak took the wheel and dropped him off. When he parked the jeep at their apartment house a soldier was waiting outside the entrance.

"Major Barak?"

"Yes."

"General Dayan wants you to report to Jerusalem Command, highest urgency."

"L'Azazel!" exclaimed Nakhama. "Inevitable. You won't even see Noah."

"I will, motek, no matter what. That's a promise."

Jerusalem's streets were lively with auto and foot traffic despite the cold, probably because of the armistice talk. He was braking the jeep outside Dayan's headquarters when Ezer Weizman came out, his aspect hangdog, his cap on straight. "You, too?" Weizman greeted him, all gaiety quenched. "When did you get here? He sent for me half an hour ago and I flew up."

"What's happening?"

"Better hear it from Moshe."

"Come on, Ezer!"

"Okay." Weizman looked around at the empty street, and his voice dropped. "B.G.'s in panic. More British bluff, a damn stiff note delivered to his sickbed about those Spitfires. Claims they were unarmed and over Egyptian territory on a photographic mission."

"Any truth to that?"

"Absolute shit! They mixed it up with us over Nirim. They tried to shoot us out of the sky. We can prove it, they crashed in our territory, what more do you want? There's the wreckage! The American ambassador can come and see for himself in the morning! But the British are demanding compensation and threatening war again."

"What did you expect?" said Barak, keeping out of his voice, as well as he could, his own alarm. "That the British Empire wouldn't react to losing five warplanes to some flying Jews?"

"They can go to hell! I don't believe the Americans will let them enter the war. Or if they do attack, well, we'll shoot down more planes! We'll stop their damn troops, too, at our borders. Leave it to Allon to do that!" He punched Barak on the chest. "And *you'll* help him do it!" The aviator jumped into an army car and roared away.

In Dayan's map-lined office Sam Pasternak was shouting in English on the telephone.

"Ah, there you are, Zev," said Dayan. "A plane is standing by to take you to Rafah. I've already spoken to Allon. On the Prime

Minister's orders, you're to stop personally all attack preparations, see to an immediate general retreat of all forces from the position, and report compliance directly to him."

"Why? Why the panic?" Barak expostulated. "Ezer told me about the British note, but still —"

"They're massing troops at Aqaba. That's not a threat, it's a fact. Army intelligence has just issued a war warning."

Slight pause. "Well, Moshe, a fact can be a bluff, too."

Pasternak was hanging up. "Hi, Zev. I just got hold of Christian Cunningham. Luckily he was at home. I told him Weizman's version of the dogfight. He wrote it all down and read it back to me, and he promised that the State Department and the White House will have it right away."

"This CIA man has such high connections?" Dayan asked incredulously. "This Cunningham? I've never heard of him."

Pasternak shook his head. "You wouldn't have. He knows the right staff people. That's how Washington works."

"He's a friend, then," said Dayan.

"We'll see." Pasternak's face lightened in a grin at Barak. "Actually he was having tea with that daughter of his when I called. It's four in the afternoon there. She wants to know whether Wolf Lightning received her poem."

"What poem? I never got a poem."

"She sent you a poem about a firefly or something."

Dayan's eye lit up and he crookedly smiled. "Wolf Lightning? A firefly? Just how old is this daughter, Zev?"

"Don't be ridiculous. Maybe she's ten, twelve."

"They grow up," said Pasternak.

"Zev, get on that plane, get down there and report compliance to B.G.," said Dayan. "Any time of the night, just call him! Understood?"

"Understood, sir."

Dayan walked out. Pasternak said soberly, "Nasty, the last British note."

"But they can't really intervene, can they, Sam, at this point? It's unreal." Barak was still clinging to the hope that the Rafah junction could be captured "by mistake"; as Guderian had dashed to the Channel in 1940 "by mistake," forced the French to surrender, and driven the British into the sea at Dunkirk.

"Why unreal? Their troops are at our borders right now," returned Pasternak somberly. "In force."

"Look, just think about it! Surely the British public won't put up with more casualties in Palestine. That's why they had to give up the Mandate! The Attlee government would fall."

"You're talking common sense. Attlee's got a mad bull of a Foreign Minister, that Bevin, and Bevin's furious enough at us for surviving and winning to do something very stupid. Attlee can't control him. That's what B.G.'s gut is warning him, Zev, and he's the boss."

Barak raced home, and found Nakhama in an unlooked-for cheery mood, having just retrieved Noah from a neighbor and put him to bed. He peeped in on the sleeping boy, then told her he was off to Sinai again. She shrugged, laughed, and stroked his face. "You're so lean and brown now. Ah, well, I guess peace will come before we're too old to fulfill *that* commandment." It was the old Jewish euphemism for marital sex, God's command to Adam and Eve, "Be fruitful and multiply."

"There's peace now, Nakhama. An armistice, anyway. Ben Gurion's nerves are shot, that's all. He's won a great victory and he's desperate to secure it at any price. I'm sorry, sweetheart."

"Well, as you say, it's the dog leash again. But how he relies on you! You'll be the Chief of Staff one day. Remember I said it."

"Nakhama, when and how did you learn to do the Highland fling?"

Her look turned sly. "Why do you ask, my love?"

"Well, it was quite unexpected."

"Oh? Do you think you and Sam were the first soldiers who ever came to Papa's place to eat? Some British Tommies also liked our cooking."

"Interesting! You'll have to tell me more."

"That's all you'll ever know," said Nakhama with mischievous pleasure, "about the Highland fling. If you like, I'll teach it to you. Do you want to eat something? Have you time?"

"I'd better go. I have to pick up my crazy driver."

*

By the harsh light of naked bulbs in a chandelier over the dining table, he found his brother Michael helping Shayna with her homework, though it was near midnight. She was so intent on solving an equation, dark hair falling about her face, that she did not glance up as he walked in. Kishote was curled in a morris chair, fast asleep.

"Wolfgang! Ma nishma?" his brother exclaimed. "Is the war really over?"

"For the moment, Michael, yes."

The brother adjusted the skullcap on his bushy hair, and made the blessing on good news.

"Amen," said Barak, and Shayna echoed him, not ceasing her work.

Michael Berkowitz was in every way so different from his desert-bronzed army brother that people sometimes had trouble connecting the two. Michael was slight, pale, with thick glasses and a studious stoop, and he usually dressed in faded jeans and an old sweater. His two canes leaned on a chair, for he was a congenital cripple. Younger than Zev, he was the sole religious Berkowitz, the "white sheep," as their joke went, in a hard-bitten socialist family. At twelve he had requested a bar mitzvah, because a friend was having one, and the teacher had instilled in him a love for Talmud and ritual. At sixteen he had been admitted to the Technion, a prodigy in mathematics and physics. He sometimes came to Jerusalem to attend advanced seminars and lectures, so Barak had told him to look up Reb Shmuel, and Michael now and then studied Talmud with the old tailor.

"Don't let me interrupt you," Barak said to his brother. "Her homework's important. I'm just here to pick up this sleeping warrior."

"I'm finished," said Shayna, jumping up, "and I promised the sleeping fool some supper." She went off into the kitchen. Kishote slept on, oblivious.

"What are you helping her with?"

"Calculus."

"That little girl? Is she that bright?"

"Mathematically, very! She also has a broad outlook and an

inquiring mind. I don't know how she got that way in the Old City. However, she also has a razor tongue."

"Amen," put in Yossi, without opening his eyes.

"Kishote, we're leaving by plane soon."

No response.

Michael said, "I have a letter from Mama. Father is better, but he's not going back to the UN until February. Doctor's orders." He recounted the letter, and they talked about their parents' problems. Meyer Berkowitz had suffered a stroke in an angry exchange at the UN with the Saudi representative. "They've taken an apartment in Manhattan for the time being," Michael said, "and she's crazy about it. Almost as cultured as Vienna, she writes."

"Well, that's Mama. She may never come back."

"What's the real word on this armistice, Zev? Can it lead to peace?"

"No, not now. We've beaten them off again, that's all. Stalemate without gunfire for a while. That's my view. I'm considered a pessimist."

"No hope for peace at all, ever?"

"Oh, yes. Two hopes, Michael. Long range, the Arabs get tired of losing lives to no purpose and decide to leave us alone. Short range, the powers let us finish a war, just once, and convince the Arabs that we're here to stay."

"Wake up, fool," said Shayna, walking in with a plate of smoking potato pancakes, and prodding Kishote with an elbow, "if you really want to eat."

He sat up brightly. "Shiga'on!"

Barak said, "We have to get going, Yossi."

"No time for some pancakes, sir? She made them special for me."

"I certainly did not," said Shayna. "Dr. Berkowitz and I were hungry, and you happened to be here."

"Didn't I ask her to make them" — Kishote appealed to Michael — "because they were so good on Hanukkah?"

Michael grinned and said nothing.

"I had the potatoes anyway. They were getting spoiled, sprouting eyes," said Shayna. "It's a sin to throw food away."

"Well, those pancakes do smell good," said Barak, pulling up a chair.

"Imagine, flying off God knows where in the middle of the night!" exclaimed Shayna, dishing out pancakes for them. "What a crazy life! Now that there's peace, you'll have to find some way to make yourself useful, Kishote. Maybe collect Jerusalem's garbage. . . . Just a minute! Make a blessing before you eat that pancake." Kishote clapped a hand to his hair. She struck his shoulder. "None of that. With a hat!"

Meekly he put on his army beret, made the blessing, and ate. "Mm, excellent," he said. "Peace will make no difference to me, Shayna, I'm a soldier."

"You mean that's what you're going to *do*? Be a soldier? A regular soldier?"

"A regular soldier, and why are you making such a funny face?"

The girl was in fact grimacing like a gargoyle.

"A *goyishe parnosseh*!" ("A gentile trade!") Nose in the air, she marched out, leaving them looking at each other over pancakes.

"You heard her, Zev," said Michael. "Better go back to chemistry."

"Not me, Michael. That's finished. The gentile trade for me. For good."

"Truly? Kol ha'kavod," said Michael.

The Weizman version of the air battle prevailed. President Truman issued a sharp note criticizing the British for venturing combat aircraft into a war zone and blaming Israel for their loss. In the House of Commons the Attlee government took a storm of criticism and backed off from its threats. So the War of Independence ended, the guns falling silent early in January 1949, though disengagement talks went on for months. Israel existed, and all the Arab invaders one by one signed armistice agreements with the country that, they stoutly maintained, wasn't there.

PART TWO

———

Suez

12

Lee Bloom

In the four years that followed the war, the country that wasn't
there had a hard struggle continuing not to be there.

Those years from 1949 to 1953 were the worst of times,
Moshe Dayan writes in his memoirs. The army more or less fell
apart. The scratched-together force of incompatible militias plus
reservists, draftees, immigrants, and foreign volunteers could cope
better with Arabs than with victory. Though impotent to fight on,
the Arab governments would consider no treaty with the invisible
country. Armistice brought not peace but siege. Terrorists called
fedayeen crossed ill-guarded borders to derail trains, burn busses,
blow up buildings, and murder unwary civilians. Housing, cars,
clothes, food, and fuel were scarce. Life was shabby and precarious.
Israelis left in droves for places like Canada and Los Angeles. In
1953 Dayan was appointed Army Chief of Staff, and he writes that
then things began to improve.

Those same four years, 1949 to 1953, were the best of times,
Ben Gurion writes in his memoirs; Israel's heroic years, "the greatest years in our history since the Maccabee victory over the Greeks,
2,300 years ago," because in those four years the Jewish population
of Israel more than doubled. The wondrous Return, the Ingather-
ing of the Exiles, the radiant core vision of Zionism, began to come

true. All around the Mediterranean the frustrated Arab governments turned on their Jews and drove them out, and the beleaguered new Jewish State of 600,000 took in 700,000 Jewish
refugees! This happening, perhaps unprecedented in the history of
the world, caused the shortages, the empty treasury, the black market, the rationing, and the disillusionment of the fainthearted. Israel
nevertheless survived and even flourished, until in 1953 Ben Gurion
resigned as Prime Minister and Minister of Defense. Then, he
writes, things began to deteriorate. They deteriorated so badly, in
fact, that late in 1955 the people had to recall him to power, and
none too soon.

For within the year the Egyptian dictator Gamal Abdel Nasser
nationalized the Suez Canal, infuriating the British and the French
governments, and once again the Middle East was on the front
pages. Israel was barred by Egypt from using the Canal anyway, but
the possibility of another all-out war sent a seismic shudder through
the region.

*   *   *

Christian Cunningham had noticed the young man on the New
York-to-Paris Stratocruiser, sitting alone in the crowded lower-
deck bar, reading a magazine and taking no part in the drunken
joking as the huge plane jolted through a North Atlantic October
thunderstorm. On the El Al flight from Paris to Tel Aviv two days
later, there he was again; same gray flannel trousers and natty blue
blazer, reading reports and magazines from the same calfskin case.
He ate little, drank club soda, and did not banter with the stewardess. He conducted himself, in fact, much as Cunningham himself
did on long flights. Air passengers were time users or time killers,
and this fellow was a time user. A Hollywood type, Cunningham
would have guessed from his modish dress, heavy gold jewelry, and
full wavy black hair, except that the magazines he read were about
aviation, armaments, and real estate.

For his part Don Kishote's brother was wondering about the
gaunt gentile in a three-piece suit who had showed up again on the
El Al flight, watch chain across the vest and all, reading the *Journal*

of Biblical Archaeology. The two men had the first-class section to themselves. The crowd in tourist class were mostly Israelis, for tourism was way down, and Lee Bloom — as he was now known — wondered at an archaeologist venturing to visit Israel in this tense time. After a while the watch-chain man drifted off to sleep, horn-rimmed glasses pushed up on his forehead. Lee Bloom took out and reviewed Sheva Leavis's handwritten memorandum, went over and over it, then in the lavatory tore it up and stuffed the pieces in the towel disposal.

The pilot's grating announcement in harsh Hebrew and awkward English woke them both, and Cunningham spoke first, peering out the window. "Well, there's the Holy Land at last."

Lee Bloom craned his neck to glance ahead. The descent through broken clouds offered glimpses of a gray jagged urban sprawl along the blue sea. "Doesn't look all that holy, does it? Amazing how it's been built up."

"You've been here before?"

"Once, for a short while." Lee Bloom gestured at the magazine on the other man's lap. "Does archaeology go on during a war?"

"There's always trouble in this region. The digging is done where it's quiet. You think there'll be a war?"

"Well, how can the French and British sit still and let this Nasser fellow get away with grabbing the Canal?"

"Nationalizing it, you mean."

"Same difference, sir."

"What can they do about it?"

"Land troops and take the Canal back. I think they'll do it, too. Just a question of time."

"And the Russians?"

"It should all be over in forty-eight hours. Then the Russians can make all the nasty noises they want to in the UN. It won't amount to a hill of beans."

Lee Bloom's English was only faintly accented, but he said "a hill of beans" with the quote marks of a foreigner.

"You may well be right." Cunningham opened the archaeology magazine. Kishote's brother made no effort to prolong the conversation. Upper-class goy, he surmised, not California, maybe East Coast.

At the gate to the baggage area of the grimy chilly little terminal of Lydda airport, now Hebraized to Lod, Lee Bloom recognized Zev Barak waiting in uniform, somewhat heavier, his hair prematurely dusted with gray. "Adon Barak!" he hailed him with a touch of irony.

Barak stared, trying to fit this dapper figure to the scrawny deserter he had left in the Los Angeles airport eight years before. "Is this Blumenthal?" Leopold grinned and they shook hands. "Sam," Barak said to Pasternak, who was beside him peering into the passport queue, "meet Lee Bloom. I guess you've read about him."

"Lee Bloom? Hi there, who hasn't? I understand you and Sheva Leavis between you own half of Los Angeles."

"Ha! Three buildings. The papers here really write crazy stories." Lee Bloom scanned the people beyond the barrier, who were waving and calling to the passengers. "My brother said he'd meet me, but — oh, there he is. Joe! Yossi!"

Kishote was coming in through the police entrance, and as the brothers embraced, Barak noted how much bigger he was than Leopold. His long lean frame had filled out, and his paratrooper boots added more height. Leopold by contrast was thin and a bit stooped.

"Okay, Zev, there comes Cunningham." Pasternak strode to greet the CIA man. "Hello, Chris. You remember Zev Barak?"

"Well, well. Wolf Lightning! Hello!" Cunningham gave Barak a brief bony grip. "Now where do I pick up my bags?"

"Come with me," said Barak.

Pasternak approached Lee Bloom, and despite the echoing passenger clamor and flight announcements, spoke very quietly. "Blumenthal, that problem of yours that Sheva Leavis phoned me about from Paris —"

"Yes?" Leopold turned alert and anxious.

"I've looked into it. I was going to call you at your hotel, but here you are, so . . ." He pulled a card from a pocket and handed it to Yossi. "Kishote, you know where to find this guy? Manpower Section, Kirya?"

"Sure," Yossi said at a glance.

"Take your brother straight there from here." Pasternak smiled at Leopold. "That's that. Now, is Sheva bluffing about the rolling mill, or is there something to it?" Though Pasternak was now Dayan's deputy chief of intelligence, military procurement in gray zones of legality remained a province of his.

Leopold responded, all business, "It's for real. There's this Jewish firm in Canton, Ohio. Four brothers. Their father started in the junk business, now they're in iron and steel. They've got the finance, and the production experience. That's clear. They're very tough negotiators, and they're no Zionists. We could have a deal if the tax picture here is on the up and up. They think it sounds too good, and therefore must have a big catch. I'm here to check that, among other things."

"Let me know if I can help. And Yossi, call me if you hit a snag at Manpower." He went off to join Cunningham.

Lee Bloom hefted the despatch case and a valise. "This is all I brought, Yossi. I left the rest in Paris."

"Then let's go. How long will you stay here?"

"Depends." Leopold followed him through the crowd. "Three or four days, the most. You've put on thirty pounds, haven't you? All muscle, looks like."

"They work us hard in the paratroops."

"Seen a lot of action? You never write."

"Neither do you."

"I know."

Outside, a strong damp wind blew dust and sand across an almost empty parking lot. From an army car a blond female soldier in the back seat waved at Yossi. "There's Yael Luria. Remember her?"

"Sure, the hard-nosed girl I met that time in the King David Hotel."

"That's her. She's Lieutenant Colonel Pasternak's aide."

"Not married?"

"No. She has special friends off and on."

"Including you?"

Yossi burst out laughing. "Fat chance. She's a terror. Anyway, as you well know, I've got a girl."

At an open rickety car rental booth Leopold gave a stout gum-chewing girl a voucher, and she blasted machine-gun Hebrew at the brothers. "Your driver has a toothache," Yossi said. "They're calling for another one."

Leopold looked him up and down, taking in the red beret, the shoulder ornaments, and the heavy reddish boots. "Three bars. What's that, like an American major?"

"Captain. *Seren,* it's called. I'm a platoon leader, up for company commander."

"You have to tell me your adventures."

"You have to tell me how you come to own half of Los Angeles." Yossi pushed his glasses up on his nose and grinned at his brother. "Any truth in all that bullshit?"

"Enough so that I'm inviting you and your girl to Paris. Hey, how about it? Did you get your leave? And will she come?"

"I'm working on the leave. Shayna's dying to go. Her parents are giving her trouble. You remember, they're very religious."

"Is Shayna, still?"

"Mister, here's your car," called the girl in English. A faded blue Peugeot rattled up, driven by an old man with a three-day gray beard, wearing a torn wool hat, who greeted them in indistinct toothless Hebrew.

"What is this?" Leopold challenged the woman. "My voucher guarantees a new Oldsmobile, with an English-speaking chauffeur."

Harsh rat-tat-tat Hebrew, which Kishote translated. "The new Oldsmobile is in the garage. The English speaker has the toothache. You can have the Oldsmobile Thursday."

"Nothing changes here. Let's go."

"Kirya," Yossi said to the driver, who nodded and started off. "Is Shayna still religious? Absolutely. Won't travel on Saturday, strict about food and holidays, studies the Bible every day. But she's okay, if you know what I mean. Wants to be an aeronautical engineer. Wears blue jeans, and in her *dati* [Orthodox] crowd that's scandalous. She doesn't care."

"And she's really all that pretty now? I remember her as a skinny little snotnose."

"You'll see for yourself. You go to Jerusalem first, right?"

"Yes, one day there, probably two days in Tel Aviv, back to Paris."

"Good, we'll pick her up at the university. She's just finishing her exams."

As Barak was loading the CIA man's worn suitcases into the army car, Pasternak said to Cunningham, "Chris, meet Captain Luria, my right hand."

With a prim smile and handshake, Yael said in agreeable tones, "I'm at your service, Mr. Cunningham, for as long as you're here."

"Charming of you," said Cunningham, and she felt that this old American had read her relationship with Pasternak at once through those thick eyeglasses. Pasternak had not wanted her to come, but having heard so much about Cunningham, and perhaps just to throw her weight around, she had insisted and prevailed. Pasternak saved his whip-cracking for serious matters, and she knew when she could push him. With her in the car, substantive talk was impossible. They rode through ploughed fields and orange groves in constrained silence until Cunningham spoke.

"Last time I was here was in 1936. The Mandate was an interesting place. Beautiful, elegant, and so peaceful, too! The British had the touch, you must give them that. But then the Arab riots broke out again. Very bad, very sad."

"I was five years old in 1936," piped up Yael. "I remember the riots. Papa left the moshav and fought for months. We kids were all frightened. It's a different world now."

"Not different enough," Cunningham said. This extinguished the small talk until they left off Yael at the Kirya, the army head-quarters compound in central Tel Aviv, and drove on.

"Very handsome young woman," said Cunningham.

"Anything you want done, Yael will get it done," said Pasternak.

Cunningham put a lean fist on his mouth to yawn. "Does this driver understand English?"

"No," said Barak.

"Very well. Our intelligence is that the Israeli army is ready to march to the Suez Canal at twenty-four hours' notice. Is that accurate?"

Pasternak and Barak looked at each other. "That's a big compliment," said Pasternak. "Nice if it were true. Is President Eisenhower making United States policy, Chris, or Secretary of State Dulles?"

"Well, that's a large topic. I need a nap, just an hour or so, then let's meet and talk. All right, Sam?"

"Of course." As the car drew up at a downtown seaside hotel, Pasternak added, "Meantime the Prime Minister may wonder whether you've brought a message from your government."

"No doubt." Cunningham got out of the car. "By the way, Barak, my Emily asked me to give her regards to Wolf Lightning, if I ran into you."

"Really? Nice of her to remember me."

"Oh, she does. She's at the Sorbonne, getting her master's. She has acquired a boyfriend, a French poet. Mrs. Cunningham and I have been visiting them. Do you have daughters?"

"One."

"I daresay she seems sweet, and simple to manage."

"Very. She's a year old."

"Just wait." He consulted the vest pocket watch at arm's length. "Suppose we meet at four?"

Barak said as the car drove away from the hotel, "Sam, did we need Yael?"

"Do you know Yael?" growled Pasternak.

The plasterboard walls of the cramped bleak office in the Manpower Section were covered with organizational diagrams and mimeographed personnel lists, and Ben Gurion in an open-necked shirt scowled down from an old photograph. The almost bald lieutenant behind the narrow ink-stained desk gestured at two hard chairs, donned horn-rimmed glasses, and fumbled through a pile of varicolored folders. "You speak Hebrew?" he asked Leopold.

"Of course, though I'm a bit rusty."

"All right, here we are. Blumenthal, Leopold." He flipped through papers fastened in a scuffed yellow file, nodding and nodding. "Well, the record is in order. No problem." He rested clasped hands on the folder and glanced at the brothers, his aspect official, remote, arid. "So. What can I do for you?"

Leopold looked to Kishote, then in hesitant Hebrew replied, "I would appreciate knowing my exact present status."

"Your exact present status." The lieutenant opened the folder and read from the top sheet: " *'Summary: no record found of this person's enlistment or service in Zahal. Many records of 1948 are incomplete or missing. That he fought with the Seventh Brigade at Latrun in an immigrant unit, as he states, is unconfirmed. He arrived in Israel on the vessel* Nordau *from Cyprus on May 20th, 1948, and left six weeks later for the United States of America, where he remained and became a citizen. No military obligation or penalty exists. His reported combat service, and his interest in having his Zahal record in order, are appreciated.'* That's it. Did I read it too fast for you?"

"Not at all." Leopold darted an emphatic finger at the folder. "I'd like a copy of that paper."

"Why not?" He carefully lifted the sheet from bent prongs. "Dora! Duplicate." A woman soldier in sweater and slacks popped in, ran a similar form into a typewriter, and clattered away. Smiling at Leopold, the lieutenant removed his glasses. "So! You're Lee Bloom, the real estate wizard of Los Angeles." His entire aspect changed. He was an inquisitive admiring young man without much hair. It was as though he had shed his uniform with the glasses. "I have a cousin in Toronto in real estate. Nothing like you and Sheva Leavis, of course."

Leopold's aspect also changed. Self-assured man of the world again, he asked about the cousin in Toronto, said he knew him, and chatted about real estate until the clerk handed the lieutenant the typed-in form and left. The lieutenant scanned the sheet, corrected it here and there in ink, and initialled it. "Not a great typist, Dora."

"This is perfect, thanks." Leopold folded the paper inside a breast pocket. When the brothers went out into the sunshine he said hesitantly, "Yossi, you know how sorry I was not to come to Papa's funeral. It was this business, you realize. I'm mighty grateful to Sam Pasternak."

"Nothing to be grateful for," said Yossi, his face a blank. "Your file was in order."

As the Peugeot rolled down the long curving hill into the Ayalon valley, Lee Bloom was describing to Kishote how he and Leavis had gotten into the building business. He broke off, pointing at a distant hill. "Well, well, there's that damned Latrun."

"Yes. We never took it. The new highway has to detour around it. So, you say it was cheaper to build your own warehouse than to pay rent?"

"Definitely. They're all robbers, those warehouse guys. Sheva Leavis was buying up tons of surplus army stuff. We were travelling to Manila, Tokyo, Hong Kong, Singapore, three times a year. Lot of stuff from Europe, too. You need a place to hold such quantities while you look for buyers. That's the whole idea — buy for pennies, hold, and sell for dollars. That's how we also moved into textiles, baskets, toys, hats — I tell you, Joe, buying in quantities in the Orient is fantastic, if you have the cash and know what you're doing." He punched his brother lightly. "But look, business is boring. I want to hear about the paratroops."

"You've built only three warehouses, you say?"

"So far. Pretty big ones. Actually the last one we just sold for a factory. We've bought a lot of land, too, but not half of Los Angeles. That's Israeli newspaper nonsense. Good locations, right price. I watched the first construction, saw where the contractors were wasting money or plain skimming it off. I asked Sheva to let me contract for the second building, and I brought it in at almost half the cost per square foot. The hell with all that, do you know a guy in the paratroops named Ben Menachem?"

Kishote was lounging on an elbow in the back seat, eating sunflower seeds from a paper bag. He sat up straight and blinked at Leopold, pushing his glasses up on his nose. "Why do you ask?"

"The United Jewish Appeal brought this big tall incredibly handsome guy to a dinner in Los Angeles. Not a good speaker, but we heard terrific stories about him."

"He gave speeches all over America. He was ordered to," said Yossi. "He hated it. He said he'd rather go on raids into Syria alone than do that tour again."

"Well, I'd like to meet him."

"He's dead." Yossi resumed eating the seeds.

"Oh? Sorry. Good friend of yours, this Ben Menachem?"

"We called him Gulliver. The fact is, they still call me Don Kishote. They used to make jokes about Don Kishote and Gulliver."

"Don Kishote. Right." Leopold ventured a smile at his brother. "I remember that. Was your friend killed in action?"

Kishote had absorbed into his bones the Israeli soldier's distaste for discussing combat with civilians, especially foreigners. His brother had become Lee Bloom of Los Angeles, and he did not want to share his memories of Gulliver with Lee Bloom. His laconic response was, "Reprisal raid, Syrian side of the Sea of Galilee. I was on that raid. He was in command. He went in first as always. He had bad luck." Yossi slouched and resumed eating seeds. "But don't think Gulliver wasn't a good speaker. He'd been to law school. He loved history. He could recite Abraham Lincoln speeches by heart. Very educated. He didn't like talking at American banquets."

It was drizzling in Jerusalem when they got there, and the driver was reaching out with his wool hat to mop the windshield. "There she is," Yossi said, as the Peugeot sputtered toward students huddled under a shed at the university bus stop.

"Which one?"

"White sweatshirt and jeans."

"That one? Why, she's tall."

"She doesn't smoke, so she grew."

Shayna did not kiss Kishote when she got into the back seat with them, but the look she gave him stirred envy in Leopold Bloom. He had had his casual flings and passionate affairs, but such a pure loving look from such shining girlish eyes he had not had. "So, this is Leopold!" She held a slim hand out to him. "Hello, Lee Bloom! That's my whole plan, you know, to marry a fellow with a rich American brother."

"Why not just a rich American?"

"Fine! Please introduce me to one." She rubbed her face against Yossi's uniform, and Leopold felt a sharper pang of envy. "I can't stand soldiers, especially paratroopers. They're all out for only one thing."

"Isn't she sophisticated?" Yossi said, and he gave the driver Shayna's address.

"Is there a telephone in your flat?" Leopold asked her. "I have to confirm some appointments."

"Our neighbor has one. Her uncle is a Knesset member. On the waiting list it takes seven years."

"Driver," Leopold switched to Hebrew, "do you know where the Defense Ministry and the Treasury are?"

The driver said mushily, "Me knows, take mister there," and turned to beam bare-gummed pride at his language proficiency.

"So, you've got an English-speaking driver after all," said Kishote.

"I thought you two looked alike," said Shayna, studying Leopold's face. "You don't. Not anymore."

"He has glamor now, he has polish," said Yossi. "A rich American."

"That's exactly right," said Shayna, lightly caressing his brown face. "And you're nothing but a dirty soldier. Ugh! With whiskers." She smiled at Leopold. Her mouth was rather wide, her teeth perfect, her lips thin and very red. She wore no makeup. "When I told my mother you were coming, she said, 'Oh yes, he's the one who ate the cake with no blessing and no hat.' Have you met many movie stars?" She asked this in a bright naive tone.

"A few. Are you coming to Paris?"

Her face fell. "I hope so. Grandpa says I should. Mama's worried. Papa's impossible."

"Worried about what?" said Leopold. "You're a big girl."

"Papa wants to know whether you're married, Leopold, and whether your wife is with you, and where I would be staying in Paris. He's working in Tiberias. There's been a lot of telephoning. You're not married, are you?"

"My girlfriend came with me. She's in Paris now."

"I see. Well, would I stay with her? . . . Here we are."

The brothers exchanged a glance and shook their heads as they left the car. In the narrow street of old two-story houses, little boys in skullcaps and earlocks were chasing each other, and twittering little girls wearing long dresses were playing a kind of hopscotch.

"It isn't as though we're even engaged," Shayna went on to Leopold, leading them into a dark narrow hall and up creaky stairs. "Yossi's just a pest I put up with. No engagement till I graduate, if then. My parents insist, and they're not wrong."

"Who mentioned an engagement?" said Yossi. "You're just going to Paris for a few days. You will, and no nonsense, Shayna. *Paris!*"

"We'll see," said Shayna. She introduced Leopold to her neighbor, a harried-looking plain woman with a kerchiefed head, who opened wide inquisitive eyes at the real estate wizard of Los Angeles, and led him to the telephone.

Later as they sat around the table in Shayna's flat talking in Yiddish, her mother, now quite white-haired, brought in tea and cake. Leopold put a palm on his head and muttered a blessing, his first in some years. The old lady smiled. "Well, that's nice, Leopold. But we have free-thinking friends, we're used to all kinds."

He was relieved that she did not bring up the Paris trip. A minor actress named Isobel Connors was sharing his suite at the Georges Cinq, so discussing who would stay where could have been awkward. While Reb Shmuel, in a threadbare bathrobe and looking not in the least different after eight years, expounded a Torah passage to Yossi — this was an invariable practice whenever the paratrooper came to the flat — the mother talked about her cousins in Los Angeles, asking questions about their neighborhood, and the climate, and Jewish life there. "It's Yossi's birthday tomorrow, you know," she said. "We're having family in this evening, cousins of our Los Angeles cousins, just a few people. Please stay."

"So it is," said Leopold. "I'd forgotten, but I'm afraid I'll be busy. I've just gotten here."

"It's nothing," said Shayna. "Of course you're busy."

Yossi walked out with his brother to the car. "I'm staying for dinner," he said, "and I'll nail down Paris. Worried! Did you ever hear of anything so ridiculous?"

Leopold gave him a skeptical look. "My boy, I've heard things back in L.A. about paratroopers. In fact, about you. She's lovely, and fresh as a rose, and she's crazy about you. So they're worried."

With an angry dismissive gesture Yossi exclaimed, "L'Azazel, what are they afraid of, that I'll screw Shayna in Paris? *Shayna?* Would I have to take her to Paris for that? I'm just as crazy about her, and I'd no more try that — First of all I couldn't succeed. Anyway, look, Leopold, a girl is what she is. Some girls like to play around, so you play. Why not? But Shayna? Foolishness!"

"Okay, then nail down Paris."

"Don't worry, I will. Tell me about your girlfriend."

"You'll see her in Paris. Isobel's a movie actress. Shayna, she isn't. Maybe I'll make a real birthday party for you tomorrow night in Tel Aviv."

"Why not?"

Leopold got into the Peugeot. The driver munched his gums at Yossi in a grin, and the car sputtered off.

Christian Cunningham was drinking coffee alone in the dining room, at a window overlooking the harbor. It was mid-afternoon, and like most hotels this one was nearly empty. The boots of the two officers made echoing noises on the marble floor. "Isn't that where the gunrunning ship ran aground," Cunningham said, pointing, "and you almost had a civil war? And now that gentleman Mr. Begin is the minority leader in the Knesset."

"All true," said Pasternak, signalling to a hovering waiter to bring more coffee.

"There are no people like the Jews," said Cunningham. " *'A people that dwells alone, not to be considered as among the nations.'* Balaam said that, you know. Balaam was a seer."

"I don't know about Balaam," said Pasternak. "Balaam's ass saw more than he did, had to give him a talking to. The Prime Minister told me to inquire, would you like to see him?"

Cunningham stuffed a pipe from a red-white-and-blue-striped pouch and lit it in slow deliberate moves. "I'm far too lowly a functionary for that. My wife and I came to Paris to meet the fellow our daughter is in love with." The long bony face gloomily lengthened. "I thought I would visit the dig at Capernaum, to salvage the trip, while my wife consoles herself by buying Paris hats."

He puffed in silence, then took a hard tone. "The British and the French will make a fearsome blunder, Sam, if they attack Egypt.

So will Israel, if she plays along with them. I hope you people don't think Eisenhower is really lovable old Ike with the big grin. He's steel and ice, Dwight Eisenhower is, and he doesn't like to be crossed. In anger he's fearsome. He once sent millions of men to face death. Don't ever forget that."

Under Cunningham's severe stare, Pasternak responded, "If in fact the British and French are planning an attack, and if in fact they don't clear it first with Mr. Ike, that might indeed be quite risky for them. So?"

The three men were silent for a while, their cups clinking. Cunningham spoke up. "Early this year the French cleared with our State Department the sale to Israel of twelve fighter planes, Mystères. Well-named! They're mysteriously multiplying here, like amoebas. We know you may now have close to a hundred." Long pause, many puffs. No comment by Pasternak. "Doesn't that suggest that Israel may take part in an attack on Suez?"

Pasternak said, "Which would make Mr. Ike very displeased with little Israel."

"Very."

"Chris, that Secretary of State of yours, Mr. Dulles, is a disaster. '*Massive retaliation . . . going to the brink . . .*'" Cunningham winced and wryly smiled as Pasternak ground out the quotes. "Talk, talk, while Russia makes that 'Czech arms deal' with Egypt! *Twelve* Mystères! What are we supposed to do while Nasser trains up pilots for those two hundred Russian planes, and the crews for the five hundred Russian tanks — recite psalms? That's what the Jews did in Poland, getting into the trains."

"The target of the Russians is not Israel," said Cunningham.

"No, of course not. They're playing the old Great Game, only now not against Disraeli, but John Foster Dulles. Why in God's name does Mr. Ike let that pompous old lady run your foreign policy?"

Cunningham took a long time to answer. The words came slowly and carefully. "Mr. Dulles regards the Soviet Union as the great menace to western civilization. About that he's right. About how to deal with the menace, he's an innocent. He's a corporation lawyer, a drafter of plans and treaties."

"He was defeated for the Senate in New York by a Jew, Herbert Lehman," Barak put in. "That's not good for us, possibly."

"Well, the French are not exactly Jew-lovers, are they?" Cunningham's manner turned very sharp. "Israel might in fact help a Suez operation to succeed. In that case the Americans will condemn you. The Russians may intervene and take military action against you. Moreover, at the first setback, you can count on the British and French to abandon you. That's the guess of a low functionary. The one thing I'm sure of is the wrath of Eisenhower."

"He's busy running for reelection," said Pasternak, "and New York is a big state with many Jews."

"That's stupid thinking, Sam. A war crisis will at once bring out the D-Day commander inside the nice guy with the big grin, election or no election." He took out his watch and squinted at it. "I had hoped to drive up to Jerusalem, for the sunset on the Old City walls. It's getting late for that."

"You might be disappointed at the view," said Barak. "Wooden barricades, sandbags, barbed wire sort of spoil it."

Cunningham walked down to the lobby with them. Barak said, "Sir, my regards to your daughter, and please tell her the firefly poem was very nice."

"Firefly poem?"

"She sent it to me after our visit to you about the Constellation. It showed up after a year and a half. Israel postal service at the time. It's better now."

"I'll be sure to tell her. She writes poems in French these days." Watching them go out through a revolving door, Cunningham felt his personal sadness come back strongly to mind. What a difference between these fellows and Emily's pasty long-haired midnight lingerer in trendy cafés in a Sartre trench coat, with Sartre eyeglasses and no Sartre talent!

Barak was saying to Pasternak as they left, "Inconclusive chat! Can you tell me why I was shlepped away from my brigade for this?"

"The Old Man wanted to have your reaction."

*

"He was speaking for his government?" asked Ben Gurion. They were in the underground map room of the Kirya, and he stood with Dayan at a large wall map of the Sinai Peninsula, slashed with the heavy lines, arrows, and unit symbols of Operation KADESH. The code name was printed in bold black crayon on a lower corner.

"I can't say," replied Pasternak, "but the State Department is bound to know of his visit. Was he carrying a message? I don't think so. As he says, he's too low a functionary."

Ben Gurion looked at Barak, who said, "I'm not sure how low he is, but I'd say he talked as a friend — a very worried friend — not as an emissary."

"Is that all? Then why did he bother? We've had plenty of nasty warnings straight from Eisenhower and Dulles. This was nothing new. I'm a lot more worried than this Mr. Cunningham is."

It hurt Barak to see how unwell and very aged the Prime Minister was looking. Dayan on the other hand had good color and radiated high spirits. He had been advocating an attack on Sinai for more than a year, ever since the "Czech arms deal"; smash the Egyptian army, he had urged, before it could absorb the vast influx of Soviet weapons and turn them on Israel! Ben Gurion dropped heavily, despondently, into a chair. "That the British and the French will abandon us at the first setback goes without saying. And how does the war end? Who replaces Nasser, but another Nasser?"

"Whatever happens, it's a political opportunity for us, Prime Minister," insisted Dayan. "We can wipe out the terrorist bases in Sinai, open the Straits of Tiran, and secure passage through the Canal. And we're gaining a major arms supplier in France. That's plenty for one war."

For as long as a minute Ben Gurion sat silent, breathing noisily, his eyes filmy and vacant. "I will go to Paris myself," he said at last, "meet with the British and French Prime Ministers face to face there, and find out what's what. If they will not meet me, I will assume bad faith and I will cancel Operation KADESH." His bleary look turned on Pasternak and Barak. "Moshe will accompany me, of course, and so will you gentlemen."

13

On to Paris

At the little engagement party in the home of Shayna's cousin Faiga, the boys without exception wore yarmulkes, and the girls long-sleeved dresses with skirts well below the knees. Religious Jewish families tend to favor early marriage, and this was especially true among Shayna's Jerusalem friends, who were pairing off like turtledoves. Shayna's dark blue midcalf silk dress, which she had made herself, was the best she had, for she was going on to Lee Bloom's party for Don Kishote at the Dan Hotel in Tel Aviv; a prospect as dismal as this gathering was joyous.

These young people were her bunch from childhood days. She might wear jeans and go out with a paratrooper, yet she had never broken away and did not want to. The others regarded Don Kishote askance, but there was always the hope that she would make a mentsch of him; though many a skullcapped boy there hoped instead that she would come to her senses and drop the paratrooper. She had had her decorous romances with one or another of them, but none had lasted long.

"Must you go so soon?" Glowing with the excitement of her betrothal, Faiga gave Shayna a reluctant goodbye kiss at the door.

"I wish I didn't have to go at all. You know that." Faiga was her confidante, and Shayna had told her about the Tel Aviv party.

The cousin pulled her aside and whispered, eyes agleam, "And what about Paris? Shayna, will you really do it?"

With a heavy noncommittal sigh, Shayna left.

It would have to be raining and windy, she thought, as she wrestled with a gyrating umbrella on her way to catch the *sherut,* the jitney taxi, to Tel Aviv. She was sorry her mother had ever mentioned Yossi's birthday to Lee Bloom. He wasn't giving a party for his brother. That was his excuse for inviting big shots to his hotel and mingling with them. They were coming because Sheva Leavis had been written up in the Hebrew press as an Israeli who was making a fortune in the world outside, a topic always good for feature stories in the weekend editions, and Lee Bloom usually figured in those stories as Leavis's sharp young associate who had fought at Latrun. Such write-ups did not wholly skirt the touchy aspect of Bloom as a possible army deserter. Israeli journalists were masters of the wounding innuendo, and the hints were there.

The hem of her dress thoroughly bedraggled because it hung beneath her coat, she climbed into the crowded sherut, and landed in a jump seat facing a black-bearded black-hatted Hassid, who was at great annoyed pains to make no contact with her knees. She sympathized and did her best to cooperate, but as the sherut careened and bumped wildly roaring downhill from Jerusalem, the Hassid had to endure a few repellent contacts through her coat and skirt. Not that Shayna was herself repellent; had the Hassid allowed himself to notice such things, he would have conceded that she had a lovely face and beautiful dark eyes. He might then have noticed, too, an anxious gloomy look in those eyes. In fact, Shayna felt almost as though she were on the way to be hanged, for she was about to tell Don Kishote that she would not go with him to Paris. Ordinarily she could handle her antic paratrooper, but she had seen him tough and angry — with others, never yet with her — and that side of him cowed her.

Don Kishote had burst into her life again only during the past year, after she had all but forgotten him. He had changed so much that, except for the way he pushed his glasses up on his nose, she might not at first have been sure it was he. Her neighborhood synagogue was providing meals after the Yom Kippur fast for *hay-*

alim bodedim — "lone soldiers," foreign volunteers, and soldiers far from home or with no family — and the women and girls did the serving. There he was, with another soldier who had brought him: tall, muscular, brown, erect, and solemn-faced as of old until she said tentatively to him, "Is this Kishote?" Whereupon he looked at her puzzled, pushed up his glasses, and gave her the unchanged prankish grin. She had grown a foot or more since the siege days and acquired a woman's body, but taking no note of that, he replied, "As you see, in a gentile trade." That had been that, once he asked about her family, and acknowledged that yes, the Lee Bloom of the newspaper stories was his brother Leopold. There had been no spark.

The spark had leaped months later at the university, where the army sent him to give a recruiting talk. All able-bodied boys and girls were liable to the draft, unless they had religious or other exemption, but the army wanted the best youngsters to enlist as regulars. Seeing his name on the bulletin board, she went to hear him speak. The paratroopers were becoming an infantry elite almost on a par with fighter pilots, for their night reprisal raids were destroying fedayeen bases in Sinai and Jordan, reducing terrorist episodes, and going far to restore national morale.

Kishote spoke vividly and with much humor about his service in the fabled Unit 101 led by Ariel Sharon, which Moshe Dayan had created to activate the reprisal policy. The paratrooper force had absorbed 101, and with it, he said, much of the spirit of the legendary Palmakh. He did not gloss over the risks and the high casualties of the night raids. When he spoke of the empty seats in the cars returning from the raids, and of friends who had died, his voice hoarsened, and his young listeners grew very still. After the prolonged applause she went up to congratulate him. "Oh, you again? Good. Take me home with you. I want to see old Reb Shmuel." But his eyes told her that this time she had fetched him, as he had transfixed her with his soldierly presence and colorful talk.

Shayna was really not too sorry that her father had put his foot down and forbidden Paris, though she hated having to tell Kishote. She had never ventured outside the Holy Land, and Gay Paree was a big scary leap into the unknown. How would she dress? What could she eat? How would she manage with Kishote? It was murmured in her set, and the murmurs had reached her, that as soon as Shayna had put on blue jeans she was on the slide, and anything could happen to her next; and a *hevrehman* (wise guy) like that paratrooper was certainly bad business. She had heard more than she wanted to know about Don Kishote's escapades and amours, in a notorious room he had rented with some other platoon leaders, on a crooked old street in downtown Tel Aviv.

Yet a girl in love sheds such talk as a duck sheds water. Besides, her parents liked Yossi, who retained enough religion to mind his ways around them, and Reb Shmuel loved him because he listened to and enjoyed his Torah talk. Shayna still could scarcely face the notion of one day marrying someone in "the gentile trade," but by now she knew that Israel lived or died by its soldiers, and the inescapable truth was that she adored Don Kishote in his red beret and heavy red boots, and couldn't look or think beyond an infatuation verging on the besotted.

Now her father had spoken, Paris was off, and Shayna was not feeling too abused or deprived, just apprehensive. In a way she was getting out of a corner. Shayna was no innocent. She had avidly read authors like Balzac, Zola, Lawrence, and Joyce; Boccaccio too, also Hemingway, Colette, and plenty of more trivial fare. Deep within her, strong passions were banked by upbringing and conviction. Some nights she could not sleep for thinking of Don Kishote and bitterly wondering what devilry he was up to in that room on Karl Netter Street in Tel Aviv, while his religious love lay alone and wide-eyed in a narrow bed in Jerusalem. Suppose they were alone together in Gay Paree? Would she herself behave? Oh, how she could *astound* that rakish Kishote, if she once put her mind to it! Riotous pictures of what might happen in Gay Paree had been haunting her imagination, not to be disclosed even to Faiga.

Fortunately, she had exams on the days they had been planning to go. That was true, and that she would tell Yossi. She had inquired about taking them later, and as a straight-A student she had been granted exceptional permission. That she would not tell him. A girl was entitled — and sometimes badly needed — to fib.

*

"There's probably nothing you'll eat," said Kishote, cleaving his way through the chatter and tobacco haze of the party to hug and kiss her while she still wore her coat and held her umbrella. He gestured at the buffet table, where amid various meats and salads fat pink shrimps, which to her looked like amputated thumbs, were piled high in an iced bowl. "I told Leopold no *shratzim* [swarming sea things], because you were coming. He says he told the hotel, but —"

"Look there, will you?" Shayna interrupted. At the buffet Benny Luria in air force uniform, his heavily pregnant wife, and his sister Yael were helping themselves to platefuls of swarming sea things. "Isn't that Benny's third, on the way?"

Kishote grinned. "Yes. These moshavniks don't waste much time. And neither does Leopold. He's bought the Paris tickets! How about that? El Al, leave Sunday morning, return Thursday. No Shabbat problem, isn't that fine?"

Shayna kept a timorous silence. Flushed with party host elation, Lee Bloom came and took his brother's elbow. "Guess what, the American ambassador showed up with the manager of El Al! Shayna, come and meet the ambassador."

"In a minute, Leopold," she said, for Benny Luria was smiling at her and beckoning with a swarming sea thing on a fork. "Benny, do you know I haven't met your wife?"

"My fault, I almost never leave Nahalal," said the wife. "I'm Irit." Hands folded on her huge stomach, she had the attractive outdoors look of so many moshav women.

Shayna and Yael exchanged cool party smiles. "So, it's raining in Jerusalem," Yael said.

"It hasn't stopped for a week."

"Nice that you could get away from the university for Yossi's party."

"Yossi's party," echoed Shayna, with a satiric look around that sufficed to show she was no fool.

Benny laughed. "That brother of Kishote is something."

"He does business with the army, that's all," Yael said shortly. "Sheva Leavis's business."

"I was with him for an hour this afternoon," said the aviator.

He was a Mustang pilot about to graduate to jet fighters, much on the climb, the straightest of straight sabras. "Sheva Leavis has amazing sources of supply. For the air force these fellows are a godsend. And they're appreciated. Lot of army stars here."

"Oh, who won't show up for food and drinks in this town, Benny? What else is there to do?" Yael snapped at her brother, and in an evil mood stalked off to the bar for a glass of cognac. Pasternak had brought his wife; only to be expected, but mighty irksome. The woman had returned from London with her two children when Dayan had become Army Chief of Staff and had selected Pasternak as a deputy. Their son, Amos, by their agreement, was coming back to Israel for his education, and she had come, too, no doubt because Sam's army career was taking off. The marriage was holding solely for their children's sake. At least, so Pasternak kept saying. Yet the pestiferous woman had recently had another baby! Just one of those things, Pasternak had rather lamely explained.

To Yael, nursing her cognac and her mood at the bar, the world for the moment seemed all babies, wives, and fresh-faced girls under twenty like that religious Jerusalem kid who had hooked Don Kishote. Not that she envied Shayna her conquest. As a paratrooper leader he was said to be fearless and able, if a bit crazy, but immigrants seldom rose in the army the way the sabras did; unless, like Pasternak and Zev Barak, they had been brought to Palestine as children long ago.

Two brilliant sabra officers, a kibbutznik and a Jerusalemite, had courted Yael while she had been dallying with Pasternak; hesitating between them and him for a couple of years, she had lost them both. Now they were on the climb like her brother, like him married and producing babies, and she was Pasternak's aide and girlfriend. But she knew Sam's passion for her, she knew plenty about Ruth Pasternak, and she thought — and planned — that despite the three children she would one day rope him. Meantime here was Ruth Pasternak in a New York original, looking vexingly slim again after the third baby, another girl.

"That's a grim frown, Yael," Zev Barak said, coming to the bar and ordering orange soda.

"It's a grim party."

"Agreed."

He went off with his soda and stood with his back to the wall. Because he knew so much of what was happening, he was taking no part in the repetitious Hebrew and English babble about the Suez crisis. Barak had gnawing reservations about Operation KADESH; also, about Lee Bloom. He knew, because Pasternak had told him, that Bloom's record with Zahal was clear. He was not sure how that had come about. He had not asked. In his mind Lee Bloom was still Leopold Blumenthal, the insouciant deserter in the Los Angeles airport. *Gold purifies bastards,* the proverb went, and for Barak that was the theme of this gathering. The pretense that it celebrated a good paratrooper's birthday was ludicrous.

"Come along, Zevi," said Ruthie Pasternak, approaching Barak and diffusing expensive scent. "Why are you being such a snob?" She linked an arm in his. "Lee Bloom is going to toast his brother."

"I can hear him from here," said Barak, but he allowed himself to be led toward the circle of guests forming at the other end of the room.

"Where's Nakhama?"

"She's not well, you know, Ruthie. And she hates to leave the baby."

"Oh, so do I! Sam dragged me out."

Barak let that pass. Circulation in the party scene was Ruthie's delight, as everyone knew. Almost as open as Pasternak's relationship with Yael was Ruthie's involvement with a minor foreign ambassador. In Israel's small pressure-cooker society, liaisons could not be long hidden. There was no place to go, and everybody talked about everybody else. By common courtesy, therefore, "friendships" between men and women, often married to other men and women, were more or less accepted, and in fact relished as topics of small talk along with war, politics, and rising prices. Ruthie Pasternak, like her husband, had been in and out of a couple of such friendships, though nothing like his love affair with Yael Luria.

Lee Bloom was already starting his toast as Ruthie and Barak came into the group around him; buoyant flowery talk about his pride in his brother which made Barak cringe. Didn't the fellow know when to leave well enough alone? But the toast brought calls of *"L'hayim!"* and some hand-clapping. Kishote raised both hands for quiet so that he could respond.

"I have to thank two people," he said, speaking English because the American ambassador stood close by. "First of all my brother Leopold, I mean Lee, of course" — that brought chuckles — "for this nice party, and even more for my birthday present, a round-trip on El Al first class to Paris, for me and my girl." He put an arm around Shayna. Amid the excited comments, and the curious glances at her, she did her best not to look appalled. "Second, my company commander, Ari Cohen, who went to my battalion commander, and then my brigade commander, and got me leave for four days. Thanks, Ari!"

He gestured to a burly officer, who responded in Hebrew, in a deep rough voice, "Be ready to come back at an hour's notice, or it's my ass." Barks of laughter from the army men.

"Well," said the El Al manager to Shayna, almost at her elbow, "El Al will give you both the royal treatment. That I promise you."

Shayna exclaimed, "But I'm not going."

Yossi turned on her in ludicrous stupefaction, pushing his glasses up on his nose. "You're *WHAT*?"

"I have this exam," she said. "I can't get out of it."

"An exam? Are you crazy?"

Already regretting her naive blurt before a roomful of onlookers, she rattled at him in swift Hebrew, "Please, please, drop it for now, will you? We'll talk about it later. I'm honestly sorry, but I just can't make it."

He angrily muttered, "The devil you can't. Tell them that you were joking. Quickly!"

Undertone: *"I can't, I can't, Yossi."*

Same: *"Do you realize what you're doing?"*

"Translation, please," called the American ambassador, and the gathering broke into laughter.

"Not necessary," said Yossi, unsmiling. He turned to his brother. "Well, I guess you just return those tickets."

The El Al man put in jocosely, "And there goes our year's profit."

More laughter.

Lee knew what the working of his brother's jaw muscles meant. Touchy moment! "Look, Yossi, she has an exam. That's that, and she's quite right. You come anyway."

"What, without a girl," said Kishote, "in Gay Paree? No thanks!"

A sweet voice called out, "I volunteer." Yael Luria stepped out of the group with a demure little smile. "That is, if I'll do."

Kishote peered at her through pushed-up glasses, and said in Hebrew, forcing a grin, "Well, Yael, let's have a talk about that later. Just you and me."

"Translation, please." The ambassador got a second laugh, and this time Yael coyly translated.

"Why, there's a happy ending," the ambassador said, and the pleasantry broke up the scene, with nobody knowing, least of all Shayna, whether either Yael or Kishote had really meant it.

The luminous dial on Yael's bedside clock showed half-past two when the telephone woke her. Her immediate thought, knowing all she did as Pasternak's aide, was that this could be mobilization for war. But it was only Don Kishote, sounding brusque and tired. "Yael? Sorry to disturb you. Were you serious?"

"About what? Oh, Paris? Well, hardly. It was a joke." She yawned and added, "Maybe half serious. Why? Surely she can get that exam postponed! She'd be crazy not to go."

"Well, we've been having a little disagreement about just that. A five-hour disagreement, with weeping and hair-tearing, the whole exercise. El Al flight 43, seven-thirty Sunday morning. Will you come?"

"Look, can't this wait until the morning?" Yael's mind was clicking into gear. El Al, first class! Paris! Give Pasternak a bone to choke on! Yossi was nobody to take seriously, but he was fun in his loony way.

"Come on, will you? Will Pasternak let you go?"

It was just the right prod in the tender spot. Wide-awake, Yael said, "I suppose it's cold in Paris?"

"No colder than Jerusalem, Lee says."

"Well, I don't know. Call me at the office in the morning. I've never been to Paris. Rome, Athens, not Paris. Suppose Shayna changes her mind?"

"Not in the picture. I'll call you at nine."

Yael lay open-eyed thinking about clothes, and how to handle Pasternak, and the Paris of movies and books. Then she went back to sleep; a steady-nerved sort, not given to undue worry or excitement. She had added it all up and decided she might as well do it.

She had not, however, added in one factor. David Ben Gurion was making an ultra-secret trip to Paris, and his small entourage included Pasternak. She knew almost everything about Pasternak's schedule, but not that.

All Nakhama knew was that Zev was going abroad, because she had had to dig out his passport, unused since his tour of duty in a French command school at Saint-Cyr. That it was serious business she gathered from his abstracted air when they met with Noah's teacher. The boy was studious enough, the woman said, but given to pranks like bringing frogs into class and hiding them in girls' desks. "Zev, you have to give him a talking-to," she said as they drove home.

"Let that be his worst offense."

In their apartment his brother Michael was drinking tea and working on papers at the dining room table. He now had a teaching job at Hebrew University and was living with the Baraks while looking for digs. Michael had allowed his hair to grow out in a great brown bush, and looked more like the violinist he had once wanted to be than the mathematician he had become. He moved aside his canes and poured Zev a cup of tea. "Nakhama says you're leaving?"

"Well, I may. Incidentally, you got the Matisdorf girl into plenty of trouble."

"Me? How could I? She's number one in the class."

"Trouble with her boyfriend." As Barak sipped tea and recounted the episode at Lee Bloom's party, Michael looked more and more puzzled.

"But she asked to take the exam a few days late, and I agreed."

"You *did*?"

"Why not? Whenever she sits down to it, she'll whip through it in an hour. I didn't know she wanted to go to Paris. It's all news to me."

"Well, he's taking another girl, or at least I think so, and it's a mess."

"Is he that big paratrooper I've seen her with? The one with glasses they call Don Kishote?"

"That's him."

"She's better off not going to Paris with that one."

"I know him well. I think you're wrong. Anyway, she blamed your exam."

"Okay with me. She's a modest nice girl, very religious. She'll go places as an engineer, if she follows that track. I think she should be a mathematician, and one thing's sure, she doesn't need a paratrooper complicating her life. Good riddance."

"I didn't say they'd broken off. That's a heavy love affair." Barak smiled at his brother. "And your love life? Any hope?"

Michael Berkowitz adjusted his small knitted skullcap, which had a precarious purchase on his thicket of hair. "It's not going to work out." Barak's glance at the canes was involuntary. "Nothing to do with that. Lena's been wonderful about my problem. The thing is, she really, deeply doesn't believe in God, Zev. She wants no part of Yiddishkeit. Born and grew up on a Mapam kibbutz. Loves music. She'll get her Ph.D. in Russian literature without question." Michael threw up his hands. "But she's inflexible. She isn't angry at God, or rebellious, or anything. She just thinks it's all nonsense. Primitive mumbo-jumbo. She feels totally Jewish, she says, without it. We've talked about this for weeks. We're on opposite sides of a line that can't be crossed."

"I like Lena. Too bad."

"I love her," said Michael mournfully. "It was so great at first, and I don't attract many women."

"You'll attract one that'll put up with God. Or let's say God will send you one."

"All I ask of God," said Michael, "is to go to work on Lena."

"Don't. If he's in the mood to work miracles, Israel needs them all."

Nakhama was banging around in the kitchen, and by the sound of the impacts not in the friendliest of humors. He went in there, disarmed her of two frying pans, and embraced her. She did not respond at first, then she did, grudgingly.

"It won't be for long, *hamoodah* [darling]. It can't be. I have to return to my brigade."

"Oh? Good to know. The army's bad enough. These mystery trips, let me tell you, I can do without."

The airplane thrumming through black night was like none Barak had ever flown in. President Truman had presented it to De Gaulle, the story went, as a victory gift after the war, and now that De Gaulle sulked in retirement writing memoirs, it was a French government plane; fitted up for ministerial journeys with beds, galley, and a darkened conference area where the Israelis were relaxing, while their French hosts sat up late over wine at the table up front.

"Anyway," Dayan had remarked to Barak when they came aboard, "it doesn't smell of horses. We're making slow progress." Pasternak, Dayan, and other officials were now stretched out asleep. Ben Gurion was reading a thick volume in a cone of light, and Barak was rapidly scrawling Hebrew hen tracks on a pad.

October 21, 1956

Paris Meeting — Analysis

(Sorting out my thoughts on this grotesque Suez "scenario," as the British call it, in case B.G. turns to me and asks for an opinion.)

A. The British-French Proposal

    1. Israel invades Sinai and threatens the Suez Canal.

    2. It is assumed that Nasser mobilizes his army to defend the Canal.

    3. The British and French issue an ultimatum "to both sides" to withdraw armed forces from the Canal area. It is assumed that Nasser will refuse. Whereupon they land troops in the Canal Zone to "restore peace."

    4. Once there, they march to Cairo and get rid of Nasser. Reduced to bare bones, that is it.

B. Colonel Nasser

A flamboyant revolutionary nationalist. What the Americans call a "tinhorn," that is, a noisy bluffer, yet to us he's a real threat. He can't destroy France or England, but in that bombastic book of his, *The Philosophy of the Revolution,* he proclaims that he'll unite the Arabs in one great nation, revenge their defeat in 1948, and wipe out "the Zionist entity" once for all, as soon as . . .

"Zev! Come here." Ben Gurion calling with a wide-awake smile at one in the morning. "See what this fellow writes."

Barak laid aside his pad. B.G.'s book was a Victorian edition with dense double-columned small print, and looking over his shoulder Barak could hardly make out the words the thick forefinger indicated. "Isn't Sharm el Sheikh your brigade's objective, if I go ahead with KADESH?"

"Yes, Prime Minister."

"Well, just look here. *Yotvat!* That's the Bible name for the main island in the Straits of Tiran, and he says it was a Jewish settlement! That's how far back in history *we* belong at Sharm el Sheikh. This is Procopius, writing in early Byzantine times, around the year 500 — nearly fifteen hundred years ago. A century before Mohammed was even born! So much for Arab claims that it's always been theirs."

The big bald head bent again over the book, and Barak returned to his seat. It was just like the Old Man to be reading ancient history on the way to a meeting that could shape modern history, and possibly lead to World War III. To Barak the outcome of this venturesome show of force was absolutely unknowable, and at best not promising.

He picked up the pad and went on with his scrawling for well over an hour, then tried to sleep; but he could not, so he showed Sam Pasternak his many pages of notes. Pasternak read them with care, now and then wryly grinning, and handed them back without a word. Barak waited, and when Pasternak yawned and closed his eyes he snapped, "Well?"

"Well, what? Waste of time. He's already decided to do it, or we wouldn't be on this plane. The rest is haggling."

14

Les Folies-Bergère

In the crowded ladies' cloakroom of Les Folies-Bergère, at a big mirror amid swirls of cigarette smoke and a twittering din in French, Yael and Isobel Connors were freshening their makeup between the acts, side by side. Lee Bloom's girlfriend was a stylish redhead half a head taller than Yael, with a perfectly shaped Hollywood face — high cheekbones, sunken cheeks, wide-apart eyes, and a slightly pouting mouth. Yael judged her to be past thirty and somewhat worn by the film life; she had never heard of the actress, but believed Lee's assertion that she had played big parts and had once been nominated for an Oscar. So she was suitably impressed, and becoming glad after all that she had accompanied Kishote to Paris, mostly to burn up Sam Pasternak.

On the long bumpy plane ride, through most of which Kishote had slept, Yael had been having glum second thoughts about this wayward excursion. Pasternak had nastily growled at her about it, and that had been satisfying. Still, at heart she was afraid of him, and especially afraid of losing him. Don Kishote was no replacement, younger than she was and hardly a great catch, and anyway he loved that little Jerusalem prude. Yael was not enjoying the show much; she was desperately tired, and Kishote too had kept yawning despite all the nude cavorters of the Folies-Bergère. He did not promise to be much fun, but Paris might still be. The Champs Élysées was stunning in its blaze of light, and this naughty Folies-Bergère would make a good story back home, and so would Isobel Connors.

"How do you like the Folies so far?" The actress looked at Yael in the mirror. Her voice was husky, almost hoarse; she was one of many replicas of Marlene Dietrich floating around the movie business.

"Well, the costumes and the sets are unbelievable. Such extravagance! I guess the men enjoy all the naked girls running around. Maybe I don't exactly follow the skits, with all the slang, but aren't they very dirty?"

Isobel Connors's lips curled in a salacious grin. "Which ones, dear?"

"For instance, that scene in the tailor shop. The tailor fixing the comedian's zipper. All that stuff. The audience was howling and howling, and if I got it, it was really dirty."

"You got it," said the actress, uttering a laugh right out of *The Blue Angel*. "Say, that brother of Lee's is cute, but he can't seem to stay awake."

"We had a bad plane trip, and the army's been working him hard. He's a paratrooper."

"So Lee told me. I think that's terrific. Ready? Let's get back to the boys." As they strolled among the lobby promenaders Isobel Connors said, with a slantwise glance at Yael, "You're a soldier too, aren't you?"

"I'm in the army, yes."

"I envy you." The Dietrich voice went vibrato. "Those Israeli army men are something, aren't they?"

"Some of them."

"Do you happen to know a fellow named Sam Pasternak?"

Yael barely managed not to leap a foot in the air, which was her impulse. "Sam Pasternak? Yes, why?"

"I met him years ago, in Beverly Hills. He was raising funds or something. Ugly brute. Short, barrel-chested, funny eyes. But charming! Wow. Is he a general by now? That man was going places."

Yael at first thought she was being baited, but the actress clearly was only gossiping. "I believe he's a colonel. We don't have many generals."

"There are the fellows," said Isobel, heading through the crowd and waving.

When they came outside after the show the night had turned misty, with a chilly drizzle which enhanced the magic of the lights. All Paris seemed to glow cold and white as the limousine crawled through thick traffic to Le Tour d'Argent.

"Isn't that the most expensive restaurant in Paris?" Yael artlessly asked Lee Bloom.

"It's the best."

"I could use some coffee," said Kishote, sitting up front with the driver.

"Yes, about a gallon." Yael's tone was tart. Kishote had fallen asleep during the spectacular finale about Messalina, an orgy in a Roman bath with troops of naked youths and maidens splashing in and out of a vast real pool, amid much simulation of intercourse, all to Debussy's *Afternoon of a Faun*.

Isobel Connors giggled, and said, "I guess Yossi's bored by Roman history."

"I'll tell you about the Folies-Bergère," said Kishote. "One girl with her clothes off can be the greatest thing in life. Twenty of them are like big chickens with the feathers off."

"Why, Yossi, you're a philosopher," said Isobel.

Waiting behind the velvet rope for the headwaiter of Le Tour d'Argent to seat them were several couples in smart clothes looking self-important and impatient. Across the restaurant, over the heads of the thronged diners and through huge picture windows, Yael could glimpse Notre Dame looming illuminated in the mist. What a city! What a restaurant! And what a man of the world this Leopold Bloom was, in his dark sharply tailored suit, with protruding white shirt cuffs fastened by big gold links, an American every bit as elegant as these Frenchmen all around him! By contrast Don Kishote appeared decidedly shabby and oafish, though seeming quite at ease and unaware of it, in an ill-fitting gray suit badly wrinkled by the plane trip, standing away from the faded blue shirt he hadn't changed, his big wrists dangling and without cuffs because it was a short-sleeved shirt. In his paratrooper uniform he cut a good figure, though there was always a slightly clownish air to him, but in Israeli street clothes nobody could take him for a regular patron of Le Tour d'Argent. The headwaiter looked him over with half-closed eyes before showing them to a table at a window, with a grandiose view of the cathedral's flying buttresses and lit-up towers, magnificent in the frostily glowing mist.

"Oo-ah, how do we rate this table?" Yael exclaimed.

"Sheva Leavis's name," said Lee, rubbing thumb and forefinger together. "That maître d' has reason to remember it."

"There's a fellow who's dressed worse than I am," said Kishote, nodding his head toward another window table, where a large man with long dishevelled hair, in a rumpled stained shiny blue serge suit, sat with a slim beautiful woman. "I guess that headwaiter is no snob. I thought he might be, the way he looked at me."

"That's Diego Rivera," said Isobel Connors, "and he's with Paulette Goddard."

"Is she the one who was Charlie Chaplin's mistress?" Yael was proud of knowing the spicy rumor.

"His among others," said the actress. "She's had more men than Messalina."

"Can I get some coffee right away?" said Kishote,

The waiter brought menus handwritten in French, which Yael knew well enough to follow Lee's suave orders. He ended by ordering coffee for Yossi *"toute suite,"* at which the waiter hesitated and blinked incredulously, as though he had asked for a roast cat, before bowing and departing. Delicious grilled fish garnished with mussels came along after a lengthy wait, and then enormous white asparagus, and then exquisite tiny strawberries, but no bread and no coffee. The pale yellow wine was the best Yael had ever tasted, and she drank a lot of it, and found herself feeling more kindly toward poor Kishote, who was weaving in his seat and ate almost nothing until the bread and butter came along, when he ate it all while the others watched Diego Rivera and Paulette Goddard quarreling in Spanish.

"This is good bread," he said. "I like this restaurant, but it's slow with the coffee."

When the actress and Yael went off to the lounge, and Kishote was drinking a tiny demitasse, Lee said, "Look, I'm sorry about the hotel, and putting you on different floors. I didn't realize Paris was all jammed up for the auto show. We were lucky to get two rooms for you in the same place."

"It's not a bad hotel, Leopold. Only thing is, Yael's hall light is out, and she had to grope her way to the toilet with her cigarette lighter. I complained, and now she has candles. The French are very accommodating."

"I tell you what." Lee tossed a key on the table. "You take that. Extra key to the suite, Isobel has one. I have to fly to Frankfurt with Sheva tomorrow, just overnight, and Isobel's going to Cannes for two days. She has movie friends there. Our suite is big and very fancy, and you two can use it."

"What for?"

"For whatever you want." Lee faintly leered. "There's a bar with everything, and a great view of the Arc de Triomphe. It's nice."

Yossi shook his head. "You're off track. Yael is madly in love with someone else, and I'm in love with Shayna, you know that." He sighed. "I'm disgusted with her, that's all."

Lee shrugged. "Shayna still has to mature."

"Yes, for a decade or so." Kishote took the key. "Well, at that I suppose Yael will get a kick out of seeing a suite in the Georges Cinq. She's enjoying all this. Thanks."

The two couples emerged in the frigid mist as the cathedral bells were chiming midnight. The drizzle had stopped. Lee said with smoking breath, "This is when Paris begins to wake up. Let's go on to Montmartre."

"Great idea," said Isobel.

Huddled in his army coat, Kishote groaned, "Yael, you go."

"Not without you."

"Come on, it's a perfect night for Montmartre," said Lee. "The mist, the chill. Right out of Toulouse-Lautrec."

But Yael begged off too. The limousine dropped them at a

dingy hostelry on a blind alley, L'Hôtel Feydeau, and the actress and Lee went on to Montmartre. "See you day after tomorrow," he said in farewell. "Have fun." He had pressed on Yossi a fistful of francs, saying that Paris cost like sin unless you had dollars to exchange, and he knew Yossi had no dollars. Yossi took the money because he had Yael on his hands, felt he owed her a good time, and couldn't otherwise deliver.

The hotel elevator, no larger than a telephone booth, squealed up inside the stairwell with jerks and shudders. Kishote and Yael, standing face to face, were perforce in violent body contact like overeager lovers, their grins of embarrassment barely visible in the dim glow of an overhead bulb like a mushroom. When the elevator stopped a foot or so above her landing, Yael jumped out and Kishote followed her. "I'll walk up from here," he said. "The next jump could be worse, and I'm a coward."

She laughed and kissed his cheek. "What do we do tomorrow, and when do we start?"

"Anything you say."

Kishote struck Yael, all at once, as very young and forlorn, no Sam Pasternak by a light year. "Sorry I'm not Shayna Matisdorf."

"Well, so am I, Yael, but you're a good sport."

"Know what? Let's climb the Eiffel Tower, Kishote." She put on a gay air. "And maybe have breakfast up there, if there's a restaurant."

"You're on. Call my room in the morning."

"There are no room phones, just one on each floor."

"Right. Like the toilets. Okay, bang on my door. It's number 517, just two away from the toilet. Real luxury."

Barak and Pasternak shared a room in a hotel off the Étoile, about halfway in quality between the Georges Cinq and L'Hôtel Feydeau. For instance, the room had a toilet, and Pasternak plunged straight for it when he got back from a conference in a suburban villa about midnight. Barak was lounging on a twin bed in underwear and a heavy bathrobe, reading *Paris-Soir*. Without explanation, a Dayan aide had told him he would not be needed at the conference. "Well, what happened?" he called. "Are we going to war?"

"Hold on." Pasternak came out after a while shaking his head. "The Frenchmen served us some strange creatures for dinner with claws and feelers, sort of like scorpions. Écrevisses. In a rich sauce. I almost died during the second meeting. Or maybe it was just nervous stomach. The Old Man staggered everybody, even Dayan." He lay back on a bed, cradling his head on his arms. "What about your dinner with Chris Cunningham? How did you explain being in Paris?"

"I didn't explain. He didn't ask. His wife's charming, an aristocrat."

"Yes, a noble lady, Caroline. How about the daughter and her boyfriend? That poet?"

"The girl's grown up sort of striking, in a strange skinny way. All bones. The boyfriend showed up after dinner, had Cointreau and coffee with us, then took her away."

"What's he like?"

"A catastrophe. Hiroshima in a trench coat. I'm having breakfast with the daughter tomorrow, unless I'm wanted out at the villa. I'm supposed to reason with her about life and love. That emerged from the dinner. The girl's idea."

"Well, it looks like we're not going to war. I couldn't have been more wrong." Pasternak sat up. "I'm feeling better. In fact, hungry. Either the Old Man is a political genius beyond my understanding, or he's clear off his head. Why don't we go to Montmartre? Have some drinks and something to eat?"

"Sam, I don't want to go to Montmartre. It's full of tourists and weird characters staring at each other. There are bistros around here."

"Not open now. Get dressed."

"Okay. Tell me about the conference."

"You won't believe me, though I'll tell God's truth and nothing else. This whole Suez thing's like a comedy written by a guy smoking hashish."

"It has been right along."

"Well yes, but it's getting crazier. I don't think anybody knows what he's doing, except maybe B.G. He baffles me." He glanced around at the walls and lowered his voice. "More, outside."

When they emerged into a silent foggy side street and walked toward the nearest boulevard, Pasternak resumed his account. The three top men of France had shown up at the villa first — Prime Minister, Foreign Minister, Defense Minister; smooth, gracious, well-disposed to Israel, even admiring. In return for their arms supplies they had been learning many secrets about Israel's military capabilities, and they seemed a bit dazzled, Pasternak said, probably because they hadn't expected much from a country of little over a million people. The conference had begun with chitchat about Suez, Nasser, the Americans, and so on. Then the Frenchmen had invited Ben Gurion to speak first about the proposed operations.

"You know the Old Man," said Pasternak. "It took him a while to get wound up. But when those Frenchmen grasped what he was driving at, they looked at each other stunned. Absolutely flattened. First he asserted that Egypt's grabbing the Suez Canal was just a detail. A comprehensive solution of the regional problem was needed, so he would offer a new concept that would restore British and French power in the region. Then Nasser would wither on the vine, or easily get forced out."

Pasternak stopped walking and touched Barak's arm. "Now what comes next beats everything."

"Well, at this point nothing will surprise me."

"Okay, then listen. B.G.'s great concept was that Jordan wasn't a real country and should be partitioned! It was just a diagram on the map of Ottoman Palestine, drawn by mistake by the British Foreign Office. Everything east of the Jordan River should go to Iraq, everything west to Israel. The British sphere of influence would be Greater Iraq, Iran, and Egypt. For the French, the solid bloc of Syria, Lebanon, and Israel. Zev, he seemed dead serious with this *meshugas*."

Barak shook his head. "I believe he was. I've known him since I was a boy. Finding himself sitting with the three most powerful men in France — talking to them as an equal, a Prime Minister, just went to his head. He was intoxicated. He thought he was Roosevelt at Yalta, carving up the world."

"Either that, or he was throwing them off balance, talking deliberate nonsense," Pasternak said, "while he took their measure, and got ready to make his real demand — that all three forces attack simultaneously."

Standing under a haloed streetlight, Pasternak hailed a passing cab. The driver looked about eighty years old, with a bushy Clemenceau mustache, and eyebrows like two more mustaches. *"Ata m'daber ivrit?"* Pasternak inquired. The driver's unfocussed blank look satisfied Pasternak that he didn't know Hebrew. *"Bien.* Montmartre."

They got in, and he went on. "Well, their Prime Minister said they had better stick to the Suez question. The English might pull out unless we moved fast, because Eden was already catching hell in Parliament, and his Foreign Office opposed any action that might irritate the Arabs. We only had Anthony Eden with us, and he was a sick man and weakening."

"Anthony Eden," spoke up the driver in hoarse French, "is an enemy of France and a homosexual."

"Justement," said Barak.

"The guy B.G. really angered was the Foreign Minister," Pasternak continued. "That man got vehement. If the British were provoked to back out at this crucial moment by such bizarre proposals, he said, Nasser would become unshakeable, stronger than ever, and out to become the new Saladin by destroying Israel. He urged B.G. to bear that in mind. That's when the Englishmen arrived at the villa."

The cab stopped at the foot of the Montmartre hill. Inquiry in crack-voiced French: "Monsieur desires that I ascend?"

"No, from here we walk." They got out and Pasternak paid the fare.

With a glittery look and a snarling lift of his mustache, the driver said, "Monsieur, Dreyfus was guilty." The cab jolted away.

"Cognac, right now," said Pasternak, and they went into a dark little boîte and sat as far as they could from the only other customers, two dim bulky shapes talking in American accents.

"When I say the Englishmen arrived," Pasternak resumed, "I mean there was a lot of bustling in and out of the big main room, and some British voices off in another part of the villa. We could hear two words being repeated over and over: *'No collusion, no collusion.'* The English wouldn't come into the same room with us. The French ministers had to go running back and forth, one end of the villa to the other, and it's a big villa. The British were like rabbis, we were like ladies, and the villa was an Orthodox synagogue. Strict separation."

Barak ruefully laughed. "Are you saying Ben Gurion never met them face to face?"

"Oh, leave it to the Old Man. This crazy shuttling by the Frenchmen went on for about an hour. Finally B.G. said there was no point going on with this peculiar business, it was a deadlock, and he'd fly home in the morning. That brought the rabbis into the ladies' section. They even shook hands."

"Through a handkerchief, no doubt," said Barak.

"This is pretty raw cognac. Let's move on. Let's eat something."

As they started to climb the crooked cobbled street, Pasternak said, "There was a point after that when I thought Ben Gurion really would walk out. He looked within an inch of it. You know, when that jaw juts forward and he turns all pink and can't sit still —"

"I know it well."

"He was urging the English Foreign Minister, Selwyn Lloyd — square face, a cold fish, or maybe he just felt chilly in the ladies' section — to advance the date of the landing in Suez. The French were all for that. But the British insist they won't land until about a week after we invade Sinai. B.G. argued that we'd be fighting alone all that time. The Egyptians could bomb our cities. The Russians might even intervene. Well, Lloyd said he was sorry about that, but England couldn't be seen as starting a war, her allies would disapprove. B.G. was gripping the arms of his chair with white knuckles, the way he does, when fortunately the French invited us to dine on those écrevisses."

Pasternak halted and peered through an open doorway into a brightly lit smoky place, where an accordion played and a few people at the tables discordantly sang. "La Vache Heureuse," he said. "The Happy Cow. I once had a good steak here. Off an unhappy cow, I guess. Feel like a steak?"

"If you do."

Pasternak was almost through the door when he stopped. "No. I see that fellow Lee Bloom in there. No need for him to know we're in Paris." He stood squinting through the smoke. "Very pretty redhead he's with. I think I recognize her."

"Sam, I think you recognize most women."

"No, I met that woman in California. Yes, that's her. Connors. Isobel Connors, she's an actress. She was a blonde then. I'm sure it's her. Well, let's move on."

Seven or eight young people came roistering down the hill, laughing and shouting in German. The two Israelis trudged up past them in silence. Then Barak asked, "So, the outcome?"

"Deadlock. The British want us to commit a real act of war. The Old Man will only do a raid against the fedayeen, and he wants them to start bombing the Egyptian airfields the day after we go. The British say no, that'll look like collusion."

"Then we fly home in the morning?"

"Not yet. Dayan ad-libbed a compromise plan that they'll take up tomorrow. Ah, here we are, Les Rieurs Amants, The Laughing Lovers. Great place. I once saw Hemingway in here. While I was eating, a lion leaped in through the door and he killed it. They do very good coq au vin."

"He had a rifle with him?"

"A rifle in Montmartre? Are you crazy? No, he strangled it with a checkered tablecloth."

"All right, let's have coq au vin. Did you really see Hemingway in here?"

"Well, a guy who looked like Hemingway."

"In what way did Dayan alter KADESH?"

"Let's go in and order our coq au vin. It takes nearly an hour, though."

"Sam, let's get a cheese sandwich."

"If they make them, sure."

Over the sandwiches and a bottle of superb red wine, Pasternak ticked off Dayan's scheme in a low voice, in quick Hebrew military jargon. The few diners at other tables were almost out of earshot, and none looked like a Hebrew speaker, or like Hemingway. "Dayan has his heart set on KADESH, hasn't he?" Barak commented, shaking his head. "Wants his Sinai war."

"He's right," Pasternak replied with sudden asperity. "Moshe's sense of priorities is incomparable. If we have to fight Nasser sooner or later — and I see no alternative — the best way is with the British and the French, not alone. If this is the only way to bring in the British, okay."

"With Israel the foil for their comedy act, taking all the blame in the United Nations?"

"Zev, our choices are few."

Next morning Barak sat in the posh busy lobby of the Georges Cinq, waiting for Emily Cunningham. His mind was on the Dayan plan, and he paid little heed to the prosperous guests, mostly American by their dress and chatter, coming and going. The military attaché of the embassy, his platoon leader in the old Haganah days, had awakened him with a telephone call. Ben Gurion wanted him at the villa by half-past ten, so the breakfast with Emily would have to be short. Barak had no idea what the girl wanted, and was not very interested, but he had been unable to reach her to call it off.

Through the street door came the poet he had called Hiroshima in a trench coat, hatless and smoking a pipe; a short doughy fellow of twenty-five or so, with long hair around a bald spot. They made eye contact, and the poet gave him a crinkly eye-shutting smile and sank into an armchair across the lobby, pulling a newspaper from his pocket. Soon Emily Cunningham came catapulting out of an elevator straight at Barak, dressed in the American collegiate skirt-and-sweater uniform, the skirt a loud tartan, the sweater loose, hairy, and bright blue. "Oh, God," she said, falling on the couch beside him before he could get up, "I'm late as hell, and there's no time for breakfast. André and I have to go to a lecture. I clean forgot. I'm so sorry I could die. Mother and Dad leave this afternoon. I just had coffee upstairs with them. Have you had coffee? Oh, God, there's André."

"Emily, I really haven't time for breakfast, either, so it's just as well —"

"Oh, God, you're not just saying that? Thanks." She took his hand with large bony fingers. Her touch was cold and gentle. "Why do I keep saying 'Oh God' like a schoolgirl? I keep hearing myself being an idiot. You fluster me. Can we have a drink? Say at five, here in the bar?"

"Look, Emily, it's not important, I'd have enjoyed talking to you, but —"

"Not important? It's desperately important. How long will you be in Paris?" She was staring at him through large glasses. The black pupils of her gray eyes were enormous, like a cat's in a dark room.

"Not long at all, a day or so, and I'm pretty well tied up, so —"

Her grip tightened, her voice dropped and became charged. "I'll be here in the bar at five. If you can't make it I'll completely understand. I'll wait till five-thirty and then leave. I just don't believe it's completely accidental that we've met again. It can't be. You look much older. Remember the fireflies? How many children do you have, Wolf Lightning?"

"Two, Emily."

"Oh, God, here comes André. Oh, God, that's my fourth 'Oh God.' Zev, André knows more about Lamartine than anybody alive, and he writes gorgeous poetry. I'm doing my master's on Lamartine. You must think André's a creep." She jumped up, and he stood too.

"I don't know him at all."

"He's a crashing creep, truth to tell, but fascinating. My parents would like him better if he were a Ubangi with wooden plates for lips — André, *cheri!*" She kissed Hiroshima, and they chattered in rapid French. André closed his eyes at Barak, and they made off together, still rattling away.

Left with time on his hands, Zev Barak sank back on the couch, more than a little bemused by the girl's eccentric appearance and disappearance in a minute or two, and by her bizarre manner. Emily Cunningham radiated high voltage and some kind of distress, and though she was only passably pretty — the excited eyes with the big black cat pupils, the face all bones and angles like her father's, a nice girlish figure vaguely discernible inside the loose outfit — she amazingly attracted him, and he was not sure why.

"Adon Barak!" Lee Bloom stood there with an overnight bag and a despatch case, both of softly gleaming leather. "We meet again!"

15

The French Whore

Yossi and Yael climbed the Eiffel Tower in a balmy sunny autumn morning, rewarded as they ascended through the giant gaunt girders by an ever-broadening view of Paris and the crooked Seine crossbarred by bridges; a great sprawl to the horizon of brown and gray buildings and spiderweb avenues, except where parks and gardens flamed with October color. They found a café on the lower platform, but Yael wanted to go all the way up first, so they climbed to the top.

"This is what the ground looks like, Yael," said Kishote, raising his voice over the wind whining through the steel struts and railings, "when you jump."

She was clutching the rail with one hand, and peering down at the vertiginous view. "Oo-ah! It gets me *here*." She pressed a palm between her thighs. "I've thought of asking for parachute training. I believe I won't."

"Aah, this is worse. Something about looking over the rail, and seeing the tower curving away below, makes you want to dive over and kill yourself," Yossi said. "God knows why."

"That's it. That's just how I feel."

"Well, in a chute you float down, it's all different, it's exhilarating, it's great."

"I'll take your word for it, Kishote. I'm ready for breakfast." Yael shuddered. He put an arm around her.

"Cold?"

"Not exactly."

"It was your idea to come up here."

"I wouldn't have missed it. If you're going to climb a tower, you climb it. Let's get down out of here."

The coffee *à l'Américain* in the almost deserted café was fresh and strong, with a different European taste, and it came in large cups. "Well, if you want a good cup of coffee in Paris," said Kishote, "you evidently don't go to Le Tour d'Argent, you just climb the Eiffel Tower."

"It was exhilarating at that, up there," said Yael, laughing as she heaped butter on a flaky croissant. "Something to do once."

He grinned at her. "Your color's coming back. You looked green for a while."

"I felt green. Funny. Heights never bothered me before."

"Never mind. You look lovely now."

She shot him a skeptical glance. In a leather jacket and wool cap she felt comfortable, but far from lovely. "Thanks. I hardly slept. Did you have bedbugs?"

"What! No. Did you?"

"Maybe it's that hotel. My skin crawled all night. I never saw one, no."

"Why don't we start with the Louvre?" He was thumbing a guidebook he had bought in the café. "Then take the boat ride on the Seine? The book gives them both four stars."

"Anything you say. Tonight I want to go to the Comédie Française. I saw in the paper that they're doing *Tartuffe*."

"Sure, but is your French that good? Mine isn't."

"Pretty good. When I was a kid I read all the Molière I could find in Hebrew, and then in French."

"You're still a kid."

"Ho! Look who's talking . . ."

They smiled at each other. The early start, the hard climb in the morning air, the disturbing thrills at the top, the jolts of coffee, had put them both in high spirits. He really was a kid, she was thinking. In a green army sweater, his curly hair tousled by the wind, his eyes boyishly playful through the rimless glasses, he was no longer a shabby Israeli out of place in Paris. He was Don Kishote. And it crossed her mind that Shayna or no Shayna, Pasternak or no Pasternak, there might be jolly harmless doings with the Don while they were in Gay Paree together. Nothing to plan or to work at, just play the situation as it unfolded.

"Yael, you're looking me over like the headwaiter at Le Tour d'Argent."

"I am? No, I'm not. You spilled coffee on your sweater." She pointed. "If we're going to start doing all the four-stars, let's go."

They raced through the Louvre, touching base at the Mona Lisa, which they found startlingly small, and then at the Venus de Milo. They walked all around the Venus, contemplating it in reverence. At least that was Yael's mood, and she thought it was Yossi's until he spoke up. "You know, if this statue had arms, nobody would ever have heard of it. That's what makes it. No arms."

"Kishote, don't be idiotic. It's the most beautiful woman's figure in the world."

"What? Look at those fat thighs, that thick waist, and those dinky little breasts! Why, you've got better breasts. She has a lousy figure. Yours is nicer, but you have arms, so you're not that special."

"You're not only a fool, you're an ignorant fool." In Yael's tone there was amused kindly music. However ridiculous the fellow was, it was not displeasing to be favorably compared to the Venus de Milo.

"What I want to do besides all these four-star things," said Kishote, as they left the Louvre, "is ride in a carriage in the Bois de Boulogne, and eat there at a restaurant among the trees. I read about that once in a book. Then I saw the movie. It was with Ingrid Bergman. And it was in the autumn like now. She was an older Frenchwoman in love with an American college boy, a big romance, but they were giving each other up, as the autumn leaves drifted down on them."

"You've got me crying," said Yael. "The way we're dressed, though, I don't think a carriage will stop for us in the Bois de Boulogne, or a restaurant let us in. Anyway, how do you pay for all this? You're not spending that kind of money on me, even if you've got it."

He told her about his brother's largesse. "Lee wants us to have fun, so why not? He won't take back the francs."

"Well then, that's different. All right."

In the Bois de Boulogne a carriage driver reined in his horse so abruptly, when Kishote waved one of the larger and more colorful French bank notes at him, that sparks flew from the creature's hooves. The headwaiter at a restaurant tucked among the scarlet and yellow trees gave them a long Tour d'Argent scrutiny before conducting them through many empty tables to a small one in an inconspicuous corner.

"*Quel vin monsieur désire-t-il?*" inquired a waiter in a purple velvet vest, with a gold chain around his neck, approaching with a large leather book, after Yael had ordered in French from another waiter a lunch climaxing in roast duckling. Kishote looked to her inquiringly.

"He says, 'What wine does Monsieur desire?' "

"Not *do* I desire wine — *what* wine do I desire?"

"That's right."

"Well, at that, Ingrid Bergman drank wine with that boy at lunch. In fact, they drank champagne. Champagne," Kishote said to the waiter. The man opened the book to a middle page and extended it to show him a long list of champagnes. "Yael, just tell him the best champagne they've got."

"Are you crazy? That can cost the price of an automobile. Anyway, champagne in the middle of the day?"

"We go next to Napoleon's tomb and then the Bastille. We need cheering up."

The wine steward was grimacing at the rapid exchange in Hebrew, as though he too suspected Dreyfus was guilty. Yael ordered a modestly priced red wine which seemed to show great connoisseurship, for the waiter brightened, bowed, offered a fast smiling compliment, and went off rethinking Dreyfus.

The food was quite as exquisite as the best French food was supposed to be, and this unaccustomed midday feasting and drinking lifted them both into the giddiest of moods, laughing at the French, at Israel's problems, at the world, and at themselves.

"Poor Shayna," said Yael. "What she's missed!"

"Yael, I want you to keep notes and tell her about it. Tell her everything."

"Ha. She'll scratch my eyes out. You tell her."

"If I ever talk to her again," said Kishote, in a sudden drop to bitterness.

"Come on. She's a nice religious girl, and you knew that right along."

Signalling to the waiter and pulling out Lee's wad, he growled, "Let's go to Napoleon's tomb."

The last thing they did that afternoon as the sun was sinking was to walk in the Tuileries Gardens, where the children still played in brightly colored warm clothes under the chestnut trees, and gossiping nannies wrapped in cloaks were starting to wheel home the prams. The breeze had freshened, and leaves were whirling down on the lawns, on the pools, and on afternoon strollers like the two young Israelis. "The guidebook says we're supposed to feed the carp, or we're not allowed to feed them, I forget which," said Yossi. "Anyhow, I'm for feeding them." He pulled a roll from a trouser pocket, broke it in half, and gave half to her. "For what that lunch cost, I figured I could take a roll for the carp."

"You think of everything, don't you?" Yael laughed. Children gathered to watch as they threw out bread bits and the fat fish rose to gulp them. "Paris is glorious, Kishote. Unbelievable! Tomorrow let's just walk. Let's walk everywhere."

"Sure. Now, Lee said the concierge at the Georges Cinq would get us tickets for anything we want. Is it still the Comédie Française?"

"Why? Would you rather see more big chickens with the feathers off?"

"No. I thought you might be tired."

"I couldn't be fresher. I'm walking on clouds."

The concierge, a gray-headed roly-poly man with the dignity of a cardinal, in a wing collar and dress coat, was all condescending grace to Yossi. Ah, yes, Monsieur Bloom had arranged to take care of whatever entertainment Monsieur might desire to book. Moreover, Monsieur Bloom had left instructions that Monsieur might care to dine in his penthouse suite or in the Georges Cinq Grill, and all that too would be taken care of.

"Let's look at Lee's suite," said Kishote. "He says it's nice."

"Fine, but I don't want to dine in any grill. I look like a peddler woman. Anyway, I'm not hungry after that lunch."

As they walked through the ornate double doors into the suite, Yael exclaimed, "Oo-*wah!*" The sitting room was a rich long vista of antique-style furnishings and real paintings, not famous but to their unpracticed eyes serious art. They wandered through to the bedroom, where she uttered another "Oo-*wah!*" The bed was draped from the ceiling to the floor in swathes of rust silk, and the spread was a pattern of Chinese characters, in black and white.

"Look!" Yael peeked into the bathroom. "Marble. Gold faucets! My God, what does this cost? How rich is your brother?"

"Rich enough. How about a drink?"

"No, no, I've had plenty today, I don't want to sleep through *Tartuffe*. Let's look at the view."

Yossi had to pull hard on the tasselled cords of the heavy drapes. The floor-to-ceiling windows looked out over the Arc de Triomphe to the Eiffel Tower. Paris glowed below in a rosy sunset arching all over the sky. "Ah, God," Yael murmured.

"You know something, Yael?" he said quietly, as they stood there side by side, both reddened by the sunset glow, "I still have that handkerchief you gave me, when we went into Lod and Ramle. The blood's all black. I never washed it out, just kept it."

"Why, you crazy thing? Why keep that rag?"

"Because I thought you were a goddess. A girl soldier, the first I ever knew, beautiful and tough and so far above me! I never threw it away. It's in my stuff somewhere." Yossi felt a sharp tug at his elbow that spun him half around to face Yael. She was looking at him with intense glittering eyes, and a small tight-lipped smile.

"A goddess, hey? And what's the difference, again, between me and the Venus de Milo?"

"You have arms," said Kishote, through a constricted throat.

"Exactly so," said Yael, and she held them out to him in the leather jacket sleeves. The gesture was an impulse, like the offer to go to Paris with him. It was a long moment before Yossi made his move, while Yael wondered half-embarrassed whether he would. The move when he made it was crushing and inflaming. So far as that went, as she should have known if she did not, Don Kishote was no kid.

Furious kissing and caressing for a while, then Yael appeared to shrug out of her clothes; one moment all dressed if disordered, the next naked as Eve.

"By God, I was right about you and that Venus," gasped Don Kishote, startled by this sudden unveiling of stark beauty. "No comparison whatever. None! Especially the breasts."

"My best points," said Yael, posing with chest thrust out and arms concealed behind her back, Venus de Milo fashion.

"Yes, both of them," said Yossi, and as happens at such moments they both laughed and laughed at nothing while he peeled as fast as he could, seized her, and rolled with her into the bedroom and onto the canopied bed.

In the bar below, Emily Cunningham was waiting for Barak at a narrow table. Beside her, two Germans, one portly and black-haired, the other a bronzed blond ski-instructor type, were smoking heavy cigars and talking heavy business. It was twenty-five past five. The smoke was choking her, but the bar was very crowded, and she did not want to move until she had given the Israeli his five more minutes. And in fact here came Wolf Lightning, striding through the shorter men standing three deep at the bar, looking around for her. She waved, and he came and sat down.

"Traffic was unbelievable," he said. "I drove in from out of town."

"I'm saved. Five minutes, and my life would have lain in ruins."

"You have a ridiculous way of putting things, Emily."

"I'm absolutely serious." She coughed as a cloud of cigar smoke rolled in her face.

"This is no place to talk," said Barak. "Come with me."

"Where to?" They both stood up.

"There's this American I know who has a suite here. He's gone out of town, and he said I could use it, the concierge would give Monsieur Barak the key. It'll be quiet, at least."

"Sounds lovely," said Emily Cunningham, picking up her fur-trimmed coat. She wore a rough skirt and a blue shirtwaist that showed something of a barely existent bosom. She took his arm as they left the bar. "Five minutes! I'm so happy that I didn't give up! Deliriously happy."

"Stop talking nonsense."

In Lee's suite, Yael and Kishote had been going at it explosively, and were side by side under the canopy, still breathing hard. Yael lay face down, her head on her arms. He was sitting up, his back against the headboard, his body vibrating with pleasure, his brain in tumult. Now what? He knew about Yael and Pasternak, as so many people did. He had made the remark about the handkerchief in all innocence. He could not tell whether that, or the whole dreamy day financed by Lee's francs, had brought on Yael's pass at him, or whatever it had been. Nobody had been seduced. It had simply happened.

She turned her head and wanly smiled at him. "Wow. I don't love you, Kishote." Low husky tender voice. "You know that."

"Something to do once," he said.

"Well, ah . . ." She left the rest unspoken, they both burst out laughing, and he swept an arm around her shoulders to pull her close. At that moment they heard the double doors bang open, and the voices of a man and a woman.

"Oh, l'Azazel," exclaimed Yael, and she panicked out of the bed and into the bathroom. Zev Barak came into the bedroom and halted in stupefaction.

"Kishote! What the devil!"

"Just having a nap," said Don Kishote airily, though extremely startled. "What are you doing in Paris, Zev? And in Lee's suite?"

"Never mind. Your brother's as feather-headed as you are. Where's Yael Luria?"

"I guess I bore her. She took off and went shopping." Barak was heading for the bathroom. "We've got tickets for the Comédie Française tonight — I wouldn't go in there, Zev."

"Why not?"

Yossi had hoped Yael would have the presence of mind to lock the door, but obviously she had not, because Barak was opening it. "Well, I just used it. It stinks in there."

"Who cares?" Barak went in, and was starting to unzip when a low female voice half snarled, from behind a thick flowered shower curtain, *"Monsieur, monsieur, pour l'amour de Dieu — allez-vous en!"* ("For the love of God, get out of here!")

As surprised as he had ever been in his life, Barak hastily closed his trousers and ran out of the bathroom, slamming the door.

"You mad dog," he snapped at Yossi, who sat up naked on the bed looking singularly stupid, "why the hell didn't you tell me you had a French whore in there? By God, you work fast."

"She's no whore," Yossi said. "She's the daughter of a Sorbonne professor. He teaches medieval philosophy."

"Where did you meet her?"

"I picked her up in the bar."

"You're a lunatic."

"Do you have a whore out there?"

"What, are you mad? She's a child."

"I caught a glimpse of her. Pretty big child, Zev."

Barak closed the bedroom door hard as he went out.

"Somebody's here, I gather," Emily said. She was at the window. The lights of Paris were coming on one by one. The long lines of streetlamps already shone.

"Yes, that American has a crazy Israeli brother. He's in there."

"Fantastic view, Wolf. Come and see."

"Yes, very nice." He had brought the girl here to talk in peace, but that French trollop might well come popping out for a drink at the bar, possibly stark naked. "Let's go somewhere else, Emily."

"Mother and Dad would usually have tea about this time on the mezzanine."

"Now you're talking. Tea on the mezzanine it is. Come on." Barak closed the doors noisily on the way out.

Softly giggling, a towel draped bewitchingly on her, Yael poked a naked shoulder out of the bathroom. "Did I hear them leave?"

"They're gone."

"Oo-ah! It's a miracle he didn't recognize my voice."

Yossi repeated, "*Monsieur, monsieur, pour l'amour de Dieu. . . .* That was great, Yael. He took you for a French whore."

Yael looked disconcerted, then in a burst of husky laughter she cast the towel aside, with the flirtatious flourish of a stripteaser. "A French whore! Well, I'll tell you something, Don Kishote. In the mood I'm in, that's almost a compliment." She leaped back into the bed. "One girl with all her clothes off, you said, can be the greatest thing in life. I'm the wrong girl, I guess, but —"

"But you're the one that's here." Kishote pulled her into an embrace.

"Now that's no compliment at all," she tried to protest, but "no compliment at all" was smothered in a kiss.

The mezzanine was as spacious and quiet as the bar had been small and noisy. One old lady with blue hair, wearing a large hearing aid, was having tea alone, feeding bits of cake to a very fat brown poodle tied up beside her. Barak and Emily sat down at some distance from her, and Emily ordered *thé à l'Anglais* from a starchily uniformed waitress. She peered at Barak with wide dark-pupiled eyes. "It's dim in here, and if you haven't guessed, I'm blind as a bat without my glasses. Mind if I wear them?"

"Why not?"

She said, taking a case from her purse, pulling out thick-lensed glasses and carefully putting them on, "Because men seldom make passes at girls who wear glasses." He looked blankly at her. "Oh, that's meant to be humorous. It's a couplet everybody knows in America. By a popular verse writer. I've tried to imitate her — Dorothy Parker is her name — and I've even sold a few things to magazines, but I'm no good at light verse. Or poetry, either, English *or* French. I'm finding that out. It's sad, but also liberating. Writing is torture. I'll have to do something else with my life." All this came out in a rush while she looked intently at him. "Hm. Gray hairs, Wolf?"

"Just a few. They come along."

"Are you happy?"

"Emily, you asked to talk to me. What about?"

"How do you come to be in Paris, Wolf? Dad says a war is about to break out over the Suez Canal, and Israel will probably be in it." Barak did not comment. "Well, I know better than to ask such questions. I'm just prattling. I'm nervous."

"I have no idea why."

"Haven't you? Well, maybe I'll tell you. André, by the way, is very impressed with you."

"That makes me feel bad."

"Why should it?"

"I'm afraid I've been describing him as Hiroshima in a trench coat."

Emily scowled and flared. "That's utterly disgusting."

"Sorry."

"I mean, aside from the slur on poor André, who's talented and harmless, it's in vile taste. Hiroshima is a tragic horror of history. It's no subject for jokes."

"True."

"Very cruel and crude, Wolf."

"Okay."

Her mouth wrinkled, and she gnawed her lips.

"What's the matter, Emily?"

"I'm trying not to laugh."

The waitress brought the tea service. Emily ceremoniously poured for Barak, asked how many sugar lumps he wanted, milk or lemon, cakes or bread and butter, serving him in a prim formal way that scarcely went with her disorderly cloud of dark hair and casual shirt and skirt.

"You make me nervous," she said abruptly, "because I'm not sure this is happening. I can't tell you how strange it is. You know about fantasies. Maybe you have them."

"Everybody does."

"Well, here goes the probable quenching of any spark in our relationship, but I'm going to tell the truth. Since the night you came to our house — eight years ago now — the night of the fireflies, as I think of it — you've been in nearly all my fantasies. This crossing of paths in Paris seems just like one of them, and when you asked me to come up to that suite, I almost had to pinch myself, because I must tell you some of those fantasies have been hot stuff. Now there it is."

"And now you've made me nervous."

"Oh, yes, I'll bet. You? The strange thing is you're *exactly* the way I remember you, the way I've been picturing you. Even, in the last few years, to the gray hairs."

They looked at each other over the teacups in silence, Emily's eyes almost all black behind the glasses. Quite at a loss as to how to handle this turn, Barak was sure of one thing. The quirky girl was cutting all the way inside his self-possession, and kindling an electric interest such as he did not remember feeling since his first meeting with Nakhama. How was it happening to him? She did not compare to Nakhama in looks, and scrawny women had never attracted him. He had once read a book of Dorothy Parker's verse; the last word, he thought, in sophisticated New York wit. This odd twenty-year-old had dashed off and even sold such cosmopolitan poems, and was writing a thesis on Lamartine; very nice, but what did that have to do with sexual magnetism, with the stirring in his whole body?

"I'm a virgin," she said.

At that the lady with blue hair, who sat far down the mezzanine, turned and looked at her before feeding her dog a whole éclair. Emily caught the move and said to Barak, "Did I yell that?"

"She's been fiddling with her hearing aid since we sat down. I think she's heard every word so far."

Emily dropped her voice. "Well, I hope she's amused."

"What's the matter with André? I understood it was a wild love affair."

"Oh, nothing's wrong with André. I've had a good Christian upbringing, and it's stayed with me. I'm repressed as hell, and he can't do anything but argue and whine. I've had no experience. At William and Mary, I was a greasy grind, Phi Bete, all A's. I joined a sorority, and depledged after the first pajama party when they sneaked the boys in. I'm a total loner. I've never met a guy who could hold a candle to my father. Hence, I suppose, fantasies. Very unhealthy, no doubt." She put a hand on his, and the touch was unexpected and sweet. "If I came to Israel, could I meet your wife? I'm obviously innocuous. I'm very curious."

"Nakhama doesn't speak English."

"Oh? Well, that wouldn't matter much. And I'd like to see your kids."

"Emily, you're not a dumb girl. Your parents hoped I would talk you out of André, or at least try to."

"Well, go ahead." For the first time, Emily Cunningham gave him a whole-souled smile. She had beautiful teeth and her smile had an odd satiric shape to it, better suited to a much older person, perhaps to a man. "I'd love to hear how you do it."

"I have a feeling it's not necessary."

The smile vanished. "I'm crazy about André."

"For your own reasons, you want to worry your parents. You've succeeded. When do you graduate?"

Emily took a notebook and pencil from her bag and handed them to Barak. "Write your address in Israel, and telephone number."

More and more stirred — so much so that he thought for a moment of refusing — he scrawled the information. "I don't advise you to come to Israel in the near future."

"Is my father right?"

"It's a beautiful country, and when you do come, Nakhama and I will be glad to show you around."

"More tea?"

"I have to go."

She jumped up. "What a date! I do believe I'm cured."

"Of André?"

"That's my business. Of fantasies."

"Yael," said Kishote, snapping out of an exhausted doze, "what time is it?"

She looked at her wristwatch, moving her arm as though it were broken, or coming loose in the socket. "Quarter to seven."

"Do we still go to the Comédie Française?"

"Of course . . . Oh, no. No. Not again. No!" The double doors into the suite, which tended to stick, were audibly opening. "Not again! I can't stand it."

A man's voice, cheerful and gravelly, resounding through the apartment: "Well, I call this luxury, Isobel. Your sweetie Lee Bloom has the right idea."

"God in heaven." Yael went rigid, seizing Kishote by the shoulders. "That's Sam Pasternak."

"You're sure?"

"He must have come to Paris with Barak," Yael whispered. "It's a military mission, of course. Kishote!" It was a frantic hiss. "On your life, get him out of this apartment. *On your life.*"

She darted into the dressing closet where she had hung her clothes. Kishote picked up the towel she had flung aside, fastened it around his middle, and walked into the living room, where Sam Pasternak was hugging and kissing Isobel Connors. She saw Kishote over Pasternak's shoulder. "Eee-eek!" She pulled away, rounding astounded eyes at him.

"Hello, Isobel," said Kishote. "I thought you were in Cannes."

"Oh, yes. Well, I'm flying there tonight, and —"

Pasternak exclaimed, "Kishote! What are you doing naked, and where the devil is Yael?"

"Can I talk to you, sir?" He took Pasternak by the arm and walked a little away from Isobel, who was pouring herself whiskey at the bar, looking very shaken. "Yael's at a department store, I think it's called the Lafayette something —"

"Galeries Lafayette."

"That's it, and the fact is, I've got a French *zonah* in there."

Sam Pasternak's truculent look relaxed in an approving grin. "French *zonah*, hey? How is she?"

"I'm about to find out. I'm meeting Yael at the Comédie Française. If you and Isobel care to join us —"

"No, no, she has to fly to Cannes, and I'm busy. How much longer will you be here?"

"Say a half hour."

"That's just fine."

Isobel Connors said with recovered aplomb, "So, Yossi, having a nap? You see, I missed my plane to Cannes this morning. Mr. Pasternak is an old friend. We just happened to bump into each other in a restaurant, and —"

"Right, right," said Pasternak. "Let's let our young friend finish his nap, Isobel. He's done a lot of sightseeing today. I'll buy you a drink in the bar."

As soon as they left, Yael came out of the bedroom in a slip, her blond hair wildly tumbled. "Wonderful. How did you do it?"

"I said you were a French whore."

"Again? I'll begin to believe it. Who was that woman with him, the dirty swine?"

"I have no idea," said Don Kishote, on general principles.

"Poor Ruthie. What a scoundrel he is! Well," said Yael through her teeth, "I can't accuse him, obviously, but he'll pay for this. I have my ways."

"I've got to shower," said Yossi, "and are my clothes okay for the Comédie Française?"

"Doesn't matter. We'll go as we are." Yossi looked down at his towel-wrapped body, and she guffawed. "As we soon will be." He was standing near the windows, and on a warm impulse of gratified desire she flung herself at him for an affectionate hug and kiss. "Ah, look out there, Don Kishote. Paris is everything the books say it is. Isn't it? It casts a spell. I've been in a dream. You've been a nice, nice part of it. I almost wish I loved you, but there's just no room. And you've got Shayna."

"On to *Tartuffe*," said Don Kishote, a shade more casually than she might have wished, so soon after their shared raptures. "Who's first in the shower?"

16

Mitla Pass

The villa where Ben Gurion was staying and meeting with the French and British ministers was a drive of a half hour or so from Paris. Pasternak and Barak arrived there next day close to noon, and found him in an old sweater and an open shirt collar, reading Procopius amid fruit trees losing their yellowed leaves. His cheery aspect, and the serene way he greeted them, suggested to Zev Barak that he had made up his mind, and that the decision was for war. If Ben Gurion were about to turn down his hosts, the French, and return to Israel out of the game, he would be wearing the stern thin-lipped worried look with which he faced unpleasant confrontations.

"It's amazing," he greeted them, brandishing the book, "what I'm reading here. This fellow, look you, wrote the official history of Byzantium under Justinian. Praised his emperor as a giant, a genius, and so on. Then later he wrote a 'Secret History,' which is included in this book. In it he attacks Justinian the way our newspapers attack me. Nothing is permanent in history, but nothing changes very much, either — Ah, here's Moshe now."

Dayan appeared eating an apple, followed by aides. Ben Gurion pulled from his shirt pocket and unfolded a yellow paper covered on both sides with his writing. "Moshe, I've been thinking overnight about your compromise. Tell me again in simple words what the new plan is and why the British should accept it. And if *they* do, why *I* should. Isn't that *tartai d'satrai* [a contradiction]?"

"Sam, did you prepare an operational map?" inquired Dayan. In his hasty review of the change of KADESH plan with Ben Gurion the night before, the Chief of Staff had merely sketched the new strategy on the inside of a cigarette package.

"Small scale," said Pasternak, handing him a page pulled out of a history book he had found in the embassy.

Dayan rapidly scanned the little map, all scarred up in pencil with arrows and troop symbols, and passed it to Ben Gurion. "Good enough. The change is mainly in the timing, Prime Minister, as you see." Dayan briskly gestured at the map. "The enemy's main Sinai forces are in the north, so I was originally going to attack there first. Instead we'll start on the central axis with a parachute drop in battalion force at the Mitla Pass, where Sam has put a star. That's more than a hundred miles behind the Egyptian border, less than forty miles from the Canal. So it can surely be called the act of war the British want, but *we* can call it a major reprisal raid, and if the situation doesn't develop favorably — for instance, if the British renege after all — we can easily pull the boys out. Certainly it's a big tactical surprise. So far from our airfields, so close to theirs."

"And supposing," replied Ben Gurion, squinting shrewdly at Dayan, "Nasser also calls it an act of war, and sends his fifty Ilyushin bombers to set fire to Tel Aviv and Haifa? Hah? What then?"

"Sir, the French have promised to put three fighter squadrons on our airfields. If they don't deliver by S-hour, we can stand down. But they want us to march, sir, and they'll deliver."

Consulting his yellow sheet, the Prime Minister shot questions at Dayan. Obviously he had grasped the plan, and had asked for the "simple" explanation to hear how Dayan would sum it up again for the British. Dayan fielded the Prime Minister's searching questions with crisp facts and figures. He would not tell the British, he said, exactly where Israel would attack, except that it would be a drop so deep behind the Egyptian lines that it would menace the Canal in sufficient force to be taken as an act of war. For this they would have to accept Ben Gurion's word.

"Well, they had better take my word, if they want me to help them throw out Nasser. It's a good plan, Moshe. It'll save lives. Now let's see how the British respond. Zev, come with me" — he put away his question sheet and pushed himself out of the garden chair — "while I dress up for the meeting."

His bedroom had furnishings almost of museum quality, for the villa belonged to an old family of great wealth and reliable discretion. The old bald paunchy Jew, with his desert-browned face and white tufts of side hair, made an odd figure in this setting, pottering around in his underwear as he laid out a dark suit, a white shirt, and a red tie, talking the while. "Now pay attention, Zev. A memorandum of agreement will have to be written today. Whenever and wherever that's done, you must be there, monitoring the wording. The typing will be a job for aides," he said, hauling on capacious trousers, "but it's very important. One wrong word can be very dangerous. Assuming we come to an understanding, everything after that will go quickly. The Englishmen will be on fire to leave. It will be very hard to change the language once it's on paper. See to it that our side doesn't have to change a word! Understand? That's your job."

"I understand, Prime Minister."

After hours of tough talk the British did take Ben Gurion's word, and they accepted Dayan's "act of war." Ben Gurion in return accepted their grudging concession to move up their ultimatum, and their attack on Nasser's airfields, by a few hours. In the small bedroom where the memorandum was being typed up, Barak paced and listened as the British, French, and Israeli aides dictated in English line by line, from notes taken at the meeting, to a British aide at a portable typewriter. Several times Barak called aside the Israeli aide to correct vital cloudy wording before it was written down, and each time his change went through.

At last the three French ministers, the two British diplomats, Ben Gurion, and Dayan sat down around a conference table for a reading of the text by the aide. Ben Gurion held up the process, often pausing to reflect, and repeating some sentences aloud, while the others exhibited marked impatience to be done and be gone.

When the reading ended, the conferees looked at each other and nodded. Ben Gurion lifted the paper from the aide's hand, signed it, and passed it to the French Defense Minister, who pursed his lips, raised his eyebrows, and signed it, too. Ben Gurion slid the paper across the table to the senior Englishman, a diplomat of lower rank than Selwyn Lloyd. Lloyd had not returned.

"There is nothing official about all this," said the diplomat, making a very wry face. "Why signatures?"

His Russian accent thicker than usual, Ben Gurion said with a cold smile, "Surely ve need a record of vot ve agreed to. Odderwise vot heff ve accomplished here?"

"Well, as a matter of record only," said the Englishman, and he signed. Ben Gurion folded the paper and put it in his breast pocket. Within minutes, everyone had left the villa but the Israelis.

Ben Gurion looked around at the others, his mobile face as grave, Zev Barak thought, as it had been when he had read the Declaration of the State eight years ago. "So, gentlemen, ve go to var," he said.

*   *   *

Now the country that wasn't there broke out of its nonexistence, and the children of Israel went marching once more into the Sinai desert as in olden days, only this time going the other way.

Colonel Nasser's land did not much resemble Pharaoh's Egypt, except in geographical location and ancient magnificent monuments; not in language, not in religion, not in customs, not in culture, and not in its Arab populace. But after three millennia the Jews were exactly the same quarrelsome Israelites of the Exodus, with the same God, the same language, and the same national character, including the same ineradicable tendency to veer forever between the sublime and the balagan. Of such was the Battle of Mitla Pass; half sublime, half balagan, a heroic fiasco, an inside-out Thermopylae fought to no purpose whatever.

The paratrooper battalion was duly dropped at the Mitla Pass as the detonator for an international bombshell, the French and

British landings in Suez. That was its sole mission. It had no other. But the brigade commander, Ariel Sharon, was not told of this secret larger strategy. He therefore thought his force was leapfrogging a hundred miles behind the enemy lines to fight, an understandable misapprehension.

*   *   *

Five days after David Ben Gurion folded the agreement into his pocket, sixteen transport planes, twenty-five paratroopers to an aircraft, soared forth toward the sinking sun over Sinai. This was the battalion scheduled to jump into Mitla Pass and sit there until Ben Gurion could weigh the Egyptian response and the British good faith. Of the French he had no doubt. Their three fighter squadrons, as promised, were poised on his airfields.

Skimming the flat sands to avoid radar detection, the sixteen Dakotas gave paratroopers like Don Kishote who glanced down through the narrow windows a sense of rocketing toward battle, but in fact these machines were old lumbering workhorse DC-3s, making about two hundred miles an hour. They had less than two hundred miles to go, and thirty minutes after takeoff they were already climbing to jump altitude.

That was a long half hour for Don Kishote, a buzzing tense whiz into the unknown. No well-defined line of retreat as in the night raids, kept open by blocking units and covering fire, not this time; the battalion would be dropping far out in mountainous desert into a hornet's nest of enemy armor, so far as they knew utterly dependent on parachuted supplies of food, fuel, water, and weapons until the main body of Arik Sharon's brigade could fight its way to them, past enemy strongholds and through rugged desert terrain. Cumbersomely weighted with his gear, which he had checked and checked to boredom, uncomfortable and nervy, Yossi passed the worrisome grinding minutes thinking over his touchy meeting yesterday with Shayna, and trying to sort out his feelings after the bizarre doings in Gay Paree.

*

Shayna had come on the telephone with a tremendous sneeze, and then a surprisingly cheery, "Well, so you're back! How was Paris, and where are you?"

"Paris was okay. I'm calling from the Falafel King outside my base. You have a cold?"

"The worst! But I'm getting over it. I caught it the night of that party, in all that rain. Just as well I didn't go with you, I'd have stayed in bed with fever there, same as here. Come and tell me all about Paris." It seemed to Yossi from her tone that she was taking in stride their quarrel and his going off with Yael, and was her affectionate self.

"I can't." He was talking on a public phone outside the gate of the air force base, where aviators and paratroopers sat with wives or sweethearts, murmuring tentative goodbyes over falafels and beer, for the impending action was in the air. He dropped his voice. "High alert."

"I'll come there, then."

"Not if you're sick."

"Foolishness. What's a good time?"

"I've given my company an *after* [time off] at seven."

"I'll be there."

Still her reticent self, she hung up without endearments. Shayna had her obscure depths! He did want to see her, to be with her before he went off to battle. He also dreaded it. That crazy business in Paris with Yael had been nothing like his casual fooleries in the flat on Karl Netter Street. How could he talk to Shayna about Paris and leave that out? That was what had happened in Paris.

When he came in at seven to the Falafel King stand, there she was huddled in a coat. "What's the matter?" were her first words, followed by a sneeze.

"God bless! Nothing." He fell in the chair beside her. A grim briefing in the chilly bleak base assembly hall, with tall maps of Sinai and heavily arrowed transparent overlays, had just given the Mitla force its picture of the mission. Hairy! It was a relief to push aside war thoughts for love thoughts. He did love this girl; one look at her and he knew it. Paris didn't matter. Even the reddened nose was endearing because he felt sorry for her. When she smiled her cheeks curved in a way peculiar to her, a beautiful shape, and her eyes shone for him, as Yael's had never done in Paris. But as Yael had said, she wasn't in love with him.

"Everybody is saying it's war. They're starting to hoard again in Jerusalem," Shayna said. "Mama's as bad as anybody, our cupboards are all piled up. The stores are emptying. But I'm not asking questions." Her sharp look searched his face.

"Good. Don't."

"So?" She clasped his hand in hers. "Tell me about Paris. Was it fun?"

A perfectly innocent question; or was it? Her face showed the usual transparent joy at being with him. And yet, wasn't she being a little too free and easy? She squeezed his hand and went on. "All right, that was a terrible fight we had. I'll talk first. I'm sorry, Yossi. Didn't you tell me about paratroopers who freeze and won't jump? That was it. Paris was a jump, and I froze. I could have fought it out with my father, I guess. But I didn't, and it's past and gone. As it happens I got sick, so it was for the best. I'd have just been a nuisance. And my parents were so relieved that I didn't go!"

"Paris is overrated," said Yossi.

"Come on, now. In what way?"

"Well, maybe I was out of the mood. I missed you." *There* was a needed little touch of truth.

Her cheeks curved enchantingly. "Oh, did you? How nice. Start at the beginning. Tell me everything you and Yael did."

(To all the devils!)

"Well, the first night Lee treated us to the Folies-Bergère."

"Oo-ah. Folies-Bergère. Do the actresses really dance around with nothing on?"

"Yes, or else with the most gorgeous costumes you ever saw. I liked them better dressed."

With a side-glance of old-lady wisdom she said, "No doubt. And then?"

He made her laugh with his description of the headwaiter at Le Tour d'Argent, and then of the fleabag hotel. She was envious of the Eiffel Tower climb — "That sounds like the most fun" — and listened with wide eager eyes to his account of the four-star sights and the performance of *Tartuffe*. "That was about it," he said. "When we got back to that miserable hotel, there were the cables ordering us home on the first plane."

"What about the Georges Cinq Hotel?" she said.

"What about it?" He was very startled. "Do you want a falafel?"

"That swanky suite your brother had. What happened there?"

"I think I'll have a falafel."

"Well, I will too, then."

He glanced at her covertly as he waited for the counterman to throw together the falafels. She sat there with a composed countenance, showing no trace of jealousy, anger, or suspicion. What did she know? Could she have talked to Yael? But Yael had come with him straight to the Ramle base, where Sam Pasternak had set up Moshe Dayan's general headquarters, and she had been working day and night ever since. He had met her once in a corridor, looking pale and dishevelled, and she had barely said a friendly hello in passing. Anyway, Yael would never breathe a word. Or would she? Yael was a hard lady with sharp claws. What was behind the sweet face of this nineteen-year-old sphinx?

"Didn't you go to his hotel?" she asked as he brought the falafels. "Your brother told me about the suite at the party. He said he would let you use it. It sounded fantastic."

"Oh, Lee likes to show off. Yes, we went up there for a drink. It had a nice view, but to me it looked like a movie set. Phony."

"I'll bet Yael enjoyed it." He looked dumbly at her. "She's got a taste for luxury, I'm sure."

"Well, by that time we were both pretty tired. She took a nap."

"There? In the suite? How peculiar. Why not in your hotel?"

"She claimed it had bedbugs."

"Bedbugs! Ugh!"

"Just a short nap, then we went on to the Comédie Française."

"What did you do while she napped?"

"Lee had some dirty French magazines there. I read them."

"You would." She looked at him in silence, by now with more than a trace of skepticism.

"Another falafel, Shayna?"

"I can't finish this one."

To Yossi it seemed plain that she had caught on or already knew somehow. Why had he been so clumsy in his lying? Why Yael's nap, l'Azazel? Why the dirty magazines?

"I'll tell you, Yossi, I'm getting suspicious."

"What? How so?"

"I think you had a marvellous time, and you just don't want me to feel bad. But don't be a fool, we'll go to Paris together one day. How much time have you got? Can you walk me to the bus station? It's due in fifteen minutes."

"Let's go."

He wanted to kiss her in the darkness. "Don't. You'll catch my cold."

"Never mind."

"No, I mean it. Don't."

He knew when she meant it. With Shayna's blue jeans went a certain limited willingness for endearments, but clearly not tonight. They walked in silence for a while, then she said, "Listen, Yossi, my cousin Faiga's getting married soon. Any chance that you could come with me to the wedding?"

With the maps of the Mitla drop fresh in his mind, Yossi said, "If I can, I will."

"It scares me how my friends are getting married right and left." Shayna laughed merrily in the gloom. "I'll be the old maid of the bunch in a year. Not that I care. Do you know, while you were in Paris I got a proposal? Think what I'd have missed by going!"

This stung Kishote. "Who now?"

"What do you mean, who now? Do I get that many? Bertram Packer, his name is. He came around to see me when I was laid up. Actually he asked me two years ago, and now bang, he went and asked me again."

"And is this one of those yeshiva friends of yours, exempt from the army?"

"Oh, no, Bert's very religious, but he's B'nai Akiva. Did his three years and he's a reserve artilleryman. Don't worry, I didn't accept." She took Yossi's hand. "So don't snarl like that. You went off to Paris with that beautiful Yael Luria, and do you hear me snarling?"

"Final check!" Harsh call of the jump master over the twin-engine roar. Rattle of buckles, creak of bucket seats, clank of Uzis, tense joking among the younger paratroopers, set businesslike faces of the veteran jumpers as they tested their straps, back chute, safety chute, overhead cords, leg-sack fastenings. No more puzzling over Shayna, at least for a while!

"Dvukah Aleph!" ("First hookup!")

Yossi and the five men linked with him stood up and sidled forward, overhead cords hooked to the cable, left leg forward, right leg back. Side door sliding open, wild rush and howl of icy air, red sunset light striking through the gloomy Dakota, crimsoning young faces. No joking now.

"Kfotze!" ("Jump!")

Yossi had placed himself third in the hookup, to see the jump get off to a normal start. First jumper, a good boy. Out, gone! Second jumper, hint of a freeze, hanging there too long.

"Kfotze!" An ungentle shove in the small of the back by the NCO. Gone!

Yossi's turn. Into the opening, the wind, the roar! Red sun half-sunk behind black mountains. Different from the Negev, really high mountains. Maybe Mount Sinai out there, who could be sure? Moses, Ten Commandments . . .

"Kfotze!"

With a laugh Don Kishote threw himself out, turning over and over in rushing cold air. Brief straight fall, expected queer feeling in the balls — jolt of the straps! Slow swing, slow swing, parachute flapping and swelling beautifully overhead. Peaceful silence, bare whiffle of parachute. Parachutes floating here and there in the dark blue sky. Release the leg sack, release the chest chute, let them dangle well clear . . .

There it was far below and to the west, the lone pillar of the Parker Memorial just visible in the dusk, the marker of the entrance to the Mitla Pass. He and the other troops dotting the sky were all falling short, two or three miles to the east. So much Yossi observed, then the gray-brown sand strewn with rock rubble was coming up at him. Not much ground wind. Good. He hit hard and well, feet clamped together, easy tumble over, best jump yet! Now for the Egyptians! All around him paratroopers were landing, some clumsily, some deftly, one nearby groaning with pain and writhing, his leg twisted awry on the sand, youngster from another company. Yossi freed himself from his chute and gear and ran to help him.

The evening star was a gem in the sunset, the air was growing cooler and the breeze fresher, and in the purple twilight the memorial was a dark small hump due west, where the horizon was still streaked orange. The battalion commander, Raful Eitan, a small leathery moshavnik who could smile charmingly or be coldly cruel, rounded up and mustered his troops; a good drop, only a dozen light injuries among four hundred jumpers. Raful marched the three companies westward on a vague road like a camel track across the chilly silent desert. Not a living creature or growing thing in sight. Of Egyptians, no sign. Four hundred marching men, looking like a lost patrol in the empty expanse of sand and rock under a vast dark bowl of sky.

At the memorial, by the last fading light and brightening starlight, they quickly laid out their defense perimeter, digging themselves in, setting up blocking positions and ambushes along the camel track, and activating the air guidance beams. As the soldiers were eating field rations, welcome black shapes came droning in under the stars, and down floated clusters of parachutes bringing jeeps, mortars, ammunition, guns, food, water, and medicine to paratrooper cheers. The aircraft sounds died off in the night, and the battalion was marooned in the wilderness, a small lightly armed parachute force, meat for any armored attack.

"Ben Gurion has a high fever."

Clean-shaven and bright of eye, Moshe Dayan strode next morning in the small hours into Pasternak's inner office in the command headquarters, housed in a decrepit hut on the old British air base outside Ramle. There were newly dug command bunkers on the base too, but Sam Pasternak did not intend to use those holes. So far the Egyptian air force had not stirred, and if it did, he said, he would stay where he was and count on Egyptian marksmanship for his safety.

"The Old Man's been under a great strain," said Pasternak.

"All the same he's plenty alert, and he wants to know what's happening."

Pasternak wearily gestured at the transparency over the big wall map of Sinai. A large red circle designated the paratroops far out at Mitla, and two stubby black arrows at the Egyptian border, north and center, showed infantry incursions that could be pulled back fast. Dayan asked, rapping his knuckle at the Mitla marking, "Has Arik Sharon moved yet to join them?"

"He signalled half an hour ago, *'I'm going.'* He hadn't received half the six-wheelers we promised him, so he commandeered every civilian bus and automobile he could lay hands on."

"That's Arik. Now you track down those six-wheelers, Sam, and order them to rendezvous with him!"

"I've done that. Meantime he's rolling." Pasternak pressed a buzzer on his intercom. "Yael, bring me that despatch from Raful. . . . First word from Mitla, Moshe, and it's disturbing. His signal equipment was knocked out by the drop, and just came on again —"

Despatch board in hand, hair flying, Yael hurried in. Dayan glanced at the top sheet and initialled it. "So, a couple of Egyptian patrol jeeps came upon Raful in the dark, and got away. So what? They won't know what to make of it. Neither will Cairo. Not until there's air reconnaissance — Yael, you need sleep."

She was slumped against the map, red-eyed and yawning. "Sam needs sleep. Coffee, Dode Moshe?"

Dayan shook his head.

"I'll have more," said Pasternak, and she went out.

"After I talk to B.G., I'm flying south," Dayan said.

"Where in the south?"

"Where they're fighting."

"Moshe, you're needed here."

"I need to see the soldiers, and it's good for them to see me. The campaign is all laid out. Stay in touch, let me know of anything

I have to act on." Dayan was peering at a time chart on the wall, displaying the projected day-by-day actions of the next two weeks in four vertical columns — Israel, France, Britain, and the United Nations. "You're very optimistic about the UN, aren't you? No decisive vote for ten days? Cut it in half."

"Why, Moshe? Everything depends on the Americans. The Russians will scream and threaten, but do you suppose Eisenhower will throw over his allies? He'll cry, 'Shame, shame,' yes. Hard action, no."

Dayan vigorously shook his head. "That fellow Dulles will throw over England and France, all right. We're in a race against that old nag, if in fact *this* happens today." His stiff finger pointed at two entries in the French and British columns: *Ultimatum.* "Otherwise we're doing KADESH alone. Which is okay, too. Let's have a look in the war room."

At the center of the wide room lined with operational charts, female soldiers at a broad table map were pushing here and there markers symbolizing Egyptian and Israeli brigades or battalions, and moving pins that showed front lines. Young officers at desks or at the charts, many wearing earphones on long wires, were tracking events in a busy hum of talk punctuated by telephone rings and much barking into receivers. Pasternak and Dayan walked around the room, querying the officers and encountering from one after another, responses such as, *"There's no reply"* . . . *"We can't get through"* . . . *"The signal was garbled"* . . . *"I'm only guessing. . . ."*

When Yael handed Pasternak coffee, he put the cup to his mouth without thanking or looking at her. "The fact is, Moshe," Pasternak growled, "communications are terrible. Bad equipment, insufficient training."

"All the more reason for me to go to the front." Dayan swept an arm at the animated staff room. "As for the picture that's forming, so far so good. I want a plane standing by at 0430 hours."

"It will be there."

Dayan left. Yael approached Pasternak with a meat sandwich on a paper plate. He said shortly, "I'm not hungry."

"You don't know whether you're hungry or not." She spoke in low familiar tones. "You don't know what you're doing. It's a wonder you're standing up. You haven't slept in forty hours, do you realize that?"

"You're keeping score?"

"I've made up the cot in the underground room."

"It smells like a grave. I'm not going down in that hole."

"Yes, you are. Moshe said to me, 'Take care of Sam, he's doing a wonderful job, he's irreplaceable.' That's what he said, word for word."

"All right." Pasternak took the sandwich. "I'll eat."

"You'll sleep," said Yael in a bossy half-whisper, "right now. I'll wake you in an hour — or sooner if anything important comes through."

"Well, then check on those six-wheelers that were supposed to join Sharon, you hear? And tell Uri to warn the officer in charge that if they don't rendezvous with Sharon, he can start preparing for his court-martial."

In the bunker, instead of getting under the coarse blanket on the cot, Pasternak lay down with an army coat over him, and pulled a string to turn off the naked light bulb overhead. Yael came down the steps with a flashlight, and ignoring his grumbles took off his boots. "It does smell like a grave," she said. "Nice and peaceful. The Rehovot six-wheelers will meet Arik, in fact they'll get to the rendezvous first."

"What did you buy at the Galeries Lafayette?" he muttered, half-asleep.

"Huh?" Half-asleep herself, Yael took a moment to grasp the question. "Oh? You mean in Paris?" It all seemed to have happened months ago.

"Where then? In the Mitla Pass?"

"Well, if you really want to know, some oo-la-la French underwear."

"Ah! So? That's something to look forward to." He tried to fondle her as she wrapped the coat more closely around him, and she struck his hand away.

"Oh, you think so? You can just go on looking forward."

"You're keeping up that nonsense?"

Yael had not been sleeping with Pasternak for a couple of

months, as her dissatisfaction with her status had become acute. Such a freeze had happened before, it had melted in a return of passion, and now it was on again.

"No, I've put a stop to all nonsense, once for all. Never mind that stuff, Sam, rest."

She found her brother Benny in Sam's office, wearing a fleece-lined cap, rakishly tilted, World War II movie style. Unlike most officers in the command hut he looked rested and cheerful. "Here's the report Dode Moshe wanted, on my mission," he said.

"Moshe's come and gone. The story we heard about you is pretty wild, Benny."

"Well, you read it and see."

She slid out from the envelope a flimsy sheet of air force stationery, filled with single-spaced typing.

October 29, 1956

Interim Action Report — Urgent

Subject: Failure of Equipment.

1. My group was assigned the mission of interfering with enemy communications, to prevent reports of the parachute drop at Mitla by cutting overhead telephone wires in Sinai. Four Mustangs were specially equipped for this task with weighted hooked cables to wrench wires from poles.

2. The mission was flown on schedule. However the hooked cables were torn from the planes by the wires, or were lost en route to the objective. Equipment proved too flimsy for the purpose.

3. Therefore it was decided to attempt severing the wires by means of our wings and propellers. This was done, and the mission was accomplished. All assigned lines were cut.

4. However this method is hazardous, since aircraft must fly within 4 meters of the ground and possibility exists of wires wrapping around propellers or damaging wings. It is suggested that stronger cable hooks or some more effective cutting device be used.

Benny Luria, Major
Commanding

Yael stared at her brother, who was finishing Pasternak's half-eaten meat sandwich. "You actually flew this mission?"

"Me and three other guys. Why?"

"Whose raving mad idea was that propeller business? And how could you take such a risk?"

"Well, the fact is, Yael, last month a student pilot on the base flew into some telephone wires by mistake and cut them. He and his plane survived. So we knew it was possible. And it wasn't so bad. Just a heavy bump and a shaking up. I missed my wires twice before I cut them."

"Were the planes damaged?"

"Some dents and scrapes. My plane's propeller was nicked. Mustangs are tough workhorses."

They were both doing movie acting; the pilot feigning nonchalance, Yael pretending to be indignant. In fact she was bursting with admiration for her brother, and Benny with admiration of himself. Flying into those wires had been a nasty sweat.

Pasternak came in with Zev Barak, who had just arrived all tuckered out and badly needing a shave. "Yael, I couldn't sleep. Hello, Benny — You know about this guy's wire-cutting lunacy?" he remarked to Barak.

"I heard something."

"Sam, why aren't we attacking the Egyptian airfields, do you know?" Benny brashly inquired. "By dawn they'll all scramble for sure. They outnumber us four to one. We're missing the best chance we'll have."

"Don't ask questions that aren't your business."

"Whose business is it to fight the Egyptian air force? Anyway, there's my report."

Yael said, "Two kids and another on the way, and he does a crazy thing like that."

"Crazy family," said Pasternak. The brother and sister went out together, smiling.

When they were out of the room Barak said, "You could have told Benny in general what's doing."

"Told him what?" Pasternak snapped. "That an air strike is an outright act of war, and until the British move we have to pretend all this is just a raid? You tell him *in general* without violating security, if you can! You have my permission."

Barak was studying the transparency over the wall chart, with markings of the projected advances into Sinai. He moved his finger along the southern axis, which began at Eilat, the southernmost point in Israel, and ran two hundred miles down the eastern Sinai coast to Sharm el Sheikh, the lower tip of the peninsula. "Sharon's got a tough job, but my brigade's may be harder. We have poorer vehicles, our troops are older reservists, and it's no terrain for six-wheelers. We can't carry enough supplies to take us all the way to Sharm el Sheikh. That's clear."

"Those are your problems and Yoffe's," said Pasternak. Barak was Colonel Avraham Yoffe's deputy commander. "Our whole objective in this war is to reopen the Straits of Tiran, no matter what the French and British do, so don't talk nonsense, just find a way to solve your supply situation."

"Well, I asked the navy about resupplying us at Dahab. That's about halfway to Sharm. Unfortunately, the landing craft that could carry the supplies from Eilat are in Haifa."

"In Haifa? Why in Haifa? Why aren't they in Eilat, when we've had terrorist action and war plans in the south for months?"

"That remains a question. Balagan. Ask the navy."

"Bring the craft to Eilat overland."

"I've just been looking into that."

"Well?"

"Actually it's feasible. They could go by rail from Haifa to Beersheba. There they could be loaded on flatcar trucks and taken to Eilat."

"Then there's your answer."

"No. I took the trouble to check the route. It's obvious that the craft can't get past some structures along the way — stations, sheds, warehouses, the usual."

"Demolish them."

Barak's worried face relaxed in a grin. "Really? And who gives permission for such destruction? And who pays?"

"That will be attended to. You do it."

Yael returned, her face somber, and handed a despatch to Pasternak. "New word from Mitla."

"Hm!" Pasternak initialled it and showed Barak the message. ARMORED ATTACK ON THIS FORCE AT DAWN ANTICIPATED. URGENTLY REQUEST AIR COVER.

"Rouse the French liaison officer," Pasternak ordered Yael. "It's getting warm for your friend Don Kishote."

"Him? He'll brush off the shells like dandruff," said Yael, going out to the war room, which was now in tumult.

Barak and Pasternak looked at each other. "Long way from that fancy French villa," said Pasternak.

"Long way to Sharm el Sheikh," said Barak.

17

Musketeers and Omelettes

Don Kishote lay on his back in a foxhole, looking up at the brilliant desert stars and thinking a tired soldier's thoughts — flickers of awe at the black endless universe, flickers of longing for Shayna, for her slim body in his arms, flickers of concern about that puzzling last meeting with her, flickers of recollection of the crazy time with Yael in Paris, which made him laugh out loud in the dark. French whore, indeed! That Yael was something, though he wanted no more of her than he had had. A she-leopard! *"Something to do once . . ."* Exactly so, Yael!

The Egyptian armored column heading for Mitla Pass had been knocked out by the air force; so far, so good. But after a day of hard labor piling gun emplacements of rock and sand, and of enemy air attacks that had done no damage but broken up the work, he was worn out. The rumored news from elsewhere was all cheering; victories up north, and Sharon's relief brigade well on the way, capturing or bypassing fortified outposts and due sometime tomorrow. Snugged down for an hour of sleep before going back on watch, well sheltered from a brisk cold wind by high sand heaps ringing the hole, he was drowsing off when prickling nerves roused him. What was that? Faint rumble; on the ground, or in the air? Night attack? He grabbed his gun and jumped out of his hole. All around him shadowy paratroopers were emerging from the earth with their weapons. Then somebody shouted, "Arik!" The cry went up here and there, and he discerned a crawl of black beetles in the starlight, a column miles long under a drifting dust cloud, far off to the northeast.

"Arik! Arik!"

He too joined the yells that greeted the riders on the trucks, busses, tanks, and half-tracks, as they came clanking and roaring in, many with hissing radiators and thumping flat tires. Jubilant paratroopers capered alongside them, shouting hurrahs. Soldiers jumped down from the vehicles, bewhiskered, greasy, and sandy, embracing and kissing others just as dirty and unkempt. Amid the reunions none was more joyous than that of Don Kishote and a big pudgy redheaded soldier. They pounded each other's backs, and tasted grease and dust in breathless kisses on bristly cheeks.

Kishote loved Aharon Stein, this fat not-too-bright kibbutznik, called Jinji for his red hair. Jinji had nearly failed the paratroop course and the platoon leader's course, and he loved Kishote for helping him pull through both. In background they were unlikely buddies; Kishote a Polish Cyprus immigrant, Jinji a son and grandson of Deganya Aleph pioneers. A total sabra speaking only thick native Hebrew, ignorant alike of the outside world and of the Jewish religion, Jinji knew only simple Zionist socialism as an outlook, and competition with Deganya Aleph peers as a way of life. He had twisted an ankle in a harness jump, and then cracked two ribs on a rock in his first airplane drop. The course commander had advised him to try artillery or armor instead. But he was from Deganya Aleph, he was going to be a paratrooper or die, and he was a paratrooper, though still a platoon leader, while Yossi had advanced to company command.

"What a march! You'll go down in history," Yossi exclaimed. "From the Jordan to Mitla in a night and a day!"

"Biggest balagan you ever saw," said Jinji hoarsely. "We won a couple of good fights, that part was all right, but planning, supply, maintenance, spare parts — nothing! I'm dying for water. Can you spare a drop?" Kishote pressed his canteen on him. "Punctures, breakdowns, engines conking out, I can't begin to tell you. We were mobilized at such short notice, we got going so fast, that nothing was organized. I changed vehicles four times on the way, and —"

"But you're here."

"I'm here, and you're right, we'll go down in history! You were under air attack, hey?"

"No problem. Our air cover showed up. When they saw our planes they skedaddled."

Jinji dug an elbow into Kishote's side. "Look there." On the hood of a jeep nearby, Raful Eitan and Arik Sharon had spread a map and were bent over it, conferring by flashlight. Sharon held the wind-whipped map down with a long knife from his hip sheath. A burly blond sabra with a gory repute earned in planning and leading ruthless reprisal actions, Sharon looked as begrimed as any of his men. "What next, do you suppose?" Jinji asked.

"If I know these two guys," said Kishote — and as a company commander he had had much contact with both — "we go for Suez at dawn. Right through there." He jerked a thumb toward the defile leading into Mitla, humped black against the stars. "Arik Sharon is going to beat everyone to the Canal or kill us all on the way."

"Has the pass been reconnoitered, Yossi?"

"By air, yes. No Egyptians there."

At the map, Sharon was tracing a course with the knife. "It'll be slow going through these two defiles, Raful, but in this saucer" — the knife swept around the broad central stretch of the pass — "and that's most of the way, there's plenty of room to maneuver." His voice was down to a croak, his eyes were swollen almost shut in a mask of grease and sand, but his teeth showed in an uncivilized grin, and his cloth hat was set at a jaunty angle. "Once we debouch from the other end, we're more than halfway there."

"At your orders," said Eitan, who knew but didn't fathom — any more than Sharon did — the command from general headquarters forbidding any move westward into the pass.

*

For the shell-game world politics of the Anglo-French alliance had still not been disclosed to any of the field commanders. An armored brigade in the north had jumped the gun and crossed the border in a night attack, whereupon Dayan had arrived by plane, blazing mad, and had dressed down the commanders of the brigade and the northern front; deeply puzzling them both, since Dayan himself had created at Lod and Ramle a legend for ambitious officers to emulate, the tradition of disregarding orders and dashing into combat. To Arik Sharon the Mitla Pass was plainly his chance to eclipse Lod and Ramle by getting to the Canal first, and Kishote's surmise was correct; nothing was going to stop him.

In the morning Sharon asked General Staff headquarters, via a communication aircraft, for permission to advance through the pass. *Denied*. He next asked approval to send "a patrol" to reconnoiter just the nearby eastern defile, with a view to occupying higher ground at the entrance. This permission was brought by a staff officer from HQ, who briefly landed in a Piper Cub with very specific and limiting orders. When the plane flew off Sharon organized and sent out "a patrol" in battalion strength, capable of capturing the entire seventeen-mile pass against any anticipated opposition. These troops set out on a beautiful desert noonday in a long column of half-tracks, trucks, tanks, and heavy mortars, heading for the shallow barren hills of the defile, while Raful's paratroopers stayed dug in where they were.

Perched outside his foxhole, submachine gun in hand, Don Kishote watched the column grinding by, and shouted "I envy you!" to Jinji, who went past waving from a truck and grinning. Many a time Kishote had set out in such a column, rolling to the jump-off point of a reprisal raid. But this was war, and the objective was nothing less than the Suez Canal! The barren rocky scenery around him, rising sunward in ragged eroded cliffs and mountains, stirred his blood; this was the Sinai of the manna, the golden calf, and the thundering Voice, just as he had pictured it as a child. Of the larger strategic concept, of course, he knew absolutely nothing, any more than Sharon or Raful did. Nor did Kishote have any inkling that this advance in force into the pass was a violation of express orders; and he could not know, any more than Raful or Sharon did, that during the night a sizable Egyptian detachment had occupied the Mitla Pass, armed with high-powered weapons, and had ensconced itself in the caves and rock pits on the sides of the cliffs.

His broad shoulders wallowing, Sam Pasternak was pacing like a zoo bear. He growled at Barak, just returned from reconnoitering the entire length of the railroad to Beersheba, "Well, good, at least *you're* here. What about those landing craft? Did you start the railroad demolitions?"

"How could I? I never got your authorization document."

"I'll strangle Yael."

"Where is she?"

"Collecting that Colonel Simon, Ben Gurion's liaison with the French government. We're going to B.G.'s house — he's still in bed with fever — as soon as Dayan gets here. That plane is long overdue." Pasternak glanced at a wall clock, his forehead wrinkled with worry. "The Old Man has received a letter from Eisenhower that he doesn't like."

The telephone rang. "Yes? Right away." He hung up and said to Barak, pointing a thumb at the war room, "Okay. Dayan's arrived this minute, and he's out there raising hell over Mitla."

"Mitla? What's happened at Mitla?"

"You haven't heard about Sharon? You will. Come."

Zev Barak was appalled at the way Dayan's eye was popping with rage under the webbed helmet, the white showing in a wide rim all around the pupil. The Chief of Staff's uniform was covered with dust, his face was dirty and perspiring. Angry questions pelted Pasternak: How had this happened? Who had given Sharon permission to advance into the Mitla Pass? Where were the despatches? What was going on right now? And what was all this insanity about Ben Gurion wanting to call off the KADESH operation?

It was Pasternak's turn to be mild. Arik had been authorized only to send a patrol into the defile. How a whole battalion was trapped there under heavy fire, he was still trying to find out. As for Ben Gurion, the British ultimatum had expired hours ago, and they had not bombed the Egyptian airfields as agreed, so the Old Man feared they were backing out of the war. The Americans and the Russians were calling a session of the UN General Assembly, and he intended to announce before the assembly meeting began — probably by cabling Eisenhower — that Israel's reprisal raids had accomplished their purpose and the troops were being withdrawn. He was calling in the French colonel to warn him of this intention.

"Where are those Mitla communications?" roared Dayan. A young officer with a scared face rushed up to hand him a despatch board. As he was flipping through the flimsy sheets, another officer brought Pasternak a telephone on a long cord. The conversation at his end was a grunt or two. Hanging up, he said, "Well, Yael's got hold of that French colonel, Moshe, so you're due at B.G.'s house."

"Good!" Dayan dropped the despatches on the table. "Courts-martial will be busy when this is over. The lapses of discipline are intolerable. Arik's got himself into a mess, and whatever happens, he's to bring out every single killed or wounded soldier! Let him know that, Sam, from me!"

"Yes, Moshe."

"Zev, meet me outside in five minutes. We'll go to the Prime Minister in your car."

When Dayan was gone Barak asked Pasternak, "What caused the delay with Colonel Simon?"

"He was having his lunch. For a Frenchman that can mean three hours. I knew Yael would fetch him, she says he can't take his eyes off her shirt front. She told me he makes her chest feel funny."

"Well, it's covered, that's what," said Barak. "He's used to the Folies-Bergère."

In Barak's commandeered car, an old Mercedes with an irregular cough that made it jolt forward, Dayan asked Barak, "If your brigade leaves Eilat tonight, can it get to Sharm in three days?"

"Avraham Yoffe's commanding us, sir. He's the one to ask."

"I'm asking his deputy, so let's hear."

Barak drummed his fingers on the wheel, taking his time to answer. "We're still mobilizing. We're a reserve brigade, guys leaving their homes and their jobs. Transport vehicles are still below allotment. Supply problems unsolved, such as —"

"The thing is," broke in Dayan with dry professional calm, "we may have no more than three days. I believe the UN can be stalled that long, even if the Brits and French pull out — which incidentally I don't believe they're doing. But our objective for KADESH has always been Sharm, and it still is. We've already lost a lot of boys, and Sharon is losing more." Pause. Different, lighter tone. "So, three days? Yes, or no, Zev?"

"Remember, sir, I went on Operation YARKON."

"Remember? I pinned a decoration on you myself."

"So you did, sir, and I'm the wrong man to say yes to three days."

Dayan fell glumly silent, while buried memories of the YARKON ordeal rose in Barak's mind. More than a year ago he had served in a patrol that had landed by rubber boat far down in the Sinai, to reconnoiter the burning wastes on foot and map a route for a surprise motorized thrust from Eilat to Sharm, in case war should come. Code-named YARKON, the patrol had been sent out after Nasser had installed at Sharm el Sheikh heavy guns which could block the Straits of Tiran. It had been as close a brush with death or captivity as Barak ever wanted to endure. In three days and nights of summertime inferno the patrol had trudged the Sinai, until a Bedouin band had chanced on their footprints and alerted an Egyptian camel patrol, which came after them. In desperation they had signalled for rescue, and were airlifted out by two-seater planes making hairbreadth landings and takeoffs on level patches of sand. For a long time afterward Barak had been deathly sick from dehydration, coming much closer to being killed by the sun than by the enemy.

After a pause Dayan spoke up brusquely. "Time factor aside — any other major difficulties?"

"There is one, sir." Barak described the problem of transporting the landing craft.

"Is it hopeless?"

"I'm still working on it, sir."

"Well, and if the demolitions can't be done in time, Zev — will your brigade be able to fight on to Sharm, assuming it isn't replenished by sea?"

"No, it won't. It can't possibly reach Sharm. Mankilling terrain, murder on machines, seventy miles of it uphill."

"Then the supply problem has to be licked," said Dayan, "because even if the Old Man calls off the rest of KADESH, Zev, at this point we must go on to Sharm el Sheikh. Now, you can tell him more about YARKON than I can."

"Tell him what?"

"Tell him, speaking from YARKON experience, that your brigade can make it in three days, no matter what."

"You want me to lie, sir?"

With a shrug and a shrewd one-eyed glance Dayan said, "Look, it's an estimate. Any man can make a mistake. Once we go we'll keep going until we take Sharm. Then he can sort out the politics. That's his job. Even if we're forced to withdraw, we can bargain to get the straits reopened, and free passage guaranteed by the Americans — but only if we're holding Sharm, Zev."

"Fifteen minutes, no more," said Paula Ben Gurion. She stood outside the bedroom in her usual shapeless black dress, confronting Dayan and Barak. "That French fellow is in there now with little Yael. They just got here."

"How is Ben Gurion?" asked Dayan.

"A hundred-and-four fever. A terrible flu. Fifteen minutes! Whatever has to be decided, you'll have to decide in a quarter of an hour. Do you understand, Moshe?"

"A quarter of an hour, Paula."

Ben Gurion lay back on heaped pillows in a white nightshirt, which with his disorderly white flares of hair accentuated the bright pink flush of the aged face. His eyes were closed, his arms extended on the blanket. Colonel Simon stood by the window, hands clasped behind his back, a portly gray-mustached military figure in a gorgeous gold-braided French officer's cap, with banks of parti-colored medals and ribbons on his tailored uniform. He looked extremely uneasy. Yael was at his elbow.

"Moshe is here, Ben Gurion," said Paula, whereupon the Prime Minister opened glittering eyes and sat up, raising his arms stiffly to get leverage.

"What is happening at Mitla?" he inquired in a weak hoarse voice.

Dayan tersely summarized the despatches. Ben Gurion turned to the French colonel, and spoke in English. "You see? We dropped those boys so near the Canal only because your governments wanted an 'act of war.' " His tone was wearily sarcastic. "Now my boys are under heavy ground attack, and what if the Egyptian air force attacks them next? Where is the good faith of your governments? The British promised to bomb the Egyptian airfields long before this. What has happened?"

As Yael translated, Ben Gurion muttered to the Israeli officers, "Hebrew I didn't expect him to understand. But English?"

Unexpectedly the French colonel interrupted Yael in a heavy accent. "Meestair Prime Meenistair, pardonne, for matters grave my English eet eez not entirely reliable." He listened intently until Yael finished, and then responded at length, with sweeping Gallic gestures. Barak's French was good, but to him the colonel seemed to be wandering, and talking to no purpose about omelettes and musketeers. He felt he must be missing something. Dayan looked baffled, too.

Paula was listening with a furrowed brow. "He keeps talking about an omelette. Is he hungry? Should I make him an omelette? Only after this meeting." She glanced at the alarm clock on the bedside.

"Musketeer is the code name for their landing operation, I know that," said Ben Gurion, "but what is all this about omelettes?"

Yael explained in rapid Hebrew that an operation called OM-ELETTE was superseding or modifying Operation MUSKETEER. It involved a complicated change of landing plans, so with one thing and another, the airfields would be bombed, but probably not till that evening.

Heavily, angrily, Ben Gurion shook his head. "Not satisfactory. I am bitterly disappointed. We are already standing condemned before the UN and all the world as an aggressor, whereas Nasser made war on us first with his blockade and his fedayeen attacks. We have smashed two fedayeen bases, and that is enough. Your governments have betrayed my trust, Colonel. I have summoned my Chief of Staff," he gestured at Moshe Dayan, "to end the reprisal operations and withdraw my soldiers from Sinai."

Colonel Simon's face grew longer and sadder as Yael put this to him in clear French. Watching him, Barak did not see him glance once at her shirt front, which happened to be bulging perkily. That was Yael Luria for you, he thought. To her, world affairs revolved around her tits.

"He says," she translated the colonel's agitated response, "that he wants to telephone his government at once."

"Paula, show him the phone in my office."

"All right. So he doesn't want an omelette? If he does he can have one."

"No omelette," said the Prime Minister.

"Nine minutes," said his wife, beckoning to the Frenchman, who followed her out.

From among the papers strewn on his bed, Ben Gurion picked up a teletype sheet and handed it to Dayan. "That came from Washington an hour ago. Rabbi Abba Hillel Silver was called to the White House, and told to bring it to our embassy." A quick glance, and Dayan passed it to Barak with a shrug. Ben Gurion said, "Dulles wrote it or dictated it, that's his style. But Eisenhower put his name to it. It's much worse than the last one."

Couched in stiffly polite phrases and personally in care of the rabbi, the letter in effect threatened a total cutoff of American military and economic aid to Israel, prohibition of fund-raising, and sanctions that might include an embargo on vital imports, unless the Israeli "aggression" was at once terminated and the troops withdrawn to the armistice lines. *"It is to be hoped and expected,"* the writer piously continued, *"that none of these grave eventualities will come to pass, due to the Israeli government's maturer reflection on recent developments."* The letter closed with protestations of friendship for the Jewish nation.

"In London people are rioting in Trafalgar Square against Anthony Eden's policy." Ben Gurion's voice was weaker. "The General Assembly will meet tonight to condemn us, and maybe to expel us. The Egyptian navy is bombarding Haifa and moving into the Gulf of Aqaba. Their air force is attacking our troops on all fronts.

There's intelligence that Iraq and Jordan may be mobilizing." He turned his fever-flushed face at Dayan. "And you want to go on with KADESH? Why?"

"Because we're winning everywhere, Prime Minister," Dayan returned forcefully, "and I believe what Colonel Simon says. Once the bombing of the airfields begins the whole Egyptian front in Sinai will fall apart. We are winning a great victory and must not stop." Ben Gurion made a very Jewish skeptical grimace, humping his shoulders and inclining his head. "And at all cost we must capture Sharm el Sheikh."

Ben Gurion tiredly turned to Barak. "How long will it take you to get to Sharm?"

"Once we start," said Barak, "three days."

"When can you start?"

"If we are so ordered, right away."

Ben Gurion looked to Dayan, whose face was blank and his eye dull, then back to Barak. "Wolfgang, you are telling me a bobbeh-myseh. Why are you telling me a bobbeh-myseh?"

Paula came in, followed by Colonel Simon and Yael. In a spate of speedy French, his face alight with relief, the colonel spoke again of omelettes and musketeers, adding several obscure references to telescopes. Yael explained that the latest modification to the plan, code name TELESCOPE, advanced the landings by two days, and called for the massive bombing of the airfields without fail at dusk that very evening. The French Defense Minister was ready to confirm this to Ben Gurion by telephone, if need be. The Old Man nodded and nodded, and smiled at the colonel.

"I won't shake hands with you," he said, "you might catch my flu. I accept your word and I'll take no further action until tonight. Tell that to your Defense Minister."

Yael translated. Paula said, "The time is up. Ben Gurion, rest! Yael, ask the Frenchman if he's sure he wouldn't like an omelette."

"Or a telescope," murmured Barak to Dayan.

Ben Gurion overheard this and his eyes flashed humorously and craftily at them. "Wolfgang, no more bobbeh-mysehs. Get your brigade good and ready. That is a terrible route. Don't push when you're not prepared. We have had enough of that." He let his glance rest on Dayan, then lay back. "I want to hear at once any news that comes in about the Mitla Pass. If you must, wake me up."

The news about Mitla was much worse than anybody who wasn't there knew.

The hills at the entrance to the defile looked like all the others in the Negev and in Sinai: brown, barren, wind-eroded, boulder-strewn, and void of visible life, except for here and there a tough clump of scrub brush. The trouble was with the invisible life. From these silent dead shallow heights were bursting great volleys that had caught the advance combat unit by surprise, sent its ammunition truck exploding sky-high, ignited the fuel carrier in a tower of flame and billowing black smoke, knocked out two tanks, and shut a trap on the force commander and his troops. Behind, burning vehicles and unseen guns; ahead, unknown surprises; from the hills of the defile killing cross fire, whenever the trapped soldiers moved out of the cover of their halted vehicles, or raised their heads from the shelter of wadis, the foxholes of nature. On the wireless, garbled frantic overlapping communications:

"Uri, Uri, cease fire, you're firing on us —"

"Negative, Motta, negative, negative, we're not firing —"

". . . Yes, yes, we're trying to come back and help you" — this from a half-track company that had outrun the commander — *"but we're taking a shit rain of bullets —"*

And so on, a continuous jumble of harsh voice signals drowned out now and again by crackling whistling bullets, roars of mortars, and thin cries of the wounded.

Out of range of the enemy fusillades were the strung-out vehicles of two parachute companies, sent in by Sharon to rescue the ambushed unit. Sharon was staying outside, preparing to fight an enemy armored force reported approaching from the north. The parachutists who had come to the rescue were setting up a battery of heavy mortars; the question was, where to fire them? In the bright afternoon sunlight, and the drifting smoke and dust of the entrapment, the enemy gun bursts seemed to come from everywhere and nowhere.

How then, to counterattack this invisible ambuscade? The commander of the rescue force decided on the desperate expedient of sending a jeep ahead through the defile, to draw fire while spotters watched the hills with binoculars to pinpoint the firing positions. At his call for a volunteer, Don Kishote was one of several who responded, and Raful Eitan, who was there to observe the rescue, himself offered to drive the jeep. The one chosen was Yehuda Kan-Dror, the commander's own driver. Kishote hated to see him go, for he knew Kan-Dror had lost a brother in the War of Independence.

It was all over in a few minutes, but very long minutes they were, as the jeep bounced along the rough track into the defile, leaving a plume of dust and drawing down a deafening continuous drumfire from the hills. Through his binoculars, when he should have been watching the hills, Kishote could not help following Kan-Dror's weaving course. He could see dark bullet holes appear all over the vehicle, could see the wince of the driver's helmet as he was hit and hit again. The jeep halted at the turn of the defile, the engine smoking. Kan-Dror lurched from the driver's seat, staggered some paces, and vanished from sight into a wadi.

"*Gibor hayil* [Man of valor]," someone said in a hushed voice, and he spoke for all who watched. But the valor was in vain. The far-spread shallow hills to the north and south were pitted with caves, and there was no telling — so the spotters claimed — from which of them the voluminous all-around fire had come. Kishote wondered how many of them had really been able to take their eyes off the ride of Yehuda Kan-Dror.

The rescue units were under orders to bring out all the casualties, at any cost. This was the rule of the Israeli army, dating back to Palmakh days, when the squads had been made up of boyhood friends. A soldier like Yehuda Kan-Dror, setting out with the white rigid face of a man who believed he was going to his death — Don Kishote would never forget his glimpse of that face as the jeep started off — knew that if wounded he would probably reach a hospital; and if killed, he would have a grave in Israel for his parents to visit. But the caves still commanded the defile, and the casualties could not be retrieved under their guns. There remained only a single laborious and perilous alternative: to clear out the gun pits one by one with small-squad attacks.

This process began after Kan-Dror's ride, and went on all afternoon and into the twilight, when locating the guns by their fire became easier. Squads climbed the hills to the ridges by roundabout routes, crawling through areas that might be exposed to the enemy guns, plodding by the hour up steep rocky slopes that took them to the caves from below, above, or the side, but out of the lines of fire. As the dusk deepened to a few stars above, it became clear that the southern ridge had the most and the heaviest weapons; they were raking the squads moving along the north ridge with long-range fire and piling up the Jewish casualties.

With six picked soldiers of his company, Don Kishote went edging along the south ridge on a narrow outcrop, where poor rubbly footing and deep drops on either side made for slow going, toward an emplacement that was pouring out bright noisy volleys. The ground broadened, he saw vague shapes ahead, and his sharp challenge brought quick shouts in Hebrew. It was Jinji's platoon, and they pointed out to him the slope falling away below, and a long meandering path toward the gun cave. "He tried to lead us down there. He went first and he got it," said Jinji's number-two man, a lean shape with a beard. "I tried to reach him, but they've got this path covered. I had bullets screaming past my ears."

"Is he alive? Do you know?"

"For a while he was yelling to us. He's down on a ledge there. I don't know whether they shot him again. Lately he's been quiet."

"Did you try to get at them from the other side?"

"Not possible. It's a sheer drop. No footholds."

"I'll have a look."

In the flickering light of the gunfire from the cave, and the distant glow of a burning vehicle, Kishote saw that on the other side there was in fact a nasty drop. Overhanging rocks concealed the cave itself. Peering here and there, leading his squad with slow care along the ridge, watching the drop in the gun flashes, he thought he saw a way down. It needed a long slide on the almost vertical rubbly slope, a jump to a shelf projecting beyond the cave and then with luck a leap back into the cave. The Egyptian gun crew was watching the other way down, that was sure. From this side they might be surprised.

Kishote had taken many risks in the night on reprisal raids. But here were soldiers, not fedayeen, armed with powerful weapons and on full desperate alert, for the trappers were becoming the trapped. Without reenforcements, and with Arik's troops in a grim methodical attack on the caves, these gun crews had to stand to their guns till they were killed, or else take their chances on fleeing into the night. Some had tried to flee and had been seen and shot. Others had escaped. The squads were reporting finding empty emplacements with guns intact and live ammunition piled up. This one, however, was going strong.

"I think I'll give it a try," Kishote said to the others.

His master sergeant said shakily, "Sir, don't. It's crazy."

"Well, we've got to get Jinji out of there."

He placed his men to cover him, and waited for the light and noise of the next fusillade. Not the kind of risk Kan-Dror had taken, but risk enough. Scared, exhilarated, his blood up, he waited for his moment.

Bursts of gunfire. Light, light, and more light! Down he went, automatic gun swinging on a strap, hands tearing on the rocks. Here was the ledge. A long-legged jump, another jump, and he landed in the cave with a thump, a rattle, and a frightening yell! He was near a dim oil lamp by a heap of automatic magazines, face to face with amazed Egyptians, six or seven of them, cowering at the sight of the tall gun-bearing apparition fallen from the sky. He barely had time to think how much they looked like his own squad, a bunch of young guys in uniform, and to see the soldier with his back to him, who was guarding the path where Jinji had been shot, swing around with his automatic at the ready. Yossi shot him, and then shot them all. As they sprawled and writhed in blood, crying out in strange words, he edged through the emplacement to the path, on the watch for any Egyptians he had missed, his pulse racing. Nobody, and no sound but the screams and groans of the gunned-down gun crew.

"Hey!" he yelled up the path. "It's Yossi. The objective is secured. Find Jinji!"

Hooded flares marked the improvised landing strip near the Parker Memorial, the only patch of flat ground in the area not hopelessly rough and wadi-scarred. As one Dakota took off with a full load of wounded, the exhaust of its two engines casting a blue glare on the strip, another was circling to land. The air force had sent an engineer to inspect the area, and he had reported that there was no place a Dakota could come down, that nothing larger than a Piper Cub could safely land at the Mitla Pass. But Arik Sharon had "talked down" a Dakota bearing medical supplies and stretchers for the wounded, and now they were arriving one after the other in the small hours to evacuate the casualties: more than a hundred found so far, more than thirty of them dead.

Kishote's company had the job of bringing the casualties aboard and quickly refitting the Dakotas as hospital planes, pulling out the bucket seats and installing makeshift pallets and safety lines to secure the wounded. In this mournful task, performed by flashlight and flares, Yossi was surprised to find that Yehuda Kan-Dror was alive; white as paper from loss of blood and barely conscious, but alive. Given up for lost, he had managed to crawl out of the deep wadi and collapse in the path of a patrol seeking the wounded. Jinji too was alive, and showing more life than Kan-Dror when he recognized Kishote in the light of the flares. He was heavily bandaged about the head and one leg, and a medic was holding an intravenous bottle over him. "Kishote! They say I owe you my life," he gasped with a feeble wave, as his stretcher was handed into the plane.

"Get well, Jinji, and we'll figure out what you owe me."

All around him, stretcher bearers were carrying up the wounded and handing them aboard. On a few of the stretchers the faces were covered; the soldiers had died while being rescued. This Dakota was the same aircraft that had carried his company to the parachute jump; the planes were all more or less the same, but in this one some wag had stencilled a Bambi on the forward bulkhead.

"So, Bambi," murmured Don Kishote, "it's not much fun going home after the party, is it?"

18

The Race

As the morning reports poured in, all the officers in the war room were looking cheerful for a change. Even the dour bone-weary Pasternak was studying the big table map with something resembling a smile. The girls were moving pins and unit symbols far into Sinai, except for Colonel Yoffe's brigade, which had not yet budged.

Operation KADESH was finally unfolding as Dayan had foreseen. The laggard British bombing of the airfields had done the job, eliminating the enemy air force from the fast-moving war; and the Egyptian troops that had been pouring into Sinai were in a headlong rush back to the Canal Zone. So at last — and this was why Pasternak was almost smiling — Yoffe's brigade could start down the track mapped out by the YARKON patrol along the Sinai's east coast; heretofore it would have been too vulnerable from the air. Yoffe had to go mighty fast, however, to capture Sharm before the United Nations voted on an American cease-fire resolution already under debate in the General Assembly. There were two enemies now, the Egyptians and the clock.

A soldier at the table: "Sir, telephone for you."

"Hello, Pasternak here."

"Crazy balagan," were Zev Barak's first words. "No use giving you a long story. I want your authorization to buy eighty-seven cows."

"Eighty-seven cows? Is this a joke?"

"Do you want an explanation, or will you just give me an okay? We have a serious problem."

"Let's hear it."

Barak glanced out the open farmhouse window at the stumpy white-haired figure keeping the bulldozers at bay. The smell from the barns was oppressing his city-bred nose. "Okay, it seems there's this old guy whose cow barns extend a few feet into the railroad right-of-way. Actually one very long barn, all along the track. The trains cleared it, so he got away with it for years. There are eighty-seven cows in that barn. He's one of these old Russian Jews, built like a rock, a demented individualist. He says the rotten socialist kibbutz system is behind all this, he's made all the rotten kibbutzim look sick with his successful private dairy, and they're out to get him."

"So what? Knock the barn down."

"He's got an Uzi, and he's ready to shoot the bulldozer drivers."

"Well, then, disarm the old lunatic! That's hard?"

"Sam, we got to talking. Turns out he knew my grandfather in Plonsk, in fact, he says he was once in love with my grandmother. I feel sorry for him."

"Zev, what the devil will the army do with eighty-seven dairy cows?"

"We can eat them, can't we?"

"By my life, you're as crazy as he is. You don't eat dairy cows, you milk them. Demolish the barn, I say, and fast. Tell him Solel Boneh will build him a brand-new one." Solel Boneh was the giant governmental road-building and construction corporation.

"All right, I can try that."

"Zev, you sound light in the head. What about your brigade? Is it on the move?"

"Definitely. Yoffe has started south, and I'll catch up with him when I've cleared this snag. The landing craft are loaded on flatcars in Haifa ready to go. The other demolitions have been done. There's just this cow barn."

Barak was in fact light-headed, not having slept all night in the hard push to get the brigade ready to roll. He found the barn impasse weirdly amusing, and enjoyed baiting Pasternak with it. Moreover, short of using force on the old man, he really was at a loss.

"Do whatever you think best," snapped Pasternak. "Buy the cows, shoot the old guy in the leg by accident, I don't care. The UN may vote today or tomorrow on the cease-fire. *Move!*"

Barak approached the dairyman, who, except for a bristly white beard, rather resembled the Prime Minister in his pugnacious jaw, heavy nose, and fierce eyes under bushy snowy brows. When Barak made the Solel Boneh proposal, the Russian exploded. "Solel Boneh? I *worked* for Solel Boneh! I *quit* Solel Boneh! The only thing in this country worse than the kibbutzim is Solel Boneh. Before Solel Boneh gets around to it, the Messiah will build me a barn."

"The army will buy your cows, then."

"And what will I do without cows? Go back to work for Solel Boneh? I *fart* on Solel Boneh!"

Barak took from a pouch his operation map of KADESH. "Look, Reb Shloimeh, here is how things stand." In quick sentences he sketched the war picture, making as clear as he could the mission of Yoffe's brigade, the reason for the demolition, and the race against the UN vote. "Without the replenishment by sea, Reb Shloimeh, the boys won't take Sharm el Sheikh, because the tanks and trucks won't have the fuel to get them there. And your barn is in the way of the boats I have to freight to Eilat. *Zeh mah she'yaish.*" ("That's how it is.")

The dairyman listened, looking hard at the map and nodding. "Why didn't those fellows on the bulldozers tell me all that?"

"They're just drivers, they had their orders. We're racing the UN."

"I *fart* on the UN," said the farmer, lowering his gun. "Let me get my cows out into the field."

"I'll give you a document, showing that the government will rebuild your barn."

"Wipe your ass with the document. I'll rebuild my own barn."

*

Colonel Avraham Yoffe, the big burly brigade commander, had requested Zev Barak as his deputy because he knew him from the Jewish Brigade days. As Sergeant Wolfgang Berkowitz, Zev had been adept at coping with the deep sand and balky machines of the North African desert. Also, Barak had been on the YARKON patrol, so he understood that the challenge to the brigade was as much making it down the Sinai coast, as taking Sharm el Sheikh.

Barak had risen to the job, had drawn up formidable lists of requirements, and had sleeplessly checked their delivery and distribution, driving Yoffe's staff to exhaustion and accepting no report except, "Done!" Now, as the long column of the Ninth crawled out of the Negev into enemy territory, there was no lack of spare parts and repair equipment in the ten-mile-long serpentine on wheels, nor of water, food, extra fuel, spare tires, and the thousand small items of a mechanized force on the march through a wasteland, carrying its own means of life support like a fleet putting to sea.

Miles ahead of the main body, Barak rode with a jeep-mounted company of engineers and mortar troops, scouting the mapped route for ambushes and minefields. As the sun climbed and the level open desert sloped up toward the mountains, the ground became more broken. Next his company ran into the dunes, great rolling waves of sand piling upward to the horizon, and behind him Yoffe's column came ploughing on into the dunes, where its speed of advance dropped close to zero.

Spurred by urgent messages from headquarters to make haste, Colonel Yoffe lashed his force onward with a rough tongue and scary willpower. Half-tracks churned grooves through the all-encompassing sand, and the trucks were ordered to drive in those tracks, but still they sank in to the wheel hubs, while the mortars half-buried themselves in the sand thrown up by their own wheels. Under a killing sun soldiers all along the march got off their vehicles to drag and heave at them. Overheating motors steamed and screeched, wheels spun showers of stinging sand, and half-tracks roared up and down the line to hitch up and tow stalled vehicles.

At headquarters Sam Pasternak got this picture all too vividly from the flimsy Piper Cubs of air communication: the column bogged in the sands, lying baking and inert on the gray-brown sands of Sinai, a dotted line of black machines paralleling the rocky coast along the sparkling sea. Meanwhile the political sands were running out in New York. The delaying tactics of the French and British diplomats could stave off the cease-fire vote at most for another day or so, yet their landing forces were still at sea, a good way from Suez. The London riots were threatening to bring down the Eden government. The chances kept dwindling that Yoffe would get to Sharm on time.

Dayan had been right, Pasternak bitterly realized, to hold back Yoffe until the enemy air had been knocked out, but the British had delayed the bombing too long, and now John Foster Dulles was hell-bent on stamping out the Suez campaign. While up north the Egyptians were in retreat and collapse, the real prize of the war, Sharm el Sheikh, was at hazard, and slipping by the hour beyond Israel's grasp.

"What do you mean," Pasternak all but snarled at Yael, "they can't find Dayan? Has his plane gone down? I *must* talk to him."

The Chief of Staff was hopping from front to front, Yael retorted, and no sooner was he located than he was gone and in the air again. His plane's radio was not working or not answering. Pasternak sat at his desk, unshaven and grim. "I see only one way through this balagan," he said, munching on a sandwich she had put in his hand, unaware of what he was eating. "Sharon's brigade is doing nothing now at Mitla but licking its wounds. Raful's paratroopers are still in good shape. They could get off their backsides, and make an end run around Mitla Pass to the other coast of Sinai. It's nothing like that terrain Yoffe's bogged in. The roads are pretty good, some are even tarred. Raful could capture an airfield with a parachute drop, and get heavy assault equipment delivered to him by air. That battalion could roll right to Sharm, and if Yoffe doesn't get there in time, Raful might. I want to recommend this to Moshe for immediate decision, but where is he?"

"Go ahead and do it," said Yael.

"What?"

"Do it, Sam."

He stared at her, and managed a sour grin. "Just like that? On my own? Change the tactics of my superior's campaign?"

"Is it the right thing? Is it urgent?"

"Urgent? It's the only thing. Possibly Yoffe and Barak will make it through, but it's looking worse by the hour."

"What have you got to lose by issuing this order, compared to losing Sharm el Sheikh?"

Pasternak was used to Yael's quasi-wifely effrontery, which she was not careful enough to conceal from the staff. She looked drawn and depressed, almost ill, but the brass was all there. "Well, we'll see. Tell Uri to come in here. And bring me the schedule of reserve airborne armor."

"All right, and I'll keep trying to contact Moshe."

"Do that." He startled her by harshly laughing. "Do you know what the biggest risk is? If I give this order, and then Raful Eitan beats Avraham Yoffe into Sharm, Avraham will have my liver on a skewer. With onions."

So now it was becoming a strange three-way race: Raful Eitan's paratroopers making a run for Sharm down the peninsula's west coast, and Avraham Yoffe's brigade climbing through the dunes on the east coast, both converging toward the southern point of the Sinai triangle at Sharm el Sheikh; and in New York, Eisenhower's UN delegation, in unlikely partnership with the Russians, forcing the pace toward an assembly vote for a cease-fire. Red Army tanks at that very moment were bloodily crushing an uprising against the Soviet puppet regime in Hungary, and the Americans were mildly reproving the Kremlin for this disorderly conduct, but reserving their indignation for Israel and to a lesser degree, for their allies, the British and French. To Sam Pasternak, who at the hub of these things was as aware of the whole picture as anybody, world politics wore the surrealistic look of Salvador Dali's melting watches, but these nightmare watches were recording the disappearing hours of Israel's opportunity to open the Straits of Tiran.

"Keep going," Pasternak signalled to Avraham Yoffe, who reported around midnight that the brigade had at last struggled over the top of the seventy-mile rise, but was strung far out of sight along the slope up to the watershed, and needed a respite. "I tell you, *keep going*! The political situation is deteriorating fast. For insurance, Raful is on his way down the west coast to help you take Sharm, if need be."

This dug spurs, just as Pasternak figured, into the brigade commander. He allowed his troops only two hours of rest and machine maintenance under the stars, while to the rear half-tracks and mechanics labored to extricate vehicles still stuck or disabled. Then the ten-mile line of overtaxed machines and two thousand exhausted men was back on the move, bumping and groaning downhill in the black hours before the dawn, through wadis criss-crossed with kidney-jarring crevices.

The sky brightened and a blinding orange sun rose on the strange iron caravan traversing camel tracks old as Genesis among the precipices. The great question now was, would the landing craft make the rendezvous? Battling the sand and the uphill grade, the column had burned up most of its fuel, as Barak had calculated. Without replenishment from the sea it would sputter to a halt far short of Sharm. So as Barak's first reconnaissance jeeps emerged from a steep arid brown canyon, he and his troops cheered at the sight of waving palm trees, shining blue water, and three vessels approaching on the sea.

But this exhilaration was brief. Out of small silent oasis buildings under the palm trees came the crack and whine of bullets, and this first encounter with a human habitation brought the first brigade deaths. By the time an organized search flushed out and killed the snipers, Yoffe was arriving with the main body of the brigade, and frogmen Barak had brought were snorkeling off the beach, searching for mines and underwater obstacles. The soldiers swarmed off their vehicles to dive into the water, and Barak allowed his own reconnaissance troops a swim, then summoned them back to the jeeps as the landing craft were easing up on the beach.

"Are we going to beat Raful?" His uniform blackened by sweat, Avraham Yoffe towered beside Barak's jeep, which was loaded up with jerricans of fuel, the motor running.

"It'll be close. Wadi Kyd's our problem."

"I'll tell you what," said Yoffe with an angry half-smile, "sending Raful was a sensible precaution, no argument. But if he takes

Sharm, I'll *kill* him." He waved a thick hairy arm at the serried lines of vehicles drawn up for refueling, covering the desert clear to the canyon defile. "Sharm el Sheikh is *my* objective!"

Like the YARKON exploration, Barak's scouting trek to Wadi Kyd was an awesome passage through Bible wilderness; and his line of vehicles, which made the primeval cliffs echo with mechanical racket, seemed a weird anachronism, as in a time-travel movie. Those brief days in Paris, he was reflecting, those farcical meetings of a few old men in the Sèvres villa, had launched a fantastic turmoil in faraway places. There was no telling how the British and the French would come out of their dilatory operation, with their landings still days away, the Russians dropping horrid hints about intervening in Sinai with troops and using rockets on Paris and London, and the Americans making no horrid counternoises, but rather agreeing with the Soviet position and merely asking for cooler heads, except about the inexcusable Israeli aggression.

Meantime Israel was close to conquering a peninsula three times the size of the sliver of coast that was all its territory. If some things had gone wrong in KADESH, Dayan on the whole had been right, Barak perceived; and if the Old Man with all his weaknesses was a political genius, the one-eyed moshavnik with all his faults was emerging as a military genius. The brigades to the north had already routed the Egyptians and swept all the way to Suez. There remained only Sharm to capture. Barak's long-range feeling of doom about the preposterously tiny Jewish sandbar in the sullen threatening sea of Islam — a feeling that he never voiced, but that was an unceasing gnaw — was lifting in the dazzle of this triumphant campaign.

The recollections of Paris brought to mind, as Barak's jeep rocked and jolted under the blazing sun and on into the starry night, memories of the gawky garrulous Emily Cunningham. Ever since his return, flashes of the strange girl had come and gone in his thoughts. The puzzling thing was that he had not quite forgotten her in his hard-pressed, day-and-night toils to get Yoffe's brigade mobilized, supplied, and ready to roll. He remembered even small things — the impatient quick waves of her long thin hands, the sudden way she widened her eyes at words that struck her, the untidy brown tumble of her hair, the cheap big American wristwatch she wore — above all, the desire she woke in him, the sort of youthful appetite he had buried under a dozen deep-layered years of happy marriage and fatherhood. The Cunningham girl couldn't compare to Nakhama in looks or in charm — skinny where his wife was voluptuous, acerb where his wife was sweet, brusque and forward where his wife, however tired or out of sorts, was soft and womanly. True enough, Emily was a clever creature, wholly of the great world outside Zion. War tended to blot out that world, but Emily was managing to intrude on him even here, amid the Sinai crags and dunes. A man was never too old for foolishness, it would seem, or at least *he* was not.

At Wadi Kyd, as he had feared, the ravine walls narrowed to a defile passable by camels but not by military vehicles. Shrugging off the risk of mines or ambush, he took a small patrol on foot through the bottleneck in the dark, and decided on blasting it open, for there was neither time nor fuel to turn back the brigade and explore another way to Sharm el Sheikh. This was no cow barn demolition, but like that job it had to be done.

Colonel Yoffe responded to his urgent report by speeding engineers with high explosives ahead to the site. They went straight to work. The terrific rolling thunderclaps and the pillars of flame that lit up the night gave Zev Barak an even eerier sense that he was living a Bible scene. When the long train of the brigade came winding through the wadi, visible in crimson flashes, the rubble from the explosions lay piled high in the defile, with more crashing down in cloud, fire, and pungent fumes at each reechoing BANG!

He put the entire brigade, as it came up, to clearing the broken rock with bare hands and levelling it out in a makeshift roadbed. Four thousand hands are a lot of hands, and in an astoundingly short time — though Colonel Yoffe paced and bellowed through every minute of it — a half-track and then a heavy tank truck tested the road and got through. Thereupon, Barak ran his scouting unit on ahead, while the brigade started to move again. A mile or so beyond the defile his jeep struck a mine. In a howl of sudden flame he was thrown clear, so was his driver, and heavy random cross fire assailed the patrol in the darkness. Stunned and bleeding, he pulled his men and vehicles together and retreated to await the daylight. He had found out what he sought: ambush ahead needing air attack, mines ahead needing sappers.

By contrast Raful's paratrooper battalion was having a breeze, after a long circuitous desert journey that avoided the Mitla Pass. The convoy stopped long enough to collect heavy guns and ammunition delivered by airdrop at a captured airfield, and from there — at least for Don Kishote, in a jeep at the head of the leading company — the journey down a good tarred road along the deep blue Gulf of Suez was something of a joyride; all the more so, as his exploit in rescuing Jinji had already won him a rough good word and a slap on the shoulder from the taciturn Raful Eitan.

The convoy rounded the southern tip of Sinai in the dead of night. Heading northward to Sharm, it encountered at last a fire-fight in dark morning hours, at a defile that led directly to the fortress. Here Kishote, whose jeep was near Raful Eitan's command car, heard him call up Colonel Yoffe to let him know he was within wireless range, and ready to battle through to Sharm el Sheikh.

"*Negative, negative! I am attacking now from the north,*" came the rough voice of Yoffe, somewhat garbled but the point very clear. "*Advance to within one mile of the enemy's southern gun emplacements and halt! I say again, halt! Let's not have another balagan like they've just had up north!*" He was referring to a bad business in which two armored brigades approaching the same objective had started knocking out each other's tanks.

Colonel Yoffe was senior officer at the scene, a brigade commander. Raful Eitan, a battalion commander, was in theory bound to comply with this harsh growl over the wireless channel, reenforced by a message sent in a Piper Cub that came whiffling to a landing on the flat sands near the battalion. The pilot jumped out and ran to Raful's jeep with a flapping despatch in hand. Not far off in the dawn light, rapid multiple flashes of heavy gunfire were visible. Kishote overheard Raful and his second in command, a tall bearded major as aggressive as Raful, discussing the despatch. "Well, there it is in writing," said the deputy. "*'Halt, do not repeat* NOT *advance.'* So do we still go?"

"Of course! At once! How do we know how the situation's changed since he sent it?" Raful gestured toward the distant thumping artillery blaze. "Sounds like he's having a very hard time. He'll probably be delighted to see us."

Their white teeth showed in an exchange of grins on brown dusty faces, and the battalion set on to Sharm el Sheikh.

And so the Egyptian commander of the fortress found himself under heavy attack north and south. After a fight of several hours, he sent an emissary to surrender to Yoffe's more powerful force. When Don Kishote chugged into Sharm el Sheikh in the jeep behind Raful's, the sight that greeted them was a makeshift blue-and-white Star of David flag and pole being planted atop a fortress building by Yoffe's soldiers. Riding in with Raful was Moshe Dayan himself. He had flown partway, and then riskily raced alone down the west coast in a command car to be in at the fun of Sharm el Sheikh's fall, passing through frantic mobs of fleeing Egyptian soldiers who could easily have killed him.

"So, we meet again," said Don Kishote to Barak, coming on him by chance during the cleanup of snipers in the ruins of the fortress, which the air force had reduced to rubble before the ground onslaught. Bodies of Egyptian soldiers lay sprawled in the sun or half-buried by debris, still oozing blood, and smoke drifted over the dismal sight, framed in wild harbor scenery of blue water and red rocks.

"Small world," said Barak, whose head and right hand were bloodily bandaged.

"Are you okay?"

"Yes. Hit a mine. Nothing too serious."

"Better view here than from the Georges Cinq," said Kishote, looking out at the craggy red-brown islands of the Straits of Tiran, rising out of the purple sea.

"Matter of taste."

"Who won, Zev?"

"Who won what, the war? What a question! Ask the Egyptians!"

Kishote gestured at the flapping flag. "No, I mean the race for Sharm — Yoffe or Raful?"

Barak did not answer at once, glancing around at the wreckage, the carnage, and the beautiful setting. He had led a failed attack at two in the morning, falling back in the face of a stiff barrage of cannon and machine gun fire. Yoffe had been out to beat Raful into Sharm, no matter what, but for Barak beating Raful had had no such urgency. What mattered was taking the objective with minimum casualties. Still, he had exulted as his half-tracks rolled into the fortress behind the Egyptian command car showing the white flag, and he saw no sign of Raful. Nakhama often accused him of enjoying war games and combat. "You do Luna Park out there," she would sometimes say. Smart lady.

"Well, Kishote," he said, "that will depend on who writes the story. As an honest historian, I'd call it a tie. As Yoffe's deputy, I'll maintain that we won in a walk."

Kishote laughed, eyes agleam with triumph, and trotted off. Barak saw Raful, Dayan, and Yoffe in earnest converse nearby, their faces too bearing the grim joy of conquerors.

But for him, the flush of victory was ebbing in the sight and smell of the Egyptian dead. He had encountered such sights and smells before, in North Africa and in Israel's battles; but this time they came hard upon a supreme lifting of spirit, a soaring sense of mission accomplished. This was a letdown which those three conquerors did not feel, or managed to suppress. Maybe that was because the three were sabras, and had been fighting off the Arabs all their lives. It made Zev Barak wonder whether, after all, he had the makings of a future Israeli general or was at heart a misplaced Viennese Jew.

19

The Foreign Minister

On a small door in a dim corridor outside the war room, a tacked-up hand-crayoned sign read *Hayalot* (female soldiers). Yael opened the door and very quickly closed it as she stepped in, for the Foreign Minister of Israel was standing there with her black skirt hiked up on one side, displaying capacious pink wool bloomers. "Do you have a safety pin on you?" inquired the Foreign Minister, in her cigarette-roughened voice.

Yael was dumbfounded. She had just returned from Ramat Gan HQ, where she had been collecting some secret documents for Pasternak. He was now conferring with Ben Gurion and other cabinet ministers at the large table map of the campaign.

"Ah, I can get you one, Madame Minister."

"Many thanks." Golda Meyerson fumbled at the elastic of her bloomers. "Of all times to have a problem."

Yael whisked out to the cubby where she kept her things. She was used to important people, but she had never been at such close quarters with "the American," as she had often heard Mrs. Meyerson referred to. She had heard other epithets, too. Mrs. Meyerson had recently been promoted from the Labor Ministry to the Foreign Office post in a devious political shuffle by Ben Gurion. She had Hebraized her name at his insistence, and people were still getting used to calling her Golda Meir. Golda was Yael Luria's idea of a woman, handling the biggest men on equal terms in politics and — so the talk went — in bed, and playing as strong a part in Israel's business as any of them.

"You're very pretty," said Golda Meir with a long keen appraising look, as she used the pin, shook down and straightened her long skirt, and touched at her dark braids by a small square mirror nailed to the plywood wall. "You're Nahum Luria's daughter, aren't you? Sam Pasternak's aide?" Golda had risen through the Labor Party and knew all the kibbutz and moshav leaders.

"Yes, I'm Yael Luria." Possibly Golda knew about Pasternak and herself; and if so, no surprise.

"Last time I saw you, you were a little girl. I'm hearing wonders about your brother, the aviator." Golda's stern worried face relaxed in a brief smile. She lit a cigarette and inhaled like a truck driver. "Sam looks as though he hasn't slept since the war started."

"He really hasn't."

"Well, now he can sleep — we hope."

Actually, as he gave the briefing at the table map, Sam Pasternak was feeling pretty good. His eyes looked glassy in deep dark hollows, and Yael feared he would fall asleep as he stood and topple over. But on hearing that the Old Man was coming with his top ministers, he had managed a reviving shower and shave, and a change of uniform. He had been through several slumps of killing fatigue, had caught a second and a third wind, and now the adrenaline of victory was keeping him going.

"Not one inch!" Ben Gurion was saying when Yael came to the table map, beckoned there by Pasternak. "Not one inch backwards!" A stiff finger was thrusting at the ministers, Golda among them, and their aides. The Prime Minister's jaw stuck out, his mouth was a black line of resolve, and his eyes flashed anger, real or assumed. He looked in the best of health, rested and of good color. Pasternak whispered to Yael that the French liaison officer was coming, and that she should stand by to translate.

A minister with bushy gray hair ventured mildly, "Ben Gurion, the cease-fire and withdrawal vote went eighty-five to one against us, and there's serious talk of expelling us from the United Nations."

"There's talk!" With a broad gesture at the situation map, and a sudden change to merry affability, Ben Gurion said, "Why are you all so worried? While they talk and talk in New York, and we are sitting in Sinai, things are not so bad."

"And Bulganin's letter?" Golda's interjection was almost belligerent. "What about that letter?"

"Golda, I'm not a Jew with trembling knees. That I think you know. He wrote letters to the British and the French, too. They are going right on with the landings, aren't they? They're not frightened, either."

"He didn't write them in the same terms: '. . . *calls into question the very existence of Israel as a state. . . .*' That is hard language." Golda waved her cigarette like an admonishing finger. "That's a military threat."

"And the intelligence from Moscow?" the bushy-haired minister put in. " *'If Israel doesn't withdraw, the Soviet Union is preparing to squash it in the next twenty-four hours'?*"

"You must learn to look at a map, Pinkhas." Ben Gurion pointed to a wall map of Europe and the Middle East. "That is only scare talk, planted propaganda. Twenty-four hours! It's not physically possible. The Russians are trying to cover their murderous actions in Hungary. And to grab credit for stopping the Suez campaign, in case Eisenhower does stop it."

"Prime Minister, Colonel Simon is here," said Pasternak, at a sign from the duty officer at a distant desk.

"Well, the briefing is finished. Golda, you will stay." To the others he said as they left that they would meet again in the evening. "So, Golda," he remarked, "now you will hear all about omelettes and telescopes." He chuckled at her mystified reaction.

The French officer came striding in, erect as a large paunch would permit, his much-bemedalled uniform spic and span, a fine martial figure in contrast to the rumpled and mostly unshaven Israeli officers in the situation room, some of them wearing old sweaters. *"Monsieur le Premier,"* he began without any other greeting, *"vous nous avez faites tous des dindons."*

Yael translated. "Mr. Prime Minister, you have made turkeys of all of us." Ben Gurion raised heavy eyebrows at her. She shrugged and added in Hebrew, "It's exactly what he said, Prime Minister. *Dindons.* That's French for *hodim* [turkeys]."

"Turkeys?" Ben Gurion addressed Simon directly. "How turkeys, Monsieur Colonel?"

Maintaining the aggrieved tone, Colonel Simon declared that Israel had let down its allies by accepting the General Assembly's cease-fire resolution, when the landings were only beginning. Egypt of course had jumped at both cease-fire votes, in the Security Council and in the General Assembly. What justification was there now for continuing the assault, which was supposed to "restore peace"? *Malheureusement* — the colonel repeated the word with extravagant gestures — *malheureusement* there was no veto in the General Assembly. The landings were proceeding "brilliantly," but they might have to be aborted and the scoundrel Nasser would survive, unless Israel reconsidered and continued to fight.

"But fight for what, Colonel?" Ben Gurion pointed to the table. "Your governments instructed us to halt ten miles short of the Canal Zone. Well, we are there, all along the line. In the south we are in Sharm el Sheikh. What now? Shall we march on Cairo?"

As Yael translated the colonel reluctantly smiled. *"Monsieur le Premier,"* of course I admire your successes, but I am reporting the grave dilemma of my government."

"But consider *my* dilemma," said Ben Gurion, sounding a shade pathetic. "The Americans have threatened us with ruinous economic sanctions. The Russians have actually threatened to annihilate us as a state! Haven't they, Golda?"

"We have received a terrifying letter from Bulganin, Colonel," she said. "Absolutely frightening."

"You see, Colonel? We are a very little country, squeezed by mighty superpowers. Thanks to gallant France, and only thanks to France, our soldiers have been able to clean out the terrorists in Sinai, and free our passage to the sea. That we will always remember."

"I shall report those gratifying words to my government. However, *Monsieur le Premier* —"

"Colonel, only the folly of England insisting on delaying the landings for a week — to maintain an empty pretext that the whole world now laughs at — has created your dilemma. Surely you know that. By the French plan you would have landed six days ago. You would now hold the Canal, and Nasser would be a fugitive in Switzerland."

"*Hélas,* how true," said Simon. "Once more England has made a turkey of France. It is 1940 all over again. The betrayal at Dunkerque! You cannot then reconsider?"

Ben Gurion spread both palms upward and looked at Golda, who sadly shook her head. "I am helpless to do that, Colonel."

"*Monsieur le Premier,* I have done my duty as an emissary. I shall at once report your most regrettable response." The French colonel drew himself very erect, pulling in his stomach. "I now speak as an individual and a soldier. Yes, France has aided you, but the lightning conquest of Sinai is Israel's glory. With this hundred-hour victory, you enter modern history, no longer a nation of victims but of warriors. I salute you, and I salute the Jews." He did salute, very formally.

Ben Gurion too drew himself up, pulled in his own paunch insofar as he could, and returned the salute. "I pledge Israel's eternal gratitude to France. For your ally, England, I feel only sorrow. Whatever else has happened, the British made possible the Jewish State, and we Jews will never forget that."

"Ah, the British." Colonel Simon shrugged. "*Hélas,* I fear the British lion exits from history a turkey. *C'est la guerre.*" With a brief bow to Golda Meir, he marched out, pausing to blink in surprise at a filthy bandaged figure entering by the same wide door.

"There's Zev Barak now," said Sam Pasternak.

"Good." Ben Gurion turned to Golda Meir. His face hardened into deep worry lines, and his voice was harsh. "The Bulganin letter is an insulting and very dangerous communication. What do we do?"

"I know the man. In Moscow I met him often." Golda Meyerson had been Israel's first ambassador to Moscow, where she had angered the Russians by attracting crowds of singing cheering Jews.

"He is just another Soviet politician. They are all alike. They only understand when they get as good as they give. I'm going to draft an answer as rough as his letter."

"Be as rough as you please, and I'll sign it. Just don't dare him to squash us. I don't think we can beat the Red Army."

"I'll bear it in mind." She said to Yael as she left, "Thanks for the pin."

"What pin?" Ben Gurion asked Yael, with his usual insatiable inquisitiveness. "You gave Golda a pin? What did she want with a pin?"

Yael was still groping for a reply — "To hold up her bloomers" seemed not quite the thing to say to Ben Gurion — when Zev Barak approached, greasy and sandy from head to foot. "The Piper Cub came with your message, Prime Minister, and I got on it as I was. My apologies."

"That's Sharm el Sheikh dirt," said Ben Gurion. "Beautiful dirt. Those bandages, nothing serious?"

"No, I'm all right. When I left, we were spiking the cannons. Even if the Egyptians come back tomorrow, they'll be a long time closing the straits again."

"They'll never come back. Never!" Out came the Ben Gurion jaw, and the brows heavily lowered. "Sharm el Sheikh is just a rocky point on the Straits of Tiran. Historically it's all Yotvat. The main island in the straits was an ancient Jewish settlement, and we were there two thousand years ago, it's all described in Procopius, I showed it to you. We have returned. There we stay. That is unchangeable."

He fired rapid questions at Barak about the breakthrough battle, the demeanor of the Egyptian commanders, the handling of prisoners, the condition of the Israeli troops, the level of supplies, and the restoration of the ruined fortress as a defensive position. "Zev, I talked with Moshe this morning. Avraham Yoffe is recommending you for a *tziyun l'shvakh* [distinguished citation]."

"Why me? He's the one. Who else would the men have followed all the way through that Gehenna?"

"You saw Moshe at Sharm?"

"Yes, he came in with Raful."

"He was everywhere but here, Sam, right?" The Prime Minister smiled at Pasternak. "All through the war."

There was no response but an unfocussed stare. Yael touched Pasternak's arm, and he started. "What? Sorry," he mumbled, blinking.

"Sam, I order you to rest!" Ben Gurion exclaimed. "I know what you've done here. Moshe Dayan himself told me, *'What we messed up in the morning in the field, Sammy straightened out at headquarters in the afternoon.'* You've been outstanding."

"I never heard a gun go off," Pasternak muttered.

Ben Gurion took his arm. "You'll come with me in my car."

"Tell Uri," said Pasternak to Yael, as the Prime Minister led him away.

"I want to telephone Nakhama," Barak said to her.

"Use Sam's office."

When Yael came into the office Barak was on the phone, laughing. The jubilant tones of his wife rattled in the receiver. "Well," he said as he hung up, "she's pleasantly surprised that I'm back already."

"I can imagine."

"Your friend Kishote, by the way, is a big hero. You've heard about it?"

"He's not my friend."

At the quick edgy words, Barak gave her a quizzical glance. "Your travelling companion, then. Whatever you please. He'll be up for a commendation, without a doubt."

"Why, what did he do?"

The feat had reached Barak embellished in the way of battlefield stories. Don Kishote's leap had become a mountain goat bound beyond human strength, he had wiped out an entire platoon of Egyptians and — a touch of pure fantasy — he had climbed down to the ledge where Jinji lay, and had carried him up to safety in his arms. "I'm not sure about most of that," said Barak, "but I know he saved the man's life and knocked out a gun cave. Raful told me as much."

"Well, he took a crazy chance. Do you admire that?" Yael's comment was snappish and, Barak thought, peculiarly frosty. "How long will he last doing such things, and what kind of leadership is that?"

Barak stood up. "Avraham Yoffe has told me to take seventy-two hours. Three days with my wife and kids! *That's* leadership."

"Was Kishote hurt? Did you see him?"

"Yes. Not a scratch."

"Then all I can say is, *'God watches over the simple.'*" It was a byword from the Psalms.

"I'll tell you, Yael. Kishote is a bit crazy. So was his friend Gulliver. So was Theodor Herzl. So is Ben Gurion. Kishote's a soldier, a fighter, and he'll be a player, if he lives, right to the top."

Barak left Yael crouched over a paper cup of tepid coffee, in an agitated quandary.

She was a very regular female, and therefore damnably worried. Once, only once, had she ever missed, in a tense time of high school examinations. Then she had been a virgin and there had been no other possible explanation but tension. This time the other explanation was all too plain; high jinks in the penthouse of the Georges Cinq Hotel. She had thought it a safe time of the month, it had just been impulsive foolery with distracting interruptions, and the long and short of it was — either war tension was making her miss, or the French whore was in trouble.

The unlikelihood of it, the sheer *injustice* of it, aggravated Yael Luria. Years of passionate lovemaking with Sam Pasternak, sometimes occurring in a storm of quarrelling or reunion when precautions were forgotten, and yet — nothing! Had it happened with Sam, a lever of a sort would have been placed in her hand. At least she loved him! But by the worst luck, she had been giving Sam the old freeze lately, so it just couldn't be Sam. She couldn't even pretend she thought so. What a trap! It had to be the stress of war — of course it could be the war — or else she was actually pregnant by that foolhardy Don Kishote, who with his other drawbacks had that religious Jerusalem girlfriend. An appalling possibility, that it might be Don Kishote! To be shut from mind until the next time had come and gone.

All during KADESH, as she had worked night and day at headquarters, the mounting number of missed days had kept unnerving pace for Yael with the accumulating victories. One cheering ray in the gloom had been the thought that if the worst should come to the worst, she would know she was fertile. Yael had done too much sterile lovemaking, with Pasternak and before him, not to have a suppressed gnaw about this. And now Barak had offered another cheering ray in her quandary. If Yossi was no Sam Pasternak, he was emerging from the pack. He had scored high in KADESH, after all. *"A player to the top, if he lives!"*

Still it had better be tension. As the man in her life she wanted no part of that beguiling daredevil, Don Kishote.

"You're hurt!" Nakhama exclaimed, as she opened the door to Barak.

"Mostly I'm dirty." He held his wife at arm's length to kiss her, but she thrust past his arms to hug and kiss him hungrily. She then touched the bandages. "Zev, what happened?"

"Scrapes and a sprain. Nothing more. Very lucky, my jeep hit a mine. I have to shower, and you'll change the dressings."

Noah appeared in scout uniform, a lean brown sharp-eyed boy carrying a newspaper. Almost twelve, he was on his dignity, and well past scampering and dancing when his soldier father came home. "Look, Abba!"

A three-column picture on the front page of *Ha'aretz* (*The Land*) showed the Egyptian command car flying a white flag, and behind it Barak at the wheel of his jeep, with a helmeted soldier manning the machine gun.

Michael Berkowitz limped out of a bedroom in hat and over-coat, a thick briefcase under his arm. "Wolfgang, welcome home! You're all right?" He threw an arm around Barak's shoulders, kissed his sandy cheek, and pointed at *Ha'aretz*. "You're the talk of the university."

"Aren't classes suspended?"

"They're resuming Monday. I'm doing backed-up paperwork. That girl Shayna is helping me."

"Good, tell her that her paratrooper is okay. I saw him at Sharm el Sheikh. He distinguished himself in battle."

"Ah, she'll be happy! She hasn't said anything, but she's been in a fog of worry. So, we'll have a good talk tonight."

But the brothers did not talk that night. Nakhama made an early dinner and put the baby, Galia, to bed. Noah balked, insisting that he wanted to hear all about the march to Sharm el Sheikh. His father had gotten as far as the arrival at the oasis of the landing craft and the search for the snipers who had killed his soldiers, when Nakhama interfered. "Abba is exhausted, be off with you, Noah. He'll be here for three days, you'll hear it all." With her husband absent so much she ruled the family, an old-fashioned Moroccan-style mother.

Barak tumbled into bed between fresh sheets, revelling in the comfort and in being clean, but disoriented by the unexpected transit from the beautiful battle-torn Sharm El Sheikh vistas, to the narrow walls of the flat, the warm quiet music of family talk, and the fragrance of his wife's spicy cooking and of Nakhama herself. She had been strictly business as he sat nude in the bathroom and she changed his bandages, a chore she was used to; and she maintained that manner when she brought the radio into the bedroom and pulled down the shades on a window violet with twilight. "You're absolutely worn out. You'll hear the six o'clock news and you'll go to sleep. None of that," she said, deflecting the arm he reached for her. "Let's listen to the news, I say."

She sat on the bed and they clasped hands as the bulletins came thick and fast, the international news first. The French and British landing forces were advancing down the Canal Zone against weak Egyptian opposition, but the political situation was turning catastrophic. In London spreading street riots and an uproar in Parliament had the Eden government near collapse. In the UN a rising howl against France, England, and Israel was being stirred up and directed by the Americans. The Russians were openly preparing to land troops in Egypt, and were inviting the Americans to join them in an expedition to "crush the aggressors." The Bulganin letter to Ben Gurion was making world headlines. The announcer quoted samples: *"Russia Will Crush Israel — Bulganin"* and *"Final Eradication of Zionism by USSR!"*

Nakhama's hand tightened on her husband's at these items. "Zev —" she murmured.

"None of that will happen. The Americans are out to stop the landings, and they will probably do it. The Russians are making noise."

"Horrible noise!"

"Well, Soviet noise."

The Israel news was the ebullient other side of the coin. More details of victorious battles, stories of heroism, casualty figures low though sad enough: fewer than two hundred killed and missing, where the Egyptians were admitting many thousands. The broadcast included a recorded interview with Colonel Yoffe by a correspondent in Sharm el Sheikh. When Yoffe mentioned the "heroic" efforts of his deputy, Lieutenant Colonel Barak, she turned to hug him and found herself pulled down on the bed.

"No! No, I say. You have to rest. Time enough for that. No." Unsuccessful protest, slight struggle, a frantic whisper: "Now look, this pillow is wet, and it's blood. I told you."

"The scab pulled loose. It's nothing."

"Come, I'll fix it up and change the pillowcase." She turned on a dim bed lamp. "God, it's only half-past seven. What a scandal. Suppose Michael came home and found us like this? Hurry." She dressed his head wound again, firmly put him to bed, and bent over to kiss him. "Welcome home, hero. Sleep well."

Next morning when he came blinking into the strong sunlight of the kitchen in a bathrobe, his wife was putting away dishes. A King David Hotel envelope lay on the kitchen table. "What's this, now?"

"Sorry, I forgot it. A girl brought it yesterday afternoon. American archaeologist's daughter. A message from her father."

"Archaeologist?" He was opening the letter.

"I think so. We talked French, and didn't get far."

Nov. 6, '56

Hi, Wolf Lightning —

Am scrawling this over tea and cake at the King David. Lieutenant Colonel Pasternak has a sealed letter that my father sent to me in Paris, instructing me to fly here and deliver it to him, hand to hand. Most of Wednesday I'll be at the Ramat Rakhel excavation that Dad helps to finance. Wait-listed on a plane back to Paris Thursday. Pasternak said you're somewhere in Sinai but I intend to see your wife and kids anyway. Amazing victory of Israel, however my father is very negative about it. Sorry as hell to miss you, but everything always happens for the best, my mother likes to say. Possibly.

Emily C.

Over the splutter of frying eggs Nakhama said, "Sam Pasternak called. He told me to let you sleep, but you're to call him once you're up."

"I'll eat first."

"That girl talked to Noah, and said his English is *merveilleux*. Nice girl. Is she an archaeologist, too?"

"I don't know. I met her father in America."

In the gun battles for Sharm el Sheikh, Barak's aberrant thoughts of Emily Cunningham had quite faded. A letter from Cunningham, brought hand to hand from Paris! Worrisome. The bold choppy note made him wonder at those peculiar musings about the girl on the long Sinai trek; product of boredom, fatigue, and stress, he thought, a kind of meaningless wakeful dreaming. Nakhama glowed as she put his breakfast before him. He had seen that radiance often when he returned from battle or a long absence. She wore a plain blue housedress, and her hair was a rich careless pile on her head. He said, "You look wonderful."

She kissed his forehead below the bandage. "Eat, and call Sam. He sounded concerned, I don't know why. The news is all good, except the British and French are stopping their troops, and the UN may occupy the Canal Zone. It's all up in the air."

20

Issur Yikhud

Golda Meir chain-lit a cigarette as she read Cunningham's two-page letter straight through without comment, now and then glancing over her desk from Pasternak to Barak, who had never been in her office before. It was a bare little workplace for a Foreign Minister, its walls unadorned except for pictures of Ben Gurion and the gaunt President Ben Zvi, both in open-collared shirts, and a large map of Israel with the occupied Sinai hatched in red ink. Smoke drifted out of the small half-open window, and an ashtray heaped with butts sent up a stale smell. "Tell me again who this man is." She took off her glasses and dropped the letter on the desk.

"A friend," said Pasternak. "High in the Central Intelligence Agency."

"In the CIA? A serious person? Then what is all this unprofessional *hugger-mugger*" (Golda used the English words), "sending a personal letter to his daughter in Paris by diplomatic pouch, for her to bring here by plane during a war?"

"I guess he didn't trust cable or telephone, Madame Minister, or the pouch direct to Tel Aviv." Pasternak shrugged. "Mr. Cunningham's somewhat meshuga on security. Like others in intelligence."

"And a lot meshuga on the Russians," said Golda, with a

dismissive wave at the letter. "I was born in Kiev, you know. I can assure you a Russian puts on his pants one leg at a time. A Russian is not ten feet tall. You walk in Moscow, you see a lot of short Russians. Some Americans have strange ideas about Russians." She peered at Barak, who sat blank-faced. Pasternak had brought him along to give his view of Cunningham and of the letter if asked. "You know this man, Barak?"

"Not as well as Sam does."

"What do you think of him?"

"Strange person, keen mind, and extremely well connected."

Wrinkling her large bold nose, Golda picked up the letter and read out the opening sentences in a sardonic tone.

Dear Sam:

I write this during a sleepless night. I'm confoundedly worried. Your victory is militarily admirable, but politically it can prove suicidal. The American shield is down. All Israeli policy decisions must turn on that fact. With her American background, your foreign minister should understand this. The intelligence from Russia is appalling, and we're taking it very, very seriously here . . .

"American shield?" Golda almost snorted. "*What* American shield? What have the Americans done for us in this business but make trouble?" She tossed the letter to the desk as the two men looked at each other. "Go ahead, Sam, explain to me about the American shield."

Pasternak made an inviting gesture at Barak, which was also an order. "Zev's heard Christian Cunningham expound. Quite recently, in fact."

The half-closed eyes in her strong face shifted to Barak with cold challenge.

"In a sentence or two, Foreign Minister," Barak said, "I can't explain."

"But what this man says makes sense to you?"

"Yes."

"Then let's hear it, and take your time."

Why had Sam put him on this spot? Here was no relationship

such as Barak had with the Ben Gurions, to whom he could speak almost like one of the family. He had to talk geopolitics on the spur of the moment with this woman who made foreign policy — insofar as anyone did besides David Ben Gurion — and who had a formidable reputation for not suffering fools. What could he say that she did not already know? This had to be a probe in the Old Man's style.

He summoned up nerve, and began. The "shield" obviously meant, he said, the friendship of a great power. In Cunningham's way of thinking, Zionism had "slipped into history" — Golda Meir worked her dark eyebrows at the phrase — in 1917 with the Balfour Declaration, behind the shield of England. That shield had lasted until the Arab uprisings and the UN partition vote, which had gone through behind the American shield, specifically President Truman's intervention. Otherwise Israel would not exist. The threat to Israel's survival came less from the Arabs than from a great power's policy of penetrating the Arab world by means of an unfriendly, sometimes menacing stance toward Zionism. Russia was now playing that gambit in the old Great Game, and the American shield alone had been restraining it. But with Eisenhower furious at Israel, its political predicament, always precarious, had overnight turned extremely grave. That, said Barak, was the Cunningham view behind the letter.

"Well said, Zev. Chris also makes two material points there," added Pasternak, jabbing two fingers toward the letter. "Point one. Dulles has gone into the hospital with cancer, so Eisenhower is directing policy himself. He's not a diplomat but a military man used to ruthless quick action. Point two. The State Department has let it be known through channels that a Russian attack on England or France will bring American retaliation." Pasternak paused. "And Chris emphasizes, Madame Minister, that *Israel is omitted from that warning.*"

"Yes. '*Israel is not — repeat not — mentioned.*' I saw that." Golda Meir slid the letter across the desk to Pasternak. "Well, now I understand you both, and I couldn't disagree more. Your CIA friend is saying we should tremble at the Russian threat, obey the UN, and withdraw from Sinai forthwith. Not a chance. Rotten advice." She turned on Barak. "Shields, shmields! What's the matter with you? That makes sense? What shields? We Zionists have done it ourselves! We've built up and fought for and won this land, and *that's* why Israel exists! When a great power befriends us, it's to serve its own interest in the region, nothing more. For the British we were a buffer against the French, until the Arabs made it too hot for them to stay here. As for the Americans, what kind of a shield have they been, embargoing arms to us while Russia armed Egypt? If not for the French, whose interest is to throw out Nasser, he could be overrunning us now, instead of the other way around. Then would *he* withdraw? Hah, Sam?"

"Not very likely, Madame Minister."

"No, not very. So let the Egyptians show peaceful intentions and start talking to us! If we back out of Sinai, shaking in our shoes, will that make them talk peace? What a joke! And as for the Russians, well, they're a long way from here, and they're very busy at the moment crushing Hungarian women and children under their tanks." She stood up, smoothing her dress and glancing at her watch. "Ben Gurion will be speaking on the radio in an hour. I advise you to listen to him. I'm going to see him now."

"Did you expect anything different?" Barak asked Pasternak as they emerged into a cloudy drizzly afternoon.

"Hardly, but Chris's letter alarmed me, and I thought she should see it. She has her mind made up, so that's that. Or I should say the Old Man has his mind made up. Same thing, and we may be in for a disaster."

Walking past the King David Hotel after going to the bank, Barak remembered that Emily Cunningham was leaving today, probably had already left. Go in and check? Why bother? Time to get home for B.G.'s broadcast. But on an irrational impulse he did go in, and there she was at the reception desk handing in her key, in a squirrel coat and a gray shawl, with a blue leather bag at her feet. He felt an instant stir of delight. When she saw him her eyes popped comically, and her mouth fell open in an audible gasp. "You! You're supposed to be in Sharm el Sheikh! I saw your picture in the paper!"

"You're leaving now?"

"I have hours, but I hate sitting all packed in a hotel room."

"Does your room have a radio?"

"Yes."

"Take back your key." He picked up her bag. "The Prime Minister will speak soon. I want to hear him. It will be in Hebrew, and I'll give you the gist. Okay?"

"Why, sure."

She kept stealing saucer-eyed looks at him as they walked up the broad staircase to the second floor in silence. In the narrow room she waved at the window. "Depressing view. All that barbed wire, and the Old City beyond. More depressing when the sun shines on the walls. Then Old Jerusalem looks like Paradise Lost."

The small radio whistled, squealed, and gargled static until he got it tuned to rapid talk in Hebrew. "He'll be on in a few minutes," Barak said.

She threw the coat and shawl on a chair. "You know that I visited your family?"

"Yes."

"Your injuries aren't serious, are they?"

"The bandages will be off in a week."

She made an awkward gesture with a stiff arm and a slightly bent elbow. "You still move your arm that funny way. Are you aware of it? I noticed it in Paris."

"Nobody else notices it. Or at least comments on it."

She smiled the grown-up smile that satirically creased and dimpled her girlish face, and he began to remember why he had found her piquant. "Terrible manners."

"How's André?"

"Oh, all right." The smile disappeared. "Look, can you tell me — give me a hint — what was in my father's sealed letter? A weird business! Are things here that serious?"

"We're not easily frightened. We can't afford to be. We've won a big victory, that much is sure. Sit down, stop scampering around like a cat in a cage." He gestured at the radio. "Sorry if this Hebrew bores you. It's political comment. It bores me too."

She flopped on the bed, propped on her elbows. "My God,

you have a beautiful wife and fantastic children. The baby girl is lovely, and that boy Noah will be a leader."

"Nakhama said you're a nice girl."

"*Ha!*" An explosive sound. "Did she? We could hardly communicate. Is that her name — Nakkama? Sounds American Indian. Daughter of the Moon, or something. Like Wolf Lightning. Maybe the Indians really are the Lost Tribe of Israel."

"You're babbling, Emily. And it's Na*kh*ama."

"What does that mean, Na*кн*ama?" She forced the guttural thickly.

"Consolation."

A shadow passed over the girl's face. "I may as well tell you, or warn you, that I have occult powers. Don't laugh, I very rarely use them, but when I do they scare me, the way they work. I willed you through the revolving door of the hotel just now. I did! I said to myself, 'I know he's in Sharm el Sheikh, all the same *I will him to come into this lobby right now.*' And you came. Do you believe me? I'll swear it on the Bible. There's a Gideon Bible there in that drawer, and I'm a believer."

"Look, our bank is just down the street, and Nakhama needed cash. Did you will all that?"

"Don't make fun of me. I tell you, I've done this before. Once in college I needed twenty dollars to get out of a terrible money scrape, a horrible disgrace. I willed to find a twenty-dollar bill, and I found it in an old purse I'd been meaning to throw out. I've done it other times, too."

"Suppose I hadn't walked in? What about those occult powers?"

"Ah, but you did!"

On the radio, a burst of harsh, different Hebrew. "There he is." Barak fine-tuned the dial.

"Do you think I'm crazy?"

"Not exactly."

"Pretty?" She kicked her legs, which were lean but well-shaped.

"Shut up, I want to hear him."

"God in heaven, Wolf Lightning, I'm glad you came through that revolving door."

"All right."

"You know, you wouldn't tell me to shut up if you didn't feel at home with me. Interesting."

Ben Gurion was only getting started, but Barak did not want to miss a word. He went and put a hand over her mouth. She nipped it with sharp teeth. "Sorry, I'll be quiet."

He shook his head at the coltish girl, and pushed aside her squirrel coat to sit in the armchair. Emily walked to the window and stood with her arms folded, looking out at the Old City. She was dressed in the same sweater and skirt she had worn in Paris. As the voice rushed on, strident and emphatic enough to make the radio rattle, Barak sank lower in the chair, feeling burdened and weary.

For it was a resounding victory speech, rigid, high-spirited, uncompromising, the same attitude Golda Meir had taken at the meeting. The old armistice agreements were dead. Egypt's acts of war had killed them. The former armistice lines no longer existed. As for the proposed UN force in the disputed areas, Israel would allow no foreign troops on her soil, *or on any territory she occupied!* (When Barak heard these words, spoken with defiance, he cringed and put a hand to his forehead. "What?" Emily whispered. "What did he just say? It's pure Chinese to me." Barak put a finger to his lips.) When Egypt and the other neighbors showed a disposition to discuss peace, they would find Israel surprisingly forthcoming. Meantime Israel could rely on her soldiers, as she had amply illustrated, to rebuff all intruders. The vast buildup of fortifications and arms caches they had uncovered in Sinai proved that Israel had acted in self-defense just in the nick of time.

"You didn't like the speech," she said as he turned off the radio.

"Your father won't like it. Here's what Ben Gurion said, in a few words." Barak summarized the talk, and his gloom deepened as he did so, though the presence of the girl was both distracting and charming.

"You're probably right, Chris will be appalled. But I'm an awful ignoramus about politics."

"How are you doing with your thesis on Lamartine, Emily?"

"I don't feel like talking about it."

"I see." An awkward pause. "Well, I guess I'll be on my way. Thank you for the use of the radio."

"I don't have to leave just yet."

"I have things to do."

"Okay." She shrugged on her coat and tied the shawl over her hair. "You're right. If I kiss you once I'm lost, so let's get out of here."

As they faced each other, well apart, the twenty-year-old American girl in the squirrel coat and the bandaged Israeli officer in his early thirties, Barak incongruously thought of a religious rule he and Michael had argued a lot about in their teens, *issur yikhud*. Strict Talmudic law prohibited a male person and a female — down to a ridiculously low age for both of them — who weren't related, to be alone together in a closed room. Zev had maintained that in modern times issur yikhud was nonsensical and unenforceable. Michael, a sober yeshiva student, had replied that it was unenforceable, except by willpower; nonsensical, not at all. Barak had never paid the slightest attention to it, of course, much to his gain in enjoyment over the years. Until this moment, it had not crossed his mind again.

"Foolishness," he said. He took her by the forearms and gave her a casual kiss on the mouth. "Okay? Big deal?"

"That was inevitable," she said, "since the night of the fireflies. You did it, not I. Remember that. You'll have to, one day."

She darted through the door, grabbing her bag as she left. He went out after her. "Let me carry that."

"Oh, please. Don't be so damn polite. It's ridiculous." In the hallway she turned her face to him. It was streaming tears.

"What the hell? *Now* why are you unhappy?"

"My God, that's how much you know. I'm trying not to expire with joy."

His throat tightening, Zev Barak said, "Next time we meet, if we do, you'll probably be married with two kids, like Nakhama, and just as happy."

"I very much doubt that, but if I am, it won't make the slightest difference." She put a tissue to her eyes. "Talk about fantasies! Wow! Was the speech that awful, really? The taxi guy at the airport took francs. Will they take them here?"

"I'll put you in a cab."

"Oh, right, you're fresh from the bank, you're flush. Thanks."

As they walked down the staircase she said, "I broke off with André. No doubt that amazes you! Ha! You knew I would, the instant you laid eyes on him. God knows why my parents carried on so. Poor André! And I won't finish my master's in Paris, since you ask. I'm going home. I'll finish it there, maybe at Georgetown."

"You want to teach?"

"Yes. In a girl's school. There are several around Washington, out in the country. I love girls. They're realistic and tough. Boys are nearly all vain soft slobs."

"You're reversing the sexes, aren't you?"

"No, that's the truth, the reverse is a trashy cliché." She took his arm. They were about to enter the lobby. "Listen to me. If I could be your dog, just your dog, I'd find a way to live in Jerusalem. It's hopeless, that's very plain. So put me in the cab and say goodbye until we meet again."

He forced a light manner. "You'll use your occult powers, I suppose, to make sure we do."

"I won't have to." She suddenly smiled, a different, loving smile. She had beautiful white teeth and wide red lips that curled oddly at the corners. "Hiroshima in a trench coat! How coarse, how brutish. But that did it, in a way."

He put the bag into the cab, at her feet. "I love you," she said.

"I believe you think so. Wait till you meet him. The man you'll marry. Then you'll know what love is." He held the door open, despite himself not wanting to see the last of Emily Cunningham.

"I know exactly what love is, and it's everything. I know you and Nakhama love each other and are perfectly happy. She's spectacularly beautiful and sweet, and I daresay smart. We couldn't make contact at all. Well, close that door, and say goodbye. No help for it."

"I guess you are crazy. Or maybe just *yotzet dofan*."

The cabdriver, a swarthy man in a conical wool cap, looked around at the words.

"And what's that, *yotzet dofan*?"

" 'Emerging from the side.' In English, cesarean birth. In Hebrew that too, but it's also come to mean 'out of the ordinary.' "

The satiric smile again. She held out her hand, and gripped his with slender fingers. "You bet, kiddo," she said. "As it happens, I actually was born by cesarean section. *'From my mother's womb untimely ripped.'* "

Her dramatic reading made him laugh. " *'Lay on, Macduff'*?" he said. "Doesn't that come next? *'And damned be him that first cries, "Hold, enough!"'* "

"Nope! Nice try, but it's *'Accursed be the tongue that tells me so.'* You have to brush up your Shakespeare, old scout. Maybe I can help someday." Her eyes brilliantly flashed at him. "Bye-bye for now, Wolf Lightning."

That law of *issur yikhud* was very much on Shayna Matisdorf's mind, as she sat outside the closed bedroom door of her cousin Faiga right after the wedding ceremony.

From the parlor the joyful tumult of the nuptial festivities — singing, joking, laughing, dancing, arguing, and the clamorous klezmer music of two saxophones and a bass fiddle — went on full blast, while she, another girl, and two yeshiva youths stood in the hallway, to bear witness that Faiga was alone inside with her bridegroom Fyvel long enough for the thing to happen, theoretically. This brief *yikhud* of newlyweds was a pure formality, but so strictly observed in Shayna's milieu that she took it for granted and saw nothing in the least odd or colorful about it. Faiga and Fyvel would spend the prescribed eight or ten minutes in there, drinking tea and eating cake — with huge appetite, because they had fasted all day — and they would of course emerge as virginal, both of them, as they had gone in. Knowing how shy Fyvel was, Shayna thought Faiga might not even get kissed behind that door. Nevertheless this act of *yikhud* was a true seal of the marriage, as much as the ceremony under the canopy and the breaking of the glass.

The door opened and out came the happy pair, the pallid groom in his white *kittel* and Faiga a-swirl in the creamy veils and lace of her bridal dress. She was scarlet-faced and laughing, and the wispy-bearded Fyvel had an unfocussed bemused look, as though from a hard blow on the head, so Shayna surmised that there had been a kiss after all. Good sign, and unquestionably Faiga's doing. Faiga was all right.

In that short vigil outside the bedroom door Shayna reached a momentous decision, and riding home on the bus she kept reviewing it. She left the wedding immediately after the yikhud, though the merrymaking would go on for hours; because Yossi's battalion was being rotated back from Sinai after six long weeks there, punctuated by rare weekend leaves. He had just missed the wedding, alas, but she was counting on a call from him, possibly tonight. Shayna had suffered agonies during the brief war, and now knew beyond doubt that she was lovesick, maddened with love for the paratrooper they called Don Kishote; and that it was time, more than time, to do something about it.

Shayna had managed their confrontation at the Falafel King as well as she could, though wretched with a cold and torn by jealousy and suspicion. Inexperienced as she was in such involvements, she was easily smart enough to realize that being casual and pleasant, while finding out all she could about the Gay Paree episode, was her best course after the way she had botched it. Yossi had not reassured her much with his stumblebum answers to her questions. She would never know, probably, what had gone on, but one thing she did know; she loathed Yael Luria, and had to regard her henceforth as a menace. The talk about Yael and Pasternak had never reached Shayna; the army and her little clique hardly intersected. All she knew was that Yael was beautiful, strong-willed, and liberated, and — unless instinct was grossly misleading her — a worrisome rival.

Perhaps in her secret heart Shayna had loved Kishote since she had met him as a little girl, when she had baited and snubbed him. She remembered her first laughable sight of him in split trousers; she remembered beating him with her fists when he showered himself with her pail of water, and feeling even then some inchoate attraction to him. She dated her conscious falling in love to the talk he had given at the university when he had spoken with such reticent emotion about Gulliver, and about the empty seats in the bus carrying the raiding party back to camp. That skinny immigrant boy of the Jerusalem siege had grown into a tall well-built soldier, the papers had carried the story of his exploit in the Mitla Pass, and he was *her* Yossi and nobody else's. Certainly not that Yael Luria's! In a word, Shayna wanted to get married.

There was something of a snag in that Don Kishote had not proposed. He had simply been seeing a lot of her. She had made it clear — perhaps a bit too clear, she now thought — that she wasn't ready for marriage, and anyway had her doubts about him because she was religious and meant to remain so, and he was a wild one; knowledgeable about the religion, but far from observant. In her fashion, actually, Shayna had herself always held to issur yikhud, with other young men as a matter of course, and with Kishote by laying down the law from the start. "B'seder, issur yikhud, no problem," he said, and what endearments she accepted occurred on evening walks or in his jeep, and relatively innocuous at that, though to Shayna all this had been new and deliciously shocking. To her religious set Shayna was a bold borderline trifler with the rules, but her own mind and conscience were clear. Love allowed for certain sweet freedoms, but issur yikhud was the uncrossable red line.

It therefore occurred to Shayna, as she mulled the matter over during the long ride home on the bus, that if she allowed herself to be alone with Yossi in a closed room, it would be the boldest of hints that she wanted him to propose. Really, it was the most a modest religious girl could do. Of course nothing would happen, any more than it had with Faiga and Fyvel, but he would surely get the idea. For Shayna decision meant action. When the telephone rang she sprang at it. He was calling from the apartment on Karl Netter Street, and after some greetings and sweet talk she said she wanted to come to see him there.

"Here? Why here?" he inquired, astonished. She had never yet visited his den of iniquity. "I'll come to Jerusalem."

"No, you must be exhausted, and you haven't got much time. I'll be there about seven o'clock. Don't argue, I'm going now to the sherut station."

Yossi hung up and said to his two paratrooper roommates, Shmuel and Amir, "Well, this is a new one. Shayna's coming here."

Shmuel, a very big Turkish Jew with a heavy black beard, was entangled at the moment on their broken-down sofa with his light of love, a hefty signal corps sergeant named Miriam. Amir was frying salami and eggs in the small kitchen, causing much smoke and pleasant smells. "Well, what do we do," said Amir, "make ourselves scarce?"

"No, no, on the contrary, you have to stay here. All of you."

He briefly explained issur yikhud. Shmuel had heard of it in his religious boyhood in Turkey, but to Amir, a Mapam kibbutznik, it was complete news, of a piece with all religious nonsense. Miriam said she was glad to know of it, and would have to remember it. When some of those fresh officers tried to take advantage of her, she would plead issur yikhud. She was sorry she had to get back to her barracks, because she would like to meet a girl who was that scrupulous. In Haifa, the free-thinking town where she grew up and where the busses ran on Saturdays, there was no way of finding out such things. Issur yikhud as a dodge certainly beat pleading the time of the month. It was less embarrassing.

Shmuel said, as he gave her a farewell hug and kiss, "Just so you don't try that issur yikhud on me."

"On you? What would work on you? A kitchen knife didn't."

"Well, that time I knew you were just being coy."

"A Turk is a Turk," said Miriam, and she left.

So when Shayna arrived at Karl Netter Street she found in the flat of sin not only her bespectacled hero but two other uniformed paratroopers, red boots and all, with whom he shared the place. Here was another snag. They both seemed strangely obtuse, sitting side by side on a decrepit sofa, making no move to leave and give her a chance to proceed with the scenario fixed in her mind: to wit yikhud, leading to some passionate but limited carrying on, and then down to serious business. She was annoyed with Yossi. Couldn't he have arranged privacy for this first rendezvous of theirs in his flat? He had greeted her with a decorous kiss, and now he too was just sitting in an armchair, looking browned and glorious, but oddly stupid.

The talk was halting and constrained. The huge black-bearded fellow asked if she had ever been to Turkey.

"No, I've never been outside Israel."

"I'm from Turkey. Beautiful country, Turkey. No place for a Jew, though."

Shayna knew that soldiers back from the front disliked to talk about the fighting, so that was no topic to start. Anyway, she had no desire to make conversation. She sat mum, looking around at the small dingy flat of evil usage, waiting for them to go away. What was the matter with them? They knew she was Yossi's girl!

"Would you like some salami and eggs?" Amir inquired.

She declined.

"I guess I'll make myself a salami sandwich," said Yossi, jumping up. He was baffled by Shayna's coming here, and yearned to take the lovely slender figure in his arms, but was at a loss how to proceed. When he was in the kitchen, Shayna, who had had quite enough of this, made an unmistakable gesture at the two paratroopers to clear out. The big blackbeard, who was only a foot or so from her chair, hissed softly, "What about issur yikhud?"

Staggered, Shayna hissed back, "In Turkey you observe it?"

"Well, some of us," hissed Shmuel.

"It's all superstition," said Amir in a natural tone.

"What's all superstition?" called Kishote from the kitchen.

"Nothing," said Shmuel, as Shayna repeated her emphatic thumb gesture of dismissal. He pulled up Amir by an elbow. "We're just leaving."

"Why?" Yossi put his head out of the kitchen. "Stick around! Please!"

But they were going through the door and closing it behind them. Thereupon Shayna went to him, threw her arms around his neck, and gave him one hell of a kiss; thinking even as she did it that Faiga could not have kissed Fyvel like this. But Fyvel was not Don Kishote, and she was not Faiga. For his part, Yossi reacted with battlefield quickness to the new state of things, ill though he understood it. When Yael had thrown herself at him in the Georges Cinq, that had been a surprise, but nothing too novel except that she was a colonel's girlfriend. But this was *Shayna,* all different, infinitely sweeter, and altogether a glimpse of a promised heaven. Before long Shayna strong-armed him off in a loving way. "All right, enough! Do you know I almost died worrying about you? I'm so proud of you! You look so handsome, so wonderful. You came home safe! The Holy One, blessed be He, answered my prayers."

This may have struck the wrong note. Yossi inquired, "Shall I open the door?"

"Oh, for heaven's sake, Yossi! Give me a salami sandwich. I want to talk to you. Seriously."

Walking into the gate of the Ramle air base, Shmuel and Amir met Yael Luria coming out. "Hello there!" she said. "So, your battalion's back? Where's Don Kishote?"

They looked at each other, and simultaneously Shmuel said, "I haven't the faintest idea," and Amir said, "We just left him in Karl Netter Street."

Yael looked at them with a twisted smile, quite used to the self-protective conspiracy of men. "Karl Netter Street, eh? Is he coming back to base tonight?"

Neither one answered. In the gloom of the gate, lit only by the sentry's lamp, Amir had received a nasty elbow dig from the Turk, who had no notion what Yael wanted of Kishote, but never told the truth to a woman about another man or indeed about anything, as a matter of Ottoman wisdom absorbed by osmosis.

"Well, thanks," she said. "Your battalion did wonders. All honor to you." She turned and went back to headquarters. More than two months had now passed, and Yael definitely had to have a word with Yossi. The creaky telephone system of Tel Aviv was overloaded with postwar calls of returning soldiers, and it was half an hour or so before she got past the busy signal of the whole area to a ring of the Karl Netter number.

"Hello, Yossi? It's Yael. Welcome back! Congratulations! Here at headquarters they say you performed wonders on the battlefield."

"Oh, hello there," said Yossi in a neutral tone, since Shayna was sitting near the telephone with an inquisitive look on her face. "Nice to hear from you."

"Yossi, I have to see you. We have to talk. It's rather urgent."

No doubt Yossi was being dense, but the probable reason for this call did not cross his mind. Yael was Colonel Pasternak's lady-love, as nearly everyone knew; a freakish, impulsive person, and for all he could guess she wanted to bask a bit in the glory of his battlefield wonders, or flirt with him, or who could say what?

"Why sure. I'll be in touch with you one of these days."

"Who is that?" inquired Shayna, who clearly heard feminine timbre in the receiver sounds.

"One of these days, *nothing!*" exclaimed Yael, and the receiver sang with the womanly resonance. "Tomorrow morning! Here at the base, or in your flat?"

"I said, *who is that?*"

Shayna's yikhud with Yossi had gone according to plan. She had really disarmed and won him. They weren't exactly engaged, because she said she wanted first to get the approval of her parents and Reb Shmuel; but she was already feeling proprietary, and losing no time in asserting it. As for Yossi, he was deeply smitten with her, knew there was no way to bed down with her except in marriage, and powerfully desired her — certainly at the moment! Also, he was beginning to wish for kids. So, let it be Shayna. She was by far the best ever, and she had yielded him all of her virtue she was going to yield before a wedding, that was as sure as sunrise. He put his hand over the receiver. "Oh, you know, just one of those girls. Sorry about this."

Shayna's response was a fierce frown and a stern head shake.

"Yossi, are you there? Have you hung up on me? Don't you *dare!*"

"I'm here, I'm here. Sorry. I'm going back to the base tonight."

"Then I'll see you at the Falafel King at seven in the morning. You hear? *Be there.*"

Shayna said, "What on earth is that *shmata* [rag] going on and on about? Just hang up. You're finished with all that."

"Okay," said Yossi, which served as a response to both of them, and he did hang up. Shayna turned loving again, and some time passed before she declared she had to go home. He walked with her through the crooked streets of old downtown Tel Aviv, both of them vibrant with the afterglow of advanced intimacy. At the sherut station they kissed before she got into the jitney.

"No more shmatas," was her whispered final word. "I'm yours and you're mine, and that's that."

"No more shmatas," said Don Kishote, and he walked back to Karl Netter Street in a fog of excited happiness. He had never experienced such adoration for a girl as had flooded him upon modest Shayna's yielding; well, semi-yielding. Life was just beginning. Victory, perhaps a decoration, and Shayna!

21

The Shmata

The coffee in the Falafel King's open café was not bad, but the cakes tended to be old and not wholly free of Ramle's ever-floating dust. Yossi was there on the stroke of seven, the military habit in his bones, and he ate two of these while waiting, warmed by a strong morning sun, for Yael to show up. That she was late did not surprise him; a woman officer, and a spoiled one at that, the colonel's pet. Planes practicing landings roared into the base and roared off, trucks full of soldiers came and went through the sentry gate, and the small café became crowded while Kishote sat washing down dusty cake with coffee and thinking not about Yael at all, but about Shayna.

She had taken his position by storm, and good for her! He had fallen for her months ago and had gotten pretty involved, no argument, but in his happy-go-lucky way he had counted on her standoffishness to keep the matter indefinitely on hold. In a flash she had changed all that. Well, so be it. Time to jump. It had to come, sooner or later. Kfotze, Kishote! She wasn't the prettiest girl he knew, not even as pretty as some he had fooled with, by no means as striking as Yael Luria; slight, dark, her face a bit sharp and her fresh smooth skin, maybe because she was so young, not entirely clear. Beautiful hair, deep eyes that could flare with controlled passion, quick brain, and a radiant enchantment about her beyond resistance, at least for him. She would make a great mother, character like rock. They had talked about children, and he had not opposed her flat ruling that their upbringing would be extremely religious. Kishote liked the religion, and thought kids should have it. What they did about it afterward, as in his own case, was their business. He had left that cavil unstated to Shayna.

"Sorry, sorry, sorry! Big rush, big mess." Yael bustled into the café, every blond hair in place, her uniform crisp, her color natural and high. "Can't stay, either."

"No? Have a cup of coffee, at least."

"Well. . . ." She stepped to the counter, and the King, a fat greasy man in an apron and a cardboard hat, served her with deference ahead of others waiting. "Not a mark on you," she said, dropping beside him, "after all you went through!"

"Yael, what's up? What can I do for you?"

She glanced at tables within earshot, full of chattering young soldiers. With a strange laugh she said, "How do you think I look?"

"As usual, a knockout."

"Do I? Thanks. I feel — well, I've never felt exactly like this. Kind of marvellous, and kind of horrible." She sipped coffee and looked around again. "Oh, this is impossible, this was a mistake. Anyway there's no time. Is your battalion on duty, on reserve, what?"

"Three days off duty, then back on reserve."

"Can I meet you down at Karl Netter Street? Say this afternoon? Say three o'clock?"

"Why? What's it all about?"

"Well, hamood —" She put her hand on his.

Honk, honk, honk! At the wheel of an army car, Sam Pasternak was hitting the horn. "Where are the charts," he shouted at her, "and what to all the devils are you doing out here? Hello, Kishote."

"Everything's about ready, sir," she called back. "Just the last map, Uri is going over it, and —"

"*About* ready? You get in here! I meet the Prime Minister in an hour."

"Karl Netter Street at three o'clock," she murmured, "don't fail me," and she hurried to the car.

At this point Yossi might well have guessed what was afoot, had he been less preoccupied with Shayna's bombshell. But maybe not. To him, Yael was Yael, Benny Luria's high-flying sister, an old story. They had had a few laughs in Paris and a z'beng v'gamarnu, a fleeting toss. After Mitla Pass and Sharm el Sheikh, the Georges Cinq Hotel was faded nonsense. The question was, how about next month's rent on Karl Netter Street? Amir and Shmuel couldn't keep the flat unless he paid his share, but Shayna had laid down the law: goodbye to Karl Netter Street! Serious decision.

Pasternak was confronting a different Ben Gurion: gone the buoyancy, the confidence, the smile of victory. The faces of Dayan, Golda Meir, and their aides around the table all reflected the Old Man's somber mien. As Yael set up the charts of Sinai on a rack, Pasternak was thinking of the Friday afternoon in the Tel Aviv Museum when Ben Gurion had read the Declaration of the State to crowded rows of Zionist leaders. This was how he had looked then: resolved, defiant, grave.

And then and there the State had been born in balagan! When he finished the reading the musicians had missed their cue to strike up "Hatikvah," so the Old Man started it solo, the audience laggardly joined in, and then the orchestra straggled along, in a mighty discordant send-off to the Jewish State. Afterward Sam had joined the young people dancing in the streets, but that sober Ben Gurion expression had stayed with him. Here it was again, and in a way the whole enterprise, for good or ill, was still a B.G. solo, with a discordant chorus trying to follow him.

"Why four charts?" inquired Ben Gurion, who noticed everything. "Three withdrawal proposals, we decided."

After weeks of skillful delaying tactics by Abba Eban, Israel's ambassador to Washington, the Israeli government was at last, under implacable pressure from the Americans, coming forward with maps specifying possible stages of withdrawal from Sinai.

Golda Meir said, "Moshe Dayan and I asked for another one."

"We just finished it up this morning," said Pasternak. "It's not too detailed."

"To what purpose?" Ben Gurion asked Golda.

She looked to Moshe Dayan. "Longer withdrawal time, Prime Minister." Dayan too was less than his forceful self. "Longer interval before withdrawals begin."

Ben Gurion sighed. "Wasted effort."

"Who knows?" said Dayan. "Every day brings something new. The longer we can hold on, the more options may open up."

"If there were any justice," said Golda Meir, "there would be no discussion of withdrawal at all without linkage to peace."

"*Yoisher* [Justice]?" Ben Gurion spoke the old Yiddish word with vibrant overtones of ghetto wisdom, sadness, and mockery. "Yoisher she wants? From the Oom [UN]? So, Sam, let's hear the plans."

Pasternak took up his pointer and began with the minimum proposal meant for negotiating purposes; it had little chance of acceptance, but would test the pressure. The room for maneuver was already narrow. The very day after his triumphant speech, Ben Gurion had utterly caved in to Eisenhower's angry threats that his newly reelected administration was prepared to support UN sanctions against Israel, going as far as blockade; and that if Ben Gurion still persisted in his unrealistic intransigence, and the Soviet Union took military action against Israel, the United States would not intervene!

Chris Cunningham had called the turn, Pasternak realized, the American shield was down; and B.G. too had swiftly and sadly come to that recognition. His cabinet had accepted at once and publicly the principle of total withdrawal from Sinai, as soon as arrangements with a UN peacekeeping force could be worked out; the same basis on which the French and British were exiting Suez with their tails between their legs.

So what was left was playing for time, for assurances that the fedayeen would not return, above all for guarantees that the Straits of Tiran would remain open for Israeli shipping. Since then Pasternak had been working on various maps, stages, and time frames for getting the army out of Sinai, an action not unlike pulling a hand out of a basket of fishhooks. The last hook was Sharm el Sheikh. All the plans called for staying there to the final moment.

"The American Jews failed us," Golda Meir remarked as Yael was changing charts on the rack. "Where were they? He carried New York by the biggest vote ever!"

"They have no conception of our strategic realities," said Dayan. "Most of them don't know where the Sinai is. That's a fact we live with."

Hours later, when Pasternak had answered multitudinous questions on the four plans, and the air was thick with smoke, Ben Gurion said wearily, rubbing his hands over his face, and looking around with reddened eyes, "This withdrawal, made by us in good faith, will pay large dividends one day. Now it's painful. We've been through other painful times. We have the best soldiers in the world. We've shown that, and it won't be forgotten by anyone."

"I received yesterday," Moshe Dayan put in, "a copy of an article by the British expert Liddell Hart on our campaign. He calls it *'a classic of the military art.'*"

The Prime Minister nodded, with a melancholy smile. "That's very nice. And true. But this little country can't defy the two superpowers. Look you, France and England couldn't." He turned his palms upward in a gesture of resignation. "Zeh mah she'yaish. Now. Who takes these plans to New York?"

"Sam should go. Nobody else," said Golda.

"I want Sam here," Moshe Dayan rapped out.

"Then detach Zev Barak for this mission," Pasternak said. "That's my recommendation. I'll put him in the picture."

Ben Gurion looked at Moshe Dayan, who nodded, then at Golda. She shrugged. "I don't know Lieutenant Colonel Barak that well. If Moshe says so, all right."

"Wolfgang's b'seder," said the Prime Minister. "I know him. So. Sam you send him to New York with that stuff, and while he's over there, he can take some private messages of mine to Washington."

Yael drove Pasternak back to the Ramle base. They had had to talk about the briefing on the way over, so he had not used his regular driver. After starting out in a long glum silence she said, not looking at him, "So KADESH was all for nothing! Hundred-Hours War, hah? Classic of the military art, hah? Round-trip to Sinai, in and out."

"Don't talk foolishly. Nasser broke the armistice terms when he blocked the Straits of Tiran, but the UN did nothing, and the Americans did nothing. They thought we didn't matter. Israel just wasn't there on the map. No problem! But now a UN force will take station in Suez, Sinai, and Gaza, so that'll prevent fedayeen raids. And the straits will remain open with American guarantees."

"For how long?"

"Who can tell? The main thing," he added through his teeth, "Israel is on the map now."

"You're making the best of a rotten deal."

"Exactly."

"Can you spare me for a couple of hours this afternoon?"

"Today? When we're so jammed up? No."

She turned to look him in the eye. "You mean yes."

"What for?"

"Things."

He did not answer. When she glanced at him again, he sourly nodded.

At the Karl Netter flat, where he arrived early to pay the back rent and clear out rubbish, Yossi fell to wondering at last just what the devil Yael Luria could want of him. He was waiting to hear from Shayna, and trying in vain to get through to her in Jerusalem. Meantime, here was Yael on the way. The real reason actually did cross his mind, but it seemed preposterous. First of all, in that dimming z'beng v'gamarnu in Paris, Yael herself had assured him as they dove into bed that there was no risk. He had inquired with a look and a gesture. She had laughingly whispered, "*Zeh b'seder* [It's okay]." But if by chance that actually was her fix, well, Sam Pasternak had to be the lucky or unlucky guy — depending on the viewpoint — in the way of nature and on the law of averages. No? Yael knew that as well as he. She would hardly try such a farfetched bluff on him. So what was she after? Nothing to do but wait and see, and meantime try Shayna's number again.

Yael meantime doffed her uniform and put on a pretty pink dress for the visit to Karl Netter Street, after showering and making up with care. This was serious business, handling Don Kishote, and it required looking peachy. *Les jeux sont faits,* as the French would say. The chips were down. Yael had given much thought to her options, and they were three, or possibly four. At 2 A.M. of a sleepless night, she had listed and rated them in her methodical fashion, and then torn the paper to scraps.

1. Abortion. Absolutely out, I will have this baby!
2. Marry Kishote. Best alternative by far. A first-class soldier, smart enough under the crazy streak, and that's already fading down as he advances in the army and matures. Not my type, God knows, but he has a future, at least. And anyway he's my baby's father!
3. Try to force things with Sam. Hopeless. I'll lose. Carrying another man's baby, I'm in a bad, bad position. Got myself into a trap. Zeh mah she'yaish. Bye-bye, poor Sam! But he's had this coming to him long enough. Enjoy your Ruthie, Sam!
4. Other guys? Jacob? Ariel? Ron? Desperation, only if all else fails.

Such was Yael's hardheaded appraisal of her fix. Left out, however, was the least foreseen aspect of it. In the doctor's office when all doubts had been resolved, and she knew, an astounding thrill of happiness had shot through her turmoil and trouble. Words unspoken had resounded in her soul like brave music. *I am a woman!*

At a wedding in the moshav, long ago, the itinerant rabbi had once talked about a Bible figure, maybe Lot or Lamech, who had two wives, one for pleasure and one for childbearing. On hearing this Yael had decided, with the cynicism of sixteen, that *she* would be the pleasure wife, but by now she had come to have a fierce craving to be the other kind. Don Kishote had opened for her that door of life, and she meant to drag him through it with her, whether by allure or by force of will.

He greeted her with his usual puckish grin, shoving his glasses up on his nose. "Hey, you look nice, Yael. Different."

"You mean, not in uniform."

"Why, you look swell in uniform, too, but that's a nice dress. Come in, come into the old pigsty."

She hoped that when she stepped into the flat, invitingly close to him, he would take her in his arms. They stood toe to toe but it didn't happen. "Can I offer you something? A cold drink? There's orange soda."

"No thanks."

"Tea?"

"Well . . . a cup of tea, why not?"

He went into the kitchen and began clattering and banging. Wrong move, she thought. Bad move. He was saying, "I never know where those guys put anything. We do have tea bags, I swear, I bought them myself —"

"Oh, never mind the tea." She came to the kitchen door.

"You want tea, you'll have tea. Look, here's crackers. No. All moldy. Those guys —"

"Yossi, I'm pregnant."

That stopped the fuss and the chatter. It stopped Don Kishote in his tracks. He peered at her and pushed up the glasses.

"You are?"

"I am."

"Well! Mazel tov."

"Thanks. Mazel tov to you, too, dear. You're the baby's father."

They stared at each other through the kitchen door. Second chance for him to take her in his arms. He did nothing of the kind. Yael had a qualm of doubt. Should she have worn the dress, after all? Had it alarmed him, put him on his guard? He was used to her in uniform. Don Kishote came out of the kitchen, took her elbow, and led her to the sofa. Ah, this might be more like it — but he only said, "Sit down, Yael," with a little push, and sat well clear of her.

"Look, don't be so solicitous," she laughed. "I'm in great shape and it's only been a couple of months."

He took his time to respond, looking intently at her. "How do you know, Yael?"

"How do I know *what*?" Despite herself she turned testy. "That I'm pregnant? The angel Gabriel came to me in a dream, announced it, and told me to call him Emmanuel!" Then, more lightly, with an effort, "Simple, dear, I missed two periods, and took a test, and that's it. I'm pregnant."

"Don't be angry, Yael."

"I'm not in the least angry."

"What I meant was — now you said you're not angry — how do you know it's me?"

She bit her lip, and hoped she hadn't bitten it through. It hurt terribly, and she tasted blood. "What do you mean? I *know*."

"Now, you say you're not angry."

"I'm not, I'm not angry, Yossi, for God's sake. Go ahead! Say what's on your mind. We have to be honest with each other."

"You're talking about the Georges Cinq Hotel."

"What else?" She produced a merry chuckle. *(Keep it light, Yael!)* "The French whore, remember?"

"Sure, and I remember you said, 'Zeh b'seder.' "

"Did I say that?" An innocent blink of big eyes.

"You did."

"Zeh b'seder?"

"Those were your words."

"Well, all right, I suppose I thought so, then. My mistake." She smiled. "But I'm *happy* about this baby, Kishote, and what's done is done."

"You truly aren't angry, Yael?"

"Why should I be?"

Kishote hesitated, but there was no other way, he had to come out with it. "Then just tell me this. What about Sam Pasternak?" Her answer was a cold dangerous stare. He bumbled on, "I mean, how can you be so positive?"

Yael jumped up. "Oh, what a mess! I'm not going to cry, I'm not!" She rapidly paced around the room, her hips swinging in a way Kishote thought fantastically exciting, though she wasn't trying for this particular effect at all. "But *you're* the father, and I'm going to have this baby, and what are we going to do about it?"

She came over to him, and Yossi too was on his feet. Once more they were toe to toe. Her tone softened. "As for Sam, that's been over between us for months. Don't ask me why. It has. This is nothing I'd lie about, surely you must know that. I'm absolutely certain, Don Kishote. It's you." She looked up at him, putting all the allure she had into her eyes and her voice. "You said I was a goddess. That was why it happened. And now? Am I so utterly repulsive to you?"

"Repulsive? God, Yael —" He took her in his arms, no help for it. The telephone rang. It was on a small table right beside them, and he picked it up. "Hello?"

"Yossi, it's all right!" Shayna's voice rang with jubilation. "Mama and Papa are happy, and Reb Shmuel says our children will be great men in Israel! Yossi? Hello? Yossi?"

Yael made an exaggerated face and stepped away from him. She heard the tones, though not the words. It was not hard to guess who was on the line. Kishote made a feeble gesture at her, a mere noncommittal wave.

"Well, what's the matter?" inquired Shayna.

"Nothing at all. That's great," he said. "Really great."

"You sound funny, Yossi. And not very happy, or am I crazy?"

"Of course I'm happy. Why shouldn't I be? That's great."

"Yossi," said Shayna, her voice hardening, her instinct almost infallible. "You've got a shmata there with you. Haven't you? How dare you!"

"What makes you say that? There's nobody here."

"That's good. Then when can I see you? Can you come to Jerusalem now?"

"To Jerusalem? Now?"

Yael was pacing, her hips sinuously swaying. She stage-whispered, "No! We have to talk."

It was a bit too loud, and Shayna was too alert. "Who was that? Yossi, I heard that shmata! You throw her out, do you hear? Throw out that shmata *now*! I'll hold the line."

The repeated word "shmata" came through the buzzing of the receiver, and Yael flared, though still whispering, "Who's she calling a shmata! The mother of your child? Let me talk to her!"

"Darling, there's somebody at the door," said Yossi. "I'll have to call you back."

"There's *nobody* at the door. There's a shmata in your flat, and if you ever want to see me again, tell her to leave!"

Yossi pounded his fist on the wall. "It must be the landlord. Our rent's overdue. He's breaking down the door, Shayna! I swear I'll call you right back."

"Yossi —"

He hung up, and faced into Yael Luria's infuriated glare. She was radiantly beautiful, a wrathful goddess indeed. "That's more like it, and you're *not* calling her back. Not until we've talked all this out. Maybe not then."

But Yossi had had enough. "You don't love me, Yael. Whatever's going on between you at the moment, you love Sam Pasternak. You're his woman."

"I have been. I'm not denying that."

"I love Shayna Matisdorf. She's my woman, and I mean to marry her."

"Shayna wouldn't go with you to Paris, Don Kishote. I did."

The towers of Manhattan, spiking up through dirty haze as the plane descended, brought to Barak's mind his last arrival in New York. He decided at that moment to visit Marcus's grave. There was time, he had three days in all, plenty for this wretched UN errand. Visiting Marcus would at least be a mitzvah, a good deed, however sad.

The long, long hours on the plane had dragged by like one interminable hour of 3 A.M. thoughts, as he studied the different withdrawal plans and charts to keep them distinct in his mind. The woman beside him was an overperfumed dumpy sort in her fifties, leafing through fashion magazines when she wasn't sleeping or eating, not likely to peek at blurry Hebrew mimeographing. Withdraw, withdraw, withdraw; that brilliant victory, the terrific march of the Ninth to Sharm, which now reverberated in his memory, like his advance over the Roman road in 1948, as a brief burst of glorious hours balancing and justifying long plodding years in uniform; and now this crawl-out! Dog leash again, this time with choke chain. Obey, or suffocate.

During the next two days the working sessions with Israel's UN delegation were a bitter business, the morning-after headache from the brief intoxication of victory. It was a wretched change from life in the field with his brigade, another damnable courier job, a fate that seemed to pursue him. He was glad to escape on the second day, in a train bowling along the majestic Hudson through a misty landscape, the autumn colors all faded to brown. The West Point graveyard with its well-tended grass and stands of firs was still green. As he passed through the rows of markers he saw one thin army officer standing with folded arms and bent head far from Marcus's grave. Otherwise the cemetery was deserted. At Marcus's stone he recited a halting half-remembered *Ayl molay* (prayer for the dead), then on an impulse began to whisper, his eyes moistening:

"Situation report, Colonel Stone. We're a lot better off than we were when you died. We won the Negev, and some vital ground in the center and around Jerusalem. You'd be amazed the way the country's built up. The population's more than doubled. We never took Latrun, so the highway runs around it. But we've just won a big victory, we conquered the whole Sinai, though the politics won't let us keep it. Anyway, the beachhead is holding. So rest well, Mickey, and —"

Footsteps on gravel. He fell silent, brushing fingers at his eyes. The footsteps halted, approached, halted again. Barak stood with bowed head for long moments, then looked around. The officer was a major, dark-haired and athletic-looking, with a round friendly face. "Colonel Marcus, eh? You knew him?"

"Very well."

"You're from Israel?"

Barak was wearing civilian clothes to be inconspicuous on this trip. He held out his hand. "Zev Barak. Israel Defense Force."

"John Smith." The officer faintly smiled as they shook hands. "That's my real name."

"Why shouldn't it be?"

"Well, it's so common here people make jokes about it." He gestured toward a car parked in the distance. "I saw you come in a taxi. I can give you a lift. Not all the way to New York, I'm heading for Washington."

"That's where I'm going now, Washington, but I'm figuring on flying."

"Come along." They started to walk side by side. "Like to talk to you about your Sinai campaign. My war is Korea. Certain parallels. Military brilliance, political washout."

"How long is the drive?"

"Five or six hours. By the time you get to the airport, and catch your plane, and fly in this weather, you won't do much better."

The parallel of Korea and Sinai had never occurred to Barak. It interested him, and Major Smith had a pleasant no-nonsense manner. "Well, I accept. Many thanks."

Barak's reminiscences of Marcus intrigued the American, especially the account of the "Burma Road." He had never heard of it, and the use of the name made him smile and nod. Thereafter the drive went by in searching comparisons of experiences in Korea and Sinai. In Korea even mighty America had been brought up short, so Major Smith maintained, on a political dog leash. MacArthur could have won the war. UN and home-front politics had stopped him, and eventually gotten him fired. Smith drove at high speed with skill. He was in armor and wanted nothing else, he said. Using force internationally these days meant moving armor, Sinai had once more shown that. He got Barak to describe the Ninth Brigade's operation at length.

"Very impressive, like the Jap march down Malaya to Singapore," he observed. "Surprise via an overland route considered impassable."

"Well, but in three days, not seventy."

"Your theater of operations is small. Like your 'Burma Road.' A few miles instead of seven hundred miles, but the same idea. The principles of war don't change." By this time they had passed Baltimore and were approaching Washington. "Now Barak, can I ask you a frank question?"

"Why not?"

Smith's tone changed; dry and careful, just short of hostile. "You Jews say you've returned to your homeland. You claim you were there before the Arabs. Suppose the American Indians raised a claim that they were here first and wanted it all back? What then?"

Such talk was not new to Barak. He too changed tone, deliberate and cool. "Two answers. If they had the force to take it back, they would, and the world would probably marvel and approve. But that's too hypothetical, like your question, and it's not the real answer. After what has happened to my people, we need a state of our own, strong enough to make sure that nothing like it will ever happen again. So we've gone back to where we came from. Where else?"

"There are eighty million Arabs. Eight hundred million Moslems. They don't want you there, don't believe you belong there. Think you can hack it in the long run?"

"We're trying. It's our one shot left. *'No choice'* is a good motive."

Smith nodded, his face impassive, and they did not speak for a while. He was driving to a house in McLean not far from where the Cunninghams lived, staying there with a married brother in army intelligence, while seeking a bachelor flat in Washington. Just back from duty in Germany, he had lectured that day at West Point on Soviet armor, before visiting the grave of his academy roommate killed in Korea.

Pasternak had ordered Barak to telephone Cunningham and see him if possible, so the CIA man was expecting him. Over the phone the father had not mentioned Emily, and Barak had not asked about her, though among his dark airplane thoughts he had wryly wondered whether the girl had willed him into making this trip, with her marvellous occult powers. As it turned out, she wasn't there; still in Paris, not returning until January, and her mother was with her. In the foyer of the house a large oil painting of Emily pleasantly jolted Barak.

"Who's that?" inquired Major Smith on the way out. Cunningham had invited him in for a drink.

"My daughter. Bad likeness, painted by a girlfriend in college."

"Looks like a girl who turned me down when I graduated from West Point. Sue Funston."

"No relation," said Cunningham. When Smith left, Cunningham asked Barak what he thought of the man.

"Well, on that long drive we talked a lot. He's a smart professional. Why do you ask?"

"I know him. He's going places in the army."

"Well, I'll say this, he's not sympathetic to Israel."

"The army isn't. Or hasn't been, I should say. That may

change." Chris Cunningham did not elaborate. He liked to deliver enigmatic pronouncements, and Barak let it go at that. With a rare smile, Cunningham rapped a knuckle on the portrait. "Barak, her mother believes you rescued Em from that little fat Frenchman. We're in your debt."

They had cocktails in a glass-enclosed porch full of potted greenery. "Crazy end to the war, that was," said Cunningham as he quaffed a large martini while Barak sipped sherry, "and it's a damned good thing your Mr. Ben Gurion backed off from that light-headed victory speech of his. You people were on the brink of an abyss, Barak. Did you realize it? Eisenhower was fit to be tied. The Russians had snookered him with the rocket-rattling, and hogged the credit for stopping the war, whereas it was he and Dulles who stopped it, of course. Squelched the French and British, made you quit, and saved Nasser's bacon."

"Well, Chris, the Russians did threaten to flatten us in twenty-four hours if we didn't stop. That wasn't pleasant."

"Noise. And now they're making noise about your withdrawing. But you'll withdraw because Ike threatens sanctions and means it." He finished his drink and stood up. "Let's have a bite to eat. I tell you though, there's another side to Ike, if that's any comfort. He's a warrior. He'll understand that he's forcing you to sacrifice a victory you won fair and square, and he'll probably remember it."

When Barak met again with Abba Eban in New York before flying home — Eban had a dual job as Israel's ambassador in Washington and UN representative — he ventured to quote these views of "an astute friendly CIA man," as he put it. The tall highly intellectual Abba Eban was an unlikely but ideal Israeli diplomat, Barak thought, for the UN post; speaking better English than the British representative, expressing his sharp points in mellifluous flawless sentences, the embodiment of what Americans called an egghead, complete to his almost perfectly oval head. Eban listened to him with a magisterial smile, now and then nodding. "We shall gradually withdraw, of course," he commented. "En brera! And under American, not Russian, pressure. That is true. But we shall emerge with substantial gains, after very difficult parleying for which I shall be responsible. I believe we shall put a long quietus to the fedayeen raids from Gaza and Sinai. We shall obtain an American guarantee of free passage through the Straits of Tiran, our main casus belli. And the menace of a combined attack of Arab armies on us will be lifted for a term of years, perhaps as long as ten. That too is victory, or victory enough, shall I say, in our constrained circumstances."

*   *   *

Sharm el Sheikh, March 1957, four months after the end of the war. Troops and vehicles of the last Yoffe battalion to leave the base are lined up in formal array on the parade ground in blazing sunshine. Opposite them, the battalion of incoming Egyptian troops in almost a mirror formation. Band music, shouted orders.

"Why, Abba? Why do we have to give it back?" Noah's voice, choking with anger. "We won the war."

Barak is not in charge of the ceremony. That is the battalion commander's mournful task. He has come to observe as a senior officer of the Ninth Brigade, and Yoffe has granted him permission to bring Noah and his scout troop. Though the youngsters know what they are about to witness, they are staring with shocked faces as the Star of David flag comes down, and the Egyptian soldiers spring to hoist their green banner with white crescent and stars. Barak looks at his son, whose face is set in a peculiarly hard grown-up expression.

"Why, Abba?" he repeats. "Why, when we beat them?"

"We're doing it for peace, Noah."

"But they hate us. Look at them."

The faces of the Egyptians, to be sure, wear unfriendly grins of triumph.

"That may change in time."

A soldier walks past them carrying the folded blue-and-white flag.

"We'll get it back, you'll see." Noah sets his little jaw and lifts his head, looking around at the base, the cliffs, and the sparkling blue waters. "*I'll* get it back."

PART THREE

Missions to America

22

Emily's Letters

After the Suez fiasco, Great Britain and France were no longer serious players in the Middle East, and Israel was tarred as their co-conspirator in a failed last gasp of imperialism. Colonel Nasser, on the other hand, gained immense prestige as a giant-killer. For had he not seized the Suez Canal, defied the two great colonial empires, weathered the storm, and brought them down? Riding high, Nasser launched a confederation of Syria and Egypt called the United Arab Republic, proclaiming it as his first step toward creating and leading a strong bloc of all the Arab nations. American planners perforce turned to wooing him, but he showed much smiling skill in remaining noncommittal while accepting the largesse of both superpowers; from the Americans economic aid, from the Russians massive new weaponry.

Israel meantime was left once more with the haunting problem of military supply. France was in deep political turmoil, and a cutoff sooner or later of that source had to be reckoned with. Certain British munitions could be had in controlled quantities, strictly for cash on the barrelhead. As for the U.S.A., some army strategists saw in Israel's "classic of the military art" a new factor in the region, a possible offset to Nasser should he tilt all the way to the Soviets. The notion of using a million Jews, however, as a counterpoise to the hero of eighty million Arabs made slow headway. By and large the State Department and the Pentagon hewed to the old British policy in the Middle East: firm ties with the Arabs and a cool shoulder to Israel.

After some two years of this ongoing problem, Zev Barak, a rising armor commander, wrote Christian Cunningham for a confidential appraisal of a possible change in American policy regarding tanks for the Jewish State. The CIA man was slow in replying. When Barak opened the thick envelope that at last arrived, a scrawl on yellow ruled paper in Emily's writing fell out of the wad of Cunningham's typed pages. Barak read her letter first, shaking his head over it and smiling.

> Foxdale School
> Middleburg, Va.
> Sept. 15, 1958

Dear Wolf Lightning —

Hi! Voice from the past! I don't think of myself as a sneaky sort, but this is pretty damn sneaky, tucking a billet-doux of mine into my father's letter to you. He gave me the letter to mail and it wasn't sealed too well. On impulse I pried it open — didn't read it, of course — and am hastily scratching off these unpremeditated and no doubt dopey words. I just can't help it. I've ached to write to you for well over a year. When I think I missed your flying visit after the war when you brought Jack Smith to the house, I grind my teeth with frustration.

The thing is, I don't know whether Nakhama can read English, though she can hardly say ten words in it. If I were your wife I sure as hell would be inquisitive about a letter arriving from America addressed in a feminine (sort of) hand! I should have thought long ago of using Dad's stationery and typing an address, but as I say I'm really not the sneaky sort. It never occurred to me. So if Nakhama opens your mail (which I kind of doubt) and sees this, folded inside Dad's impeccably typed pages, you've got a problem. But not much of one, and I have a very bad problem being utterly cut off from you. So I'm taking this chance. If I embarrass you send me a short snarl or ignore me and that'll be that. I'll wait. I'll wait until you come here again or our paths cross in your country or in Europe or for all I know in Madagascar. It will happen.

All right, now that I've done this fell deed what can I say to you?

I'll just let 'er rip. For me there's been one event in my meager life in the past couple of years, Wolf, *mon vieux* — one event — your kissing me in that dingy room in the King David Hotel. Before it I had a dishevelled random existence and a small craziness about an Israeli army man I glimpsed as a girl of twelve. Since then I've been your *"yotze dofen"* (is that nearly right?), untimely ripped and getting through the days with one poignant life-nourishing memory.

There's nothing either of us can do about it. *How well I know that!* Perhaps come to think of it you've done more than you realize, by providing me with a way out of this cul-de-sac, if I want out. Guess what? Major Jack Smith has become a beau! Or a suitor, or a swain, or anything you please except boyfriend. I've never had a boyfriend unless you count old Hiroshima, who by the way continues to write me long letters in exquisite French enclosing fine poems. (Although he now lives with another poet, an Indian from Trinidad, who I gather is *his* boyfriend. Modern times.) I keep up the correspondence, André was and is delightful, very funny when he's in the mood and an absolute mandarin about literature, and in his way he goes on loving me. It's nice to be loved. I hope you agree with that simple proposition.

It's quite unlikely I'd have come to know Major Smith if you hadn't delivered him to my doorstep, as it were. I've never met his older brother who lives near here. Jack stayed with him only a week or two before moving into digs in Arlington. But thanks to you Jack saw that portrait of me in the foyer that Hester Laroche painted (she was for a long time — chastely but passionately — my girlfriend), and it reminded him of his girl who got away. He's been paying me rather prim low-key court ever since. I think the girl who got away damaged his spirit for romance. He's no Hiroshima for ineffectuality, but truly girl-shy, and that's strange because Dad reports he's regarded in the army as a fireball.

There's no way I could love Jack, amiable and manly as he is. For concerts, theater, tennis, horseback, and such he's just great, and he's a good dancer, too. I've never danced much before. I date very little. Most guys are nuisances. As for you and me, these things at bottom make no sense, I daresay, but I've pretty well puzzled it out so far as one can. It's all one-sided, obviously, except for an eerie and possibly wishful sense I have that it won't always be.

You were the first Israeli I ever laid eyes on or talked to. You correspond with Dad, so I'm sure you've sized him up by now. He's a Jekyll and Hyde, a tough brilliant intelligence man, totally down-to-earth and infinitely skeptical, suspicious, and cynical, with an obsession about the Soviet Union. He is also a religious visionary who some people would consider a nut, his ideas are so fundamentalist and millenarian. What my comparative religion prof used to call "chiliastic." Dad thinks we're in the Latter Days, and that the return of the Jews to the Holy Land is the Sign, the Hope. He is wholly mystical about the way the Jews have risen from the ashes of Auschwitz and marched back to Jerusalem as Joshua's warriors reborn. There's nothing in history to match it, he maintains, nothing natural about it, it's the religious turn in world affairs called forth by the nuclear age. Those views aren't in his intelligence estimates of course, but that's the man. It's what I've been hearing ever since Israel was founded.

And on the famous night of the fireflies, there you were; also Major Pasternak, but I saw only you with your bent arm, invested with all the glory and glamor of my father's visions. That was before you spoke a word. Then when you talked up to him at the table, and after that when we had that conversation on the terrace — which I could write out to this day, word for word — I was hooked, or more exactly transfixed, shot through with Cupid's arrow, a poor skinny nothing of a mouthy little twelve-year-old.

Now, what do I want of you?

Just to correspond. Okay? Do you believe me? Hester Laroche went back to Oregon after college, married a local banker's son, and already has two children, but we still write to each other at least once a week, sometimes more often. I'm her secret life while she goes on with what's expected of her in her hometown, and what on the whole she enjoys and is happy with. Not much talk of Mahler or Laura Riding or John Donne (we used to read Donne aloud to each other, sweet thunder that is!) or Plutarch, who we discovered together is endlessly deep, wise, and entertaining. We tell each other small things too about dresses and cooking and the weather and what's blooming in the gardens. It's lovely. A letter arriving from Hester brightens my day.

Can't we try to do that, Wolf? Is there anything harmful in it? You may not have much to write about to me, but I'm dying to write to you. I seem to be going nowhere with Jack Smith, but soon or late I know I'll do just what Hester has done, find some guy who'll do. Meantime I'm in no hurry at all. I love the girls at Foxdale and I love my work there. It's an enchanting place. If you answer and we start to write I'll tell you about it. I just want to know that you're there. I'm here.

Love,
Emily Cunningham

Same hurried almost vertical hand, *t*'s uncrossed and letters skipped, yet quite clear, with generous wide curves of the loops. The girl's claim that one kiss in a hotel room was a watershed in her life struck him as affected, a bit laughable, and a bit sad. By this time Emily was far from his thoughts, though he had never entirely forgotten her. A year and a half of intense army reorganization and field exercises based on the lessons of the Sinai campaign, the press of family matters — the move to a larger flat, the illnesses and schooling of the children, a failed pregnancy of Nakhama's, Michael's troubled courtship of his irreligious Lena — and the border incidents and internal political shenanigans that filled the days in Israel: all these things had long since eclipsed the strange moods and incidents of the faded KADESH time.

"What's funny, Abba?" Noah popped into the tiny back room Barak used as an office, and found him still smiling.

"Oh, nothing. Comical letter from a friend in America."

"Here's another reason to smile, then. I've been accepted in the Reale School."

The father jumped up and hugged the boy, who had grown a foot since his bar mitzvah and now had the suspicion of a mustache. His face was changing too. The Berkowitz bones were beginning to show through Nakhama's oval soft features; lengthening jaw, deepening eye sockets, and the brown eyes looking wiser, yet with a new touch of adolescent shyness. The Haifa premilitary academy was the best in Israel, the doorway to the army elite.

"They told me in school today. Proud of me?" Noah still peered up at his father, though at the rate he was growing Barak thought his son might look him straight in the eye in a year or so. The fresh-colored boyish face glowed.

"Couldn't be prouder."

When Noah left, Barak sat down at his desk and studied Cunningham's response about tanks. It was not encouraging. Containment of the Soviet Union was now the one theme of American policy, he wrote, and the Arabs were such a weak link in that policy that the planners had to be wary of any move that might offend them. On this point Cunningham quoted at some length Major John Smith, who was now in army war plans. Smith was not pro-Jewish or anti-Jewish, the CIA man wrote, and he was quite hard-headed about Nasser, seeing him as a mere charismatic upstart riding a streak of political luck. But, Cunningham went on,

Jack calls Israel "a small thorn in the flesh of the Arab world, causing some political pus and bound to be extruded after some years of inflammation and pain." Jack's prevailing school of thought at the Pentagon considers Israel a passing historical accident in the Middle East, created by world revulsion at the Nazi massacres and President Truman's pro-Jewish sympathies. When I try to argue that the Jews themselves are a historical accident that's lasted three thousand years and more, and ordinary logic doesn't apply to them, Jack smiles at what he considers my religious loose screw.

You should get to know Smith. He's a sound fellow, and a comer in the army. Israel has to reckon with such officers and their ideas. They are pragmatic patriots in the mold of George Marshall, a very great man who thought Truman's policy in Israel a serious mistake and opposed it to the last. In fact, I think you or somebody like you should enroll here in any army course they'll admit you to — something nonclassified like armor or artillery. There's a professional respect here for your Sinai victory. Once here, you could start softening the hard-frozen ground for a small initial purchase of stockpiled old Shermans. Even that could take years. Ike is essentially unforgiving about Suez, though in casual comment he has grudgingly commended Israel's good-faith withdrawal, and the technical skill of the campaign.

Barak showed Cunningham's reply to Dayan, who had finished his tour as Chief of Staff and was studying Middle Eastern affairs at Hebrew University. General or civilian, Dayan remained the number-one army figure. "Good idea," said Dayan. "We could use those Shermans. Go ahead and do as he suggests."

"Apply to armor school, you mean?"

"Absolutely. The Americans lead the field. Professional advancement for you, Zev, and maybe you'll break the ice on procuring tanks, at that." Dayan gave him an appraising glance with a half-closed eye. "You're a fellow who might just do it."

"You flatter me, sir."

"No, I don't," said Dayan.

So Barak applied to the armor school at Fort Knox, Kentucky, for the next opening, a course starting in 1960, nearly two years off. Command of his brigade now happily preoccupied him; much could happen in two years, so he put the prospect from mind.

As for Emily's "billet-doux," Barak tore it up and tried to put it from mind as well. But he could picture the girl's disappointment — not that she was exactly a girl anymore, must be getting into her twenties — at finding not a word of acknowledgment from him, day by day and week by week. Her acerb charm had pervaded the letter. Almost, as he had read the words, he had heard her tense hurried voice. That voice continued to echo at odd moments, self-assured yet plaintive: *"I just want to know you're there. I'm here . . ."*

At last he sat down to dash off something.

Dear Emily:

I got your very nice "billet-doux." When I delivered Jack Smith to your doorstep, as you put it, he and I had quite a talk, driving down from West Point. He's an able man, and I can't think he'll be "girl-shy" any longer than he deems proper. He's also quite good-looking. My guess would be that you'll decide he'll do.

I now command an armor brigade, and am out to make it the best in the army. My son Noah, whom you liked, has been admitted to our most select high school. All is well with us.

Interesting that two American college girls discovered Plutarch together. I still read Plutarch almost every night. The paperbound copy I picked up in the British army is falling apart. If I had to choose three books to have with me on a desert island, no problem. Bible in Hebrew, Shakespeare, Plutarch.

I'm not much of a letter writer, but I'll be glad to hear from you once in a great while. Why not? You can address your own envelopes. Nakhama isn't nosy about my mail, she has enough on her mind without that. Two children, a new larger apartment we can't really afford on army pay, and so on. I don't consider your father a nut, but you're not far from one. If I took you seriously I wouldn't be answering you. You're very lovely, and very nice, and the fellow to make you happy is on his way to you, if he isn't Major Smith.

Sincerely,

Barak didn't like this letter much, but to cut off the echoing voice he mailed it, and it worked. "That girl" dimmed from mind.

*   *   *

After a year their correspondence was an ongoing if sporadic one, consisting mostly of her letters.

September 22, 1960

Dearest Zev —

I've a world to tell you this time — Hester tried to kill herself and I've been out in Oregon visiting her — but before I get into that, I'm sorry as hell that you have to drop out of that armor course. I've been counting the months and lately the weeks, but you've done the right thing, no choice. Of course you can't leave Nakhama at such a time. At least she has a chance to keep the baby, although staying bedridden for months is a lousy prospect. Please please give her my deepest wishes for full recovery and a marvellous baby. Sorry, I'm not interested in meeting the officer who's coming in your stead. He's not you. Finis.

Well, about Hester, what a mess! I can't imagine that you've saved my letters, but if you have, tear them up! I never think when I write, I just pour it out, as you know by now. Her husband came on a packet of our correspondence and was scandalized, mostly by an unfinished letter of hers which was very warm. "Wish I could feel your dear arms around me," and such. Also a sweet poem. Doesn't mean a thing, Zev, girl stuff, but it doesn't go in Eugene, Oregon. There was a big fight, and Hester tried to hang herself on a chandelier that you couldn't hang a dog on, and it came down with a crash on top of her. I don't mean hang a collie, I mean a poodle, I saw the chandelier, it's been put back, really flimsy. Well, then Bruce, that's the husband, was all tears and contrition. The thing was hushed up, and he bought her a Mercedes convertible, and I was invited out there to show that he understood and there were no hard feelings or suspicions left.

He's a nice enough man but very dull. Hester has painted about a thousand canvases, I guess to keep from going crazy, they're piled waist-high in her attic. Portraits of her kids, landscapes of Oregon scenery — a fabulous state, Oregon — but most of them are ghastly abstracts that hint at a disordered mind. Hester was never thin, the girls at school used to call us Laurel and Hardy, but she's really ballooned. But that's not why the chandelier came down. She couldn't have been serious, heavy as she is, jumping off a chair and expecting that chandelier to do her in. It's a mercy she didn't bring down the whole ceiling. Hester just isn't happy.

SO, my fine feathered friend, as we used to say as kids, don't you dare keep on with this stuff about my getting married! What's the matter, guilty conscience about these stupid letters, four of mine to every one of yours? I'll get married when I'm goddamn good and ready, and that may be never! I'm quite okay as I am. So stop harping on that dreary note, it's the one thing in your cautious avuncular letters that really burns me up. I'm delighted that your armor brigade won the

Defense Ministry citation for excellence, but that must occur with everything you touch.

Your dropping out of the armor course is the tip-off on you and me. Pure fate! We're destined to conduct a Shaw-Terry correspondence, no more — I hesitate to say Héloïse and Abélard — which gets torn up as it goes, so that only we two get to enjoy it, not the whole bloody snoopy world. Shaw met Terry just once backstage in a crowd, you know. There's no record that he kissed her, so I'm one up on Ellen Terry, and can let it go at that. The truth is I absolutely love loving you from a distance. I've gotten used to it. So stay away since that's how the good Lord clearly wants it, and just lay off the marriage jazz, okay?

Jack Smith, by the way, is back in the picture. He got to squiring a beautiful army brat after he and I drifted apart, and it surely looked like orange blossoms for half a year. Jack was sort of old for her, but he's making a name in the army, and I suppose she was flattered and just enjoyed gaffing him and then throwing him back. It takes all kinds. So now he's been burned twice, a shaken fellow, but it isn't affecting his career. I suppose I rate as an old friend who at least won't hurt him, and we do have good times.

Are you following our election over there? Kennedy is all glamor and grace but I'm not sure of his specific gravity. Nixon is a glowering climber nobody likes, he's just Ike's boy. But he's able. Years ago, running with Ike for vice president, he got in a corner with the uncovering of some kind of illegal fund he had, and he looked to be finished. But he battled his way out with a mushy TV speech about his wife and his dog Checkers, a right slick performance. The Jews here are all against him, being mostly liberals, so I guess you Israelis also are for Kennedy. Though I'm not sure how you relate to American Jews, you really seem different breeds of cat.

By the way, not that it's my business, but is there anything to all this newspaper talk about an Israeli nuclear reactor? Big vague fuss here. Nasser threatening to mobilize six million men and march in to destroy it, and all that. Should I worry?

Well, that's it for now. You have no idea, dear old Zev, how much reluctant affection seeps through those few careful lines of yours. By now you believe me. You know I'm neither ordinary nor silly, and you value my regard. As you should. Love is the rarest gift this melancholy existence affords. You should hear my father read romantic poetry out loud sometimes, Shakespeare's sonnets, Browning, Swinburne. He seems a stick, but I believe he and I have much the same nature. He's channelled it into patriotism, and he's happy enough with my mother, but there's capped turbulence there.

Anyhow I herewith sign off with unchanged reasonably pure love. My dreams are my own affair. I'll give *Anatomy of Melancholy* a try, since you urge me, but the title has always put me off. Anyway I don't really believe there's a book to compare to Plutarch. However, since Uncle Zev says so —

All yours,
Emily

31 December 1960

Dearest Emily:

There, I break down and call you dearest. Enough already with the caution.

Nakhama's had a girl, a big beautiful kid, eight and a half pounds, and they're both fine! So now we have one boy and two girls, and that's it for Nakhama. She had a rotten time, but now we're very happy, though we both wanted another boy. The girls fight in this country but it's the boys we hand the torch to. I hope by the time this baby grows up the Arabs will have gotten over their delusion that we will ever leave, or that they can drive us out. But it looks like a long pull, and it may soon be Noah's turn to take up the torch. If he has to, he'll hold it high.

I'm writing at 11 at night and snow is falling on Jerusalem outside my window. You call this New Year's Eve. It's not a holiday here for us, we had our New Year in September, in fact the day you wrote me about Hester Laroche and the chandelier. Here this day is called Sylvester, some minor saint's day. The American tourists get drunk, blow horns, and throw colored paper around. We go about our business.

That's a real horror story about your poor fat friend and the chandelier, her thousand paintings, and her boring husband, but the way you wrote it I kept laughing. That's very Israeli, you know, making laughter out of the awful things that go on here. I'm happy enough and fulfilled enough, at this moment, to tell you that I return your affection, not at all in the same way, not with the tricksiness (is that good English?) which is your trademark, and not at all like my love for Nakhama, which is my life. I couldn't have predicted you, but I appreciate your letters and your feelings. George Bernard Shaw I'm not. Abélard God forbid I should be. I haven't much to say to you, Emily, for obvious reasons, and if you sense affection between the lines let it go at that.

With these few lines I say goodbye for now, a joyful father and

Your faraway friend,
Zev

P.S. — About the reactor, it's a French design for electric power, and years away from completion. Newspaper nonsense.

Z.B.

(A card of congratulation on the birth of a girl, printed in Hebrew and English. On the blank space folded inside, this scrawl:)

January 10th, 1961

Zev, my love — I went to a Jewish bookstore in D.C. to get this card. I'm crying as I write these words because you and Nakhama have a new baby, because I'm happy in your happiness, and because in your fashion you love me. It's a black freezing midnight in McLean, and against all nature the night is winking with fireflies.

Your Emily

23

A Turkish Fantasy

"Kfotze!" As the master sergeant's hand hit his shoulder the Gambian colonel leaped, and the other jumpers in the dvukah, the hookup, shuffled up toward the slipstream roar and the blaze of sunshine at the open port.

"Kfotze!" Out leaped a trainee Don Kishote especially liked and admired: the brigadier general from the Ivory Coast, stout, serious-minded, black as coal, sedulous in calisthenics, always reading political science books in his off-time for an unfinished master's degree at Johns Hopkins.

"Kfotze!" Turn of the joking colonel from Cameroon, who had brought his exotically robed pretty wife along to Israel, and played strange tunes on an instrument like an elongated piccolo. "Goodbye, cruel world!" he shouted in a French accent, laughing as he jumped.

"Kfotze!"

"No."

"Kfotze!"

"Absolutely not!"

"*Kfotze!*"

"I won't! MY PARACHUTE'S LOOSE!" A bellow by a very tall fat officer, clutching at the sides of the port. "I'M NOT JUMPING!"

The sergeant went behind the trainee and planted a heavy boot on his rear end. *"KFOTZE!"*

"No! Listen, you kick me, you starting a war with Uganda!"

"Unhook him, Uri." Don Kishote had expected trouble with this one, a swaggerer who towered over the others, and had done childish monkeyshines in the harness jumps to show his courage. The small gnarled master sergeant gave Kishote a dirty look, hating to excuse a freezer. But he unhooked the Ugandan officer and pushed him away from the port.

"Kfotze! . . . Kfotze! . . . Kfotze!"

The last three African officers leaped one, two, three, proud of their nerve after Idi Amin's freeze. Pointing a thick shaking finger at the sergeant, who was sliding the port door shut, Idi Amin shouted over the engine roar, "Major, I want this fellow reported for insubordinate behavior, for threatening a military personage of a friendly power, and for putting a boot on my ass! Feel my parachute. It's loose!"

In this unwelcome assignment Yossi had checked each parachute himself, not wanting the death of an African big shot on his record or his conscience, and he knew that the parachute was on as tightly as if it were glued to that enormous fat back. He gave the parachute a perfunctory feel. "Yes, practically falling off. The sergeant didn't notice. Sorry." Idi Amin smiled toothily at Yossi, and the sergeant made a gagging noise.

That same afternoon Kishote confronted the Foreign Minister in her office. "Sit down, Major Nitzan." *Nitzan*, meaning bloom or blossom, was now Yossi's name, Hebraized from Blumenthal when he married. "This conversation is under four eyes," she went on. "I'm bypassing army channels for sufficient reason."

"Yes, Madame Minister."

"Now, what's all this about the Uganda officer? Uganda's important to us, and this man's a bull with horns there."

Yossi described the episode. Golda Meir wearily nodded, her eyes distant and glazed. "Yes, well take him up again tomorrow, and make sure that he jumps this time. Understand? That will be all." She picked up a paper on her desk.

"Madame Foreign Minister," said Yossi, "the man will not

jump. Or if he jumps, he will die." Golda put down the paper and scowled at him, her reddened eyes now alert. "He may be a bull with horns, but he wasn't born to jump with a parachute."

Golda pursed her lips. "But I've heard he's a champion boxer. Are you saying he's a coward?"

"He's as great a coward as I've ever seen."

She regarded him through wreathing smoke, half closing her eyes. "Major Yossi Nitzan, I've heard good reports of you. I've heard you referred to as Don Kishote. I know about your *tziyun l'shvakh*. You weren't assigned this duty by chance. Tomorrow at this time you will report to me again. Your report will consist of two words. 'He jumped.' "

"Yes, Madame Foreign Minister."

"If he dies, that will be bad for Israel. And for you, not exactly a tziyun l'shvakh."

"I understand."

"Two words. 'He jumped.' "

"*Ken, ha'm'fakedet.*" Kishote ventured this formal army response and a salute. It was as much irony as he could allow himself with the imposing Golda. She did not smile, and she returned the salute with the hand holding the cigarette.

In a room almost bare of furniture, a curly-headed toddler was clumsily chasing Yossi Nitzan round and round a table that was a plank on two sawhorses. "Bow wow! *Ani kelev, Abba hatool!*" ("I'm dog, Daddy cat!")

"Miaow! I'm scared, I'm scared!" Kishote turned, hissed, and spat, humping up his shoulders.

His son shrieked with delight. "Nice cat! Now Abba elephant."

Kishote put an arm to his nose like a trunk, and trumpeted, swaying from side to side.

"Now lion, lion!" cried the boy. Dropping on all fours, his father uttered a fearsome roar.

The child shrank back, his face wrinkling up. "Bad Abba. 'Fraid Abba."

"No! Aryeh Nitzan is never afraid. Doesn't Aryeh mean the same as *ari* [lion]?"

"Ken, Abba."

"Well, is a lion afraid of a lion?"

The child's big gray eyes brightened. "No."

"Then let's see." Yossi roared again, eyes glaring, teeth bared. The child trembled but stood his ground, then fell on his hands and knees and gave a soprano roar in his father's face. They were roaring so, nose to nose, when a door slammed. "Yossi, are you here? We have a big problem — *Ai!* Now what's all this?"

"The lioness!" exclaimed Kishote. "She brings food!" They both turned to roar at Aryeh's mother, who put aside groceries, pulled her skirt far up on silk-clad legs and went down on the floor. The three of them roared and snarled at each other until the child rolled on his back laughing and breathless.

"What's the problem?" Kishote helped her up.

"Who do you suppose walked into the shop today?" Yael was out of the army and managing, very successfully, a bridal shop on Dizengoff Avenue.

"I don't know. Golda?"

"Ha! Golda, a bride? Hardly. Hint! An old friend of yours."

"Shayna," said Yossi at once.

A nod and a vinegary grin. "Nobody but Shayna Matisdorf."

"So she's getting married, finally."

"Don't look so heartbroken, please."

"Nonsense, I'm very glad for her. Who's her guy?"

"It wasn't her guy, and she's not getting married. She was with her boss, Professor Berkowitz, and —"

"Zev's lame brother?"

"Yes, and he brought his intended, Lena something. She's the bride, and she couldn't get fitted in Haifa, so they came to Tel Aviv. And the problem is I did something idiotic. I invited the three of them to come here."

"Here? And Shayna accepted?"

"She did. All three did."

Kishote looked around at the sawhorse table and three folding chairs, all the furniture in the room. "Well, no problem, I'll get a few more chairs. They'll understand. You're a busy lady, and I'm in the field so much —"

"They'll understand *nothing,* we're going to furnish up this place fast. *Chick-chack!* It's a disgrace. We moved in months ago." Yael glared around. "The thing is, Shayna has a friend whose kid is in Aryeh's kindergarten, and she told me she'd heard Aryeh was the smartest and the handsomest child ever. She couldn't have been nicer, very genuine, and without thinking I said, 'Well, come see him.' And Professor Berkowitz asked to see him too, and he'll bring that Lena, of course."

"When are they coming?"

"Friday."

"Where's your brother?"

"Benny? What's he got to do with it?"

"I have to talk to him. It's urgent. He's not at the air base."

"That's right, it's his youngest's birthday. He must be at the moshav. Try there." She picked up Aryeh and carried him into his room, which unlike the rest of the flat was amply furnished, even crowded, with bed, chairs, table, toys, and rocking horse, all new and of the best. "Undress. Bath time."

"No. Eat."

"Bath." Hard motherly note. Aryeh unbuttoned his jumper.

Later when they were eating at the sawhorse table, and Aryeh was smearily and greedily feeding himself mashed potatoes, she asked, "How did it go with the Africans?"

"All right."

"Is it finished?"

"Not quite."

"Did you reach Benny?"

"Yes, I'm going to see him after dinner."

"Tonight? At Nahalal?" Kishote nodded, his face sober. "So you'll stay there overnight?"

"Probably. I'll see."

"Try to get back." Yael's voice dropped almost to a purr. "I'll miss you . . ."

He looked at her askance, and faintly grinned. "Why is this night different from all other nights?"

"Is that a complaint?"

His taut expression warmed. Wry affection and secret amusement glinted in his eyes.

"More," said Aryeh. Yael wiped the child's messy face and refilled his plate.

"I'll try to get back," said Don Kishote.

"Yes, try." She put a hand on his. "I don't know, today I got to thinking of Paris . . . the Eiffel Tower, Venus de Milo, the Georges Cinq, all that . . . things you should never forget, but you do, you get busy —"

"Well, you saw Shayna."

She gave him an uneasy glance. "She looks *very* well. If anything, thinner. Can't say that about me, can you?" A rueful pat at her aproned figure.

"I like them overweight and dumpy."

She struck his arm hard with a fist. "Swine."

Don Kishote stood up, pulled her to her feet, and embraced her. Yael's yielding figure was in fact a lot more curvy than it had been in Paris, somewhat on the Venus side. "Okay, I'll come back."

"You will? Good! But not on my account, really. Four hours on the road —"

"The thing is," said Kishote, "I have this late date with a French whore."

Yael chuckled. "There's a store near mine that rents furniture. I'll try that. Waste of money, but simple."

"Rent a bed, at least. For appearance's sake. They won't know I like sleeping on a cement floor on a mattress."

"Complaints, complaints! Hurry back. Love to Benny and Irit, and happy birthday to Danny."

Don Kishote did not much enjoy the long drive to Nahalal. Too much time to think. Shayna coming to their apartment! Here was a turn! Since the fearsome night of their breakup, which he had tried to bury out of memory, he had only glimpsed Shayna now and then at a distance in Jerusalem gatherings, and once they had un-expectedly come face to face in a lobby outside a lecture hall. She had been with some guy in a yarmulke, and with casual hellos they had passed each other by.

Regret was not one of Yossi Nitzan's natural feelings, nor was guilt. Life was a sort of tactical battlefield for him, which perhaps made him a good soldier. Size up the situation, make a decision, act! The action once past, on to the next thing. Yael's catastrophic surprise had created a new situation, calling for judgment, decision, and action. Tell Yael to stew in her self-cooked soup, and go on with Shayna? On two counts not possible.

First of all, whatever his devilries in Karl Netter Street, he was at bottom a good Jewish boy; having a baby was a marvellous thing, and the baby — his first! — would need a father, and its mother a husband. Second, he could not go on with Shayna any-way, much as he might yearn to do so. He would have to tell all to her. She was a good Jewish girl, religious to the bone, and her quick irrevocable judgment would be that of course he *had* to marry Yael, and she would throw him out.

So exactly it had happened, and he had put it behind him, but for a long time he had been haunted by her stricken look when he had told her about Yael, the horror in her wide staring tear-filled eyes, as though she were watching him bleed to death as he talked. What he least wanted to remember was his oafish stumbling last mistake; starting to say to Shayna that he and Yael could not really last long together, that he would marry her because it was the right thing, but that maybe one day —

"*Stop right there!*" With those strident words and a single gasp-ing sob she had cut him off. "Yossi, what you are is an overgrown stupid child. There's nothing more to say. It's over. You've nearly killed me. It's *over,* forever and absolutely, get that into your head! We must never, never, never see each other again." With that she had hurried off into the night, leaving him standing there at the Yemin Mosheh windmill overlooking the Old City; the romantic picturesque spot where they had first kissed, where newlyweds came to have their pictures taken, and where she had asked him to meet her so that they could talk over wedding plans, since her parents had given consent. Minutes after Yael had departed from his apartment, returning Shayna's call, he had dumbly agreed to come and meet her there. Tactical instinct; if it had to be done, do it and get it over with.

Kfotze, Kishote!

Much time had passed. He had forgotten much. Aryeh was the joy of his days, and his army career was going well. As for Yael, she was quite a woman, and he was fond of her in a way, though he did not and could not love her. Since they were both young, healthy, and attractive, and sharing a life together, sex was part of it, but he was careful to have no more children with her. And now Shayna was coming back after all, if only to visit Aryeh! A surprise eruption from the past, unsettling and obscurely exciting; how would it go? What could she really want? *"Never, never, never"* had been her last words, years ago.

He drove into the moshav close to midnight, and found Yael's aviator brother in a bathrobe, reading the small Bible that the army distributed free, and that gathered dust on many an Israeli shelf. "Getting religion, Benny?"

Luria put aside the book with a humorous grunt. "Hi. Moshe Dayan says that we have to live by the Tanakh [Scripture] in this country. Of course he means the history part, not the religion, that guy! And he's right, you know? At least in this book you learn why we're here."

"We're here because we've been chased and murdered pretty near everywhere else."

"That's not all of it. Not by a long shot. What can I do for you, Kishote?"

When he returned from Nahalal, Yael was sleeping on the floor like the dead. He woke her, dropping on the cold cement and crawling under the covers. "Oh, you're back." She yawned, then, "Oo-wah, it's light outside."

"Five o'clock."

"How's Benny?"

"Fine. I had a piece of Danny's cake."

"Lovely. You must be exhausted." He pulled her into his arms. Her resistance was sleepy and minimal. "Look, get some rest. We can do this anytime."

"No. Something to do at once."

This provoked a husky laugh, but the late date did not come off because Aryeh, awakened by his father's return, danced into the bedroom in pink pajamas, chanting a song learned in kindergarten:

" *The Lord of the World, who reigned before anything was created* — ' "

"Oi! Get the lord of the world out of here," said Kishote, "and wake me in two hours. Your brother is flying down to meet me."

The sun was high and hot when the aviator picked him up in an army car and drove to the paratrooper base. "Benny, will this actually work?" Yossi asked. "I'm getting shaky."

"Best idea I could think of, Kishote. It should."

Benny was a full colonel, shorter than Kishote but considerably better looking; rugged sunburned features suited to a cowboy movie, very thick-necked, erect posture even at the wheel of a car. Close-cropped hair and intent eyes gave him a hard look, but he could smile and seem friendly, even fatherly, all at once. He had three children, he commanded a fighter squadron, and he was very much the military paragon and a model family man; that is, he kept his young mistress in Tel Aviv under wraps, in a respectable job as a hotel receptionist, and held dalliance with a few girlfriends to a discreet minimum. His Bible reading, such as it was, evidently did not interfere with this part of life, any more than Moshe Dayan's did. His cherished wife Irit was unaware of all this, or acted as though she was.

"He won't hang up on the tail, Benny, and kill himself?"

"Not if he remembers to count to three. Then he has to remember to pull the cord. By the way, he can count to three?"

"Yes, I checked him out on that."

"Excellent. You're set then. If he freezes, we do the other. That's all been arranged."

"I'm much obliged, Benny."

"No problem."

Idi Amin was half an hour late getting to the base. A limousine used by the Foreign Ministry, one of the few in all Israel, brought him there, caparisoned in white dress uniform with banks of medals and ribbons, gold epaulettes, and splashes of gold trim. "This is my lucky day," he said to Kishote. "Today we do it."

Yossi introduced him to Benny Luria. Idi Amin looked down at the airman to smile as they shook hands. "Colonel Luria is my brother-in-law," said Kishote. "He'll pilot the plane, and there'll be just the three of us."

It was a four-seater trainer with a large side door. Suited up for the jump, the parachute fastened and tightened on him by Yossi, the Ugandan climbed in first, and took a seat beside a large sandbag. "What's this for?" he inquired a shade anxiously.

"Ballast," said Colonel Luria.

"Ah, ballast," said Idi Amin. "Yes. Ballast is very important."

The plane climbed swiftly and levelled off at jump altitude over green farmland bordered by the sparkling Mediterranean. "This is it, sir," said Kishote. "Ready?"

"Here? I'll land in the water," protested Amin, his eyes bulging and showing the whites.

"Wind is off the sea at ten knots," said Colonel Luria. "You'll drift inland."

"Anytime, sir," said Kishote, gesturing at the door. "Jump, count to three, pull the cord and" — he gestured at the silver parachute emblem on his chest — "you're one of us."

Idi Amin stared down at the ground, out at the sea, at Colonel Luria, at Major Nitzan, then slowly, emphatically shook his head.

"Sir," said Yossi, "I'm under strict orders from the Foreign Minister to report that you jumped, and *I'm going to*. So make up your mind, sir."

The parachute blossomed white in the azure sky, and the plane circled in a steep descent. Soon Don Kishote drove the army car to the deserted potato field where the parachute lay flattened, a snowy blob fluttering gently in the light wind. "Let's pick up your chute, sir," Kishote said to Idi Amin, stopping the car, "so you can turn it in."

With a wily unembarrassed grin, the Ugandan got out and

gathered the bundle of cords and silk in his long arms. Kishote helped him. "What about that?" inquired Amin, as Yossi unfastened cords from the sandbag.

"Served its purpose," said Yossi.

With the parachute crumpled into the back seat, Yossi drove west on a dirt road, and pulled up on the edge of a grassy embankment. Below was the sandy beach, six or seven feet down. Clear waves quietly lapped at the sand. Idi Amin stared at him. "Now what's this about?"

"Sir, I have to report to the Foreign Minister in two words, *'He jumped.'* I intend to do just that. So jump, and you'll turn that in" — a thumb gesture at the back seat — "and you've got your silver parachute."

Idi Amin's big dark moon face broke out in a charming, delighted smile, that in an eerie way reminded Kishote of Aryeh. "Ha ha! I understand! The Foreign Minister, she wants you to say, 'He jumped!' So we fool her! I jump, and you tell her the truth. 'He jumped!' "

"That's exactly right, sir."

"Major, you're a clever one. Here goes." Amin bent his knees once or twice on the edge, then jumped, hit the sand, and tumbled. "Damn, ow, that hurt!" he yelled. "I think I sprained my ankle."

"All the better, sir. You'll be limping back. Realistic! So don't brush off that sand."

After returning Idi Amin to his limousine, Don Kishote drove straight to the Foreign Ministry. Golda Meir's secretary passed him into her office, where she was conferring with several staff men in short-sleeved shirts.

"Nu?" she greeted Kishote, without ceremony.

"He jumped."

She nodded grimly. "I hear he injured his ankle and is limping."

"The doctor taped it up. Nothing serious."

"Asita hayil." ("Well done.")

"Ken, ha'm'fakedet." The edgy tone made the staff men's heads turn. Don Kishote turned on his heel and walked out. No salute.

*

After a two-day brigade exercise in the Negev in night parachuting, Kishote came home late in the evening and found Yael sitting on a worn yellow sofa, looking disconsolate. The flat was all furnished: dining set, bedroom set, rugs, chairs and armchairs, coffee table, lamps on side tables, even pictures on the walls; a wolf howling at the moon, a rabbi clutching a Torah. The effect was bleak and seedy, a mishmash of secondhand odds and ends. "Well anyway," Yael greeted him, "now the place doesn't look as though you haven't got a wife."

"When did you say they're coming?"

"Tomorrow for tea, then they drive back to Haifa."

"Do we have any wine?"

"What's the matter? Have you eaten dinner?"

"Just a glass of wine."

He talked about the exercise as he drank two glasses of the Adom Atik they kept in the house for Shabbat kiddush. He wanted Aryeh to get used to the ritual, and a bottle usually lasted a month or so, but Don Kishote was in a rare embittered mood. Deputy commander of the brigade, he had argued with the commander against scheduling a night drill. "I told Doron, I said, 'Look, we'll probably never jump again in a combat situation, it's an obsolete tactic. Certainly never at night, so why do it?' You know what his answer was? 'The exercise is on.'" Kishote finished the wine at a gulp. "We had a lot of injuries. Parachute training is fine, it creates an elite in the infantry, I believe in it, but there's a limit."

"I can buy flowers," said Yael, glancing around, "and some books. Flowers and books make a big difference."

He put an arm around her. "How's Aryeh?"

"He wants a dog. I bought him a new suit. He looks so handsome in it!"

"Yael, they know I've got a wife."

She looked straight at him. "I'll tell you something. Sam Pasternak's always said you should go into armor. He thinks you've got a great future, and tanks are the service, tanks are what decide wars. Tanks and the air."

Somehow it still irked Yossi when she spoke about Pasternak.

"I've been in tanks. I'm a paratrooper. I love my brigade, and I don't think about the future."

"I do. You should."

"The Africans have their graduation ceremony day after tomorrow. I may call in sick. . . . Flowers and books are a nice idea."

She hurried home early in a taxi next day to get ready for the visitors. Outside their garden apartment house in Ramat Aviv soldiers were unloading furnishings from an army truck and streaming in and out of their ground-floor flat. "What to all the *devils* —!" she exclaimed, rushing inside. Don Kishote and his old friend Shmuel from the Karl Netter days, the big bearded Turk, were in the living room, both in uniform, directing the soldiers to lug furniture here and there.

"We're almost finished," said Kishote. "The flowers and the books came, by the way. We'll put them around last."

Shmuel said, "Doesn't it look nice, Yael?"

"Nice!" she gasped.

Shmuel's father was a wealthy furniture dealer, and on his son's marriage to a buxom air force corporal from Argentina, he had furnished up a magnificent flat for them. This opulence now engulfed Yael: a gorgeous plushy Turkish carpet, figured draperies and silk cushions masking the seedy furniture; also rich brocades and tapestries on the wall instead of the wolf and the rabbi, and wherever the eye turned, a clutter of fine objets d'art.

"By your life, Kishote, what have you done?"

"Yael, my love, what you want is for Shayna Matisdorf to drop dead. This should do it. No?"

"You're a madman. I don't want anything of the kind!"

"You don't like it?" inquired Shmuel a shade anxiously. "We can take it all out."

"Why, it's all great. It's just, well Shmuel, it's so, so *Turkish.*" As his face fell she added quickly, "Not that I don't like Turkish style, I love it."

"It's all going back tomorrow," said Don Kishote, "This is just so Shayna should drop dead."

"Stop saying that. You know I'm not like that." Yael burst out laughing. "Look, Shmuel, I could easily get used to these things, they're beautiful. Thanks!"

"No problem," said Shmuel with a hirsute grin.

"I'll fetch Aryeh from kindergarten," said Kishote.

Yael said, "All right, you crazy man. Now where are the flowers? The books? And are you going to wear that wrinkled uniform?"

Little Aryeh took for granted the Turkish transformation of his home, since nearly everything in his life was a novelty. When Professor Berkowitz and Lena arrived, he exhibited a precocious sense of occasion, sitting quietly on a low chair in his new suit, munching a cookie, and observing the visitors with sharp eyes. Seeing him focus on the professor's canes when he arrived Kishote winced, but his son looked up at him, saw his warning frown and slight head shake, and ignored the canes thereafter.

"Shayna will be along," said Michael. "Charming place you've got here."

"Tasteful," said Lena, a plump lady in her late twenties, with a round face, a broad peasant nose, and a clever good-humored look. "Sort of Turkish, isn't it?"

"Sort of," said Kishote. "I had an uncle in Ankara. He died and left me these things. He was in figs. Quite well off."

"I really love my bridal gown," Lena said to Yael. "Nothing like it in Haifa."

"I'm glad."

They were making such awkward small talk when the doorbell rang. Don Kishote went and opened the door. Shayna stood there in the same old black raincoat, and she looked no different than she had at the windmill, even to the pained wide eyes. For Yossi, seeing her at his door was almost like being hit by a car, the impact was so startling and hurt so much. Her dark eyes met his, and it was all still there; the depth, the fatally wounded love, and all the agony of their last parting. In nearly three years nothing had changed between them! That was the real shock. Not for her, that truth was in her expression; and not for him, by the power of that truth to shake him. Her face was pale and composed. "Hello, Yossi." She offered her hand, and stepped inside. "So that's Aryeh. Hello, Yael. Well! He looks like you, Yossi, doesn't he?"

"So they say."

She went to Aryeh and bent down. "My name is Shayna."

For the first time the child spoke. "Teacher Shayna."

"That's right," said Yael. "His kindergarten teacher is Shayna, too."

Lena said, "We've heard such nice things about you, Aryeh. You sing and dance, don't you? Will you do it for us?"

Aryeh brusquely shook his head.

"He hasn't been this quiet since he had his tonsils out," said Kishote, "under ether."

"Let's have tea," said Yael, "and forget him for a while. That will do it."

After the political chit-chat usual in Israel, Michael Berkowitz disclosed, over the tea, that the army had recruited him, with the rank of captain. "My profile is about sixty percent, but the army wants my physics, not my physique." He chuckled at his academic joke, and fumbled with his knitted skullcap. "That nuclear reactor the Americans sold us is just a small laboratory thing. All kinds of American inspectors and controls. The French are talking business about a serious reactor. An installation we'll build and run ourselves."

" *'Exalted and praised be the living God . . .'* " Aryeh piped up in song, getting off his chair.

"Ah, here we go," said Yael. "Inattention is what activates him."

" *'He exists, but His existence is outside time . . .'* " The tune to these grave words was gaily syncopated, and Aryeh showed off with lively hops and turns.

"What on earth is that child singing?" inquired Lena.

"Surely you know it," said Shayna. "That's 'Yigdal.' The morning synagogue hymn."

"I haven't been inside a synagogue in my life."

" *'He is One, and there is no unity like His unity . . .'* "

As the child capered, looking around for applause, Lena persisted, "But does he have the faintest idea what the words mean? Does he go to some super-religious kindergarten?"

"It isn't religious at all. Just a neighborhood kindergarten," said Kishote.

" *'He is a mystery, and there is no end to His Oneness . . .'* "

"What a memory, Aryeh!" Shayna clapped in time to his song, and he danced in front of her, eyes alight.

"Michael, dear," said Lena, her brow knitted with worry, "will our kids have to learn such things?"

"They're bound to, my love, unless we farm them out to a Marxist kibbutz." He shrugged and smiled at the others. "Talk about your marriage of opposites!"

"Well, I'll stick to our deal," said Lena, "but I'll certainly insist that they learn some regular nursery rhymes, too."

Shayna caught up the little boy and kissed him. He put his hands on her face, and kissed her forehead.

"Well, he's a joy," said Professor Berkowitz, glancing at Lena and at his watch. *"Halevai af unz."* ("May we be so blessed.")

"Amen," she said, "and we should be thinking of going."

Shayna put down the boy, and they were all making their farewells when he came in from the bedroom in helmet and sword. "Shayna, Judah Maccabee," he said, and commenced a Hanukkah act of fierce swordplay for her. She picked him up again, and with a kiss handed him to Yael, shaking her head and smiling. "A treasure," she whispered. Yael held Aryeh close and returned a deprecating shrug, as though to say, *"If you only knew, he's just a big nuisance."*

Kishote walked out with them. Michael limped to a rusty small car and Lena helped him in. Shayna lingered behind, strolling side by side with Yossi.

"Shayna," said Don Kishote with uncharacteristic gentleness, "this was a big surprise. A very nice one."

"Well, Yossi, a lot of time has gone by, hasn't it? I heard about Aryeh, and I wanted to see him."

"I'm very glad you came, Shayna."

"So am I. He's a wonderful child. And Yael looks like a Renoir."

"Are you happy, Shayna?"

She halted. He glanced at her, and the depths in her eyes

shook him as before. "I'm fine. And now you're a father. I still find
that strange."

"Did you think I'd never grow up?"

"Have you?"

"Hey, I'm a major, Shayna."

"I know. Major Nitzan. I like Nitzan." She gave him her hand.
"I love Aryeh." He wanted to hold on to her hand and exchange
more words, but she withdrew it and got into the car. "Goodbye,
Major."

"Shayna didn't drop dead," Yael said when he came back to
the apartment. "I don't believe she noticed the furniture."

"Lena did. That Lena is okay," Yossi said. "A forthright lady."

Yael began picking up the tea things. "Well, she drives a hard
bargain, I'll tell you that." Still in his helmet, Aryeh was filching a
cream cake. Yael yanked it from him, mashing it. Aryeh wrinkled up
his face at her in hurt anger. "Dinnertime. You'll kill your appetite."

Yossi took his hand, "Come, Judah Maccabee, party's over. I'll
bathe you."

A band played and a red-bereted paratroop battalion in dress uniform paraded in fierce sunshine, then stood at attention for the
ceremony of awarding silver parachutes to the African officers. Major Nitzan walked behind the Ramatkhal (Chief of Staff), General
Tzur, as he passed down their line, pinned the emblems on them,
and shook hands, one by one. Idi Amin, when Kishote went by,
gave him a broad wink.

Zev Barak was there, watching the ceremony. Afterward, as
the Ramatkhal chatted with the Africans and the paratroopers noisily dispersed, he beckoned to Yossi, who was striding off the parade
ground. "Don Kishote! *Ma nishma?* I spoke to my brother Michael
on the phone yesterday. He says you and Yael have a wunderkind."

"Zev, when can I have a talk with you?"

"What's wrong with right now? I'm just waiting for the Ramatkhal. We're planning an air-and-armor war game for later this
year."

"That's what I want to talk to you about, armor."

Yael sat up late, wondering where her husband was. Usually

he called when he had to change plans, but dinnertime had come and gone, and the chicken she had roasted was cold and uneaten in the oven. When he was not there she dined on cottage cheese and a cracker. The apartment was shabby again, the Turkish fantasia cleared away. The Shayna visit had come and gone like a summer storm, brief and tumultuous but wreaking no damage. Or had it? Yossi had sat up reading that night until she fell asleep, and had slipped into the other rented twin bed without disturbing her.

The door opened and he came in smiling. "Sorry, business. I'm hungry."

"There's a chicken all cooked. I'll heat it up."

He ate with appetite, putting down half the chicken and most of a bread loaf, talking inconsequentially about politics. She put at his elbow the large pot of tea he would drink after a good meal. "Well, there's news," he said as he poured his first cup. "You know that Zev Barak's the operations officer of the Armored Corps."

"Yes?"

"I met him today at that — that *ceremony*." He bit out the word. "He needs a deputy, it turns out. We got to talking. I said I was interested in maybe transferring to armor. Like *that,* he offered me the job."

"You accepted?"

"I couldn't, straight off. It's a decision. I know tanks, but I'd still have to take the armor course. Maybe a special command course, too."

"Accept his offer, Yossi."

"It's a staff post. I'd rather be in the field."

"I tell you, take that job." Strong tone, just short of bossy. "I know what I'm talking about. So do you."

"You're probably right."

She came around the table to hug and kiss him. They made love that night in her twin bed. He spoke up in the darkness after a silence. "You know something? A bed beats the floor, after all."

Yael, feeling foxy, and somewhat reassured after the turmoil of Shayna's visit, said, "A great leap forward, as Chairman Mao would say."

"Something exciting about a narrow bed, too," he said. "It's the precariousness. You're hanging on to each other not just for love, but so as not to fall out on the floor."

A long pause. Yael, cool and quiet: "Shayna Matisdorf will never get married."

"You're crazy."

"You'll see. Not while you're alive."

"Shayna got over me long ago. I was never religious enough for her, anyway."

"Ha!" She leaned over him, her breasts brushing his chest, her scented hair falling on his face. "I've got you, and I've got Aryeh, and tough for Shayna. Want to stay the night in this bed? You're welcome, but it's close quarters."

"Let's give it a try."

She lay back, hesitated, then permitted herself to say it. "Shayna should have gone to Paris."

"Enough about Shayna, all right?" said Don Kishotc, carefully rolling over.

24

Missions to America

A very little thing decided Zev Barak to withdraw, if he could, from a mission to Washington with Pasternak.

He was sitting at the small desk in his den at 1 A.M., with a late moon wanly shining through his black window, trying to finish a letter to Emily Cunningham before Sam picked him up for a visit to an armor exercise in the Negev. Propped against the desk lamp was the last snapshot Emily had sent him; inscription on the back, *"New assistant headmistress of Foxdale School, with beloved friend Zev."* Zev was a big red horse. In brown baggy riding clothes and glasses, Emily Cunningham was an unglamorous figure, lean and almost plain. The second page of his letter ran so:

> . . . You give me hell, Emily dearest, whenever I bring up marriage again, but I swear I worry about you. What a fooler that photograph is! Just a spinster assistant headmistress, to the life. You're burning away in secret, consuming yourself. Not only could you make a man very happy with your power to love, you'd find out for the first time what happiness can be. The ultimate joy in life is children, but the ultimate sweet part is passionate love, and since your upbringing or your fastidiousness, I'm not sure which, won't let you have casual relationships, you must put up with my nagging. Remember how Shakespeare in the sonnets keeps telling that mysterious handsome friend of his to get married and have

children? So many of those lines apply to you, and "the bird of time is on the wing." The other day, I can't tell you why, I read the *Rubaiyat* again — it only takes ten minutes, you know — and my eyes were dropping tears when I finished. And I kept thinking of you . . .

He had written all that the night before with Nakhama sitting near him, reading a new Hebrew novel by the same floor lamp. She knew about the correspondence. He had shown her, as they came in over the years, snapshots of the peculiar girl who had once briefly visited her. Nakhama had long since apparently accepted his story that the CIA man's daughter had had a schoolgirl crush on him, and that it had evolved into an interesting letter-friendship. She genially said she saw nothing wrong with it. In truth there was nothing wrong, except that of late Barak was falling in love with the schoolteacherish creature who wrote the letters. He was still trying to puzzle through this bizarre development, which he could no longer laugh off or put from mind, and meantime here was the letter to finish.

And I kept thinking of you, no doubt because you wrote me last year that your father had read the *Rubaiyat* aloud to you, and said it was a rhymed version of the Book of Ecclesiastes. That parallel has occurred to me, but I've never read it anywhere or heard anyone else point it out. Your father . . .

"What will you have for breakfast?" Nakhama startled him, standing there at his side in a woolen robe.

"Oh, you're up? I didn't think I woke you."

"I guess your desk lamp did. It doesn't matter." She peered at the propped-up photograph. "Your friend is really losing her looks, isn't she? How old is she now?"

"Twenty-three, twenty-four."

"She should get married."

He gestured at his letter. "I keep writing her exactly that. She has a sort of complex, I think, about her brilliant father. Probably no fellow her age compares to him. Can I have some hot cereal and tea? It's a long way to Sde Boker."

"Sde Boker? Aren't you going to armor maneuvers?"

"Ben Gurion wants to observe them."

"Okay, oatmeal, tea, and I'll make you toast."

He snatched the photograph when she left, and tossed it with his pages in a drawer, feeling rotten for no reason traceable to any word, tone, or act of his wife. Whatever problem existed, it could only be in his own mind. What was going on?

All right, he decided as he put on his uniform, it was no great mystery. Between the army and his family, and in the confines of little Israel, he lived a straitjacketed life. Emily was an escape, a daydream; but also a living woman beyond the broad ocean, and *that* was the reason he was hesitating about going to Washington. Emily Cunningham sometimes called herself his pen pal, and that was her niche. The transoceanic paper romance was a poignant delight, and he wanted to keep it unpoisoned. He had had one extramarital affair long ago, and had felt rotten then. When he saw Sam, he would ask out. He had enough on his mind.

Hours later, after flying down to Beersheba together, Barak and Pasternak sat in the back seat of a command car speeding to the Sde Boker kibbutz in a chilly dawn. Wide awake, his mind in a churn, Barak thought Pasternak was dozing until he said abruptly, "Zev, why don't you want to go with me to Washington?"

"Have I refused?"

"You haven't agreed." Pasternak looked out at the hills reddening in the dawn, and gestured toward the narrow tarred strip cutting through the empty Negev desert ahead. "Remember when this was a dirt track, and we needed a machine gun jeep as escort? KADESH accomplished that much, at least. The Negev is safe."

"KADESH accomplished plenty."

"Did it?" Pasternak yawned. "I had dinner with Dayan last night. He still thinks we didn't have to leave Sharm el Sheikh. Not without a peace treaty."

"Easy to say now, by hindsight."

"Maybe. His view is that the Russians were bluffing, and Eisenhower and Dulles wouldn't have pushed through sanctions and a blockade. The Congress would have stopped it. The Old Man got trembly in the knees."

"Moshe didn't have the responsibility. The Old Man did."

"Why does Ben Gurion want to watch this tank exercise, Zev? Isn't it routine?"

"Well, he's down at Sde Boker anyway, and he likes to visit the soldiers," said Barak. "And since you've brought it up, Sam, please take someone else with you to Washington if you can."

"Aha. There you go. Why? You're great with Americans, and you know more about tanks than I do."

"Just let me out of it." Barak spoke in low hard tones.

Pasternak gave a noncommittal shrug, but he thought Barak was acting strangely. Zev Barak was now deputy chief of the armored corps, and the unending army speculation already had him marked for eventual command of the Northern or Central Front, a crucial upward leap on the *maslul,* the career path. The promotion pyramid was steeply narrowing for colonels, and so far Zev was holding his own. Unfriendly gossip ascribed Barak's rise to favoritism by Ben Gurion and by Dayan, a straight Ben Gurion man, but Pasternak considered him a sound and brainy officer; no ruthless flashy charger like Arik or Raful, but a solid candidate for general rank, if he played the game right and had no very bad luck.

"Okay, but you surprise me. I thought you'd enjoy a trip to Washington." Short pause. "Just a change."

The tone was level, no trace of insinuation; but a troubling notion crossed Barak's mind: namely, that Pasternak, now chief of military intelligence, might know of his correspondence with Emily Cunningham. There was no reason for intelligence to have intercepted the letters. He had made no effort at concealment. Still, the contents were far from casual, and not for other eyes. Pointless anxiety, no doubt.

"Look, Sam, we're doing an armor doctrine review, and I want to stay with it. Also Noah's coming home for the summer break. You're the negotiator. We have plenty of tank experts, you can take your pick."

"We'll see."

In the khakis tailored for him, David Ben Gurion stood waiting outside his cottage on the kibbutz grounds. A red sun giving no warmth was poking over the mountains of Moab in Jordan, lighting up the green fields and orchards of Sde Boker and the stone-strewn sands stretching all around to far horizons.

Here were the Old Man's dream and reality, thought Zev Barak, contrasted in stark morning light and long shadows. With awesome willpower he had tried to make the desert bloom, and to bring the world's Jews back to Zion. So far he had achieved small watered patches like this in the desert wastes, and most of the Jews were outside Zion, with every apparent intention of remaining there. Ben Gurion looked old and worn. Instead of thinning he was becoming paunchier. In army khaki his short stature and bulging waistline made him a funny figure. He tried to compensate, when he remembered, by sucking in his stomach and looking fierce. But Ben Gurion's fierceness came out in small committee meetings, where he broke men and turned political tides.

He said with no greeting, "Sam, how does it stand with your mission to Washington?"

"We leave Sunday."

"Then we must talk." He turned to Barak. "When will the exercise be over?"

"Ten o'clock."

"We'll come back then to Sde Boker." Ben Gurion settled down in his seat and dozed off.

He climbed nimbly enough to the top of a hill overlooking the war game area, where the broad-shouldered chief of armor, David "Dado" Elazar, waited for them, a brisk wind tousling his thick black hair. An extensive simulated Egyptian strongpoint was laid out on the gray-brown sands below: belts of antitank ditches, marked minefields, zigzagging interlocking trenches, stone breast-works, sandbagged artillery emplacements on high ground, and dug-in tanks barely showing gun muzzles; all strictly according to Soviet doctrine. Inside the fortifications, the machines defending the "Blue Force" were crawling about, and foot soldiers en masse were moving into the trenches. An attack by the "Red Force," Elazar told the Prime Minister, would soon come from the north.

The Prime Minister squinted around in the bright sunlight, looking very dissatisfied. "So, Dado, what's going on down there?"

B.G. tapped Elazar's shoulder and pointed to a dust cloud to the southeast, directly under the sun.

"What the devil!" Elazar turned on Barak, who was peering through large German binoculars at the cloud. "That can't be the Red Force."

"But it is," said Barak.

Standing up in the turret, recognizable through the fog of dust and exhaust by his stature and the sun glint on his glasses, Yossi Nitzan was leading his battalion to the attack; coming from a direction not only unscheduled but unreachable, given his starting point and the range of his British Centurion tanks. Ben Gurion asked for the binoculars, and stared through them. "So where are the tanks?" Only four tanks were visible in the oncoming formation, followed by many jeeps and half-tracks. The Blue defenders below also had only four tanks. "I thought this was to be a tank battle!"

"Skeletal exercise," said Dado Elazar. "We can't accept the wear and tear on tanks and tank carriers in games. We don't have enough, and they're too old, and the breakdown rate is too high. We have to conserve and maintain them for war."

Barak added, "The depot is months behind now on repairs. Especially to Centurions."

"This is no good. The Egyptians won't attack you with a skeletal force," said Ben Gurion. "They have more Russian tanks than they know what to do with."

"Exactly, Prime Minister, they don't know what to do with them," Pasternak said. "We rate their tank crews as ill-trained, and their maneuvers as chaotic."

"But they have plenty of tanks for their chaotic maneuvers, hah?"

Dado Elazar was on the wireless, suspending the exercise until the umpires could rule on Don Kishote's unauthorized maneuver. Ben Gurion interrupted Elazar's stream of jargon. "Who's this fellow, Don Kishote, you're talking about?"

"He's commanding the Red Force, sir," said Elazar.

"Order him up here."

"I've done that."

"What's the matter with him, Dado? Is he irresponsible?"

"Well, he's a fine officer, Prime Minister." Dado glanced at Barak. "A bit of a nonconformist, one might say."

"A bit meshuga, one might say," Barak growled. Kishote was a protégé of his, and he was very annoyed. As the Prime Minister watched with a grim expression, Yossi Nitzan came bounding up the rocky slope.

"You've disobeyed orders, Nitzan," Dado greeted him, barely returning his salute, "and thrown off the whole exercise."

"Sir, direction of approach was left up to me."

"Yes, within parameters of range."

"Sir, my Centurions carried sufficient additional fuel for this approach."

"Loaded outside the tank?"

"Why, yes. No room inside, sir."

"Then you led into hostile territory a force of moving torches waiting to be lit. The umpires will rule you've lost the battle before it starts."

"Sir, we consumed all interior fuel outside enemy gunfire range. We refueled from the jerricans in black night. The exercise stipulates no enemy night air activity."

Barak, Elazar, and the Old Man glanced at each other. Ben Gurion seemed faintly amused.

"Kishote, what's the point of these *kuntzen* [tricks]?" snapped Barak.

"Training in tactical surprise, Colonel. For my battalion, and for them." He gestured down at the Blue Force, where despite the order to suspend, frantic redeployment was going on from north to southeast.

Three army umpires, bald older officers, arrived on the hilltop to consult with Dado and Barak. As they argued, Ben Gurion asked Nitzan, "Why are you called Don Kishote? Do you fight windmills?"

"Living in this land, Prime Minister, who doesn't?"

"True enough." Ben Gurion gave him a tired wise smile. "What are we but a collective Don Kishote, hah, young fellow?" The smile faded. He wanted to know what country Yossi was from, whether he was married, and to whom. "Yael Luria? Her father's a great Zionist. Her brother may head the air force one day. You married well."

The umpires concluded that Nitzan's surprise approach was fair. The war game proceeded, raising a great fog of dust and causing a reverberating motor racket in the hills as jeeps and half-tracks roared here and there. But no live ammunition was being used, and a sense of unreal confusion pervaded. Even for Barak, who had been through many such exercises, the make-believe fight was hard to follow. That was up to the umpires, he figured. At least the tank captains and unit leaders were being pressed to think in field combat conditions, however abstractly the game was played. Ben Gurion was sitting on a rough low reddish rock, yawning and paying scant attention. "Well worth seeing," he remarked to Barak, holding out a hand to be helped to his feet. "Now we go back. Come, Sam." In the car he said, "That Don Kishote, Zev, tell me about him."

"He transferred from paratroopers, Prime Minister, took the required courses, and inside of a year he had the best battalion in the armored corps. Very tough on maintenance, very hard driller, rain or shine. The men follow him, because he does everything, however tough, that he asks them to do."

Sam Pasternak sat silent through this talk about Yael's husband. Ben Gurion tilted his head at him, with a sly look. "Somehow I never heard that Yael Luria got married. And to a fellow who came in from Cyprus!"

"Yes, and they have a son," said Pasternak, in a tone that closed the topic.

When they came into the Sde Boker cottage, Paula emerged from the kitchen, wiping her hands on a gray apron over her long black dress. "They're killing the chickens now. You'll stay for lunch, both of you," she said to Barak and Pasternak. "When did you last taste fresh-killed chicken? Really fresh-killed?"

Pasternak glanced uneasily at the Old Man. "I have a conference in Beersheba at noon, Paula. A helicopter's coming for me."

"And I have to get back to the war game," Barak said, "for the debriefings."

Paula flipped a scornful hand. "You both work like dogs, you deserve a treat. You'll stay. Fresh-killed!"

"Argue with her," said Ben Gurion. He went into the bathroom.

She looked at them with a changed expression. "He's not well. He doesn't sleep. He's losing his appetite. So stay! Please! Maybe he'll eat a good lunch. And then tell me when you last ate such chicken. I make it with paprika."

Ben Gurion took them into his study, and sank wearily into the seat at a desk stacked higgledy-piggledy with newspapers, magazines, and correspondence. Behind him was a solid wall of books, and there were books on other shelves and on the floor. He gestured them to chairs and looked from one to the other in a long silence.

"I'm frightened," he said at last. "Skeleton exercises! We won't fight skeleton wars."

Another silence. He picked up a book from his desk. "Plato. It's a month since I read any Greek. I promised myself to read some Greek every day. A man who can't manage his time is in trouble."

Paula came in with three glasses of tea. Her husband scowled, and she left without a word.

"I met with President Kennedy last year," B.G. said, sipping tea. "I also met him before, when he was a senator. He has a new skin now. Impressive. No Eisenhower yet, no De Gaulle. No Adenauer, even. Those are great men, you only have to be in a room with one and you know. Kennedy, well, I wondered when he was elected how such a boy could become the American President. But he's the President, and we have to convince him to supply us with tanks." He turned to Pasternak. "What's the word from Abe Harman about your mission?" This was the ambassador in Washington. "Will the Secretary of Defense receive you?"

"No. In that respect, Prime Minister, no change from the Eisenhower policy. They'll give us a meeting with State Department and intelligence people, to discuss minor weapons of defense only, and no weapons new to the region. For major supplies we have to look to Europe. No financial aid. The main difference, Abe reports, is that these Kennedy people seem more willing to talk to us."

Ben Gurion heavily sighed. "KADESH was good, in that Israel is now regarded as a serious state. It was bad in that De Gaulle could tell me that no matter what superiority the Arabs acquire in weapons, Israel is invincible. He said that to my face when I visited him. Whether he believes it is another matter. The message I heard was that French supplies can't be counted on anymore."

He stared at them, and held out a stubby palm.

"I shook hands with Adenauer in New York. I did that. The Prime Minister of Israel shook the hand of the German Prime Minister. Ever since, I've been hearing about the Jewish blood on this hand." He clenched it to a fist, and let it fall on the table. "That handshake meant half a billion dollars in aid, when the reparations were running out. When I get to the next world, I'll try to explain to the European Jews why I shook the German's hand. I have to think about the living Jews, and the Jewish State. Maybe in that world they already understand." A pause, and a keen look at Pasternak. "I'm still awaiting the army's word on the Egyptian rockets. Are German scientists involved, or aren't they? The Mossad report says flat out that Germans are building and test-firing them."

Pasternak moved his lips, as though rehearsing an answer to himself. "Indications, yes, Prime Minister. Proof, not yet. The test-fired missiles were inaccurate, our people report, and there have been misfires."

"If German scientists are doing it, and the story comes out," said Ben Gurion, "my German policy will be in ruins. I'll fall."

Impulsively Barak said, "You will not fall, B.G. There's nobody else."

The Old Man shook his head and tightened his mouth in an expressive skeptical gesture. He sipped tea in silence, his look faraway and sad. "So. What equipment will you discuss with the Americans?"

"Not tanks. They're ruled out as being offensive weapons," said Pasternak.

"Never mind, discuss them! Say the words, at least. Don't we need tanks to defend ourselves from invading tanks? Now let's see."

He found a paper amid the pile on his desk, and read off his priority list of weapons. Meantime, he said, combing of the scrap steel market for junked tanks had to be intensified. There were thousands rusting around the world. Israel would have to fix them up and make do with them, until a breakthrough came with at least one great power, as a reliable supplier of new tanks.

"We are surrounded," he said. "We have not one ally. Nasser is arousing the Arab masses, and Russia is arming him. De Gaulle said to me, *'I will not let Israel be annihilated.'* Eisenhower said the same thing when he turned me down on tanks. I told De Gaulle, 'By the time you fine gentlemen decide we're being annihilated, it may be a little late to do anything about it.' "

For all this gloomy talk, Barak saw that Ben Gurion livened up as he talked, and his filmy eyes cleared. Delicious odors were wafting in from the kitchen as the Old Man gave Pasternak his emphatic final instruction about the Washington visit. The Kennedy people had reluctantly agreed to sell Israel the Hawk antiaircraft missile system, but now they were pressuring him to accept instead a British missile, the Bloodhound.

"The answer is *no*. We hold them to the Hawk!" B.G. struck the desk with the hand that had shaken Adenauer's. "It's all a dodging game, to let the *other* fellow offend the Arabs. We need the Hawk to defend against Ilyushin bombers, don't we? We need it even more to get the Americans to supply us with one serious weapon, and break the ice." He stared hard at Pasternak, then at Barak. "Do you both understand that?"

Pasternak said, "Zev has asked to be let out of this mission."

The Old Man turned an inquiring look to Barak.

"Family reasons, Prime Minister."

"Is Nakhama all right? And the children?"

"They're all right."

Ben Gurion waited for him to elaborate, but he said no more. "Well, Sam, get someone else, then. There will be other missions, more important yet."

"You've never tasted such chicken in your life," said Paula through the door. "Come!"

"The fact is, I'm starved," said the Prime Minister, jumping up.

Zev Barak was experiencing surprise at his own reaction to

being released from going to Washington. Regret! Belated irrational regret. He was also relieved, his decision had been sensible, but
he wished he had not propped that damned snapshot of that
damned Emily where Nakhama had seen it.

Paula Ben Gurion slipped her arm through Barak's. "You see,
Zev? It did him good that you stayed. He could talk out his heart."
She patted her shapeless bodice. "He carries the whole country
right in here."

"You really don't mind if I go to the wedding?" said Yael. "By
myself?"

"Well, Aryeh will be taken care of, as you say, and what else
matters?"

Yael would have preferred a different response; a protest, an
argument, even a masterful turndown. She was clearing away the
plates of a late supper. Still in a dusty uniform, Kishote was writing
on a clipboard, with the mimeographed exercise order out on the
kitchen table, turned to a middle page. Beside it lay the invitation,
and a picture of Lee Bloom's bride-to-be.

"We've never been to America, either of us," she said.
"Wouldn't it be nice to go together? All expenses paid, Yossi!"

"Not possible. Go ahead, enjoy yourself."

"The thing is" — her tone sharpened a bit — "once I'm in
California, I wouldn't want to rush back. There's so much to see!"

"God, I was starved." Kishote put aside the clipboard and
stood up. "Now a shower."

"She's beautiful, isn't she?"

Yossi picked up the photograph, a studio glamor shot, and
wrinkled his nose over it. "How old does he say she is, nineteen?
She doesn't even look that." He read from the thick creamy wedding announcement engraved in lace-thin italics, "Mary Macready.
Hm. Old Hassidic name."

"He says her mother's Jewish. They're getting married in a
temple, anyway."

"Lee is a fool." He dropped the picture as though discarding
a playing card.

"Worth how many million dollars now?"

"Yes, he can afford her." Kishote went into Aryeh's room to look at the boy asleep. Soon the shower noisily gushed.

Yael undressed with some haste and threw on a peach satin negligee from Paris, damaged in her shop and bought cheap. At a mirror she gave herself a hard looking-over. Nothing wrong with what she saw. Most men she knew would want that, some of them pretty badly. Some still approached her. This Don Kishote, after five years of married life, baffled Yael. He could make love or not when he came home, more or less as she pleased. If invited by gesture, look, or word, sure; otherwise even after a week or two in the field he would go to sleep, or read, or work on army papers. Would he take the negligee as an invitation? She slapped on perfume. "The question is," he emerged from the hallway in a bathrobe, drying his head, "whether Aryeh won't tear Nahalal apart. Does Benny know what he'd be taking on? Does Irit? Does the moshav council?"

"Irit handles whole nurseries. Aryeh won't be so wild when he has all those moshav children to play with."

"Maybe not."

"Why can't you come? It's been ages since you've had leave."

"My unit was a disgrace in the exercise. I have to drill their heads off and make staff changes."

Yael hesitated. Then, as he got the clipboard and sat down in an armchair, she said very casually, "Why, Sam Pasternak told me you were the star of the war game. Said that even Ben Gurion commended you."

The shot at least grazed him. He did look up, eyebrows raised. "Sam? You talked to Sam Pasternak? When? How come?"

"Well, it was quite accidental." Yael sat, crossing her shapely legs so that the satin skirt fell away. "I was in the El Al office, checking on reservations to Los Angeles. It's a mess. You have to keep changing airlines."

Full stop.

He said after a moment, "And Sam Pasternak?"

"Oh yes. Sam. He's going to Washington soon. No details, of course. You know Sam. He was getting his ticket. Anyway, your unit did extremely well, he said."

"The others were worse, that's all. Pretty nightgown."

"This thing? Shopworn."

"Let's go to bed."

"You have work to do, don't you?" He put aside the clipboard, pulled her to her feet, and swept a hard muscular arm around her shoulders. She added, "And you must be dead tired."

"Come quietly," he said. "Don't wake Aryeh."

The lovemaking was always satisfying; different from Sam Pasternak's rough ways, which she could not forget, and which had often shocked and roused her to her very bones. Their bed experience really continued their first encounter in the Georges Cinq; fun and games between two people who did not love each other, but enjoyed uncomplicated sex. Yael's trouble was that for her it was getting complicated.

Not for her husband. He openly joked about their marriage even to others, calling it, "Raise Aryeh Incorporated." Don Kishote was capable of the deepest feeling. That, she knew. He adored the boy, and instinct told her, though she had no way to prove it, that he had adored that prudish mathematician, Shayna Matisdorf, and perhaps still did. He never talked about Shayna. So far as Yael knew, he had not seen her since her one visit to their briefly Turkish flat, in which they still lived.

"Are you sure of this?" she whispered, as Kishote reached for her after a while in the dark, and pulled her close. "You don't have to impress me. I'm impressed." Now what had done this, Yael wondered, as she yielded. That negligee? Good investment, if so, at thirty-nine lira! The mention of Sam Pasternak? The prospect of her going off to California? How could she know?

He was whispering the right endearments, doing all the right things, it was lively fun with this husband of hers. And yet, wrapped in her arms and legs, sweetly excitingly loving her, Don Kishote remained — in a way impossible to accuse him of — unattached, inscrutable, not hers. They kissed and said goodnight. He was soon asleep. Yael lay wide awake, thinking with some resentment of a trip to America by herself; and feeling, as she too often felt, like a married shmata.

25

Dorothy in Oz

In her office overlooking the field where green-bloomered summer session girls were playing hockey with screams, squeals, and ferocious clacking of sticks, Emily Cunningham contemplated the picture of Zev Barak which she customarily set on the desk when she wrote to him. Taken for an army journal on his promotion to colonel two years ago, it showed some gray in his thick hair, but otherwise the strong-chinned round face and the wise faintly worried brown eyes had not changed since the famous night of the fireflies.

FOXDALE SCHOOL
MIDDLEBURG, VIRGINIA

Letter #26

Wolf! You wretched Gray Wolf!

Did you imagine that I wouldn't find out?! Do you think that I'm the daughter of the greatest intelligence man in the USA for nothing? You could have come to Washington, you were ordered to come, *and you begged off!* I must have an explanation, full, convincing, and grovelling, or this correspondence — this entire peculiarly luminous and enchanting friendship of ours — gets the axe. I mean this, I'm dead serious. I will not be dodged. I will not be scorned. And I will know — *why?* Why did you pass up the chance to see me?

Having vented her disappointment she was unsure how to proceed, and thought of a brusque sign-off with *Yours, Emily.* But writing to Zev Barak was a joy, like receiving a letter from him or cantering alone through cool woods in autumn. So after a pause to take thought, she went on:

> Okay, I choke off my wrath for old times' sake, and await your excuse. My news is that, incredible as it seems, I may become headmistress here soon, though I'm ridiculously young and unsuited! Our headmistress, Fiona Salmeter, is an excellent educator and administrator, wonderful with girls and parents alike, and genuinely religious, which is important in a school supposedly nondenominational but really Christian through and through, with regular chapel and such. Our star visiting minister has been the Reverend Wentworth, a splendid speaker, a serious Old Testament scholar. He's published many articles on the Book of Amos.
>
> Well, Fiona seems to have shot Reverend Wentworth in the groin. They've been having a discreet affair for about fifteen years. Now the Reverend Wentworth has been trying to break it off, because he was recently widowed, and he wants to marry again, and his new lady doesn't approve of Fiona. His late wife Millicent didn't mind Fiona at all. They used to ride the trails together a lot, and play knock rummy at night and drink Kahlúa. Millicent was an atheist at heart and not too happy about being married to Reverend Wentworth, though she didn't dislike him, exactly. She was just glad that Fiona did for him, as you might say, in certain ways. I knew this Millicent and liked her, if her religious obtuseness somewhat put me off. She loved poetry, especially by women. Sometimes she and I would read Elizabeth Barrett Browning or Elinor Wylie to each other. When Fiona didn't play knock rummy with Millicent, she played gitchi-gitchi with Reverend Wentworth, and then Millie and I would read poetry. That's what Hester and I called hanky-panky at college, gitchi-gitchi. It's interesting that in all the years the English language has been evolving since Beowulf, no polite usage has ever emerged for that simple business. As a career virgin I'm unlikely to improvise one, so I'll make do with gitchi-gitchi. Anyway, the Reverend Wentworth is in no danger, but for some time he will not be interested in gitchi-gitchi. The story he and Fiona have told the sheriff and the school board is that she asked him to clean her gun, and he inadvertently peppered himself in the groin. Since it happened in her bedroom the tale is faintly fishy, and all that is up in the air right now.
>
> What else? Oh, Hester's show in that New York gallery was a surprising success. Did I write you that she developed her own way of

abstract painting, in the vein of Jackson Pollock? She makes holes in the sides of closed fresh paint tubes, and so when she squeezes a tube the paint squirts on the canvas in utterly random ways. Hester calls this "Stochastic Holism." There was a big article in the *New York Times* making elephantine fun of stochastic holism, but as a result Hester Laroche was news, and collectors started to come and buy. Modest prices, but the stuff sold. People put bets on new painters, you know. Long-shot horses. I went to the opening, and there was old Hester in a Buster Brown haircut and a pink satin tent dress, and her husband in a tuxedo looking proud and baffled. Hester may never go back to Eugene, Oregon. Unlike these smart New Yorkers, those squares in Eugene don't appreciate stochastic holism.

So much and no more. You deserve no more! Remember hereafter, you wretched Gray Wolf, that Christian Cunningham knows everything that is happening everywhere in the world, and about Israel he knows *absolutely everything.* Assume that and you won't be caught out again. No lovey-dovey sign-off, I am angry with you. For what it's worth, CC thinks the world of Sam Pasternak and expects the mission to have some success. You were a fool to pull out. Why, *why?* Will I eat you?

> Your outraged
> Emily

The Air France plane was thrumming smoothly over the black ocean. The lights had just been turned off after the movie, and moonlight shone through the small square window on Yael's face.

"Sam, don't be ridiculous." Yael took the familiar hairy hand off her thigh and dropped it back in his lap.

Sam spoke genially from the darkness beside her. "Aren't we friends?"

"What a stupid movie," Yael said. "I should have gone to sleep. You, too."

"Yael, I'm thinking of jumping to Los Angeles for that wedding. I was invited, you know."

"And your business in Washington?"

"It's the weekend. The State Department shuts down every Saturday and Sunday, the way we do for Yom Kippur. Even stricter."

"Suit yourself."

Silence. Darkness makes for intimate conversation, and after a while Sam said, "That husband of yours is quite a guy, that Don Kishote."

"I think so."

"He's going places."

No response.

"You're happy?"

"Very. Sam, if you're not sleepy, I am."

"How is it you don't have more kids, then, just the one? Do you have a problem?"

"Me? Certainly not. He doesn't want more."

"Funny. Ruth and I don't get along, never have, but we've got three. It happens." No response. "You know, Yael, I'm not much of a believer, but I do believe marriages are made in heaven."

Yael was piqued. "You do?"

"Absolutely. Such botches have to be the work of a Jewish bureaucracy."

Despite herself she burst out laughing, too loudly for a darkened plane. She put a hand to her mouth, then said, "Well, hamood, sticking to Ruth — for five very long years, friend, while I was around — was your idea."

"I know, I know." Heavy bump of the airplane. Louder engine noise, flash of seat belt sign. He said, fastening his belt, "Incidentally, I spent last weekend in Tiberias. Just a breather before this trip. The Pension Geffen is gone, Yael, did you know that? All torn down, and they're building a big hotel there."

"Well, nothing lasts forever, Sam. That's a choice waterfront spot."

"Some things last. Memories."

"They fade, too."

"Do they?" He took her hand. "You mean to tell me you don't remember the Geffen? St. Peter's fish for breakfast with a bottle of Carmel hock? Rowing on the Sea of Galilee?"

"I certainly remember that you made me do the rowing, you monster."

"Your superior officer. Besides, I'd had a rough night."

She snatched away her hand and hit him with it. "All right, that'll do. Did Ruthie go with you to Tiberias?"

"Ruthie's back in her London flat, didn't you know that?"

"How should I?"

"Well, she is. Amos and Ilana are staying with me. She took Leah."

"Imagine that. Chief of military intelligence wasn't important enough for Ruthie, hey?"

"That wasn't it. Porfirio got posted to London as ambassador." Porfirio had been the Colombian chargé d'affaires in Tel Aviv.

"Oh, I see. How convenient that she has a flat there."

"Don't be unkind. Ruthie's really a mess. She and I won't make it much longer, Yael."

"I wish this plane would stop bouncing around, don't you?"

"Look, I'll come to Los Angeles. Where will you be staying?"

"I don't know. Lee Bloom made the arrangements. Don't bother on my account, it's pointless. Sam, shut up or I'll move. I'm tired."

Silence. Plane motors murmuring, small bumps, then smooth flying. After a while the seat belt sign went off.

"Sam" — low voice, high charge — "you'll need it at the State Department for shaking hands with diplomats. You don't want it broken off. Last warning. No more! . . . That's better."

A baritone chuckle. "Sleep well."

"Same to you."

On a Sunday morning the Manhattan financial district looks not only shut down but plague-stricken, so deserted are the steep stone canyons. Yael and Pasternak got out of the Hertz car and their footsteps echoed as they walked along Broad Street, in white sunshine slanting steeply through the silent empty towers.

"My God," said Yael, halting and pointing round-eyed at a block-lettered street sign, WALL STREET, white on blue.

"What about it?"

"Sam, when I was a kid in Nahalal, our teachers were socialists, Marxists. Wall Street was the evil center of the capitalist hell. Here it is. Wall Street!"

"Just a street, you see," said Pasternak. "What we should do is go up on the Empire State Building. From there you'll see it all."

"But when's your plane?"

"There are always planes to Washington."

Yael shakily laughed. "Kishote once took me up on the Eiffel Tower and I got the horrors. Which is higher?"

"This is. But you won't get the horrors."

The wind was strong on the Empire State's observation platform, so he took her to the glassed-in area. "There it is," he said, with a grand gesture of one arm, "not only Manhattan. All of New York. There's Long Island, there's New Jersey, there's Brooklyn. Exceptionally clear day. Sometimes it's all muck and you can't even see the Statue of Liberty. Looks like a toy down there, doesn't it?"

She stared around, then pulled a silk scarf from her purse, tied up her hair, and walked out in the wind. "It all really exists, doesn't it?" She seemed to be talking to herself. Following her, he had to strain to hear her. "It's really here. It's not a movie and it's not a dream. Sam, why should anyone want to live anywhere in the world but here? What other place is like this? Paris is *nothing*."

"Wait till you see Los Angeles."

"It can't compare."

"You're wrong. That's the place New Yorkers move to. They either die, or they go to Los Angeles. I'll see you there next week, then we'll make comparisons." He glanced at his watch, and raised his voice over the wail of the wind. "I'd better put you on your plane."

As the elevator dropped he said, noting her bemused look, "Yael, I think you're discovering America. Mrs. Columbus."

She gave him a wry smile.

Yael's bemusement deepened as she flew westward. Hours and hours of droning plane engines, more than enough to fly from Tel Aviv to Paris, and still they flew on! The descent to Chicago in a crashing electrical storm, with blue-white lightning zigzagging and cracking past her window, should have frightened her, as it obviously did the passengers around her. Children cried, people vomited, stewardesses scurried and staggered in the aisles, the lights went on and off, and Yael felt only drunken exaltation; Mrs. Columbus on the pitching deck of the *Santa Maria*, impervious to seasickness, sighting the New World.

She had to change planes in Chicago. All flights were delayed. Enjoying the mere vast size of the terminal and the variety of the shops, she wandered for hours amid disgruntled wet throngs. The sun was out again when her plane took off over high waves crashing and spraying against a shore lined with tall buildings. There was nothing beyond the shore but blue water, clear to the horizon; Lake Michigan, an inland Mediterranean Sea, and not even the largest of the Great Lakes! So it went, hour after hour; limitless panoramas of green farmland, splotches of big cities, more farmland as far as the eye could see through drifting clouds. The pilot made a full circle over the Grand Canyon. *Oo-ah!* A wadi, nothing else, but when America produced a wadi, it staggered the soul with its depth, its breadth, its majesty, its ragged meandering colossal frightening red bleakness. Mars on earth, tucked in a corner of one state with a beautiful name, *Arizona* . . .

A crayoned sign held by a short Oriental in a black chauffeur's uniform standing at the plane gate read NITZAN. Yael was not expecting to be met. Had the free spender Lee Bloom ordered a car for her?

"I'm Mrs. Nitzan."

"Yes, madame."

He bobbed his head, showed great teeth in a smile and took her handbag, then helped get her luggage, and led her through automatic doors to a parked silver Rolls-Royce, out of which stepped a lean little man with close-cropped thin gray hair. "Welcome to Los Angeles, Yael." A peculiar grin curled up his mouth in a U-shape. "I'm Sheva Leavis, Lee's partner. I'm just off to Hong Kong. I'll be back for Lee's wedding. Wang will drive you into town." His English was only slightly accented.

Utterly startled, hypnotized by the gleaming Rolls, Yael tried to act composed. "Why, thank you. How nice of you. Where will I be staying?"

"Well, that's up to you. Lee has booked you into the Beverly Wilshire. But I have a little place here, and my wife's in Vancouver, she's not well, so nobody's home at the moment. You're welcome to stay in the guesthouse. Wang and his wife will take good care of you."

"Mr. Leavis, I wouldn't think of imposing. I'd better go to the hotel."

"Madame, please come, it will give us pleasure," spoke up the chauffeur, his *l*'s and *r*'s blurry. "My wife very good cook. All strictly kosher."

Yael now wondered whether this was some elaborate practical joke of Lee Bloom's. She had of course heard of Sheva Leavis, the Iraqi man of mystery. But he was never photographed, and this plain little fellow in slacks and a polo shirt was nothing like her idea of a tycoon. She glanced at him, and the strange smile came and went with sudden upsliding mouth corners. "You won't be uncomfortable, Yael. Hotels are cold."

It was the kind of decision Yael was apt to make, like going to Paris with Don Kishote. She held out her hand to Leavis, who shook it with a dry cool grip. "Okay, Mr. Leavis. I can hardly refuse."

He opened the car door for her. "Excellent. I'll see you on Friday. It will be nice to have company for Shabbat dinner. Wang will be with you shortly. How nice that we meet on such a happy occasion." A sliding smile, and he closed the door and went off with the chauffeur, leaving Yael inhaling the rich odors of a Silver Cloud Rolls-Royce interior, marvelling at the inlaid wood trim and enjoying the caress of soft leather under her thighs.

The automobile rode, or rather floated, much like a cloud, through a fantastic forest of oil well derricks and on into a green palm-lined dreamland of mansions topping grounds like small parks, on a sharply curving highway called Sunset Boulevard. Wang turned off through a stone archway and wound up a knoll all smooth lawns and bright flowers, toward a sprawling structure with a red-tiled roof. Partway up the knoll, half-hidden by a hedge with immense red blooms, was a white cottage. "Here is the guesthouse, Madame." Wang brought her bags inside, gave her keys, and inquired whether she would like a drink, perhaps a glass of champagne.

"Why, I guess champagne would be nice."

Left alone, she sank into a pink plushy armchair, kicked off her shoes, and peered around at her surroundings; a large living-dining room furnished in modern style, a rough-hewn stone fireplace with large real logs, unfamiliar paintings on the walls that were not reproductions, she could see the impasto ridges. Yael was no longer Mrs. Columbus. She was Dorothy in Oz.

Barak had a hard time starting a reply to Emily Cunningham's letter #26. He considered leaving it unanswered, and letting the thing die off so. But he could not, and once he began writing, he wrote several pages late at night, after Nakhama and the children were asleep. When he read over the outpouring he knew he must either go back to his first idea, tear it up, and choke off the relationship at this point, or send it and plunge ahead into risky waters. The letter ended:

> . . . and there you have it. You demanded an explanation, and now you know why I pulled out of the military procurement mission. In the army we always review an operation or a campaign to see where the mistakes were, where we did well, what we failed to foresee, and what new ideas or doctrines we can derive. I guess my mind is used to working that way. I've learned strange lessons from this experience. First and foremost, and hardest for me as yet to grasp, a man can really love two women, love them in completely different ways. Next, it seems that love between man and woman can fire up without sex or the possibility of sex, because there you are and have been for years, far around the bulge of the earth, and here I am, yet it's happened.
>
> So I find that mere letters can create love. It's no illusion, that's sure. I know what love is — far more than you do — because I've loved Nakhama for years and years, and you claim to have had only this one unfulfilled infatuation with a distant foreigner, if we don't count old Hiroshima. Of the two of us, I now think I'm the crazier one. You have the excuse of your inexperience. I have no excuse. I'm just in love with you, and your ridiculously funny yet moving letters, and your eccentric sharp mind, and your darting hands, and your laughing eyes, and your lean figure that looks so sweet, even in those schoolmarmish pictures you send me. Good camouflage, but I see right through it to *Emily*, the charmer and the haunt.
>
> Therefore, child, I will continue avoiding any assignment to Washington until you're safely married. All right? Just be damned sure of that. Nakhama is not only the love of my life, the mother of my kids, she's my best truest friend. You're no siren by character or intent, but still you and I had better keep an ocean between us, or — as you threaten — we

must axe this "luminous" and most unlikely relationship. Those are the
terms. Have it your way. Either way. As we say here, *zeh mah she'yaish.*
That's it.

Wolfgang

He had never before signed his former name. Nor did he
know why he did so now. He read the letter over and over, tucked
it in a desk drawer, slept on it, and after breakfasting as usual in the
morning with Nakhama, he stopped at the post office on the way to
the Ministry of Defense, and mailed it.

26

Lee Bloom's Wedding

Yael was almost gasping, so thick was the cigarette smoke in Herschel Rosenzweig's apartment on Fairfax Avenue. It was hard to hear what her old school friend Osnat Friedkin was saying, because of the animated Hebrew talk in the crowded room. "Enjoying this? Everybody knows Herschel and Bluma, and we all drop in on Friday night."

"I feel I'm back in Tel Aviv," Yael shouted.

"You are," said Osnat. She worked in a travel agency catering to Israelis arriving in or departing from Los Angeles, mostly arriving.

It was a far more familiar scene for Yael, in fact, than the Shabbat meal she had just eaten with Sheva Leavis, waited on by Wang in a white coat, at a long polished table where Leavis had invited her to light the candles and make the blessing. These people smoking cigarettes, drinking tea or soda, nibbling shrimps and crackers as they chatted or argued, were more her sort. Herschel Rosenzweig, a portly journalist with a grizzled beard, sat in a corner on a large armchair that commanded the room, feet up on the ottoman, smoking a long cigar, and expounding a familiar theme; to wit, that David Ben Gurion was a fascist dictator with a natural affinity for the Germans, and that Israel's hope of creating a just socialist society, a light to the nations, had long since gone down the drain. Zionism had lost its soul, and the Arabs now held the moral high ground. People nearest him were listening, the others were all talking at once.

Green cards, from what Yael could overhear, were topic number one. These Israelis either had green cards, or were waiting for green cards, or had been refused green cards, or were riskily working without green cards. There was also much violent disputation about who was and who wasn't a snob, and why. Osnat Friedkin had married her American dentist, had since divorced, but meantime had acquired two children and citizenship, so she did not need a green card.

"Hello there, Yael." Rosenzweig had loudly greeted her, not stirring from his armchair when she and Osnat arrived. He was a Nahalal expatriate, and his *yerida*, "descent," from Israel to Los Angeles, was still an embarrassment in the moshav; especially since he had once written fervent nationalist poetry, and his songs were still sung by soldiers on the march. "How's your Don Kishote? I hear he's a star in the armor. I was in the armor, you know."

"Yossi is fine."

"So! You've come for the big wedding, and you're staying with old Sheva Leavis." To that extent, thought Yael, Israeli Los Angeles was certainly like Tel Aviv; everybody tended to know everything about everybody else. Osnat had already filled her in with all the gossip, mainly deleterious, about the people in the room.

"That's where I'm staying."

"Well, Sheva is no snob. That's all right. That brother-in-law of yours, now there's a snob. Is it true that Frank Sinatra is coming to the wedding?"

"I have no idea."

Yael had seen Lee Bloom just once, when he had visited her for a hurried half hour in the guesthouse, looking stout, sleek, and nervous. The first thing he had said, before he sat down, was that Frank Sinatra was coming to the wedding. A plane chartered by Lee would bring him from Las Vegas and return him there. Sinatra was appearing at one of the big hotels, and could not miss a performance. He planned to come to the temple, as well as to the reception at the Bel-Air Hotel. "Frank's a great guy, good Catholic but very tolerant," was Lee's thumbnail sketch of the towering celebrity. Yael was well aware that Mary Macready at eighteen had been much photographed at parties and nightclubs with the great Sinatra. Weather forecasts for the weekend were still uncertain, said Lee, that was the only problem, but it was a four-motor plane and they were counting on Sinatra. He was a good friend of Mary's and the weather was seldom bad this time of year.

Bluma Rosenzweig stopped passing soft drinks and canapés long enough to throw a cushion beside Yael's chair and plop down to chat. A Nahalal farm girl a few years older than Yael, she had kept her muscular figure, and the charcoal American pants suit looked good on her. The makeup was still Israeli, too much green around the eyes, too much black on the eyebrows. She remarked on how well Yael looked and was explaining that she insisted on speaking Hebrew at home for the sake of the children, when Sam Pasternak appeared through the swirling smoke. Herschel Rosenzweig lumbered out of his chair.

"Sam, what a surprise!"

Talk of movies, parties, snobs, and green cards ceased, and in the fall of noise the room focussed on Pasternak. So Yael had seen an army conference room change from chaotic chatter to sharp attention to one arrival, when the arrival was Ben Gurion or Dayan. She felt herself the target of covert glances and of whispering behind hands. Those who didn't already know she was the old girlfriend of the chief of military intelligence had been filled in, she could assume, by Osnat Friedkin.

"I figured I might find you here," Pasternak managed to mutter to her, as Rosenzweig led him to the commanding armchair, where he asked for club soda. The Israelis clustered around him in a disorderly semicircle, pulling up chairs or standing, firing questions at him — about new terrorist border incursions, a bomb explosion in a Jerusalem marketplace, a reported fistfight of politicians in a committee room of the Knesset, the rumor that Ben Gurion might resign again — and over and over, *"Mah b'emet ha'matzav?"* ("What's really the situation?") The tumbling questions and his short answers went on until Rosenzweig's rough voice cut through the others: "Sam, what about the Egyptian rockets?"

Abrupt quiet. Pasternak sipped soda, with the heavy-lidded look that was his trademark.

"What about them?" he responded after a pause, in the gravelly tone that was a warning not to press him.

"Nasser says — he said it on television and we all saw it — that those rockets can hit any target south of Beirut."

Pasternak growled, "Nasser says a lot of things. Nasser suffers no shortage of mouth."

"Is there any truth to it at all?" ventured Osnat Friedkin, perhaps bolder than the rest because she did not need a green card.

"You saw the movies of the rockets on TV," said Pasternak. "There are rockets in Egypt. Whether the Egyptians can hit anything with them" — he shrugged his thick broad shoulders — "is the question. I mean, intentionally." This brought an uneasy laugh in the room. "Well, rockets are nothing to laugh at, but let me just say we have bigger problems right now."

"Like what?" inquired Bluma Rosenzweig.

Pasternak's large head swung here and there, taking in the whole room. "Well, like yerida." Thick silence. "Nothing personal, comrades, but the Arabs don't really need rockets, do they? They need patience. They just have to wait while Israel gradually leaks away to America, with or without green cards."

"Don't look at me," said a bushy-haired thin young man with a pencil mustache. "I finish my doctorate next June and I go home. My wife's back there now with the kids."

A burly red-faced man said, "I fought in two wars. When I got out of the army, no jobs. What was I supposed to do? Eat pictures of Herzl?"

"We all fought," said an angry voice, "that's no argument. And there are jobs back home. Only a dishwasher here makes more than a bank manager there. That's the fact of it."

"And spends it all, with these prices" — another voice — "and he's no better off, and he's just washing dishes. *That's* the fact of it. Sam is right, and Sarah and I are talking about going back as soon as Irma finishes high school."

Arguments broke out all over the room, so vehement and cacophonous that the departure of Pasternak and Yael, slipping out one after the other, went almost unnoticed.

"Not very tactful," she said, getting into the front seat of a rented Ford.

"I was tired. Let them chew on the truth, for once." He drove up Fairfax Avenue too fast, and jammed on brakes at a red light.

"You're in a bad mood."

"My nephew Uri was there. Did you see him? Red sweater, glasses? Brilliant mechanical engineer. Wouldn't look me in the eye. Sat in a corner eating pumpkin seeds."

"It didn't go well in Washington?"

He gave her the heavy-lidded look, and said no more until they were speeding along Sunset Boulevard. "I don't blame those State Department guys. They haven't changed their line since the Balfour Declaration. There are seven hundred million Moslems, and after Hitler about ten million Jews. There are eighty million Arabs, and maybe a million Israelis — the ones who haven't leaked away yet. The Arabs have oil, the Jews have bopkess. Where does the interest of America lie? Any question? That's assuming the striped-pants boys, as Truman called them, aren't anti-Semites. Some are, but that's beside the point."

"You were right about Los Angeles, Sam. It's the Garden of Eden. If I leak away, this is where I drip to."

That brought an affectionate side-glance. "Seen a lot?"

"Sheva Leavis has this Chinese houseman. He drove me all over in a Silver Cloud Rolls-Royce. You just have to drive up to the Griffith Observatory at night, Sam, to decide on yerida, if you're going to."

"Never been there."

"Tell me about Leavis. How can a man be that rich? Own a gorgeous estate in Beverly Hills that he stays in maybe ten days a year? Equipped with a Rolls and a Chinese couple?"

Pasternak grunted. "Beverly Hills real estate is oil land. The Rolls too keeps going up in value. He has the use, and while it all stands idle he makes money. That's Sheva."

"He seems to be really religious."

"So were the first Rothschilds."

Stop-and-go as the lights changed, they drove a long way west without further words, into the sharper curves of Sunset Boulevard through shadowy trees and scattered lamplit mansions. Yael had half expected a hand on her knee (or higher) along the way, and would not much have minded, actually. It was always good to know that Sam's desire was there. She had not forgotten his remark in the darkened plane that his marriage might not last.

"So President Kennedy makes no difference?" She broke the silence. "None at all?"

He held up a hand. "I didn't say we had a failure. There's a difference. But you know, Kennedy said that the biggest surprise in his presidency so far is that he gives orders and nothing happens."

"Then he's a weak President."

"Yael, Presidents come and Presidents go. The bureaucrats sit there, and fudge orders they don't like. At fudging, these State Department guys are world masters. They wait the Presidents out. So far this time they're like viziers handling a boy king. I think he'll surprise them if he's reelected. He got in by a hair, so he isn't sure of himself or his power."

"Sheva's place is just past this light, to the left."

"I know where Sheva's place is." He pulled under the stone archway, stopped, and turned to her with his old crafty grin, barely visible in the archway lamplight. "Too bad you're not in the hotel."

"Why?"

"I'd try banging on the door."

"You'd just get sore knuckles."

"I've never changed, Yael."

"The guesthouse is up there. Do I walk?"

He started the car, drove up the knoll, and braked with the engine running. "There. Could Wang do better?"

"Thanks." She gave him a cool kiss on the cheek, pressing his hand. "Israel isn't leaking away, thanks to guys like you."

He said, "And Don Kishote."

"See you in the temple, Sam."

Pasternak took the curves of Sunset Boulevard too fast as he drove off to his dingy motel, perturbed by a hunch that Yael might well leak to America; not on this trip, but someday when she could work it all out. She was good at that, and in the end Yael did what she wanted to. The notion of Israel without Yael there — even as Don Kishote's wife — gave Sam Pasternak a disagreeable feeling of emptiness. The rented car swerved and rocked down the winding boulevard, and coming around a curve he had to jam on squealing brakes at a red light. He sat there wondering why lights in America took so bloody long to change, thinking of Yael and of that hard night long ago in Tiberias.

The fast-dancing wipers could not keep up with thick rain beating against the windshield, and Wang had to slow down. A few yards ahead of the Rolls, Sunset Boulevard was a gray blur of blowing water.

"Well, no Frank Sinatra, I guess," said Yael.

Sheva Leavis's reply was a brief upsliding smile. Arriving from Hong Kong on Friday evening just before sundown he had looked dead-white and decrepit, and his dinner talk had lapsed into long silences. Today at breakfast he had been in high spirits, and he was looking healthier.

"We be late for ceremony, Mr. Leavis," said Wang, "but faster dangerous."

"They'll delay it, Wang." To Yael he added, "Or if Sinatra can't come, they'll postpone it."

She looked to see whether he was smiling. He was not, but his eyes were crinkled. "Sheva, *when* were you in my Dizengoff shop, anyway? I feel such a fool, not to remember it."

"Why should you? I brought my niece there, two years ago. An orphan, I married her off, gave her money and let her pay the bills. You run a nice shop. Efficient. Good value."

"I have to do something."

"Yes, army pay is not much anywhere, but in Israel it's bad."

"Probably I married the wrong brother."

He grinned at her. "Your husband is a great fighter for our people. Lee buys and sells real estate."

"That's all Lee does now?"

"Lee does several things. Some with me, some on his own. He does well." Leavis shrugged. "He likes Las Vegas too much."

Limousines were piling up at the temple entrance. In a raincoat and bareheaded, Sam Pasternak leaned against a tall pillar of the portico, smoking a cigarette. "Ah, there you are, Yael. You're to go right to the bride's room. Lee is running around without a head. He's afraid Sinatra's plane has gone down. Hello, Sheva."

"You're not serious," said Leavis.

"Well, the charter company told him Sinatra took off in the rain, and now they can't contact the pilot. Lee is phoning them every five minutes. Come, Yael."

"Why the bride's room?"

"You're his only relative at this thing. She asked to meet you."

In the foyer Lee Bloom came pushing through the crowd in a morning coat and striped trousers, his ascot tie askew, his hair disordered. "They heard from the pilot! Frankie is safe! The storm messed up the aircraft frequencies."

"That's a relief," said Pasternak.

"Yes, isn't it? Everybody's late anyway. What a day! The organist and the choir have plenty of music to kill time, so that's no problem. Sheva, you'll be sitting up on the stage with the rabbi, Congressman Milstein, State Senator Harrigan, and Frankie. Come, Yael, Mary keeps asking for you."

Leavis reached into a breast pocket of an exquisitely tailored black suit, and put on a small skullcap.

"You won't need that here, Sheva," said Pasternak. "It's Reform."

"Well, there are Torahs in the building," said Leavis.

Lee Bloom led Yael through the noisy foyer and down a pink-carpeted corridor. "Why am I the only relative, Lee? What about all those Blumenthal cousins in Buffalo?"

"Look, I offered to fly them out, three families! They're Orthodox, they wouldn't come to a Reform temple. Crazy. So I'm damn glad you're here. Why didn't Yossi come?"

"The army, Lee."

Lee shook his head. "He'll never get to the top in that army. He's not a Palmakhnik, he's not a kibbutznik or moshavnik, he's not a B.G. protégé, he's an outsider, he's nobody. Maybe he'll make brigadier. Maybe! Both of you should come here, you can do more for Israel here. This is the bride's room. Go on in, I'm not supposed to see her."

Mary Macready threw her arms around Yael. "My sister-in-law! Mama, here's Yael Nitzan, she came all the way from Tel Aviv!"

The mother, a small woman in a floor-length dress, said, "Hello. I'm Jewish."

"So I understand," said Yael.

The bridesmaids fussing at Mary were so pretty that Yael supposed they were showgirls. But none compared to Mary Macready. Lee had picked himself an exquisite piece of work: immense green eyes set in her head like slanted emeralds, a small uptilted nose, a lovely mouth with a full underlip, a cascade of glossy black hair, and an improbable figure, tiny-waisted, slim, and big-bosomed.

"If only Bill had lived for this," said Mrs. Macready. "Bill was my husband, Methodist but very tolerant. Bill was a great fan of Frank Sinatra."

The ceremony was not long delayed by the storm. Sinatra came walking down the center aisle of the nearly full temple in a white skullcap, greeting the buzzing wedding guests with smiles, waves, and handshakes. The rabbi left the platform to escort him up carpeted steps to a high-backed chair between the Holy Ark and Sheva Leavis.

"Why on earth has he got on that yarmulke?" Yael asked Pasternak. They sat together in a front row. "Can't he see nobody else has one, except Sheva?"

"At a Jewish function that's what he wears, I guess."

"And who are all these people anyhow?" She looked around at the rows on rows of guests.

"Lee does a lot of business in Los Angeles. And he flew down two planes full from Las Vegas."

The happy couple were soon standing under the flower-banked canopy with the rabbi. The cantor, a handsome black-robed young man, was pouring out a rich Hebrew nuptial song, backed by an unseen choir.

"If Ruth and I can't go on," Pasternak murmured, touching Yael's fingers, "is there any chance for us?"

She pushed his hand away, muttering, "Oh, Sam, shut up."

"I'm absolutely serious."

"I have a husband, thank you. A wonderful one. Quiet!"

"I know why Don Kishote married you."

Badly jarred, keeping a straight face, she said, "I like this music. Sh!"

Someone behind them echoed, "Sh!"

Sheva left before the wedding brunch began, in a social hall where a large jazz band played and long tables were piled with a lavish buffet. Lee started the dancing with Mary Bloom to great applause, which redoubled when Sinatra, skullcap gone, next twirled the bride. Waiters continuously passed champagne. Pasternak and Yael drank a lot of champagne, ate heartily, and even danced. "You're stepping all over my feet," Yael said. "Why did you drag me out on the floor? You know I can't dance. Neither can you."

"I can with any other woman."

"Thanks."

They continued to clomp around. Afterward he drove her to Sheva Leavis's guest cottage. "You can come in if you want to," she said, as he shut off the ignition.

"I have to turn in this car." He glanced at his watch. "We stayed too long at that balagan. My plane's at one."

"What did you mean, you know why Yossi married me? What kind of nonsense was that?"

The strong face went grave. The heavy eyes drooped almost shut. "I knew long ago."

Yael's mind raced through the possibilities of some disclosure, inadvertent or not, to Sam Pasternak. Yossi would never talk about it, of course. Shayna Matisdorf knew, and might well hate her, but she was not capable of injuring her in that way. What then? Aryeh's early arrival? Sam Pasternak was not guessing. When he said he knew something, he knew.

"I haven't the faintest idea of what you're talking about."

"After KADESH, Yael — months later — we were talking about your trip to Paris. I asked you how you liked the Galeries Lafayette. You said you didn't go to Paris to waste time in a department store. But during KADESH, when I was about to take a nap in the bunker, you told me you'd bought some oo-la-la underwear there." They looked hard into each other's eyes. "Yossi didn't have a French whore in that Georges Cinq bedroom."

With a light laugh, Yael replied, "If you think I slept with Yossi in Paris, fine. It didn't have to be the Georges Cinq, Sam, we were in the same third-rate hotel for two nights."

Pasternak nodded, the half-closed eyes not leaving her face. "So, I'll see you back home. Or are you leaking to Los Angeles here and now?"

"I wouldn't blame Ruth for throwing you out." She leaned to him, kissed his mouth, and let the kiss linger. "You're an animal and a pain. Quite a wedding, wasn't it? Worth the trip."

"Definitely." He started the car. "When will we get that close again to Frank Sinatra?"

Pasternak was used to the unfolding grandeur of America under a transcontinental flight. Shutting out thoughts of Yael and that teasing kiss — she was a fiend at getting her own back — he passed the hours of his return to Washington scribbling a first draft of a report for Ben Gurion, which he meant to show to Christian Cunningham first. It ended:

Conclusion

Accomplishments of this mission, nil except for keeping Hawk AA missile negotiation on track. Bloodhound diversion successfully eliminated. In time we will get this crucial American weapon, but to avoid offending the Arabs, delivery will be put off as long as possible, and we will be asked to soft-pedal the whole matter.

The State Department negotiators could not argue against their own intelligence, which confirms ours, that the Soviet delivery of bombers and fighters to Arab countries threatens our national survival. But the fundamental American position is unchanged: (1) they will not introduce any major new weapons systems into our region (2) we will have to look elsewhere for our main source of supplies (3) they will under no circumstances supply us with weapons of offense. Translation, tanks.

Still, it is not all negative. There has been a change. They have reviewed our entire defense posture with us, and that in itself is a development. They are willing to listen, and to have another review "if and when the situation warrants." Probably the real difference is a different President. However, by the time the will of the President filters down through the bureaucracy, it is diluted and fogged over. Direct contact with President Kennedy on these matters might help. Of that there seems to be no present prospect.

27

The Yellow Flowers

Knuckles rapping at the door of Shayna Matisdorf's hot windowless office in the Technion Institute. "Come in!" She glanced up from the design manual of the Mirage aircraft and fell back in her chair, pulling off black round glasses. "You!"

"Come with me for a ride in the country," said Don Kishote. "You look pale."

Speechless, she stared. In the more than two years since the visit to Aryeh, she had not seen Yossi Nitzan or heard from him. She habitually scanned military stories in the papers for his name, and leafed through each issue of the army journal in the Technion library, so she knew of his promotions; and she had cut out and kept one picture of him, half-hidden among armor officers standing with hands on hips around a map on a jeep hood.

Now here bursting on her was this same antic Kishote, glowing with health, lean, looking no older, bewitching her with a grin. She was appalled that he should see her shiny with sweat and unkempt from the futile blowing of a noisy fan, in a sleeveless old dress so thin as to be scarcely decent; her brown brassiere at least was opaque, however obtrusively ugly. She had not come to the Technion planning to charm anyone, just to stay cool if she could in a third day of hamsin.

"What the devil are you doing in Haifa?" she managed to say without gasping.

"I'll tell you on the way. Come on, a nice ride will cool you off."

"How's your wife?"

"That's it, she's coming home, so I have to pick up Aryeh at Nahalal. It's not far, we'll be back in a couple of hours. Wouldn't you like to see Aryeh? He's all grown up."

"She's coming home? From where?"

"California. She went to my brother's wedding. We talked on the phone today. Frank Sinatra was at the wedding. He didn't sing, though. I asked."

Shayna shook her head at him, exasperated, excited, at a loss. "Look, go along to Nahalal." She gestured at her desk. "I'm working. Falling in on me like this is preposterous, it's just like you, couldn't you have phoned? You phoned Yael in California."

"She phoned me, from some rich guy's house. I can't afford to call California. Aren't you glad to see me? I've missed you, Shayna. It's stupid to be so out of touch."

Resisting an urge to jump up and throttle this fellow, Shayna said, "You picked the wrong day, sorry. I have to help Michael with his pots."

"What pots?"

"Oh, he and Lena have separate cooking pots in their kitchen. He keeps kosher and she doesn't. She had a party and used his pots, and they had a big fight. I said I'd help him make his pots kosher again. His cutlery, too."

"But that takes no time at all."

"That's how much you know. It's very complicated."

"Where's Dr. Berkowitz?"

"Next door."

"Come with me."

Michael sat by an open window, in a breeze so strong that it flapped the collar of his sport shirt and tousled his thinning hair under the skullcap. Beyond the window the blue bay sparkled, and two patrol boats were heading out to sea. The desk papers were held down by a paperweight, a pair of binoculars, and a framed picture of Lena. But it was a hot wind, and his shirt was sweated through. He listened to Yossi, pursing his lips and nodding.

"Yes, that'll do it," he said, taking keys from a drawer. "Shayna, you know where my pots are, red for meat, blue for milk. Lena's pots are white, never mind those. Thanks, Yossi."

Shayna said, "You mean I should go with him?"

"Why not? It should be cooler around Nazareth. Look, Yossi, figure on having dinner with us. My brother Zev may come. He's touring factories in the north."

"I'll have my five-year-old son with me."

"Aryeh? Beautiful."

The pots bumped and clanked in the trunk as Yossi's driver sped them eastward on the narrowing tar road. "This is almost like the old days," said Yossi. "Remember when we used to go climbing the hills around Nazareth?"

"I'm engaged to be married," said Shayna. His look of shock pleased her.

"Well! Mazel tov. Who is he?"

"You'll meet him at dinner tonight. He's the son of Haifa's chief rabbi. He won't eat, though. He's very strict. He'll only eat his mother's cooking." Short pause. An added sentence like a stiletto. "And mine, now."

"Hm! When are you getting married?"

"Chaim has to finish his Ph.D. He's a math genius. The army deferred him. He's twenty-two."

"Much younger than you, eh?"

Stiletto tone. "More mature than some people much older."

"So it won't be for years yet."

"Not necessarily. The army may let him do his service at the Technion."

Looking at her with frank rue, he said, "Well, I wish you happiness, that you know."

She turned away from him and pointed. "There's a whole hillside of those yellow flowers we used to pick. What was the name?"

"We never found out, Shayna. You said you would, but you didn't."

"Couldn't ever count on me, could you?"

He threw an arm around her slender shoulders, gave her a rough hug, and withdrew it before she could object. "Turn off here," he told the driver.

A winding one-lane dirt road led to a fenced army camp where the commandant, a paratrooper friend of Kishote's, waited at the gate. "You're in luck, Kishote," he said, getting into the front seat, "it's cleanup day, the vats are boiling." He directed the driver to the long wooden dining hut. Shayna, Yossi, and the driver carried Michael's stuff through rows of wet tables to the back, where half-naked soldiers were scouring and mopping out the stifling kitchen. When Shayna appeared, a babble of obscenities faded down.

"No problem," said the fat blond-bearded cook in charge. He dumped the cutlery into a coarse net, dropped it into a steaming vat, and immersed pot after pot with a large iron hook. "The rabbi makes us do this before Passover. Also when our pots get mixed up. Don't ask me why. I'm Hashomer Hatza'ir." This was a very radical irreligious Zionist faction, the Young Guardian.

"Aren't you curious? You could at least ask," said Shayna. "Then you'd know what you were doing."

"Excuse me," said the cook. "Asking our rabbi a question can kill an afternoon. He says dunk pots, I dunk pots, and finish." The cook shrugged and rolled his eyes at Don Kishote. A major's girlfriend who was strict about dunking pots! Weird.

At Nahalal they drove past orchards, fields of corn and vegetables, farmhouses, and communal buildings to Benny Luria's home, one of the oldest on the moshav, inherited from his father. There was nobody in the plain small cottage, where children's toys were scattered around a washing machine on a badly weathered sagging porch. "They must be out working," said Yossi. He took the wheel to drive here and there through the concentric circles of the Nahalal layout. "There they are! See him, Shayna? The curly-head? Kid needs a haircut!" Several children were hoeing beside Benny Luria, in a fallow patch of broken brown clods amid green fields. The aviator wore threadbare shorts, a canvas hat, and sneakers, and sweat was rolling down his thick neck and hairy brown chest.

Aryeh shouted, "Abba, Abba," dropped the hoe and came

running. Shayna had last seen a toddler, but this was a stoutish good-sized boy who sprang up into his father's outstretched arms. "Abba, *ani eh'yeh tayass* [I'm going to be a pilot]!"

"Why does Yael say he's a terror?" asked Luria. "He's a good boy, he likes to work. Hello, Shayna."

She forced a smile, feeling like a fool. It had not occurred to Shayna, until it was too late, that of course Yael's whole family would be at Nahalal. Don Kishote had swept her along, and it had all happened too fast. Not that Benny Luria so much as lifted an eyebrow, but she knew well that Israeli army men, as a matter of mutual courtesy, took in stride all pairings.

"Shayna's engaged to the son of Haifa's chief rabbi," said Kishote in an offhand way.

"Mazel tov! Great guy, Rabbi Poupko. He comes to the base sometimes and talks about Talmud and cabala. The fellows like him."

"Remember me?" Shayna said to Aryeh, who was still in Yossi's arms and inspecting her with sharp bright eyes.

He put a hand to her face, and said with a smile that melted and hurt her, "Aunt Shayna."

"That's right! Aunt Shayna."

Aryeh demanded that Luria's oldest son come in the car while the other children started to walk back. This was Dov, a weedy tanned youngster much resembling Benny, even to the sneakers, shorts, and canvas hat.

"Dov is going to be a pilot," said Aryeh, sitting on his father's lap. "So am I. Can't I stay for Dov's bar mitzvah next week? Or come back?"

"Bar mitzvah?" Kishote looked to Luria in surprise. Moshavniks were not much for ritual, and Benny Luria, he thought, was as freethinking as Yael, despite his nosing in the Bible.

"It can't harm him," said the airman. "Why are we here, after all, in this land? Let him pick up a little tradition."

Dov spoke from the front seat without turning around. "Rabbi Poupko talked Abba into it, so I had to learn it." Matter-of-fact words, not resentful.

Yossi gathered up Aryeh's clothes from a bedroom where two

double-decker wooden bunks left little room to move around. Luria's cheerful wife Irit showed up with hay in her hair and on her cotton dress, and pressed cakes and cold soda on the visitors. While Dov and Aryeh turned cartwheels and handsprings on the grass outside, Yossi told the Lurias about the ex-Nahalal people Yael had met in California.

"Listen, Los Angeles can have Herschel Rosenzweig," said Irit. "And that Bluma. She's the one who wanted America. It's a shame about those three beautiful children."

"Yael talked to the kids. They miss the moshav."

"I'll bet both boys come back," Benny said. "They were Dov's pals. They still write, and their Hebrew's perfect."

"What do you say about Dov's bar mitzvah?" Irit addressed Yossi. "Next thing I know, Benny will make me wear a wig, you'll see." By tradition strictly pious married women wore their hair short under a wig or a cloth, or both.

"Why? Here's Shayna," said Kishote, "engaged to Rabbi Poupko's son. She doesn't wear a wig."

"Engaged to that Chaim? Congratulations." Irit looked at her with interest. "Well, once you're married you'll wear a wig. Pity, you have such nice hair."

"We'll see," said Shayna.

They left Nahalal, and the car was threading down through grassy hills when Yossi told the driver to stop. "Aryeh, want to pick flowers?"

"Yes, yes." The boy bounced on the car seat.

"Yossi, let's not waste time, I have to get back to Haifa," said Shayna. But she went with them, climbing the rocky hill and picking yellow flowers, with fuzzy stems that slightly stung the fingers.

"Pick plenty," Yossi said to his son. "We'll bring some home for Mama."

The faint wild sweet scent shattered Shayna with total recall of her first real kisses, when they had gone climbing long ago in these hills. Not like the first shy pecks at the windmill. Kisses! She could hardly bear to look at Yossi, but she could see that — however many girls he had kissed, and more than kissed, before her — it was hitting him hard, too.

"Enough, enough," she said. "Let's go!" All three had their arms full of the fragrant yellow wildflowers.

"I want to pick more," said Aryeh.

"No, we go now," barked his father.

They were five for dinner in the Berkowitz flat. Aryeh had eaten early and voraciously, and was napping. Shayna and Zev Barak took the peculiar table setting for granted, but it was all new to Don Kishote: two tablecloths, red and white, two sets of differently colored dishes, and two kinds of cutlery; metal on the red side, wooden-handled on the white side. Lena tersely and acidly explained that the red side was kosher, and gave him his choice. He sat with her.

"How's your factory tour going?" Michael asked Barak, in a heavily obvious change of subject. "Are you encouraged? Discouraged? What?"

Barak shook his head. " '*The Eternal of Israel will not deal falsely,*' " he quoted the Book of Samuel, an Israeli byword of despairing bravado. "Otherwise we have problems." Barak was reviewing the arms manufacturing capacity of the country as projected for the next ten years; purpose, to explore feasibility of manufacturing tanks in Israel.

"What about that French 155-millimeter howitzer, Zev?" Kishote inquired. "Will they be able to mount it on the Sherman chassis?" Israel had a number of old Shermans, bought from war surplus and scrap wherever available.

"Not without modifying the Sherman drastically. It may not be feasible at all. The study's still going on."

"The answer had better be yes!" Kishote looked and sounded grim, shaking his head. "Or we'll be outgunned in the field before we ever engage the enemy. Half our tanks will be blown up by Soviet artillery, firing outside our combat range."

"Well, we have more immediate problems," said Barak. "The turret of the Centurion can't handle the German cannon we ordered. The contract has to be cancelled."

As they ate dinner, Professor Berkowitz joined in the officers' quick terse exchange of jargon and acronyms about the state of munitions supply. Like most academics he had a defense task, analysis and design of weaponry, a subject he taught at the Technion. Shayna was struck by an aspect of Yossi Nitzan new to her. That he was an able combat soldier she knew, but he was dealing here with technology for which he had no academic training. His face and manner changed as he talked. When he pushed up his glasses, the humorous glint was gone from his eyes, and the other men were paying close heed to his analytical battlefield thinking.

"You could do worse, Kishote," Barak said, spooning up fish soup, "than to apply for the course at the Army Industrial College in Washington. They'd admit you, I'm sure."

"I'm not leaving my brigade to sit in American classrooms."

"There you speak emptily," said Berkowitz. "You're top-heavy with field know-how and combat experience. There's more to command in war than being a fighting man."

"In the end that's what it all rests on," retorted Kishote. "Seasoned fighters leading young fighters. The new thing about Israel is that Jews fight. Nothing else."

"The new thing about Israel," exclaimed Lena, restless at having been quiet so long, "is that the Jews have come home after two thousand years."

"The Arabs dispute that this is our home, and they have their viewpoint," said Shayna. "So far they can't dispute that here we Jews fight."

"Exactly, and if they dispute that successfully just once, Shayna," said Kishote, with somber mien and an approving nod, "it'll all be over. My job, and maybe Aryeh's job, is to make sure that they don't! If necessary, for a hundred years."

"Bluster," said Barak. "You want to stay at brigade level, that's up to you. Leadership beyond that needs training, no less than platoon leadership did."

"Anyway, don't talk about my going to America around Yael," said Kishote. "That Beverly Hills fragrance is in her nose already, believe me."

Shayna jumped up as the doorbell rang. "There's Chaim."

Kishote expected her rabbi fiancé to look like the usual yeshiva product: pallid, stooping, undernourished, shabby, or the alternate florid, pear-shaped version. Into the apartment there strode instead a tall straight fellow all in neat black, with an extremely bushy black beard that left visible below his forehead only his mouth, nose, and eyes, and a black felt hat perched on heavy long black hair growing down into the beard. The nose was big and imperious, the brown eyes somewhat fiery. Barbered and dressed Vienna style, Chaim Poupko might have looked not unlike Herzl. Invited by Lena, he sat down in the white unkosher area, declining tea with a smile.

"What's wrong with my tea?" demanded Lena, still bellicose. "Not kosher enough?"

"Thank you, Lena, I'll have tea." He left it untouched.

Shayna said to him with an affectionate grin, "Dr. Berkowitz showed me the written outline of your thesis, and he agrees with me. You're biting off more than you can chew."

"Riemann or Gauss, Chaim," said Michael. "Not both."

"My theme links them," said Poupko. "The link created differential geometry."

"It's not unoriginal," said Michael, "but it'll take a few hundred pages full of equations, and I'm not sure it'll work, even so."

"It won't," said Shayna. "Two cats in one sack."

Rapid-fire mathematical cabalisms ensued among the three, and Kishote could observe an unmistakable warmth between Shayna and Poupko. He wondered whether he should have yielded, after all, to the haphazard notion of dropping in on her en route to Nahalal. As a consequence his nose was being rubbed in the good fortune of this hairy son of a chief rabbi, and Shayna's evident fondness for him.

"We'll be late for Alterman," Poupko said abruptly, standing up. "They close the doors, and we'll miss the first half."

"I love Alterman's poetry," Lena said. "But I hate poetry readings. Poets can't read their own stuff."

"Let's go." Shayna held out a hand to Kishote. "Give Aryeh a goodbye kiss from Aunt Shayna."

As the door closed, Kishote said, "Quite a fellow."

"Excellent brain. Talmudic vigor, mathematical gift," said Berkowitz. "And it isn't every black hat who'll go to hear Natan Alterman."

"And he'll do his army service at the Technion? Too bad," Kishote said. "Looks like he could make a soldier."

"Doing it at the Technion is Shayna's idea, not his," said Berkowitz. "He's talked to me, in fact, about putting off his thesis and serving his two and a half years in the field."

"Well, she's right and he's crazy," said Lena. "What's he going to eat? He won't trust the army's kosher food. He won't even eat Michael's. He'll starve."

"I don't see that fellow starving," said Zev Barak.

"If he decides to put on a uniform, tell him to ask for armor," said Kishote to Berkowitz. "I'd like him in my brigade. I'll see to it that he eats." He went and woke Aryeh. "Come, we're going home."

Aryeh inquired, stretching, "Where's Aunt Shayna?"

"This is from Aunt Shayna." The father kissed him. "She's gone."

"Don't forget Mama's flowers. They smell nice, Abba."

"Very nice." Kishote lifted the bouquet dripping from a vase. "Come and say goodbye."

"Well, Aryeh! They grow up fast, don't they?" Zev Barak said as Kishote came in with the yawning boy. "I visited my son at the Reale School today. He graduates next year, and he wants the navy."

"The navy?" Kishote wrinkled his brow. "Why the navy? That's a dead end."

"This is a navy town," said Lena, clearing both areas of the table.

"So far that's Noah's choice," said Barak, "but a year's a long time."

"I'm going to be a fighter pilot like Dov Luria," said Aryeh.

Zev Barak's melancholy eyes brightened at Aryeh. "I believe you."

The small hall where Alterman read his poems was only half full. "Haifa is not a town for poetry," remarked Poupko, walking out with Shayna to the smoky lobby during the interval. Some people were leaving.

"It's too hot for poetry," she said. "But let's stay. The poems are worth it. Bitter, irreligious. Good."

"By all means." After a silence he said, "So that was your famous Don Kishote." It was his first reference to Nitzan. On the way to the hall they had talked about his thesis.

"Not *my* Don Kishote," she shot back. "Not a word in two years, then he drops out of the sky to give me a ride to Nahalal, can you imagine, and pick up his son. Sorry you didn't see Aryeh, he's sweet."

"Nitzan's a good-looking man. Quiet sort."

"Ha! Quiet? Kishote?" Shayna gave a harsh laugh. "He was looking you over, very hard. I think he approved. Not that I care."

"Does he have any religion?"

Shayna coughed and coughed. "Let's go outside. I'm choking."

The stars were bright over the dark nearly empty street. "Religion? Yossi isn't observant, but he's a Jew all right, he's nothing else. He loves Israel, loves the ground he walks on here. Just before you came in, he rejected a suggestion that he go to an American army college. He was in the camps, you know, as a kid. Maybe that's why he's a crazy fighter. I really never figured him out. Never got to know him that well. By your terms no, Don Kishote's not religious."

"Sounds like my grandfather."

"Your *grandfather*? The Ezrakh?" This Jerusalem-born sage, still hale at eighty, was popularly called the Ezrakh, "the Native," because in his lifetime he had not set foot outside the Holy Land. "Chaim, you'll have to explain that, if it's not a silly joke."

The lobby bell rang. "Time for more poetry," said Poupko. Afterward when he took her home he did not explain, and she did not bring up the subject of Nitzan again. Alone in her flat, she buried her nose in the flowers by her bedside, then fell face down on the bed.

The weather had something to do with Yael's mood as she went through immigration in the terminal: gray, heavy, sticky, blowy, drizzly, the worst kind of Tel Aviv summer climate, when everybody who could do so went somewhere else. Also, the flight over the Mediterranean had been rocky, and the pilot, briefly her boyfriend in high school, had invited her into the cockpit and had bored her by boasting about his five children. The Lod terminal, after the airports in America, looked to Yael like a Nahalal cow shed. Almost, she could smell the cow manure, the confining depressing odor of childhood chores.

"There you are! Aryeh, Aryeh!" The boy was running to her, and her spirits lifted as she lifted him. He looked brown as a soldier, and he was heavier than she remembered. Don Kishote came sauntering behind their son, and he too was a gladdening sight, this powerful bespectacled figure in uniform with the fetching grin. They kissed heartily.

"Welcome!" he said. "I figured you'd come back from Los Angeles, but who can be sure?"

"Don't be ridiculous."

He drove his army car out of the terminal with her beside him, the boy on her lap. On the way to Ramat Gan she told him about Sheva Leavis's estate, the wedding, and Sinatra; also a lot more about the Rosenzweig evening. Their phone talk had been hurried, for she had not wanted to run up a bill, even if to Leavis it would have been pennies. Yossi laughed a lot. "Well it was an adventure. Pasternak really let the *yordim* [emigrants] have it, eh?"

"It rolled off them."

But Yael was thinking that the yordim had a point, as she encountered again the narrow asphalt roads full of potholes, after those smooth ten-lane California freeways. The few billboard signs on the weed-choked roadside were bleached by the sun, the frames blown askew by the wind. In the shopping streets of Ramat Gan, half the miserable little stores were closed, with dusty bedraggled window displays or TO LET signs, because of another *mitun,* recession. How tacky, how dreary, how familiar, how small, how altogether Israeli! She said abruptly as the car turned into their street, "I'm back in Lilliput."

He gave her a swift sharp glance. "So you are. Glad to be back?"

Hugging her son, she said, switching to English, "Home, sweet home."

The yellow flowers caught her eye as they entered the flat; in a vase on the hall table, with a childishly printed Hebrew sign in three crayon colors on torn cardboard, WELCOME, MAMA.

"Beautiful," she said. "Thanks, Aryeh."

"We picked them coming back from Nahalal," said Kishote.

"Aunt Shayna didn't pick many," said Aryeh. "She's lazy."

"Shayna?" Inquiring casual tone, as Yael smelled the flowers.

"She's marrying the son of Haifa's chief rabbi," said Kishote. "I brought her along to see Aryeh."

"Ah. How did she look?"

"Hot."

Aryeh ran off to his room.

"Did you meet her fellow?"

"Yes. Big black beard, math genius, younger than she is. I liked him."

"Wildflowers don't last. The scent's gone."

"Well, get rid of them."

"Aryeh won't like that. I'll throw them out tomorrow."

Whatever her irritation, or perhaps it was cloudy jealousy, at this business of the wildflowers and Aunt Shayna, Yael had no cause to complain of her welcome in bed that night; for a long-married pair, there were happy doings. Yael was never quite sure whether this enigmatic man of hers had shmatas, so to say, or girlfriends; if so he was more discreet than she thought he could be. Of Shayna Matisdorf there was of course no question. Certainly Kishote now acted like a husband deprived, and gave her quite a workout.

"What's the matter? Still not sleepy?" he inquired, with a rub of a hairy leg on hers. "It's after three."

She was sitting up in the gloom, her back against the headboard, deliciously aglow and exhausted. "In Los Angeles it's mid-afternoon, or something. I'm all turned around."

"Have some wine."

"You know something, Yossi? We don't have to live like this."

"Like what?"

"This." A hand circled in the air. "Two cramped bedrooms,

one bathroom always full of Aryeh's junk, no washing machine, and so on. This."

"What do we do about it?"

"I have ideas. We can talk tomorrow."

"No, go ahead and talk now."

"Well, it's nothing substantial, not yet. Sheva Leavis and your brother own a building in Beverly Hills on Wilshire Boulevard. Very fancy district. A bridal shop in it may go bankrupt, and they took me to have a look at it. Gorgeous shop, perfect location, terrific inventory, but two silly Frenchwomen are running it into the ground, and —"

"You want us to move to California so you can take over that shop?"

"Easy, dear, don't snap like that. If I went there, just me, just for a couple of years, I know I could turn that shop into a money-maker. I *know* it. Leavis said if I accomplished that I could put in a manager and come home with a part ownership. A steady income in dollars, Yossi."

"And Aryeh? What about him during those years? Does he do without a mother? Or does he go with you to Los Angeles and catch the virus, God forbid?"

"Okay, okay. I didn't say there weren't problems, hamood. Let it go at that for now. I'll try the wine."

28

President Kennedy Will Deliver

"Ben Gurion resigned not a day too soon. He should have resigned months ago," said the Foreign Minister, peeling onions at her kitchen sink, a food-stained white apron over her housedress. "If he expects the Labor Party to beg him to come back this time, he can forget it. He's finished, *kaput*, OUT! For good!" With a quick glance over her shoulder, Golda caught Barak and Pasternak exchanging wry looks as they sat drinking orange soda at the kitchen table. "Listen, it breaks my heart!" she exclaimed. "That I've been his strongest supporter, ever since I got dragged into politics — by *him,* and no one else — everybody knows."

Two dirt-streaked boys came tumbling into the kitchen, loudly arguing about who had won a leg-wrestle. They snatched handfuls of cookies from a jar and scurried out, still yelling at each other.

"Oy, grandchildren! I'm just a sitter, while Menahem and his wife go to Salzburg for the Mozart Festival." She dropped the onions into a pot on the stove. "Well, they're darlings, but spoiled? Pioneers they aren't. A new generation."

"Madame Minister, has the State Department finally agreed?" Pasternak asked cautiously. "And if so, when do we go?"

"Agreed. The date isn't set yet. October or November." Golda hung the apron on a hook and shook her finger at Zev Barak. "Now listen, last year you backed out of the mission, I understand. This time you go. No nonsense! The Mossad has it from the CIA that you're well regarded in Washington."

"Probably because I haven't been there for years," said Barak, thinking this must be Chris Cunningham's doing.

"Never mind. Yitzhak Rabin will head this mission. No fooling around, the Deputy Chief of Staff will be letting them know that *we must have tanks*. And President Kennedy will deliver the goods, you'll see." She sat down at the table and took a pear from the fruit bowl. "The pears are in season. Delicious! We can't fight new Soviet tanks with patched-up surplus from World War II. I told Kennedy that in Florida. He listened. You've read the report of my meeting with him? It was amazing. It was historic. What he said to me, what he promised me, Ben Gurion never got from him. Not from *any* President. They all found him obnoxious, which he always has been, even at his best. David, King of Israel!" She bit into the pear. "So sweet, so juicy. Fruit of the land. He treated me shabbily for six years, sending me off to Africa, Asia, God knows where, to keep me out of sight while *he* ran foreign affairs. For your information, gentlemen, the Foreign Ministry is now headed by the Foreign Minister."

Barak had heard about the tumultuous Labor Party meeting, where Golda had denounced Ben Gurion in the bitterest terms to his face, when he was already reeling from a flare-up of old political squabbles, and a new newspaper storm over leaked reports — only too true — that Israeli soldiers were in Germany, secretly training with advanced equipment. What choice did the army or Ben Gurion have, when only the Germans would sell Israel a few state-of-the-art systems? But the old lion was down, and they were all rending him. What disconcerted Barak was Golda's part and pleasure in his fall.

"It's graven in my mind," Golda went on, "what President Kennedy said to me." She changed her voice to a grotesque caricature of Kennedy's Harvard accent, quoting in English: " *'Madame Minister, the United States has a special relationship with Israel in the Middle East, really comparable only to that which it has with Britain over a wide range of world affairs.'* You look again at the report, you'll see I've got it word for word. What a declaration! What a change from Eisenhower rebuffing Ben Gurion!"

"It will be a great day," said Pasternak, "when you can declassify that report."

"Oh, not for years! The Arabs would raise a howl! What's the difference? His advisers were there on the porch with us. So were mine. It's all on the record in Washington." She smiled a far-off smile, finishing the pear and wiping away juice with a handkerchief. "Have some fruit, gentlemen."

They both declined.

"Yes, I can just see Kennedy there on his rocking chair, in his shirt sleeves, no tie, the ocean breaking on the sand. . . . He looks like a college boy, you know. I had to keep telling myself, *'This is the President of the United States, with all that power!'* " Golda abruptly laughed. "Maybe he had to keep telling himself, *'This old yenta is a Foreign Minister.'* "

Turning serious, she again shook a finger at Barak. "Now while you're there, you're to stay in closest touch with our military attaché. Keep him in the picture. If you ask me, he's our most important man in Washington. The ambassador just bangs his head against the State Department stone wall. The United States Army has respect for us. We get hints! I know what their military planners are starting to think. *'Maybe little Israel, down there on NATO's southern flank, can be useful to us one of these days!'* Even if Dulles deceived and betrayed us, that was a big gain from our Sinai victory." She lit a cigarette and squinted at Barak through the smoke. "How would you feel about serving in that job one day?"

"Since you ask me, I'd hate it, Madame Minister."

"You're a fool. It's a tremendous career leap, and you'd be right for it. But that's far off. Well, I have to cook supper for those kids, they eat like wolves." The officers jumped up. "So both of you work with Rabin and his staff on the agenda for the mission. I want to see it next week."

"Yes, Madame Minister," said Pasternak.

She put a thick arm around his shoulder. "See? This is what Kennedy did when I left. Just like this, Sam! And he said, *'Mrs.*

Meir, don't worry, nothing will happen to Israel!' So earnest, so sincere! You must plan this mission right, present the facts, do a job. You won't see or hear from the President, but he'll know everything, and we'll get the tanks."

Outside it was a cool clear Jerusalem afternoon, such as the Holy City can offer in August while Tel Aviv swelters in seacoast steam. "Well, she's in the saddle again," said Pasternak, "with a crash."

"Listen, Sam, if I go on the mission, what does that do to the October armor exercises?"

"Why, what's the problem? Nitzan can take over your brigade, can't he? He'll be fine." Pasternak looked at his watch. "I have to meet my lawyer in Tel Aviv."

"I'll come with you, if you won't be too long. Then we can talk to Rabin."

"Gemacht!" ("It's a deal!")

"Sorry about you and Ruth," Barak said as they got into Pasternak's car.

"No choice. Look, I haven't been an angel. She says this Colombian fellow wants to marry her." He turned up his hands. "At least Amos is going into the army, so that's that. About the girls, well, my guess is that in the end the guy will skedaddle back to Bogotá, and she'll come home and throw her parties for her Tel Aviv bohemians again, and look for a new diplomat. She's got all the Loeb money, no problem."

Barak let Pasternak thread his way through the thick traffic to the highway before he spoke again. "Look here, Golda gave me the horrors, Sam. Military attaché in Washington!"

"It's a top spot, Zev."

"It's paper-pushing. Don't tell me otherwise."

"Well, she was just talking. I understand you're slated for deputy, Central Command."

"So I've heard, but you know the army. Sam, what's Golda's vindictiveness toward the Old Man all about?"

A shrug and a sidelong look. "There are those who say it started in bed." Few remarks on any Israeli subject could surprise Zev Barak, but this jolted an incredulous laugh from him. "Long ago, of course. Otherwise, you can take her at her word. He pulled her out of the Labor Ministry, which she loved, put her in the Foreign Ministry, which she didn't want, and then sent her junketing to places like Burma and Liberia while he took over foreign relations."

Most cars they passed were rattling old European miniatures, gasping up the hills and racing down them, leaving contrails of black exhaust. Fifteen years after the Jerusalem siege the mountain road was still littered with wrecked vehicles from Kastel to Latrun, war memorials preserved with red primer paint. Down on the flat the two-lane highway took a tortuous bend around the Latrun fortress. "A bone in our throat," said Pasternak, gesturing. "We should have captured it in 1948, and we could have."

"Ben Gurion couldn't bear to shed any more Jewish blood," Barak said, "and I've never blamed him."

The first lines in Emily's latest note, which fell out of a letter of her father's, were a surprise and a relief.

> Letter #33 (Right? Or am I losing track?)

Old Wolf—

    I hasten to share big news in a quick scrawl which I'll stick in a letter that Chris is about to mail to you. Nothing sneaky, natch, just haste. Come October first I'm off on a South Seas cruise with Hester! Christmas in Tahiti, back in January.

So she would not be there . . . one concern (and one anticipation) less . . .

    Wangling a leave of absence from Foxdale took some doing, but in the end Fiona was gracious and helpful. She should be, I lied like a trooper at the school board inquiry into the matter of Reverend Wentworth's groin. Perjured my soul (though I didn't happily have to take my oath on a Bible) to assert that they were both pure as the driven snow. As her closest associate I was believed. The Reverend healed up, and now they are both enjoying gitchi-gitchi once more on odd Sundays. His intended new bride, no doubt put off by L'Affaire Groin, gave him the old heave-ho.

    Hester and hubby have booked on a Matson liner, and Hester

invited me along. As she put it to me she does love him, he's a dear, but he bores her into murderous insanity, and on a long cruise she would be bound on one dark night to throw him over the side. She doesn't want to do that, it would be hard on their three kids. So be advised now that a silence between October and January will NOT signal any break in our bond. I'll just be out of touch.

My other piece of news, kiddo, is that I may be working around to the Jack Smith alternative. Surprised? Jealous? Overjoyed? I'm going to give that a long THINK in the South Seas. Jack and I have a strangely old-fashioned relationship, rather out of a Thackeray novel. I don't know what if anything poor Jack does about gitchi-gitchi — he's got no Nakhama, like a certain having-it-both-ways louse of my acquaintance — but he's been waiting me out a long time now and who knows, who knows? I'm getting on.

Yours *quand même,*
Emily

Big news indeed! The cruise, not Jack Smith; that was mere Emily piffle. It would keep the great circle distance between Emily Cunningham and himself roughly the same while he was in Washington. He went into his tiny workroom and closed the door, to read Cunningham's letter, which was long and strange. He sat in his threadbare armchair eating pistachios, a vice that was making his trousers tight; partly a nervous habit, but also he loved the damnably fattening green nuts from Persia. Then he started to write an answer to the CIA man, but his thoughts kept wandering back to Emily.

He had dug himself in too deep with her. That was the nub of it. Writing affectionate letters had become a minor vice, an indulgence like pistachio nuts and even less advisable. Once the newlywed Nakhama had enjoyed such mush, and she still liked to be petted and complimented, but she was a no-nonsense woman; there was a time for everything, and the time for mush had ended with the birth of Noah. No doubt she was right. Blessings, therefore, thought Barak, on the blubbery Hester Laroche, and her South Seas cruise.

His unguarded outpourings to Emily had paralleled a less frequent exchange with her father. What both relationships had in common was escape from the submarine-like quarters of Israel, as

Barak sometimes thought of it, to the great surface world beyond. Father and daughter offered him two different escape hatches. Cunningham had an offbeat challenging mind, and writing to Emily took Barak out of a marriage happy enough, yet circumscribed by his wife's interests and nature.

Nakhama had never been one for European or American books, plays, poetry, or serious music. She knew very little English, and even her childhood French, acquired from immigrant Moroccan parents, had rusted with disuse. Unless outside literature was translated into Hebrew she was unaware of it, and no longer very interested. As the years passed she had narrowed her focus down to raising two girls and a boy, and keeping a decent household going on an Israeli army salary.

By contrast Emily Cunningham consumed books old and new, made weekend forays to New York to take in plays, concerts, and art shows, and she commented amusingly on these. She stimulated him. For a year they had written back and forth about Sartre. One cold desert night, out on a field exercise and sitting up on a tank, Barak had scrawled by flashlight a disenchanted outburst; Sartre was after all an adroit eclectic with nothing new to say, a borrower and a self-promoter, whose "existentialism" was mainly a gimmick cribbed from Heidegger and other Germans. Emily's quick admiring concurrence had warmed his heart. To Nakhama, even in Hebrew translation, Sartre would be as opaque as Egyptian hieroglyphics.

He tore up Emily's note, and set about finishing his answer to her father.

> . . . . Now as a Jew of course, I'm moved by your view of this century's travails as "the thundering tread of Gog and Magog," and our return to the Holy Land as "the new Beginning in history, the Hope, the first faint sounding of the Great Horn heralding the Messiah." *Halevai,* we say in Hebrew; would it were so!
>
> But to me it's all the tread of a passing monstrosity, totalitarianism. Once the old regimes fell apart freedom seemed in sight, Chris, but bad men grabbed power and seized on all the new technology to clamp fear and stunned obedience on their people. That's Leninism, that's Hitlerism, that's Maoism. But I think the people will take heart and throw off the new kings and dukes in their disguise of cloth caps and Mao collars. Maybe even in our lifetimes.

Unlike you, Chris, I've never seen Marxism as an apocalyptic new faith menacing the West. It has no great prophetic figure. Marx was a bourgeois self-indulgent curmudgeon, and Lenin, the nearest thing to their ikon, was a self-righteous slaughterer, a Slav Robespierre. As it wanes, I imagine Marxism will remain the status quo where the reds have got the government and the guns; and where they haven't, a rationale for upheavals to confiscate and redistribute wealth, if governments are shortsighted or rotten.

But yes, you're dead right about the Soviets as the real threat to Israel's existence. They'll keep encouraging the Arabs to wipe us out, simply because it suits their book to penetrate the region. They'll keep sending deluded young Arabs to their deaths maybe for half a century before the Arabs get wise, and stop playing expendable Russian pawns in the old Great Game. That is all quite irrelevant to Marxism. And meantime we have to hang on, hence our desperate ongoing quest for arms. Our young fighters are as good as the best in the world, and they're highly motivated. But there's no contest between spears and artillery. It's not that one-sided yet, but it's tending that way. We really need tanks, Chris!

I share your concern about Ben Gurion's fall. You're right about that, too. Though in form he resigned, he was deposed. His successor, Eshkol, is not in his mold. He's as gray as a cloudy day. He lacks world vision. Israel's a small place, but it happens to be at the fulcrum of a giant world happening, the facedown between America and Russia. Ben Gurion knew that. Eshkol knows about pipelines and electric plants. He's a Labor Party man from year one, and he's quietly done many crucial things in building the country, so maybe he'll work out . . .

As he wrote, Barak could hear Nakhama coming in, and then one after another the girls, aged eight and three, both merry today, he was glad to hear. The usual afternoon sounds included much bickering and some sharp motherly commands. A rap at his door, and Nakhama's voice: "Zev, supper!"

"All right."

Well, down to earth from world visions. I'm called to the table. There's a lot more I could tell you about the new Eshkol government. Was it Churchill who said that democracy is a terrible system, worse than all others except those that have been tried? Something like that. Anyway, the Israeli system is no damn good, that's for certain, but we're like people in a leaky boat in a storm. If we take the time to fix the leaks we'll sink. We just have to bail and bail and keep bailing until the storm passes . . .

When Barak came into the kitchen and sat down Nakhama was at the stove, peculiarly smiling. The girls were seated around the table, all titters and side-glances at one chair that remained vacant. "So who's this for?" Barak inquired.

"For me," said Noah, entering in uniform, tall as his father but leaner, the boyish face stern and serious, then breaking into a grin at Barak's amazement. "Navy recruits sign in early."

Zev Barak jumped up and embraced his son. Noah's grip around his shoulders was hard and prolonged. "Then it's the navy, after all."

"I know you wanted me to go into armor."

Barak held his son at arm's length, savoring the joy and the faint fear of seeing him in fighting dress. All services wore the Zahal uniform, the differences were in caps and emblems. "You're the man who has to serve. Serve where you want to, and where you can."

"He arrived while you were in there, working." Nakhama's plump face was radiant, and tears stood in her eyes. "I almost fainted, I thought he was still in Haifa."

"Noah is handsomer than Abba," said Galia, the eight-year-old.

Noah sat down. "I'm starved," he said in his old boyish tones, "and nobody's handsomer than Abba."

"You know," Barak said that night in their bedroom, "Galia's right. I'm a fat old workhorse. Once I could have gotten into that uniform of his. No more!" He was sitting up in bed, reading with glasses, his first pair. He had told the optometrist that he could see perfectly well, only his eyes felt tired at night. The optometrist had nodded and put glasses on him, and suddenly print looked twice as black and the optometrist had red veins in his nose.

"Don't talk fat to me." Nakhama in a bathrobe was brushing out her hair. "I'm a hippopotamus." She had put on a few pounds.

"I have to stop eating pistachio nuts."

"I have to stop eating."

Barak told her about the mission to Washington. "It's not till October or November, and I won't be gone more than ten days, if that." He closed the Evelyn Waugh novel and took off his glasses. "Nakhama, Golda talked about my going there as military attaché. Not now, of course, but she has it in her mind."

Nakhama stopped brushing to glance at him. "Would you want that?"

"Would you?"

Pursing of lips, Nakhama's hard-thinking mannerism. "It might be valuable for the girls. They'd pick up good English once for all. Even Noah's isn't very good, and I'm just a dummy. It's terrible. I'd work on it if we went."

"But Sam thinks I have a chance at Central Command. So do I."

Central Command confronted Jordan, weak and quiescent ever since the expulsion of its British army officers during the Suez fiasco. It was the junior of the three sector commands, with its back to the Mediterranean and its front running through divided Jerusalem, along the jagged armistice line — the "Green Line" — which in places was in sight of Tel Aviv and the sea. Northern Command faced Syria, Southern Command held down the front with Egypt; star assignments for future chiefs of staff. He was not yet on that level, but he had fought up and down the central sector in his youth, he knew every stone, and it was the post he aspired to next.

Nakhama got into bed, and they talked as they often did about his competitors for general rank and sector command: all veterans of 1948, all decorated and steadily advancing, all with intensely scrutinized abilities, defects, and positioning in army politics. Maybe he was too thoughtful and a shade too fatalistic, Barak sometimes felt, to be a really fierce career charger. Sam Pasternak had once remarked that he was possibly a shade too civilized. If so, he couldn't change what he was.

As she turned out the light Nakhama said, "Well, then, you go to Washington in October or November for a week or so, eh? I guess you'll see your friend Emily there."

"No. She'll be on a cruise in the South Pacific. Sort of a sabbatical from her job."

"Oh? Too bad." Nakhama's voice in the dark had no trace of guile, relief, or indeed any feeling. "It's not a honeymoon, is it?"

"No. It ought to be. She's an old maid, just about."

Pause. "When I saw Noah today, Zev, I remembered you, coming into Papa's food shop in your British uniform. Noah looks the way you did then." She leaned over to give him a gentle kiss. "He's not handsomer than you. Go on eating pistachio nuts. You work hard. You're entitled."

Dusk falling, the first stars showing. On a dark ridge, shadowy Centurion tanks, jeeps, and armored carriers lined up. The sentry stopped Barak's car at rifle point, then saluted and directed him to Kishote's tent. Before leaving for Washington, Barak was paying a last visit to his brigade. He stepped out into crunching snow and icy wind for which he was ill clad, having driven up from Jerusalem in a sunny temperate afternoon. The snowfall here in November was freakishly early, but what was not freakish in Israel these days?

Chaim Poupko, in grease-streaked fatigues, was saying as Barak entered the tent, "The slope gives you the derivative, sir, you see." He stood before Don Kishote, who sat at a plank table under the harsh light of a naked bulb, studying a graph on plotting paper.

"Zev! You're off to America?" Kishote got up. Poupko snapped to attention and saluted. In uniform the mathematician looked thinner and decidedly odd, with the skullcap and untrimmed beard.

"So Poupko," said Barak, "you're an armor man, after all. Doing what?"

"Sir, in training for tank driver." Awkward soldierly deference.

"I'm trying a self-study course in calculus," said Kishote, pointing at the graph. "As long as I've got a math whiz in the brigade, I have him check my work."

Barak smiled at the rabbi's son. "How's the lieutenant colonel doing?"

"Straight A's, sir."

"A diplomat," said Kishote.

Barak inquired, "Are you eating well?"

"No problem, sir."

At a nod from Kishote, Poupko saluted them both and went out. "He's surviving on hard-boiled eggs and baked potatoes," said Kishote. "His big treat is sardines. Shayna brings them to him, also fresh vegetables, and now and then a cooked chicken. He'll eat what she cooks."

"They didn't get married, Michael told me."

"Well, it seems to be off, at least for now." Kishote's tone went flat. "I'm not sure. You're leaving when?"

"Sunday. How's the exercise going?"

A female soldier in a heavy green sweater, baggy lined pants, and earmuffs brought them mugs of coffee and meat sandwiches. Kishote told him a skeletal force was acting as the Syrians in a war game of the Northern Command. The extremely unseasonal cold snap and snowfall were a great break. Maneuvers in subzero temperature and snow had shown up real problems in these units transferred from the southern desert: gun sights icing up, lubricants thickening so that motors failed to start, and so on. "A lucky learning experience," said Kishote. "How do we know we won't be pulled up north in an emergency? It's opened my eyes, Zev. We're going to have to prepare a complete freezing-conditions doctrine."

"Good. Make a start on it. Why calculus, by the way?"

"Oh, I keep running into calculus when I try to check R&D reports, weapons specifications, even game theory analysis. You know calculus?"

"I learned it. It comes down to a few mechanical operations that aren't hard."

"Once you know what you're doing, maybe."

They went out and walked among the machines in the snow, talking about brigade problems: performance of officers, changes of personnel, equipment deficiencies, training schedules, and the like. Barak had long since noted how tough and unrelenting Kishote was about these nuts-and-bolts matters. However erratic in his personal life, Yossi Nitzan had another face as a soldier. Barak was confidently leaving the brigade to him, and meant to recommend him as its next commander.

They came on Poupko, joking with the others in his crew as they worked on a track they had removed from the wheels and flattened in the snow. Barak climbed up and dropped into the tank for a surprise inspection. Maintenance excellent, to the eye; no rubbish, equipment clean, stowage in order, and the cramped space, the whiffs of diesel oil, metal, and electronics, gave him a nostalgic twinge. The field, the field! Damn Washington.

"I'll be off," he said, back in the tent. "Long ride to Jerusalem."

Kishote made a rapid scribble on a despatch form. "Look, here's Yael's telephone number and address in Los Angeles. Give her a ring, will you?"

"Sure." Barak scanned the form. "How long will she be there?"

"Not definite. She's looking into a business proposition. Another thing, ask to talk to Aryeh. He knows you. He likes Uncle Zev." Kishote hesitated. "You can tell a lot by the sound of a child's voice."

"Okay, I'll talk to Aryeh."

Kishote gratefully stuck out his hand. As they walked out to the car in moonlight the thin layer of glittery dry snow squeaked under their boots. "Don't come back without four hundred tanks," he said.

In Washington too, a freakish November snow was falling, snarling the evening traffic. The Washington Monument loomed through the fluttering flakes, the top out of sight in glowing mist. Barak had last glimpsed this great obelisk right after the march on Sharm el Sheikh. If Dulles had snatched away the fruits of victory, a victory it had been, after all; yet seven years later the struggle went on and on, and here he was in Washington to beg for arms.

"Not a bad first meeting," said Pasternak. The taxi was taking them from the State Department to Christian Cunningham's home in McLean, its progress across the jammed slushy Potomac bridge very slow. "At least we were talking to soldiers as well as cookie-pushers."

"No commitments," said Barak. "Zero."

Pasternak held up a palm. "I'm talking atmosphere. Tone. You weren't along last time. Deep freeze! Rabin is doing well. We're going to make progress."

The loudspeaker in the cupola over Cunningham's porch responded sepulchrally to the doorbell. "Would that be Colonel Pasternak?"

"Hello, Chris."

Another voice, a young woman's: "And would that be the Gray Wolf?"

29

Queenie

"What the hell?" murmured Barak to Emily in the foyer, halting her by the elbow at her garish portrait while Pasternak went on into the library with Cunningham. "Why aren't you in Samoa or Bali-Bali?"

"My God, Zev, you're getting gray! But it's nice. Distinguished." She wore a dark tailored suit and a frilled blue shirtwaist, with a gold wolf's-head pin on her shoulder. A new stylish Emily! When he had last seen her seven years ago, she had still been doing the sloppy college girl; and in the snapshots she had sent since, the dowdy schoolmistress.

"Emily, come on, what's happened?"

"I'll explain, I'll explain." She was breathless, radiant, and laughing. "We've got to meet and talk."

"Okay, when? Where?"

"The Lincoln Memorial. Tonight."

"Tonight? Are you crazy? And why the Lincoln Memorial?"

"It's lovely in snow. Be there, Wolf. Ten o'clock. By the statue. Don't you dare disappoint me. Come along, sherry time."

"Now look, Emily —" but she was darting off into the library.

During dinner Barak had trouble concentrating on what Christian Cunningham had to say about their mission. The CIA man already knew that General Rabin, in his opening presentation at the State Department, had talked of a range of new weaponry as well as tanks. "It won't fly, gentlemen," Cunningham said. "This isn't a bargaining situation where you ask for the moon and settle for a crescent. You can end up with nothing at all, you know."

Emily appeared to be listening, but Barak knew better. He caught the subtle swift shifts of her eyes at him, and could only hope that the others did not. Pasternak seemed oblivious. Cunningham as always was inscrutable, with his cold lean countenance and thick glasses. He disconcerted Barak by turning on him. "And that was pretty ridiculous, Zev, that last letter of yours. Artillery versus spears, indeed! Don't talk that way in the meetings. You Israelis spoil your case by overstating it."

"Figure of speech, you know."

"Way off the mark. We rate you as still militarily equal to the Arabs, or slightly superior."

"First of all that's wrong, Chris," said Pasternak, "on plain count of weapons. Most of all, tanks. On that we can produce hard intelligence. In any case, an equal balance is for us very dangerous."

"I don't follow that," said Emily. After her father's reproach to Barak she was paying attention. "Am I being dense?"

"In a war in our region, Emily," Pasternak said patiently, "the available munitions tend to get shot off, burned up, put out of action in a short time."

"True enough," she said. "So?"

"So, the Arabs have an infinite ready reserve close by in Russia, you see. Planes, tanks, shells, artillery, all they need, deliverable overnight. We have exactly one source, the French. Now that they've lost Algeria, we're less important to them. Resupply from them is seaborne and slow. And subject to strong Arab pressures and changeable French politics, especially with De Gaulle back in the picture."

Emily looked to her father, who gave a short sober nod.

"Sam's talking facts, and that was my point," Barak said to him. "After the blow-off of what's on hand, it can in fact become spears versus artillery for us. You know that, Chris."

"You'd better win the war during the blow-off, then," said Cunningham.

"We live and plan by that rule. The Arabs can lose ten wars, but we can't wipe them out. They not only can wipe us out, it's their openly stated war aim. We have to be too strong for them to try it."

"Well, *that's* clear, Zev," said Emily, smoothing her chin with a gesture that pantomimed Abraham Lincoln's beard. Barak made the briefest possible frowning head shake at her.

Cunningham said, "It's far from clear, Emily. An arms race just brings the Soviets ever deeper into the region. They've heavily penetrated Egypt and Syria already. Some fine day Russia will crush Israel with one swipe of a bear paw, unless the Jews find a way to live in peace with the Arabs. Soon!"

"Tell us how," said Pasternak. "The Moslem world knows only one sovereignty, Islam. We face not just the Arabs, not just the Soviet Union, but more than half a billion Moslems, don't we?"

"In a way, yes."

"That's something of a puzzlement, no?"

"A puzzle you must solve. The glory of the Moslem world," returned Cunningham, "will be that they'll eventually accept and protect God's people, after the Christian world came too damnably close to murdering you all."

"You lose me there," said Pasternak. "It sounds wonderful. I hope you have some information I don't."

"Emily, let's have our brandy and coffee in the library."

"Yes, Father. Then I'll peel off and go back to Foxdale."

Seen from a taxi window through falling snow, Emily was a small dark figure by the monumental spotlighted pedestal of the memorial. "Wait," Barak said as he paid the driver, then climbed the freshly snowed-over stairs as fast as he could. "You have a car?" he shouted. At her nod he waved at the taxi, which disappeared.

She was holding out her arms. "Seven years," she said. "Seven years."

Her fur coat and his army greatcoat kept them some distance

apart as they kissed. "Emily, what the devil happened to that cruise?"

Emily took off a black glove to twine cold fingers in his. "Hester got pregnant. Would you believe it of her poor hubby? Amazing feat of mountaineering."

Despite himself Barak burst out laughing. "Is she all right?"

"Flourishing. Why did you ask whether I have a car?"

"I'd rather not walk back to my hotel."

"Are you sharing a room with Pasternak?"

"No, he's staying with our military attaché, in fact."

"Perfect." Her fingers tightened on his, her nails sharp on his palm. "Let's go for a little walk."

"Here? In the snow?"

"Of course. It's quiet and beautiful, isn't it?"

"And then?"

"Why, then we'll go to your hotel and make love."

"We'll do what?"

"You heard me. Gitchi-gitchi. We'll screw."

"Emily, honestly!"

"Is that vulgar, dear? You know I'm new at this. 'Screw' is in all the books, in fact the more usual word is —"

"Hold it. Right there!" Barak freed his hand and held it up.

"That's my car, dear, under the lamp. We'll just walk a bit and then on to your hotel. Don't you love me?"

"Sure I do. Let's go now. We can have a drink, talk, get out of this cold. I have to make an early start tomorrow."

"Gray Wolf, we're going to make love."

"Emily, stop the foolishness. Not on your life."

"Why not? Are you impotent?"

He could not help it, he laughed again, then thought he might as well go that route as any, to cut off this spinsterish aberration. "Well, it's very embarrassing, but you've wormed it out of me."

"Then why are you laughing? That's very sad."

"Yes, it's been tough for Nakhama. But we love each other, and when you're older, Emily, you find it doesn't matter all that much. We have our family, after all."

She was peering at him, the black pupils of her eyes enormous.

"Liar! I bet you still screw, ten times a night. I bet she begs you to let her sleep."

He threw an arm around her. "You're shocking Abe Lincoln. Let's go for our walk."

They took a turn around the memorial, saying no more. Snow caked their coats. She held his hand tight. In the car she put the key in the ignition, then turned to him. "That was no kiss up there. Come on."

He kissed her. No change in seven years. A long kiss, sweet as in the King David.

"That's more like it," she gasped, breaking free.

"Start that engine."

She obeyed, lifting her voice above the whirring of the cold motor. "You know, I wondered and wondered how this would go tonight. So far I think we're okay. We're off a knife edge." The engine caught, and she shifted into gear. "I didn't really expect you to take me to your hotel room."

"That's good."

"What I wanted was to get you used to the idea." Before he could object she changed tone and subject, straining her eyes through the semicircles in the snowflakes swept by the windshield wipers. "Zev, I'd guess your mission will be a success. My father's super-cautious. That's his business. There's great sympathy here for Israel. Not just because of the Holocaust. That's a negative thing. It's the resonance with American history."

"How's that?"

"Well, it's one of my father's themes. He can go to town with it when he's in the mood. You've landed on a hostile shore, trying to bring forth a new nation conceived in liberty, haven't you? You and we both started as colonies that threw out the British. Both had early years of dangerous adversity, only yours are still going on. Almost a mirror image, Chris will sometimes argue."

"Pretty forced, Emily. Your Pilgrim Fathers had no history of living here, and that's the mainspring of Zionism. If another million Jews would come, the Arabs might believe in it, and make peace — look out!"

A yellow cab trying to pass went skidding in front of them,

and stalled half turned around in their path. Emily calmly used brake and wheel to run up over the curb onto the snow-covered grass beside the highway, and slithered back down on the road well past the cab.

"Oo-ah," said Barak, "you know what you're doing."

"Usually."

As they walked into the small hotel near Union Station, Emily looked around like an exploring cat. "I've never been in this place before."

"It's cheap. Even so, my travel allowance doesn't cover it."

In the gloomy sour-smelling bar, three men and three women at a round table were making the uproarious noise of call girls and their customers in jocose foreplay. "I don't know about this," said Barak.

"Fine, let's go to your room."

"Nothing doing. You sit down."

A rat-faced waiter in a dirty red coat came up with a rag and wiped slop off their little table. "What'll it be, folks?"

She said, "Zev?"

"Me? Oh, beer."

"Beer? Coming in from the snow?"

"Well, I don't drink much. Coca-Cola's just as good. You?"

"Double Jack Daniel's on the rocks with a twist."

The waiter bared his fangs at her in friendly appreciation of her patronage. "Okay, Queenie." Emily might not look like a call girl, but they came in various guises.

"Are you working at shocking me?" Barak inquired. "You have to drive to Middleburg."

"As you remarked, I know what I'm doing."

At the round table a heavy-set john with a hoarse midwestern voice was telling a joke. ". . . So the bartender says, 'Look mister, in this bar we don't talk religion.' The guy says, 'How about politics?' 'We don't talk politics, either.' 'Well, how about sex?' 'Sex, sure, talk about sex all you want.' So the drunk says, 'Okay, what do you think of our fucking Catholic President?' "

The girls whooped, the men hee-hawed. The heavy man started another joke, and the waiter brought the Coca-Cola and the double bourbon. Emily raised her glass. "Cheers. Now you listen to me, Gray Wolf, I've spent a bloody fortune and a lot of time this past year going to a psychiatrist. Don't you suppose I realize I'm strange? The upshot was that according to him, what I needed was a good screwing. Moreover he more or less volunteered to supply same. A short fat guy with a droopy mustache and pince-nez glasses. You're not drinking your Coke." She took a deep gulp of the bourbon.

Barak sipped, staring at her. "Did all this really happen?"

"Certainly."

"Was the man serious?"

"Well, I began to think so, about the time he came over to the couch and began patting me on the leg. On both legs, sort of high up. Where they join, you know?"

Baritone guffaws and high giggles at the other table. Barak broke into laughter, too. "Yes, I know. What did you do?"

She frowned. "Don't laugh, I'm telling the truth. He said I was the most charming patient he'd ever had, and I had gorgeous legs, he couldn't help noticing that, the way I tossed and turned on the couch, and I really did need to get over my father fixation. Otherwise I might end up an old maid, and that would be too bad, because I'd make a wonderful wife and mother. For that matter I believe him. He's helped me. I'm still seeing him."

"But how did you get him to stop that patting, or whatever?"

"Oh, no problem. His wristwatch buzzed, the fifty minutes were up, so that was that. Next patient."

The girls and their clients were leaving the bar in a merry babble. Sudden quiet, except for the clink of glasses and bottles being collected by the waiter.

"Ray has a wife and five kids," Emily went on.

"Ray?"

"Raymond Sapphire. His real name is Shapiro. He started practice in West Virginia where there are no Jews, so he called himself Sapphire. The fact is, I like Ray, but physically he's as revolting as a horned toad. Zev, to me most men are. Ray didn't cure me of that, and I guess he realized it. No more passes by the horned toad, anyway."

"Did you tell him about us? About the letters?"

"Of course."

"What did he make of that?"

"Oh, elementary. You're a father figure, pure and simple, and I can allow myself to love you because you're six thousand miles away and there's no risk of actual sex." She put a hand on his, and looked deep into his eyes. "Ha!"

"Drink up, folks," called the bartender. "Last call."

"Yes, I'll have another," said Emily.

"No you won't," said Barak. He paid, and helped her on with her coat.

The bartender showed his little sharp teeth at her, and patted her arm. "Come again, Queenie."

In the grimy lobby a gray-haired clerk was asleep at the desk, and a sailor was kissing a girl in the telephone booth. "Where did he get Queenie?" Emily said. "It sounds so lowbrow and whorish. I'm flattered."

The snowfall had almost stopped. Barak walked her to the car, parked on a dark side street. There she unbuttoned her coat, then his, and thrust herself close to kiss him. Her voice was muffled, her face on his shoulder. "Have I scared you off? Wolf, I love you, I love being in your arms, there's nothing wrong with it, is there? It's marvellous, it's so *sweet*. Say what you will, it beats letters seven ways."

"What's the telephone number of the Foxdale School, Queenie?"

When a morning strategy session at the embassy broke up, Barak lingered in the conference room, and once the others were gone, he picked up the telephone. Emily had been haunting him all during the bleak three-hour discussion. Time to do something about this.

"Hello, this is Miss Cunningham." Businesslike teacherish tones, almost another voice.

"Hi there, Queenie."

Pause. A burst of rich joyous laughter, and a drop of half an octave. "It's you! Oh, Wolf, it's you! My God, talk of my occult powers! How —"

He broke in, "Listen! I'm talking on an embassy line through a switchboard, so let me make it simple and short. Understand?"

"Understood, sir."

"I'm not interrupting anything?"

"Glory, no. I'm just sitting here correcting goddamned senior French exams. Or trying to, with about ten percent of my brain engaged. What can I do for you, sir?"

"How about meeting me tomorrow night? Not at Abe's place again. Where we went afterward."

"Tomorrow night?" An audible catch of breath. A silence. Voice down another half-octave, and close to a whisper. "Are we perchance talking gitchi-gitchi, *mon vieux*?"

"Well, there is this unfinished business we should attend to. I won't be here long, you know."

"Oh, absolutely. I couldn't agree more. Say, how about this afternoon? I could arrange that, and —"

"Sorry, I can't."

"Pity. Tonight then? It is rather urgent, as you say."

"Tomorrow night, Miss Cunningham. My first clear time. Say eight o'clock?"

"Whiz bang! You're on! Eight o'clock! Bye!"

Barak hung up, hoping the switchboard girls were very busy, or that they thought he was one of the uninteresting good husbands.

In the hotel bar next night, the clock crept past eight, then past nine as he worked on papers by the meager amber light. So, was their date off? Case of virginal last-minute flutters? If so he was probably well out of it. Meantime, plenty to do! Never mind the unexpected pounding of his heart. At his age, too stupid! These papers were deeply discouraging. In a small chilly conference room of the State Department at a meeting that afternoon, the Americans had sharply challenged the Israeli assertions about the large and growing Arab array of Soviet and British tanks. He now had to compile a document of intelligence excerpts to support the position, and General Rabin wanted it done by morning. Of course he should have called off this rendezvous, but Emily in the flesh was proving too tantalizing a temptation.

The bartender brought him a second Coca-Cola. "Waiting for Queenie, mister?" Barak nodded. "She's high-class. You can tell. They're usually late." He dropped his voice and gestured. "We get some real bimbos in here."

A real bimbo in a tight red dress sat cross-legged on one of the two barstools, showing fat thighs and ruffled blue garters. Nobody else was in the bar but the waiter, so Barak worked on as well as he could, making pencil notes on his documents until Emily at last arrived in a rush. "Here I am, here I am. Fiona had one of her migraines. I had to stay late." She fell into the chair beside him, and seized his hand in a clammy clutch. "Zev, did you really mean what you said on the telephone? I didn't sleep all night. Not a wink."

He squeezed her hand hard. "Hi. Let me put away this silly bumf, and we'll get down to business."

"Oh, wow! It's on, my love? Truly on?"

He freed his hand to stow the papers, smiling at her. "Unless you've changed your mind, always a lady's privilege."

She stared at him with lemur eyes, then looked around ruefully at the bar, the bartender, and the bimbo. "The thing is, Old Wolf, this isn't how I thought it would be. So help me, it's like a dentist's appointment."

He burst out laughing. "Really? Why, what did you expect, Queenie?"

"Oh, who knows? In my fantasies we'd be in some magical terrifically elegant private place, and there'd be champagne in a bucket, and candles, and roses, and all that, and you'd sweet-talk me into it."

"Talk you into it? I can't talk you out of it. That's obvious. You're preposterous. Dr. Sapphire has the answer, so let's go." He zipped shut the briefcase, a loud rasp in the almost empty bar.

"You're right, you're right, you're absolutely right. Get it over with." Her voice was tremulous. "On second thought, may I have a drink first? Sort of like laughing gas?"

"By all means." He beckoned to the bartender. It was beginning to look as if Emily would balk and back out, after all. So be it! Her choice. He would not press her, though her slender young figure in a black suit was an inflaming presence, and everything else about her enchanted him: her slightly breathless way of talking, her knack for crazily funny narration with a straight face, her swift curving hand movements and an especially emphatic gesture with all ten fingers shaken straight at him; these were just a few of the snaring graces of this fey spinster who was drinking off half the Jack Daniel's at a gulp. "Ah! That's better. Wolf, when were you last unfaithful to Nakhama?"

"God, you're impossible, Emily. You shouldn't have said that."

"I guess not. Sorry. Tell me you've never been, and the dentistry is off. I mean that, darling. I *mean* it. A homewrecker I'm not."

"You're not wrecking anything, but . . ." He hesitated. "Oh, hell — fair enough, I'll tell you about the only time that mattered."

"Great." She finished the drink with a second gulp, and signalled to the bartender for a refill.

"Emily, where on earth did you learn to drink like that?"

"From Fiona, really. She's the next thing to a barfly. Always ladylike, but when things get rough at school she goes into Middleburg, to the Red Fox bar, and tanks up on bourbon. I used to drink sherry with her. I've switched. Go ahead. The only time that mattered . . ."

"Well, if this will impress you, she was a marchesa. Italy, 1945."

"A marchesa! Oh, wow."

He told it sparely, but the memories flooded in on him, and as he spoke he could almost smell the climbing roses on the balcony outside the marchesa's boudoir overlooking the purple Adriatic.

"Then she was the one who really did it," exclaimed Emily. "What a fellow you are, I swear! We have to hurl ourselves at you, don't we? She sent the bottle of wine to your table, and you hadn't so much as noticed her!"

"For a fact, I hadn't. But I was twenty-one, and I guess not that bad-looking. Not fat and gray, anyhow. So she noticed me."

"Brunello, you say."

"Yes. It was excellent wine, by the way. The waiter brought it with the marchesa's compliments to the victorious British soldier. From her own vineyard."

"She was pretty?"

"Emily, she was thin and blond. She was thirty-seven. Sort of stringy. Extraordinary woman, spoke several languages, very witty, very chic. She truly fascinated me, and I had trouble looking Nakhama in the eye when I got home." He shrugged. "After a while, I managed."

"And the other times? The times that didn't matter? Tell me."

"Oh, Emily, shut up."

With a sudden sober mien, she said, "Wolf, my very dear, do you want to call this off?"

"God, no. Come on."

In the elevator his arm was around her, and he could feel her shivering. There was peculiar excitement in that; he felt at once sorry for her and shaky with a hunger for her.

"So this is where it's going to happen?" Emily's voice shook as they entered a room smelling of Lysol, lit by the red glow of the hotel's neon sign through the window. "The historical society will be putting up a plaque."

"Come here, Queenie." He tossed their coats on the bed and embraced her, in the blinking crimson light. She responded to his kiss with real enough passion. Virginal nerves going by the board! Gently he began unbuttoning her shirtwaist, passing his hands over slight breasts, beautifully firm under the white silk. She peered at him with great round eyes as his hand moved down a slippery row of pearl buttons. Suddenly she burst into wild giggles, choking, "Sorry, sorry."

"*Now* what?"

"Two things, darling. You're tickling me, and you smell like Coca-Cola. Not that it's an unpleasant smell," she added hastily, trying to stifle her laughter with a small fist on her mouth. "Come on, why are you stopping? I'm deliriously happy, honestly."

The telephone rang. The room was so small that he could reach out and pick it up without releasing her. "Yes, put him on."

"Saved by the bell?" she inquired, softly kissing his cheek and his ear.

"Yes . . . hello, Sam. . . . Really? Is that good or bad?" Long pause. He glanced at his wristwatch, holding it up to the red light. "I see. But look, that's in half an hour. . . . Well, I may be a few minutes late. Quite a turn of events."

He hung up and looked at her.

"I know, Doc," she said. "You're not going to drill after all."

"I love you, Emily," he said, "God help me, I love you, but no drilling. Not tonight. I'm wanted at the embassy."

"It's just as well. This is too squalid even for Queenie. We'll try again in the Growlery."

"Growlery? What's that?"

"You'll find out."

Sam Pasternak was pacing under a streetlamp outside the embassy. "There you are," he greeted Barak with smoking breath. "The guy changed his mind, we're to meet him at his house, not here. Rabin's already there. It's not far, we can walk."

They trudged together along Connecticut Avenue through dirty slush. "Did you manage to reach Yael?" Barak asked.

"Finally. I gather she's going ahead with that Beverly Hills shop. The problem is still Aryeh."

"I promised Kishote I'd talk to the boy. Did you?"

"He wouldn't come to the phone."

The President's deputy special counsel lived in a narrow old brownstone on a side street off Dupont Circle. A prominent Washington lawyer, he was Kennedy's Jew, so to say, though in print and on television nobody said it. Rabin and the attaché were having drinks with him in a very small book-lined room on the second floor when Barak and Pasternak arrived. Like them, Rabin wore a suit and tie. The attaché, a stout general Barak had served under in the training and doctrine section, was in uniform and looked extremely weary.

"I don't suppose you have those excerpts ready," Rabin said, glancing at Barak's briefcase.

"I've selected them. They'll be ready for presentation at our morning meeting" — he turned to the attaché — "if your office will print them up."

A growl. "It'll be done."

"What is their thrust?" inquired the counsel. "Do they make a solid case?"

Barak looked to Pasternak, whose gesture signalled that he talk openly. The discussion of Israeli intelligence that followed was singularly candid. The counsel, a lean man in his forties dressed collegiate style — gray flannel trousers, brown tweed jacket, black knitted tie — got up and walked back and forth in the constricted space. General Rabin, in a characteristic crouch over his perpetual cigarette, said nothing until the counsel turned to him and asked, "Well, I'm convinced, but will this convince the Defense and State people?"

In his slow low way Rabin replied, "Their job is not to be convinced."

"True. I spoke to the President not two hours ago. He's been following this business very closely."

"Well, that's good news," said Rabin to the others, managing to sound joyless.

"Mind you" — the counsel picked up the bottle of Scotch, offered it to the others, who declined, and poured some for himself — "it's a matter of extreme delicacy. He has to take a world view. Arab good will is crucial to many United States interests."

"So we've been hearing," said Rabin from his crouch.

"Still, you fellows have three things going for you." The counsel ticked them off on spread fingers. "First, he made a promise to Golda Meir that he'd be sympathetic to Israel's situation. He keeps his promises. Second, he's a World War II man, and he remembers how the Arabs played along with Hitler. He doesn't expect ever to count on them, and he thinks Israel may one day be our ace in the hole in the Mediterranean. Third, he believes the Jewish vote swung the election to him."

Faintly brightening, Rabin said, "Then we have a chance, perhaps?"

"A lot depends on your meeting next Monday with the State and Defense people. They're sending pretty senior persons to that one. By then they'll have had a chance to digest Colonel Barak's presentation, and so will the President." The counsel gave Barak a friendly yet distant smile. "So, Colonel, deliver!"

"I'll do my best, sir."

When the meeting was breaking up, Barak said to the counsel, "You'd probably know the answer to this. What's a Growlery?"

"Growlery . . . ?" The counsel's sharp eyes brightened. He snapped back like a contestant on a television quiz show, "Growlery. Dickens. *Bleak House.* A place where you hole up when you get hopping mad. Why?"

"Thanks." Barak shook his hand. "You're amazing."

"English major, Harvard," said the counsel, smoothing his hair with both hands.

The embassy car took off with General Rabin. Pasternak and Barak got into a cab with the military attaché. "Why are you so beat?" Barak asked the attaché, who slumped back on the seat, eyes closed. They were going to his apartment to talk over the intelligence excerpts, and the best way to present them to the Americans.

"You'll find out. You'll be up for this job one day."

"Not if I can fight it off."

The attaché opened his eyes and rolled his head at Barak. "There you're mistaken. The ambassador makes the official noises, the missions come and go, but this section delivers the goods."

30

The Growlery

On Monday morning Barak left the hotel in an uneasy frame of mind. Over the weekend there had been no reaction whatever from the Americans to his hard-wrought aide-mémoire, not even hints about its effect from friendly lower-level contacts at State and in the Pentagon. Nor had the President's special counsel returned General Rabin's calls. As for Emily, not a peep from her, and telephoning the school had raised only a custodian with a ripe southern accent and no information about Miz Cunningham.

His unease was not about the aide-mémoire. It presented, he felt, a conclusive well-documented argument for obtaining the tanks. The usual Washington stall about supplying Israel, that her military prowess guaranteed victory in any defensive war, was crumbling in the face of the brute mass of Soviet weapons pouring into Arab countries, and the hard intelligence of Arab officers training in the USSR. In the air the balance was shifting especially rapidly: a hundred Ilyushin bombers newly delivered to Egypt, and MiG-18s and MiG-21s piling up on twenty-seven Arab airfields, far outnumbering the French Mirages based on Israel's seven fields. On the ground Israel's Centurion tanks — numerical disparity aside — were no match for the T-54s and T-55s arriving in Egypt and Syria.

A dangerous incentive was developing for a surprise attack on the Jewish State, and a timely supply of American tanks — however few at first — would not only reduce the asymmetry, but send a signal that would cool the atmosphere in the region, and lessen the odds of all-out war. Such was Barak's case, backed by a sheaf of intelligence annexes and exhibits. It was unchallengeable, he thought, if President Kennedy's assurances to Golda Meir counted for anything at all. That was the question.

As the participants walked into a brightly sunny State Department conference room for the showdown meeting, Barak was struck by the sheer pictorial contrast between the sides. He was the tallest of the Israelis, and all the Americans but one State aide were taller than he. The gray-headed, pink-faced army general towered well over six feet; the Assistant Secretary of State was a lean pallid funereal figure at least as tall; and their mostly blond aides and deputies appeared to have been purposely selected to make the Israelis look like squat dark troglodytes, making outrageous demands out of primitive ignorance. Or so it seemed to Zev Barak that morning, and he thought that the Americans' greetings were ominously toothy and glassy-eyed. He had no feeling of contact with any of them except the general, whose smile was brief and uncomfortable as he shook hands.

The State man opened by saying that alas, the CIA's Middle East arms balance estimate directly contradicted Colonel Barak's eloquent aide-mémoire. He went on to review recent favors shown Israel by the United States, at much risk to its relations with Arab countries: release of the Hawk antiaircraft missile (although delivery would take a while), support of the Jordan water project (although Arab threats to prevent it by force were causing some delay), and so on. About the specific arms requests, he deferred to the army general.

Next the general informed them that the U.S.A. had no missile boats and no plans to make them; so Israel would have to look elsewhere to counter the Russian missile boats that the Arabs were receiving. As for ground-to-ground missiles, the American weapons were designed for nuclear warheads and not modifiable for conventional warheads, hence unfortunately not available for Israel. Regarding tanks, any transfer of various American models under discussion would have to be subject in the end to political judgments, which were State Department turf, as the general put it, with a gesture at the gloomy Assistant Secretary of State, who sat sucking at a cold pipe.

These two statements, punctuated by readings aloud of many technical document excerpts, consumed over an hour. In a break for coffee and cookies the black-clad State official, reaching for an amicable tone, brought up his gardening hobby; the unseasonable warm spell that had melted the snow, he feared, might mislead his crocuses into coming up and then being frozen. Pasternak commented that around Washington getting misled by a warm spell and then getting frozen was always a hazard. His gravelly voice and ursine roll of the shoulders brought chuckles, but the Assistant Secretary of State did not laugh, and Barak thought Sam had talked out of turn. When they lined up again at the table in facing chairs, the State man asked an aide to read out a draft protocol summing up the talks and the department's recommendations, which would go via channels to the President. Of course, he said, he would welcome the Israelis' comments before finalizing the text. During the reading he gnawed at his pipe, his eyes resting on Rabin's dour face.

At the end of the reading, silence.

"General Rabin?" inquired the Assistant Secretary.

"Deeply disappointing."

"Why? That's a substantial concession we've recommended on the tanks, isn't it? We thought you'd be pleased."

"Forgive me, sir, I'm a blunt soldier. What concession? You require hard intelligence from us on Egyptian tank types and numbers. Meantime, if I understand what I just heard, no tanks for us. How do you define *hard* intelligence?"

The Assistant Secretary looked at the handsome blond aide who had read the protocol. The aide said in a Bostonian accent, "Intelligence which the CIA will confirm or accept."

"Which could take months to develop," Pasternak put in. "Or a year, and it's an elusive criterion at best."

"And the proposal to assemble the tanks in Europe, sir," Barak said, "could mean a delay of years in delivery."

"No other way," declared the general, looking glum, "in existing political circumstances."

Walking out of the State Department building into the sunlight, Rabin said, "The mission is not a success, gentlemen." He added to Barak, "Your memorandum was excellent. The result was decided beforehand."

Returning to the hotel after an unhappy postmortem afternoon in the embassy, Zev Barak was astonished by the slam of his own pulse at the sight of a telephone slip in his message box. He read the scrawl and crumpled it.

"Where can I rent a car?" he asked the desk clerk.

She stopped filing her nails to stab in the air with the file. "Union Station."

Emily's auto was waiting in front of the Middleburg post office with lights turned off. He parked the rented car and got in beside her. "Hi, Wolf." She started the motor. "You made amazing time."

"Clear directions."

"How goes your mission, dear? I decided not to bother you over the weekend."

"That was sensible. On the mission, no comment."

"Understood. How much time have we got?"

"I should be back by ten."

"Right. We're off to the Growlery." She turned up a dark narrow street, twisted around a couple of corners, and skidded into a two-lane road. "The ice hasn't quite melted out here yet. Fear not. The school isn't far."

"Emily, what is the Growlery?"

"Gatehouse of the estate that the school bought. The last headmistress lived in it. Fiona and I use it to get away. Relax, or work, or whatever. We play cards there. It's nice. There's a fireplace." She put a dank hand on his. "Nervous, dear?"

"Me? Why should I be?"

"Lovely. *I'm* not. Cool as a cucumber. Fit as a fiddle. Happy as a clam."

"Clams are happy?"

"Why not? They're hermaphrodites, aren't they? They screw themselves. What a wise system! No complications."

"Oysters are hermaphrodites, I think," said Barak. "Not clams. Anyway, hermaphrodites don't self-fertilize. Not as a rule."

"Wow, you're well-informed! All the straight dope on hermaphrodites. I'm weak on biology. French lit's my game. Say, guess what? Hiroshima has won a poetry prize. No kidding! He sent me a copy of the book. You won't recognize his picture on the jacket. He broke his nose in an auto accident, and he's bald. He looks like Socrates."

"Emily, for God's sake watch the road." She kept looking at him as she prattled, with eyes that gleamed when cars came the other way.

"I can drive this road in my sleep. I love you, Wolf. I'm astounded that you came. You Israeli army men are all up to no good. Everybody knows that. I was afraid you might be different."

"Shut up, Queenie."

"I can't. This time it's on for sure, I know, and to tell the truth I'm in acute panic. Here's the school. See? Just a hop, skip, and jump." She drove through a stone gateway lit by wrought-iron lamps, and whirled the car to a stop by a wooden cottage. "Growlery. The school's up there." She flipped a hand at a large rambling moonlit structure atop a hill, at the end of a winding gravel road.

Barak was taking off his coat as she crouched by the fireplace, touching off a bright flare of paper and kindling. He said, "So, is this where Fiona and her Reverend do their hootchy-kootchy?"

"That's gitchi-gitchi, dear. No, no, Fiona has a house down the road. Her own house, very charming. Make yourself at home." She turned on one standing lamp and slipped out. The fire took hold, brightening and crackling, with a pleasant woodsmoke smell. The cottage had an angular wooden ceiling from which a wagon-wheel chandelier hung, and this main room was lined with books slanting higgledy-piggledy on the shelves. He sat down on a worn upholstered couch facing the fire, and saw on the low table before him a crystal bowl heaped high with pistachio nuts.

"I shouldn't have told you," he called. "I'm fat enough."

"Oh, the pistachios? Enjoy, enjoy." A crash of glass. "Oh, bloody damn, Zev!"

"Here I come." In a small kitchen broken glass lay in a pool of red wine. She handed him a bottle. "Here, open this one while I clean up the mess. Some start on our tryst, hey? Egad, do I ever have the shakes!"

"Brunello, I see."

"What else? Go ahead, take it inside. Here are glasses, there's the corkscrew. We're going to have a beautiful unforgettable time, even though I'm no marchesa, and there are no candles or roses."

As they drank wine by firelight, she gave a lively account of Jack Smith's wedding in Washington Cathedral to the daughter of one of the town's rich lawyers. The romance had burgeoned quickly, and the ceremony had been the event of the fall for old Washingtonians. "Patricia's very gentle and pretty, I'd say she's beautiful. I like her." Emily sat on the floor, resting her head against Barak's knee. "A good horsewoman. The only thing is, she's crazy. Not crazy like me, I mean that she should be locked away. Once she and I got back from a hunt all sweaty, and we sat in a corner of the club bar drinking Pimm's Cups, and she told me she had seen a spaceship."

He was caressing her hair. "Come on, she must have been kidding."

"Positively not. She said she was off by herself looking for shells on a beach in Tortola — that's the British Virgin Islands — and this flying saucer came whooshing down and threw up clouds of water and sand. Then it landed, and aliens came out."

"And what did they look like, little green creatures?"

"Well, she was just starting on that — she said they were sort of round and doughy — when she saw Jack coming over. She whispered, 'Not a word to Jack, not on your life, he'll think I'm ga-ga.' Well, then they got engaged, and she's hardly spoken to me since. But she meant every word, Zev. Her eyes got that funny shiny look, you know? Poor Jack!"

A flaming log tumbled forward, smoking into the room. Barak shoved it back with a poker, then dropped on the floor beside her and took her in his arms.

"There's another bottle of Brunello," she quavered. "I bought three."

"I've had enough wine."

"Well, have some pistachio nuts."

"Not just now."

He kissed and caressed her, at first gently, then with rising passion. She was shyly and inexpertly responding, and he pulled her to her feet. "Come, Queenie."

Breathlessly, "Where, dear?"

Clasping her icy hand, he led her toward an open bedroom door. "Oh, there," she said. "Well, bless my soul."

A patch of moonlight fell through a tall window on the double bed. He took off his jacket.

"I see. I guess this is it," Emily said. "Well, I'm all for it. Here goes nothing!" With a determined yank at a zipper, she shrugged herself out of her woolen dress. It lay in a puddle at her feet. She stood in a lacy slip, bare arms crossed over her chest. "So, what do you think so far? Pretty stringy, like the marchesa?"

"Beautiful, young, glorious."

"Thanks, but Wolf, this feels damn funny. I'm not at all embarrassed. It's as though you're another girl, almost. Now why should that be?"

"Are you saying you're not in the mood?"

"Darling, can't you tell I'm seething with passion? But my gosh, you're undressing fast! Army training, hey? Now under this slip," she said, picking up the frothy hem, "everything is French. Incredibly yummy. You'll go out of your mind."

"I can't wait, but how about pulling down the shade?"

"Oh, yes, yes, to be sure. Nobody's out there, still, good idea. I'm sort of — Christ on a bicycle!"

"What?"

"Fiona."

"Fiona!"

"Wolf, she's heading this way. I left her at the Red Fox, she should have been good for hours!" She thrust all ten fingers wildly at him. "Put on your clothes! Or get under the bed! Jump into the closet! Do *something!*" With great speed she pulled on her dress and zipped it up.

"Now listen, Emily" — Barak seized his trousers — "you just go out there and tell Fiona you've got a guy in here."

"A guy? She won't believe me. She'll think I'm doing something truly horrible. Cooking frankfurters in the fire! She's murder on frankfurters, because of all the dripping grease. We had a hair-pull about that once."

"Do as I say, Emily. Just go on out there." He propelled her by the elbow toward the door.

"You really think I should do that? All right, I will. But dress, dress, in case she barges in! She's a rhinoceros, Fiona."

As Barak dressed he heard voices outside, then hysterical giggling. He went to the couch, took a fistful of pistachios and ate, tossing the shells in the fire. The high-pitched hilarious chatter outside went on and on. It was after nine o'clock. His amorous mood waned, and he began to feel like a fool, sitting and cracking pistachio nuts in a cottage on the grounds of a girls school in Virginia, at the end of a failed mission for armaments, waiting and waiting for the chance to be unfaithful to his wife. Emily came in at last, laughing, and slammed the door.

"Well?"

"You were so right!" She dropped on the couch. "When I told her, you know what she did? She went, 'Whoopee!' and threw her arms around me, and laughed fit to bust. She's three sheets to the wind, and then some! She cross-examined me about you, wanted to come in and just say howdy, and I had a hell of a time getting her to vamoose. She's gone now, and — Oh, blast, Zev, stop eating those stupid pistachios!" She embraced him, and pushed him back on the couch for a desperate amateurish kiss. "Where were we, now? Shall I open the other Brunello?"

"Never mind the Brunello." He pulled her close, and kissed and kissed her delicious thin mouth.

"Ah, that's the spirit," she murmured against his lips. "Come on now, hotshot."

But it was just talk. Her response was forced and clumsy, and her elbows and legs kept getting between them. After a while, holding her a little away by the shoulders, he said, "Now, Queenie, is it on? We get undressed again, go through all that business, okay?"

"Why not? I'm all on fire, aren't you? Only, I'm thinking you have to be back by ten, don't you? And it's after nine already. Would we be rushing it too much? How long does it actually take, dear?"

"Depends on how quickly the novocaine works." With a wry grin, Barak sat up. That she too had been jarred out of the mood was all too plain, and her inexperienced effort to conceal it was rather sweet. "Darling, I think Fiona dumped a pail of wet sand on you."

Emily sat up with a sad laugh. "Okay, she sure to Christ did. But how could you tell? Wasn't I kissing you like Garbo? Zev, I'm still willing, honest."

"You're adorable and I love you," said Barak. "You and Fiona enjoy the Brunello."

"All right. I was afraid of this as soon as she showed up. God, was she ever amused. You know what she said, Wolf? She said, 'Well, well, Snow White earns a scarlet letter.' "

"Not yet." He helped her to her feet. "Drive me back to my car. Nice try."

Sam Pasternak flew to California at the invitation of Sheva Leavis to discuss weapons available on the open market, while Barak visited an armor general at Fort Knox whom he had kept in touch with for years. Unluckily the general's new young wife, slim and hoydenish, reminded him of Emily, and Barak's idea had been to get away from Emily and, if he could, from thoughts of her. He was in too deep already, he felt, and to what possible good end?

Pasternak telephoned him at Fort Knox from Los Angeles. "You promised Kishote to talk to Aryeh? He's right here, in Sheva's guesthouse. Yael sends regards. She's out at the moment. Here's the boy."

In the doleful way Aryeh said, *"Mah shlomkha, Dode Zev?"* ("How are you, Uncle Zev?") Barak got the instant whole picture.

Did he like California? Yes, it was nice. Any friends? Yes, but he could only see them after they came home from school, and when they spoke English he couldn't understand them. Did he feel well? Yes, but he would be glad to go home. He missed Abba.

Pasternak came back on the phone. "He was putting that on for you. He gives Yael a hard time, too. But he swims in Sheva's pool, and plays with the Chinese houseman's dogs, and usually he's in fine spirits. He does want to go home, and good for him."

"How's Yael?"

"Very busy. I'm coming back tonight. Is that farewell reception for us on at the embassy?"

"Yes, and Rabin invited all those guys from State and Defense we were dealing with."

"That'll be a jolly gathering."

To Barak's enormous surprise, it was. The plane out of Fort Knox was delayed, and when he got to the embassy he found a cheery party going on. Everyone had a glass in hand, but mere alcohol could not account for this extraordinary ambiance of good feeling, and certainly not for General Rabin's smiles and banter with the lanky black-clad Assistant Secretary of State. Pasternak took Barak off into a library out of sight of the reception room, and sat him down in a corner couch under bronze busts of Ben Gurion and Herzl.

"In strict confidence, Zev, something wonderful has happened. Turnaround! The special counsel met privately with Rabin this afternoon, with a message from President Kennedy. The President has read State's protocol, and he's going to overrule it. We'll get the tanks by executive order!"

"Oo-ah! Blessed be the Name! When? Which types? How many?"

"All that will be negotiated. The decision is the main thing, and it's taken. The counsel's working on the presidential order, and he told me to tell you he's making good use of your aide-mémoire. Kennedy will issue the order when he gets back from a speaking trip."

Barak set down his Coca-Cola, and put out his hand to Pasternak. Nodding and grinning, Pasternak clasped his hand. "And those guys out there have no inkling of this," he added, "and are giving us credit because we're such good sports about being turned down."

Returning to the reception, Barak saw Christian Cunningham putting on his hat and coat. He had not spoken to the CIA man, but thought Cunningham had given him odd looks across the room. Then again, he was in such turmoil about the Cunningham connection that it might have been his imagination. He stayed on at the embassy for dinner, and midway through the meal an aide called him to the telephone.

"Wolf, how are you? I'm calling for my father." Amiable light tone. The sound of her voice shook his nerves with pleasure.

"I'm okay. I've been out of town."

"So the embassy told me. You go back to Israel day after tomorrow, don't you? Dad hopes you can come for a farewell lunch here early tomorrow. Say around noon?"

"Sam Pasternak, too?"

"Just you this time."

"I'll be there."

"Anything special you'd like? I'll be cooking. I make good pepper omelettes."

"Sounds fine. How've you been, Emily?"

"Wonderful. Fiona and I finished off the Brunello, all right. She kept drinking to 'the guy.'" Emily laughed charmingly. "We got wildly soused, and I've gone up a hundred percent in Fiona's esteem. Ray is pleased, too."

"Ray? Pleased about what? What the devil did you tell that quack?"

"See you at lunch. Ray's no quack. He says you're what the doctor ordered. He's right. Bye, Wolf."

The cab brought Barak to McLean on a windy gray November day, with brown leaves whirling past the windshield and dancing along the road. He rang the bell of the house, expecting Cunningham's ghostly voice from the cupola. Instead the door opened, and there stood Emily in an oyster-gray negligee, her eyes glistening, a tremulous smile on her very pale face.

"Come in, Wolf. I lied. My father's gone to New York." She

closed the door behind him. "He didn't invite you to lunch. We're alone. Now. Would you like a pepper omelette?"

Issur yikhud!

And so it happened, in Emily's bedroom on the second floor, overlooking the terrace where fifteen years ago they had watched the fireflies. She lay on her stomach, her face buried in her arms for a long time, while he foggily wondered at his own feelings — somewhat as though he had been electrocuted and survived — and at her worrisome silence. At last she rolled over and looked at him owlishly. In a very hoarse voice: "You know that all this is absolutely new to me."

"Yes, I know."

"Well, how many times do we do it? I don't want you to strain yourself, but I feel like doing it a lot more."

"Really?" He gathered the slim body in his arms. "That's good. Dr. Sapphire will be pleased."

"I ought to feel terrible about Nakhama. Why don't I? Have I hurt her? You'll fly away, and I'll not see you for another seven years. Maybe never. Maybe I'll get married now." Her hands moved softly over his back. "My God, Zev, gitchi-gitchi is not overrated. I always thought it was, I thought there was something cloacal or nasty about it. It's the most beautiful thing, it's unutterably beautiful, ineffably —" She kissed him again and again, covering his face with kisses.

"I hope you fall in love and marry, Emily. I want to know that you're happy —"

"Fall in love?" She put fingers on his mouth. "Old Emily D. wrote a quatrain that takes care of that, sweetie."

> *I've known her from an ample nation*
> *Choose one;*
> *Then close the valves of her attention*
> *Like stone.*

"Which doesn't mean I can't be a good wife and mother. I will be, I promise you, Wolf, but those valves are shut."

Later they were really eating pepper omelettes, in a large old-fashioned kitchen looking out on barren trees and brown shrubs, when the telephone rang. Emily answered it, rounded her eyes at Barak, and put her hand over the mouthpiece. "Sam Pasternak?" she murmured.

"Sure. He knows I came here for a lunch." He reached for the telephone. "Little does he know what else was on the menu — any more than I did. . . . Hello, Sam. Yes, I said I'd be back around two, but — *What?*" At the startling change in Barak's face, Emily jumped up and came to him, putting an arm around him. "Okay. Yes. By all means." He hung up and snapped on the kitchen radio.

"Zev, what is it?"

He held up a hand, his face a mask of shock. "Let's just listen."

It was a small old set that whined as it warmed up slowly. When the whine cleared off, an announcer was saying in a shaky voice, stammering and repeating himself, that President Kennedy had been shot, and nobody yet knew whether he was alive or dead.

"Oh, my God. Kennedy!" Emily choked on her words. "No, no! Not President Kennedy! It can't be happening. Not the *President.*"

"Sh-h-h!"

For a few minutes the announcer's talk was a disjointed hoarse description of crowds, cars, policemen, motorcycles, an ambulance, a glimpse of a body on a stretcher, more crowds. Pulling himself together, he gave a more coherent story of the President's arrival in Dallas, of the motorcade, and of the shots which had gravely wounded him and the Governor of Texas, possibly coming from the top of a building. He went on with repetitious graphic chatter about stampedes of shouting people around a line of automobiles, which disclosed nothing of what had actually happened to the President. Going back in time, he began recapitulating his impressions of the hatless smiling Kennedy waving from the back of the open car, with his wife beside him in a pink tailored suit and pillbox hat.

"Oh God, Zev. That radiant young man, that goddess of a wife at his side — struck down! It's something out of Plutarch. Jack Kennedy! Jackie Kennedy!" Emily sobbed, dashing tears from her eyes with a fist.

Struck mute, Barak was thinking that this frightful American catastrophe was also an immeasurable disaster for Israel. He could only hope that the early reports were panicky, that the young President would live.

"Emily, I must go to the embassy."

"I know."

"Call a taxi."

"Of course."

At the door, as the cab honked, she clung to him and kissed him, tears running down her face. "Will I ever see you again?"

"I'll call you, Emily, before I leave."

"Listen to me, Wolf, at this terrible moment I want you to know that if this morning was all, it's enough. It will last out my life, it'll never fade . . ."

Gripping her in his arms, the bulky army coat between them, he said, "And I'll forget nothing, not the Lincoln Memorial, not the Growlery, not your white lie about lunch —"

"Scarlet lie —"

"Snow-white lie, Queenie, Emily, Snow White, God bless you. I love you. God make you happy. Goodbye."

"Write, Wolf! Write! Let's write, always!"

Cold wind swept in as he opened the door.

Summertime. Fighter planes were landing and taking off in a hazy day in the Negev as Barak and Benny Luria watched from the control tower. Now and then Luria barked air force jargon into the microphone, and more jargon gargled back at him from the loudspeaker. Though Barak had picked up some of this talk from combined air-and-armor exercises, he still felt like an outsider on any air base. Heyl Ha'avir, the air force, was a tough little asteroid in orbit near the small planet Israel, so Barak sometimes thought; the gravitational connection was there, but minimal.

"Sorry, I had to get this drill over with," Benny said as they climbed down the ladder. "It was scheduled before I knew you were coming. We'll give you a decent lunch, anyway."

"Will your staff have the air annex of the exercise ready before I leave?"

"If not, they'll hear from me."

As they sat in Luria's office, eating fried chicken and assorted vegetables, they got to talking about aircraft procurement, and that led to Barak's tale of the arrest to the tank program. Pasternak and the Mossad, he told Luria, after half a year, were still on the quest for "hard" intelligence of Egypt's tank forces, since President Johnson had accepted the State Department's protocol. Luria was wrinkling up his handsome face so grotesquely that Barak inquired what was the matter with him.

"With *me*! What's the matter with Pasternak? With the Mossad? With this crazy country? Did anybody think of asking the air force about Egypt's tank force?"

"Why, what would the air force know about their tanks?"

Luria pressed a button on his desk. "Do you by chance remember Rotem?"

"Rotem?"

"Yes, Zev, Rotem."

This was the massive surprise incursion by Nasser into the Sinai three years before with armor and infantry divisions. Incredibly, the move had gone undetected by Israel for days. The first shocking reports had set off secret war alerts and first steps toward mobilization. After two weeks Nasser had withdrawn his forces, trumpeting that he had forestalled Israeli plans to attack Syria over a border dispute. With the Mossad and army intelligence blaming each other for the fiasco, shake-ups had ensued in both services, heads had rolled, Pasternak had risen to his present post, and doctrines had been drastically revised.

"I remember Rotem," Barak said with a shade of irony.

A girl soldier entered, neater and prettier than most of those in the armor division. Barak did not begrudge Luria the comelier girls, the snappier uniforms, the more comfortable barracks, or any other perquisite of the air force, with its simple fateful mission, *Clear skies over Israel.*

"Mira, tell Yoram in photographic to pull the Rotem folios for us to look at."

"B'seder." As she left, Mira managed an arch glance at the husky armor general with the gray-sprinkled hair.

By the harsh light of a magnifier, in a gloomy stuffy record storage room, the two officers studied aerial desert photographs from a large stiff folder labelled ROTEM — EGYPTIAN ARMOR. "The whole picture," said Luria, "formed up west of Jebel Libni. What more do you want?"

"Fantastic," muttered Barak.

"I flew some of those missions." The young soldier Yoram spoke with pride, his curly black hair dangling over the magnifier. "This is a shot I took myself, this panoramic one. We've got telescopic shots that identify types, even show regiment markings. We had German lenses, you know, the real stuff."

"Well?" Luria poked Barak with an elbow.

"I've got to phone Sam."

Pasternak was not at the army intelligence HQ. "Track him down," Barak told the duty officer, "highest urgency, and tell him I'm in Benny Luria's office."

Soon Pasternak called back. *"Gott in himmel,"* he exclaimed, as Barak described the find. "How could we have missed that? Army intelligence has been even stupider than the Mossad, and that takes a lot of doing."

*   *   *

The most convincing photographs, with precise and exhaustive technical evaluations and extrapolations, went off by army intelligence courier to Washington. Three weeks later, a jubilant report from the military attaché: the CIA was convinced! So was the Defense Department. Even the State Department conceded that the Soviet Union might well be upsetting the balance of armed force in the Middle East, and that countervailing steps might be considered.

State's proposal, emerging laggardly, was that West Germany sell Sherman and Patton tanks to Israel, and the United States would resupply the Germans. The Bonn government, dependent on the United States for weaponry and for protection from the heavy Soviet forces in East Germany, cheerlessly agreed. With little delay, Arab threats were forthcoming against West Germany of economic boycott and a possible oil embargo. Thereupon the Germans, expressing much sympathy for the unfortunate predicament of Israel, pulled out of the deal.

The next State Department idea was to provide elements of tanks to several European countries — chassis here, turret there, gun and fire control elsewhere — and have them assembled in such a way as to diffuse and fuzz the responsibility of supplying Israel with tanks, leaving America in the clear with the touchy Arabs.

31

The Queenie-Wolf Letters

22 November 1964

Dear Old Wolf:

Has a whole year really blitzed by? The papers today are full of backward glances at the assassination, with copious pictures and a general elegiac tone. For me this day is forever a day of mingled joy and horror, a strangeness which will haunt me while I last. The rest is silence, my love. I know I've been laggard all year in writing, I who importuned you to write, *write*! And you've been a dear. If your epistles read a wee bit like army reports, long on fact and short on sugar, well, that's my Israeli Spartan.

I didn't want to tell you until it was definite, but most of the year I've been in the throes of taking over from Fiona as headmistress. You see, at long last Reverend Wentworth has doffed the cloth. Fiona has said to me a million times that she would *never* be a minister's wife, and indeed with her hollow leg she's not quite the type, so the Reverend has packed in the divinity thing, and has got himself a job as an editor in a Christian publishing house. They tied the knot back in September. I guess they're happy, but Fiona seems to lack the old fizz lately, so help me. Can it be that authorized gitchi-gitchi turns out to be a bit of a bore, compared to the sneaky article? No spice like a sense of sin, hey toots? Is that it? Will she have to shoot him in the other groin to recapture that old magic?

Answering the query in your October letter about Hester, I'm sure I told you that I went out to Oregon for the christening of their girl baby. I was godmother, she even named the poor helpless mite Emily.

Well, next I heard Hester was in a severe post-parturition depression, and hinting at trying the chandelier caper again, only this time on a magnificent old oak in their garden, which must have been standing there when Lewis and Clark trekked by. Even Hester couldn't bring down one of those branches, sure as hell she would hang. So her hubby begged me to come out again and cheer her up.

I went and did my best. We gossiped and played Mahler records and read aloud John Donne and Plutarch, and got roaring drunk a few nights (much the most effective recourse), and she loosened up and let me into her attic studio, where she is now into painting insects. She stupefies them with cigar smoke — she's taken to smoking black stogies — then looks at them through a magnifier and paints them. I believe Hester's found her metier as the Audubon of the creepy-crawlies. She did the most alarming spider! I thought it would leap right off the canvas with those hairy legs and sink fangs into me. My visit did the trick, especially my reaction to the spider. She's now doing spiders like mad, and is positively lovey-dovey with her maddeningly bland hubby, who reports to me that she's no longer studying the oak tree for the best place to sling a noose.

Now Old Wolf, I don't want to hex the thing by being too hopeful or explicit, but a new guy may be entering my picture. He's a classmate of Jack Smith's, and before Jack married Pat he took me to a reunion of their West Point class, dinner and dancing, and I met this Lieutenant Colonel Bradford Halliday. He's in Germany now on an air force base. I had no idea I'd made the *slightest* impression on him, Wolf, and out of the blue a couple of weeks ago here comes this stiff letter saying that since his wife died (some tropical plague in the Philippines did her in, despite all the shots) I'm the only lady who has ever . . . etc., etc., and he hoped I wouldn't mind his getting in touch when he comes Stateside again.

I do remember the man well. Extremely tall, an intelligent talker, and with something melancholy yet pleasant about him. Jack told me that "Bud" Halliday has a red-hot rep in the air force. Don't get jealous now, *mon vieux,* so far this is just mostly imagination. But you've always been after me to get married, and since that wonderful and ghastly morning, exactly a year ago today, the possibility now at least exists for me.

My God, let me quit this scrawling before I burst out with futile love talk and tears.

All my love,
Queenie

The correspondence continued, infrequent but steady, and a year later, Barak wrote one of his longest letters.

22 November 1965

My dearest Queenie:

First of all, my condolences on your mother's death. I'm writing separately to your father. May she rest in peace. I met her only twice, but I remember her as an elegant lady with a subtle sense of humor and a hint of depth, a lady out of a Henry James book almost. I know what a blow it can be, having lost both my parents not too long ago, within a short time of each other.

It happens to be exactly "that day" again, doesn't it? Yet another year gone by! I just realized that, writing down the date. In my life the months seem to flash by like hours. We've had much terrorist activity in Central Command, and I've been in the thick of preventive and reprisal raids, less said the better. You destroy my letters, I'm sure, as I do yours. I have a lot to tell you, but forget what I'll now write about Germany as it pertains to our rearmament problems. I set foot on that accursed ground last week, after vowing long ago that I never again would.

No country on earth will openly sell us front-line battle tanks, Queenie, but we're due to get some American tanks through a devious process of international assembly which compels us to deal with the Germans. I was sent on the first mission, German being my language and armor my service branch. No escape. Well, when the airplane door opened and we walked out on the ramp, there on the tarmac was an honor guard of Wehrmacht troops, with the German and the Israeli flags flapping in the breeze side by side. A stomach-churning moment, I tell you! My father got us all out of Vienna well before Hitler came, but the Nazis were already strutting in the streets. Long-buried memories rose up and overwhelmed me, with a sickness of soul that nobody can know who wasn't a Jew in Europe then. The strained politeness of our encounter with the Germans, from the first handshakes (how could we avoid exchanging salutes and shaking hands?) was simply awful, and the awfulness went on to the last. I'll sum it all up in one story.

We were invited to cocktails and dinner at some senior officers club. To warm the atmosphere, I guess, the waiters kept refilling our wineglasses, while we chattered about everything but what was really on all our minds; on the Israelis' certainly, and by the artificial very forced good humor of the Germans, on theirs too. But all that wine backfired.

One of the wives at my end of the long table, middle-aged and all painted up and loaded with jewelry, suddenly burst out in a loud voice, "What's going on here? How long can we keep on pretending? You were all in on it, all you officers, and you know it! Let's at least be honest with these Jews, tell them we're sorry. Or even if we aren't, at least talk about what happened instead of all this gibble-gabble —" Something like that she managed to yell out before her husband grabbed her and hustled her away from the table, shouting over her voice that she wasn't well and hadn't been for some time.

The mission itself didn't go badly, though the Germans drove cold hard bargains at every point. Bad conscience or not, no easy terms for the Jews! However, as to the tank work, they know what they're doing. They always know, whether it's tanks, rockets, or crematoriums. When the door of our special El Al plane closed on Germany, I drew my first full breath in four days. The evening we got back Leonard Bernstein was conducting the Israel Philharmonic, and seats were reserved for our party up front. Nakhama and I found ourselves first row center. I tell you, Queenie, when the concert began, and Bernstein and that magnificent orchestra struck up "Hatikvah," The Hope, and the packed hall stood up as one man, I was swept by a sense of what we Jews have accomplished here in the Holy Land, a feeling of pride and strength in our new beginning, that made all the hard times and sacrifices seem endurable.

But the rest of the evening didn't stay on that high emotional plane. You and Hester make a fetish of Mahler, and I too love his huge beautiful mishmashes, but for Nakhama, who tends to fall asleep at concerts anyway, Mahler is straight chloroform. Sixteen bars and she's under. We were in the front row, not two feet from the first violinist, who happens to be my old friend Pinkhas, a fine musician, and Pinkhas kept scowling at poor Nakhama as he scraped along through that stupendous First Symphony. I tried a pinch or two and an elbow jab, but she only muttered. I was damned tired myself, anyway, so during the Brahms piano concerto that followed, I too nodded off. I haven't run into Pinkhas since, and don't especially want to.

Aside from her low tolerance for classical music Nakhama is just great. So are my children. Noah's about to go to sea in a patrol boat, and I, Queenie, may be coming to Washington as our military attaché.

I put this baldly, just as a possibility. I've tried and tried to dodge this assignment, it's a dubious sidewise career move. But General Rabin (a) thinks that I'm effective with the Americans and (b) assumes that Nasser is preparing for a military showdown with us. If I resist hard enough, I can probably get out of it and stay in my deputy post in this Central Command, aiming for the next upward rung of the army ladder, commander of the sector. But the experience in Germany gave me pause. Israel has existed only seventeen years so far, by the skin of her teeth. The more I come to understand things, the more I perceive how our miracle of the Return is linked to your older miracle of America. Your father's been talking that line for years. I've just begun to grasp it. Two world titans confront each other, America and Russia, freedom versus despotism, and square in the middle of the battle zone is this precarious little nonsense called Israel, to me the most precious patch of ground on earth. If General Rabin is right, and I can best serve over there, why should I fight it any longer?

So I tell myself, and then again I tell myself cut the bullshit, what you mean is that Queenie is in Washington.

More soon.

Deep love,
Zev

P.S. One of our best officers, Lieutenant Colonel Nitzan, my former brigade deputy, is now at the Army Industrial College at Fort McNair outside Washington. He's married to a mighty attractive Israeli lady, so he's no alternative to your Lieutenant Colonel Halliday, who sounds promising. But if your paths cross you'll like Yossi, he's funny and bright.

Z.

*   *   *

Yael left the busy bridal shop and hurried to her rented house in Westwood. The instructions she had left for lunch were peculiar: *"Cook for two, set the table for three."* She found all in order, and her Peruvian maid starting the chicken Kiev which Lee Bloom fancied. The other guest had a diet problem, according to Lee, and would bring his own sustenance.

She was changing her dress when she heard a throaty engine sound in her driveway, and then a cutoff. Damn, were they half an hour early? She threw on a robe and saw through the window a fiery-red convertible Cadillac, out of which emerged not Lee Bloom but — to her utter stupefaction — Don Kishote in uniform, pulling luggage with him! Three days earlier he had telephoned her that his course was over, and he was flying back to Israel that same evening. He came into the house, dumped suitcases and canvas bags in the hall, and greeted her with an exhausted grin and a quick kiss. "Hi. When does Aryeh get out of school?"

"Kishote, what the devil . . . ?"

"Yes, yes, long story. That car out there belongs to my friend Alvaro, a Mexican colonel who was in my course. Alvaro is rich as Korah, nice guy, he mentioned he wanted to hire somebody to drive his Cadillac to L.A., and I said I'd do it for him, no charge, just to get myself out here. I couldn't afford to rent a car to cross the country, but this way —"

"For God's sake, was that a problem? I'd have sent you money —"

"Yael, who wants your money? When does the boy come home? Three, four o'clock? My plane leaves at nine."

"Your plane?"

"Sure, for Tel Aviv, via New York."

"Listen, *listen to me,* you crazy man! Why didn't you call me at least? What kind of business is this, just falling in on me, and why must you leave tonight? You must be dead, and —"

"I'm all right. I tried calling you twice." He glanced at his watch. "Fascinating, driving across America! Washington to Los Angeles, sixty-three and a half hours. Now I have to get the car to Alvaro's hotel, the Beverly Wilshire. How do I get there?"

"Yossi, your brother Lee is coming to lunch here with a film producer. Why not join us? Aryeh won't be home until four."

He waved her off. "Your business is your business. Lee and I have talked by phone. I'll say hello when I come back, then I want a bath and a nap."

She gave him directions to the hotel, staring at him incredulously. "You drove clear across the country to see Aryeh for an hour or so before you fly off to Israel?"

"And to see you, of course, and talk a bit. We didn't resolve anything in Washington, you were busy showing Aryeh the sights and the course didn't leave me much time. Tell Lee I'll be back soon."

Shortly after he left, Lee arrived with one of the strangest persons Yael had ever seen; a man so fat that he shook all over as he waddled in, dressed entirely in black, including a black shirt and a black neckerchief. "Mrs. Nitzan, Mr. Greengrass," said Lee, whereupon the fat man smiled and said through his teeth, "I'm Jeff. If you have any straws, Mrs. Nitzan, I'm all set for lunch." His diet problem was at once obvious, for his upper and lower teeth were wired together, and he was carrying two purple cans of liquid nourishment. "My secretary stupidly forgot to give me my straws."

"I have straws."

"Fabulous."

While Yael and Lee ate chicken Kiev, Jeff Greengrass sucked at his lunch and described the film for which he sought Sheva Leavis's financing. The industry was in the bust end of its perpetual cycle, he explained, and bank money was unobtainable except for the big stars and directors. This would be a small-budget film starring a rising stand-up comedian named Cookie Freeman, who would write and direct it.

"Cookie's dying to make pictures," said Greengrass, reasonably clearly through clamped jaws, "so we can get him for spit. It's a very cute idea. *Two-Gun Teitlebaum,* he calls it, all about a Jewish tailor in Brooklyn who inherits a piece of property out in a Wild West town, where his uncle came as a peddler and stayed to run a saloon. This town is run by the bad guys and nobody wants to be sheriff, see? So they make this Jew, Hymie Teitlebaum, sheriff the day he arrives. Well, I swear to Christ, Cookie Freeman milks that idea for comedy like you wouldn't believe. Mr. Leavis can read the script, of course. Or you can, Yael, if I may call you that? It's a winner."

"Mr. Leavis can't judge a movie script, and neither can I. Lee sent me your proposal and I read it carefully. I have some questions."

"Hit me."

The trouble with Greengrass's answers were that they were so voluble and detailed. Yael got lost in all the industry jargon: above the line, below the line, negative cost, one-year write-off, investment credit, distributor's gross, producer's net, and so on and on, all sprayed through Greengrass's teeth as by a fogging machine. What she thought she discerned was that Greengrass as producer could not lose, and that Cookie Freeman might well wind up working for nothing. As for the risk, it would be all Sheva Leavis's, or Lee's too if he participated. Kishote reappeared while this was going on. The brothers briefly embraced, then he went off to bathe.

"How's your little boy?" Yael asked Lee when the fat man wobbled out after lunch, leaving two empty cans.

The buoyant manner Lee had been maintaining faded away. "Okay, but that ear infection hangs on. The doctor says it's not unusual in three-year-olds. It would help if his mother were around more, but what makes her happy is playing the clubs, so her agent gets her the bookings, and she goes out and sings. What did you think of Jeff's pitch? He's sort of a freak, but he's made two successful small films."

"Well, he seems to know his business. Maybe *Two-Gun Teitlebaum* could make money. Sort of a Jewish parody of *High Noon*, isn't it?"

Lee Bloom smiled and patted her shoulder. "Yael, that's pretty sharp, that's just what Cookie calls it, a Jewish *High Noon*."

"Well, but, Lee, Sheva doesn't approve of your getting into the movie business, and he's very leery of venturing money himself."

"Sheva's a business genius, but he's old-fashioned. The tax write-offs in films are the point he misses."

"Sheva doesn't miss anything. He says movies are dreams, and manufacturing dreams isn't for serious people."

Lee Bloom shook his head. His high-styled mane of graying hair fell away from his bald spot, and he smoothed the hair back in place. "Wrong. Making film product is a serious business, Yael, like land development. Very similar, actually, as I see it. You need a piece of ground, that's the story property. A construction plan, that's the script. Building materials, that's stars, actors, settings. A builder, that's the director. And a client, that's the distributor." Lee was speaking now in great earnest, piercing the air with a forefinger. "And money, of course. That's the same. The one-year write-off, *there's* the big difference! It's tremendous, Yael. If the risk goes sour, you write off the film fast, it's gone, and the IRS has taken most of the gamble. Whereas an empty building stands there, eating taxes and deteriorating. Sheva won't see it, but — well, Joe, feeling better?"

He and Yael both chuckled as Kishote appeared in a fuzzy yellow bathrobe much too short for him, his head damp and unkempt. "So, Lee, what's this I hear, you're going into the movie business now?"

"It's a possibility." Lee turned solemn. "Nowadays you have to diversify."

"Look here, Yossi," said Yael, "if your flight departs at nine, that's the height of the rush hour. We'll have to leave here at five, and you'll have no time at all with Aryeh. Why don't I go and get him out of school early?"

"Do it."

She left the brothers looking at each other in an awkward silence. Lee spoke first. "Kind of a wild trip, Joe. Just like you."

"What's Yael got to do with movies, Lee?"

"Nothing. She has a good business head, and Sheva wanted her to size up Greengrass."

"Quite a house she's rented here," Kishote said, glancing around.

"Actually, she's buying it."

"She is?" Yossi yawned.

"Joe, I think you should get some sleep."

"I will. Is she making that kind of money?"

"I'm cosigning the mortgage."

"That's nice of you."

"Well, Sheva has an iron rule against going on notes, and I know she's valuable to him. Sheva's a deep one. I suspect he's more interested in films than he lets on. He'll listen to Yael, and Greengrass made an impression on her."

"He made an impression on me. He should be rendered down for whale oil."

"Well, he wouldn't qualify for your tank brigade," Lee returned jovially, "but he's a nice Jewish boy and he's going places." Kishote yawned widely and rubbed his eyes. "Joe, go lie down. I'm leaving. It's great seeing you again. I don't have to say how proud of you I am. We all are. Sheva thinks the world of you. Have a good flight."

Alone, Kishote went wandering through the house. Ten times the space of their flat back home, fine new furniture (was she buying that, too?), several bedrooms and baths, a smooth front lawn bordered by red-flowering bushes, a walled garden with a pool and a slide, swings, palm trees, and lemon and orange trees studded with fruit. In the biggest bedroom, pictures on the dresser: himself and Benny, in uniform and much younger, an inscribed picture of Moshe Dayan — *"To pretty Yael, from Uncle Moshe"* — and not too surprisingly, an early picture of Sam Pasternak, thin and with plenty of hair. Drop in on a woman without warning, and accept the consequences! The largest picture was of Aryeh as a baby in her arms, in a silver frame. Kishote did not snoop in closets or drawers. From what was visible, Yael either had no fellow or she made her trysts elsewhere.

Aryeh's room cheered Kishote. His latest picture, taken on his promotion to lieutenant colonel, was on the boy's little desk. There was no other in the room. On the walls were bright El Al posters of Jerusalem, Eilat, and Haifa. Noticing the edge of a photograph that was tucked under the desk blotter, he pulled it out and it gave him a turn; an old yellowed boardwalk snapshot of himself and Shayna on the Tel Aviv beachfront.

"*ABBA!*" Aryeh leaped on him, waking him from an involuntary doze in an armchair. "Abba! Abba!" The boy hugged and kissed him, babbling his joy in Hebrew. Yael stood regarding them with a melancholy smile. "Kishote, don't sit around in that silly bathrobe. If you're not going to sleep —"

"I'll sleep on the plane, what else is there to do? Come with me, Aryeh, while I get dressed."

"I got all A's on my report card, except in American history," exulted Aryeh. "It's a stupid school, and the kids are all stupid, all they talk about is sports and television. I even got the third highest mark in English, and besides —"

"Talk to Abba in English, why don't you?" said Yael. "Show him what you've learned."

Ignoring her, Aryeh said, "Abba, are you really flying home tonight? Why? Stay with us."

"You'll ride with me to the airport," said Kishote. "I have to go back to my brigade, Aryeh."

"He's not riding with us," said Yael, "unless he does some homework first."

"You hear Imma? Go to your room, Aryeh, and get busy," said Kishote. "We'll still have time to talk."

"Abba, I hate it here." Aryeh kissed him again and scrambled out.

"He knows what you want him to say," Yael observed with a twist of her mouth. "Are you hungry?"

"Sit down, Yael. Lee says you're buying this house."

"I told you about it in Washington."

"Not that I recall. So you're settling here for good?"

"What makes you say that? In California you buy a house and sell it two years later, motek, for a fifty percent profit. It makes more sense than renting, that's all."

"Okay, two more years. That'll make four years in all. You're definitely coming home then?"

Yael sat on the edge of the long modernistic beige couch, looking at him and not replying. All at once she burst out, "Stop trying to pin me down, Yossi! If I make enough so that we don't have to live like dogs anymore, yes! Otherwise, what's another year or so? I can't get anything done back home, I choke among those shleppers! Here it's like a gold rush, you don't know which opportunity to grab at first! I'll come home when I'm good and ready, all right? When I can provide us and Aryeh with a decent life, which an army officer, much as I respect the army, can't do."

"Wouldn't you rather have a divorce? Then you wouldn't have to choke among the shleppers at all."

Yael's face showed real shock; wide eyes, open mouth, sudden pallor. "Is that what you want?"

"I want my boy home with his mother."

"Yossi, we made an agreement, and —"

"That was temporary."

"Did Shayna Matisdorf ever marry that rabbi's son?"

Kishote's turn to look startled. "What kind of idiotic side issue is that?"

"Well, did she or didn't she? He's in your brigade, or he was."

"He served his *sadir,* and he's out. I think I'd have heard if they married."

"I suggest you get a little rest, then we'll have a bite." Yael stood up. "You're very, very tired. You look worn out. Talk like this hurts me, but I'm happy to see you. Aryeh loves you and so do I, whatever you may think —"

"Then don't buy this place. Come home. We live modestly in the army but not like dogs. That's no way to talk, and never talk that way around my son, Yael, do you hear?"

"Yossi, listen, this sudden jump in and out of Los Angeles is plain craziness. Surely the army will extend your leave! Put off your flight and let's talk when your head is a little clearer. And Aryeh will be so happy!"

He got up and clumsily put an arm around her. "You have a point, but I can't do it. Trouble in my sector again."

"What, the water war? You told me the Syrians were beaten and quit."

"They're trying something new. Look, I'll go talk with Aryeh in his room. Okay? Forgive the homework. He'll get it done."

"He's your son. Go ahead."

Later the cook-maid went looking for Yael, and found her at her dressing-table mirror, staring at herself. In her broken Spanish-English she inquired whether the colonel would be staying for dinner. Yael made no sign of having heard, so the puzzled woman repeated the question. Turning a drawn face to her, Yael told her to forget about dinner, they were all going to the airport and would have a bite there before the colonel flew off.

20 July 1966

Dearest Queenie:

Well, it's on. The die is cast. I report to our Washington embassy in October, and Nakhama and the girls will join me in January.

I've written you before about our bizarre "War for the Water" with Syria, and it appears to be coming to a climax. General Rabin is insistent that I'll be particularly useful in Washington in this precarious time, so I've saluted and said, "At your orders, sir." There's a sort of understanding that I'll get commander, Central Command, as my next post, but it's nothing to count on.

To borrow your colorful phrase, Nakhama is happy as a clam about this. It's a struggle for her to run a decent home here and also dress and cope with two growing girls on army wages. She's had to take a part-time job in a jewelry shop, actually, to make ends meet. On the living and housing allowances of the attaché she feels she'll be rolling in luxury, though by U.S. standards the money is still pretty modest. The girls too are excited about America, though not so happy about leaving their friends. Their English is passable, so we'll put them straight into school, and I'm sure they'll make new friends quickly. The other embassy kids usually do.

There you have it, Queenie, and unless your Lieutenant Colonel Halliday shows up meantime, we'll be seeing a little more of each other than heretofore. Will our relationship survive this, or does it thrive only on starvation, distance, and pen and ink? We'll soon know, won't we?

Yours,
Wolf

August 1st, 1966

Wolf!

I'm all but wordless with shocked joy. No hair nor hide of Lt. Col. Halliday, though it wouldn't matter a curse if he were camping on my doorstep. You know that. A Mahler cycle is on for the National Symphony, Sept.–Dec., and I do believe I'll subscribe for the two of us, okay? Word out to all Virginia fireflies: *"New orders, flash in the fall."*

A toi,
Queenie

PART FOUR

———

Six Days

32

Casus Belli

The so-called War for the Water went on sporadically for years, and if one gropes for the origins of the famous Six-Day War of 1967 it is not a bad starting point.

In 1964, three years before that celebrated war exploded, the Israelis completed their National Water Carrier, a north-to-south conduit of canals, tunnels, and pipelines some eighty miles long, bringing River Jordan water to the Negev Desert. The Arabs perceived this as a threat, for it would increase the usable land in Israel and therefore the influx of Jews; so the Syrians set to work diverting the Jordan tributaries in their territory in order to dry up the carrier.

Tank duels across the border ensued. As the Israeli marksmanship improved, knocking out the tractors and dredgers digging the diversion canals, the Syrians moved their machines farther and farther from the Israeli border, until the equipment was beyond the range of tank guns and could dig away at dams and canals with impunity. For there was a tacit understanding in the region that activation of the Israeli air force in the water conflict might lead to real war.

Enter Colonel Israel Tal, a wiry dark sabra no taller than Napoleon, who took over the armored corps from Dado Elazar, and improved and trained up his tanks to shoot and hit the earth-moving machinery far outside their tested range. After some furious gun battles that ensued the diversion project was dropped, but the water war did not end there. The balked Syrians instead turned to intensive shelling of the Galilee farms and kibbutzim from the lofty cliffs of the Golan Heights, where Israeli tanks could not readily hit them back. Ben Gurion's cautious successor, Levi Eshkol, at last sent the air force to suppress once for all the artillery bombardment of the Galilee villages, knowingly risking war with the Arabs and even possible Soviet intervention.

The date of this reprisal attack was April 7, 1967. The Syrian air force did in fact scramble its MiG-21s, the most powerful Soviet fighter plane at the time, and an Israeli squadron of lighter French Mirages shot down six of them without loss. This news caused a world stir. The Russians lost face, the UN scolded, the Arabs raged and threatened.

*   *   *

And in mid-May, in consequence, the Mirage squadron leader, Benny Luria, found himself in Los Angeles, as a star attraction at a United Jewish Appeal black-tie dinner dance for a thousand people. He was seated up on a long dais, flanked left and right by big givers, in UJA parlance. His sister Yael, at a front table with poor yawning Aryeh, was looking up at him with smiles which he could not return, for the situation at home was turning very ugly; and here he was, listening to UJA speeches and having to make one, too. His victory had touched off escalation on escalation. Egyptian armored divisions were now pouring into the Sinai Peninsula, Nasser was demanding that the UN peacekeeping force get out of its positions along the armistice lines, and on the TV, street mobs in Cairo, Baghdad, and Damascus were howling, "Death to the Jews!" But the commander of a Mirage squadron had yet to go on speaking after the cherries jubilee, at dinners like this one in San Francisco, Chicago, and Washington. Benny had telephoned Zev Barak just before the dinner, to make sure no orders for his return had come in on the embassy teleprinter. No, nothing.

The other main speaker, a tall bald U.S. senator, was waving his arms and pounding the podium. "Now my friends, just a word about these new troop movements in Sinai. Three American Presidents — Eisenhower, Kennedy, and Johnson — have pledged that America will never let Israel be destroyed. This loud-mouthed Colonel Nasser is bluffing, as usual, and in my view the crisis will blow over, unless he makes the mistake of his life. In that case Israel will prevail!" *(Standing ovation.)*

The air ace, in a light dress uniform with no medals, rose to speak after a long flowery introduction by the banquet chairman. "I ask you all in this audience," he began, "to rearrange your country a bit in your imagination. Start with Rhode Island, and surround it with some real big states. Say put Texas to the south, Illinois on the north, California on the west. The fourth border is the Atlantic Ocean, as now.

"Good, then behind those three states, my friends, put Michigan, Pennsylvania, New York; and let's say all six are at war with Rhode Island, all in a pact to wipe it out and drive its people into the ocean." Benny turned to the senator sitting beside him. "Mr. Senator, given that picture, it's nice to have your assurance that Rhode Island will prevail." The senator gave him a nonplussed half-smile. "Especially since to complete the picture, I'd have to put north of Illinois a superpower violently hostile to Rhode Island and committed to all-out military support for its enemies." A pause. Sober faces all over the ballroom. "Fine. Now I'll make my speech. Like the senator, my friends, I just wanted to cheer you up." At his easy wide grin, the audience broke into laughter and applause.

"He's good," Lee Bloom said to Yael. "Where'd your brother learn to speak English like that?"

"A year in England. RAF staff college and engineering courses."

"His accent is so charming," said Mary Macready. "Like Charles Boyer."

"Sh!" Sheva Leavis put a finger to his lips. He was not on the dais with the big givers. What Leavis gave for any cause was never announced.

Benny Luria delivered his standard UJA talk, calculated to give American Jews a lift; old stuff, but not untrue. His theme: Israel had no strategic depth in territory, but the love and support of the world's Jews provided a unique strategic depth of spirit and resources. Benny knew it was no use urging his hearers, as Ben Gurion interminably had done, to be real Zionists and come to Israel with their goods and their children. There sat his own sister, gone from Israel for years, and considering a divorce so that she could stay in America; Yael Luria of Nahalal, a reserve captain in the army, who called General Dayan "Dode Moshe"! What then was to be expected of these fortunate American Jews? Benny marvelled that they turned out in such vast numbers in city after city, and pledged so much money, and listened to an Israeli fighter pilot with such rapt faces and shining eyes.

He closed with a few terse words about his squadron's victory. The Syrian MiGs were good warplanes and the Syrian pilots were competent and brave, but they had no strong motive to risk death. Their country was safe. Up there in the sky, everything depended on the pilot's motivation, alone in his cockpit. Israeli pilots knew that their country could live or die by their own victories or defeats in the air. That was their edge in combat; that, and the training that went with it. No matter what the current crisis might bring, the air force would fulfill its mission, *Clear skies over Israel*.

The audience rose in prolonged applause, then the orchestra struck up a frug, and the ballroom floor became crowded with wriggling couples. Even Lee Bloom, somewhat on the paunchy side, was soon out there with his pretty wife, frugging away, and Aryeh was dancing with a gawky little girl in an evening dress. Yael turned to Sheva Leavis with a grin. "Well, this just leaves us."

He held up a hand. Leavis was one of the few men in the ballroom who wore a skullcap, though in business hours and travelling he went bareheaded. With his lipless sliding smile he said, "Don't suggest it. Don't even think it."

"You, Sheva, doing the frug? You're more likely to do skydiving."

"I once did a parachute jump, Yael. Just to do it."

"You did? How was it?"

"Expensive. I was making large pledges all the way down."

Later Benny Luria and Yael sat on the balcony of an apartment on Sunset Boulevard. Below them the million lights of Los Angeles twinkled under an unusually clear starry sky. They talked about the chances of war until Aryeh went off to bed. "So, you were going to make a pile in three years, Yael," her brother said, "and come back to live like a queen. What happened?"

She shrugged. "One thing and another."

"Are you ever coming back?"

"Who knows? Yossi talks divorce, off and on, but we just drift along, because of Aryeh."

"Yes, I'm sorry about that. I admire Yossi." He glanced around at the terrace and the large living room behind the french doors. "You're doing all right here, I'll say that."

"No complaints."

"Yossi told me you were buying a house."

"It got him angry, so I pulled out. Just as well! Aryeh went back home for a whole year — that was our agreement — and I'd have gone mad in that big place. We're comfortable here."

"What do you do for a love life?"

"Is it any of your business?"

"No."

Yael hesitated. "Oh, well, I have friends. As I'm sure Yossi has. You too, for that matter."

"Not as much as you might think. Not nowadays."

The brother and sister looked at each other in the vague orange light of one terrace lamp.

"Oh?"

"The squadron takes time and energy."

"No doubt." Skeptical tone, lopsided grin.

"Dov's started basic training in the pilot course."

"That, you wrote me. So?"

"I'm finding I'm like all the other parents of pilots. I worry. I worry like anything." After a silence Benny said, "You've heard of the old rabbi they call the Ezrakh?"

"Of course. The one who's never set foot outside Israel. Son-in-law's the chief rabbi in Haifa."

"That's him. I went to see him about a boy who got killed in flight school. The parents asked me to." Benny lit a cigarette and was briefly silent. "Lives like a beggar in a hole in the wall in Jerusalem, this Ezrakh, surrounded by books. He asked me amazingly sharp questions about flying, and about plane maintenance and performance. Not a word about religion, except when he talked of the dead boy. Interesting guy, the Ezrakh. I've taken to visiting him now and then."

Yael cocked her head at him, smiling. "Are you telling me, Benny Luria, that you're getting religion and laying off the ladies?"

Long pause. The answer was slow and thoughtful. "Lots of time to think, Yael, up in the sky. Lots of solitude. We keep over-flying the Sinai, where Moses received the Commandments. Talking to our flight controllers three thousand years later, we use the same language he did. That's interesting, isn't it? . . . Do you have some more soda?"

A gentle breeze blew on the terrace, wafting the scent of orange blossoms from dwarf trees in tubs. The smell made Benny homesick, for he had done unending picking and sorting of oranges as a boy. Yael handed him a tall glass tinkling with ice. "Come on. Are you giving up Eva, too?"

"Who's Eva?"

She laughed. "I see. They say that this Ezrakh is a wonder worker. If you give up Eva I'll believe it."

"How do you feel about giving up Aryeh?" No answer. "Is he packed and ready? Our plane's at seven A.M."

"He's ready. Look, I made a deal with Yossi, so once more he's going home."

"I've talked to that kid, Yael. He won't come back here again. He's growing up, and he hates it."

"Did you see him dancing? He seemed not too unhappy or out of place."

"What's this Sheva Leavis like, Yael? Man of mystery, hey?"

"He's a giant and a gentleman. Now look, Benny, will there be a war? If I thought so I'd come home now with you and Aryeh."

"Why?"

"Just to be there."

"It takes a war?"

Yael shook her head impatiently. "I asked you a question."

"How do I know? It's all up to Nasser. He's grabbed the initiative, that's for sure. Since B.G. stepped down, our politicians are all just Yiddisheh mammehs."

"Of all the times for Aryeh to go back," Yael fretted, "when there may be a war! And if I know Don Kishote, he'll ride the first tank into Sinai."

"Who else?"

Next day toward evening Luria sat on another terrace, this one overlooking the Potomac, with Zev Barak and a bony-faced old CIA man in a gray suit with a vest and a watch chain. "What you're saying about the MiG-21 in combat confirms our intelligence," said Cunningham. "Especially the vulnerability of the fuel tanks."

"Yes, that's a definite weak spot, sir, where the wing joins the fuselage."

"Colonel, we'd be glad to have a written report on your encounter with the MiGs, for very restricted use and no attribution."

Benny's eyes went to the military attaché. "No problem, Chris," said Barak. "Also you'll get the raw pilot debriefings and prints of the combat films."

"Most helpful, all that."

"Now ask Benny any questions you want."

"That wide turning circle of the MiGs in dogfighting, Colonel — limits of the plane or excessive pilot caution?"

"It's not the plane, sir. I've test-flown a MiG."

Cunningham put down his drink and stared. "How the Sam Hill did you do that?"

But this was too much for the aviator, and he hesitated, though Barak had assured him that Christian Cunningham was a trusted friend. Obsessive secrecy was ingrained in the air force.

"An Iraqi pilot was induced to defect, Chris," Barak said, "and bring us the plane."

"Really?" Cunningham's heavy eyebrows arched over thick glasses. "Remarkable coup."

"Yes, it was mainly Pasternak's doing, and took more than a year."

"Well! Any other weaknesses, Colonel, from where the pilot sits?"

"Some blind spots, sir. Not three-hundred-sixty-degree vision, as in the Mirage. And the firing of the guns is erratic. But it's a fine aircraft."

Trotting down the brick stairs, a thin bespectacled young woman in a sleeveless summer dress gave Benny a glass of soda, and handed Christian Cunningham a large sealed envelope. "From your office, Father."

Cunningham unfolded and read a Teletype sheet. "Well! So far so good. Nasser has not yet closed the Straits of Tiran. Sharm el Sheikh's full of Egyptian soldiers now, but your traffic is still going through."

"Closing the straits is a casus belli," said Luria. "He knows that."

Barak glanced at his wristwatch. "U Thant's flying to Cairo right now. Maybe Nasser's waiting to see what the UN's offering him not to close the straits."

"Sir, my turn," Luria spoke up in a silence. "Can I ask you a question?"

"Shoot."

"What's Nasser really up to, in the CIA view? Does he calculate the Arabs can pull it off this time?"

Short cold laugh. "Emily, may I have another old-fashioned?"

She jumped up. "Colonel?"

"No, thank you."

"Zev?"

Barak shook his head. As she brushed past Benny Luria he caught a whiff of sweet scent, which with the oddly familiar "Zev," stirred his interest in her.

"What's Nasser up to? Well, one can speculate, Colonel, but

the real question is, what are the Russians up to? They're obviously fomenting all this. Lately Russian prestige in the Third World has been sinking," said Cunningham, his cool colorless voice taking on subtle overtones of delight, "what with Marxist regimes getting overthrown one after another — Sukarno, Nkrumah, Ben Bella — and we in the agency, may I say, have not been totally uninvolved."

Barak put in, "Sam Pasternak says you've done wonders."

"Well! From Sam, praise indeed. At any rate, Syria is now the star on Russia's bedraggled Third World Christmas tree, so they're out to build her up, perhaps even to grab Arab leadership for this dictator Assad from Nasser, who's an unreliable cuss. So we estimate, but who knows? Those fellows in the Kremlin are like sideshow magicians, they pour red wine and white wine from the same bottle."

Cunningham took a long swig at the old-fashioned his daughter brought him, letting that image sink in.

"Brilliant moves *and* boneheaded mistakes! Czars, commissars, no difference, same Russian nature. And there's the key to the enigma that baffled Churchill. One can try to guess their next brilliant move, but who can anticipate the folly of a fool?" A plane came roaring overhead, and Cunningham paused.

"What are those little flashes on your lawn?" inquired Luria as the noise died off.

"Those are fireflies," said Barak. "Summer insects that light up."

"Beautiful. Part of the mating process, hey?"

The voice of Cunningham's daughter in the gloom. "Exactly, Colonel Luria."

"Chris, this is not a mere crisis over prestige," said Barak. "Nasser's armor is rolling up to our Negev border. That's another casus belli, and he knows it."

The CIA man nodded. "It's getting out of control because of stupid Soviet tactics. They've told Nasser that you've got twelve brigades poised to invade Syria. Nasser's protecting his own Arab leadership role by sending the armor into Sinai. He has to do that much."

"Then it's Rotem again!" Benny Luria exclaimed to Barak.

"Same exact damn thing as Rotem, Nasser sending in the armor because he claims we're about to attack Syria. Both times, complete fabrications."

"Of course," said Cunningham, "or the Russians would have taken up Israel's invitation to inspect your border with Syria. We know what their ambassador replied, though it's not public."

Emily asked, "Well, what *did* he say?"

"That the Soviet Union had no need to verify facts."

The airman restlessly turned in his chair. "Sir, can I use your phone?"

"Of course. Come with me."

Luria followed Cunningham up the stairs.

Barak and Emily looked at each other. He said quietly, "Hi."

"Wolf, how's Galia?" Low intimate tone.

"Her arm's in a cast. Not a serious fracture, thank God."

"What happened? All you said over the phone was you wouldn't be at the Growlery because you had to take her to the hospital."

"She fell off her bike."

"Is that all?"

"Why do you ask?"

"There's a thick veil of gloom enveloping you. I feel shut out, and I know you feel rotten about not being in Israel now. It's written all over you."

"My government wants me here."

"There's a fresh pile of pistachios in the Growlery, if that's any comfort. And plenty of Brunello. Bear it in mind, love."

"Sure enough, Queenie."

With a rattle of gravel, Barak's car pulled away from the house up a steep curving driveway through leafy trees. "Look Benny, relax. If you're called back before the banquet tomorrow night, the ambassador will make the speech or I will."

"Interesting guy, Christian Cunningham. What about that daughter? What does she do?"

"Headmistress of a girls school."

"Does she live with him?"

"He's a widower, so she's there a lot."

The car crossed a bridge over the Potomac, slowed by heavy traffic both ways. The lit-up monuments and Capitol dome came in sight. Benny asked, "How do you like it here?"

"It's fine."

"You seem depressed."

"I'm just hoping there's no war."

"It's inevitable now. Of all times, damn it, that there had to be four UJA banquets in a week! And for me to get stuck with them!"

"Maybe that's why Nasser moved on the fifteenth, Benny. To catch us off guard, celebrating Independence Day."

"Funny about that daughter, Zev. She's no beauty, but there's something sexy about her."

Barak grunted. "You've just been away from Irit too long. And from Eva."

"Could be."

Getting out of the elevator, they heard music in Barak's apartment. Aryeh was teaching the frug to a skinny girl with her arm in a sling, and a smaller girl was clumsily frugging by herself. Nakhama jumped up and turned off the music. "Darling, Noah just phoned from Haifa. His ship's gone on full war alert."

"That's it," said Luria. "I'll be called back."

Barak said, "Not necessarily, the navy's the jumpy service."

"And guess what, Zev?" Nakhama said. "You've got a nephew! Lena had a boy, Noah says, and your brother Michael's in heaven."

"Well, well!" said Benny. "Let's put him down for pilot training in 1985."

Nakhama laughed. Barak said, "Let's get through 1967 first."

"To bed, Aryeh," the airman said. "We may have to make an early start." He led away the protesting boy, and Barak's daughters went off to their room.

"So what does Mr. Cunningham say, Zev?" Nakhama put on an apron. "Does the CIA know anything? Is it going to be war?"

"He says it's all out of control now."

"Was Emily there?"

"She came in for a drink."

"Noah says people are starting to hoard gasoline, Zev, and

buying out the food stores and markets. Scout troops are on civil defense duty, cleaning and stocking up the air raid shelters, piling sandbags at the schools. . . ." Nakhama sighed, and shook her head. "Back to 1948, hah?"

When Benny Luria was shaken awake he could not at first remember which city he was in. "Well, Benny, this time you were right." Bare-chested, in undershorts, Barak switched on a lamp. "The embassy phoned. Teletype calls you home at once. Nasser has closed the straits."

Benny sat up alertly on the living room couch, saying, "What's the time?"

"After two. An embassy car will take you to New York. It's your best chance. Pan Am flies to London at nine. Nakhama's making breakfast. Aryeh's getting dressed."

"Flags up, Zev!"

"Looks that way."

Speaking without a note that night at the Washington Hilton in Luria's place, Zev Barak talked as though he had planned, written, and revised a speech for weeks, ending up after an impassioned half hour punctuated by applause:

"We don't want one more inch of territory than we have! Let our neighbors only make real peace with us, and we Jews will shove our planes and tanks into the sea!" Applause again interrupted him. When it subsided he went on with quiet intensity. "Fighting isn't a Jewish occupation. It hasn't been since the time of the Maccabees. But in Europe we learned two bitter lessons we'll never forget. We must have a home, and we must be able to defend it. Now we have a home, and if it's attacked, we'll beat our enemies to their knees as we've done before, whatever the cost, because EN BRERA — unlike our enemies, we have no choice! No choice but victory!"

He stepped back from the podium. At a front table with Cunningham, Nakhama, and two U.S. army generals, Emily leaped up, ardently applauding like the others in the ballroom, while her father and the generals stayed in their seats, whispering to each other. Nakhama too sat without clapping (let others applaud her husband!) and Christian Cunningham leaned to her and spoke through the applause. "Mrs. Barak, your husband's an orator! An unsuspected talent."

"Well, he's a quiet man. But when he has something to say, he can say it." As Emily sat down Nakhama added, "Mr. Cunningham, you and Emily must come to dinner at our flat someday soon."

"With pleasure. Emily, you arrange it."

"Yes, Father," said Emily, with an odd churn at her heart.

In a London airport hotel, where Aryeh fell asleep at once, Luria watched television until the test pattern squealed. The final pictures were of the Middle East crisis: Nasser all smiles as he fielded press questions about his political triumph in closing the Straits of Tiran; a grim-faced Israeli government spokesman in an open-necked white shirt, making flustered responses to a barrage of shouted queries; more footage of screaming fist-shaking mobs in Arab capitals; and to Luria most convincing and worrisome, shots of darkened deserted streets in Tel Aviv and Jerusalem, of sandbagged shops and school buildings, of children being herded down into shelters carrying their nightclothes, of man-on-the-street interviews selected to convey fright and despair among the Israelis.

Setting foot in Israel later that day, Benny Luria saw at once how accurate the TV news had been about the people's mood. The blue-uniformed woman at the immigration window looked up from his passport with scared eyes. "So, Colonel, you've come back for the war, eh?"

"Just in case there is one."

"I lost a brother in 1956."

"Terrible. I'm sorry."

"I can't take any more. I've just had another baby, and my husband's in tanks." As she stamped and returned the passport she managed a woeful smile. "Well, Colonel, if we do have to fight, with God's help please break their bones this time. Once for all!"

He was relieved to see only people dressed like tourists lined up at exit gates or sitting around the desolate terminal. When trouble threatened, they were best out from underfoot. So far as he could judge, Israelis were not fleeing. However alarmed, they were staying to face it.

Aryeh suddenly said as they walked out into the sunshine, "Dode Benny, I'm so glad to be home! When do I see Abba?"

"As soon as I can find him."

"I want to see Dov, too."

"Him you may see right away." He waved to his driver, approaching in an army car. On the front pages of the papers the driver handed him, Benny discerned the same lugubrious state of mind, heightened by the hysterical calamity-mongering of Israeli journalism. Disaster sold papers in this country, and the bigger and blacker or redder the headlines, the faster copies were snapped up. It seemed to Benny sometimes that his people were hooked on the adrenaline of crisis. In combat flying that adrenaline worked to quicken response, sharpen perception, rouse fighting anger. Bottled up with no outlet of action, it was a shot of chemical that gave a flush to civilian nerves at once scary, pleasurable, futile, and addictive.

In the towns the car passed through, he saw more and more evidence of public disarray and funk in the shuttered shops, empty store windows, littered streets, and only a few pedestrians hurrying here and there on usually crowded sidewalks. Mobilizing the reserves had half emptied the normal walks of life. The heaviest vehicle traffic was of army personnel trucks, tank and gun carriers, and he was glad to observe that at least the young soldiers looked cheerful.

Passing through the sentry gate of the Tel Nof air base was like flying out of overcast into sunshine. Heyl Ha'avir! Straight streets, smooth-cut lawns, smart-stepping squads of trainees, pert uniformed young women zipping past at the wheels of jeeps or striding along the walks with erect bosomy posture. Almost, it might be a time of peace, except for the heightening of pace, the charge in the air.

Benny left Aryeh with Dov at his quarters, and made a quick round of the hangars. Pilots were hovering near their planes in G-suits, ground crews were fussing at the Mirages, and one and all were complaining about the hesitancy of the government. *"What are we waiting for?"* The words were flung at him over and over. As he went from hangar to hangar he flung back standard drill questions about the strike plan code-named MOKADE (Focus).

"Chaim, what's your target in the first wave?"

"Inchas, Colonel."

"When do you take off? What's your position in the flight? What altitude? Primary target?"

Snapped accurate answers from the pilot.

This was what had been haunting Benny since Nasser's first move, making him edgier by the day as he flew around the States delivering UJA speeches. It was a hair-trigger plan, timing was everything, and if war came Israel might well stand or fall with that operation.

To another pilot: "Tali, time of arrival over target?"

"0745, Colonel."

"Secondary target? Assignment on first pass? Next pass? Emergency options?"

Even if awakened at midnight they were expected to shoot back the answers. With the entire op plan in his head, Benny Luria found no flaw in their nervy responses. Now, he thought, if only the politicians will unleash them! Years of work were at stake. As facts changed, individual missions were updated, but the MOKADE plan stood: *Surprise and smash the Egyptian air force in the first hours of the war.*

33

The Wait

Now began the countdown to war, remembered in the chronicles of Israel as the *Hamtana* (the Wait).

Israeli strategic doctrine set out three conditions that could escalate a crisis to full-scale war: two regional, one international.

1. An imminent military threat to the nation created by the massing of troops on Israel's borders.
2. A reversal of the status quo which Israel could not leave unchallenged without losing its military credibility.
3. An abandonment of Israel to its fate by the international community.

Two of these conditions had now been fully met. A hundred thousand Egyptian troops and hundreds of tanks had poured across the Suez Canal into Sinai; and Nasser had ordered out all the UN peacekeepers in the region, and closed the Straits of Tiran, choking off Israel's southern access to the sea. The Soviet Union of course was publicly backing all Nasser's moves, so there remained but one fateful question: Would the western powers and the UN induce or compel the Egyptian dictator to reopen the straits and remove the troops from Sinai, or would they confine themselves to disapproving statements and leave Israel to extricate itself from its peril?

To seek an answer Abba Eban, now Israel's Foreign Minister, made a flying round of the three western capitals that mattered. In Paris he was greeted, as he walked into the office of President Charles de Gaulle, by the Frenchman's booming warning, *"Ne faites pas la guerre!"* De Gaulle was vague about how Nasser might be persuaded to change his naughty course, but exceedingly clear on one point: if Israel fired the first shot, it would forfeit in toto and for good the friendship and assistance of France. In London, Eban fared better, receiving no such threat from Prime Minister Harold Wilson; but Wilson was just as foggy about what could be done to dissuade Nasser from his regrettable bellicosity.

Only in America did Eban encounter a concrete proposal. Receiving him cordially, President Lyndon Johnson told him he would try to create an "international flotilla" of warships, which would force its way through the straits if the UN reproof of Nasser, and the very existence of this flotilla, did not cause the Egyptian dictator to reconsider and call off the blockade. Forming such a flotilla would of course take time, the American President said, and he asked the Israeli government meantime to use forbearance — and *wait.*

*   *   *

Sam Pasternak sat drinking coffee in the office of Motti Hod, the air force chief, a tall balding lean man with a small mustache, in a trim blue uniform. "Sam, Sam, are you telling me we don't act for two to three weeks? With the whole country paralyzed, the Arabs mobilized at our borders, and —"

"Motti, Lyndon Johnson wants time to create an *'international flotilla'* " — Pasternak's tone was ironic, and his face skeptical — "so Eban reported, to force the straits open. The cabinet vote was close, but the decision was to play it Johnson's way and wait. The idea is that the maritime powers will demand free passage for *'all nations,'* that is, including us. If Nasser backs down, fine. If not, this international flotilla will enter the straits, so that —"

"But what maritime powers? De Gaulle's gone over to the Arabs, that we know. From England we can as usual expect bop-kess. America's tied up in Vietnam. I ask you, what powers?"

"Well, maybe Holland, maybe Canada, maybe Sweden, maybe even Australia. Eban isn't quite clear on that."

"Maybe nobody?"

"Maybe nobody."

Hod poured water from a large carafe and drank off a glassful, the only clue that he was tense. The joke about the air force chief was that his engine was water-cooled. He had drunk several glasses since Pasternak had arrived before dawn, red-eyed and unshaven, from the all-night government debate about going to war. "Does anyone in the cabinet believe in this flotilla? Does Eban?"

"It's hard to tell what Eban believes, he's so articulate," said Pasternak. Hod grunted and almost smiled. "But he's against going to war now, he made that plain."

"Listen to me, Sam. Nasser openly proclaimed that he's legally justified in closing the straits because he's in a state of war with us. Correct?"

"Hundred percent."

"Well, if we're at war, why can't we strike?"

"That's what Rabin kept urging until his voice gave out. Going through three packs of cigarettes didn't help."

"How is he, honestly?" There were disquieting rumors about the Chief of Staff's health.

"Rabin? Okay, from what I could see through the smoke."

Hod's voice dropped. "And the talk of his collapse?"

"Look, I was with him when he visited Ben Gurion. The Old Man may be out to grass, but he was his old self, absolutely furious at Rabin for calling up the reserves. He roared that Rabin was provoking the Egyptians, that we couldn't fight such a war alone, that he, Yitzhak Rabin, would be personally responsible for the end of the Jewish State after only nineteen years. Rabin went into a black hole for two days. I didn't feel so hot myself, after that. Ben Gurion was terrifying."

After a silence Hod said, "A great man, but he lives in the past. Not calling up the reserves would have been criminal neglect."

"I agree." Pasternak glanced at his watch. "So, where's Luria?"

"Benny drives fast. He'll be along. I thought the Prime Minister was coming for this briefing, Sam."

"Eshkol asked me to take the briefing instead and report to him. He must work on his radio speech. The whole country will be hanging on it tonight."

"I don't envy him."

"Nor do I. The politicos are out for his head. It's a crime."

"You've always been an Eshkol man."

"For good reason! All the years Ben Gurion was the star, I tell you Eshkol was the worker. This country's infrastructure is Levi Eshkol's doing."

"You don't have to sell Eshkol to me. We'll be flying Skyhawks soon because he went to America and got Lyndon Johnson to send them." The buzzer sounded. "Yes? . . . Good. . . . Okay, Benny's here. Let's go." They walked to the briefing room down a long corridor lined with pictures of Mirages and Skyhawks in flight, pictures of previous air chiefs, and recruiting posters of handsome pilots and beautiful air force girls.

Benny Luria was astonished to see General Hod come into the briefing room not with the Prime Minister but with Sam Pasternak, whom he deeply disliked. Pasternak had all but ruined his sister Yael's life, he thought, by consuming her youth in nonsense. Now he was some kind of intelligence big shot, his status obscure, except that he was very close to Eshkol.

"Benny, brief General Pasternak on the mission of your squadron in MOKADE," said Hod, "and on the overall picture of the first wave."

Luria knew Hod well enough, and in any case was brassy enough, to blurt, "Motti, do we go tomorrow or don't we?" Since his return he had been sensing, with a heavy heart, a slackness in the air force, an absence of the expected electricity before a strike.

"Never mind. Proceed." The generals sat down in armchairs.

Luria's crisp presentation of MOKADE aroused Pasternak, weary as he was, to towering enthusiasm. A tremendous thing! The succession of colorful maps and overlays, the minute-by-minute schedules of action, were worked out in stunning convincing detail.

The Prime Minister would be cheered, and he could use some good news.

"Well done, Benny," Pasternak said as the three men walked out afterward. "Did you see your sister in Los Angeles?"

"Of course."

"How is she?"

"Too comfortable. Making too much money." Luria stalked away.

"Benny's beside himself," said the air chief. "He thought the strike was on for sure today or tomorrow, and he's frantic at the risk of delaying much longer."

"Why? It's a great operation, Motti, whenever it happens."

"Wrong, *wrong*! If Nasser strikes first at our airfields, all that work, all that planning and rehearsing, go up in smoke! Sam, for God's sake, you tell Eshkol that."

"Don't you think I will?"

In pajamas and a bathrobe, Levi Eshkol was breakfasting on a large broiled St. Peter's fish, a dish of scrambled eggs, and a loaf of black bread. The bald big-bellied Prime Minister peered at Pasternak through thick rimless glasses. "Sam, *kumt essen* [come eat]." An old Yiddish greeting, and Pasternak declined in the old Yiddish way, "*Ess gezunt* [Eat in health]."

"Well, sit down. This is a delicious fish. They woke me after only an hour's sleep with a letter from Kosygin. Food is fuel and I need it. Read that letter."

Pasternak skimmed the Hebrew translation lying on the desk. Eshkol observed, "Not as bad as the letter we got from Khrushchev in 1956, hah? That was a real bombshell."

"No. This is not good, though."

"Not good at all. Now, what about the air strike plan?"

"Prime Minister, it's masterly. I was totally won over. I went to the hangars, too. I talked to the pilots and the ground crews. They're sharp as razors, all of them, eager to go."

"So, let's hear." While Pasternak summed up MOKADE, Eshkol ate the fish down to the bones, then broke open the head for the morsels. "It sounds complicated," he commented with a worried head shake. "Like a ballet. One performer makes a mistake and it'll become a terrible balagan."

Slowly he wiped his mouth with a napkin. "And meantime, Sam, such *tzoress* [troubles]! Menachem Begin's been on the phone, urging me to step aside, and for Ben Gurion to return as Prime Minister!" He stared at Pasternak. "You hear? *Begin* wanting Ben Gurion! Then there's Dayan! Out of the army for eleven years, he's demanding to return and take immediate command of the Southern Front! My head is spinning, I'll tell you the truth."

All too aware of the growing ground swell for Dayan's return — there was even newspaper talk of his replacing Eshkol — Pasternak shied off. "Have you finished the radio speech, Prime Minister?"

"That speech! *Oy vavoi!* No, I haven't. Do you suppose I could postpone it?"

"Impossible!" Pasternak blurted with alarm. "The effect on the country —"

"I know, I know. Still, I dread it. And first I must answer Kosygin, and then meet with the generals, who are all in a boil over the Hamtana." He got up and paced with slow heavy steps, his bald head bent. "But Sam, the Washington situation is the worst of it!" He turned a haggard face on Pasternak. "Eban comes back and says one thing, and the American ambassador here says something else entirely. Our ambassador there can't get a straight word from the State Department. Secretary Rusk makes puzzling statements to the press. From President Johnson I hear nothing, and I thought I had good relations with him! Sam, *to this minute I don't know what's really going on in Washington!* You hear?"

"Prime Minister, launch the air force now. Today, tomorrow!" Eshkol blinked at him. "Go! Fight! I tell you the MOKADE plan will work. It's brilliant, down to the last detail. There will be a cost, but we'll win. After the fact the Americans will applaud you, Johnson included."

"I can't." With a deep sigh, Eshkol sat down at his desk. "The cabinet gave me no mandate to go to war. A shaky tie vote, no will to act. Besides" — he squinted sidewise at Pasternak, and spoke in a strange voice — "maybe this Hamtana is not so bad. Gives us time to get good and ready. Though I can't say that in this cursed speech." He flourished papers full of scrawls, and added with a foxy side-glance. "Listen, Shafan [Rabbit]." This had been Pasternak's code name in the underground. "You may have to fly to Washington yet. I must know where Johnson stands before I can move. I must *know!*"

Pasternak came back with Eshkol's code name. "I'm ready now, Layish [Lion]."

"Oy vavoi!" Eshkol groaned and smiled. "Such a decrepit old lion!"

In the Berkowitz apartment in Haifa, crowded with Lena's kibbutznik relatives and the professor's academic friends for the newborn's circumcision, all was noisy anxious speculation about what Levi Eshkol would say in his radio speech. Surely this Hamtana, the nerve-wracking time of no war and no peace, with an ever-mounting Arab threat at the borders, could not be endured much longer! Because Don Kishote was there in uniform he was pestered for his views. He replied with shrugs and grunts.

In the bedroom Shayna was trying to calm and comfort Lena Berkowitz, who cowered with her sleeping eight-day-old son on her lap, complaining, "Why don't they get this barbaric business over with? If they have to mutilate the poor thing let them do it and finish!" Lena had grown up on a Marxist kibbutz, where all the boys had been circumcised as they were born. All the kibbutzniks had agreed that this was a primitive bloody rite that should be abolished, and no parents had omitted the circumcision.

"They're not here yet," said Shayna, glancing out the door. "Who's 'they'?"

"Colonel Luria and the Ezrakh. They're coming together."

"Well, so what? The Ezrakh is just religious window dressing, isn't he?" Lena fretted. "And Colonel Luria may be a big hero, but if he's late, too bad, let them do it already, for heaven's sake."

Shayna explained that they were the two designated honorees of the *brit* ritual. Colonel Luria would take the baby from his mother's arms and ceremonially deliver him to the Ezrakh, and he would be circumcised on the Ezrakh's knees, a great distinction for the family. "Actually it's the baby that's being honored," Shayna said, "by two such important participants."

"Yes, I'm sure he'll be absolutely thrilled," said Lena, hugging him close. "Poor sweetheart."

Don Kishote looked into the room. "Shayna, they're arriving."

"Oh, God," said Lena.

Shayna came to the doorway. Benny Luria was walking in with an erect little white-bearded man in a threadbare long black coat and a rusty broad-brimmed hat. They were followed by a blond girl in a new beige army uniform, black cap perched on her neat coiffure.

"Who is that creature?" Kishote asked Shayna.

"You don't recognize her? That's Daphna Luria."

"What, snotty little Daphna with the buckteeth, running around Nahalal? That's her?"

"Pretty now, isn't she?" Shayna said. Daphna was smiling at Noah Barak, who emerged in uniform from among the guests to kiss her cheek. The teeth had obviously been fixed.

"A child," said Yossi. In fact, to him she seemed Yael reincarnate, the warrior goddess he had been smitten with on the Latrun battlefield. "Are she and Noah engaged, or something?"

"She's stationed at Ramat David," said Shayna, "and they see each other. Envious, Yossi?"

Kishote ignored the dig. "Shayna, I must talk to you about Aryeh." The boy was staying with her during the Hamtana emergency, for Kishote was encamped in the field with his mobilized brigade.

"Why not?" She tried to keep her manner light. "Drive me and Aryeh home afterward. We can talk on the way."

The noise in the flat was rising to a great hubbub, with much gesticulating and arguing among the men clustering around the Ezrakh and Luria.

"Shayna, I'm going out of my mind," said Lena, clutching the baby. "Find out what's happening."

"I'll try." She went shouldering into the disorder and Kishote saw her talking to her former fiancé, the black-bearded Chaim Poupko, long since married, with two children. His father, the chief

rabbi of Haifa, loomed tall and stout at the center of the distur-
bance, expostulating with the Ezrakh. Soon Shayna came back,
saying, "Here we go. It's all settled." The noise was fading away
into muffled ritual chanting.

Lena quavered, "What's been the trouble?"

"No trouble."

The guests were making way for the Ezrakh, who was approaching the bedroom wrapped to his ankles in a yellowed black-
striped prayer shawl. With a kindly smile he held out his arms to
Lena, who hissed at Shayna, "So what's this?"

"Give him the baby."

"But I thought Colonel Luria —"

"It's been reversed. Go ahead, everything's fine, it's beginning."

Lena handed the child on a pillow to the Ezrakh. He nodded,
still smiling, and walked away with stately steps. In a reluctant tone
Lena said, "By my life, the man has a nice face."

"He lives downstairs from my mother in Jerusalem," said
Shayna, as the chief rabbi and the *mohel,* a very short man in a white
coat and surgical mask, began chanting the liturgy. Benny Luria sat
in an armchair between them, looking solemn and a little confused,
a prayer shawl over his uniform, the baby in his lap. "He's very
poor, the Ezrakh, his apartment is just a cellar, but the greatest
Torah scholars come there to consult him."

"Will they do it to my baby now?" choked Lena.

"Any minute."

"Tell me when it happens." She dropped on the bed, her hands
over her ears.

More chanting, Michael Berkowitz's hoarse voice reciting a
blessing, sudden quiet, then general shouts of "Mazel tov!"

"So! His name's Reuven!" exclaimed Shayna, kissing Lena.
"Mazel tov! It's a lovely name."

"It's over? He didn't scream?"

"Not that I could hear. Just *wah, wah,* and quiet. They give the
baby wine, you know."

"I want to see him!"

"They'll bring him."

"What happened? Why did the colonel and the Ezrakh change places?"

"The Ezrakh wanted it so."

"So Reuven was circumcised on the knees of a fighter pilot from Nahalal? Suits me!" Lena burst out in a hysterical laugh. "Something to remember, isn't it?"

Hungry after all the delays, the guests fell to with cheery appetite on the food and drink laid out on long tables. Benny Luria and the Ezrakh drank a toast with the pale happy father, and left. Daphna Luria and Noah Barak also departed forthwith. The other guests remained and became reasonably merry, considering their previous glum Hamtana mood. "The question is," Michael Berkowitz called out over the jocund singing and chatter, as the party wore on into the evening and the blackout curtains were drawn, "do we or don't we watch the news from Jordan? Do we want to be depressed? Eshkol will be on in an hour."

Israel had no TV station, but the Berkowitzes' small black-and-white set picked up the Arab broadcasts. During the Hamtana anxious Israelis were congregating in flats and shops that had sets, for the pictures from Jordan were morbidly fascinating. Everyone wanted the professor to turn on the TV, and in a moment the same scary stuff of recent days filled the tiny screen: Arab crowds in city squares burning Israeli flags and howling for the extermination of the Jews; big squat Russian tanks ranged by the hundreds in Sinai as far as the camera could show, manned by black-mustached crews in spruce uniforms; masses of bombers and fighter planes darkening the sky over a jubilant Nasser and his smiling staff officers.

The Jordanian narrator: *"Egypt's brave armed forces stand poised and ready for the final battle to reverse by force the fait accompli imposed on the Arab nation by force, by American imperialism, the Zionist excrescence on Arab soil."* Shots of Syrian, Iraqi, and Jordanian forces on the march. Nasser addressing a cheering assembly of trade union workers, the tall handsome Egyptian radiating confidence and power, his impassioned rhetoric ominous even in his rapid mellifluous Arabic, roughly conveyed by English subtitles.

"We have been waiting for the day when we would be fully pre-

pared to liberate Palestine. It has come! Taking over Sharm el Sheikh meant confronting Israel, but it is no longer a question of the Gulf of Aqaba. . . . The battle will be a general one, and our basic objective will be TO DESTROY ISRAEL."

A woman guest's shaky voice: "It's a second Holocaust."

While Nasser was still talking Kishote walked to the set and snapped it off. "Nonsense! If we had a TV station it wouldn't be showing our armed forces, but they're ready, I promise you. Haifa's streets are empty because we're at battle stations out of sight all over the country, on highest alert. And that's where Reuven Berkowitz will be eighteen years from now, if by then the Arabs haven't come to their senses and left us alone. So in his honor let's drink and enjoy!"

"Will there be a war, Colonel?" A voice from the gloom, the lights being off for better viewing. Michael flipped them on and the guests blinked.

"You've heard Nasser," said Yossi. "Next you'll hear Eshkol, and I think you'll know. What's happened to the wine, Shayna?"

Israelis are not usually drinkers, but wine bottles went round and round, and the talk grew animated as the guests shook off the stunned dejection that had followed the Jordan broadcast.

"Five minutes till Eshkol speaks," said Lena. "Turn on the radio already, Michael."

"This will be Eshkol's greatest hour," said Chief Rabbi Poupko. "Mark my words."

Sitting not far from Eshkol in the small dimly lit broadcasting studio, Pasternak leaped to retrieve a page of the speech that fell to the floor from the Prime Minister's trembling hands, while the aides and the radio men just stared in frozen disbelief. Eshkol gave him the grateful look of a drowning man rescued, and resumed trying to read aloud, through thick glasses, jargon he could not possibly have written himself.

"In the cabinet meeting today the government laid down principles for the . . . uh, uh, continuation of political activities which are designed to . . . uh, uh, induce the international factions — uh, factors — to adopt affecting measures — effective measures — to safeguard the . . ." he held

the page to his eyes, painfully peering "*. . . freedom of international shipping in the Tiran Straits . . .*"

L'Azazel, what had become of Eshkol's own speech? So Pasternak angrily wondered. What dismal shlepper had concocted this turgid stuff and handed it to the bedeviled old man fighting for his political life? What criminal shlepper had put him at a low narrow microphone table, placed wrong for the single overhead light? What sheep-headed shlepper had failed to insist on a rehearsal, failed to think of making a recording in which stumbles and hesitations could be edited out? Shleppers, shleppers, shleppers, the collective soft underbelly of Israel!

As the Prime Minister stammered on, Sam Pasternak was already calculating the damage of this fiasco. The Americans and the Arabs must be monitoring every word, and Eshkol sounded like a man in terror, unable to control his voice or his tongue, lapsing into mere "uh, uh" while trying to make out the words.

"*Uh, uh, lines of action have also been adopted for the . . . uh, uh, removal of military considerations — uh, uh, concentrations from Israel's southern border . . .*"

Not my responsibility, this shattering balagan, thought Pasternak, but whose? He had arrived only five minutes before the broadcast, to accompany Eshkol afterward to the parley with the generals. It had already been, he knew, a calamitous day for the Prime Minister. The murky political maneuvering to force him out had boiled up in meetings, phone calls, corridor whisperings, offers, counteroffers, threats of resignation. His oldest friends were deserting him. A cabled letter from Lyndon Johnson, warning him that if the Israelis commenced hostilities they would have to go it alone, had stampeded a new cabinet vote to take no military action while the American President tried to assemble his flotilla. Eshkol next had to face his generals, knowing the postponement might push them near mutiny, for how much longer could their outnumbered troops sit and wait for the foe to strike on three fronts? How much longer could the economy endure this paralysis? Beset on all sides, Eshkol had apparently assigned an aide to rewrite his speech, and had not had time to look it over before he went on the air.

"*. . . action to safeguard our . . . uh, uh, sufficient — uh, uh, our* *sovereign rights and security on the frontiers and the prevention of aggression . . ."*

In a coffee shop outside the naval base, Noah Barak and Daphna Luria stood with sailors, officers, and navy girls around an old radio set, which further garbled Eshkol's talk with static and whistles. Wondering, dismayed looks passed among the young listeners.

"What is this?"

"Is he sick? Is he having a heart attack?"

"Can you understand him?"

"This is not possible!"

Noah seized Daphna's hand and led her out of the shop. "I can't take it. Anyway, my captain gave me only two hours off to go to the Berkowitzes. I have to get back on board."

"Noah, what ails the Prime Minister, do you suppose? He sounds panic-stricken."

"Who knows? If he's frightened, the navy isn't. We'll continue our argument about Zionism, Daphna, maybe after a war."

"You really think there'll be war?"

"After what we've just heard? If I were Nasser I'd strike at dawn."

They lingered under the sentry's blue light at the base gate. "You look awful," she laughed, "like a dead man."

"Even in this light, you look beautiful."

"Come off it." She struck a small fist on his shoulder. "And no more arguments, understand? You're a Zionist? Fine, all honor to you. I'm a Daphna-ist, first and last. End of discussion."

"No, just the beginning."

"Oh, well." She gave him her hand. "You mustn't overstay your leave, Noah. If there's war, come back safe."

He did not release her hand. "And call you?"

"Why not?" With a slight squeeze, she disengaged her fingers and hurried off into the dark.

In the Berkowitz flat when Eshkol finished, silence. All faces were somber. Somebody groaned, *"Ayzeh gimgoom!"* ("What stuttering!")

The chief rabbi spoke up with hollow cheer. "He's been under a heavy strain, that's all. It was a good speech."

"I'm taking my family down to the shelter tonight," said a philosophy professor.

"Don't be like that, Alex," said his wife. "We're not going to the shelter." She turned to Yossi Nitzan. "What did you think, Colonel?"

"He's no speaker," said Yossi, "but he warned the Arabs we'll win if they start something. That's the main thing, and that's the truth."

The guests made hurried goodbyes and left in a murmur of dejected comment.

"Ben Gurion has to come back."

"Dayan! We need Dayan!"

"No, Allon! Allon is worth ten Dayans."

"I still believe in Eshkol."

"Eshkol? He'll be out of office in two days."

"He's got to step aside as Minister of Defense, at least."

When the red light went out over the door of the broadcasting studio, Levi Eshkol took off his glasses and rubbed his eyes hard, his large head hanging down. "My eyes itch so! They itch!" He put on the glasses and shuffled the papers together. A young bearded aide accepted them, looking doleful. Eshkol pushed himself to his feet, and trudged to Pasternak. "Thanks for picking up the paper. You saved me. How was it?"

"Well, Prime Minister, you warned the Arabs to beware of attacking." Pasternak spoke as forcibly as he could. "And you let the Americans know that the Hamtana from now on is their doing, and we expect them to act responsibly. The record's clear. The elements were there. It was all right."

"You think so? Good." The others came around him — the shleppers, Pasternak thought with angry contempt, who had probably destroyed the man — with empty congratulations. "So, Sam, what next? Yes, now I meet the generals. All right, we move."

As they went down a flight of stairs, Eshkol missed a step and clutched at a banister. Pasternak caught his elbow and kept him from tumbling. In the back seat of his car, Eshkol leaned his head back and closed his eyes. "Better make an air reservation, Shafan."

"It's made, Layish."

The Prime Minister's eyes opened, and the old foxy Eshkol was smiling tiredly at him. "Bad, wasn't it?"

"Prime Minister, you were in a tough spot."

Eshkol shook his head. "All my fault. I should have shut out everything else and concentrated on that speech. Now I realize it."

"There was too much happening. You couldn't."

"Well, it's over. Now for the generals."

As Yossi drove Shayna through the blue-lit streets of Haifa, a ghost city at nine o'clock, she rattled on about the Ezrakh, for the Prime Minister's debacle had shaken her nerves, and sitting with Don Kishote in a car always perturbed her. Their strained relationship was all the more tense now that she was caring for Aryeh. "In the Old City we kids played in his yard," she was saying. "He'd call us into this room full of huge old books, and give us candy. He looked just the same then. I'd swear he wore those same clothes. And he did nothing but learn Torah, day and night."

"Was he captured when the Old City fell?"

"No, a month before the vote for partition he moved out, books and all, to a hole in the New City, in Geula. There was a lot of criticism, questioning his piety. Then after the war people said he was a prophet. He ignores what anyone says about him. We moved out right after he did, Grandpa's tailor shop too. Grandpa said if the Ezrakh could go we could go, and we did."

"How does the Ezrakh live?"

"In those days he sold kerosene. Now he sells candles. Not many, so as not to hurt the business of other candle sellers. People would buy a lot more than he sells. It's a big thing to have the Ezrakh's candles for Shabbat. When he gets in a new stock it's all gone in a day or two. He won't accept support or gifts."

Yossi turned into the road winding up Mount Carmel. "I'll tell you, Shayna, that old man impressed me, putting Benny in the chair, and all of us obeying him, mohel, rabbis, Benny! Leadership. If he were eighteen and in my brigade I'd give him a platoon."

"Well, that story will certainly get out, the Ezrakh yielding that honor to an air force colonel! He's already an odd man among the *haredim* [pious], because he's a Zionist. He calls Israel the beginning of the Redemption, the footsteps of the Messiah, the Great Era. He's not openly attacked, since the greatest sages consult him. They consider him a walking Mount Sinai." The jeep bumped and roared up a steep cobbled street to the old tenement where she lived. "Wake up, Aryeh, we're here," she called.

Yawning, Aryeh jumped out to the dark windy street. "It's cold here, Abba."

"Let me come up with you, Shayna," said Yossi. "Give me a cup of tea."

"By your life, no."

"Why not? I've never seen your flat."

"No!"

"Why not? Issur yikhud? Aryeh's your protection."

"Don Kishote, go and fight the war, if there's one coming. Leave me be. I'll take good care of Aryeh."

He lowered his voice so that the boy, taking shelter in the doorway, could not hear. "You may not see me again. Ever. You realize that?"

"Don't! Elohim, you're unfair, you're disgusting."

"Ten minutes."

"Oh, wait here then. You and Aryeh both."

She went running up four flights of black-dark stairs, snapped on the lights, and drew the blackout curtains. From a clothesline strung between the transom and the window she frenziedly snatched off cheap underwear she had hung up to dry — stockings, nightgowns, panties, brassieres, the washing of a two-week pileup. Shayna lived alone, brought home much academic work, and tended to let housekeeping lag — laundry, dishes, bills — and now and then go at the mess in one whirlwind night. She dumped the stuff in her tiny spare bedroom, swept books and test papers off the kitchen table, and cleared her desk of stacked bills and mathematical journals. Two framed photographs stood there, usually half out of sight: the fading blowup of herself and Kishote on the Tel Aviv boardwalk, and one of her latest swain, his skullcap almost invisible, his beard close-trimmed, his smile charming. Shayna slung the boardwalk picture into the other room, pulled down the clothesline, and opened the window. "All right! Come up!"

"Coming!"

Aryeh went to bed, and as they drank tea in the kitchen, Shayna's unease lessened, for she saw that Yossi was all business. He talked about the prospects of war. If it came, and he now saw it as a fifty-fifty chance, his armor brigade would be in the forefront. He had confidence in his men and in himself, but war was chancy, and he had to think ahead. "There's Aryeh's education, Shayna. I want him to have some Yiddishkeit. I've named you for his religious guide in my will, and left money. Yael knows all about this. If he goes back to Los Angeles . . ." Yossi shrugged and pushed up his glasses. "Well, I don't think he will."

Shayna found her voice after a moment. "I'm touched, and I agree about Aryeh."

"Good. Thank you. Please give me more tea." As she poured he went on, "Lee and I both started in a yeshiva, you see, because that was how my mother wanted it. He rebelled and they sent him to a Zionist school, but I liked it. I tried to keep up the religion even in the camps. It was too hard. Aryeh won't be an Ezrakh, but he shouldn't be an ignoramus. I pity some of the sabra boys in my brigade. Wonderful kids, but of Yiddishkeit they know nothing."

"Aryeh already knows quite a bit, Yossi."

"I'm glad you think so. Next thing, that fellow on your desk. Is that the new one? The Canadian?"

"Oh, you noticed. Yes, that's Paul."

"How far has it gone?"

"Yossi, don't start that —"

"Shayna, I think it's over with Yael and me. I've tried to make it go for Aryeh's sake, but —"

Shayna's reserve broke. "Oh, for heaven's sake, Yossi, how great a fool can you be? Yael will never let you go. You're a star of the armor force. What's more, she'll never give up Aryeh, and neither will you. You're talking nonsense."

"What you don't understand," he said with an effort at patience, "is what Los Angeles is like. Yael wants to stay there."

"She says so?"

"Her brother Benny just came back from there. She's in a luxury flat in Beverly Hills, and up to her neck in moneymaking."

"Is there another man?"

"I don't know, and one trouble is, I don't much care."

Aryeh appeared in his pajamas. "Aunt Shayna, this was on my bed."

Kishote took the boardwalk picture, and glanced from it to Shayna. It was the same photograph Aryeh had had in his room in Los Angeles. Yossi wondered just how perceptive this ten-year-old of his might be. "Aryeh, I'm going now. Give me a kiss, be a good lad, and obey Aunt Shayna. Back to bed."

Aryeh hugged and kissed his father, and went out.

Kishote said, tapping the picture, "Those were the days, eh?"

"Yossi, people say if a war starts the Iraqi or Syrian air force may bomb Haifa right away. Should I take Aryeh someplace else?" The awkward change of subject failed. He came and leaned over to kiss her cheek. "Goodbye. Stay where you are. Shayna, what if Yael sets me free? I tell you it's coming. It has to."

Hoarsely she quoted Ecclesiastes. " '*What's crooked can't be made straight.*' "

"Motek, scrap that Canadian."

"Go, or I'll push you down the stairs."

"I love you, Shayna."

"We're not on the Tel Aviv boardwalk, Kishote. That was a million years ago. God protect your going."

*   *   *

Next morning in Israel's leading newspaper, *Ha'aretz,* a front-page editorial:

> . . . If we could believe that Eshkol was really capable of navigating the ship of state in these critical days, we would willingly

follow him. But we have no such belief after Eshkol's radio address last night. . . . The proposal that Ben Gurion be entrusted with the premiership and Moshe Dayan with the Ministry of Defense, while Eshkol is given charge of domestic affairs, seems to us a wise one. . . .

In the press, on the radio, in street rallies, such was the unvarying reaction to Eshkol's speech. The mounting cry was *"Dayan!"* Moshe Dayan, of the legendary dash through Lod and Ramle; Moshe Dayan, the fourth Ramatkhal, who had turned Zahal into a real army; Moshe Dayan, the victor of Sinai, moshavnik, ice-blooded fighter, war correspondent, farmer, Minister of Agriculture, Knesset member, world figure with the eye patch — Moshe Dayan for Minister of Defense! And let bumbling deflated Eshkol linger on as a figurehead Prime Minister, while the national hero took power . . .

Nasser addressed the Egyptian National Assembly that same day. The confident exuberant speech proclaimed that the time was now ripe to *"restore conditions in Palestine to what they were in 1948"*; that is, before Israel existed. This made a sensation in Arab lands. King Hussein of Jordan flew to Cairo to embrace and kiss Nasser on world television. They had been attacking each other for years, right up to the day of the speech. The milder terms traded had been *coward, oppressor, robber, scoundrel, lackey, spy, dog,* and so on. The more eloquent Nasser had had the better of the exchange, with *the Hashemite harlot* and *the treacherous dwarf.* Overnight all that changed. They signed a military pact, and the treacherous dwarf brought an Egyptian general back to Jordan to command his army.

The PLO leader, one Ahmed Shukairy, his bearded face radiant with delight, now spoke up from the Old City on world TV. His forces would join the war, he vowed, and after a swift Arab victory all Jews not born in Palestine would be sent back where they came from. As for those born there — the sabras, about half the Israelis — those who survived would be permitted to stay. *"I estimate, however,"* he added, *"that none will survive."*

34

Pasternak's Mission

At a desk piled with letters, cables, invoices, all the paper blizzard of the crisis, Zev Barak was on the telephone with a dealer in Brazil, a fellow far on the shady side, who could however deliver certain weapons in quantity, reliably and fast. Barak and his staff were urgently lining up not only resupply of munitions and matériel from every available source, plus ways and means of delivering them, but also foreign airfields where despite Arab threats cargo planes could land and refuel. Just as urgently, he was staying in touch with the Pentagon, where a few high officers were all-out for Israel and others were dragging their feet like State Department functionaries. Barak was getting things done, and the ambassador had already commended him in the cables, but the job was what the Bible called "sitting on the weaponry," not facing the enemy. That gnawed at him, and keeping very busy was the best way to dull the gnaw.

His private line rang. That could be only Nakhama, or a certain Pentagon insider, or possibly Emily. He put the Brazilian on hold long enough to pick it up. "Oh, it's you. Call you back, Queenie."

"Please, dear. At school."

The conversation with the man in Brazil on the open international line, laced with cabalism, code, hints, and double-talk, took a while to conclude.

"Emily? What's up?"

"I'll tell you, dear. I don't think I'll be able to come to dinner tonight. I'm terribly sorry. Father's coming, and he's the one Nakhama really invited, so —"

"And you, why not?"

"Well, there's this girl, Ethel Windom. She fell off a horse. It may be serious. I'd better stick around until I hear from the hospital."

"Emily, you're lying."

"I am not. She got thrown headfirst on a stone fence and broke her nose. Lost a front tooth, too. Question is whether she also has a concussion."

"I'll expect you at seven. Be there."

"Zev Barak, confound you, I believed you when you said Galia fell off a bike and broke her wrist."

"That was the truth."

"Was it? Maybe you were just out of the mood. How am I to know?"

"Emily, when you lie, which is seldom, your voice goes queer, like Donald Duck. Nakhama's working hard, making a nice couscous dinner. See you at seven."

"No, no, Wolf! And I *don't* sound like Donald Duck."

"Yes, yes, on both points, Queenie. Goodbye."

The horse excuse had been one of several Emily had been weighing: a fire in the school kitchen, a robbery in the dormitory, and the too banal splitting headache. Of all things she did not want to have dinner in Nakhama Barak's flat. No good could come of it. So spoke her gut. When the school day was over she went to the Growlery, showered, and lay down, hoping to fall asleep, wake up well into dinnertime, and telephone abject apologies, explaining that Ethel Windom was showing symptoms of a brain hemorrhage. After an hour of sleepless tossing she dressed in a hurry and rocketed to the apartment house on Connecticut Avenue. As she drove, the first item on the radio news was of more Arab countries, small ones on the Persian Gulf and also Saudi Arabia, joining Nasser's military pact to *"surgically remove the Zionist cancer from Palestine."*

"Superb couscous," Cunningham said to Nakhama, digging in with appetite. "The first time I met Sam Pasternak we ate couscous. Marseilles, May '44. The OSS was doing advance work for the landings in southern France. The Jewish underground was a big help."

Watching her austere, usually laconic father play up to the dark fleshy woman as he rambled on about the sabotaging of German troop trains, Emily could see that he really liked Zev's wife. Not too hard to understand! She exuded natural warmth, her black-brown eyes were very clever, her smiles alert and appreciative. Her English was now passable, and her accent piquant. Altogether an attractive lucky woman; yet Emily realized that she truly did not envy Nakhama Barak, and had no yearning to supplant her. In that respect at least she was not quite the guilty "other woman." The place she held in Barak's life, though passionate, was minor. Israel, his wife, his children, and the army owned most of him. That was that.

Incomplete though her love life was, Emily was grateful for it as a sheer grant from heaven; so she was thinking as she sat mum at Nakhama Barak's table, waiting for the first chance to get away. She had other loves. She loved teaching French literature, she loved the girls, and she loved nature, so close at hand in Middleburg. She loved the horses. Riding through the woods and over the green or snowy fields was a durable joy. So were the deer, the foxes, and the birds: cardinals, jays, martins, grosbeaks, nuthatches, robins, red-headed woodpeckers, all those darts of singing color. Above all was her love for her unique, lonely father.

In however limited and sporadic a manner, Gray Wolf did fill a void as the man in her life. The letters had been lovely, his presence was lovelier, and everything was okay, in short — except when she had to confront the man's wife eyeball to eyeball, as it were. Also, Zev Barak seemed subtly different in the presence of his wife, a big good-looking somewhat graying man on the heavy side, this lady's husband. Altogether Emily was not enjoying this plunge into the brute reality of her love affair, as she had known she would not. She yearned to skedaddle, and she had never liked couscous, anyhow. It was a tremendous relief when Zev looked at his watch and said to her father, "Well, time to go and pick up Sam."

Nakhama asked as they left the table, "Mr. Cunningham, how does the CIA truly see our situation? What is Colonel Nasser up to? Will he make war on us?"

"There's a war already on, Nakhama. The Arabs have never made peace, you know. If you ask will another big battle break out soon —" he glanced at Barak " — well, maybe we're about to hear something about that."

"And how will it all ever end?"

"Now that's a very large question. For an answer, you must invite me again for couscous. Best I've ever eaten." With as friendly a smile to a woman as Emily had ever seen on her father's gaunt face, he shook hands with Nakhama, and he and Barak left.

Restraining an impulse to bolt, Emily said, "Let me help you with the dishes."

"Oh, no, no, I have two big strong girls. They're just doing homework." Nakhama called and they came running in. Galia, with her wrist in a cast (so that had been the truth), was by far the prettier; the younger, Ruti, was a meager little creature with a sullen look. Galia said to Emily, "Your school really has horses?"

"Yes, we teach riding."

The sullen Ruti broke out in smiles. "Oh, could we ride your horses? Could we? We know how, we ride at our uncle's kibbutz —"

Nakhama rapped out a smiling rebuke in Hebrew, and the girls began clearing the table. "Will you stay and have tea? Or whiskey? We have Bell's twelve-year-old Scotch."

"Oh, no, no, thank you. I must go."

"Must you? Zev knows you so much better than I do. Your letters have given him so much pleasure, for such a long time and —"

(*I should have bolted!*) "He's an outstanding man, and your girls are sweet. I'm afraid I must be going. Thank you for a delicious dinner."

"You're welcome. Could I really bring my girls out to your school someday, so they could see the horses? They'd love that. Maybe we could talk a bit."

"Someday, why not? Goodbye."

"Goodbye. How about tomorrow?"

"I'm afraid we have graduation tomorrow."

"Sunday?"

"Sorry. Not Sunday."

"Maybe Monday, then?"

(These Israelis! It's how they survive, no doubt.) "Well, yes, I guess so. I'll have to check my calendar."

"All right, I'll telephone you tomorrow to make sure. Zev has the number?"

"Yes, he does." *(Let me out of here, dear God!)*

Nakhama spoke in Hebrew to the girls, who were doing the dishes in the kitchen. They came romping out, "Oh, that's wonderful! We love horses! You're so kind! We can't wait till Monday!"

"Yes, well, as I say, I'll have to check my calendar. Now I must hurry. . . ." Emily shook Nakhama's hand and at last got the hell out of there.

As Barak edged his small Chevrolet into the heavy Connecticut Avenue traffic, he said, "Were you kidding my wife, Chris, or do you actually have an idea of how it will all end? If so, I'm listening."

Cunningham grunted or chuckled, hard to say which. "I once wrote out my notions on that theme for Admiral Redman when he headed the CIA. My answer had nothing to do with intelligence. A short memo, perfectly serious. He returned it with an unserious comment, so I dropped it in my FORGET FOR NOW file. I review that file now and then. I find interesting things."

"What was his comment?"

"Just a red-ink scribble, *'Chris, you should live so long.'*"

"I'd like to read that memo."

"Barak, any idea of what Sam wants of me?"

"No, the cable read, *'Imperative I meet our friend.'* That's all. He's coming from the Prime Minister, I can tell you that."

"Able but unlucky man, your Levi Eshkol. Will he survive?"

"As Prime Minister? Certainly. The government can't fall at such a time. He may have to give up the Minister of Defense portfolio, which will be a body blow to him."

"Who'll get it?"

"Dayan."

Not till they were crossing the Memorial Bridge did Cunningham speak again. "Your wife is an engaging lady."

"She's a good listener."

"My chatterbox daughter was mighty quiet. Cat got her tongue. I talked enough for both of us, I daresay."

No response. Cat had Barak's tongue, too.

Pasternak was one of the first passengers out of the plane gate. In a seersucker suit he looked very ordinary, a burly middle-aged businessman, possibly seeking contracts in Washington. He had no luggage but a despatch case. After an exchange of pleasantries they walked out of the terminal in silence.

"Well, Sam, what can I do for you?" Cunningham inquired, when they were away from the crowd and heading for the diplomatic parking lot.

"Can you arrange for me to meet with your Secretary of Defense?"

"That's all? Nothing easier."

Pasternak said, "I'm serious, Chris."

"I'm serious, Sam."

When Barak returned to the apartment Nakhama was in a nightgown combing out her heavy black hair, where a few silver wires now showed when he looked close. She said lightly, "What do you think? Your friend Emily has invited me to bring the girls out to her school to see the horses."

"She has? That's nice." Barak's mind was on heavier matters, but the high-strung Queenie must have been well over her anxiety about coming to dinner, if she could be so amiable to Nakhama and the girls. Good move, good sign.

"Yes. Monday. She has to check her calendar, so I'm to call her tomorrow. You have the number?"

"Sure."

Accustomed to Zev's reticence, Nakhama fell asleep without a word about Pasternak. He lay awake digesting Sam's news: the country grinding to a panicky halt in the Hamtana, a new national unity government formed, Begin entering the cabinet, the clamor for Dayan still rising. If Chris Cunningham could get Pasternak to the Secretary of Defense, he had more clout than Barak knew. As to what Pasternak had to say to the Secretary, he could only guess.

"I'm told he'll be in his office at ten o'clock," Cunningham said next morning. "I'll call him then. That's simplest, just a straight phone call."

Barak asked, "He'll take your call?"

"Oh, he'll talk to Chris," said Pasternak. They were drinking coffee on Cunningham's terrace. The balmy morning air, the distant quietly flowing Potomac, the fragrance of the gardenias blooming in tubs, and of trees rained on during the night, created an illusory sense of peace, of everything right with the world. "What about the international flotilla?" Pasternak asked Cunningham. "Could you find out anything last night?"

"Not much to find out. It doesn't exist."

Pasternak glanced at Barak, who said, "You mean it can't be formed in time."

"Don't tell me what I mean. It's a phantom, a nothing. Forget it."

Pasternak almost growled, "Are you saying it's been a hoax?"

"Oh, come on!" Christian Cunningham got up and paced, cup and saucer in hand. "Remember how Eisenhower and Dulles stopped the Suez war?"

"Remember it?" said Pasternak. "It cost us the Sinai."

"So do the British and French remember," said Barak. "It destroyed their empires."

"Well, do you know what happened when Selwyn Lloyd, the British Foreign Secretary, visited Dulles in the hospital not long afterward?"

They both shook their heads.

"It's interesting. We have it well documented. Dulles said to Lloyd, 'Selwyn, once you'd landed in Suez, why on earth didn't you march to Cairo and get rid of the fellow once for all?' Well, Lloyd was flabbergasted! He said, 'Foster, why on earth didn't you give us a signal, even a hint, that you and Eisenhower really were thinking that way?' *'Oh,'* says Dulles, *'we couldn't possibly do that.'* . . . Sam, aren't you chilly in that seersucker? It's breezy out here."

"I don't mind. They told me it was sweltering in Washington."

"Not by the river. Anyway, gentlemen, this flotilla thing is more or less a replay of our 'international action' proposal in the Suez crisis. That time Dulles called it *'the consortium of canal users.'* The 'maritime powers' wouldn't pay canal tolls, they'd hold the tolls in this 'consortium,' to pressure Nasser. It was vague. That was the idea, to be vague, to delay, to let things cool, to put off the use of force. It did delay the British and the French, fatally. Call the flotilla an update of the consortium. That's about it."

"A stall, then," said Barak.

The CIA man coldly smiled. "Zev, I'd venture that all the way up to the Oval Office, nobody has ever said outright that the flotilla was a stall. Nobody had to. Not like Israel, where you talk every matter to death. It can be prudent to stall sometimes, to explore ideas that will probably go nowhere, and never to spell that out in so many words as policy. This whole thing was a French notion. That should be the tip-off."

"All right, Chris," exclaimed Pasternak, "got it! 'International flotilla' is a diplomatic dodge. Contradicts all the cables we've had from the U.S.A. since Nasser closed the straits, but fine. Now what?"

Cunningham consulted his watch, and began to dial on a jack phone plugged in by his chair. "Now I'll put in the call."

Several audible long rings. "Good morning, Major. Christian Cunningham here. . . . Nice to talk to you. Is the Secretary available?" A considerable tense pause. "Oh, Mr. Secretary? . . . Thank you sir, I'm fine. Sir, here with me in my home is an Israeli general, an emissary from Prime Minister Eshkol. . . . Yes, sir, intelligence. . . . Mr. Secretary, his identity is a secret, but of course if you . . . Thank you. He comes with a message for you alone. . . . Yes, sir, I recommend that you see him urgently. . . . Understood, Mr. Secretary. We'll be waiting." He hung up. "He'll call us back."

"How did he sound?" Pasternak asked.

"Very interested. I believe he's telephoning the President."

Neither Israeli batted an eye, but Barak was astonished. Cunningham was not the head of the CIA, nowhere near the top, and the Middle East desk was by no means the biggest section. Was Pasternak as relaxed as he looked, slumped there in a puddle of seersucker, or was he too feeling the tightness of the moment?

"Sam, you missed the couscous last night at Zev's place," said the CIA man. "Better than in Marseilles."

"Nakhama's a Moroccan, Chris, it was bound to be good. I met Nakhama, you know, before this lowlife did. I told him she was the prettiest girl in Tel Aviv. Biggest mistake of my life. She'd be making couscous for me today if I'd kept my mouth shut."

"Perhaps she wouldn't have fallen for you."

"Inconceivable."

The ringing phone sounded to Barak like sudden thunder. "Hello? . . . Thanks, Major, put him on. . . . Mr. Secretary? Yes, sir . . . No, in civilian clothes, of course." Cunningham allowed himself a nod at the others, his eyes gleaming through the glasses. "The Shirley entrance. . . . Yes, Mr. Secretary." With a flourish he put down the receiver. "Let's go to the Pentagon, Sam."

"Good luck," said Barak. "I'll be at the embassy, waiting to hear."

Driving along the river in his car, Cunningham held forth on his favorite theme. Pasternak should not forget the Soviets for a minute, he warned. The Arabs were Russia's high-visibility clients. They would fight a war as planned and drilled by Russian instructors, with Russian tanks, planes, artillery, and missiles. Therefore, with things going so sour in Vietnam, it could hardly break President Johnson's heart, or the Secretary's, if Israel were driven to give Nasser a nasty biff.

"But as Dulles told Selwyn Lloyd," Cunningham reminded him, walking up the steps of the Shirley entrance, "they can't possibly say that. So pay very close attention, and whatever the words are, listen for the Russian music."

A marine major with gold shoulder loops waited for them in a foyer dominated by grand color portraits of the President and the Secretary of Defense. Pasternak was struck by the crisp gleaming splendor of the Pentagon, even here in a side entrance. America! How different from the rundown Kirya entrance, where girl soldiers gossiped, eating sunflower seeds, and the small main foyer usually needed sweeping! But there was nothing grand about the Secretary of Defense as he jumped up, crossed the spacious office, and greeted them with brisk handshakes; a natty middle-sized man in rimless glasses, with slick black hair and a ready smile. "Chris, much obliged."

"At your service, sir."

The Secretary motioned the Israeli to a couch at the far end of the room. Cunningham melted away like a wraith, and the Secretary took an armchair, his manner unhurried. All the time in the world! So far so good, thought Pasternak. He had expected a quick formal exchange across a desk top.

"Did you just get here, General?"

"I arrived last night, Mr. Secretary."

"Then you've had some rest."

"I'm fine, sir."

"We have a mighty healthy regard here for Israeli intelligence."

"Thank you. We make more than our share of dumb mistakes."

"Coffee?"

"Chris Cunningham gave me plenty, Mr. Secretary."

"You know Chris well, I gather."

"We met in the war. OSS and Zionist underground cooperated."

The Secretary smiled. "Quite a feat, getting hold of that Iraqi MiG. How did you do it?"

Not unskilled in "listening to music," Pasternak thought he heard a friendly note. Clearly Cunningham had told the Secretary, and the Secretary was letting Pasternak know that he, too, had a special relationship with the CIA man.

"Well, that's a long story, sir. We can send you a report if you wish. Mainly it was a lot of very dull hard work. Months of wasted time, false leads, disappointments, the usual. The key was making contact with a disaffected pilot. Our air force chief asked us to get him a MiG, so in the end we got him a MiG."

"We have a healthy regard for your air force, too."

"So do we, sir."

"Yes. Well now, your Prime Minister seems to have his hands pretty full these days, with one thing and another."

There it was, the cue to speak.

"I've known him since I was a boy, Mr. Secretary. Levi Eshkol can handle whatever comes. I bring a message from him, and what I have to say requires no reply from you. The Prime Minister wants you to know how matters stand from his viewpoint."

The Secretary's genial look was gone, replaced by hard attention. His lips were a line. "Go ahead, General."

"Sir, unless the United States acts soon, in a way that decisively changes the picture, Israel will have to do something." Pasternak very deliberately paused.

The Secretary's half-closed eyes behind the glasses searched his face, and he echoed in a flat voice, "Do something."

"Yes, sir. Our country can't put up indefinitely with a mobilized menace on all three borders. With repeated public threats of our imminent destruction. With the economic burden of keeping our reserves on alert, week after week. It's intolerable."

"We don't believe here," said the Secretary in slow cold tones, "that Israel's destruction is imminent."

"Nor do we, but the Arab governments are publicly threatening to destroy us, and they're in full military posture to try. We must take that seriously."

"Granted."

"So we have to do something soon."

"What do you call soon?"

"A few days."

"Cigarette?" Pasternak accepted one from the silver box. The Secretary extended his flaming lighter.

"Thank you, sir."

They smoked in a measurable silence.

"How long will it take you?"

Despite a jump of his heart Pasternak matched the Secretary's even tone. "We estimate two to three weeks."

"What casualties do you anticipate?"

"Six to eight hundred."

Pursing his lips, the Secretary looked at Pasternak for a space. "What do you want of us?"

"No military assistance, sir. Two things. One, we trust the Sixth Fleet will remain on station. Two, we expect political support after the cease-fire."

The Secretary sat back in his chair, raising his eyebrows. "Political support . . ."

"Mr. Secretary, in 1956 we withdrew from the Sinai in good faith. We took that risk, though we won a bloody war. We acted on President Eisenhower's guarantee that America would uphold the freedom of the straits and the status quo in Sinai."

The Secretary soberly nodded. "That is true."

"But that was to be the responsibility of the UN, sir, and the UN has miserably failed, as you know. We've waited nearly two weeks for an international political solution. Our enemies have been massing at our borders all that time, digging in, hardening up their positions, making their military pacts, and openly preparing to strike. The Prime Minister frankly advises you that this can't go on much longer, and trusts you will understand."

After a meditative moment, and a long hard look straight in Pasternak's face, the Secretary said, "I will tell you something, General, if you can tell me that only Levi Eshkol will hear it, and that he will not breach my confidence."

"Sir, I can give my word on that."

The Secretary spoke slowly, choosing his words. "President Johnson has received from Dwight Eisenhower a verbal communication through an intermediary. Eisenhower's message states that in view of Israel's good-faith withdrawal from Sinai in 1956, and the American guarantee of the status quo which Nasser has now abrogated, the United States should not interfere with Israel's freedom to act. Eisenhower calls this *'a debt of honor.'* That was his exact term." The Secretary stood up and offered his hand. Pasternak was on his feet on the instant. "Your Prime Minister's frankness is appreciated. Tell him from me that the messenger has well and faithfully discharged his mission."

"Thank you very much, Mr. Secretary."

In the bright sunshine outside, Chris Cunningham was waiting by his car. Before Pasternak could speak he held up a flat palm. "If anything that transpired in there is my business, I'll know about it. Where are you headed?"

"My embassy."

"Good, I'm going downtown too."

The ambassador's greeting was a tired wave from behind the desk. Stoop-shouldered, gray with fatigue, Abe Harman looked on the verge of collapse. He was as energetic and keen a man as Pasternak knew, he always looked like that, and he never collapsed. "So?" he inquired heavily, when Pasternak finished his account of the meeting, "what do you make of it?"

"You're the diplomat, Abe."

" *'How long will it take you?'* That was his first reaction?"

"Word for word."

"I believe you've accomplished more in a morning than we've managed to do here in weeks."

"Back-channel messenger, that's all."

"Yes. Frustrating for the front channel."

"Ambassador, where's Zev?"

"On the Hill. The Secretary of State is testifying on the crisis before a congressional committee. Are you going right back home?"

"I leave on the three o'clock shuttle to New York. El Al goes at six."

"If you'll write up a précis of the meeting, I'll get it to Tel Aviv at once."

"Fifteen minutes," said Pasternak.

"Okay. Use my private office."

Pasternak scrawled away in the small rather airless inner room, at a desk where the ambassador's wife smiled from a photograph. When he came out again and put the précis before the ambassador, Barak was there, looking remarkably cheerful, even excited.

"Here's Sam now!" The ambassador too appeared bucked up, and only half as stooped as usual. "Tell him, Zev!"

"Tell me what?"

"Dean Rusk just sang some amazing new music to congress," said Barak, "as Chris Cunningham might put it. He testified that the United States is now planning no action except through the UN."

Pasternak pulled down his mouth corners in incredulity. "Through the UN?"

"You hear?" exclaimed the ambassador. "The UN! Paralyzed by the Russians and the Arabs, still denying there's any emergency!"

"Bye-bye flotilla, then, eh?" said Pasternak.

"Even as rhetoric, perhaps," said the ambassador, "and that's not all. Listen to what happened afterward. Tell him, Zev."

"The media hounds outside the conference room shot questions at him," Barak said. "He brushed them off, and picked only one question to answer. Somebody yelled, 'Mr. Secretary, is America going to restrain Israel from precipitate action?' Rusk jerked a hand, said, 'I don't think it's our business to restrain anyone,' and hurried off."

Pasternak glanced from the ambassador to the attaché. "And his manner while testifying? That's important."

"I thought he was acting on brand-new instructions that he didn't like. Also, that the question might well have been a plant."

A moment's meditation. Then Pasternak said, "Defense talked to the President, and the President talked to State. The situation has changed. Eshkol's message worked. That's my estimate." About the Eisenhower message to Johnson he would not say anything, ever, except to his Prime Minister.

"Ours, too," said the ambassador.

Barak said, "Green light, Sam?"

"Amber, anyway," said Pasternak.

The three men sat in silence. Barak found himself yearning to be over there after all, in any post where he could lead troops against enemy fire. For unless Nasser could now be induced or bribed or scared into reopening the straits — and that seemed unlikely, with the Egyptian dictator riding a hysterical wave of war-fever popularity — the remaining question was when and how war would come.

"You're monitoring Arab reactions?" the ambassador asked Pasternak.

"Always." Sam glanced at his watch, and mentioned several staff intelligence people. "I have to go out for an hour. When I get back I want to meet all of them in your conference room."

"Done." The ambassador picked up the telephone.

Barak asked, "Will you stay over here?"

"No, I'll leave on schedule."

"I'll take you to the airport."

35

On the Eve

At her dressing mirror Yael Nitzan was pleased with what she saw. Something about Washington, even the hairdressers. Class. After a while in Beverly Hills all hairdos looked alike, no matter what you spent, especially if you were blond. This coiffure made her look different, fresher, younger, and it cost half what she would pay out there.

But Yael was very worried about the war, about Aryeh, and about Kishote, estranged as they were. She had no intention of vamping Pasternak, but he had telephoned her to say he was coming to Washington and wanted to see her. So he was still vulnerable. Nice! Here she was. It was her rule, whenever they met, to give him pangs of regret and make him wish that he had never let her get away, and preferably that he had never been born. She wasn't sure that he was the head of the Mossad, but since what he did now was unclear, and his last post had been chief of military intelligence, the talk might well be true. In any case he would know more about what was happening than almost anybody. He might not tell her much, but she could read Sam Pasternak from tones of his voice and shifts of his eyes.

Gravelly voice on the house phone. "It's Sam. Shall I come up?"

"No, no. I'll be right down."

They had the enormous main restaurant almost to themselves; breakfasters gone, too early for the lunch crowd. Yael ordered a cheese omelette, and devoured it with appetite while Pasternak drank coffee.

"How do you stay so thin? You look beautiful, wonderful, seventeen."

"*Shtuyot* [nonsense]. And you're getting fat. It's not good for you."

"Nobody to take care of me. So, motek, you're divorcing Yossi."

Yael halted in breaking a roll. "Who says so?"

"You're not?"

"Sam, what's going on back home? What will happen? Nasser's absolutely frightening on TV. My lawyer talked to his brother in Herzliyya yesterday. He said they've started digging a thousand new graves in blocked-off public parks, because the military cemeteries are already crowded. All the shopwindows in Tel Aviv taped up, the buses hardly running —"

"Yael, *yih'yeh b'seder* [it'll be okay]. If we have to fight, we'll win."

"We will, Sam?"

"Yes. Look, you've been away too long, getting all trembly in the knees like this. Why sit over here and worry about stupid rumors? Come home with me! I'll get you a seat tonight on El Al."

"Are you crazy? Think I came east just to see you? I have some urgent business in New York tomorrow."

"Do you have a fellow in Los Angeles?"

Yael looked him in the eye. "How can I hide anything from an intelligence genius? Yes, I do."

"Who is he?"

"Since you ask, he's my dentist."

Pasternak blinked. "Who? Your *guy*?"

"Yes. Very handsome, very sexy. Jewish, married, funny, and thin. Thin as a pole."

"A sexy dentist? *Tartai d'satrai* [Contradiction in terms]."

"And you? Still messing with all those bohemian girlfriends in Tel Aviv? How do you keep them straight?"

"The fact is, motek, I've slowed down."

She looked hard at him. "You mean you now have to be more prudent."

"Well, that's right." He gave her a sly coarse grin, and old emotions broke through layers of Yael's lost time. They had been so right for each other, a kibbutznik of the pioneer Pasternaks of Mishmar Ha'emek, and a Nahalal girl of a founding family! But he had married a rich Yekke of Swiss immigrant parentage, and she had paid for a crazy afternoon in Paris with a forced marriage to a Polish outsider. Pasternak broke into her thoughts as though they were audible. "Come on home, Yael."

"And then what?" Yael exclaimed, throwing down her knife and fork. "You don't know what America is like, Sam, really. For you it's all politics and intelligence. This is a world of mentschen, Sam, not of shleppers. At home I went crazy trying to get anything done. Here you breathe, you function. Here business is business! A promise is a promise, a contract is a contract, a phone call is a phone call, an appointment is an appointment, a deal is a deal, a yes is a yes, a no is a no. What have you got there in those four cubits of a country? An army, fine. An army, thank God! And outside the army, what? Shleppers, shleppers, *shleppers!*"

"We've built a land, we had to have it, and it's ours. You know all that," said Pasternak, his spirit sinking as he thought of Eshkol in the dim-lit studio.

"Oh, by your life don't talk Zionism to me. I'm Yael! Benny is doing great things there. So is Kishote. Maybe one day Aryeh will too, I don't know. I'm not saying we don't need a Jewish State. I say it'll survive without me."

"What actually do you do, Yael? What's your business in New York tomorrow?"

She accepted the drop to a quieter topic. "Oh, in a word, Israeli women's fashions. They're coming up, especially in leather." She looked in the mirror inside the large flap of her purse. "Horrible bags under my eyes. No sleep."

"To all the devils, you're so beautiful, Yael."

With a flash of her eyes in lieu of thanks, she said, "Well, this has been nice. Did you have anything special in mind, Sam, calling me from Tel Aviv at two in the morning?"

"More or less. If you and Yossi are really through, I would be interested to marry you."

It caught her by surprise. So did her own turbulent reaction. She looked long at him, and her voice softened. "Ten years too late, motek, but it's charming of you. You're a great Israeli, and any woman would be proud, I guess, to be asked."

"I miss you."

"You know what, Sam? I hope there's no war, I'm rotten scared, I don't sleep thinking about Benny and Kishote. And Aryeh!" Her eyes unexpectedly stung and her voice weakened. "But if we get through this mess, and you finish up whatever job you've got now, why don't you come here? Like Sheva Leavis, you could do really big things."

"Yael, you know the story of the fox and the fish."

"No."

"Yes, you do. It's from the Talmud but it was in our kibbutz primers. The fox invites the fish out on dry land, where it's so nice and sunny and all kinds of good things grow. The fish says no thanks, I have enough trouble surviving in my own element."

She reluctantly laughed. "Hamood, I'm glad you telephoned. Is Ruth still in England?"

"Well, yes. She comes to see the kids, and they visit her in London. They detest the guy, think he's an anti-Semite."

"Maybe that's what she wanted."

He paid the check, and they walked into the lobby. "I'll come up and help you with your luggage."

"*Lo, b'aleph!* [Flat no!] It's just a hatbox. Do me a favor. Find out how Aryeh is and call me. Yossi called twice, and I was out both times. Now he's down south with Tal's tanks. If you see Benny say I love him, and wish him victory. Here's my elevator."

He held her back. "Yael, surely you were fooling. There's no such thing as a sexy dentist."

"Oh, no? I'd say there's a failure in Israeli intelligence."

He burst out laughing. "What, then, is novocaine an aphrodisiac? Are they on to something?"

"Goodbye, motek." She kissed him again. "None of your business, but about Yossi and me, well, there are problems." She dove into the closing elevator.

The security guard behind the embassy's bulletproof entrance window spoke on a microphone. "General, your staff people are waiting in the conference room."

"Very good."

Pasternak's meeting with the staff was brief and encouraging. The main topic was the Arab intercepts, which so far showed no real awareness of a radical change in the Washington picture. He went into Barak's office, saying, "Ready to run for the shuttle, Zev." C-R-R-RACK! Outside the window, jagged lightning split the sky, the blue-and-white flag wildly flapped, and thunder rolled and rumbled. *"Mah pitom?"* he exclaimed. "The sun was shining when I got back here."

"Washington weather," said Barak. "Changeable."

They drove to the airport through lashing rain. In the short walk from the diplomats' parking lot to the shuttle, Barak was drenched. The waiting room was crowded with impatient passengers, and rank with a smell of wet clothes. Beyond the blurred picture window the plane was barely visible. "You're drowned," said Pasternak, off in a corner having coffee and a doughnut.

"You said you wanted to talk more."

"Yes. Have a doughnut. To me, America is coffee and doughnuts in an airport."

"Worm's-eye view." Barak put coins in the dispensers. "What will you report to the cabinet about those Arab intercepts, Sam? It's as though Rusk said nothing that mattered."

"Well, the Arabs have never taken the flotilla seriously. Smarter than our own cabinet."

"Nasser made ugly noises about it."

"Just jawing for the press." Pasternak finished his doughnut and bought another. "By the time I land, mark me, Dayan will have the Defense portfolio."

"Well, he's a great fighter."

"No doubt. Still, a guy who laughs when the bullets are flying around his head may not be the right civilian to head the Ministry of Defense. Death is nothing to laugh at."

Barak said with a wry smile, "The Eshkol man talking."

"Loading now for first section," grated the loudspeaker. Passengers went surging toward the gate.

Pasternak glanced at the streaming window and picked up his despatch case. "Hm. Brave pilot. Look, the Sinai campaign was a masterpiece, but didn't B.G. have to hold Moshe back for a year before the political chance came along? Moshe needs a boss. He's trampling Eshkol down."

"Well, Sam, Dayan really can't do much about what happens next. The war plans are set. If war comes, Rabin will run it, and it'll come the way this storm did."

They were moving toward the rear of the crowd. "Tell me," said Pasternak in an offhand way, "what does Chris Cunningham think about you and his daughter?" Barak made no reply. Pasternak looked at him with drooping eyes. "Does he know?"

"Know what?"

"Zev, we have no more important friend here than Cunningham."

"I know that. And Chris knows that Em and I are old friends. We've corresponded for years. At his request, in fact, when she was a silly kid in Paris, involved with a goofy French poet, I helped pull her out of it. His wife was alive then. They both couldn't thank me enough. That was the start."

"Not quite. She was there when I first brought you to McLean in '48, just a little string bean."

"True enough."

"The thing is, Zev, there's also your own army future to think about."

The eyes of the two men met. Nothing more had to be said. Zev Barak's shrug said all: *What will be, will be.* The words he spoke aloud were, "Ah, Sam, I wish I were getting on this plane with you."

Pasternak gripped his shoulder. "You're in exactly the right job. Love to Nakhama." The swirl of passengers pulled him away. "Yih'yeh b'seder," he called with a farewell wave.

He got back to Israel in a windy humid gray afternoon and found the cabinet sitting in its emergency identity as the Full Ministerial Defense Committee to reconsider the question of going to war. He made his report sparely, since the cabled substance was already known to them, and in fact had helped to trigger this fateful debate.

Pallid and grim, Eshkol slumped at the head of the table, flanked by his two bitterest foes, Menachem Begin and Moshe Dayan. In the few days since Sam had seen him he seemed to have aged much. National unity, indeed! This bizarre reshuffling of old enemies made Pasternak think of Hussein kissing Nasser for the cameras. When he finished speaking Eshkol roused up to say, "Sam, *asita hayil* [a valorous job]."

"Thank you, Prime Minister."

Moshe Dayan shot sharp questions at him. Like the other cabinet ministers Dayan wore an open-neck white shirt, but his old air of authority and the combative gleam in his good eye showed well that this was no civilian, but the great general back in command. All the others were deferring to him except Eshkol, sunk in silence and gloom. "Let's meet tonight, Sam, at eleven," Dayan said at last. "I'll want a full update on the latest intelligence from Cairo."

"Yes, Minister." Pasternak brought out the title with an effort. Moshe was Moshe.

Dayan acknowledged the effort with a lopsided grin, and added, "You must be tired. Get a little rest meantime."

In the falling twilight outside, Pasternak encountered the Chief of Staff walking head down, smoking a cigarette. "Yitzhak, ma nishma?"

"Oh, you're back." General Rabin looked glad to see him. "Been reporting to the cabinet?"

"Yes."

"I did before you. Your cable was tremendous. Turned the situation around."

"I'd say Moshe's appointment did that."

Rabin grunted. "Well, he thinks so. Where are you going?"

"Now? Just walking."

"So walk." Rabin fell in beside him, chain-lighting a cigarette. "Moshe called a meeting of the top generals last night. He came in late, and you know what the first thing he said was? He said, 'Do you have a plan?' "

"That's Moshe. Has your plan changed much? SPADE, wasn't it?"

"Well, yes, it's the same basic plan, modified as intelligence comes in. We've had SPADE, RAKE, PLOW, HOE, and we're running out of farm tools." A grunting laugh. "It still comes down to MOKADE and RED SHEET, as you know." Rabin stopped walking and looked sidewise at Pasternak, head bent. "The air strike worries me. Very complex, extreme risks."

"Have you talked to Motti Hod? Or to the pilots?"

"Motti runs his own show. No, I haven't."

"Listen, Yitzhak, come with me to Tel Nof. I'll notify Motti you're coming there."

"What for?"

"Just do it, Yitzhak. And if there's time, we'll visit Tal's RED SHEET HQ."

Rabin glanced at his watch. "All right."

The road was crowded with army vehicles roaring both ways, the blue headlights giving no illumination in the deepening twilight. "Strange cabinet meeting," said Rabin. "They're acting as though Dayan has the war decision to make. He doesn't, you realize. I do. The Minister of Defense gives the *political* directive to attack — when and only when I report *military readiness* to attack. Anyway, that's how it's supposed to work."

"Moshe's never been much on protocol. He doesn't change."

Rabin paused while Pasternak riskily passed a long slow transporter groaning along under two Centurion tanks. "Sam, between you and me," he resumed, "I asked Moshe if he wanted my job. He can have anything now, I realize that. I put it to him point-blank. He said absolutely no, I should remain Ramatkhal. So, he's Minister of Defense."

"Listen, Yitzhak, he's united the people. He's electrified them. I felt it when I arrived. Why, when I left, the airport was like a cemetery. Today even the customs inspectors and the porters were smiling. He's an inspiration. Like Churchill when France was falling."

"That's a very good comparison," Rabin said. "I hadn't thought of it. Churchill couldn't really do anything that wasn't already laid on. Could he? The RAF planes and pilots were ready. The radar and fighter control systems were all in place. He did nothing to win the Battle of Britain but roar like a lion and inspire the people. 'Blood, sweat, and tears,' and all that."

"Mr. Charisma," said Pasternak.

"Call it that. Crucial, too. Still, the responsibility remains mine. Remember the tongue-lashing B.G. gave me? If you don't, I do."

"I'll never forget it."

The air force chief was waiting for them at the gate to the Tel Nof base. He jumped into the car, saying without ado, "Yitzhak, I'll take you to some pilots who'll be hitting the fields in Egypt on the first wave."

"In Egypt?" Rabin said querulously. "What about the heavy bombers in Sinai? They're the main threat."

"Just so," said Motti Hod, sounding pleased. "Mighty nice of Nasser to put his bombers there! Cuts our time to target. We'll get them. Later I'll go through the op order with you."

The pilots were assembled in their hangar, awaiting the Ramatkhal. As they answered his dry probing queries — their color fresh, their readiness to fight glittering in their eyes, their grasp of mission total and eager — Pasternak could see him cheering up. Rabin also walked around the Mirages, chatting with the ground crews, who spoke to him with an engaging mixture of awe and impudence. These air force lads were the other side of the Israeli coin from the shleppers, thought Pasternak, and they could save both Israel and the shleppers.

Later, as Motti Hod was reviewing the MOKADE op order for Rabin in a map room, the Ramatkhal broke in. "In broad daylight, Motti? A quarter to eight in the morning! Where's your tactical surprise? What about the antiaircraft?"

"Good question. Decision based on intelligence." Hod turned to Pasternak. "Want to answer?"

"Sure. We know the Egyptian fighter pilots' routine, Yitzhak. They return from dawn patrol when the sun's well up. Highest alert ends at seven, then they land and eat breakfast. At seven forty-five they're having coffee, or going to their offices or homes, or to be plain about it, taking a shit. That's optimum time to strike."

"Also, Yitzhak, their airfields tend to have early ground fog," said Hod, "and by seven forty-five the sun has burned it off. As to tactical surprise, the boys will fly as close to the ground or the sea as they can, under the Egyptian radar patterns. Total radio silence. Even if a guy develops engine trouble, even if he goes down or ejects, silence."

The Ramatkhal nodded, and did not interrupt again until the air chief finished. He puffed slowly at his cigarette in silence, then he said, "Now Motti, did I understand you right? You'll leave twelve aircraft to protect the entire airspace of Israel? *Twelve?*"

"For the first three hours, yes."

"And what about *'clear skies over Israel'?*"

"En brera, Yitzhak. The Arabs outnumber us in the air two and a half to one. I intend to hit them with everything I've got, even the trainers."

"Extreme risk. Extreme."

"Yes." A silence. Motti Hod said, "Are we in extremis, Ramatkhal?"

Rabin pondered, sighed, ground out his cigarette and stood up. "Approved."

The helicopter pilot shouted to Rabin over his shoulder, pointing out the window, "There it is, sir. The Seventh Armored Brigade."

The machine tilted, the motor racket increased. Stars and a quarter-moon rotated past the window. Looking down and straining his eyes, the Ramatkhal said, "I don't see anything. Desert."

"Good camouflage," said Pasternak.

On the ground, at a long table under netting held up by poles, senior officers were finishing a map session with General Tal by the green light of a field lamp. "I hear the helicopter," Tal said, and he went outside to scan the star-strewn black sky. The machine settled to earth, the Ramatkhal and Pasternak emerged from the clouds of dust and exhaust, and Tal saluted. "Senior commanders group ready for you, sir."

The officers listened soberly to Rabin's arid summary of the strategic picture. "General Pasternak and I came to see you," he concluded, "because the Seventh Brigade is the spearhead. Ready to go?"

The officers looked at one another, and Don Kishote spoke up. "We've been ready for two weeks, sir. Is the government ready yet?"

"That's an impertinence, Nitzan," barked Tal.

"Sorry," said Kishote, not sounding too sorry. "It's what my tank crews are saying."

"Let him talk, Tallik," said the Ramatkhal. "Go ahead, Nitzan, speak your mind."

"Sir, we've always known we'd face odds of two to one in tanks, worse in artillery, and Russian tanks stronger than ours. But now the enemy's had two extra weeks to harden up the Sinai, plant minefields, dig tank ditches, build fortifications. So our task is that much tougher. Why didn't we roll at least a week ago?"

A voice from the gloom: "We've missed the boat." All along the table heads nodded.

Rabin lit a cigarette with slow gestures. "I'll let General Pasternak speak to that question."

Thanks, Yitzhak, for the hot potato, Pasternak thought.

These officers, he was well aware, faced a long slog into as vast a mass of enemy tanks as had fought in any World War II battle. They were sitting beside friends who would not live. They would take their soldiers into a meat grinder of fortifications and antitank batteries through which — in defeat or victory — they could not pass without heavy losses and horrible injuries. To such men, Yael's husband among them, he had to explain the Hamtana!

He tried. The army had captured the Sinai in the Suez war, he began, but the superpowers had forced Israel to pull out. The victory had proved empty. With this Hamtana, by forbearing to strike at once, Israel had brought the Americans around to a friendly stance. This time, therefore, the army might not have to evacuate territory it won, without a real peace. In the back of Pasternak's mind was the unmentionable Eisenhower message to Johnson.

"Are you saying, sir," inquired Yossi, raising his hand again — shutting from mind that he was addressing his wife's longtime lover — "that we pay the cost in blood and bones of smashing them once more, in order to give up the Sinai for a treaty, a piece of paper?"

"A piece of paper," put in General Tal severely, "counter-signed by America, Nitzan, is pretty good paper."

Returning to the helicopter, Rabin detoured through the arrays of camouflaged tanks stretching out of sight into the darkness. Crews huddling under the stars murmured, as waiting soldiers do, about girls, food, future plans, sports, officers' shortcomings, and the like. Such visits were an old Dayan custom, but for the remote Rabin it was a novelty, and the soldiers clearly were excited and gladdened. Over the clamor of the helicopter's motor as it struggled into the air Rabin shouted in Pasternak's ear, "Let Moshe give his directive. I'm ready."

The Tel Aviv beach was crowded next day with elderly sunbathers, frisking children, and shouting teenagers playing volleyball and paddleball in steamy sunshine. On the terrace where Pasternak sat with his son, Amos, uniformed soldiers were eating falafels and drinking beer, or spooning up ice cream. Tanned and hard-bodied, Amos Pasternak looked like a soldier even in his red swimming briefs. He was completing his obligatory army years in the elite unit called *Sayeret Matkhal* (Staff Reconnaissance). "I'm for a swim before I eat something, Abba," he said. "You really want a falafel right now?"

"Right now. I mean it. That's what I feel like having, Amos."

"Coming." Soon the son returned with the falafel, and handed it to his father with a grin and a head shake. "Not diet food, Abba."

He vaulted off the terrace, loped to the water and dove in, reappearing far out beyond the bathers.

Pasternak wanted the falafel for the nostalgia the taste evoked. He had not eaten one in years, not since he had been as lean as Amos, and had skylarked on this same beach with girls like those gambolling on the sand below. Tel Aviv then had been a smallish seaside town of tree-lined boulevards, no tall hotels, few big buildings, more or less tranquil under the British Mandate. Sporadic Arab unruliness, occasional Haganah reprisal. Otherwise peace, sunlight, music, cafés, girls, water, dancing, fun.

He remembered, too, sitting with Yael Luria on this same terrace when their relationship was just a flirtation; magnificent figure she had had then, and he too had still looked passable. Nor had the city yet been much different. But what a change in the years that he had put on all the weight! A beleaguered metropolis with a long jagged skyline, choked now by army traffic, its crowded-together buildings boarded up and sandbagged, temporary air raid shelters garishly placarded, digging of more shelters still going on. Squadrons of enemy bombers minutes away in Sinai. At the border a colossal confrontation of more than a thousand tanks. A fragile anachronism, this carefree seaside scene!

"General, late despatches." A runner from the Mossad. His office always knew where he was.

> At 1000 tomorrow President de Gaulle will announce full embargo on arms to Israel. Delivery of planes and arms already paid for will be quote delayed unquote.

Bad, bad news, but not too startling, not from De Gaulle.

> Cabinet resumes at 1300 hours.

End of beach interlude, but he would finish his falafel, and to all the devils, have a beer, too. Well, Motti Hod's boys would be flying mostly French aircraft, upgraded to Israeli specifications, with some smart Israeli stuff installed. France had been a good friend for ten years. Ben Gurion was fond of saying, "Nothing is permanent in history." Next despatch:

Order of the Day by Commander of Egyptian Forces in Sinai: The eyes of the world are upon you in your most glorious war against Israeli imperialist aggression on the soil of your fatherland. . . . Your holy war is for the recapture of the rights of the Arab nation. Reconquer anew the robbed land of Palestine . . . ! By the power of your weapons and the unity of your faith . . . !

Old General Murtagi sounded like he meant business this time. On the other hand, the ultra-secret Cairo sources had not sent the code signal for WAR NOW, with time of attack; and the morning report had showed no unusual tank or troop movements overnight.

Downing his beer, Pasternak watched Amos disporting in the water. The beach was crowded with much darker Sephardic youngsters, "the second Israel" of the *mabarot* (transit camps), children of refugees from the Arab countries who had flooded in and almost overwhelmed the old Yishuv. So far the wars had been fought mainly by the sons of sabras and Europeans. These Sephardim with little grasp of historic Zionism, this huge lump of different Jews who hardly knew of Hitler and Auschwitz, had been absorbed into the army because bodies were needed. Would they be equal to machine war? Did they care enough about Israel to risk dying for it, these mabarot Jews?

He stood up and waved. Amos saw him, left the water, and came scampering up on the beach. "So soon, Abba? Had your falafel and you're running off, are you?"

"Exactly. Amos, if I don't see you for a while, good luck."

"Hoping for the best," said Amos, "but ready for anything."

It was the showdown cabinet meeting. Every member knew it. On their faces was the foreboding look of the Zionist notables who had listened to Ben Gurion declare the State nineteen years ago. The historic pictures of that scene showed some of these same faces, now almost unrecognizably older.

All the latest intelligence tended to gloom. An exchange of vice presidential visits between Washington and Cairo was in the wind. It was said in Cairo that the American ambassador had assured Nasser his government was not on Israel's side. French arms shipments to the Jewish State had been halted at the dock. Iraqi forces were on the march toward the Jordanian border. Eshkol sat like a Buddha, nodding and writing notes, while Dayan shifted in his chair, yawning.

Pasternak knew that Eshkol, Dayan, Allon, and Foreign Minister Eban — the players who mattered — had already met at midnight and decided on war. By their looks the rest of the cabinet members either knew or sensed that. But they were Israeli politicians, and they were going to have their say. One after another they talked and talked and talked. At last it ended. Eshkol looked to Abba Eban, who raised his hand.

"Foreign Minister?" said Eshkol.

In his unique Oxonian-accented Hebrew, the plump young Eban put forward a motion very convoluted in language, in effect delegating the government's warmaking power to Moshe Dayan, with Eshkol as consultant. Eshkol called for a vote. Laggardly, sixteen hands went up over sixteen grave faces. Two ministers of the far left, who had been holding the dove line with the Foreign Minister, stared in dismay at the sprouting hawk's talons on Eban's upraised hand, and they abstained.

When the meeting broke up, Dayan called Pasternak aside. "Sam, I pledged to the Rafi executive committee that I would stay linked to Ben Gurion. He was right there in the chair. I had to." Rafi was the splinter party that Ben Gurion had formed, and Dayan had needed the party's approval to accept the Defense Ministry.

"I'm aware of that, Moshe."

"Well, are you returning to Tel Aviv now?" Pasternak nodded. "Good. Drop in on B.G. and tell him what's been decided. Say I've got a lot to do now, but I can come and see him for five minutes."

Sam Pasternak was not under the Defense Ministry, but bypassing protocol was Moshe's way, and he was back in charge. "B'seder, Minister."

Ben Gurion opened the door of his flat himself. His glad smile dimmed as he said, "Come in, Sam, come in. I thought it might be Moshe. He's due to report to me after the meeting. Sit down. How about tea?"

"Thank you, Ben Gurion. I have to get on to my office, and —"

"You're doing fine work, Sam. I told Eshkol you were the man for the job. That's one time he did listen to me, the fool. He's not cut out to be Prime Minister. He's a number-two man. I never made a bigger mistake, pushing him forward."

Ben Gurion sat down behind a desk, the one place where he looked and evidently felt natural. Pasternak would not argue about Eshkol with the Old Man, whose enmity for his successor was unshakeable.

"I'm waiting anxiously to hear Dayan's report. They'd better not vote for war!" Ben Gurion rapped the desk. "I told Moshe that this isn't 1956. Without at least one big power on our side we can't fight the Arabs. That time we had the French *and* the British. And it isn't 1948, when we had to fight or die. Our losses were terrible, terrible. It must never happen again."

The worn face, thinner now and with sunken eyes, settled into a strong withdrawn expression. Pasternak hesitated to speak. All at once the Old Man brightened. "Well, Abba Eban's been keeping his head at least, and that's crucial. They won't go to war against the Foreign Minister's advice. Eshkol has no head, so he doesn't count. Moshe pledged to stay linked to me, so that's all right, too. The others will follow his lead. I could have been Prime Minister again, you know. Even Begin was for me — Begin! — but it's best this way. I've served my time."

"Ben Gurion, the committee meeting ended an hour ago. I came straight here from there."

"So?" An alert look flashed from the dulled eyes. "What was the upshot?"

"Dayan will decide what resistance to make to Egypt, according to military necessity, and consulting with Eshkol. The Foreign Minister made the motion, and it passed."

"Eban made the motion? But that's a motion for war."

"Yes."

"What was the vote?"

"Unanimous. Two Mapam abstentions. They told me afterward that they'll change their vote to yes."

Ben Gurion's large white-fringed head drooped on his chest. He heaved two thick sighs, shaking his head. "It is the gravest mistake in our history. The cost in Jewish blood will be horrendous. Our cities will be bombed, our soldiers mowed down —"

"It may not happen that way, Ben Gurion. A big air strike can catch them by surprise, and —"

"No, no." Ben Gurion waved impatiently. "All this talk about air strikes! Don't you suppose Nasser's on highest alert? Is he crazy? Anyhow airplanes are wasps, they can sting and hurt, but you fight a war on the ground, with guns, tanks, *blood*. Look at Germany! Pounded to pieces from the air for two years. Not one stone left on another, and what beat Hitler? Ground forces! Tanks, infantry, Russians, Americans, British, smashing in from east and west, fighting and dying by the tens of thousands. Well, I'll be hearing from Moshe any minute. He listens to me, I can control him, that was why we had such a success in KADESH. If it must be war, a limited action will be enough. So —"

"Ben Gurion, Moshe Dayan sent me to talk to you."

"He did?"

"The message he gave me was that he's got lots to do now. He can come and see you for five minutes."

David Ben Gurion looked thunderstruck. After a moment the thin resolute mouth curled in a slow smile. "Five minutes? Well, Sam, you tell Moshe Dayan that that will not be necessary. We can't accomplish much in five minutes."

Sam Pasternak knew Dayan had sent him to tell the Old Man that he was politically extinct, only a few days after a popular call to bring him back to power. A cruel message, but it was bracing to see the way Ben Gurion took it, with a dour smile and a few light words. For all his faults great and petty, this was the Lion of Judah who had led the Jews back home.

"Sam, you've also got a lot to do. Maybe more than Moshe." They both stood up. Ben Gurion offered his hand across the desk, then heavily sat down. "Rabin has his plans, and good generals. They'll fight the war and win. Goodbye."

At the door Pasternak stopped to glance at B.G. The Old Man sat there with a calm timeworn face and a faraway look, as though he were peering back across the years to his boyhood; or perhaps across the centuries, to the fall of the Second Temple.

36

Midway

Monday, June 5, 1967.

A broad sandy plain at the Sinai and Gaza borders is shaking and rumbling as though in an earthquake, as the diesels of General Tal's three hundred tanks turn over in dawn warm-up. These obsolescent or secondhand tanks — British Centurions, French MX-13s, and American Shermans and Pattons — are a far cry from the advanced postwar Soviet tanks massed in Sinai; but beefed up and smartened up by Israeli technology, they are the best the Jews can field.

Tal's mission, if war comes, is to break into Sinai in the north in great force, achieve surprise, and panic the enemy. Armor attacks in the center and south will follow. The northern roads into Sinai are mere narrow ribbons through towering sand dunes and deep wadis, terrain considered impassable by tanks, hence the chance for surprise. Nevertheless Russian-style defenses behind the borders — belts of minefields, trenches, earthworks, and artillery batteries, all heavily built up during the long Wait and manned by crack Egyptian armor forces — will confront Division Tal. In a late-night talk Tal has warned his senior officers that Moshe Dayan's comment to the international press about Israel going to war, *"Now is not the time. It's too late, or too early,"* was just a quick-witted obfuscation.

RED SHEET can in fact come at any moment, and since Israel has no strategic depth at all, Division Tal's battalions have no place to go but forward, and no option but to win. They are making the main thrust. The existence of Israel may well turn on how they fight.

In his level drawl, his face scored with lines that show black in the green kerosene light, the short gnarled general sums up so: "In war, nothing goes according to plan, and yet the plan is everything. Whatever happens, remember the plan! Remember your objective! Break through to the objective, fighting if necessary to the death, for the last chance for the Jews on earth. There will be no halt, no retreat. There will be only the assault and the advance."

*   *   *

Don Kishote is scrambling eggs on a spirit stove under paling stars, when Lieutenant Colonel Ehud Elad comes bumping up in a jeep through choking gray-blue exhaust clouds. He shouts over the earsplitting racket, "Yossi, why the devil doesn't your signal sergeant answer?"

"She doesn't? The cable must be grounded again."

To ensure surprise, total blackout and radio silence have been clamped on Tal's division, so communication is only via webs of cables lying on the sand. Farther south the other armor forces are freely using their lights and radio networks, amid much helicopter coming and going. This strategic deception appears to be working, for intelligence reports the Egyptians deploying for a main opening battle in the south.

Kishote dishes the smoking mess into two tin plates. "Have some eggs, Ehud."

"Thanks. I'm famished. But what's the matter, you have no cooks at headquarters?" Kishote is now the Seventh Brigade's deputy commander.

"Those clowns? Ha! Taste this. I slice bully beef into the eggs, with onions and tomatoes and avocado. It's great. We'll be eating out of cans soon enough, and living like animals. Why were you calling me?"

"I want you to address my men."

"What about?"

"What you told me last night after Tallik spoke to us."

"You tell them."

"I want them to hear it from you. Eat up and come along, Yossi."

The rising sun strikes Lieutenant Colonel Elad's mustached crimson face as he confronts his battalion, hands on hips. The fiery sunburn comes from riding in his turret exposed from the waist up amid the fumes and dust of tank maneuvers, for which war game umpires have more than once ruled him killed. Elad maintains that to fight, or even to pretend to fight, you have to see.

"Battalion, give close attention to Lieutenant Colonel Nitzan." His loud voice drives the words over the field noises of morning.

Stepping forward to face the battalion, Kishote notices Colonel Gonen, his brigade commander, standing with General Tal behind the seated semicircle of tankists. He does not like talking while his boss, Gorodish — that is, Gonen — listens, but there he is. Gorodish's Hebraized name, Gonen, has never stuck. To soldiers and generals alike he is Gorodish; a bullet-headed perfectionist, short-tempered, tough to the edge of cruelty, capable of demoting a soldier for an open button.

"Seventy-ninth Battalion, we still don't know when or if we go to war," Kishote begins, perceiving in their bored slovenly postures the low morale of the Hamtana. "What we know is that the enemy is out there" — he gestures toward the border — "and that's why we've been out here for weeks, waiting. Just waiting. I told your commander last night, and he's asked me to tell you, that only a European Jew like me can appreciate fully what it means to be an Israeli tank man. I spent years running and hiding from the Germans. Another year in a British detention camp on Cyprus. You've only read about such things. You're a new generation."

The languid young faces start to show some interest: most of them babyishly pink and smooth, a few bearded, all topped with thick shocks of hair that stir in the breeze.

"You've heard the question asked, over and over," Kishote

goes on. "Why did the Jews of Europe meekly wear those yellow stars, and go into the trains like lambs to the slaughter? Why didn't they at least put up a fight?"

He pauses, his face grave. The silence in the semicircle of green uniforms becomes heavy, amid the clanks and screeches of tank maintenance all over the bivouac ground.

"Well, I told Ehud Elad last night about three cousins of mine in Warsaw, fellows just about your age, who wore those yellow stars and climbed up the train ramps without resisting. Why? First of all, because the Germans lied to them, said they were being resettled in work camps. Was that so hard to believe? How could they believe instead that civilized Europeans, even if they were anti-Semites, actually were packing them into the train just to take them away and murder them? Now we know that that was the horrible truth, but then it was inconceivable."

Kishote has their attention now, all eyes on him.

"But even supposing they had suspected the truth, how could my cousins fight? With what? They had no weapons. They were European Jews. They relied on the gentile authorities for law and order. When a few Jews did find out the truth and took to the forests, or like the Warsaw Jews tried to fight back, it was all too late.

"Well, what I said to your commander last night was simply, thank God we're different. We're the Israel Armor Force!" He gestures at the rows of rumbling tanks. "We've got these, and we're trained to use them! We count on no government but our own government, our own Zion, our own tanks, ourselves!

"And that is why —"

A distant hum makes him break off. The faces of the soldiers are turning to the sky. The far-off specks in the blue rapidly grow into planes flying seaward in groups of four. The motor noises rise to a drumming thunder. With confused yells and cheers, the soldiers jump to their feet, waving arms and fists as the planes flash by overhead, four by four, glinting in the sun and casting fleeting shadows, flying so low that the blue Star of David shows clear on each fuselage.

"Nothing more to say!" exclaims Kishote as the planes dwindle off, the motor roars fading. "The rest is being written in the sky! Instead of the yellow star, the blue star! *Am Yisroel khai! Israel lives!*"

Lieutenant Colonel Elad strides beside him. "Attention!" Sudden rigid postures, absolute quiet among the men, their faces transformed: eager, cheerful, exultant. "Crews to tanks! All personnel to battle stations, maintain radio silence, await orders! Camouflage nets remain in place!"

A sergeant jumps out in front of the battalion: "*Alei —*"

From the battalion, a youthful bellow: "*KRAV!*" ("Battle!")

"*Alei —*"

"*KRAV!*"

"*Alei —*"

"*KRAV! KRAV! KRAV!*"

The soldiers disperse noisily at a run. Lieutenant Colonel Elad gives Yossi a bear hug and kisses his bristly cheek. "Good, excellent, perfect. Thanks! So, here we go!"

"Yes. Be careful, Ehud."

"Definitely! We meet again in El Arish, eh? Kishote, I love you." He strides away.

General Tal beckons to Yossi. He and Gorodish both appear smart and fit: tanned, bright of eye, in well-pressed uniforms and fresh caps, with heavy new tankers' goggles pushed up on their foreheads. Jewish Desert Foxes, Kishote thinks, Israeli Rommels, and not unaware of it! Tal shakes his hand and claps him on the shoulder. In mock singsong Gorodish, a former Talmud student, speaks yeshiva praise. "*Goot gezugt! Yasher koyakh!* [Well said! More power to you!] Come with me."

The airplanes have stung the whole division into violent life. Crowds of soldiers are busy around a thousand vehicles besides the tanks: signal jeeps, command half-tracks, personnel carriers, medical caravans, fuel trucks, maintenance trucks, food trucks, ammunition trucks, a supply tail much bigger than the fighting head.

In his gloomy trailer, Gorodish goes to a map hung in the back. "Now see here, Yossi. Those planes mean RED SHEET is due any minute. Southern Command gave Tal the dirtiest job, and Tal gave us the dirtiest part of it. We won't break through this morning without bad losses, but we can't stop, no matter what. I'll be up forward here" — he raps the map at a road juncture far inside the Gaza Strip — "and I want you to form a second command group, just in case. You understand?"

They look hard at each other. Gorodish is saying that he may be killed or wounded at the outset, or that in the chaos of a first assault he may become trapped. Leading the attack will then be up to Kishote.

"I understand." Yossi is eyeing the envelopes of sealed orders stacked on the table, topped by a chit with two crayoned words in Gorodish's careful Hebrew hand: SADIN ADOME (RED SHEET). "Who'll go first?"

"Ehud with his Pattons, as planned." Some eighty of these U.S. tanks were obtained by a tricky deal with the West Germans, before the Arabs caught on, howled, and stopped it. "The sharp point of the spear, column open order. I'll be close behind. You'll halt and await orders *here,* while we see how the attack develops." Gorodish bends over the map, marks a spot, and takes up a ruler and dividers. "Code name for your command group will be Karish [Shark]."

"Shark." Yossi bares his large white teeth as far as he can. "Excellent."

Not visibly amused, Gorodish says, "Move."

Flying by dead reckoning, Benny Luria is counting off the minutes before the landward turn. Silence in his earphones, but for crackle of static. The four Mirages are thrumming over the foaming wave tops at four hundred knots. The others are formed up on him as for an air show, Kalman to the right, Itzhik and Ricki to the left. *Mark!* A sweeping shallow swerve leftward, and the others follow, holding formation. Good boys, reliable as rock. Fuel okay, oil pressure and engine temperature fine, bomb switches on, strafing switches off. The engine could not be performing more sweetly. The familiar fluttering of his stomach at setting out for action has faded away. At the horizon a line of sand dunes appears, on time within five seconds. Colonel Luria is in business, coming in from the north, where least expected, too low for radar detection.

As the four planes flash over the swampy green Nile Delta's villages and canals, farmers wave, not conceiving that these are not an Egyptian patrol. There is the railroad line, with a short train puffing along. The hamlet ahead could be Faqus, the point of departure for the strike, but it is coming in sight three minutes too soon. Another village, far to the left looks more like Faqus, but if so Benny is off course. Quick review of options: *If I miss Faqus, alternate point of departure? Course, speed, rate of climb, altitude —?* He is peering far ahead for telephone poles, watch towers, any obstacle above the mud that he can smash into in one unwary second . . .

Faqus! There it is, huts, streets, canal, dirt road all in place. The time is exact, nice navigation. Ahead in the sky, not a sign of a patrolling MiG. Okay, hand signals to the others, full throttle, *climb*! And there showing up below are camouflage-painted hangars, control tower, squadron buildings, aircraft on the runways, a long-lens reconnaissance photo come to life. The Inchas interceptor base is eerily like Tel Nof, after all. An air base is an air base. Afterburner shooting the craft up like a cannon shell, ears popping, climb indicator racing round and round. Three, four, five thousand feet up into the blue, up in tumultuous steep climb. Six thousand feet! The others are right with him. From now on it is pure rehearsal. Benny Luria goes into a howling somersault, earth and sky whirl around him, and he levels out headed straight for the crowded main runway.

Nosing over to a steep thirty-five degrees, he flips the switches for the special runway-smasher bombs and dives. Sporadic AA fire begins ahead: winking yellow flashes, rising red tracers. The lined-up MiGs in his scope are growing bigger and bigger. Juicy pickings! But not on this pass. Small figures below are scuttling wildly here and there. Keep adjusting controls to dive straight, straight, *straight*! Altimeter spins down to two thousand feet. He releases the bomb, feels the slight jolt, dives on toward the ground and starts his pullout amid thickening AA explosions. Clicking switches from bombing to strafing, straightening and then swerving left, he swoops around behind the tall hangars to break the anti-aircraft fire-control lock on his plane. A quick side-glance, *Oo-ah!*

Towers of black smoke boiling up back there! The *papam* bombs have done their work, by God . . .

These bombs are a homemade product. As they fall a parachute deploys, slowing the drop. An automatic control tilts the bomb for maximum penetration, a rocket charge rams it deep below the tarmac, then a delayed-action fuse blows a gigantic hole. Years of innovative Israeli technology for these few seconds of history . . .

The others join up in an orderly climb and turn. The four planes half circle the base. Through rising smoke, they can see ruined, useless runways, pockmarked by black craters flickering with flame. The aircraft at Inchas are now pinned on the ground, trapped and helpless.

Strafing run! Luria descends at a shallow down angle, ten degrees, no more. At maximum range he opens up with nose cannon and machine guns at the MiG in his scope, his plane bucking and rattling. The fire stream stabs the MiG, and it bursts into a black-and-red bubble of smoke and flame. Not like a victory in the air; still, some spectacle! What a sight, what a reward! Another and another Russian fighter-bomber, more than a match for the Mirage in the sky, a motionless victim on the ground, blows up under Luria's guns. He is keeping grim count: another, and yet one more, all sure kills, exploding before his eyes, never to fly again. These are interceptors on permanent alert. Chances are the pilots are in them, burning up . . . hellish thought, but on with the mission. Pass complete. The orders are to make three strafing passes and depart, minutes before the second wave arrives.

As he zooms around for the next pass, the others form up still unscathed; from what he can see, not a shell hole on any fuselage. The AA barrages are thickening, red tracers and black puffs whirl past Luria's cockpit. But Israeli air doctrine is fixed and stark: ignore the AA, get the runways, then get the planes. Dropping toward the burning, smoking Inchas base for the second strafing run, Luria sees that the three other pilots have also scored heavily. On a quick count, eighteen, nineteen, twenty blackened MiGs on fire down there!

Plenty of targets left, and as he blasts one MiG and another into a flash of pale sunlit flame, he remembers the French experts who argued that a cannon is wrong for the Mirage, out of date, that missiles are the proper armament. Some experts! What havoc the nose cannon are wreaking, together with these terrific 30-millimeter machine guns, spitting a thousand bullets a minute! Luria served with the Israeli team that overbore those French engineers: Tolkowski, Weizman, Hod, great airmen, great Israelis. Great decision!

Soaring above the tumbling smoke, Benny can see no sign of the second wave coming in yet. Command decision: come around and strafe again. Pile on the destruction, annihilate this menace to the Jewish homeland. Fuel is the limiting factor. He manages two more shallow attack dives into the smoke and the AA fire, now wild and sporadic, then Luria leads his "boys" in a steep climb to ten thousand feet. No need now to slog through thick sea-level air on the return leg.

At this altitude his circle of vision takes in much of the rich green Nile valley, the gray sprawl of Cairo on both sides of the river with the toylike pyramids and Sphinx nearby, the mottled delta, the blue sea beyond, and tan desert sands stretching eastward toward the Suez Canal. Pillars of black smoke, boiling high into the translucent morning air, tell the story. Abu Sueir, Fayid, Kabrit, Cairo West, all are torched like Inchas. A thought strikes and thrills him: *By God, it's Midway!*

Benny has studied all the historic air strikes, and most vivid in his memory is the picture of Midway, the scattered Japanese carriers aflame here and there on the sea, sending skyward the funereal fire and smoke of their own immolation; a cataclysm which, in five shattering minutes, turned the course of the war and of history. "Elohim, we've won the war," he exclaims aloud, striking a fist on the bubble of the cockpit. "We've *won!*" He glances at the clock. Start to finish, they have been seven minutes over Inchas. He seizes the microphone and breaks radio silence. Why not, now?

"Tabor, Tabor, this is Slingshot Two, returning from Sunflower . . ."

*

Through the loudspeaker distortion of reports in the underground air force command post, Luria's exultant tone reverberates. Uniformed girls wearing earphones scrawl excitedly with orange grease pencils on a glass partition.

"And now Inchas!" Dayan exclaims to Rabin, as both smile and shake their heads in wonder. "If all this is accurate, Yitzhak, that makes seventy-one planes destroyed so far, just in the first wave!"

Rabin draws heavily on a cigarette. Butts are piled in the tray on his chair arm. The mortal tension in the underground command post is just starting to abate. "Encouraging, even if sixty percent true."

"Miracles and marvels!" says Ezer Weizman, the former air chief, now Rabin's chief of operations, grinning from ear to ear. "The boys sound like Arab pilots, reporting such crazy figures, but who knows?"

Motti Hod is drinking from a huge upended water jug. He puts it down with a resounding *thump* and raises a hand. The hubbub among the officers in the chamber cuts off. Officers hurrying in and out halt where they are. The air chief turns around to Rabin, who is sitting directly behind him. "In action Benny Luria is a cold fish," he almost snaps. "His report is reliable! In fact" — he waves a hand at the orange-marked partition — "you can believe all those numbers. MOKADE is going according to plan."

Pasternak at Rabin's elbow says, "I believe them."

"I must confirm RED SHEET," says Rabin, getting up.

"By all means," says Dayan. He turns to Pasternak. "Sam, call Northern and Central Command. Even if fired upon, *no advance* into Syria or Jordan."

"Moshe, those are their orders."

"Yes, yes, but Syrian artillery is bound to open up, maybe Jordan, too. Once any of our units cross the borders, it's too late to recall them. We return fire, but from static positions only."

"Yes, Moshe."

"Also report at once to Abba Eban what's going on. We're already in a new international political situation. And to Eshkol, of course."

Again Dayan is ignoring protocol, falling back into their KADESH relationship, when Pasternak was his deputy. Pasternak does not mind, though they have been going separate ways for years, while Moshe has been dabbling with little success in politics. Paunchy, getting bald, Dayan wears this morning a new majestic air. To look at him, he is not only Minister of Defense, but the real Prime Minister. Number One.

"Ben Gurion, too?" Sam inquires.

Dayan shrugs. "As you wish. Now, Arab reactions are crucial. I want to know what Radio Cairo and the others say. And the leaders will be phoning, or conferring by wireless. You're monitoring them?"

"Blanketing them. You'll get half-hour summaries. Anything special, at once."

Dayan nods and turns away. In an anteroom Pasternak shuts the door and makes the calls. Through a window he can see the girls writing up a report from the Cairo West strike.

"You catch me half-dressed," says Levi Eshkol, "but go ahead, go ahead, you sound cheerful . . . Oy, really? Sam, Sam, *mi darf makhen shekyanu* [this calls for the blessing on good news]! Should I come down to the Kirya? I guess I'll wait awhile. Have you called Abba Eban?"

"I will when I hang up."

"Yes, yes, he must tell our people in Washington and New York right away. He'll be waking them up in black night, but for this it's worth it, hah? They must get ready for a big fuss. Sam, it's wonderful! Congratulate Motti for me! Ai, Sam! It should only end as it's beginning! And listen, *call Ben Gurion.* He's entitled."

This is Levi Eshkol, Pasternak thinks; considerate of the great old man, once his boss, now his most venomous critic. He dials Ben Gurion first, then the Foreign Minister.

Gorodish emerges from the trailer. "RED SHEET!" he roars at his signal officer, in the half-track bristling with antennas. "Open all radio networks, and distribute orders!"

In a bombinating racket of engine exhaust and loudspeaker blare, runners with sealed envelopes dart through the serried lines of tanks. Camouflage nets are coming down, crews swarm into the hatches, turrets swivel back and forth, guns elevate and depress, and the tanks start to move. Helmeted commanders signal with hand-held flags half obscured by churned-up dust plumes.

Yossi Nitzan takes his command group, a platoon of Centurions with half-tracks and jeeps, to a station near the border, a mere wire fence strung along the level sand. The long column of Gorodish's brigade comes rolling up with the Pattons in the lead, tracks clanking, sand swishing into the air. Ehud Elad, erect in the turret, is shouting into his helmet microphone as his tank crushes the fence. Seeing Don Kishote in his command half-track, he waves and throws him a salute. At that moment fire flashes along the horizon, followed in seconds by the THUMP-WHUMP of heavy enemy artillery. The surprise of the air strike is over, and as Tal has said a thousand times, to win a war the armor has to capture the real estate.

Shayna's Canadian suitor is driving her to the bus terminal in Jerusalem when a scary sorrowful wail fills the air. "What's that?" he exclaims.

"It's the Egyptians," Aryeh says at once. "They're attacking Jerusalem."

She holds him close, in the back seat. "Don't be frightened, Aryeh."

"Me? I'm not afraid of Egyptians."

"Turn on your radio, Paul."

The wedding of a girlhood friend, like herself almost an old maid, has brought Shayna to Jerusalem, and now she and Aryeh are about to take the bus back to Haifa. The news is just coming on.

"The voice of Israel from Jerusalem. It's ten o'clock. This morning at 0745 hours Egyptian planes again violated Israeli airspace. The air force has driven them off and all our planes have returned safely. All forces remain on highest alert."

The rest of the news, brief and innocuous, is followed by a soft-drink commercial, which Paul shuts off. "Well, that doesn't sound exactly like war," he shouts over the continuing howl of the siren. "Does it?"

"No, it doesn't. Maybe they're testing the siren. Let's go ahead."

On the Jaffa Road shops are mostly shuttered and the usual truck jam is nonexistent, since the country's mobilized trucks are off at the borders. Distant hard thumps sound through the howl of the alarm. "Listen to that!" he calls. "Maybe it is an air raid, for a fact."

"That's artillery."

"Artillery!" The plump black-bearded face looks around at her. "You mean Jordan is attacking us?"

Shayna notes his tribal use of "us." "Well, they seem to be bombarding us."

"Maybe you'd better not try to get back to Haifa just now, Shayna. The roads will be jammed by the army, and dangerous. You and Aryeh can have my flat. I'll sleep in the yeshiva."

"Why? If we must we'll stay with my mother."

"Pretty cramped in that one room."

"We're simple people here in Jerusalem."

Off in the distance an explosion, and rising smoke. More thumps, the siren still screaming. Aryeh says, "We'll beat the Jordanians. We'll beat all the Arabs that attack us."

"Let's go to my mother's house, Paul."

"Okay."

Shayna's widowed mother lives in a thick-walled Arab house in an old religious section. The Ezrakh allows her to come down once a week to cook his Sabbath meal and clean his cellar lair, lined floor to ceiling with tomes. For this she is much envied and honored by the other old women of the shabby neighborhood. Paul turns into a side street, where laughing children are lining up at a shelter entrance. "Shayna, if it's war, what can I do, how can I serve?"

"Yeshiva boys just go on studying Torah."

"I'm not a boy."

She raises her voice over the siren. "They tell a joke about yeshiva students in wartime, Paul. The bombardment starts and the head rabbi rushes into the beit medrash, yelling, 'What's the matter with you fellows? It's war! Do something! *Zug tillim!* [Recite psalms!]' "

"Ha! Not bad."

"If you really want to sign up I can tell you where to go."

The siren is dying down. The artillery thumps sound louder. All at once the Hamtana is over, and it's war again! The first time she was a little girl, the second time she agonized over Yossi Nitzan in the paratroops. Now he is a senior armor officer, and even if she is hugging his son, she means to keep her thoughts off him. He can take care of himself, and if not, too bad, too bad! Yael's husband is not her business, and there an end.

When the car stops at her mother's house, a paunchy little man with a stubbly beard, in a tin hat and a red armband, comes running up and waves a club at the Canadian, yelling.

"What's his problem, Shayna? My Hebrew's not that good."

"That's Chaim the air raid warden. He's been dying for a war, now he's happy." She rattles back at Chaim, who walks off muttering.

Paul says, "Okay, where do I go?"

She tells him, adding, "Stay off the main avenues, Paul, there'll be army traffic. The recruiting office is on the second floor, over the restaurant."

"Got you." He drives off.

The door of the Ezrakh's airless flat, half below street level, is open. Shayna can see him at his table in shirt sleeves and a long talit katan, swaying over a small volume. The chant is not his usual Talmud singsong. The Ezrakh is reciting psalms. Shayna knows the Book of Psalms by heart, and in her mother's flat she murmurs a few psalms, despite herself, for that unchangeable madcap soldier who is not her business, Don Kishote.

37

The Road to El Arish

General Tal's mission on this first day is, while destroying all enemy forces in the north that he can, to seize the tarred road along the Mediterranean coast running from Gaza toward El Arish. For after a single day's fighting his "mailed fist" of tanks, as he likes to call it, will be like a giant mechanical toy that has run down, requiring a windup of fuel and ammunition from the supply train before it can fight on. But those "soft" machines cannot cross sand and scrub as the tanks do, so the road is a life-or-death first objective; the only way for rubber-tired supply vehicles to pass through the rocky wastes and high soft dunes, and the one safe path through the minefields.

El Arish itself, the pretty Sinai capital town on the sea with strong defenses and a major airport, lies some forty miles from Tal's jump-off point. Tal aims to crack the tough crust of the enemy's border defenses, and exploit success in the direction of El Arish, but reaching it on Day One is not a realistic goal. The coast road is blocked by a series of defenses, starting near the border by the northern anchor of the Egyptian line, the Rafah junction, which is manned by an entire tank division; and this formidable hedgehog straddles the road with artillery, tank traps, trenches, and minefields, from the sea to impassably high dunes.

Twenty miles beyond Rafah lies a second daunting barrier, the long gauntlet of the Jeradi Pass, many twisting miles of lofty dunes and broken terrain; a killing ground of yet more minefields, anti-tank guns, camouflaged tanks, and fortified trenches. Another ten miles beyond that is El Arish, but all along the way are still more strongpoints hardened up during the Hamtana.

Tal's force is the most powerful Israel can field. If it is stopped or thrown back the stunning air victory can still be vitiated, perhaps wasted, by a display of weakness on the ground in full view of the Arabs, the Russians, and a hostile United Nations. Pushing ever forward, he will get as far as he can toward El Arish, against all odds and at any cost.

*   *   *

As Kishote stands in his half-track watching Ehud Elad's Pattons rumble by in a long winding column, raising dust that veils the low sun, the sight both elates and worries him. A brave show they make, these American tanks clanking by for many minutes, manned by high-spirited helmeted kids in field green who have not yet seen battle. Sleek lines to that Patton. Low profile, smooth suspension, a great ride, a fast tank, but those gasoline engines are a bad fire hazard, and the Pattons are undergunned; they can't stand and trade long-range punches with T-55s or Stalin-3s. They'll have to do tricks to close in, or else catch them unawares. Still Ehud Elad has the nerve and the skill, if anyone does, for such extrahazardous maneuvers.

After the Pattons the Eighty-second Battalion's Centurions come lumbering, distinctly British in the staid tall look of their cast-steel hulls and turrets. Those large cannons are more like it. Years ago tankists hated the Centurions; unfit for desert war, they complained, always sanding up, breaking down, throwing their tracks, and hot enough to cook crews alive. Israel Tal and senior officers like Gorodish, Elad, and Nitzan have enforced iron rules for maintenance and brute punishments for lapses. The Centurions now work well, and their crews are happy, even envied.

Tal's voice, icy and sharp, cuts through the babble on the command network in Kishote's headphones.

"Gorodish, what's the holdup?"

Voice of Gorodish, hoarse and harassed: *"Narrow axis, many obstacles."*

"Gorodish, break through! It's only beginning!"

"Acknowledged."

In its first half hour, Kishote perceives, the operation is already in disorder. As Tal predicted, little is going according to plan. The unblooded battalions are reported blundering about under fire in the crooked streets and blind alleys of the first villages they have come to. Built to confuse and hamper invading horsemen, these mazes evidently work just as well against tanks. Kishote can see in his binoculars a stalled clutter of Centurions, and he decides to do something about this. Why wait for orders from Gorodish?

"Let's go!" He holds up a flag to summon his small command group after his half-track. Weaving past dragon's-teeth obstacles and zigzagging trenches, they drive through cultivated fields to the traffic jam of tanks outside the nearest village. Kishote sees no way to push past the vehicle jam-up. "Break through here," he orders his driver, pointing at random to a mud wall. Make a surgical cut, he figures, and see what is going on inside there. With a surprised glance and a gold-toothed grin at him, the dark little Yemenite corporal guns the motor. *Smash!* In a shower of debris the half-track is inside a gloomy dead-end alleyway of low houses, choked with halted muttering Centurions.

"To all the devils!" Kishote bellows at a tank captain, who stands in his turret, blinking at the dirt-covered lieutenant colonel bursting in at him. "Forward! Knock that house down!"

The captain shouts something about orders not to harm civilians. Jumping out, pistol in hand, Kishote darts into the one-room house at the end of the alley, shabbily furnished and to all appearances empty, then runs out and angrily waves the huge tank forward. With a roar it crashes ahead, the house collapses, and sunshine shafts through the dust into the alley. The next tanks follow over the debris, puffing blue fumes in the sunlight, and the vehicles behind them start to move.

Meantime, from the ongoing cacophony in his earphones, Yossi can hear that Tal and Gorodish are departing more and more from the plan as the battle unfolds, and the Centurion battalion assigned to hit Rafah junction is being diverted. *"Gorodish, I am going on to Rafah,"* he signals in code. Receiving no answer, he chooses to take this as enthusiastic approval. Outside the village he gathers up a company of Centurions assigned to him as a reserve force. Standing erect in the half-track, holding up a green flag, he shouts on his command net, *"Aharai!* [Follow me!]" and heads down a dusty track through the fields which lead to the highway.

A quarter hour later he is signalling from the deserted Rafah railway station, a first key objective just inside the border between the Gaza Strip and Sinai. *"Gorodish, I have captured the Vatican and await your orders."*

Gorodish, faintly, through heavy static: *"Kishote, you're where? In the Vatican? Already?"*

"In the Vatican. I've secured it. All tanks operational. Casualties minimal. When the opposition saw us coming they jumped out of their trenches and ran off like mice into the desert."

"Acknowledged. Can you see any activity in the Rafah opening?"

"Negative, dead quiet."

"That won't last. Wait for me at Naples."

Soon Gorodish and Kishote, both dust-covered and perspiring, stand side by side under the water tower on a hill code-named Naples beyond the railroad station; the highest point in the Rafah Opening, a saucer of desert seven miles wide narrowing to the junction beyond. The whole area, bisected by the black strip of highway, is apparently quiet and abandoned. Gorodish sweeps an arm around at the panorama. "God knows what's really out there, Yossi. Those damned Russians are the world's best at camouflage."

"Well, we'll soon see."

A platoon of Yossi's Centurions is crawling along the road toward the junction as a probe. When it has gone less than a thousand yards the desert erupts all around them in flame, explosions, crimson tracers, and screaming shells. Not at all surprised, Yossi is relieved to see how the intense drilling of years has taken hold. The tanks scuttle to concealment behind folds in the ground or high green castor-oil plants and return a blaze of gunfire, aiming at the flashes of hidden guns, or at enemy tanks that have thrown off their camouflage nets and are popping up from cover.

"They're good boys," shouts Gorodish over the racket. "Tell them to fall back, Yossi, the intelligence is right, that sandy ridge is where the main blocking force is."

As the patrol retreats without loss to the unit of Centurions at the foot of the hill, Kishote sweeps his binoculars clear around the horizon. Behind Naples, to the north, dust, smoke, and flashes from the continuing battle back in the Gaza villages; far, far off to the east, the rising dust plumes of Raful Eitan's mechanized paratrooper brigade, striking straight across the desert from Israel toward the Rafah junction, their mission to capture and secure it with the support of Tal's tanks; and seaward, just coming into view down the coast road, Ehud Elad's Pattons, by God! More or less, the plan is working, after all.

"Listen, Gorodish! Ehud and I together can smash through that junction," Yossi says. "Send him with me and we'll keep up the momentum."

"By your life, no. Leave an enemy pocket of this strength to our rear? We stick to the plan. Ehud's battalion will attack and destroy this blocking force before we advance."

"And I?"

"You're my reserve here. If Ehud gets in trouble you'll move when I order you."

Ehud Elad's attack on the ridge follows doctrine: one company assaulting frontally to draw the fire, two companies hooking around to surprise and smash the enemy rear. Inevitably Elad is leading the frontal attack himself. As a rule this is discouraged in battalion commanders, but Gorodish has not argued; not with Ehud Elad. In Yossi's binoculars there is Ehud, a diminutive figure edged with rainbow color, exposed as usual in the turret, leading a company of tanks up the sandy slope of the ridge. *(Down, Elud, by your life, down!)* All along the ridge enemy tanks and antitank guns are firing downward at the advancing Pattons and moving toward them. But the Egyptians cannot see behind them — and Yossi can, from his high vantage point — Elad's other two companies, a line abreast of many more Pattons, crawling over the crest of the very high soft dunes on the seaward side behind the ridge.

But Ehud's tanks climbing in the frontal assault are being hit and flashing into flames . . . one, another, a third . . . the sight saddens and sickens Yossi. Almost, he can feel the heat of those sudden fires. After years of drills and war games, here is the real thing! Crewmen are scrambling out of the flaming tanks into fusillades from machine guns above, and hitting the ground fast, perhaps okay, perhaps wounded; but a few may be getting roasted alive inside, trapped in red-hot steel! As an armor instructor, and now as a deputy brigade commander, Yossi has ordered interminable drills and more drills in fire fighting and escape. He sometimes has awakened from a never-revealed claustrophobic nightmare in a pool of sweat, thankful to God that he is in a bed and not in a burning tank. In such dark hours he has regretted leaving the paratroops, but never by day. The more he knows the tanks, the more he believes that they decide Israel's wars.

When will those approaching Pattons open up? Close the range, yes, that's doctrine! But Ehud's group is taking so many hits, and if Ehud himself —

ROAR! The entire line of Pattons coming over the dunes fires as one, making the shallow hills echo. All along the ridge Russian tanks spring into flame; eight, nine, *eleven,* stopped and smoking — what a blow! How that surprised enemy formation is falling apart, the unhurt tanks and self-propelled guns lurching here and there, some plunging down the hill, some sinking from sight, crewmen abandoning the burning tanks on the run! Again and again the rear Pattons fire as they come, hitting yet more tanks, while Ehud's force still climbs the hill, machine-gunning the concealed soldiers who come leaping out of the trenches.

Gorodish throws an arm around Kishote. "All right, it's a rout! Get ready to go for the junction. God bless Ehud! What a lion! I can't raise Raful, so I don't know how he's doing, but he's coming, I can see that from here. When Ehud's collected his wounded, he'll follow you, and I'll be with him."

"Understood."

"Once you start, Kishote, *don't stop*. I'll order some of those fellows to join you, and keep the rest in my reserve."

"Those fellows" are a long, long column of Centurions, just rolling in view from the break-in action to the north, an immensely cheering sight. "Go!"

Harassed by snipers and concealed antitank guns, Yossi's Centurions make slogging progress toward the junction. The resistance is less than before, but by Soviet doctrine a second heavy defense zone surely still lies ahead. He sends a probing patrol to the crossroads, and calls to Gorodish for an artillery barrage on the enemy positions that open fire. Gorodish complies with a rain of shells from his mobile heavy guns. Then comes the signal Kishote is impatiently awaiting: *"Advance through the junction!"*

He flags the signal, and his tanks begin to traverse the crossroads, where a large signpost bears two signs in Arabic and English: SHEIK ZWEID and EL ARISH. Eerie lack of opposition! No sound but the clank and rumble of the tanks on the pavement; has the barrage totally silenced the enemy?

Not so. When nearly all the column has passed through the junction, a hurricane of gunfire breaks upon the rolling Centurions from all sides: from hills that look bare, from camouflaged trenches, from concealed guns, a storm of explosives, steel, lead, and flame bewildering in its power and volume, paralyzing in its sudden all-encompassing noise and blaze. Tanks and half-tracks are hit and on fire. One half-track overturns. Blackened crewmen, some with their clothes aflame, come boiling out of the stricken vehicles. There are crashing collisions. The column halts. Jumping to the top of his half-track, Kishote sees his force in disarray from end to end. The Centurions are distraught elephants turning to lumber here and there, their long guns moving up and down like nervous questing trunks.

Yossi grasps his driver's shoulder. "Take me to the top of that rise."

As the half-track jolts up a nearby slope Kishote is thinking that these boys are encountering *war* now, the thing itself, and that Tal's entire attack perhaps teeters in the balance, at this unimpressive intersection of a dirt road and a tarred highway, in a waste of sand dunes weirdly sculptured by the Sinai winds. The Egyptians have held their fire to the right moment and now are letting fly with all they have. The Rafah junction is as crucial to them as to General Tal. Whatever happens next is up to Yossi's force. For all he knows, it may mean the war.

"All right, stop." The rise in a bend of the junction gives him a view of the whole disordered column, and the tank crews see Lieutenant Colonel Nitzan standing atop his half-track amid all the whistling, screeching, flaming shot and shell, holding up his command flag.

"Okay, this is what we are trained for," he speaks crisply and clearly into his helmet microphone. *"The future of Israel now depends on us. This column will drive on. If the vehicle ahead of you is on fire, help extinguish it. If it can't be done pick up its crew and go on. Leave no wounded behind. Resume formation. Resume the advance, maximum fire at all targets. We go through at all cost. Follow me."*

Still braced erect in his half-track, which he puts into line behind the first three tanks, he watches his Centurions straighten up into a moving column and advance along the road in a heavy crisscrossing fire, taking hits, but also setting on fire guns and tanks that pop briefly out of concealment to shoot.

Time ceases its usual flow in all-out combat, and he cannot say whether five minutes have passed or twenty. As the column proceeds down the road through the dunes and the volume of fire slackens, he calls for casualty and damage reports. Only then does he glance at his watch. Gorodish ordered him to move at 11:36. The minute hand is just passing 11:44. Eight minutes have gone by. He now leads a force of armor veterans. Behind are some wrecked smoking vehicles, and in them some dead.

A road sign in English and Arabic reads SHEIKH ZWEID 2 KM when Kishote first spots the dust cloud of Elad's Pattons coming up behind him on the sand. Ehud is on a parallel course more than a mile from his tracks, for otherwise if they get into melees with enemy tanks, Israelis may end up shooting at Israelis in the fog of desert combat, as actually happened in the KADESH campaign.

And shortly Kishote does run into a company of giant Stalin-3s, guarding the road outside the fortified railway stop called Sheikh Zweid. It is a brief, fierce, wide-ranging fight in clouds of dust, and he is proud to see his newly blooded tankists nimbly scatter, take cover, spot shots for each other, and pick off the Egyptian tanks like target hulks in the Negev. When ten of these have been set afire, the crews of the rest climb out and flee into the dunes; Kishote counts eleven good tanks abandoned by the roadside, great haul for the armor corps! Only, finding crews won't be easy. These Russian tanks are so cramped inside, their crews have to be almost midgets.

So it is that Ehud Elad beats him into Sheikh Zweid. The Pattons are parked far and wide at the railroad crossing, and the crews are already out of their machines, breathing fresh air after hours of choking on engine fumes and gun smoke. Some are asleep on the tanks or on the sand, others eating from cans or cooking over sooty little fires. Egyptians are still being flushed out of trenches and from under tanks and trucks, unresisting and stunned as though the Israelis have dropped on them from the skies. Sand-covered from his boots to his unhelmeted hair, goggles up on his forehead, Gorodish sits in his jeep studying a map. "What! Eleven undamaged Stalin-3s? Kol ha'kavod, Kishote. Let the Russians help carry our arms budget! You went through the junction like a storm."

"I took some bad losses."

Gorodish nods. "I'm about to call for those reports."

The senior officers of both battalions, some bloodied and bandaged, gather at his jeep. Ehud and Kishote fall on each other's necks, and hug and kiss. "By God, you're a mess," says Kishote.

"*S'ritot* [scratches]," says Ehud through a bandage, with a wry distorted grin on his badly cut mouth. One hand is caked with black blood, and fresh red blood oozes through the crude dressing.

As one by one they tell Gorodish their losses in dead and wounded, and in destroyed tanks, his face falls and his mood darkens. "Well, it's been a tough fight so far. We're making good progress. I'm satisfied. I'll now report to Tallik. Wait." He plods to the signal half-track, and in a few minutes returns looking exultant, almost radiant. "Now listen," he says to the officers, leaping into his jeep like a boy and standing up. "There's news. Aleph, the air force has in fact won the greatest victory in history. That's straight from Tallik and Tel Aviv. The Egyptian air force no longer exists!"

The officers whoop with joy. They have been picking up fragmentary reports about the air strike, but all they knew was that air support, part of all their war games, has not yet been forthcoming. They have slogged this far entirely on their own. Gorodish goes on, "The Syrians, Jordanians, and Iraqis have all opened fire on us, and our pilots are now taking care of their airfields. By nightfall there will be only one air force in the Middle East — ours! We'll finish this campaign under a powerful air umbrella." He raises a cautionary hand at their happy exclamations. "It'll be hard fighting all the same, but we'll go faster and farther with fewer losses. Now then! More good news. Raful's paratroopers are behind us, mopping up Rafah junction. He expects to report it secure very soon."

"That's news we need right now," says Ehud Elad, "more than any other!"

"Next give ear to this! Tal says that what we've done so far, breaking through to Sheikh Zweid in five hours, absolutely matches the air strike for valor. It's a historic tank march. The High Command has called off an attack on El Arish by sea and parachute drop. Unnecessary! Motta Gur's paratroop brigade is being moved from our front to Central Command, and the honor of capturing El Arish goes to the Seventh Brigade alone."

The officers glance at each other with kindling pride and excitement.

"That's the news. I'm the proudest brigade commander in this army. Prepare your units to take to the road at 1430 hours!"

He spreads his map on the jeep hood and is talking with Kishote and Elad about the attack plan for the Jeradi Pass when his signal sergeant approaches. General Tal is calling. Gorodish strides off.

"I'll go in first, Yossi," Ehud says. "The Pattons are faster. A column of American Pattons roaring into Jeradi will deliver the devil of a shock. Even if the defenders pull themselves together, you can still hammer through with your Centurions."

"What you mean is," Kishote retorts, "you want to take the

brunt of any resistance that's alerted and waiting at the entrance. Nothing doing, Ehud. If Gorodish agrees, what we'll do —"

"Here he comes."

Gorodish suddenly is his old self, all crusty business. "Things have changed. Raful is asking Tal for help. He's run into very strong resistance at Rafah junction, and he can't secure it without reenforcement. In fact, he's fighting desperately to save his brigade." Gorodish's dour look at them says the rest. Rafah junction in enemy hands at nightfall means the Seventh Brigade will be cut off without fuel and bullets, helpless prey for Egyptian armor forces, some close by.

"Well, I go back then," says Ehud. "The Pattons are faster, it's that simple." He glances at the sun. "It's only five miles. We can go and return, and still attack Jeradi before dark."

"Not if the junction is too messy," says Kishote. "I say I go through frontally with the Centurions as soon as I get there. M Brigade should be arriving about then, so —"

Tal's mechanized M Brigade has been making a wide swing southward so as to reach Jeradi for a surprise flank attack over the dunes.

"No, that's another change," says Gorodish. "M Brigade is bogged down out in the dunes low on fuel, and may not reach Jeradi today."

A silence. Kishote raps the map with a knuckle. "Gorodish, I can get through the Jeradi just with my Centurion crews. You know how they've performed. I can reach El Arish this afternoon."

Gorodish stares at him, the round sandy face a tough mask. "Yossi, you'll proceed to the Jeradi Pass," he says, "and there you'll make a judgment. It's your responsibility. No all-out battle, do you hear? It's not necessary anymore and I forbid it. We don't have to take more losses such as we've had so far today. Not with total air superiority! If it looks heavy, wait for us. Understood?"

"Understood."

The desert shakes and reverberates with the start-up of the Seventh Brigade's hundreds of machines. Exhaust fumes in clouds once more stain the clear Sinai air.

"You heard him, Kishote," says Ehud, as they part with a hug. "No battle. If the pass is hot, *wait for me*. I'll be back."

Kishote can feel the warm seepage of Ehud's blood on the bandaged face. His eyes sting. "All right, Ehud. We'll go to El Arish together. Flags up!"

The two columns of tanks rumble out of Sheikh Zweid: Ehud backtracking to Rafah junction, Don Kishote advancing to the Jeradi Pass.

38

Death of a Lion

"Zev? Sorry to wake you. Zarkhan! [Phosphorus!]" The ambassador speaks the code word for war in a sleepy croak.

"Zarkhan? Oo-ah!"

"How soon can you be at the embassy?"

"Half an hour." Empty streets this time of night.

Rising groggily on an elbow as he dons a fresh uniform, Nakhama inquires, "So? Something important?"

"This is it."

"War? Oh, God, what's happening over there?"

"I'll phone you when I know."

He speeds along River Road and whirls into dark deserted Wisconsin Avenue, where a long string of red lights is turning green. A siren wails behind him, and a revolving red light flashes in his mirror. On seeing Barak's uniform, the youthful policeman takes a polite tone. "You were doing seventy, sir, on River Road."

"I'm sorry. Diplomatic emergency."

The policeman looks for the DPL on the license plate. "Right. Just let me see your license for my records . . . Israeli, hey? I hear they're giving you a hard time over there, General."

"Well, we're still hoping for peace."

"No way! Just go all out and kick the shit out of them, sir. Like we ought to be doing in Vietnam right now. Good luck."

"Thanks, officer."

The ambassador and a few of his senior staff are gathered around a shortwave set. Genteel BBC voice: "*. . . Radio Damascus reports a quote massive Egyptian victory over the Zionist aggressor in the still raging air battle, with forty-seven Jewish planes already shot down. Unquote. As yet no Egyptian losses are reported. King Hussein has declared that Jordan quote stands shoulder to shoulder with its heroic Egyptian ally, and hails the great air victory over the Zionist aggressor that is still developing . . . unquote. . . .*"

The ambassador gives Barak an exhausted smile. "Arab bobbeh-mysehs, Zev. We've caught them on the ground, destroyed over a hundred planes so far, and we're missing two. Hard figures. And it's still going on."

Barak gasps, "Tremendous, Abe. Staggering. Thank God!"

"Yes, but now the trouble starts. Call Gideon in New York on my private line. The switchboard girl isn't here yet." As Barak dials, the ambassador groans, downing two pills, "Of all days, I have root-canal work scheduled today. Well, now I can postpone it. A silver lining."

Gideon Rafael, the ambassador to the UN, wants from Barak the latest word on the lineup of the opposed forces at the outbreak. "Though we probably won't be getting down to specifics this morning," he says. "As long as the Egyptians claim they're winning, the Soviet Union will of course just insist there's no reason for the Security Council to meet."

"Rafael, what will our position be if there is a meeting?"

"Simple enough. The Egyptians have been sending high reconnaissance flights across our borders, that's indisputable. They've been repeatedly warned that we can't tolerate it, but they claim they're at war with us, so what they're doing is kosher. Yet how are we to be sure that the flights are not heavy bombers heading for Tel Aviv? When the pips showed up again on the radar screens this morning, our air force finally was ordered to take all necessary defensive measures."

Pause. No comment from Barak.

"Clear, Zev?"

"Clear."

"A good position?"

"Fine, if we win."

"Well said." Rafael wryly laughs. "There will be a big to-do about who fired the first shot. That's what we've been hearing from the French, the British, and of course President Johnson — *'Whatever you do, don't fire the first shot!'*"

"It won't matter in the least," Barak says briskly. "The overflights aside, Nasser of course fired the first shot when he closed the straits. Blockade's an act of war under international law. I'll get on that update, and I'll send a runner with it on the first shuttle."

"Excellent. He'll be met at La Guardia."

Rubbing his eyes, the ambassador says when Barak hangs up, "The Soviets are the worry, Zev." Abe Harman is always alert to the bad side of good news. "How can they let the Arabs lose a war that they pushed them into? If it keeps on the way it's started, it'll be root-canal work for the Russians."

"Well, maybe they need it. Anyhow, Abe, en brera."

"I'll probably be called to the White House," the ambassador laments. "With all this codeine in me, I'll be a golem, a zombie. I'm so happy, Zev, it's indescribable." He points at a picture on his desk of his son in uniform. "I just hope he'll be all right."

In his lamplit office, where the windows are black dark, Barak scrawls a battle order summary, checking a marked Southern Command map spread on the desk. As he sets it all down his exhilaration ebbs. Have Syria, Jordan, and Iraq jumped on Israel's back yet? What with the seven-hour time difference and the lag in battlefield reports it will be a while before the picture clears. But the dying and maiming have certainly already begun, with Tal's armor crunching into the deep Egyptian defense works and the huge array of Russian-made tanks and artillery in the north of Sinai.

Disturbing him yet more is what the ambassador has just said about Russia. This ultimate foe — mighty, glowering, unopposed — can brush aside the Jewish State like a fly, in its grab for the oil and the globe-controlling landmass of the Middle East. The Soviet Union has been trying for years to manipulate the Arabs so as to accomplish this, but now with Nasser running out of control the Kremlin has a full-fledged war on its hands.

Where can it end, once this dazzling flare of air force heroism has died down in slow bloody land fighting? The Americans are bogged in Vietnam, and anyhow are in no way committed to defend Israel. An inconclusive cease-fire like 1956 will throw Israel back to its strip of coast with many boys dead and nothing gained. On the other hand, another rout of Egypt may well force the Soviet Union to intervene, a prospect too black to contemplate — yet will not Russia have to act to save face?

"Why do we have to give it back, Abba? We won the war," the eleven-year-old Noah protested at the flag-lowering in Sharm el Sheikh. Now he is a naval officer in the Red Sea not far from Sharm el Sheikh, temporarily transferred there and fighting in a new war . . .

The ambassador's voice on the intercom: "Zev, Sam Pasternak is calling on the scrambler phone."

The embassy is abuzz now, happy Israelis rushing here and there with exultant looks, rapid chatter, and much laughter. Behind a double-locked door stencilled in red Hebrew letters NO ADMITTANCE, female coding officers are working under a fluorescent glare.

"Hello, Sam? Zev here. It's wonderful! Is it continuing?"

The scrambler telephone makes random loud noises and whistles, then clears. "— unbelievable. The war isn't over, Zev, and yet in a way it is. We'll win." Pasternak tells him the latest air strike figures. "The rest is bloody ground fighting, and even bloodier political fighting. That's why I'm calling. This time we can't lose in the UN a war we win in the field."

"What about Syria and Jordan?"

"So far, just artillery exchanges. Eshkol has sent word to Hussein through General Odd Bull that if he stays out we won't touch him. In Sinai the tank battle so far is vicious, but —" The telephone lapses into high-pitched, whining babble.

"Sam? Sam? Hello?"

After a few seconds the voice comes through again. "— Chris

Cunningham. Call him now. Wake him up. It's vital. Here's what to tell him. Are you writing?"

"I'm writing."

Barak scribbles Pasternak's disclosures and instructions. "All this, Zev, is direct from Eshkol and Dayan," Pasternak concludes.

"I'll do my best, Sam."

"That I know. I'm terrifically glad you're there to handle this."

"I'm not. I'd give an arm to be back home."

"You're more useful where you are. Give Chris my best." Over six thousand miles and through scrambling and unscrambling, Pasternak manages to sound arch. "And to that daughter, too, if she's there."

She is. It is Emily who answers the telephone, wide awake in this black morning hour. Barak dashes out, finds his car blocked by a television network van, and hails a passing cab.

No fancy negligee this time; a brown housecoat with a dull flower pattern. "Here's Zev, Father!"

In a maroon bathrobe that hangs in folds on his skeletal frame, Cunningham sits sunken in an armchair beside a crackling short-wave set. "Hello there. Our man in Cairo telephoned a while ago. Emily, let's have some coffee. Sit down, Zev."

"Thanks. I bring word from Sam Pasternak. To begin with, some facts."

"*Ach, zo?*" Cunningham coldly smiles, turning off the set. "The Arab radios have been putting out all the facts so far. If they're facts."

"They're nonsense. Chris, we've won the greatest air victory in history." Chris Cunningham straightens in his chair and seems to grow a foot, as Barak goes on. "In less than three hours, our air force has destroyed three hundred Egyptian planes on the ground! They never got into the air. Total successful surprise."

"Your losses?"

"Minimal. Three or four planes."

"And the other Arab air forces? Syria, Jordan, Iraq?"

"As of ten A.M. over there they hadn't stirred. Maybe the

Egyptian 'facts' are lulling them, but our present hard intelligence is that they're preparing to attack our air bases about noon today. At all events my government's intent is not to cross any border but Egypt's, unless the others move first."

Chris Cunningham nods and nods. He leans to Barak, his prominent eyes magnified by the thick lenses of his eyeglasses. "What does Sam want?"

"To get a message from Eshkol to your President this morning. *'Please urge King Hussein to stay out, and convey in return a pledge from Israel not to attack him. A pledge to the United States government, as well as to him.'* "

"That's a tough one."

"Sam knows that. My government has already signalled this to Hussein through General Bull, the UN man on the spot. This would be the U.S. signing on as a guarantor, because we make the commitment directly to you."

"I'll take it up the line. It's all I can do. What's the situation in Sinai?"

"Let me show you."

The two men drink coffee, standing at a broad map of the Middle East hung on a wall. "Our tanks ran into heavy fire all along here." Barak's finger traces Tal's hook around through the Gaza Strip to attack the Rafah junction from an unexpected direction. "We may be achieving overall strategic surprise. Our big thrust is up here, but we've staged an elaborate deception down south, and the Egyptians seem to have bit. That's where they've put their main forces."

He feels decidedly queer, spilling battlefield secrets of fateful sensitivity to Christian Cunningham. His connection with this enigmatic gentile does not extend back nearly a quarter of a century, as Pasternak's does, to clandestine cooperation against the Germans. But Sam's instructions are unequivocal: *"Total disclosure, Zev, to give Chris credibility with his government. Trust his judgment and discretion. We'll be forced to communicate often via back channels. Cunningham's our safest contact, and he's a friend."*

"Is the plan to drive to the Canal?"

"The plan is to destroy the Egyptian army in Sinai. Dayan

thinks it would be suicidal to go to the Canal, the Egyptians would fight to regain it for a hundred years."

"It's not a bad water barrier."

"Dayan's been known to change his mind."

"Well!" Cunningham clinks down his coffee cup. "I'd better get going. Do I work through you?"

"Those are Sam's instructions." Barak is tired enough to add, "I'm a sufficiently inconspicuous nobody."

"That makes two of us."

"Chris, what will the Russians do?"

"Ah. Rude awakening!" Cunningham's voice takes on a ring. "They figured they had a bloodless Middle East political victory in the bag. As long as the Arabs claim success and you keep winning and clamming up, you're in good shape. Even when the truth comes out the Russians can't turn on a dime. You have a couple of days, I estimate. But the Soviet howls, pressures, and threats will come, and they'll be very ugly."

"Will they intervene?"

"I don't know."

"Chris, Sam told me to emphasize again that Israel's war aim is a cease-fire, *with no proviso for return to previous lines.* That proviso last time cost us our victory."

"That aim is exactly what the Soviet Union will snarl and breathe fire to deny you."

"Any time you have to go back, Zev, I'm ready," says Emily, looking in, clad in a dark raincoat. "If you're interested, it's pouring."

"Right now. Thanks, Em."

The driveway gravel rattles as Emily takes off with a jackrabbit start. She glances at him in the wan watery dawn light. "You look beat. No sleep?"

"Not much. And you look like a woman in a movie."

"Oh? Which film?"

"Any one of those World War II romances, darling. Pretty lady, black raincoat, slouch hat, turned-up collar, rain —"

"Your mind's on war, all right."

"That's the truth."

"I suppose Nakhama and the girls won't be coming to see the horses."

"Was that on for today?"

"I'm afraid so. Your wife is hard to say no to."

Barak utters an amused, "Hmph! No fooling." Then after a moment: "I don't know why they shouldn't go. I'm not leaving or anything. Here I am and here I stay. Putting in longer hours to shuffle papers, that'll be my war."

"You wish you were over there."

"You can understand that."

She puts a wet hand on his. "Well, you once said I really had nothing to do with your coming here. Oh, my love, how that got me down!"

"I didn't realize —"

"No, no, now I'm glad you said it. I don't want any guilty part of this burden you carry."

Rare candor surfaces through his weariness as he kisses her rainy hand. "Ah, Queenie, Queenie, why does anybody do anything? A hundred vectors go into a decision. When I took on this duty I wasn't wholly unaware that you were here. Can we leave it at that? Anyway, those were my orders."

Her hand grips his, then goes back to the wheel. After driving in silence for a while, slowing as they encounter early traffic, she asks, "Are we through?"

"What?" He is genuinely startled. "Say that again."

"You know what I said. Already you're remote, and getting more so by the minute." Emily glances at him with wide glistening eyes. She looks entrancing in her careless rain gear. "And listen, sweetie, I'm not fishing for reassurance. You're not to complicate your mind with me any longer, that's all. I can disappear with the sunrise, like the ghosts on Bald Mountain, and bless you, thank you, and love you forever. You have to fight a war. Here or there, no difference. Count me out whenever you will."

Cunningham brain! Nakhama herself cannot read him better. He has never been sure why he so loves this eccentric schoolmistress, but that is part of it. "Okay, you're counted out."

"Oh, you brute!"

"Okay, you're back in."

"Oh, you kid! However, my dearest, I mean exactly what I just said."

"I know you do, Queenie."

"Zev, are you worried about your son?"

Barak shrugs, pursing his lips. "He's on patrol in the Red Sea, transferred there from Haifa to relieve command of a gunboat. I doubt the Egyptian craft down there will venture out. Still, we all worry about our sons and daughters. As our parents worried about us."

"This will sound icky," she says, "but I swear there's a glory about your country."

"My country's an unspeakable mess, believe me, Em. Look, avoid the Chain Bridge, the Key Bridge is better this early."

Outside the embassy, Twenty-second Street is now totally blocked with television vans and press cars. The rain has let up. A new large flag, bright blue and white, flaps over the reporters and technicians crowding the entrance. "Let me off here," says Barak at the corner of Florida, glancing up the hill, "or you'll get stuck."

Her kiss is swift and light. "I know you'll be snowed under, so forget about me for now. I'll be fine."

"Look, Em, my girls can ride your quieter horsies, but keep an eye on them."

"I will."

He has to shoulder through the media people — *tanim*, as he thinks of them, jackals — just doing their wretched job. In an Israeli general's uniform, failing any real news, he is somebody, so they come yapping at him. He shrugs away the microphones, ignores the shouted queries, and darts inside.

In sheaves of teleprinter strips and despatches, the air triumph appears the more stunning as details mount. A picture is forming of Tal's attack in the north: advances, setbacks, severe fighting. Barak knows exactly what it is like out there now, at Khan Yunis and Rafah — a mixed-up racket in the earphones, red tracers crisscrossing the sandy wastes, dust clouds, cannon blasts, shell explosions, failing communications, tanks on fire, guys cursing and yelling in agony, blind maneuvering to find the enemy and avoid shooting friends. He yearns with all his soul to be out in that hell.

"Ah, Zev. Good! The thing is," says the ambassador, holding a hand to the sore tooth, "we're getting overloaded here with paperwork. Can Nakhama come and help out?"

"I'll call her." *(So much for the Foxdale horsies!)*

She comes in short order, despite the protests of the disappointed girls, and goes to work handling queries and offers of help from Jewish organizations. They are flooding in so fast that the switchboard is becoming swamped. Barak sees little of her as he fields inquiries from congressmen, military attachés, Defense and State Department acquaintances; all wanting to know — however they phrase it — who is really winning, and what the score is.

He is also tracking the UN debate. The Russian reaction is coming with unforeseen speed and harshness: immediate total condemnation of Israel, a demand for its withdrawal at once to the previous lines, and *"reservation of right to take whatever action the situation calls for."* This is diplomatic jargon for the threat to intervene. "Looks like Moscow doesn't quite believe the Arabs," Barak remarks to the ambassador at one point.

"The Russians know them," says the ambassador.

All activity comes to a standstill at noon as the embassy personnel jam the TV room to watch a press conference at the State Department. Already India, France, and most of the others are backing the Soviet Union at the UN. A few Latin American countries are talking about a cease-fire in place with no withdrawal provisos. How come? United States instigation? If so, there is hope. Where *exactly* does President Johnson stand on withdrawal to previous lines? Any hint of a friendly view? Nakhama is beside Zev, taking his hand, as the good-looking young press secretary, McCloskey, comes to the microphone. The first lines of the statement he reads are innocuous pieties about the need for a return to peace and progress in the Middle East. He pauses, looks around at the tense throng in the press room, and gives the next sentence heavy vocal underlining.

"*Let it be clearly understood that in this conflict, the United States will be neutral — in thought, word, and deed.*"

Nakhama's hand tightens to a fist, her nails digging into Barak's palm. A dismayed murmur goes through the crowded room. Back to John Foster Dulles!

The sun is still high as Don Kishote stands on a breezy dune scanning the narrow entrance to the Jeradi Pass. Hours of daylight left to drive through or shoot his way through; he can certainly wait for Ehud yet a while.

His Centurions are strung out far to the east, out of sight around bends in the high dunes. The advance from Sheikh Zweid, on the serpentine road through sandy wastes along the railroad track, has been peculiarly quiet. Almost, the force might be out on a Negev exercise. What he is viewing now through binoculars, however, is a sight never beheld in the Negev: masses of Egyptian tanks stationed hull down along the slopes on both sides of the tarred road, out of sight except for the long guns bearing on the entrance. Higher on the slopes are traces of net-covered trenches, row on row. What else is up there under the tricky camouflage? By Soviet doctrine mortars, antitank guns, and machine gun emplacements, backed by heavy artillery; this may be a tougher nut to crack than Rafah junction!

On the other hand, while the enemy's will to resist was strong at Rafah, at Sheikh Zweid it was obviously disintegrating. The Egyptian armor division back at the junction, still making things hot for Raful, is probably the best enemy force in the north. Is this monstrous silent barrier up ahead in the Jeradi even manned? Defeated troops fleeing Sheikh Zweid down the coast road may well have brought the fear-stricken cry, "*The Jews are coming!*" That was just how the Egyptians collapsed during KADESH, after putting up a brave fight at first.

The responsibility is his. "*No heavy battle, go through only if it looks easy.*" Vexing orders, and also in his mind is the last word of Israel Tal: "*In war nothing goes according to plan, but always remember the objective!*" El Arish lies only ten miles on the far side of this pass.

He has already come twenty-five miles or more since the start of RED SHEET. There is no word yet from Ehud Elad that he is returning from Rafah junction. Yossi has in fact heard nothing from him or Gorodish on the command net for over an hour.

He summons the unit leaders to an orders group, mainly to sense their spirit. Like himself, he sees, they are strangely unwearied, fired up by battle, ready to follow him anywhere. Exalting feeling! *Decision:* GO, *all guns blazing.*

The mile-long column begins to move, the tanks tightly buttoned up, gunners in all vehicles standing to their weapons. On his half-track, posted midway in the column, Kishote stands beside the gunner, bracing himself on the gun mount to strain his eyes through the binoculars for signs of enemy activity. Ahead, yellow flashes and echoing deep thunder of his leading Centurions firing right and left as they drive through the entrance. And still no response! Kishote is prepared to halt and retreat if the foe begins to put up a fight, but the column is rolling on and on through the defile unchallenged. An ambush as in the Mitla Pass? A shocked paralyzed enemy? An empty shell of abandoned war machines, the soldiers all melted away into the desert for fear of the approaching Jews?

As his own half-track speeds past the Egyptian tanks, with the machine gun rattling away to one side and the other, Kishote searches for a trace of life, of movement, of watchful crews biding their time, in those rows of bulky Soviet tanks, weirdly close by. Nothing! Closed turrets, immobile guns, silent engines in these superb T-54s, with a few giant Stalins interspersed. Should he order the Centurions to blow them all up, deny them for good to the enemy? A satisfying harvest of destruction! But that will deny them to the armored corps as well. Israel can get hold of these eminently battle-worthy tanks only by capture. Again, again, again, *the objective is El Arish!* Other fortified Jeradi positions lie ahead that may be manned and ready to do battle. Kishote makes his decision. *Leave all this behind,* keep going at full speed and charge clear through the Jeradi Pass to El Arish, no matter what.

As his last machines are passing the entrance he hears sounds of battle from behind him. Report on his headphones; a rear half-track has been hit, and a Centurion is turning to cover it and rescue the wounded. No stopping now! Onward.

In the underground command center in Tel Aviv called the Pit, the planning for a counterattack against Jordan — which has now entered the war by sending tanks across the armistice line — is interrupted by an incredible report from General Tal's field headquarters. An advance unit of seventeen Centurions led by Lieutenant Colonel Nitzan has reached El Arish! It has begun digging in, and is waiting for the rest of Gorodish's brigade to catch up. The Ramatkhal is delighted but troubled. How can that be? Is the Jeradi Pass really secured? Isn't there still trouble as far back as Rafah? Tal seems stretched out all along the coast. The staff assures him that the Rafah situation has eased, Raful's paratroopers are in control, and Gorodish is now returning to the Jeradi Pass with the Pattons. Rabin wants to believe that Tal is doing miracles, but fears the division may be overextended. El Arish by four o'clock is unbelievable!

Later the news from Tal in fact turns grim. Gorodish has almost gotten himself killed trying to enter the Jeradi Pass. The Egyptians, fully recovered from the shock of the Centurions' charge, are blocking the entrance with massive firepower, and have wreaked havoc on Elad's Pattons. Only a remnant has made it through to join up with Nitzan's Centurions. The entire advance force at El Arish is now cut off, exposed to counterattack by large armored forces nearby. Gorodish is mounting a desperate night assault to reopen the pass, so the supply echelon can reach those beleaguered tanks in time.

In the dark of the morning Kishote hears the deep clank and engine roar of an approaching armor force. He puts the weary crews of the Centurions and Pattons, still pulled in a circle for night defense, on battle alert. By the light of a lurid fire billowing over El Arish, the remaining tanks of the Gorodish brigade come rolling into the circle, decimated, smoke-streaked, and shell-pocked. Yossi runs to Gorodish, sitting bowed in his half-track, and cries, "By God, I'm glad to see you."

"Well, here we are." Gorodish lifts a sandy bristly ravaged face. With an almost deranged glare, he grates, "You know about Ehud Elad?"

In a dead voice Kishote replies, "I know he's been killed. They told me when the Pattons got here, what's left of them."

"Yes, Ehud's gone. The armored infantry finished the job at Rafah, and they're mopping up the pass now. Supplies are on their way. So is Tal. Let's have a look at your defensive positions." They walk to Yossi's jeep, and he adds, "What is that big blaze in El Arish, Kishote? Your orders were *not* to engage!" As he speaks, shells like meteors streak across the stars, and come whistling overhead.

"There's your answer, sir. They started bombarding us, so we returned fire, and we must have hit an ammunition dump. Terrific explosions. Maybe the fire spread to a fuel depot, it's never stopped burning." They get into the jeep and Kishote whirs the starter.

Gorodish tensely asks, "How's your ammunition?"

"Shells low, so tanks are holding their cannon fire. Machine gun belts are rationed. We've been killing infiltrators, but there's been no general attack."

"You're lucky. Let's hope the support echelon gets here soon."

It is bitter cold. The jeep drives past tankists littering the sand in their sleeping bags, while others scrape and hammer at tracks and engines. Some soldiers sit around little flickering fires. Yossi asks Gorodish what really happened to Ehud; for the Patton crews who came through were in shock and incoherent, and he was too busy preparing the night defenses to find out much. Gorodish still does not know the whole story, but he tells what he knows.

On encountering fierce fire at Jeradi he sent Ehud on an end run, he says, to hit the flank of the entrance over the dunes, while with another force he would try to storm the position head-on. The dunes were very steep and soft. The Pattons bogged down. The enemy poured fire on them, and Ehud Elad found himself in a killing ground. As always he forged ahead of the others into the barrage, standing up in his turret. So he perished, one moment calling orders to his driver and the battalion, the next falling into the tank, spouting blood and dead. Eighteen of his Pattons ran out of fuel, and lie abandoned in the dunes. His deputy collected their crews and with some surviving tanks pushed on through the pass.

"So after that I went in with a frontal attack of every tank I had left," Gorodish says, "which maybe I should have ordered to start with. Anyway, we broke through in force. The armored infantry came in behind us, and they're still doing hand-to-hand fighting, but the pass is open. The supply echelon has its work cut out, though, to get here. The road is jammed with wrecks all the way back to Rafah. There's a big traffic jam outside Sheikh Zweid, a lot of wounded, and —"

"I'm responsible for Ehud's death." Kishote breaks in. "I and I alone. I'll remember that as long as I live."

"Stop this jeep."

Yossi obeys. Gorodish stares at him. "Explain yourself."

In a few words, Yossi tells him about his unresisted passage through the entrance. "I made a judgment as wrong as a judgment could be. Those Egyptians were just momentarily frightened by the sight of us. They did begin to fire at the tail end of my column, and hit a half-track and a tank. By then we were through, so I kept going."

"You did the right thing."

"No, no. How can you say that? I should have destroyed those tanks while I had the chance. Blasted them to bits."

"Well, then, why didn't you?"

"I thought they were abandoned and we'd capture them. Also I wanted to get to El Arish, and I wanted to get here first."

Gorodish sits silent for long moments. More shell streaks whine across the sky. "Yossi, your advance to El Arish became the spearhead of the campaign. It made the difference, justified all the deaths and wounds, it's a sensational success. It'll be remembered, but Tallik and I will get the credit. As for Ehud, he died because we're at war. . . . Let's eat something."

General Tal arrives at dawn with his command group. Standing up on his command armored vehicle in a brilliant sunrise, he talks to the senior officers of the Seventh Brigade, and his voice goes hoarse and cracked when he speaks of the dead and the wounded. "The people of Israel are back home on their holy soil, never to be driven out again, because these heroes, your friends, my soldiers, have been willing to bleed and die like the Maccabees, like the troops of David and Joshua. Now they are immortal. We have broken the enemy here in the north. To the south our soldiers are starting to crush the strongpoints of the foe. Our fighter pilots have destroyed the enemy air forces. We won't have another day like yesterday. We have been through the worst and have won. I salute you, armor men. On to a total victory!"

After a scene of frantic replenishment, the remaining Pattons push on to capture the airfield. As Kishote watches them roll by he wonders at the stamina of these crews, on the go after more than twenty-four hours of combat and of travel back and forth between Rafah and Jeradi in their choking bumping bone-wearying deafening steel boxes, with no rest except in snatched moments.

War games are no true test of soldiers, he thinks. The game-planners have to be considerate of their physical limits, or the press and the politicians will rail at the inhuman harshness of the army. But war is no respecter of limits, it is by definition harsh and inhuman, and there is no preparing for it. He is in a slump of mood from the shock of Ehud's death, the exaltation of his charge to El Arish all quenched. He feels a hard grip on his elbow. General Tal leads him aside to his command lorry, where they drink hot coffee in mugs. "Gorodish says you feel guilty about Ehud."

"I do."

"Kishote, I've given some terrible orders in the past twenty-four hours, made close decisions, some of them appalling mistakes, as I now realize. If you can't handle such things and live with what happens you should be a civilian. No more of that, do you understand?"

"I understand, General."

"Now then. While Gorodish captures El Arish and then heads south to exploit the breakthrough, you're to prepare to race on westward as far as the Canal."

"The *Canal*, sir?"

"You heard me. We can't be sure the UN won't clamp on a cease-fire tomorrow or even today. We have to do as much damage and gain as much ground as we can in a big hurry. It's against government policy — at the moment — to reach the Canal. That may change. Some higher-ups think it might panic the UN into compelling an immediate cease-fire. But other higher-ups think it's not so terrible for us to get to the Canal. The shock can also get the Egyptians to collapse and quit, with no UN nonsense about a return to previous lines. So you should be ready to go for the Canal, after which you may be pulled back, or you may not."

Kishote's spirits are reviving. "B'seder, sir. Now suppose I actually reach it by mistake? Stupid mistakes are my specialty."

"Well, there's a thought, your reputation goes before you. So, flags up!" Tal slaps his shoulder. "As for your charge through the Jeradi, you remembered the objective. You reached it. Whatever you did to get here, that was no mistake. Never think otherwise. Ehud Elad was a lion. He's gone, and we still have to win his war."

But Don Kishote does not get far toward the Canal that morning when, standing erect in his turret, he is struck down.

39

Nakhama and Emily

Around a table map of Jerusalem in the Pit, the Ramatkhal, his General Staff, and the senior officers of Central Command gather long after midnight to discuss a momentous new challenge. The recapture of the Old City is suddenly a political possibility! For King Hussein has entered the war, despite Israel's pledge not to move against him if he stays out. Nineteen years ago, Yitzhak Rabin watched the surrender of the Jewish Quarter from a monastery roof, in Mickey Marcus's entourage. Then he commanded a Palmakh brigade. Now he commands the entire Israel Defense Force. If he is to act on this possibility, the time frame is an eyeblink; perhaps a day or two, perhaps only hours, before the inevitable yank on the cease-fire leash, now that the Arabs are perceived to be losing.

An aide approaches through the thick stale smoke. "The Prime Minister is here, General."

"Eshkol, here in the Pit?"

"In your office above, sir. He says he'll come down if it's convenient."

"I'll go up, get a breath of air." To the others he says, "The minimum objective, in short, is to seize the eastern heights, from Mount Scopus to Augusta Victoria. Then when the cease-fire does come, we'll at least dominate the Old City. Continue your work, I'll be back soon."

Wearing a dark beret and an army uniform that bulges with his fat figure, Eshkol is pacing in Rabin's office when the Ramatkhal comes in. "Good morning, Prime Minister."

"Ah, Yitzhak! I couldn't sleep, what with the bombardment and vehicle noise in Jerusalem. The sky there is all fire and smoke. So I just drove down here." Rabin opens a window to the night, letting in warm fresh sea air. "Nu, and the blackout?" Eshkol exclaims.

"No problem, Prime Minister. The Arabs won't be sending any airplanes over Tel Aviv."

"True, true, thank God! The air victory is a miracle, a marvel. It will live forever. What's going on now, Yitzhak? Will we recapture the Old City?"

"The generals want to go, but Dayan disapproves."

"So? And what's happening elsewhere?"

At a huge wall map of Sinai, Rabin reviews Tal's exploits in the north and describes Sharon's night attack at Abu Agheila, the major strongpoint of central Sinai, which is still in progress. Eshkol listens with a shrewd look in pouched sunken eyes, as Rabin tells of helicopters landing paratroops behind the Abu Agheila fortress, and the very risky complex assault by tanks and infantry. He then describes the heavy fighting around Jerusalem. "That's the biggest surprise of the war, Prime Minister. We thought Hussein wouldn't move, or at most do token harassment, like the Syrians so far. But the Jordanians are actually outfighting the Egyptians, and we're taking bad losses there."

"Are you saying we can't capture the Old City? That it would be too costly?"

"I didn't say that." Rabin automatically lights a cigarette, though one burns in a tray. "Prime Minister, if I can be frank . . ." Eshkol slowly nods his large head. "Minister of Defense Dayan has given me three don'ts, for my conduct of the war. Don't go to the Canal. Don't capture the Golan Heights. And don't take the Old City. The soul of prudence, he's become."

"Understandable, Yitzhak. Ultimate responsibility is sobering."

"Ultimate responsibility is yours, Prime Minister."

Eshkol makes a wry face. "Is it? I can summon a war cabinet meeting today to overrule those three Dayan don'ts. Would they?"

Rabin turns up his hands, drags deeply on the cigarette, and says, "He's hounding me to get to Sharm el Sheikh before a cease-fire. He calls it the prime objective of the war."

"That I find hard to understand." Eshkol strokes his chin, as though at a nonexistent rabbinic beard. "In Jerusalem we have the kind of chance that comes once in a thousand years! The Jews can return to the City of David, to Zion! Nasser has given us the chance, and Hussein by a miracle has gone along with him. If we fail to take this gift of history" — he smiles, and his tone becomes ironic — "that is, of our old Jewish God, nothing like it may ever happen again. By comparison, what is Sharm el Sheikh?"

A red telephone rings. "Yes? . . . Yes, I see . . . *What?* . . . Well, the Prime Minister, as it happens, is right here in my office. . . . Excellent, hurry." Rabin's phlegmatic countenance shows very rare excitement as he hangs up. "Sir, Sam Pasternak is coming here with a big intelligence break. He calls it the political turn of the war."

Striding up Massachusetts Avenue, Zev Barak spots Emily's red Pontiac parked under a lamppost. Her window is open. "Hi, Em. Where is he?"

She points. "Up there as agreed, waiting."

The June night is warm and starlit, and the benches in Dupont Circle are mostly occupied by crumpled drunks and entwined lovers. In his usual gray suit and homburg, Cunningham sits erect on a bench near some young guitar players lounging on the grass.

"Ah, there you are, Zev. What's this urgent word from Sam, now?"

Barak hands him an envelope. "I had a hard time tracking you to La Rive Gauche."

"My birthday," says the CIA man, opening the envelope. "Emily was treating me."

"Remember, Chris, this material was teleprinted in code. It's a hurried rough translation from the Arabic." Barak speaks softly, almost in an undertone, as Cunningham eagerly scans the typed sheets by the streetlight. "Also, the intercept was garbled by static. Still, you'll get the picture. Pasternak vouches for the voices of Nasser and Hussein. He says that they're both bound to confirm this in their morning communiqués, and your government should be forewarned, hence this urgent message. A copy of the tape is being flown here."

Cunningham finishes his quick reading, raps the papers with a knuckle, and jumps up. "Formidable! This is as hot a break as the Khrushchev secret speech was. Once again I salute Israeli intelligence. You tell Sam that. I'd better send Emily back to her school. Where will you be later, Zev?"

"At the embassy until midnight, then at home. Call me anytime, sir."

"I will, if it's necessary."

They walk together to the Pontiac. "Thanks for the birthday dinner, Em," says her father. "Sorry to cut short the celebration." He hails a cab and leaps in, saying, "White House. Southern entrance."

"Well, that was sudden," says Emily. "You must be busy as hell, dear. Can you hint how the war's going?"

"So-so. I may have to go to New York tomorrow, Emily, and I'm not sure when I'll be back, but —"

"You may? Hot diggety dog. By the merest coincidence, Hester is having a show at some Madison Avenue gallery. I've been thinking of tootling up there myself." She smiles beautifully at him.

Barak hesitates. For weeks he has had no time for Emily, and she has been sweetly understanding about it. The farthest thing from his mind right now is a romantic rendezvous in New York. "I see. Going up for the day, are you?"

"Well, puss, that all depends, you know . . . Anyway, I'll be staying at the St. Moritz, the park view is sublime."

On an impulse of rueful affection for her, he says, "Okay, then suppose I call you tomorrow about this, Queenie, when I know more?"

"Oh, scrumptious — no, wait, wait," she says. "Tomorrow is Tuesday, isn't it? Nakhama is bringing your girls to pet my horsies. No riding, the insurance doesn't allow it — but I can make a two o'clock shuttle, I guess. Now see here, Old Wolf, if you don't come to New York, or if you're busy there, never mind me, I'll see Hester's show anyway. Got me?"

"Got you."

"Lovely. Bye, sweetie. Call me tomorrow." She drives off.

He has to make his way through TV trucks, cameramen, and people lined up all the way into the embassy. In the crowded noisy foyer a tall man with iron-gray hair puts a hand on his arm. "Zev Barak!"

"Why, hello! Professor Quint, isn't it?"

"Alan Quint, yes, and look, Barak, some of us at Harvard have formed an ad hoc committee, Scholars for Middle East Peace with Justice. What can we do to help the war effort? We're not without influence, in our dry-as-dust way." He utters a dry-as-dust chuckle. Years ago, Barak recalls, this academic came to Israel to study the effect on kibbutznik soldiers of their communal upbringing. Then he did not identify himself as Jewish at all.

"That's very nice. I didn't know Harvard had many Jewish professors."

"To be frank, neither did I. Coming out of the woodwork, one might say. I'm the only one who's been to Israel, so I'm the chairman."

Barak takes Professor Quint to the cultural attaché, one Gamaliel. "Harvard? That's wonderful!" exclaims Gamaliel, a small shirt-sleeved Haifa man who needs a shave, and by his complexion a month in the sun. "Say, Professor, can you suggest a Middle East scholar for the *Today* show tomorrow morning? The Egyptians have named a Yale guy, Peterson."

"Of course. Kermit Peterson. A sound scholar," says Quint. "Total Arabist, taught in Beirut for years, Syrian wife." He ponders, and snaps his fingers. "Templeton is your man. Brooks Templeton."

"Templeton?" Gamaliel wrinkles his very pale nose. "You say Templeton?"

"His grandfather was a Polish rabbi."

"Ah."

"Yes. He told me that this morning in the commons over coffee. I hadn't the faintest idea Brooks was even Jewish. He'll wipe the studio floor with Peterson. The name is J. Brooks Templeton, professor of history, brilliant."

"Perfect, a big help." Gamaliel grins at Barak. "Thanks, Zev."

"Thank Harvard."

Barak teletypes to Pasternak, OUR FRIEND DELIGHTED WITH BIRTHDAY PRESENT. He finds Abe Harman in his office sorting through heaps of paper, in great spirits despite a distended jaw. The ambassador brandishes a fistful of yellow telegrams. "Offers of support! Zev, do you realize what money is pouring into the UJA? Millions, millions! A lot from Christians!" He taps a small brown satchel on his desk. "Look at this! A little gray-headed lady came up to me after my speech." He puts on a Yiddish accent. " *'My son is Rabbi Marcus Wax of Philadelphia, he's a good boy, I made him bring me here. There's all the money I have in the world, thirty-seven thousand dollars. It's for Israel.'* Well, Zev, what could I do? I took it, and took her address. We'll return it to her."

Barak closes the office door, hands him a copy of the Pasternak material, and reports his meeting with his unnamed CIA contact. The ambassador glances through the sheets, sits back in astonishment, then nods and nods as he reads them through, with the squint that shows he is thinking hard. "Amazing!" he exclaims. "Aside from being a gigantic political mistake, it seems so utterly naive! Imagine, accusing the Americans and the British of doing our air strike!"

"Well, Abe, at least they intend to claim that carrier planes took part in the attack. That's not quite clear from the transcript. Some of it was unintelligible."

"But good God, Zev, how ill-informed can they be? Look at this —" He points to a line. *"Nasser speaks: Do the British have aircraft carriers?"* The ambassador's face falls into familiar worry lines. "This is just too preposterous. D'you suppose the Russians have put Nasser up to this? Just as a pretext for them to jump into the war? *There's* a real evil possibility. What do you think?"

Barak knows better. Cunningham has told him, for Pasternak's information only, that the White House hot line teleprinter in the Russian alphabet came alive that day, the first time since it was installed, to signal that the Soviet Union did not intend to intervene in the war.

"Abe, I think Nasser may really believe that American or British carrier planes did it, or helped. The Egyptian air force turn-around time is about two hours, we know that. Our squadrons have it down to ten minutes. Maybe he can't conceive that we could actually have flown hundreds of sorties ourselves in one morning. Or that we'd leave our cities entirely without air defense. We had only a dozen or so planes left inside Israel, you know, during the strike."

The ambassador sits with a fist under his chin, Rodin's *Thinker* with a swollen jaw. "No. It has to be a cover-up for the world press and his people. That's all. Now, listen, Zev, Gideon Rafael will want to have air force facts and figures on hand at the UN, and an update on the ground fighting. There may be wild fireworks in New York. Better get a little sleep and make an early start." He taps the document with thick fingers. "Hussein doesn't sound too happy about going along with this accusation."

"Well, half his answers are muffled by static. Maybe the reception was better from Cairo. The Jordanians are certainly in this up to their necks. There's very bloody fighting around Jerusalem."

R-ring, r-r-ing.

"Am I calling too early, Emily? Did I wake you?" Nakhama sounds blithe and peppy.

"No, no, I've been up forever." Emily does her best not to groan the words. Her bedside clock in the Growlery shows 7 A.M.

"Fine. You are expecting us? My girls have been dancing around the flat since five o'clock."

"Of course." Emily went to bed hoping for rain, but sunlight is shafting through the curtains, naturally. "Aren't you terribly tied up with the war and all? I can send a stable hand with a car to bring out your girls, you know. You'll have trouble finding the place. It would really be much simpler. Let me do that —"

"No, no, I'll find it. We'll be there at nine o'clock."

"I'll bet you will," mutters Emily, hanging up. "On the stroke. How can I love an Israeli?"

In the kitchen she snaps on the small table TV as she starts the coffee. There is the Secretary of State, his moon face contorted with anger, proclaiming in a choked voice to a crowded press room, "*. . . utterly and maliciously false. Our Sixth Fleet is far outside flight range of the area, as the Arab leaders well know. The United States government denounces in the strongest terms these deliberate transparent lies, which can only serve to delay the untiring efforts of our delegation at the United Nations to obtain an immediate cease-fire . . .*" Even talking about Ho Chi Minh, Dean Rusk has never sounded this furious.

Over vague war pictures — tanks rolling, planes flying, artillery firing — the newscaster announces that many Arab countries are breaking relations with America and England because of their part in the air strike. He quotes Arab claims of vast successes, and notes that the Israeli army is not disclosing much. Nasser's accusations strike Emily as a sign that he is in trouble, and that is heartening. The prospect of seeing Nakhama is not.

At five minutes of nine she stands under the stone archway, dressed in white shirtwaist, plaid skirt, and clunky shoes, her hair in a bun, horn-rim glasses on her nose, no makeup, no jewelry; a dull sexless schoolmistress to the life, nerves jangling from far too much coffee, resolved to make this a mighty brisk visit. At nine o'clock Zev's car rounds the turn, crosses the bridge over the creek, and comes up the tree-lined hill to the archway. Nakhama waves and the girls yell gaily through the open windows.

"Hi. Leave the car here," says Emily. "We'll walk down to the stable."

"What a nice little house," Nakhama says, gesturing at the Growlery. "You live here?"

"Well, off and on. I spend a lot of time at home with my father."

As they descend the gravel path Galia, whose wrist is still taped, walks with dignity while Ruti goes frisking ahead. Emily now realizes she forgot to warn old Connors, the year-round stable hand, to make short work of these visitors. Unluckily, when Connors hears Nakhama's accent he pegs the daughters as diplomats' girls, potential students, and fawns on them. They pet all ten horses, and smooth all their noses, and learn all their names, and feed them all sugar. When Ruti asks whether they may ride, he says, "Why not? That's the right spirit, girls," and begins dragging two saddles from the wall hooks.

"Connors, the insurance —"

"No problem, Miss Cunningham, I'll just walk them around the paddock for a while on Brown Beauty and Frankie." The girls jump with joy. They mount the horses, and Connors leads them outside into a grassy fenced area.

"What a nice man," says Nakhama. "They'll be fine. Maybe meantime I can see that pretty little cottage of yours." She drops her voice. "I could use your bathroom."

With this, there is no arguing. But of all things, Emily has not planned on admitting Nakhama into the Growlery. While they climb the path and Nakhama praises the landscaping, Emily does a mental search of the premises for traces of Old Wolf. No, nothing. A couple of books he has loaned her would be identifiable only if dusted for fingerprints. The pullover sweater he once left behind he has since retrieved. Nothing else, all clear . . . then she remembers the pistachio nuts. There they sit — she can see them — a deep red lacquer dishful on the low table in front of the living room couch.

Well, so what, she thinks irritably. Is Zev Barak the only person in the goddamned world who eats pistachio nuts? Emily has acquired a taste for them herself. They bring tangy memories and they're fun to crack. Nothing incriminating about a few goddamned pistachios! Yet as they approach the Growlery the lacquer dish is growing in Emily Cunningham's mind to the size of the Rose Bowl, and the nuts to a capacity crowd. A sudden saving thought: she brought that dish into the kitchen last night to snack at the TV. Or did she?

"Maybe you'd like to come up and see the school, it's rather interesting." She grasps Nakhama's elbow. The path here branches uphill to the main building.

"Later, maybe," says Nakhama, drawing Emily along toward the Growlery with resolute Israeli strides. So they go in, and there on the low living room table sits the Rose Bowl. Nakhama exclaims at the charm of the place, staring up at the wagon-wheel chandelier. "There's nothing like that in Israel," she says. "That's so nice."

"Yes, isn't it! An Early American sort of thing. The bathroom is through here." Simplicity itself to whisk that dish out of sight, once Nakhama is past it.

"Thanks. So, you like pistachio nuts, too," says Nakhama, and she goes into the bedroom. Emily drops on the couch contemplating the red dish, and thinks no wonder Israel wins wars. The flush of the toilet is the sound of the bell that tolls for thee. Nakhama is all smiles as she sits down beside her. "Look, it's all right," she says.

"What's all right?"

Nakhama waves at the pistachios. Emily returns an innocent uncomprehending look. "You and Zev," says Nakhama.

"I really can't understand you. Will you have some coffee? Or a cold drink?" Maintaining the little-girl face is hard under Nakhama's clever friendly brown eyes.

"Say, a Pepsi would be very nice, thank you. Diet, if you have it. I'm busting out of all my dresses. Those embassy dinners!"

Emily brings the drink with ice, numb and waiting for Nakhama's next move, which is to take a sip and give a grateful nod. "I'll tell you, Emily, life in Israel isn't easy. For army officers it's even harder. Zev must have written you about that."

"Well, yes, he has." *(If this is just about the letters, what a relief!)*

"Yes. The pay is so low, yet they have to keep up a standard of living. They're away from home so much. There's always the wars or the danger of war. Always something going on. Always the strain. So, it's only human nature that they're not all model husbands, exactly. Israel's a very small place. Everybody knows these things. Everybody knows who's doing what. I'm not saying there aren't exceptions, of course there are. Zev is one, people don't talk about him." She smiles brightly at Emily, coming to a full stop.

(My turn to say something!) "I'm not surprised, he's decidedly unusual, your husband," Emily blurts into the pause. "Of course, you know him so much better than I do, we're just what Americans call pen pals, our correspondence somehow got started, and we've kept it up, and it's been lovely. He's very well read and witty and of

course I'm fascinated by what he writes about Israel. My father corresponds with him, too, though that's about serious matters." Once started Emily babbles until she breaks off to breathe.

"Pen pals. That's a nice expression. Still, I imagine you know Zev pretty well." Nakhama looks at the pistachio nuts, and looks at Emily. "And as I say — this is really why I wanted to talk to you, why I came out here with the girls — it's all right. When you had dinner at our house you seemed not very comfortable, and there's no reason. You've given Zev something nice. I've seen all along how he enjoys your letters, and, well, whatever else, it's all right."

To this Emily has to respond directly and fast. "Nakhama, years ago Zev wrote me about pistachio nuts. He calls them his secret vice, so —"

"That's true enough —"

"So after a while I tried them and liked them, and now I eat them. *Zev has never been here,* and those nuts are for me and me only. Okay?"

"Okay. You're lucky you stay so nice and thin, then."

"I guess I don't eat them the way he does." Emily has no idea whether Nakhama is buying her response or not. The woman's good humor is unfathomable.

"I'll bet you don't. Well, listen Emily, don't let me talk you into having a love affair with my husband!" Nakhama laughs. "By no means. If you're just pen pals, that's fine, that's better of course. I'm very old-fashioned. So is Zev, you know. But he is an army officer, and some of the other army guys are regular no-goodniks. Too many of them."

"Nakhama, I'll say this. If I were you, and even suspected Zev was playing around with another woman, I'd want to scratch her eyes out."

Nakhama makes a peculiar face. Her mouth twists sideways, and all at once she looks shockingly coarse, sad, and cynical. It is only for a moment, then her pleasant geniality returns. "Oh, our backgrounds are so different, Emily! I'm a Sephardi, a Moroccan. On my father's side I have two grandmothers. Some men in the old country still have plural marriages. I once asked Grandma Leah whether she wasn't ever jealous of Grandma Dvora. She was an old lady by that time, of course. She laughed and said why should she be? Grandma Dvora did half the work, and kept Grandpa Avram from bothering her half the time. She said she was used to it."

A knock at the door. They can hear the girls giggling. Connors tips his leather cap as he brings them in. "You've got two horse-women there, ma'am," he says to Nakhama. "I hope you'll enroll them."

"We had a race and I beat," says Ruti.

"A walking race," sniffs Galia. "I made Frankie trot."

Emily walks with them to the car, waves them off, and returns to the Growlery dazed. Nakhama is either very simple, or much too much for her. The telephone is ringing as she walks in.

Barak says, "Hi, I'm calling from the airport. Did the girls get along with the horsies?"

"Beautifully. I even got along with Nakhama."

"There you are. And I knew you were dreading it. She's okay, Nakhama."

"You can say that again."

"Well, so, how do things stand? You'll be at the St. Moritz? . . . Queenie? Queenie, are you on the line?"

"I'm here."

"Will you be at the St. Moritz? There may be a break in the UN talk at some point." A pause. "Queenie?"

"I'll be at the St. Moritz."

Barak's diplomatic credentials and his uniform readily get him through the police lines outside the UN building where a mob stands in the drizzle; a huge quiet damp gathering at the towering slab by the river, showing support for Israel just by being there. The cop who checks his documents says, "Go on in and give 'em hell, General."

In the Security Council chamber, he goes to the packed gallery to sense the tenor of the scene. One speaker after another berates Israel and calls for instant condemnation, withdrawal, and severe punishment. Nobody is paying much attention. The council members sit at a grand curved table with patient faces leaning on their hands. In the earphones the usual comic incongruity; a bearded

Algerian at the table shouting in impassioned French, and a bland woman's voice translating, phrase by cool phrase: *". . . Zionist tools of capitalist imperialism are . . . once again . . . playing the filthy game of stool pigeon for colonialism . . . in defiance of world opinion. The only suitable . . . penalty is swift expulsion and a United Nations embargo on this . . . rogue entity which is . . . no real nation at all, Mr. Chairman, but a gang of . . . marauding murderers . . ."*

At a small side table Gideon Rafael sits with two aides, busily writing. After a while Barak sends a note to him, and they meet in an anteroom. Tense but ebullient, the short wavy-haired ambassador hugs him. "Zev, once again the Arabs have saved the day for us with this lunacy about the air strike! Who could have foreseen it? The Americans are boiling. Last night, so we hear anyway, they and the Soviets just about agreed on a cease-fire draft with some fuzzy language about withdrawal, absolutely terrible for us. The Canadians were going to propose it. But this morning we hear Costa Rica or Ecuador will bring up a much better version — obviously American-inspired — that the Russians don't like at all."

"I have the entire rundown on the air strike, Gideon, if you intend to respond to this carrier foolishness."

"Only if ordered, only if the Americans ask us to. Abba Eban's flying here tomorrow to reveal our victory in a major speech. Keep me up to date on the military picture, Zev, in case of a sudden snag. Things change here by the hour."

Outside the council chamber Barak runs into a Soviet military attaché. "So, Barak, up from Washington too, are you?" This is a blond flat-faced slant-eyed colonel about Barak's age, much smaller and leaner, with ten medals to Barak's two campaign ribbons. They sometimes exchange pleasantries at embassy parties, but the Russian does not look pleasant today.

"Tell me, Golovin, do your people believe this story about the carriers?"

"Who can doubt it? Your pilot who was shot down in Egypt confessed that American planes took part, didn't he? Also Jordanian radar tracked planes coming from the direction of the Sixth Fleet. All that is well known." Golovin has the Russian diplomat's knack of saying this while conveying that he does not mean a word of it.

"Well, then, the Americans have been caught red-handed, eh?"

"You fellows think you're riding high now. Wait!" Golovin walks away abruptly.

Emily's voice on the telephone is breathless and strained. "Of course I'm here. I said I would be. How long will we have?"

"Well, say two hours."

"That much? Come along. Are you all right? How is it going? You sound sad. Am I wrong?"

"I'm not sad about coming to the St. Moritz."

"Here I am."

As the taxicab inches across town in thick rain, Zev Barak is digesting the late word from home that the government may alter policy, and unleash the army to capture the Old City and the entire West Bank. It is a Central Command campaign he has often fought in his mind, and he has run detailed sand-table exercises at the senior staff college. Capturing the Wall for Jewry, returning to that sacred place at the head of a Jewish armed force, has seemed to him a glory he would be glad to die for. Now that glory will go to Uzi Narkiss and Motta Gur, good fighters, good leaders, while he is having a rendezvous with an American woman at the St. Moritz in New York.

What has happened? How has he missed out? Sitting in that crawling cab with the rain beating, horns honking all around, and the driver's radio blasting Beatles music, he faces facts of his life that have emerged over the years: that though he is a good and brainy fighting man, possibly among the best, he has faltered in the grinding lifelong marathon on the maslul, against iron-nerved, mostly sabra competitors; that he has been a shade too thoughtful, and perhaps too gentlemanly, to play the hard Zahal game to the hilt; that there is more than a trace of the transposed Viennese Jew left in him, after all, so that he has felt hemmed in by tiny Israel's boundaries, geographical and cultural, and has hankered too much despite himself for the great world outside. Maybe that broad outlook has made him a preeminent choice as emissary to the Americans. Who can say? At any rate the event is all, and here he is on his way to Queenie, while the Jews may be on the march to the Western Wall.

When she opens the door of her suite, shiny-eyed, charming in a tailored black suit with the gold wolf's-head pin, he reaches to take that sweet slender body in his arms. At least, here is some recompense! She deflects his embrace with a deft sweep of a hand. "Easy, Old Wolf," she murmurs, and leads him inside. There stands a mountainous woman in a flowing orange sack that reaches the floor. "Here's Hester."

"Well, General Barak!" The mountain brings forth a mouse voice, small and high. "I've heard so much about you!"

Hester is even bigger than he has pictured, but he does not remember Emily mentioning that she has a mustache.

40

Now or Never

Engine sounds wake Shayna: *rumble, snort, GRIND,* going by outside, one after another. Aryeh and her mother still sleep, but she pulls on a bathrobe and goes to the roof.

In the cool starry night, a line of busses stretches down the usually deserted hill, clear to the barbed-wire barriers. Far off an artillery battle flickers, flares, and crumps. On the street below, shadowy figures come swarming out of the busses, and by the glare of a star shell she can see webbed helmets. Troops! In this old Jerusalem neighborhood, even a single soldier is a rare sight. The usual passersby are bearded men in long black coats and black hats, and kerchiefed women with bundles or babies. Now here is an attack force piling up all along the steep slope of Bar-Ilan Street, and it can only be for a thrust across no-man's-land.

After nineteen years Shayna is used to a divided Jerusalem: the rough concrete walls and high wooden barriers that cut off streets, the observation posts on the roofs of houses, the black snouts of enemy machine guns poking through sandbags on rooftops, sometimes only a few yards away. She has stopped hoping that she will ever see her childhood home in the Old City again. But from the more and more cheery words of General Herzog, the radio's military analyst, it seems that a second Holocaust is not imminent, after all; that Israel may even win, and that she may yet walk those old streets once more. As she descends the stairs a burly blond soldier is coming up from below. "Ma'am, the Ezrakh says you have a phone. Can I call my mother?"

"By all means, come."

Shayna makes a sandwich for the soldier as he tries to put his call through. It takes a while. "Yes, sorry to disturb you, ma'am, but please call Mrs. Gutman to the phone, will you? She lives on the third floor. I'm her son Shmulik. Sure, please wake her —"

Staring at the big hairy master sergeant, loaded up with battle gear and machine gun, she exclaims, "Shmulik Gutman? You're Shmulik?"

He stares back. "Yes. So?"

Shayna turns to her mother, who is making coffee. "Mama, imagine! This is Shmulik from next door on Chabad Street! Shmulik, I'm Shayna, Shayna Matisdorf."

"Shmulik!" The old lady gives him an excited hug. This huge fellow was once the frail bad boy of their Old City neighborhood, his long blond earlocks and black gabardine concealing a nine-year-old rebellious scoffer.

"So!" Shmulik gestures at Aryeh, curled asleep under an old feather comforter. "It's your son, Shayna?"

"I'm not married. I'm taking care of him. His mother's in America. His father's down in Sinai."

"That's where our brigade was supposed to go, Sinai. Some of the guys are still sore. We were all fired up to parachute into El Arish, not ride for hours and hours in busses. Me, I'm happy, it's great what we're going to do — hello? Hello? *Mama?* Shmulik! I'm fine, no, not hurt, no problems, and guess what, I'm in Shayna Matisdorf's flat. . . . That's right, Shayna from next door long ago. . . . Sure her mother's alive, she's right here, they're both fine." After a hurried affectionate talk he hangs up and glances at his watch. "Mrs. Matisdorf, Mama sends you regards. Quarter to two. It's time. Thanks!"

He is munching the sandwich as he goes downstairs. Shayna carries down a jug of coffee and some cups, and soldiers gather around her. The busses are now pulled off into side streets, and all down the hill the soldiers are getting into a column of command cars and armored personnel carriers. Through the Ezrakh's open door she sees him swaying over a tall Talmud volume. Shmulik says, "Guess what Shayna? The Ezrakh remembered my father, and he just gave me a blessing! Listen, where I'm going I can use it!"

The night is getting chilly. Shayna returns to the flat for a coat, drinks the last of the coffee, and goes to the roof. There, to her astonishment, stands the Ezrakh, looking toward the dark walls of the Old City, humming a synagogue tune. Far off to the south, artillery flashes like summer lightning amid the stars.

A sudden blue-white glare! Volleys of nearby artillery half deafen her! She claps fingers to her ears. The searchlights blaze from the top of the Histadrut building, blindingly powerful. No-man's-land far below is bright as day, a broad desert of tangled barbed wire, heaped-up rubbish, and overgrown ruins. Flaming explosions are throwing up earth, rubble, and wire, and tanks are crawling out of the black night into the glare. From the Old City walls heavy guns begin firing. The Ezrakh, a frail wisp amid this turmoil and blaze, stands stroking his beard and singing. She uncovers her ears and can barely hear the words from a Hallel psalm:

> *This is the day the Lord has made.*
> *Let us rejoice and be glad in it . . .*

The face of the girl bending over him, which is the first thing Don Kishote blurrily sees upon opening his eyes, is not pretty at all: big nose, puffy cheeks, poor complexion, and disorderly lank black hair. "Doctor, I think this one may be conscious," she exclaims. Stumbling Hebrew, American accent.

A skinny man with very bushy hair, in a bloodstained white coat, comes beside her. "Are you conscious?" he inquires, taking Yossi's wrist to feel his pulse.

"I don't know." Yossi can hardly talk, his mouth and throat are dry as dust. "Are you a bad dream? It's one or the other."

"He's conscious," says the doctor, "and snotty. Good sign. Firm pulse. Give him some more coagulant, and don't let him out of bed."

"First please some water!"

"Right, give him all he wants. I'll look him over later. They're bringing in another load from Jerusalem." He hurries away.

"You must be a nurse. Where am I?" says Kishote. She puts the cup to his lip. The water tastes marvellously sweet as he gulps it. "I have a hell of a headache."

"You're in Tel Hashomer, Colonel. You were brought from the Sinai in a helicopter. You're entitled to a headache, feel your head."

His hand encounters a mass of bandages. "Where are my glasses?"

"They were smashed. Big pieces of glass were taken out of your forehead. It's a miracle you didn't lose an eye."

"Where's my uniform?"

"You won't need it for a while."

"There are spare glasses in my pack. I have a feeling that you're very beautiful, from the sound of your voice. I'd like to see you."

"You've got some nerve, Don Kishote."

"What? Do I know you?"

She is opening a small locker at the foot of his bed. "Colonel, my brother is a tank driver in your brigade."

"He is?" Yossi says groggily. "His name?"

"Hillel Horowitz."

"I know him. Big red mustache?"

"That's Hillel."

"Good boy. What's happening in the war? What time is it? What day is it? What's your name?"

"In your pack, you say? Ah, glasses." She hands them to him. "Here you are. My name is Dora and I'm not beautiful."

He has to slide the earpieces inside the bandages, a clumsy business, but he is glad to note that his arms and fingers are working normally. He blinks at her. "You look mighty pretty to me." And so she does. Her eyes are gentle and she has a nice shy smile.

The soldier in the next bed groans, turning over in his sleep; a master sergeant in uniform, with one arm in a sling. "That fellow was wounded in Jerusalem," says Dora Horowitz. "A terrible battle's gone on there all day, the Jerusalem hospitals are so full they're sending casualties here. It's Tuesday night, the sixth, about ten o'clock." She picks up a clipboard. "Do you remember anything about getting wounded?"

"Nothing. Now that you mention it I do remember a helicopter, but it's like a dream."

"You were hit outside El Arish. The Sinai campaign is a big victory. We're just now being told that the Arab air forces were all destroyed on the ground yesterday morning. So we're winning the war, but the Jerusalem fighting is very bad."

"What about the Syrians?"

"No news."

"I feel sleepy."

"Good. Sleep."

When he opens his eyes again, the master sergeant is spooning up soup from a bowl on a tray, looking very disgruntled. Kishote says, *"B'tay'avon* [Hearty appetite]."

"Oh, you woke up? How's your head, Colonel?"

"No complaints, it's on my shoulders. How's the soup?"

"Soup! To Azazel, this soup. My brigade is going for the Old City, where I was born, and here I am in this lousy bed eating soup."

"Which brigade?"

"Fifty-fifth paratroopers."

Kishote sits up. His head swims. The darkened ward of thirty-odd beds crowded together circles slowly around him to the dissonant music of much snoring. Through an open window he sees stars.

"Going for the Old City? Truly? Miracles! In Sinai we heard only rumors."

"My arm got smashed on Ammunition Hill, we ran into a rotten fight, I tell you. We were heading for Mount Scopus, maybe the guys are there by now." On Mount Scopus, overlooking the Old City from the northeast, an enclave of abandoned Hebrew University buildings has been held by the Jews since the 1949 truce. "Me, I was saved by a miracle. It was black dark, I tripped on a stone and rolled downhill, and a second later a grenade landed right where I tripped. So I took shrapnel in my arm and that's all. I should be scattered all over Ammunition Hill, just chunks of hamburger. You heard of the Ezrakh?"

"I know the Ezrakh."

"Well, the Ezrakh blessed me before we started our break-in. That's how come I tripped, I'm sure. I'm an atheist, but all the same it was a miracle."

The soldier describes the sudden transfer of the paratroopers to the Jerusalem front in busses, and their concentration in the old religious neighborhood of the Ezrakh. From there, he says, they attacked into no-man's-land at two in the dark morning hours. In his boyhood in the Old City his family were neighbors of the Ezrakh, so he asked for his blessing before the attack. A couple of kind women in the Ezrakh's building fed him sandwiches and coffee.

Kishote alertly breaks in. "An old lady and a young one, you say?"

"Well, my age. I knew her in the old neighborhood. Why?"

"Did she have a kid with her?"

"The kid was asleep. Not hers, she's taking care of him."

"Look here," says Don Kishote, roused by this chance of war, "what the devil are we doing in these beds when the Jewish army is going to liberate Old Jerusalem?" He gets up, steadying himself to the footlocker, and pulls out his uniform. "Let's go there."

"I've been lying here thinking just that," says Shmulik. "But will they let us out?"

"Who'll stop us? They're too busy with the new casualties. We'll get a ride with an army vehicle or find ourselves some wheels."

The dim-lit corridor is empty, but the bushy-haired doctor rounds a corner with Dora Horowitz and almost runs into them. She is carrying a sloshing bedpan. The doctor asks irritably, "Where do you two think you're going?"

"Just to the bathroom," says Kishote. "He's showing me the way."

"Why are you all dressed, suddenly?"

"I'm modest."

"Get back to bed. She'll take care of you."

"I'm too modest to use a bedpan," says Kishote. "I won't do anything."

"Listen, Lieutenant Colonel Nitzan, it was just a grazing wound, luckily for you, but you have a bad concussion. You were unconscious for hours, you may have a blood clot on the brain, or God knows what. You need a lot of tests. There's no time for them now. Do you want to keel over dead?"

"No, but I do want to use a toilet."

Another doctor appears. "Avi, we need you in Ward Four right away."

"Put them back to bed, Dora." The two doctors hurry down the corridor.

"Let's go," says Dora, taking Kishote's arm.

"Hamoodah," says Kishote, "you said you're not beautiful, but I'll never forget the look in your eyes when I first came to. You have tender beautiful eyes. This guy is a fifth-generation Yerushalmi. We're going to Old Jerusalem where his brigade is fighting."

She says with a severe frown at Shmulik, and an abrupt gesture that sends a splash from the bedpan, "Sergeant, are you crazy? What can you do with one arm? This Don Kishote wants to drop dead, that's his business, but —"

"I can do more with this one arm, nurse," Shmulik flexes it, "than some guys can do with two. Shoot a gun, throw grenades —"

"Before another doctor comes, Dora," says Kishote, "help us get out of here. Which way, hamoodah?"

Her eyes fill with tears. "I should never have come to this country. My brother Hillel talked me into it. I don't have the strength. I can't stand it. . . . The entrance is guarded, you'll never get out. Follow me." She leads them down a pitch-dark staircase, and they slip out into a paved lot where command cars, jeeps, and ambulances are parked here and there.

"Ah, transportation," says Kishote. "Let's find one with keys —"

"Pick your chariot, sir," says the sergeant. "I can start anything that rolls."

"God help you both," says the nurse.

Yossi blows her a kiss. "I love you, and I'll remember your eyes." She is sobbing and smiling.

Shayna's Canadian boyfriend shows up at her flat in the dark morning hours, in a white bloody coat. "I have no medical experience whatever," he says wearily, over the cup of coffee she presses on him. "You know that."

"Then what idiot assigned you to be an orderly at Hadassah?"

"You want the whole story? I must be back at Ein Kerem by five o'clock. I just had to be sure you're all right."

"Keep it low, that's all." She looks toward the sleeping Aryeh on the couch. Her mother is in the curtained-off double bed which they share. "I was terribly worried about you, Paul, you just disappeared."

"First of all, you sent me to the wrong agency. It's for Israeli volunteers."

"God, how stupid of me."

"That's okay. So I stood in a line where everyone was speaking Hebrew. I thought it was odd, no foreign volunteers. I figured I'm the one brave galutnik, good for me. When I got up to the desk, a girl tells me to go to a different agency, different building."

"I feel terrible about that."

"That? That was nothing. I went back to my car, I'd parked it in an empty lot, and someone had stolen the wheels."

"The wheels? Not the tires?"

"The wheels. This other building wasn't far, so —"

"But the *wheels!*"

"Yes. I walked there, and got on another line, everybody talking English. Lots of brave foreigners, after all. When I finally got to that desk, there was this irritable fat lady who asked for my passport. I said it was at the yeshiva, other side of town. 'Well, go get it,' she says. 'You have a car, don't you? Americans all have cars, not like us.' I tell her yes, I have a car, but it's sitting on its axles, somebody just stole the wheels. Well, Shayna, she blew up at me. 'That's nonsense,' she snaps. 'What a lame excuse! Anybody who can steal wheels is off at the front fighting. Go get your passport, and stop holding up the line.' "

Shayna is trying not to laugh, but a subdued giggle bursts from her. "By your life, I believe it all."

"Why should I invent any of it? My car's still in that lot, only now it has no headlights or fenders. I'm insured, it's just a big nuisance. To make a long story short, I passed a building that a shell wrecked, and they were carrying injured people out. I helped the ambulance guys, and one of them was a Canadian I knew. He told me to come along to the hospital. They're very shorthanded. I've been at it night and day ever since, just doing whatever I'm told." His face grows somber. "I've seen terrible, terrible things there, Shayna. In a hospital you really see what war is all about."

A tapping at the door, and in tramp Shmulik and Don Kishote. Shayna utters a little shriek. The two rough green-clad bandaged figures seem to fill the room, bringing in a mingled smell of gunpowder, blood, and medicine. Kishote is a shocking apparition, in all truth, with his bloody bandaged head and four-day growth of black bristles, though his grin is merry and his eyes have the old untamed glint. "Shayna, ma nishma?" He glances at Paul. "Ah, the Canadian." He offers his hand. "Yossi."

"Hello, I'm Paul Rubinstein."

"Abba!" Aryeh leaps off the couch in his pajamas and runs toward him, then abruptly halts, staring at the bandages. Kishote holds out his arms. *"Ani b'seder. Kfotze!"* ("I'm fine. Jump!") The boy does jump and wraps his legs around his father as he has been doing since infancy. The legs are long and bony now, and Kishote feels with pleasure the strength in the ten-year-old's growing muscles.

"Where have you come from?" Shayna gasps. "Yossi, what happened to you?"

The mother in a nightgown peeks out from behind the curtain. "Ai! Yossele! Just a minute."

Soon she is frying a few last precious eggs she has been saving for Sabbath baking, while Yossi and the sergeant tell Shayna of their encounter, and talk lightly about their injuries. The Canadian sits silent for a while, then interjects, "Surely you weren't discharged from Tel Hashomer with those wounds. Either of you."

The soldiers look at each other. "Are you a doctor?" Yossi inquires. "I didn't know that."

"He's not," says Shayna.

"A volunteer medical orderly," says Paul Rubinstein. "I push wagons and carry trays around in Ein Kerem."

"Okay, we left," Shmulik says.

"You escaped, you mean," says Paul.

"You insist? We escaped."

"I thought so. Wounded guys keep escaping from Ein Kerem, too."

Yossi shrugs. "Do you blame him? How often does a Jewish army liberate Jerusalem? Every two thousand years? He's going back to his paratroop company, and they're fighting for the Old City right now."

"And you?" Shayna asks. "You can't go back to Sinai."

Yossi is holding Aryeh on his lap. "Of course not. Shmulik told me how you gave him a sandwich, so I thought I'd just drive up with him and see Aryeh and you."

"Come and eat," says the mother.

Shayna and Paul refuse the food. The soldiers quickly eat it all. Aryeh stands at his father's chair, his arm around his neck, watching him take every bite.

"You're a great Jewish mother," the sergeant says to the old lady, standing up. "I'll tell my mother that you fed me, and gave me the strength to fight for Jerusalem."

Kishote gets out of his chair. "You're not going, too," exclaims Shayna. "Kishote, enough!"

"Look, it's okay, Shayna. This fellow's brigade commander is Motta Gur. Motta was once my company commander, I'll only go and say hello to him at headquarters."

"No! No more craziness!" Shayna seizes his elbow.

"Colonel," says the Canadian, "with an undiagnosed head injury, is it smart to go into a firing zone?"

Aryeh takes his father's hand, looking up at him with wide eyes. "Abba, how bad is your wound?"

"I feel all right."

"But why go where there's fighting, when you're wounded?"

"Good question, Aryeh. So that for the rest of your life when anyone talks about this fight for Jerusalem, you can say 'Abba was there.' "

With a glance at Shayna, Aryeh says, "Well, then, Abba, be careful."

Yossi bends to hug Aryeh and kiss him. The sergeant says, "B'seder, we move," and walks to the door.

Kishote puts an arm around Shayna's slender shoulders for a rough yet tender hug. "Shayna, take care of him."

"What have I been doing?" Her voice is shaky and bitter. She briefly clasps his hand in both of hers. "Take care of yourself."

He kisses her mother. "Thanks for the eggs, Imma. Imagine, eggs! Luxury."

The soldiers go out. In the silent room their boots can be heard thumping down the stairs.

Sam Pasternak is almost dozing off under a tepid shower, as cold as Tel Aviv's water ever runs in June. Except for naps in the car beside his driver, he has not slept in days, nor has he been out of his uniform. Now he faces another predawn meeting with Eshkol; amazing how that heavy sedentary old man keeps going day and night, quietly and alertly following the war, while leaving in Moshe Dayan's hands the reins he has so publicly grasped. Through the drumming of the water Sam hears the doorbell, no doubt a Mossad messenger. A quick dry-off, and he lumbers to the door with the damp towel draped around his middle.

"Hello, Sam. Well! How informal." Yael Nitzan stands there in a crumpled white linen suit, the same one she was wearing in Washington, a suitcase at her feet. "Sorry to bother you."

"You again! Welcome, come in!"

"Thanks. It's ridiculous, but I can't get into my flat. I just flew in, have no key with me, and the landlord's off at the Syrian front, he drives a lorry. His wife is I don't know where." She kisses his cheek. "Ugh, bristles like on a pig, dear. Are we really winning the war? The news is improving, isn't it?"

"You came here from New York?"

"In the clothes I stood in."

"Yael, I'm due at a meeting with the Prime Minister. Want to stay here? Something I can do for you? I have to dress."

"Just let me use the telephone."

When he comes out shaved and in a fresh uniform, Yael is drinking coffee. "Ah, that's more like it. Snappy fellow. Sam, I must find Aryeh. Shayna Matisdorf's flat in Haifa doesn't answer. I called from New York, from the London airport, I'm very concerned. Monday it was awful in London, all those news reports about Haifa in flames, Tel Aviv bombed —"

"Arab nonsense. Try the Technion when the offices open. Someone should know where she is. Haifa hasn't been hit at all, and the boy should be fine." He gives her an appraising glance. "I'm off. Make yourself at home. The war is looking good. So are you, motek."

"A lie, I'm grimy and sweaty. I may take a shower myself."

"Go ahead, the place is yours."

"Thanks. You don't by chance know anything about Kishote?"

"His brigade has been smashing up the Egyptian armor in Sinai. He's a big hero, he dashed clear to El Arish on Monday afternoon with one battalion. He may be at the Canal by now."

Yael is slumped over the coffee cup. She sits up straight at this. "So! Well, that's Yossi's business, battle. It's always been."

"He'll be a general, Yael. If he lasts and steadies down, he could be on the short list for Ramatkhal. Sure you want to divorce him?"

"He doesn't love me, Sam. But my God, I hope he's all right."

"So do I. They've had hard fighting and taken heavy casualties, so I don't know." Pasternak bends and kisses her. "Here's a key. This is like the old days. Sort of."

"Sort of." She caresses his cheek lightly, her face weary and worried.

Pasternak's driver speeds him through blacked-out empty streets to a hotel near the Kirya. Eshkol is in shirt sleeves, eating a chicken leg and drinking tea in a fog of pipe smoke. A plate of cold meats lies on the table beside a heavily marked up aerial photo-map of Jerusalem. Yigal Yadin is smoking the pipe, and Yigal Allon is beside him, both studying the map.

The two eminent Yigals are in eclipse. A short week ago Allon and Dayan were neck and neck for Defense Minister, after Yadin declined the post. Eshkol wanted Allon, a favorite of his from Palmakh days. Murky backroom Labor Party politics, and the sudden public clamor for Dayan, tipped the balance. Now Allon and Yadin — and for that matter, Eshkol and Rabin — are all lost in the effulgence of Moshe Dayan, who has unmistakably sparked the country into a blaze of confident fighting spirit.

"Eat something," Eshkol says to Pasternak.

"No, thank you, Prime Minister."

"You're making a mistake. Food keeps you going. What's the word from the UN? How much time have we got left?"

"The Security Council is still talking and talking. They'll stay in session until Abba Eban gets there."

"When is his plane due in New York? Midnight, their time?"

"Maybe before. Gideon Rafael says they could vote on the cease-fire right after he talks. But Zev Barak thinks Washington will stall while President Johnson weighs the reaction to Eban's speech. A UN session has never had such a huge TV audience. All over the world, Zev says! So if Rafael is right we may have no more than twelve hours. If Barak is right, another day, maybe two."

"Assuming Nasser accepts the cease-fire," says Allon, "once it's voted."

"If he really believes what Radio Cairo is broadcasting," says Yadin, "why should he accept, when he's trouncing us? It may be his generals don't dare tell him what's happening in the field."

"How much longer can that go on?" Pasternak says.

"*Rabotai* [Gentlemen], I want to decide one thing here and now." Eshkol lays aside the leg bone and takes a bite of a chicken breast. "I meet with the cabinet at five this morning to discuss this one issue. Do we or don't we order Motta's paratroops into the Old City?"

Allon raps a forefinger on the map. "What's the question? He'll relieve Mount Scopus at first light. That's laid on. After that there's no stopping him."

"Dayan is against it," says the Prime Minister. "He argues that house-to-house fighting will be costly, and if we damage the holy places the whole world will turn against us, and right now we have some sympathy for once."

"That is a point," says Yadin.

Eshkol continues. "And Moshe claims going in is unnecessary, anyway. We'll have the Old City surrounded. White flags will be hanging out of every house. Bloodless surrender." Eshkol turns on Allon. "Is he right?"

"Right about what? About surrounding the Old City? Yes. The Jordanian armor on the West Bank is smashed. The air force will interdict any reenforcements from across the river. Just snipers and isolated units are left." Allon speaks with crisp martial authority. "Ben Ari and Amitai will close the ring north and south, Motta will take the Scopus ridge, and the white flags will be coming out, no question. About sending Motta inside to the Temple Mount, to the Wall — well, that's a question of high policy, of diplomacy, maybe of religion. Maybe even of archaeology! Militarily it can be done. Beyond that, I defer to our archaeologist."

Yadin wryly laughs. He has left the army after serving as Ramatkhal, to pursue his academic career. Except as a senior adviser to Prime Ministers, he has played no military role since.

"Prime Minister, Motta made a night attack that left the air force out of the equation," he says, "just to spare the holy places. That was well done, but we paid a very steep price. Ammunition Hill was a terrible fight, but our boys were lions and now it's ours. If the Jordanians were still there at the cease-fire, the UN would surely rule that Jerusalem remains divided on the grounds that Ammunition Hill commands the Old City. But I say the city will remain divided, Prime Minister, even with our tanks on Ammunition Hill and white flags flying on every house inside those walls, so long as Jewish feet are not on the Temple Mount."

"And what will be the losses? The cost of going in?"

Yadin glances at Allon, and puffs at his pipe.

"Light losses," says Allon. "If not for the problem of the holy places, we could call for air support and smash in with almost no losses."

"I foresee a world outcry if we go in," says Yadin, "even if every stone of the holy places is untouched. The Pope for one can't tolerate Jewish sovereignty over Jerusalem. Not until the Second Coming, when — as that previous Pope told Herzl — he'll be glad to baptize us all and welcome us back to Zion. Moshe may be right about the house-to-house fighting. Securing that maze of narrow streets could be bloody."

"Shapira says" — Eshkol is referring to the head of the Religious Party — "that it might be better not to capture the Old City. Just go on praying for it. The Messiah isn't here to lead us in, but once we've taken the Temple Mount we can never give it up."

"Shapira and the Pope aren't all that far apart," observes Allon. "Interesting."

"But speaking now as an archaeologist," says Yadin, "I find it inconceivable that a Jewish army should stand at the gates of Jerusalem, capable of marching in and restoring it to the Jewish nation after two thousand years, and should hold back. For any reason whatever!"

Eshkol looks at Pasternak. Behind the Prime Minister's head, the window is turning indigo with the first hint of dawn. "Sam?"

"Akh'shav, oh l'olam lo!" ("Now or never!") Sam Pasternak bites out the Hebrew words like gunshots. *"Akh'shav, oh l'olam lo!* In the next twelve hours, Prime Minister, or maybe not for another two thousand years."

Eshkol stands up, wiping his hands and mouth with a napkin. "I will overrule Moshe Dayan."

41

The Day of the Lord

Colonel Motta Gur, drinking hot tea on the roof of the Rockefeller Museum in the red rays of sunrise, is startled to see coming up through the trapdoor the head of nobody but his old friend Yossi Nitzan, pale and bloodily bandaged.

"Kishote, to all the devils!" Gur leaps to help him off the steep iron ladder, while his staff officers stare. "Last I heard you were down in Sinai, seizing El Arish single-handed."

Panting and dizzy from the fast climb up the winding stairs of the tower, Yossi adopts Gur's joshing tone. "Well, Motta, I have this stupid driver, he took a wrong turn, and here I am."

"I see. Happens to me all the time." Gur indicates the bandages. "Bad, Yossi?"

"Nothing much. I'm not about to lie in a bed in Tel Hashomer, my friend, while you capture the Old City single-handed."

Gur's tough moon face sobers. "If they'll give me the order."

"Is there a question? Thank you." A girl soldier, round-eyed, hands Kishote a steaming cup. "Good God, what a panorama!" It is his first glimpse of this all-around view of Old Jerusalem and its hills, bounded to the east by the high ridge from Mount Scopus to the Mount of Olives under a dazzling low sun, and on this side by the amazingly close Old City wall, which until now he has viewed only across the broad valley of no-man's-land.

"You've never been up here?"

"Motta, I came off the boat in 1948, straight to Latrun."

"Of course. Well, during the Mandate, they would bring us Jerusalem schoolkids up here. Also to the Mount of Olives. Now that's a view, and that's my mission this morning, to advance to the Mount of Olives, clear the ridge, and close the ring."

An aide, holding out a microphone: "Colonel! Central Command, about the air strike."

"Stick with my command group, Yossi, we're about to move to a better spot. And stand back from that side. Jordanian snipers are thick along the wall."

"B'seder."

More lightheaded than he wants to admit, Kishote steadies himself on the parapet. Sporadic gunfire crackles below. Half a dozen officers in webbed helmets and battle harness are on the roof, some scanning the scene with binoculars, others chattering on walkie-talkies. Like Gorodish, Gur is bareheaded; a mark, or affectation, of brigade command. Big, broad-shouldered, ambitious, Motta is a guy to liberate Jerusalem, Yossi thinks, watching him talk calmly to Central Command, his curly hair stirring in the breeze. Luck goes with Motta. What a difference between the wide-ranging desert fighting in Sinai, and combat in this hilly little bowl of a battlefield! At staff and command college he once played out the recapture of Jerusalem with Motta Gur and other officers, a war game in hundreds of meters, where the Sinai simulations were in hundreds of kilometers.

Yossi has observed evidence of the price paid for Old Jerusalem so far, as he was driving in the dawn through no-man's-land past sappers clearing mines under sniper fire, and then into eerily quiet East Jerusalem streets he has never seen before, barred as they have been to Jews since 1948. Burned-out tanks, overturned vehicles, many dead Jordanians in khaki; many Zahal boys must have died, too, but their bodies were removed immediately, an iron rule. The smells of burning and death everywhere all tell of fierce struggle. Here, however, there is no trace of the giant sullen Russian backer of the Arabs. The ruined Jordan tanks are Shermans and Pattons. The broken vehicles are Land Rovers, Mack trucks, and jeeps. And here are no wide wastes of sand, stretching to the horizon. Here around the museum roof all is close, green, built-up, beautiful, the Arab villages snugged against the hills nearby, and Jewish New Jerusalem gleaming off to the west. Directly below, the Old City is open to the eye, but of the Temple Mount just a glint of the golden Omar dome shows above the houses and trees of the Moslem Quarter. Eagerly he takes in the scene, a bit giddy from the wound, and perhaps from happiness.

In the hospital Kishote had awakened to despairing anger at his removal from the Sinai, from Gorodish, Tal, and the tank fighters. But according to the radio that battle is now nearly over. The Sinai is a graveyard of a thousand and more destroyed Egyptian tanks and vehicles. The Egyptians are abandoning their remaining equipment and streaming back across the sands by the thousands toward the Canal, barefoot and fainting from hunger and thirst. Now the crux of the war is here, in the Return to Jerusalem, and if he can't fight, he can at least see it with his own eyes.

Gur approaches. "Kishote, seriously, are you okay?"

"I'm a hundred percent. Or say ninety. Why?"

"Yaffe's up at Mount Scopus with my Sixty-sixth Battalion. Communication is rotten, I'm not sure why." Gur pulls out a pad, and sketches rapidly with a ballpoint pen as he talks. "Now this is very important, Yossi. Look here. The eastern ridge is lined with trenches and heavily mined. The Augusta Victoria Hospital — here — is the pivot —"

"It always has been."

"Right. Now then." Gur and Yossi talk in quick jargon, using few words. An air strike, Gur says, will precede the attack on the ridge by two battalions, one coming from Mount Scopus, the other from the valley below the Old City. Unless movements are coordinated and timing exact, planes or artillery may hit Jewish forces, or the tank units may end up shooting at each other, so constricted is the battle zone. Gur does not want to send one of his staff to

Mount Scopus, he needs them all. Kishote as liaison with the Scopus battalion can be a help.

"I'll do it, Motta."

"Good." Gur hands him the sketch, a cabalism of arrows, circles, and times. "Show this to Yaffe and explain it. Call me on the command net if there's confusion. We can't afford avoidable losses, the breakthrough was enough, it was very hard. Kidding aside, do you have a driver?"

"Yes. The guy who left the hospital with me. A Yerushalmi."

"Excellent, he'll know his way around. Guns?"

"Of course."

"There'll be sniping all along the road to Scopus. But Dayan went up there yesterday, so it's passable."

"I'm going now."

Gur grips his shoulder. "See you on the Mount of Olives. Ah, *there's* a view, Kishote! Keep your head down."

"Yes, that's what I forgot in Sinai." That brings a wry laugh from Gur.

Past silent shut-up Arab houses and markets, the jeep dips into the valley and winds up the steep Scopus road amid cheery birdsong. The sergeant drives one-armed. Yossi sits with his Uzi at the ready. Moshe Dayan has a peculiar tolerance, or even liking, for the whistle of bullets near his head which Don Kishote does not share; and this is the road on which Arabs once ambushed and massacred an entire convoy of doctors and nurses bound for Hadassah Hospital. Sure enough, halfway up, CRACK! A nasty whine far too close, a figure shooting from a graveyard gate. Yossi blasts at it with the Uzi and stone chips fly from the gate. Then silence, and birdsong again.

"It can't be done." Major Yaffe, the battalion commander on Mount Scopus, slaps at Gur's sketch in his palm. "Motta must postpone the air strike."

"For how long?" Kishote inquires.

"Look around you." Yaffe sweeps an arm at a huge jam of half-tracks, tanks, jeeps, and supply vehicles parked higgledy-

piggledy among the high weeds. Most of the soldiers are asleep on
the ground or in the machines. "D'you know what these guys have
been through? Heard about Ammunition Hill? Tell Motta I can
move by ten o'clock, if the rest of Uri's tanks get here."

"I will."

Soon the so-called King of Mount Scopus appears, a hard-
bitten little major with a bushy mustache and a gravel voice, who
has been up here for years. Long ago Yossi was his platoon commander, and Major Sharfman proudly shows him around his do-
main, a melancholy enclave of abandoned run-down university and
hospital buildings. "Historians will be asking for a thousand years,
Kishote, why the Jordanians didn't try to overrun me and take
Mount Scopus. The news would have shaken the world! Shattered
Israel's morale! Maybe decided the war!"

"Menakhem, you've been up here too long."

"I'm serious! Three miserable square kilometers, a hundred
guys, the Jordanians surrounding me with tanks, artillery, whole
brigades! But you know what? They had intelligence. I'm sure of it.
I've smuggled an arsenal up here that the UN doesn't dream of. Ha!
We'd have given them a bloody fight. Say, here's the Magnes Tower.
Want to climb it? Best view in the land."

"This view's not bad." Below them the Judean hills slope away
steeply eastward, and through a gap in the ridges the Dead Sea
glitters blue.

"No comparison."

Kishote peers up at the tower, named for the first president of
Hebrew University. "Judah Magnes. The guy who thought we and
the Arabs could coexist in one peaceful Palestine."

"He was crazy. Not for a thousand years."

"No, he was right, they just have to be convinced once for all
that we're here to stay. Freeing Jerusalem may do it."

"Nothing will convince them, not for a thousand years."

"How about nine hundred seventy years, Menakhem?"

The major looks taken aback, then laughs. "Well, okay. The
Arab doves could prevail by then. You see, I'm flexible."

His walkie-talkie comes to life with a message for Kishote. The
air strike will be postponed, but only until nine. Menakhem starts

to climb up in the tower. "Best spotter post," he calls to Yossi as he leaves him, "when the shooting starts."

At a huge blowup of the Jerusalem area Benny Luria is briefing his Bat Squadron, an unshaven tired-looking lot, about the strike. "Now pay attention, pilots. The General Staff is giving me a very hard time. I've denied that this squadron has ever bombed or strafed our own forces, but we all know the close call we had at Jebel Libni. Let's have no such balagan today! This target area is tiny. The opposing forces are meters apart. It's an exercise in pinpoint attack."

A hand goes up, and a freckle-faced boyish pilot says in a peevish tone, "Pinpoint with napalm? That's a contradiction."

"No, the napalm is limited to the strongpoints in this outlying sector." Benny traces red outlines on the photograph. "The strafing of the trenches here — in this pine grove along the ridge — is our main job. Now listen carefully." The pointer sweeps around and over the Old City. "*This* is a totally forbidden area. Understand? If even *one* holy place is destroyed or damaged, get ready for a world scandal, also a public general court-martial."

Luria lays the pointer down, sits on the desk top, and crookedly grins at his airmen.

"Sorry, *hevra* [comrades], that's the drill today. Day before yesterday we decided this whole damn war in three hours. Yesterday we smashed the Jordanian tank brigades coming from Jericho, and that made the freeing of Old Jerusalem possible. But memories are short at the General Staff. Today we're just those crazy aviators who can't tell Arabs from Jews. So let's be nice and careful on this sortie, b'seder?"

Innumerable times Benny Luria has overflown the diminutive diamond-shaped Old City, a maze of crooked streets, low houses, and patchy greenery enclosed by thick walls and usually looking almost deserted, except for the Temple Mount, where tiny figures drift in and out of the two grand mosques. But today as he circles before descending, it is a wild scene down there. Israeli mechanized forces crawl on all the approaches, smoke rises from the walls, artillery blinks yellow and red all along the parapets, and there is much running about in the narrow streets and on the wide plaza of the Mount. So much he sees before he dives through a dark veil of smoke billowing from the napalm attack, and commences firing.

By the time he and his aviators have noisily and repeatedly raked the deep trenches screened by the pine trees, Yaffe's battalion is formed up and moving along the ridge road, reenforced by tanks from a mechanized brigade to the north. Despite the air strike, heavy fire from the pine grove greets the advance. Super-cautious after Luria's warning, the pilots have not hit churches, mosques, or Israelis, and have not wholly quenched the dug-in Jordanians, either. Kishote sits in Yaffe's signal half-track, watching the tanks and troop carriers rumble by into the stinking black smoke of the napalm conflagration. Perched atop a passing carrier is Master Sergeant Shmulik, waving his good arm. "I'm back with my company, Colonel," he yells, "and I'm going home! Thanks for getting me out of that lousy bed."

"Keep your head down," Kishote calls back. Shmulik laughs and drops down into the vehicle.

"Kishote, Kishote, Talmid speaking. Where are you?"

Talmid (Scholar) is Motta Gur. It is part of Motta's luck or destiny, Kishote thinks, to have the perfect code name for the first Jewish commander to return to Jerusalem since Bar Kochba.

"Talmid, Kishote speaking. I'm in the dark cloud on Mount Scopus. Like Moses on Mount Sinai."

"B'seder, Moses. My command group is on the way. Meet me on the Mount of Olives in fifteen minutes."

"B'seder."

The jeep in which Kishote sets out to meet Gur goes by burning vehicles and soldiers tending to the wounded. For all the smoke and gunfire, for all the distraction of loudspeakers blatting signal jargon, Don Kishote's heart leaps when the jeep reaches the Mount of Olives and rolls out on a windy terrace cluttered with vehicles of Gur's headquarters group. Gur is surveying through large binoculars the broad terrain that lies below in clear sunshine: the entire Old City inside its walls and battlements, the grassy Temple Mount and its two grandiose mosque domes, one gold, one silver; and outside the antique walls, green hills and valleys dotted with Arab villages, and far beyond them the urban sprawl of New Jerusalem. Israeli columns are moving on the outer roads.

"Kishote, you're here! Good." Gur holds out a marked map. "Take a look at this."

"Have you got the order yet to go in?"

"No, but it's coming. My nose tells me so. I have to be ready for it. Now, this is nothing like the staff attack plan or the war games. Nothing's developed as anticipated."

Amid artillery blasts, raucous signal cacophony, and the grumbling of tanks, his eyes stinging from smoke and dust, Kishote scans the sketch. At first glance it puzzles him extremely. Gur's three paratroop battalions and a tank unit, their maneuver paths identified in different colors, will come at the Old City walls and gates in a peculiarly complicated attack. Since the few remaining Jordanian defenders face overwhelming force, why this swirl of military movement? But soon he understands — and smiles. Good old Motta! If politics delay the capture, if the order does not come in time, if the cease-fire takes effect with the Israelis occupying the ridge to the Mount of Olives, there Colonel Gur will be, on the Mount of Olives. If on the other hand, Motta's Fifty-fifth Parachute Brigade is unleashed to enter the Old City, the four forces will approach in a tangled ballet of men and machines so that the first man through the Lions Gate, the first Jew to set foot on the Temple Mount, will be Motta Gur.

"Well, what do you think?" Gur inquires, as Kishote gives back the sketch.

"Motta, *magiya l'kha* [you're entitled]."

Gur's response is a wily side-glance and a humorous grunt.

Major Sharfman now drives up in a gun-mounting jeep. Kishote borrows his binoculars to peer down at a bridge in the valley where smashed and burned Israeli tanks and vehicles lie helter-skelter. "That's the devil of a mess, Menakhem. What happened?"

"Terrible balagan. Reconnaissance guys took a wrong turn in the dark last night and piled up at the bridge. Jordanians shot them to pieces from the walls. A massacre. That place is what the Christians call Gethsemane."

"Gethsemane. *Gat shmanim* [Oil press], no? And isn't this spot where we're standing the place where Jesus preached to a multitude? Right here on the Mount of Olives?"

"Right here. Sermon on the Mount." Major Sharfman gestures at the arched facade of the Intercontinental Hotel directly behind them. "And where he preached, cocktails are served now from five to seven-thirty, with free canapés."

Kishote frowns up at the hotel. "Who ever allowed that to be built there?"

"Who was to stop it? The British were gone and we were shut out. Anyway, look down there, and ask me who allowed *that*."

Sharfman is gesturing at the slope below the terrace where they stand. The broad hillside looks like a quarry, acres and acres of broken stone and randomly scattered hewn slabs. Kishote recognizes the ancient cemetery from pictures he saw in boyhood, and he chokes up with rage.

A shout from the signal officer to Motta Gur: "Sir, Central Command! The general says he has good news."

Gur strides to the microphone. His glad demeanor, as he listens, telegraphs what he is hearing. "*Ken, ken. Mi'yad!* [Yes, yes. At once!] We're ready, and we go." He turns to the signal officer. "I will speak to all battalion and company commanders." The officer cuts in the circuits on his transmitter.

"*Paratroop Brigade Fifty-five*" — Gur in a burst of pride drops code names and speaks in the clear — "*we stand on the ridge looking to the Old City. We are about to enter ancient Jerusalem, dreamed about, yearned for, down all the generations! We will be the first to go in. Tanks, move to the Lions Gate! Battalion Twenty-eight, Battalion Seventy-five, to the gate. Battalion Sixty-six, after them. Move, move. We hold our review parade on the Temple Mount!*"

Now Gur's crude map sketch begins to unfold as a reality. In drifting dust and smoke, the battalions roll down the Mount of Olives and along the valley roads, streaming toward the walls, from which gunfire still weakly pops. Gur's command group in halftracks and jeeps takes the road which circles down southward around the desecrated graveyard, and curves back north toward the Lions Gate. Watching the advance of the battalions through binoculars, Sharfman says hoarsely, "Is it all right for a Jewish soldier to cry?"

"You've forgotten your Psalms," says Kishote. " *'When God returned us to Zion, we were as in a dream. Then were our mouths filled with laughter —'* "

Sharfman completes the verse. " *'And our tongues with song.'* Okay. No crying."

Kishote repeats, *"As in a dream. As in a dream."* He points down at the thousands of broken rifled graves, over which he is seeing the Jewish army marching toward old Jerusalem. "And *they* are all watching, I tell you, Menakhem. Watching, and laughing, and singing. This is their resurrection. This is why they wanted to be buried here. So as to be here on the great day, the Day of the Lord, and see it with their eyes. This is their day." He grips Sharfman's arm hard.

"Amen," says Sharfman, "but that's my bad arm, Yossi, wounded in KADESH."

With a laugh, Kishote lets go. "I'm out of my head and raving. Sorry."

"Raving? Do you know how I felt, up in the Magnes Tower, looking at this graveyard year in and year out? Watching them down in there with their crowbars and sledgehammers?"

With a tank leading the way, Motta Gur's command group far below is nearing the Lions Gate. A large flaming vehicle blocks the narrow road to the entrance arch. The tank shoves aside the burning machine and smashes through the massive wooden doors. Gur's half-track follows the tank through the dust and rubble of the broken entrance.

"There they go." Sharfman hands Don Kishote the binoculars. "Look. *It's happening!*" He bursts out into rollicking laughter. "Kishote, we're doing it. I've been staring at that gate for years from Mount Scopus. Now our boys are going in."

"And by God, there goes Motta," says Kishote. With the binoculars he can discern the burly figure of Colonel Gur running out on the broad plaza of the Temple Mount past the high golden Dome of the Rock, followed by other soldiers at a trot. "There they are, Menakhem, our boys on *Har Ha'bayit* [the Temple Mount]!"

Vehicles are pouring through the Lions Gate — tanks, half-tracks, troop carriers — and more and more soldiers, with guns at the ready, are running out on the broad level plaza between the two grandiose mosques.

"Unbelievable, unbelievable!" Major Sharfman's voice is low and awed. *"As in a dream!"*

Yossi is murmuring the blessing on good news. Sharfman hears him and slaps his shoulder. "Amen and amen. By God, Don Kishote, your secret is out! You're religious. Don't deny it."

"I was a yeshiva boy, Menakhem, and I'm a Jew."

The major laughs, gesturing at the scene below of soldiers thronging on the Temple Mount. "Look at this, will you! When Nasser closed Sharm el Sheikh, little did he think that this would be the outcome!"

"Nasser couldn't help himself," says Kishote. "The hand of God was on him."

Sharfman exclaims, peering through the binoculars, "Motta Gur is calling over a signal sergeant." He darts to the jeep, turns up the volume of the portable receiver, and switches rapidly through the frequencies.

"Central Command, this is Talmid, speaking from inside the Old City. I'm standing on the plaza of the Dome of the Rock. HAR HA'BAYIT B'YADENU! [Temple Mount in our hands!] HAR HA'BAYIT B'YADENU! HAR HA'BAYIT B'YADENU!"

Voice of General Narkiss at Central Command: *"I am coming there at once. All honor! All honor! Hundred percent!"*

Don Kishote and the King of Mount Scopus hug and kiss each other. The mustache is scratchy on Yossi's cheek, and Menakhem's cheek is wet with tears, though he has agreed not to cry.

הר הבית בידינו !!

TEMPLE MOUNT IN OUR HANDS!

A flame leaps through the Jewish State from the Syrian border to the Red Sea, a sunburst of national joy and glory. Fathers and sons, mothers and children, wives and husbands, sweethearts, newlyweds, comrades in arms out on the battlefield, all are fused in a once-in-a-lifetime, once-in-a-millennium surge of the spirit. Everywhere in the Holy Land

Jews embrace, dance, and sing: "This is the Day the Lord has made . . ."

הר הבית בידינו !!

Levi Eshkol puts down the telephone and turns gleaming eyes to Pasternak. *"Har Ha'bayit b'yadenu!* Let us go to Jerusalem."

"The road will be jammed with army traffic," says Pasternak. "I'll order a police escort."

"Never mind, no big *tsimmes,* we will get there." The Prime Minister looks down at his wrinkled bulging khakis. "For this I'll put on a coat and tie."

The word reaches Benny Luria as he circles Tel Nof. The flight controller droning jargon in his earphones to clear his descent breaks into a boyish jubilant shout: "All aircraft, hear this. *Har Ha'bayit b'yadenu!"*

Benny glances around and with wild whoops whirls over and over in a victory roll.

"Aunt Shayna! Aunt Shayna!" Aryeh comes running out on the roof. "Imma says hurry downstairs!"

Shayna has been watching the smoke and fire over the Old City. Here and on nearby roofs people are crowding to observe the spectacle, their portable radios making a scratchy incomprehensible din.

Her mother says as she enters the door of the flat, "Ah, there you are! An important announcement coming from the army spokesman!" And almost at once a deep not-quite-calm military voice interrupts an American rock-and-roll record: *"This is the army spokesman. The commander of Central Command has just reported 'Har Ha'bayit b'yadenu!' "*

They hug each other, and Aryeh dances around the room, shouting, "Abba was there! Abba was the first one on the Temple Mount!"

Laughing and crying, Shayna catches him in her arms. "By my life, you're probably right."

Yael hears it in her flat as she dresses after a nap. Exclaiming aloud, "Thank God I'm here!" she falls in a chair to think, but not for long. There is only one thing to do.

42

The Wall

Kishote jumps from a jeep he has commandeered, to jostle through vehicles and paratroopers jamming the Lions Gate. There above the stone archway are the legendary lions, all right, two facing moldering bas-reliefs of stiffly stylized big cats. Leopards, maybe. Pushing past the burned-out smoldering bus that still radiates heat and stink, half carried along by the rejoicing soldiers, Kishote enters the Old City.

VIA DOLOROSA, reads the street sign in the gloomy passage blocked by tanks. The paratroopers are streaming with him toward an opening in a high wooden barrier, and all at once he finds himself out on the grassy spacious plaza of the Temple Mount. The sense of being in a dream is strong on Don Kishote, and to wake up in a hospital bed would not surprise him. Right there is the grandiose blue-tiled Mosque of Omar with its huge golden dome high against the sky, and beside it unshaven rifle-slinging Israeli soldiers are clustering around the bareheaded Motta Gur. Scattered gunfire echoes below the Mount as Kishote pushes past the bobbing helmets. "Well, Motta, how does it feel to be immortal?"

Gur's face is flushed, his eyes blaze. "Hi! The boys are still hunting down snipers, Kishote, clear to the Damascus Gate. It's rotten to be taking casualties now, but the soldiers are glorious.

You know what one of them just said to me? 'Colonel, when do we settle with the Syrians?' This is a kid from the company that took Ammunition Hill!"

"Speaking of ammunition —!" Kishote pokes a thumb toward the multitudinous crates heaped perhaps fifteen feet high against the Dome of the Rock mosque. Stencilled on them in Arabic and English are British army code marks; all manner of shells, grenades, mortar rounds, flares, machine gun magazines, even dynamite. With a cynical glance at the towering ammunition dump, Gur shrugs. "Kind of careless, that, no? Listen, Kishote, Eshkol is coming. It would be a help if you are at the Lions Gate when he arrives." He gestures at Yossi's bandages. "You have a heroic look, you're picturesque, and anyway by God you are a hero. And you're reliable. Major Shimon will be there with a security detail."

"When will Eshkol arrive?"

"He's on his way from Tel Aviv. The roads are clogged with army, so it'll be a while."

"I'm yours to command, but I'm dying to see the Wall."

"You'll be disappointed. As a kid I know I was, first time. It's not much to look at. But go ahead, go down the staircase through that gate there."

Kishote descends worn stone stairs and rickety wooden steps to a dark alleyway lined with shabby Arab houses. A few soldiers wearing phylacteries are there racing through the morning service, prayer shawls over their uniforms and guns slung on their shoulders, facing gigantic shadowy blocks of weathered Jerusalem stone, with green plants hanging from high crevices. The prayer leader is chanting.

> *Let us sanctify His Name in this world, as they sanctify it in the highest heavens. As it is written by your prophet,*
> AND THEY CALLED TO EACH OTHER AND SAID —

In a yeshiva-boy reflex Kishote stops where he is, puts his feet together, and joins the chorus of response:

> HOLY, HOLY, HOLY, IS THE LORD OF HOSTS, THE WORLD IS FULL OF HIS GLORY.

Like all the soldiers he rises on tiptoe with each "holy," to simulate the flight of angels. Mighty strange, to be trapped in this old Kedushah ritual in a chilly alley open to the sky! The last response frees him to move again.

> *MAY THE LORD REIGN FOREVER, YOUR GOD, O ZION, HALLELUJAH.*

He goes to the Wall, leans on the cold stones, and kisses a projection of pinkish rock, trying to feel emotion and not succeeding when, with a swelling clatter on the stairs, into the alley bursts a short bearded figure in army uniform, carrying a velvet-covered scroll of the Law and a black ram's horn. Close behind trample news photographers and soldiers with cameras, for this is the army's chief chaplain. He kisses the Wall, puts the ram's horn to his lips, and vigorously blows. Photo bulbs flash, but no sound comes out of the horn. He tries again, and produces only a sputtering squeaking noise. "The wrong shofar!" he fumes. "Such shleppers! I told them to give me the yellow one! Satan is in this horn, nobody can blow it."

Kishote steps forward. "Rabbi, let me try, I used to blow shofar in the yeshiva."

"A yeshiva *buk'her* [lad]! Hundred percent, go ahead, try! Rip apart Satan!"

The wet mouthpiece is too narrow, Yossi sees. He blew just such a recalcitrant shofar in the Cyprus camp at the Rosh Hashanah service. He takes a deep breath, and blows a piercing shrill blast that makes the praying soldiers stop and stare, and sends a flock of birds wheeling and screaming off the wall overhead.

"Hundred percent! Health to you! Blow, blow, buk'her!"

The rabbi dances, singing the jubilant holiday song,

> *David, King of Israel,*
> *Alive, alive, and abiding . . .*

The soldiers pouring into the alley join in, ringing the dancing rabbi. "Blow, buk'her, keep blowing," he shouts. Kishote sounds blast after blast, the rabbi whirls and capers with the Torah, and the soldiers dance and sing around him. In the distance sporadic gunfire still goes on. Overhead a helicopter circles, the rotor heavily thrashing.

"Aunt Shayna, I don't *know* what the value of *x* is, and I don't *care!*"

Aryeh is being unusually mulish. Shayna is trying to drill him in algebra, and he has a keen head for it, far advanced for his age, but today he can think only of Abba, and the Har Ha'bayit flash on the radio followed by "Hatikvah" and "Jerusalem the Golden." At the double knock he jumps up and runs to the door, crying, "Abba, Abba!" It is a soldier, but not Abba; a paratrooper lieutenant, with a broad nose sunburned and peeling, and a four-day growth of red bristles.

"Shalom, boy." To Shayna he says, "Your mother is wanted downstairs, lady, by the Ezrakh."

"My mother? My mother is in bed with lumbago. She can't move. What is it?"

"Who said I can't move?" Querulous voice from behind the curtain. "The Ezrakh wants me, I'm coming, Shayna — oof! Oh!" Heavy thump on the floor.

"Mama!"

"I'm all right, I fell off the bed. Help me dress!"

But the mother is really immobilized, and Shayna puts her back to bed, violently protesting.

"My company commander is very religious," says the paratrooper to Shayna as they go downstairs. "He suggested to Colonel Gur that the Ezrakh come to the Wall. I've been sent to bring him. The Ezrakh asked for your mother to go with him."

The Ezrakh is wearing his Sabbath best, a shiny black sateen coat to his ankles, and a flat black hat somewhat less rusty than the weekday one. His long white beard is immaculately brushed out. "I'll come with you, Rabbi," Shayna says. "All right? Mama isn't well."

The Ezrakh nods, and says he will pray at the Wall for her mother's recovery.

"I'm ordered to tell you, Rabbi," says the lieutenant, "that there's still firing in the Old City. You need not risk it unless you want to."

The Ezrakh smiles and walks out of his open door to the parked jeep. Shayna follows him. "You'll have to move that equipment," she tells the lieutenant. A large field transmitter occupies the front seat. "He'll sit there."

"Why? The back's more comfortable."

"He won't sit with me."

The lieutenant grins. "Some kind of superstition?"

"Just move the stuff, all right?"

"I'd sit with you any day, lady." He hefts the equipment into the back. "But I'm no holy man, true enough."

She says as he helps the Ezrakh in, "By any chance, did you come on a Lieutenant Colonel Nitzan in there? That boy in our flat is his son."

"You mean the armor guy? Don Kishote?"

"Right. The armor guy."

"Sure. While the chief chaplain was dancing with the Torah he was blowing shofar."

"He was? One moment." Shayna runs upstairs to tell Aryeh that Abba is all right.

Soldiers are cordoning off the vast pile of munitions with barriers and ropes. "We'll be two weeks getting this stuff off the Mount," Gur says to Kishote. "There must be fifty tons."

"Better put a round-the-clock guard on it, Motta."

"I've ordered that." Gur glances at his watch. "Say, that helicopter landed a while ago. The Prime Minister should be along. Sensible to use the chopper, instead of trying to drive. Listen, tell Major Shimon to bring Eshkol here to me, and I'll escort him to the Wall myself." He gestures at the ammunition dump. "I want him to see this."

"B'seder."

Soldiers throng in the Lions Gate archway, gawking over each other's shoulders, blocking Kishote's view. *Dayan! It's Moshe Dayan! He came by helicopter!* The Minister of Defense, Chief of Staff Rabin, and Central Commander Uzi Narkiss appear through the gate, with soldiers making way and reporters and photographers crowding in behind. Dayan wears a webbed helmet with chin strap fastened, as though heading into combat. Narkiss has on a cloth cap, and Yitzhak Rabin is bareheaded. Dayan is saying to an aide, "Right this minute, get the Ramatkhal a helmet."

"Not necessary," says Rabin, looking pained, but when the aide snatches a helmet from a soldier and hands it to him, he tiredly puts it on and ties the strap.

"All right, now we go," says Dayan. In theory a civilian minister, he is in full military uniform, looking every inch the conquering commander. With Narkiss and Rabin on either side of him he marches forward, arms rigid and swinging, fists clenched, chest out. Army cameramen and news photographers walk backwards before him, shooting every stride. Watching from a doorway of the Via Dolorosa, Kishote thinks, *Magiya l'kha, Moshe* — you're entitled! Dayan's rise has made a big difference, after all. When the Hamtana frightened the country and chilled army morale, he rallied and unified the people as no one else could have.

The soldiers swarm after him to the Temple Mount. Only the security detail remains on the Via Dolorosa, waiting for the Prime Minister. Kishote walks out through the gate and looks up at the legendary lions. As sculpture they aren't much. Surprising how familiar the gate already seems, after twenty years of invisibility to Jews! Kishote's head is bothering him; the wound throbs and the dizziness comes and goes. Was that the reason the Wall left him so cold? Motta is right: a real disappointment. As a yeshiva boy he was taught, and he believed, that that Wall was the gateway to Heaven, where prayers went up straight from the earth to the Throne. But with his lips on the actual rough rock his thoughts stayed earthbound in a shady smelly alley, where a few religious soldiers were mumbling through the morning liturgy. Maybe they felt something mystical, some sense of Jews coming here to bewail the fallen Temple down the centuries. Not he. On the contrary, he thought of Ehud Elad, who had not lived to kiss those stones.

Well, that must be Eshkol, he thinks, seeing an army car winding down the road from the Rockefeller Museum. So it is. Sam Pasternak gets out of the car first, then Eshkol, in a black suit, white shirt, and blue tie. A surprise, that! Like most Labor politicians, Eshkol usually wears an open shirt collar, the badge of socialist plainness. At big events — a dignitary's funeral, a head-of-state reception, some cabinet minister's daughter's wedding — he may wear a tie. This occasion evidently calls for such full dress.

Sam Pasternak is astounded to see Kishote here, pallid and bandaged. "Yossi! Ma nishma? Prime Minister, this is one of our great fighting officers, Lieutenant Colonel Nitzan."

"What's the situation here, Yossi?" The Prime Minister sounds brisk and businesslike, but he is beaming, and his eyes in wrinkled dark sockets are joyous.

Remembering Gur's attack plan, Kishote is able to rattle off a concise picture of how things stand: which units have captured the Dung Gate, the Zion Gate, the Jaffa Gate, and which sectors they now occupy in the Old City. Eshkol nods and nods, looking up at the Lions Gate with a peculiar smile. "B'seder. I first saw those lions, Yossi, when I came to Palestine at nineteen, a nobody named Shkolnik. Now I see them again as Eshkol, the Prime Minister of the Jewish State. A big change, blessed be the Name."

"Colonel Gur is waiting for you on the Mount, Prime Minister."

"Yes? And Dayan?"

Kishote hesitates. Pasternak says, "We know he's here. We saw the helicopter go by."

"He may be at the Wall, Prime Minister."

"Well, so we go there too," says Eshkol, with faint irony.

The security detail is lounging inside the gate. There are no photographers. The Via Dolorosa is empty, the houses shuttered. From the Temple Mount comes the sound of walkie-talkies, shouted orders, and the tumult of the crowd. "This is the greatest moment of my life," says Eshkol in a matter-of-fact way, as he walks through the gate and the few soldiers salute and form up around him. On the Mount, Colonel Gur, in a helmet with chin strap fastened Dayan style, salutes the Prime Minister. Eshkol casually returns the gesture. "Now there's a fine sight, Motta." He points at the Star of David flag fluttering on an improvised pole over the plaza.

"Somebody went climbing inside the mosque, and put the flag

way up there, Prime Minister." Gur points to the top of the golden dome. "Moshe Dayan was furious. He ordered it taken down, and so I put it here."

"Yes, he has very good sense, Moshe. A tactful act. Well, well, look at this." Eshkol approaches the ammunition dump and peers at the crate markings. "Excellent, we can use it all. Very expensive stuff. High quality." He notices Gur's tart grin. "Once a treasurer, Motta, always a treasurer."

"They were lucky a shell of ours didn't land here, Prime Minister," says Pasternak. "Both mosques would be gone."

"Maybe we were the lucky ones," says Gur. "The world would have turned on us for sure."

"They will anyway," says Eshkol. "Meantime here we are."

"Some real shlepper of a Jordanian general is responsible for this," says Pasternak.

"Now to the Wall, Motta," says Eshkol.

Pasternak and Kishote trail after them. "What to all the devils happened to you, Yossi?"

"What's going on in New York, Sam, with the cease-fire?"

"They're still talky-talking. Come on, what are you doing in Jerusalem? And how did you get hurt?"

"It's a long megillah."

Pasternak thinks of telling Kishote about Yael's sudden arrival, and decides against it. Another long megillah. Let it lie, he'll find out soon enough.

"Sam, will we settle with the Syrians too? Take the Golan Heights? Or will the Galilee kibbutzniks have to go on farming under shellfire, even after this war?"

"Rabin wants to do it. Dayan won't allow it. That can bring in the Russians, he says, and we'll lose all we've gained and be much worse off."

"What does Eshkol say?"

"He isn't saying."

The noonday sun is now shafting on the Wall, bringing out its beautiful pinkish color and its peculiar weathering; some of the gigantic blocks partly disintegrated, others looking fresh from the quarry. An entire company of paratroopers is pushing into the alley, making a great noise and looking up at the sunlit Wall in happy awe. The arrival of the Prime Minister is hardly noticed.

"I should be wearing a hat, I guess," says Eshkol. At a word from Gur a soldier offers Eshkol his helmet. He puts it on with chin strap dangling, and decidedly queer it looks on the fat old man in a dark suit and tie. From a street leading off the alley comes the sound of raucously jolly male voices in a wedding song, the words from Jeremiah:

> *Then will be heard in the cities of Judah*
> *And in the streets of Jerusalem*
> *Voice of celebration and voice of joy . . .*

A handful of soldiers come dancing backwards into the alley, clapping their hands, escorting the Ezrakh to the Wailing Wall as a yeshiva bridegroom is escorted to the canopy. He is walking with slow steps, smiling, and Shayna Matisdorf is hanging back behind him in a dark plain dress, a kerchief covering her hair. Kishote waves, catches her eye, and she shyly smiles.

> *. . . Voice of bridegroom and voice of bride . . .*

The Ezrakh walks up to the Wall, and spreads out his black-clad arms on the stones. The song peters out, dies off, and all through the alley there falls a silence, except for the screams of the circling birds; a long silence, all eyes on the slight black figure embracing the Wall, and Don Kishote feels in a rush the emotion he tried in vain to work up when he kissed the stones. His spine warmly prickles.

Leaning against an Arab house in shadow, Sam Pasternak is remembering his first visit to the Wall with his kibbutznik father. The rough barrel-chested bareheaded Zionist, holding the five-year-old boy's hand, glared hostility at the wailing breast-beating Jews in black. "If I ever have the power," he said, "or if you ever get it, son, the first thing to do is tear down this wall, or blow it up. We're not victims anymore. We're workers of our land. Our history has begun anew. The past is dust." The words come back strongly, and he knows what his antireligious father would have said about this sight. It is happening because a lot of good Jewish boys died, killing many, many more good misled Arab boys. No Messiah has brought that old man here, and some goyish talk in New York may shut off the Wall again to the Jews tomorrow.

The Ezrakh turns back to the soldiers, and his wrinkled bearded face is radiant. He speaks quietly, but in the dead silence all hear him. "Why have you stopped singing, children?" He takes up the song in a weak reedy voice, holding both hands in the air.

. . . Voice of celebration and voice of joy . . .

Soon all the soldiers are singing it, roaring it, crowding around him, and he begins an unsteady little dance. Almost tottering, he shuffles through the soldiers and heads for Levi Eshkol. The Prime Minister stares in surprise, then self-consciously smiles. The Ezrakh takes his hand. The two old men link arms and go round and round in time to the singing:

. . . . Voice of celebration and voice of joy,
Voice of bridegroom and voice of bride . . .

Don Kishote darts through the jubilating paratroopers to Shayna, who stands apart at the entrance to the alley. "Come, Shayna!"

"Are you crazy?" She snatches her hand away from him. "It's no place for me."

"Why not? Look at them." Three girl soldiers who found their way into the alley are doing a round dance, arms on each other's shoulders.

"No!"

"How is Aryeh?"

"He won't do his algebra." All this is shouted over the noise.

"Good for him. It's a holiday." Don Kishote drags her toward the Wall, where Eshkol and the Ezrakh still shuffle around arm in arm. The Prime Minister has his helmeted head thrown back, and his expression is ecstatic. From a pocket Yossi pulls a handkerchief and thrusts it on her. "You'll dance with me! It's fitting! We're at a wedding, aren't we?"

Despite herself she bursts out laughing. He is offering her an East European wedding caper frowned on by the strictly pious; unmarried girls and boys sometimes dance without touching, each holding a corner of the handkerchief. The wedding song is thundering in the alley with the lung power of more than a hundred soldiers, some are happily cavorting around the Ezrakh and the Prime Minister in a ring, and Shayna Matisdorf can't hold out.

"So, all right, we'll be two lunatics instead of one, for once. Let's dance."

And so they do, twirling here and there with the handkerchief taut between them, smiling in each other's eyes. "I love you," he cries over the singing, and he falls, ripping the handkerchief from her hand.

"What's that?"

"Quiet. Don't move."

He is lying on a sort of bench; the side seat, he realizes, of a jolting command car. His head is in Shayna's lap. Another earsplitting blast nearby, and a bespectacled medical orderly on the opposite seat, fat and swarthy, says, "They're detonating mines, sir."

"Mines? What to all the devils is happening, Shayna? Where are we going, and why?"

"Quiet, I say, Yossi. We're in the no-man's-land."

"Sir, you fainted at the Wall," the orderly says. "Colonel Gur ordered me to escort you back to Tel Hashomer."

"By your life, no." Kishote tries to sit up. Shayna pushes him down. They hear more explosions, as the command car grinds and rumbles over rough terrain. "Shayna, I'm all right. I've eaten nothing for days, that's all."

"Mama gave you a big omelette this morning. You're off your head, and you're going back to the hospital."

"Right now?"

"We're taking the Ezrakh home first. So you can see Aryeh, but then to Tel Hashomer you go. I'll come along."

"Well, step one, I see Aryeh. Good. Then we'll negotiate, hamoodah." He utters a small groan.

"Sir, I can give you some painkilling medication," says the orderly.

"Not for what ails me. *'Stay me with flagons, comfort me with apples: for I am sick of love.'* How are you fixed for flagons and apples, orderly?"

"I have codeine, sir."

"Pay no attention to him." Shayna is blushing at the Song of Songs verse. She bends over and kisses his lips, a mere brush. "There. Now shut up about flagons and apples."

When the car stops at the house he sits up spryly, jumps out, and helps the Ezrakh alight from the front seat. The old man takes Kishote's head in his hands, and kisses his cheek. "Man of valor, be blessed with a swift full recovery."

"Amen," says Kishote. To the medical orderly, once the Ezrakh and Shayna are inside, he mutters, "I'll take that codeine."

He follows Shayna up the stairs. Over her shoulder, as she opens the door, he sees Yael sitting on the dingy couch with her arm around Aryeh. "Abba!" The boy jumps up and runs to him. "Imma's here, Imma came back." He hugs his father, pressing his head hard against the uniform. "Abba, were you on Har Ha'bayit?"

"I was on Har Ha'bayit, and at the Wall. I'll take you there soon."

Yael stands up. Shayna's mother is pottering in the kitchenette, where a kettle noisily steams. "Hello there, Shayna. Your mother insists on making tea. I begged her not to bother. Yossi, Aryeh told me you were injured." She comes and puts a hand gently to his face. "But I know you, you're indestructible."

"By God, this is a surprise, Yael. How did you get back? When?"

"This morning, on the first plane I could get out of New York. Oh, Kishote, what a victory! Har Ha'bayit b'yadenu! The world must be going crazy! Nasser is finished. The Arabs are routed. I'm so proud of you, of the army, of the country! I'm home, and I'll never leave again." She puts a hand on Aryeh's head. "How big he is!"

"Where are the sardines?" moans old Mrs. Matisdorf. "And the hard candies, Shayna? Why do you put things where nobody can find them?"

Nothing will do but they all have to sit down at the table. Mrs. Matisdorf, complaining at every step, ordering Shayna around, serves tea, a can of sardines, dry crackers, and a plate of red and yellow sour balls. "I wasn't expecting company," she apologizes in painful gasps, "and there's a war."

Shayna is floored as much by Yael's looks as by her thunderbolt return. This is an American beauty to the teeth, her yellow hair fashionably cut, her jewelry subdued and elegant, the white suit, though all creased, killingly of the moment. Perhaps she has put on a few pounds, but if so she is only more alluring.

While he gulps tea to wash down the codeine, Kishote too is sizing up Yael. Not looking at her with Shayna's female eye he misses the details, but he gets the idea. As the army has recaptured Jerusalem, Yael has come to recapture him. To him her beauty is an old story, and her willpower too, but this swift assault dazes him, and he is in no shape to contain it. Try to stall her, anyway! Poor beloved Shayna . . .

"Well, look, there's this medical orderly downstairs, Yael," he says, "waiting to take me back to Tel Hashomer, so — just for a checkup," he adds to Aryeh, who looks at him anxiously and stops putting sour balls in his pocket.

"Excellent. I'll go with you," says Yael. "Find out what's what. I'll talk to the doctors, I know half of them. And I'll take Aryeh home, and get the flat in shape."

Kishote glances at Shayna. She picks up a satchel of books and gives them to Yael. "He's a diligent student, Yael. I'll arrange a transfer from the Haifa school, whenever you say."

"Aunt Shayna, I finished the algebra."

"Fine. Your clothes —"

"I packed them," says Yael. "I want to thank you, Shayna. Aryeh loves you and I don't blame him. You've been like a relative. Truly, you are Aunt Shayna!"

"Well, he's a promising boy. And he's good."

"Nobody ate the sardines," grumbles the mother. "Don't Americans eat sardines, Mrs. Nitzan?"

"Goodbye, Sabta [Grandma]." Aryeh runs to her, hugs her, and returns to Yael.

Kishote holds out his hand to Shayna as Yael is closing Aryeh's little suitcase of clothing. "There's no way to thank you," he whispers. "There are no words."

"Flagons and apples," murmurs Shayna.

"Ah yes. Flagons and apples."

"For God's sake, Kishote, take care of yourself. Do what the doctors say. We've won this war."

When the Nitzans are gone, Shayna sits down at the table, pours herself more tea, and bends over the cup, leaning her head on both hands. Her dark hair falls over her face.

"Well, at least we gave them tea," groans Mrs. Matisdorf. "Guests are guests. I'm going back to bed."

"I'll clean up," says Aunt Shayna in a muffled voice, warm tears trickling over her fingers. "And I'll eat the sardines. I'm empty."

43

Banzai!

As the shuttle climbed Zev Barak was looking down again on Manhattan in morning sunlight — spiking towers, gleaming rivers, cobweb fringe of bridges and wharfs, oblong slab of the United Nations — a passing fair sight, but he had work to do after yesterday's tremendous turmoil at the UN over Israel's march to the Temple Mount. From the pile of newspapers on the seat beside him he took the *Cleveland Plain Dealer* and began to ring key excerpts in red. Under the banner headline

ISRAELIS NEAR CANAL, CAPTURE OLD JERUSALEM!
JORDAN ACCEPTS CEASE-FIRE, EGYPT FIGHTS ON

the stunning photograph appeared once more of sweaty unshaven paratroopers holding their helmets and looking up in awe and exaltation at the Wall. The lead story was a breathless paean to Israel's victories. Feature articles and the main editorial expressed incredulous admiration and total support.

"Are you that angry with me?"

He looked up, startled. Emily Cunningham stood there in a yellow summer dress and a big yellow-and-red straw hat.

"Good God. *You!*"

"You walked by me without a word. If that's how you want it from now on, okay."

"How should I know you'd be on this shuttle? I figured you'd gone home yesterday. I didn't see you under that hat."

The stewardess in a nearby seat said severely, "Madame, the seat belt sign is on."

Barak whisked the papers off the seat. "Sit, Queenie."

She did, and barked. He peered at her. "I roll over, too. As you may know." He glanced uneasily at the stewardess, who looked as though she was considering restraining the barking woman. "I went shopping yesterday, and bought this damn hat at Bonwit's, simply to cheer myself up after the Hester fiasco. It's just another fiasco. I feel as though I'm wearing a pizza."

"It's a pretty hat. Vivacious."

"Oh, you like it?" Her drawn look gave way to a tremulous smile. "Listen, I *must* explain about Hester. But you have to read all those papers, I suppose."

"Yes, we're meeting at the embassy about the press reaction to the war."

"My God, Zev, the press is magnificent. I read the *Times* in the cab. Israel, Israel, Israel! The world's new heroes."

"Emily, remember what Napoleon's old Corsican mother said when he was crowned emperor? '*Pourvu que ce dure.*' "

"It'll last, never fear. There hasn't been a story like this in our century. The Jews rising from the ashes, two million defeating seventy million —"

He pushed the papers aside, and with some effort shifted his mind from war and the fate of Israel to the nonsense at the St. Moritz. "What's there to explain about Hester? I enjoyed the visit to the gallery."

"You most certainly did not."

"Well, it got to be a lot of spiders, but they were very artistic spiders. Especially the big painting people were crowding around —"

Emily said, "*Fornicating Arachnids.*"

"That's the one."

"Well, actually, that one caused the trouble. Hester barged in on me in hysterics while you were coming from the UN, and I couldn't just kick her out —"

"What was the trouble about the *Fornicating Arachnids?*"

"Oh, to make a long story short, the Guggenheim *didn't* buy it. The docent just asked the price. Hester's agent told the *Times* critic it was sold. He printed the story and the Guggenheim denied it. So the critic took Hester's skin off in a column —"

"Big job, skinning Hester."

"Oh, shush. She came to cry on my shoulder, and then you showed up all crazed for gitchi-gitchi, but what could I do?"

"I deny being crazed for anything. I do think just the two of us would have enjoyed that Greek restaurant more."

"Dear, I felt sorry for Hester, she was so upset —"

"Upset? The woman ate a whole baby goat."

"It was a small one. Hester eats when she's upset. I'll go back to my seat, Zev. I do want to talk to you, though. Really. It's urgent."

"Give me twenty minutes or so with these papers. Why didn't you let me know you'd be on this plane?"

"I decided to take it about five A.M., when I got tired of tossing." She walked up the aisle. A trace of her scent hovered, calling up warm Growlery memories, then the air vent blew it away, and he smelled the ink of the newspapers.

The *Chicago Tribune*'s front page showed the three generals striding into the Old City: Dayan radiating stern triumph, the Ramatkhal on his left looking strained and ironic, and Uzi Narkiss on his right, where Barak could not help picturing himself. A staged photo, of course. Still, in one stark image there was the Return. The picture would go down in world history, and he was not in it. But he had the rest of his life to live, and urgent work at hand. The newspapers as he went through them spoke in a rare single voice. The underdog threatened with a second Holocaust had turned on the exterminators, routing them in battle. Sometimes stated plainly in the papers, sometimes implied, the victory was a reversal of Auschwitz, a resurgence of the Jewish people, biblical in grandeur. For once, Israel had no reason to complain of its press treatment.

The reported reaction of American Jews was striking, too.

Until now American Zionists had been a vocal but peripheral few. Now the Jews were closing up like a fist behind Israel, pouring out money, volunteering in uncounted (and unusable) numbers to fight or to serve, flooding Washington with demands for support of Israel's right to survive, against the Russian snarls and threats at the United Nations. Jordan's humiliated acceptance of the cease-fire had brought applause last night in the UN gallery, and cheers from the mob gathered outside. There had been cynical comments in the Israeli delegation: *"Nothing succeeds like success," "Americans like winners,"* and so on. But Barak thought this explosion of American Jewish support was from the grass roots and irreversible. The Return had spoken to the soul of the diaspora, and its center of gravity was shifting.

The ticket wagon came rolling down the aisle. "You're an Israeli general?" The pretty stewardess stared at the credit card and the uniform. "Why aren't you in the war?"

"I'm the military attaché in Washington."

"Do you mind if I tell the captain you're on board?"

"Not at all."

She rushed up the aisle, and returned bright-eyed and red-faced. "Captain O'Kane invites you to the flight deck, General."

Passing Emily's hat he bent to say, "Hi, go back to my seat, I'll be right with you."

"Okay, toots."

Gray-haired and plump, Captain O'Kane looked more like a bank manager than an airline pilot. "General, I flew Helldivers in the South Pacific," he said, shaking hands, "and, sir, you've got yourself one outstanding air force. What a victory! Sit down, sir." Until the Washington Monument showed above the horizon, Barak was regaled with World War II air combat tales, shouted over the signal jargon on the controller circuit. "Pleasure meeting you, General. My hat's off to your country. Sorry you have to return to your seat now."

As he came out the young stewardess said to passengers in the front seats, "Here he is." A few started to clap. He passed down the aisle amid respectful smiling faces and scattered hand-clapping. He dropped down beside Emily, muttering, *"Pourvu que ce dure."*

"Oh, come on, it's thrilling," she said.

"That it is. You wanted to talk to me?"

"We are approaching National Airport. Kindly fasten seat belts and return seat backs to their full upright position."

"Yes, listen, Zev. When Nakhama visited the school, she got into the Growlery."

"She did? How come?"

"She said she had to use the bathroom. What was I to do, tell her to go in the rhododendrons? I tried to drag her to the main building. She went for the Growlery like a bulldozer."

"Well, so what?"

"Kindly extinguish all cigarettes and prepare to land."

"She saw the pistachios."

A pause. "So? The whole world eats pistachio nuts."

"Zev, has she ever said anything to you about me? About us?"

"No. Absolutely not. She likes you."

"Yes, so she said. But she also said other things."

"What things?"

"Things. I damn near didn't come to the St. Moritz. Truth to tell, Wolf, I was *glad* Hester showed up. There now."

Barak glanced at his watch. "We'll continue this in the coffee shop, okay?"

She closed a clammy hand on his. "Great. It's good I took this plane. I'm all at sixes and sevens."

The landing was hard and bouncy. "Yikes!" she exclaimed, jumping.

"Steady on, Queenie." As he unbuckled his seat belt, he thought he should lighten her mood. "Now, about those two love-making spiders —"

"Yes, dear." She managed a smile. "What about them?"

"Why did she paint the boy spider so puny? And why does he look so miserable?"

"Zev, the male *is* puny, and the female eats him right afterward. That's spider biology. How would you like that, hey kiddo? One rapturous moment, and crunch, crunch, crunch?"

In the terminal he suddenly said to her, "Look, go ahead to the coffee shop. I'll meet you there. I see my assistant attaché at the gate."

"Right." She drifted away among the exiting passengers.

"Mordechai, ma nishma?" His assistant, a stocky muscular paratrooper captain, looked strangely glum, considering the news. "Why the sad face?"

Mordechai replied in low guttural Hebrew, "Ultra-secret. We sank a Soviet spy ship."

All was jocund excitement in the crowded street outside the embassy, even among the newsmen and the TV technicians; inside, happy scurrying and chattering in the halls and on the staircase; and in the ambassador's inner office silent gloom. "Why, none of this is conclusive!" Barak was scanning the Teletype report. "It's not even clear that the ship sank. Can't we check that?"

"The secure telephone is out," said Mordechai. "That's the latest Teletype."

The slumped ambassador groaned, "No doubt they're running around in the Kirya like poisoned mice. Our greatest day, and this happens! *Yiddisheh mazel* [Jewish luck]."

"God help us if it's true," said Mordechai.

The ambassador picked up his ringing telephone. "Yes? — Hold on. Zev, it's personal and urgent, from Philip, whoever that is."

Barak's hand shot out for the receiver. "Barak here."

"Can you meet me at the Cosmos Club in ten minutes?" Chris Cunningham sounded as perturbed as Barak had ever heard him.

"Yes." He hung up. "Abe, don't look so concerned. Such things happen, and —"

"What makes you think I'm concerned?" The ambassador laid a hand on a stack of newspapers. "Read these, and you'll believe we can beat the Soviet Union, too."

The club was a five-minute walk from the embassy. Cunningham and Barak went upstairs to the grandiose library, which at that hour was empty, and they sank into red leather chairs near a huge globe. Cunningham wore his usual gray suit and pinned collar, with the inevitable vest and watch chain, sultry though the weather was. He rubbed his hands nervously on bony knees, then burst out, "See here, Zev, are your people over there out of their minds? All fouled up? Drunk with victory? What possessed your air force to attack a United States warship?"

"American?" Barak gasped. "It was one of *your* ships?"

"An electronic surveillance vessel. It was disobeying Joint Chiefs of Staff orders, steaming off Sinai, but still —"

"But it had Russian markings, Chris."

"The hell it did."

"That's the last word we've got. It was presumed Egyptian, and it refused to identify itself, so the pilot hit it. Then he flew low and through the smoke saw Russian letters on the hull."

"Combat pilots see weird things. I'm telling you what happened. It was flying a huge American flag. Many casualties. There will be hell to pay."

"It didn't sink?"

"It didn't and it won't. However —"

"This is fearful. Let me call my embassy right now, Chris." He rushed down the great curved staircase to a booth, talked to the ambassador in spare veiled words, and hurried back to Cunningham. "Listen, we were afraid the Russians might seize the pretext to get into the war. This is a very different story. The ambassador's devastated and desperately sorry. It's a colossal mistake and my government will make amends, that's certain, but —"

"All right, all right." Cunningham was holding up both palms. "In World War II we bombed our own troops, sank our own ships, and we've had gruesome foul-ups in Vietnam. These things happen in war. That doesn't lessen your country's culpability one bit." His cold clipped tone moderated. "Now then. We're amazed that Nasser didn't accept the cease-fire. He could have halted your army halfway to the Canal. By now it's probably there. What's going on?"

"We think his generals have been lying to him."

"Yes, either that, or he's in shock." The CIA man's eyes drooped almost shut. "So what will your people do now about Syria? There are those here who want to know."

Again Barak was caught in the bind of being an unskilled

back-channel conduit. This was something Sam Pasternak should be handling. Sam was senior to him, closer to Cunningham, a professional in intelligence. "Well, I can try to find out."

"Don't stall, Zev," Cunningham almost snapped. "Nasser has handed your country a whole extra day and night for operations. Will you really let slip a chance to eliminate that menace on the Golan Heights?"

"Would your government understand such an action?"

A pause, and Cunningham barely nodded.

"Is that a message, Chris, or your opinion?"

"Of course it's only my opinion."

"Where can I reach you?"

"My office."

"I'll call you in an hour or so."

As they were walking out Cunningham said, taking Barak's arm, "You're astounding the world, you know, you Jews, by returning to your land as Isaiah prophesied you'd do. Maybe we're in the end of days, the Day of the Lord. On my low working level, you're handing Russian communism its first major setback on the battlefield and in world politics since Yalta. Only a people of God could pull that off."

"Chris, I know my ambassador's eating his heart out about that ship. I'm sick to my soul. Lord only knows what other blunders we've committed, but at least we've won the war and saved ourselves."

"No argument."

On Connecticut Avenue near the embassy, Barak and Emily sat that evening at a table in a small restaurant called Piraeus, her favorite in Washington. Emily liked Greek food, and especially Greek wine. "I'm as tense as a treed cat," she said. She was in her schoolmistress mode: no hat, hair in a bun, heavy glasses, and a brown shirtwaist and skirt. "Where's that wife of yours? I'll have another drink, if you won't." He signalled to the waiter for refills. "How could you leave the embassy, with all hell breaking loose? Will the new Soviet resolution pass?"

"Compelling us to withdraw to the armistice lines? Not if the

Americans stand firm. Otherwise . . ." He shrugged. "But it's unthinkable. The Russians are blustering to cover their disaster."

"Their ass," said Emily. "I say that, and I'm a very proper lady."

Nakhama came bustling in, wearing a wrinkled flowered housedress. "I was dressing Ruti for a birthday party and she fussed like a bride. Sorry I'm so late. Where's the ladies' room, Emily?"

"Come with me. It's hard to find, you go through the kitchen."

Off they went, smiling and chatting, leaving Barak to ponder how to handle this dinner. His notion had been to reassure Queenie that Nakhama hadn't a ghost of a suspicion about their fugitive wistful affair. A touchy business, to be gotten through quickly. By luck a call from the embassy might cut it short. When the ladies returned a waiter approached in a puffy skirt and long stockings, with a ferocious black mustache and snapping black eyes. Emily said, waving aside the menus, "I telephoned. We're having the baby goat Fársala, for three."

"Ah, madame," said the waiter, "the girl who answered was new. Baby goat on Saturday and Wednesday. Today is Thursday. Stuffed octopus."

"Oh?" Emily shrugged at Nakhama. "Sorry about this."

"No, no, it's quite all right." Nakhama turned brightly to the waiter. "Octopus stuffed with what?"

"Octopus, madame."

"How's that? You stuff a big octopus with little octopuses?"

Emily burst out in a nervous guffaw, and Nakhama giggled too.

The waiter replied with expressive gestures: "No, madame. The octopus, it is scooped out, minced with olives, grapes, lemon, and wine, and stuffed back into itself."

"Nakhama, I recommend the *katsikaki*," said Emily.

"What is that?"

The waiter said, "That is goat."

"Teenage goat, I guess," said Emily. Nakhama glanced at her and they both laughed again. There was no more tension between these two women, Barak thought, than if they worked together in an office. So far, so good!

"Ah, no, madame. Very young goat." White teeth flashed under the black mustache. The waiter was getting into the act. "Kid. Like in kid gloves."

"We Moroccans love kid," said Nakhama. "I'll try it."

They were talking about the war news when the waiter came hurrying to the table. "General, there is a telephone call for you."

Jumping up, Barak said, "Thank you. Please serve the ladies some of the wine."

"You'll like this," Emily said to Nakhama, as the waiter uncorked the bottle. "Specialty of the house. Samian. Quite a romantic wine! Byron wrote about Samian wine."

"Lord Byron! Well, that is romantic. I once tried to read Lord Byron in Hebrew, but it was hard. Maybe the translation was no good."

Emily swirled the dark red wine, sniffed, tasted, and nodded. The waiter poured for Nakhama and left. Emily raised her glass. "Well, to Israel's marvellous victory."

"The war isn't over yet," said Nakhama, "but thank you. And here's to our wonderful American friends, like your father." They could both see Barak gesticulating in the telephone booth. "Look. I think there is news."

"Do you like the wine?"

"Oh, very nice. But I better not have much."

"Wine disagrees with you?"

"Oh, no, no, just the opposite." Nakhama chuckled, looked arch, and dropped her voice. "The fact is, I don't have a head for alcohol. Even a little makes me — well, you know — very affectionate."

Emily hoped her smile did not look too uncomfortable. "Why, that's all to the good."

"Yes, unless your man happens to be too busy for affection." She gestured toward the phone booth. "Then it can be very frustrating. Better to stay sober."

Wishing she were someplace other than at this table with Nakhama Barak — at the South Pole, for instance — Emily said what came into her head, too discomposed for subtleties. "A husband shouldn't ever be that busy."

"Ah, what husbands shouldn't be, and what they are —!" Nakhama smiled, and took a healthy sip. "This is delicious. Samian
wine. I must remember."

(What the HELL *is Gray Wolf batting about on and on and on?)*

"Of all the wives I know, you must have the least to worry
about."

"I didn't say worried. I said frustrated, when I'm drunk and
he's busy. Worried? Listen, Emily, our army is full of pretty little
girls who make eyes at the officers. Elegant ladies too go after them,
especially the brilliant officers, the front-runners. Everybody knows
who they are, and Israelis idolize the army. I've learned not to
worry." She looked toward the booth, and drank more wine. "Oh,
well. So let him be busy. This is good. You're not drinking."

"Oh yes I am." Emily gulped wine.

"Of course those women are not like you, Emily." Nakhama
rambled on between sips. "Israelis are Israelis. One's like another,
more or less. You're an American woman, you're highly cultured,
you know about Lord Byron and Samian wine, you're so well read!
Zev says you can be very funny, too. I can see that. But the main
thing is, we Israelis live in a tiny world and you're from the big
world. *Ha'olam ha'gadol,* we say. Still, as I told you at the school,
I'm not worried, it's all right. Oh, my, I've finished my wine,
haven't I? Foolish of me. No more." She looked Emily in the eye.

"Ladies, you have great luck!" The waiter trotted up, smiling.
"The chef has found a baby goat! It is very, very small, we can
prepare it in forty minutes."

Nakhama said, "Well, we'll ask my husband. Meantime I'll
have some more wine, please."

"Your husband?" The waiter looked perplexed and glanced
toward the booth. "Oh. Yes. Your husband. Yes, madame, of
course." He poured wine for both and went off.

"Isn't that comical?" said Nakhama. "You arrived here with
Zev and sat around drinking, so the poor man got confused. Say,
you two could easily be a married couple."

Emily drank off her entire glass of wine, and took a desperate
plunge. "Now see here, Nakhama, let's assume General Barak and
I were having an affair, which is *wildly* impossible. Not that man of

yours. And let's assume you let me know you were on to it, but didn't object to sharing his affections, as you almost seem to be doing. That would mean swift death to the whole thing, maybe not for another woman but certainly for me. I have my pride, and I'm sure you understand that! For a lady from a tiny world, as you put it, you're okay. As we say, there are no flies on you."

"A funny expression. But I don't follow you. I haven't offered to share Zev with you, of course not, and in fact —"

"Tremendous news." Barak came striding to the table, and fell into his seat. "Egypt has quit!"

"Ah, at last," said Nakhama.

Emily said, "Quit? What's happened, exactly?"

"Sorry I was so long. Fantastic scene at the Security Council! Federenko was making the nastiest speech yet, implying that if Israel didn't withdraw at once to the old armistice lines, Russia would send troops. Then the Egyptian delegate suddenly asked for the floor, and read a few sentences from a piece of paper. He could hardly choke out the words. Egypt was agreeing to a cease-fire in place, *no withdrawal!*"

Nakhama exclaimed, "Well, well! Nasser's generals finally told him what's happened."

Emily crazily laughed. "Well, that is marvellous news! Let's have another bottle of wine."

Barak's thick graying eyebrows went up. "You two haven't polished off this one already?"

"We've made a good start, haven't we, Nakhama?"

"We certainly have." Nakhama draped an arm around her husband and gave him a long kiss on the lips. "What nice news! Let's really enjoy our dinner."

"Well, the sooner the food comes, the better," said Barak. "I'll have to rush back to the embassy."

The Baraks got into low quick Hebrew talk. "What about the Syrian front?" she asked.

"Nothing new." Plenty was new, but not her business.

"Emily's very clever. We've had a nice chat. That wine is wonderful, try it."

"Well, don't drink too much, you'll get silly."

"Don't be afraid, I won't disgrace you," Nakhama giggled.

Emily shot her a sharp look. Barak said hastily, "We're being very rude. We're just talking about the war."

"Not altogether," said Nakhama. "He told me not to drink too much wine."

"Well, he's pretty busy," said Emily. They both laughed, with the special female note and side-glances that forever exclude men.

Joking was Emily's best cover. She was hating herself for agreeing to this dinner, and yet, did it really matter that much? Once Nakhama came to Washington, how long could she have held on? No flies, indeed, on this Israeli wife! Nakhama had moved slowly, surely, like a samurai duellist in a Japanese movie. She had bided her time, taken her stance, and struck. Flash, whiz, death! What was left for Emily was only the slow-motion fall to earth, disemboweled. Barak was pouring wine. She lifted her glass.

"Nakhama, banzai!"

"Banzai?" Nakhama glanced at her husband. "Isn't that Japanese?"

He nodded. "It means 'victory.' "

"How nice. Victory over the Egyptians, yes?" She raised her glass. "Banzai, Emily."

They clinked glasses and drank. Zev Barak was delighted, if obscurely puzzled, at how well the two women were getting along. So, the dinner had worked out as planned. He could get back to the job with one worry the less.

44

The Bear Growls

Zev came home from the embassy with a sheaf of maps and documents under his arm as usual, and found his wife drooping in an armchair, a bottle of Israeli red wine beside her, and half a glassful in hand. She finished her wine at a gulp, and weaving to him, took away the maps and papers, and dropped them on a chair. "Good evening, General Barak. I thought you'd never get home. Do you love me?" She heavily embraced him, and heavily kissed him.

"Adom Atik," he said.

"Yes. Have some, and no night work! You haven't had a good night's sleep in a week."

"And you've had a lot of Adom Atik."

"A drop or two, yes. I'm going to bed, even if you aren't."

"Right with you."

"Ah, excellent." Nakhama's random walk terminated at the bedroom, and with a languid leer over her shoulder she shut the door. He took the half-empty bottle into the kitchen, and was surprised to come on another, quite empty. What was Nakhama up to? Celebrating?

Well, no wine for him. Donning his glasses, he spread maps

and papers on the dining table. On top was the coded telex he had
sent Pasternak, arguing for immediate action against Syria.

> . . . Our mutual friend Philip strongly hints that the White House
> will not be at all displeased if we end this war by giving Syria,
> Russia's main client, a well-deserved bloody nose. You know
> Philip's a sound source. I urge you to talk again to Eshkol and
> Rabin, while time remains!
>
> I understand Dayan's worry about the Russians, but when
> will we have another chance like this? From those bunkers on the
> Golan the Syrians can go on throwing ten tons of shells a minute
> on the Galilee communities, to say nothing of a rain of Katyusha
> rockets. How long can we work that fertile valley under such a
> threat? How can we ask farmers to raise families there?
>
> The whole operation can be a fait accompli in 24 hours. The
> babbling in the Security Council has hardly started. Once we hold
> the Heights, we can at least bargain for demilitarization. Dado can
> do it. He should go.

Good argument, but alas it would arrive too late, out of date!
Events had speeded up, and both Syria and Israel were condition-
ally accepting the cease-fire. He set the paper aside with a sad shrug,
and turned to the maps. The cease-fire lines with Syria marked on
them were tentative. Clouds of political gas would erupt in the UN
over every disputed meter of ground. He had to prepare to sit
behind Gideon Rafael at the council, feed him facts, back him with
authority —

The telephone rang. "Zev? Mordechai. Urgent telex from Pasternak. Plain language."

"Read it."

" 'Boss changed his mind and is going to the party as per your telex
about Philip. Urgent we talk on secure line.' "

"Call him and say I'm on my way."

He went to the bedroom to tell Nakhama; not the first time
she would be disappointed this way, nor the last. The lights were
on. The whole room smelled of Joy perfume, picked up in a duty-
free shop and worn on what she called "big nights." She was sitting
up in bed with her glossy black hair fanned out over the fancy
negligee from Garfinckel's, his birthday present, also reserved for

big nights. "Nakhama?" No use, she was dead asleep. He snapped off the light.

Hours later he got back exhausted yet exhilarated by the rush of events, and turned the light on. There she was exactly as before, not having moved a hair. Her breathing was noisy and quick. "Nakhama!"

Eyes blearily opened. "Hmmm? Oh, so you're finally coming to bed? High time." She sat up and fell back with a cry of "Ow! My head! Zevi, my head!" She put both hands to her temples. "My pulse, it's going a mile a minute! Oy! My mouth is dry as paper. Zev, I must have what they call the Hong Kong flu."

"You have what they call a hangover." He leaned over and kissed her cheek, smiling. "I'll get you something."

She gulped the fizzing Bromo-Seltzer, staring at him over the glass with huge reddened eyes. "It was the Adom Atik," she gasped between gulps. "I drank and drank while I waited for you. Zev, do I look as bad as I feel?"

"You look all right. Listen, we're attacking Syria. Dado's tanks are starting to climb the Golan Heights at Kefar Szold about now. And that isn't all the news."

"What else? Zev, why is my heart pounding so? I could be dying."

"You're not. Listen to this! It seems our Noah captured Sharm el Sheikh."

"Noah did *what*?"

"He'll get no medal, he found that the Egyptians had evacuated the position. Still, he did lead the landing party that first entered the fort. Pasternak told me this. There's a picture in *Ha-'aretz* of Noah nailing the flag over the main building."

"Beautiful! So he's all right?"

"Not a scratch. Nakhama, I need sleep. Two or three hours, then I fly to New York on the first shuttle. The Security Council will be going up in flames, and Gideon Rafael wants me there."

Nakhama gnashed her teeth, flickered her tongue, and moaned, "My mouth, the taste, the taste! It would disgust a buzzard. Well, come to bed, but don't come near me. That's wonderful about Noah."

"Isn't it? You know, when he was eleven and I brought him to the withdrawal ceremony, he told me he would take Sharm back, and by my life, he did it." Barak was stripping down to underwear.

"Syria!" Nakhama said. "And what about the Russians?"

"That's it. Dado must go like lightning, and the Golan's a nasty job. The tanks have to climb rocky cliffs a thousand feet high single file under artillery fire, then break through minefields, barbed wire, concrete bunkers, and maybe five hundred T-54s and T-55s waiting for them hull down."

"Oo-wah! Can they do it, Zev?"

"They'll have to. In one day, too."

Sitting among Rafael's staff advisers on Friday morning, Barak was unnoticeable; no uniform, just a gray tropical suit. Before the crisis he had been unable to get into it, now it was pleasantly loose. Constant strain, skipped meals, lack of sleep, and lack of appetite were thinning him down. Nor was he hungry today, though he had had but one cup of coffee on the shuttle. The berating of his country by the likes of Bulgaria, Yugoslavia, Libya, and Algeria was mere noise, but stomach-turning noise.

He had to admire the gray-haired Rafael's steady nerves and abrasive ripostes. The more Israel was attacked, the more time Rafael could gain for Dado Elazar on the Golan by responding. About noon when Federenko gave a long menacing speech comparing the "aggressor" Israel to Nazi Germany, Rafael drew gallery applause by retorting that such talk came strangely from a nation which had partitioned Poland with Hitler's Reich, occupied the Baltic states as part of the deal, and supplied Nazi Germany's war against the Allies for two years. Federenko sat glaring, twisting a pencil round and round in his hand, or talking to his staff and ignoring the speaker.

Meantime Barak was keeping track of the fighting on a marked map and passing notes to Rafael. The Security Council debate was empty drone, for the real action, the hammering out of a new cease-fire resolution, was taking place in an antechamber. The Russians wanted the Israelis to halt at once on the Golan Heights and fall back into the valley, the Americans mildly urged a simple standstill on both sides, and their surrogates in Eastern Europe and Latin

America kept floating various compromises. A news flash toward evening buzzed through the UN building, briefly animating all the worn-down talkers and negotiators. To atone for failing his people, Nasser had resigned as President of Egypt! This occasioned speeches of tribute to the incomparable Arab leader which killed more time, to Gideon Rafael's great satisfaction, and these were still going on when Barak was summoned to the secure telephone in the Israeli office.

"Zev, Dado is not going to make it today," Pasternak said straight off. "I've just been up there by helicopter, to talk to him and the brigade commanders."

"Sam, the Kirya has told us otherwise."

"Well, now I'm telling you the facts. Communications have been a mess ever since Dayan reversed himself and ordered Dado to go. Even Rabin didn't know he'd done that."

"What!"

"Zev, by my life, the Ramatkhal was asleep at home. Dayan had told everyone to go home, the war was over, and Rabin was exhausted. So he went home, and he woke up to find the war was still on."

"Why did Dayan change?"

"Nobody knows. In theory only the Ramatkhal could order that attack, but you know Dayan. Dado was asleep too, for that matter, but they got him up, the brigades were ready, and they went. A ragged start, and I tell you the heroes were the bulldozer guys, climbing those slopes to cut paths for the tanks, with artillery blasting down at them from the ridge. It's a brilliant operation, only slow going. They won't reach Kuneitra tonight. The cease-fire has to be stalled. That's straight from Eshkol. Tell Rafael."

"The Americans won't go along, Sam."

"We believe they will. Eban has sent Rafael a declaration they can back. Dado needs until about noon tomorrow. That'll barely be sunrise in New York. Are they going to jabber all night? Just let Gideon get an adjournment until morning, and that'll do it."

"What does Eshkol think of Nasser's resignation?"

"Haven't you watched TV? The street mobs in Cairo are yelling for him to retract. *Nas-ser! Nas-ser!* Smartest thing he could do.

No question, he'll stay on top. Now, have you got your map handy? Note down these positions."

When Barak returned to the chamber the council president, an amiable but harried Dane, was rapping his gavel. "The chair recognizes the representative of Israel."

"I have just been authorized by my government to declare," said Rafael, reading with slow solemnity from a telex sheet, "that Israel accepts a renewed cease-fire" (sensation in the gallery, surprise and murmurs among delegates and staff) "and requests that the UN representative on the spot, General Odd Bull, immediately contact both combatant sides to arrange for strict and mutual observance of the cease-fire."

Spotty applause broke out in the gallery. Several representatives demanded to respond. Speaking first, Federenko denounced it as a transparent delaying tactic. The British delegate said he would have to consult his government. The French delegate spoke for twenty minutes with fluent eloquence, and Barak understood every word, but when the man finished he had not the slightest idea of the French position. The American, a Jewish former Supreme Court justice, hailed the move as a serious step to end the fighting.

But the council as a whole was far from satisfied. The talk continued well beyond midnight, until the exhausted Danish president called for an adjournment for a few hours. Even Federenko was too played out to argue against it. By then it was broad day on the Golan, seven time zones to the east, and Barak's last note to Rafael said Dado's forces were again on the move. Rafael acknowledged it with a faint weary grin, and invited Barak to rest in his flat.

"I'm just leaving Washington. I'll be there in half an hour." At nine in the morning the session was on again. Cunningham's voice was muffled, and there was a peculiar roar on the line. Barak had to strain to hear him.

"How can you possibly get here so soon?"

"I'm in a military aircraft. Can you meet me at the airport?"

"Sorry. I have to stay at Gideon Rafael's elbow. Things are getting red-hot here."

"You're telling me!" The staccato noise the CIA man made

might have been a laugh. "All right. Meet me in the lounge of the American delegation at nine forty-five."

The atmosphere in the council this morning was different. Federenko was silent, his face a flat Slav mask. At the moment the Bulgarian delegate, a Soviet mouthpiece, was holding forth. The Syrian delegate kept interjecting stridently, as his staff members rushed in and out again with papers and whispered messages. Now Barak was becoming seriously concerned about the Russians. The Security Council was a place of perhaps ninety-five percent boring maneuver, duplicity, and bluff, and five percent dangerous substance. This morning danger hung in the stale air, like a cloud with interior flickers of lightning. Even the Soviet puppets were moderating their vituperation to express real fear. The spokesmen were pale and their voices shook, like this pop-eyed whiskered Bulgarian's.

"To conclude," the simultaneous translation droned in Barak's earphones, "I ask the council president to compel Israel's ambassador to disclose all he knows of the battlefield situation, so that the council can act in the light of available facts. The criminal attackers are the best source of such facts, and must reveal them."

"There is no precedent," said the Dane with tired politeness to the Bulgarian, "and I know of nothing in the charter, that enables me to compel the Israeli ambassador to make a statement of any nature."

A tap on Barak's shoulder; a fresh-faced American with a blond crew cut was beckoning. Barak picked up his map and followed him into the hall and up the broad stairway. He did not recognize Cunningham at first, standing at a window in the American lounge, looking out at the uptown skyscrapers in the rain, in a gray slouch hat and a dark poplin raincoat, wearing no glasses. The young man left them. There was no one else in the lounge.

"How much more time do you people need?" Cunningham abruptly greeted him. "It had better not be much."

Still unused to spilling secrets to this eccentric gentile, though Pasternak had pushed him into the spot, Barak temporized. "It isn't much. By the time all this talk is over, it may be that —"

"General, how much? Another hour? Two hours?" Cunningham's razor tone was something new. "If you don't know, say so. If you have to talk to Pasternak, do it. Kosygin called the President to the hot line at nine o'clock this morning. Some of his words were, *'The situation approaches a catastrophe,'* and *'Military action is imminent.'*" Cunningham squinted at Barak. "I'm here to find out the state of play in the battlefield, Zev, and no fooling. The Syrians claim you're threatening Damascus. Are you?"

"Ridiculous. The key to the plateau is Kuneitra." Barak unfolded the map, and pointed. "You know the Golan Heights topography?"

"I'm beginning to."

"Our brigades have made a three-pronged attack to clear the plateau of the Syrian army. They're closing in on Kuneitra, and by now they may have taken it."

"Then why not stop advancing and firing?"

"The fog of war is thick up there, Chris. The Syrians may be stalling General Bull on a cease-fire, hoping the Russians will push through a withdrawal resolution. Meantime they're still firing."

Cunningham nodded, gnawing his thin lips. "Very well. Now, this is for your ears. Not for Rafael. Not for Pasternak. I want *you* to grasp the gravity of what's happening, Barak. The President has responded to that hot-line message with soft words. He's also ordered the Sixth Fleet to alter its cruising pattern so as to steam twice as close to the war zone as heretofore. That's his real answer. Soviet ships monitor every course change the Sixth makes. Kosygin will get that message. What the Russians will do next is the unknown element. I'll be here till this crisis is resolved. I need from you the straight facts the minute you learn them."

"Understood."

He went back to his seat. By a vagary of UN protocol the Syrian and Israeli ambassadors sat side by side, their staffs elbow to elbow behind them. A Syrian adviser fell into the seat right beside Barak, breathing hard, and asked an aide in Arabic for a map. "No, no!" He pushed aside one offered to him of all Syria, seventy thousand square miles. "Just the Golan Heights. Don't we have a map of the accursed Golan Heights?" Another was spread before him, an army chart of Mount Hermon, the Golan plateau and the cliffs, with the old armistice lines hatched in red. "All right. Now where the hell is this place called Kuneitra?"

Nobody answered at once, so Barak leaned over, put a finger on the map, and said in his rudimentary Arabic, "There you are, sir."

Arabic: "Ah, there, eh? Thank you."

Arabic: "Not at all, sir."

Only then did the Syrian blink and stare at Barak, then turn his back.

Federenko now walked out of the chamber, puffing Stalin-like at a curved pipe, with a chilling backward glance at Rafael. Zev Barak did not believe that World War III threatened over this tiny crag called the Golan Heights, of no earthly use to Syria except for bombarding the Israeli valley below. But as a boy he had heard the grown-ups say that World War II would surely not break out over Danzig. His nerves tightened.

A commotion was starting up in the Syrian staff, with much whispering and passing of notes. The French delegate had the floor, and was pushing General de Gaulle's view that the four superpowers should act to solve the crisis. (Barak had heard of Johnson's comment on that: *"Who the hell are the other two?"*) The Syrian ambassador sent a note to the council president, who nodded and called on him, with the Frenchman's consent, to announce grave news.

"Kuneitra has fallen." The Syrian, hoarse with emotion, spoke in thickly accented English. "The road to Damascus lies open to the Israeli aggressors, since our armed forces in good faith have laid down their arms. My government demands immediate action to halt, drive back, and punish the criminal aggressors."

The American ambassador hastily left, amid murmurs in the gallery and the staffs. The Frenchman resumed explaining how the four superpowers could arrange peace. Rafael passed to Barak a rapid scrawl in Hebrew, and the paper went back and forth between them.

Can this be true?

Yes, easily.

What's our last position, again?

A few kilometers away. Our scouts reported Kuneitra abandoned hours ago. It was even announced on Syrian radio, then contradicted. Balagan knows no boundaries.

Then this could be a piece of Syrian theater to prod the Russians to act.

I think it is.

Now Rafael showed Barak a handwritten note that had just come.

> *Gideon:*
> *Imperative we meet at once.*
> *Arthur Goldberg*

Goldberg was the white-haired Jew who, at President Johnson's urging, had stepped down from the Supreme Court to head the UN delegation. He was friendly but tough, and strictly out for the American interest. "Zev, call Jerusalem," Rafael whispered as he got up, "and by your life, find out what's happening!" Barak left the chamber, and in the delegates' lounge he encountered the blond crew cut, who silently beckoned. Down one corridor and another he led Barak. Cunningham waited in a shadowy dead end by some red-painted fire-fighting equipment.

"Listen carefully, General." The CIA man put a skinny hand on Barak's arm. "The word from the President is *stop*. Stop right now. Stop where you are. Announce in the council now that your army has *stopped*. Or it will be the worse for your country's present safety, and its future relations with America."

"Rafael is meeting with Goldberg right this minute, Chris."

"Very well. Now it's not Russian military intervention that concerns the President — yet. Our surveillance is pretty good. The Russians are not yet organized to intervene. What Kosygin is up to is a replay of Suez. A saber-rattling ultimatum. The Bear growls. International bombshell! The war stops, Soviet client saved! Political masterstroke out of military disaster! Understand?"

"Very clear."

"Okay. Federenko as we talk is probably getting the text of the ultimatum by teleprinter, and scribbling up a speech to go with it. Just grasp this, General, *the war must* NOT *be ended, like the Suez war, by a Russian ultimatum!* Your ambassador has to go in there *now,* before Federenko returns to the council, and announce that the Israeli army has stopped its advance and ceased firing. *Now!*"

"Understood."

Cunningham's manner and voice relaxed. "Have you taken Kuneitra?"

"The Syrians evacuated Kuneitra this morning. Probably by now our tanks have reached it."

"Then defuse this bombshell, General, and you've won yourself a war against Red Russia and its clients. And *certain ruling circles*" — his quote of the Soviet cliché dripped with sarcasm — "will not be deeply displeased with you."

Barak hurried to Rafael's office, where he called the Foreign Ministry on the open line to Jerusalem. "Is that you, Gideon?" Abba Eban's rich Oxonian-accented Hebrew. "I've already heard from Washington, and I've talked to Dayan here —"

"It's Zev Barak, Minister."

"Ah, Zev! The very man. Let me read you what I've drafted so far."

With his usual skill, the minister was putting into dignified words a pious knuckling under to the American pressure. In substance, Dayan had already agreed with General Odd Bull to an unconditional cease-fire by Israeli forces on the Golan, at any hour and subject to any supervisory arrangement set by the UN commander. The rest was up to Bull. On Israel's side, the war was over.

"Perfect, sir," said Barak, pulling out a notebook and pen. "Let me copy that and give it to Gideon, word for word —"

"No, no, it needs a touch here and there."

"Minister, time presses. Federenko —"

"I have the picture. Tell Gideon the statement is coming."

Passing through the diplomats' lounge, Barak saw the pipe-smoking Federenko huddling with Arab and communist ambassadors and making notes. He hastened into the chamber, where the British representative was holding forth, sounding much like Abba

Eban. Barak pulled a chair beside Rafael and told him about Eban's draft statement.

"Good, great," said Rafael. "But where is it? Goldberg gave me a hell of a stern warning, straight from Johnson."

"It's coming. Eban's still polishing it. Listen, Gideon, ask to be recognized!"

"For what? Till it comes, I have nothing to say."

The British ambassador was yielding to the Frenchman, who expressed admiration for his colleague's views, but wanted to urge collective action by the four superpowers.

"Well, then say it's coming! Summarize it. Say it's being translated. If Federenko comes in here — and I just saw him in the lounge talking with his gang — he'll ask for the floor and get it."

"And if I'm challenged to produce my government's instruction, and I don't have it, then what? Do I recite psalms till it comes?"

"Better that, Gideon, than Federenko's ultimatum."

Rafael raised his hand, and requested that the representative of France yield for a crucial message from the Israeli government. "*Monsieur le President,*" the Frenchman said, "since Israel fired the first shot and caused this war, its messages are unfortunately suspect. Nevertheless, out of courtesy to my colleague I will finish my thought and then yield."

His thought was that this catastrophe could yet be turned into opportunity by timely action of the four superpowers. He was developing the point when Federenko came in, took his seat, and brusquely requested to be recognized.

"I yield to the representative of the Soviet Union," said the Frenchman promptly, sitting back in his chair.

The Danish president said, "As the Israeli ambassador has previously requested recognition, the chair will first call on him."

"My government has accepted all conditions laid down by General Bull," Rafael rapped out at once, jumping up before either Federenko or the Frenchman could argue. This raised a general buzz, and he went on. "There is complete agreement between General Odd Bull and General Dayan that General Bull will fix the hour and supervisory arrangements for the cease-fire, as soon as he has communicated with the other side. On the Israeli side, therefore, the armed conflict is at an end, in compliance with the council's resolution 211. The council can turn its efforts to securing a durable peace, which is all Israel has ever sought."

Reporters were dashing from the press section as Federenko spoke harshly over the applause in the gallery. "What is all this vague talk? Is Mr. Rafael speaking for himself? Does he have authority from his government to announce this overdue capitulation to world condemnation? If so, why doesn't he produce his instruction? Is this another clumsy delaying tactic?"

"It's hardly capitulation, considering existing facts," snapped Rafael. "And *here* is my government's instruction," he added, brandishing a paper that Barak had just slipped into his hand, delivered from the office. "I ask the council's forbearance while I translate at sight. The official text in English will be available shortly."

As Rafael slowly read out Eban's precisely worded declaration, Zev could sense the tension dissipate in the council chamber, and the cloud of fear dissolve. This was without doubt the end of the war. The ambassadors at the round table were sitting back in their seats, relaxing, glancing at each other, even smiling. The Syrian staff were exchanging relieved glances and nods; they really seemed to have feared the Israeli army was marching on Damascus. Federenko was scowling as he slashed a pencil at papers before him and scribbled insertions.

Arthur Goldberg rose to compliment the Israeli government on its unilateral termination of hostilities, and pledged the support of the United States to obtain a just and lasting peace. Federenko was still revising, so the British ambassador echoed what Goldberg said. The Frenchman then pointed out that Israel had undoubtedly made this wise move so as to appear to advantage at the peace conference headed by the four superpowers, and his government would be willing — but Federenko raised his hand, and he yielded in midsentence.

As Federenko poured bitter scorn on this futile last-ditch effort by the aggressor to escape just punishment for its crimes, Zev Barak was relaxing too, from a degree of anxiety that he only now recognized. The larger vision had been haunting him of the majestic gray carriers and cruisers of the United States Sixth Fleet changing course toward the east, the Soviet ships flashing messages to Moscow, the dour Kremlin autocrats in their slovenly clothes debating the next move; in short the old Great Game, this time a facedown between America and Russia, while on the Golan Heights the lesser game that meant life or death to Israeli and Syrian soldiers was being played out in a battlefield of a few square miles.

Rafael was responding to Federenko: "It grieves me to observe, Mr. President, that the representative of the Soviet Union does not seem too happy that the fighting has now finally come to an end." The Russian turned his head to give Rafael a contemptuous smile which came out a snarl.

A tap on Barak's shoulder; the crew cut again, with a note in Cunningham's neat up-and-down hand.

> Returning to Washington. Very well done. Bit of a close call. Hope to see you soon. Why not stop by the house to say goodbye to Emily, before she takes off on her trip around the world?

45

Encounter in the Growlery

It was a true Washington June day, dank and hot. Barak's uniform enabled him to cleave through the surprisingly big crowd in the sunshine outside the ballroom entrance of the hotel, waiting cheerily and patiently to get in. Zionist rallies as a rule were straggly affairs in half-full halls. Not today! The cynics on Rafael's staff had it right. Americans liked winners.

The capacious grand ballroom was already full and abuzz with talk. On the high wall behind the dais, a huge color blowup of Moshe Dayan on the cover of *Time* hung under crossed Israeli and American flags, flanked by smaller black-and-white pictures of Herzl and Ben Gurion. Of Prime Minister Eshkol and Chief of Staff Rabin, no sign. Barak doubted that one person in twenty in the hall had heard of them. There was only one winner in this war — the Jewish general with the black eye patch — and through him everybody here was a winner. On the dais sat eminent Zionists from all over the United States. In his speaking tours Barak had met most of them, and they greeted him by name, faces aglow with happy excitement, as he went to his chair beside the ambassador.

"Zev, you speak after me. Did those slides of the battle maps come through?"

"All set. What a mob!"

"Yes, incredible." The ambassador bleakly smiled. His face was gray, his voice was a croak, he slumped in his chair. Barak wondered whether the man could get on his feet to talk. "There's an overflow crowd in another ballroom where they've put up loudspeakers. It's happening everywhere in the country, but this is the big one."

"Are you the first speaker?"

"Well, the ZOA president will introduce me," Abe said with a little sidewise smile. "That may take a minute or two."

It took twenty, and the talking in the hall did not abate much. Barak's automatic shutoff of Zionist rhetoric cut in, and his mind wandered to the Growlery, and what he would say and do when he got there. Emily's decision to go off around the world without a word to him about it was a hard jolt. He meant to have it out with her tonight.

The ambassador got a two-minute standing ovation when he came to the podium. This crowd was avid to applaud an Israeli. "I have news for our good friends in the Kremlin," Avraham Harman began hoarsely. He paused to let the people settle down in their seats and when the hall was hushed went on. "I suspect those fine gentlemen don't quite grasp how world opinion has changed. They lost in the Security Council. Now they've called for a special session of the General Assembly. There they have the votes, so they're sure they'll overwhelm us and rob us of our victory. My news is —" He was a master at this; the audience seemed to hold its collective breath. "— Gospodin Kosygin, you're going to lose in the General Assembly, too." *(Applause and cheers.)*

As Harman launched into his speech, Barak was watching the time. In a hurried telephone call he had made yesterday from New York after the Security Council adjourned, he had promised Emily that he would be at the Growlery today not later than five.

"What's all this, Queenie?" he had challenged her. "You're really off around the world?"

"Oh, God, who told you? Oh, God, it was Chris, of course, blast him."

"It's true, then?"

"Well, it is, but —"

"Then I'll come out to see you tomorrow. I have to talk at a Zionist rally, but it'll be over by four. Say five at the Growlery?"

"Old Wolf, as it happens, that's not convenient. Day after, maybe?"

"Day after I'll be flying home, Em."

"What, to Israel? You're through as attaché?"

"No, no. Just for consultations."

Lengthy silence.

"Queenie? Would you rather not see me? Come on, what's up?"

"Five o'clock, you say?"

"Yes. There's an embassy meeting at seven, so I can't stay long, but we should at least say goodbye, shouldn't we?"

"Okay, see you at five, Zev. Not much later. The thing is, I'm having dinner with Fiona and her ex-reverend."

"Queenie, do I hear the Donald Duck voice?"

"Listen, you mangy old Gray Wolf, will you be here at five tomorrow, or won't you?"

"See you then, darling."

Four o'clock, and applause was breaking into every other sentence of the ambassador's stem-winding, fist-waving peroration.

"No more cease-fires! No more armistice lines! Peace! Let there be peace in our region at last! Our neighbors have tried terror. They have tried boycott. They have tried war. Their policies lie in ruins. Now let them try the last resort, common sense! Let them sit down with us face to face, to negotiate treaties. They cannot even dream what Israel will give up for peace. For *less* than peace, NOTH-ING. We have paid too dearly for this victory! For peace, generosity that will astound the world. Only for peace. For SHALOM!"

The audience was on its feet again, cheering. Now it was Barak's turn to give a military picture of the victory with slides, timed for half an hour. Then he could slip out, and be off and away . . . but *l'Azazel!* United States Senator Wyndham was walking into the hall, the audience was applauding him, and the chairman was hailing him to the podium for an embrace. Yielding him the mi-crophone! Damn, that windbag was good for half an hour of fiery friendship for Israel, so it would be something of a time squeeze. But what was the problem, after all, if Emily was a bit late for dinner with Fiona and her ex-reverend?

However, Barak had in fact heard the Donald Duck voice, for Emily's problem was Colonel Halliday. He was flying up from Florida in a fighter plane, and was coming to the Growlery about seven-thirty. Zev was coming at five or so, and had to be back at the embassy at seven, so there ought to be plenty of time to see both men, she was figuring, turn by turn.

And yet, as she straightened up the Growlery for her visitors, Emily was uneasy. If one was to be off with an old love and on with a new, the two gentlemen certainly should not meet, not straight off. The colonel, on leave from his post in West Germany, by chance had called her the morning after the Greek restaurant fiasco with Nakhama. On impulse she had said yes, she would be delighted to see him; so in a way Colonel Halliday would never know, he owed this date to Nakhama Barak. It was just bloody inconvenient that now Nakhama's husband was also coming. Emily almost felt herself back in a teenage girl's fix, juggling fellows.

Four-thirty. What about dressing and makeup? The maroon housecoat with blue piping she was slopping around in was all right for Zev Barak, and for him she had combed her hair and put on a rudimentary face. No glamor, no allure, they were past all that. But for a new guy, a formal sort like Halliday . . . absolute minimum for serious makeup and careful dressing, forty-five minutes. Better yet, an hour. Unknown variable: suppose that rally ran late, as rallies tended to do? Well, if by five-thirty or so Zev hadn't appeared, that would be that, he couldn't make it back to the embassy for his meeting. Sooner or later he'd call, and they'd have a telephone farewell, not the first. Meantime she had better get ready for Colonel Halliday, who had said something about dinner at the Red Fox. The main thing now was to load the fridge with beer, which she proceeded to do.

According to Jack Smith, Bud Halliday could drink more beer than anybody alive with no effect on his conduct or his waistline. The waistline she had seen for herself. One could iron a dress on it.

The conduct she could only guess at, but the man's grave dry intimidating demeanor suggested granite control. In that way he was rather like her father, but Halliday was a very tall man, with thick black hair and sharp greenish eyes. She could imagine that the wife he had lost had been happy with this imposing professional, though unlike her father he seemed void of humor. Jack Smith had denied this. Halliday loved jokes, he said, only with women he was reserved. You had to know Bud Halliday.

Emily took scissors and went out to cut fresh flowers. The sun was sinking behind the pines. Lilacs and roses were blooming in masses, and every breath she took, as she plunged her hands into the bushes and snipped, reminded her painfully of Zev Barak. Most of their love affair had been by correspondence, after all. Each year when the fireflies came and the summer flowers perfumed the night, her letters had waxed warm, and his replies too. Emily regretted nothing except that it had to end, and even that was all right. The Israeli had taught her that making love was not necessarily a nuisance of the married state, a mere nasty foolishness, but a glory of this life.

She was not in the least in love with Colonel Halliday, not yet, but — very differently from Jack Smith — the prospect of going to bed with him was not ridiculous, only remote. There would never be another Gray Wolf, but he was not hers, Nakhama had driven that nail to the board, and that was that! Maybe one day they could resume corresponding; Héloïse and Abélard to the end, sans Abélard's unfortunate disability.

"Another beer?"

"Sure."

She felt Colonel Halliday's eyes on her as she got up and walked into the kitchen. The mauve shantung was a success, no doubt of it, the skirt not too short as she had feared. Even sunk in the couch beside him she showed leg but not knee. The legs were all right.

"I feel at home here," she heard him say. "Marilyn and I had a place like this on the Blue Ridge, above Front Royal. Cathedral ceiling, wagon-wheel chandelier, fieldstone fireplace, same idea. We sold it because we used it so seldom. The squirrels and raccoons would get in, and once the hippies did. Quite a mess. That's when Marilyn said sell, so I did. . . . Thanks. What wine is that you're drinking?"

"Brunello. Like some?"

He shook his head, smiled, and sipped the beer. "Frosty cold. Great. We didn't have such pretty flowers in the Blue Ridge. Our place was a jungle."

"Well, I have the school gardeners. You were saying the Germans thought the Israelis would win."

"Yes, but nobody figured on six days, Emily. Their staff estimate was much like ours. Thirty days."

"They must have mixed feelings about the Israelis."

"The Germans? Very much so. Even in casual conversation there's a note of embarrassment, an odd look in the eyes. . . ." Halliday drank, and was silent. Emily felt no pressure to keep the talk going. It was a thing she liked about the man. After a while he said, "Your Israeli friend must feel lousy about missing the war."

Emily answered lightly and quickly, "His job here is important."

"I'm aware of that. Possibly more so than a field command. Relations with Washington have to be a main concern of the Israelis. Still . . ." He shrugged and drank.

"I've never understood this urge for combat. Is that because I'm a woman?"

"See here, Emily, you train for it, years and years. As you rise in rank you get into weapons procurement, manpower, doctrine. You manage the lives of youngsters by the thousands. It all seems like waste motion, like make-believe, until a war comes. Then all those wasted years make some sense. I'm not a war lover, war is an insanity. But conflicts of national wills occur. The use of force occurs. I've never been happier than when I was a fighter squadron commander, flying missions in Korea, which I knew then was a particularly rotten war. There it is."

She was thinking that in a brown tweed jacket and gray slacks — he had stopped in his home in Oakton to change — he looked quite as military as in uniform; straight-backed, serious, formidable. When Zev shed his uniform he shed the army to become his warm unmilitary self, a jester, a lover of music and books; in fact as he sometimes joked about himself, just another Viennese coffee-house Jew.

"Interesting," she said. "I can see that. As far as my Israeli friend goes, Colonel, incidentally, it never amounted to much, and anyway it's all over."

"Oh?" Level tone. "Has he gone back home?"

"No, he's still here, all right. But his wife and family have come. That changed everything." She poured herself more wine. "I don't really remember how much I told you about that harmless business, Colonel —"

"Bud."

She smiled, but as yet informality with this man was too much for her. "Okay. Anyway, Jack Smith was plying me with punch like mad at that class reunion dance, and then after a while, there you and I were, off in that alcove —"

"Well, I started it, Emily, talking about Marilyn. Which was strange, because I seldom do that. It wasn't that you reminded me of her. You don't. She was so mainline, you know. General's niece, old Richmond family, Junior League —"

"And I'm an overage kook."

Bud Halliday's laugh was reassuring: wholehearted, deep-chested, with an almost boyish flash in the eyes. "We can go into all that at the Red Fox. Ready for something to eat?"

"Anytime, Colonel."

"Then we go. Where's your facility?"

She pointed. "You'll see it. Through the bedroom."

In the kitchen she was turning out lights and putting away the wine when she heard the door knocker: *rap, rap, rap*. This time of night? Possibly the groundskeeper with a problem, or a telegram about her tour booking. Something. She opened the door, and Abélard stepped in and seized her. "Queenie! Did you give me up for dead? Here I am."

"Wolf! I — you — it's so late — you have a meeting, I thought —"

"Postponed. That rally will go on till midnight. Traffic coming out was murder. Now, first things first, I love you. All right?"

"Fine, but —" she tried to struggle free. "Zev, dear, you're holding me so tight. Please —"

"Why didn't you tell me you were leaving? Is something wrong? Are you angry at me? Queenie, stop wriggling like a fish." Barak was gripping her with a steely tenderness.

"Zev, listen to me —"

"I beg your pardon." Behind Emily, Colonel Halliday spoke in a parade-ground baritone.

Barak released her, and the three stood staring at one another. "Colonel Halliday, this is General Barak. You two should know each other," Emily chirruped, "you have a lot in common."

"I'm sure of that, and I would be charmed another time," said Halliday, "but as you know, I'm just going."

"The hell you are." Emily felt a surge of self-preserving instinct. This beer-guzzling air force hotshot was not stalking out of her life like that! "Sit down, Bud. Have another beer."

One heavy black eyebrow went up as she spoke the nickname. "Oh? Well, I seldom refuse."

"Zev?"

"Why not?"

She darted for the kitchen, as for the air lock in a sinking submarine. The two men sat down, Halliday on the couch, Barak on an upholstered armchair leaking stuffing.

"I have the advantage of you, General," said Halliday. "I know you're your country's military attaché. I'm back from staff duty in Wiesbaden, and I'll shortly be taking a tactical fighter air wing to Vietnam."

"Wiesbaden. I've been there. I worked with their army on acquiring and upgrading M-48s."

"You're in armor, then."

"That's my branch."

"Wasn't that a strange experience?"

"How do you mean?"

"You, an Israeli, dealing with the German army?"

Barak nodded. "Very grim."

"I'll bet."

"Beer, gentlemen."

She poured for them, looking from one to the other through horn-rimmed glasses she had put on, relieved that they had not eaten each other like Kilkenny cats. Emily was going head-down through this, discombobulated but obscurely elated. She was caught in an embarrassing moment between two splendid guys who both fancied her. Worse things could happen to a schoolmarm on the other side of thirty.

Halliday raised his glass. "To your country's fine fight, General. The air strike was a classic. We'll be studying it closely. All air forces will, for years to come."

"Thank you. For the second time in a century we were facing extermination. But this time we could defend ourselves."

"You were facing extermination?" Halliday took a dry war-college tone. "That wasn't our estimate in Wiesbaden."

"Our enemies proclaimed it as their war aim. Our people believed it, and they had a very bad time. It's true the army always thought it could protect the country. And so we did."

"So you did, and brilliantly. But how long can you hold such extended lines?"

"Against our enemies, indefinitely, until they make peace. Against the Soviet Union, it's a problem." Barak looked straight at the air force man. "We won a war in 1956, too, you know. But the Russians made threats, Eisenhower and Dulles leaned on us, and we had no choice. We had to give up all we'd gained. I can't predict what President Johnson will do. Can you?"

"He'll act in our national interest."

"Which is what, in this situation?"

"Well, there's a rising tide of world revolution, General Barak, and one could argue that with this setback to the Soviets, your country's the boy who's put his finger in the dike." Halliday drank off his beer. "If so, President Johnson might not act exactly the way Eisenhower and Dulles did. Thanks for the beer, Emily." He stood up. "General, our protocol is that the senior officer leaves a company first. You rank me, so I must beg your indulgence."

It was the first trace of humor, or at least irony, that Emily had detected in Bradford Halliday. His tone was formal, but his eyes twinkled in a sober face.

"We're a young country." Barak rose. "And we're not much on protocol."

"You're most courteous, and I'll bid you good evening."

Emily walked out with him, and came back shortly, glowering. "Wolf, why the hell did you show up two hours late? You damned inconsiderate — *Israeli,* you!"

"That's a very pretty suit." Barak took no offense, nor did he bring up her fib about dinner with Fiona. Standard lady's procedure, and he was not much surprised.

Softer tone. "Oh, you like it?"

"Listen, Queenie, I do leave in the morning. I wanted to see you, and ask you why you're off globe-trotting without a word to me."

Emily colored, looked away, then tossed her head. "I wrote you a letter. It's still here. Want it?"

"Just tell me what's in it."

"Have some Brunello."

"Okay."

Over the wine Emily said after a considerable silence, sitting on her legs on the couch, "Look, sweetums, it comes to this. I'll be a mistress but I'll not be a concubine. Nakhama *knows.* She's hinted very tolerantly and not too subtly that it's okay, and I can go right on with it. That, I won't endure."

"She can't know. She can't have told you that. It's all in your head."

"Don't infuriate me! You didn't hear our conversation at the Piraeus, Zev, while you were on the telephone for an eternity. She *knows.* You're the one who's obtuse. I don't think you understand your own wife, or for that matter me, or women in general. You're too damned charming, and we've been too easy for you."

"Was it a good letter you wrote?"

"Not very, but better than I'm doing now. Now listen, can't we go on corresponding? How can Nakhama mind that? I mean, dear Gray Wolf, that's always been the best part of it — Good God, look at the man wince!"

"I didn't wince."

"You did, too, as though I'd stabbed you with a hat pin. Male ego. God, how ridiculous. My love, I still have packing to do, so let me give you my itinerary. I'll write, and you write ahead to wherever I'll be. I'd love that."

"This Colonel Halliday seems quite a guy."

"Well, he's hard to figure out."

"I've urged you for years to get married, Queenie, you know that, and —"

"Zev Barak" — her voice choked — "get the hell out of here."

"All right, Queenie." He looked around at the familiar room. "I'll miss the Growlery. Let me have that itinerary. And your letter."

In the flower-scented darkness outside she said in a husky whisper as they kissed, "Have you ever seen so many goddamn fireflies?"

"We'll go on writing, Emily. That's for sure. At least that."

"Perfect. On your way, Gray Wolf! I don't want to weep. Tell Nakhama 'Banzai' from Emily Cunningham."

The cardinals and jays woke Emily next morning, carrying on outside her window. She had had a bad wakeful spell of the dismals in the small dark hours. Zev Barak was gone, sent off with light words to mask her pain. Colonel Halliday had left them together in the Growlery for what he undoubtedly thought was a roaring night of gitchi-gitchi. Scratch the air force. Too tall for her, anyway. Too stony. Her father loved her, otherwise what matter if on this trip she caught some horrible tropical fever like poor Marilyn Halliday, and died in five days? And so on. Emily had cut short these 3 A.M. glooms with a hooker of bourbon. Her head was fuzzy as she lay blinking at the sunshine, listening to birdsong.

R-r-ring. Gray Wolf, for a word of farewell? A good sport, Zev, an utter darling. She cleared her throat to force a cheery, "Hello?"

"Bud Halliday here. I'm not calling too early?"

"What? No, no, not at all, Colonel."

"Emily, I have a meeting in the Pentagon at noon. Then I fly back to Florida. How about breakfast at the Red Fox? Say nine o'clock? They do very good biscuits."

"Biscuits? Why — well, who could say no to biscuits? You're on, Bud."

"Splendid. Incidentally, your Israeli friend impressed me." Emily was speechless. Pause. "See you nine o'clock then, at the Red Fox."

She hung up. Scratch the tropical fever.

46

The Jeradi Pass

"Speaking of Don Kishote, isn't that him now?" Moshe Dayan squinted his good eye toward the door of Fink's Bar, a dim-lit Jerusalem haunt of the insiders, its walls lined with signed pictures of noted army officers and journalists. "With Benny Luria and an American lady?"

"Moshe, that American lady is Yael," growled Pasternak. He and Zev Barak sat with Dayan in a dark booth, at which all eyes in the crowded bar kept turning.

"Yael? Well, well!" Dayan beckoned to the threesome. "Very elegant, isn't she?"

Yael seized Benny and Yossi by the elbow. "Look, it's Dode Moshe himself, he wants us to join him. Unexpected honor!"

At a nod from Dayan, the bartender hurried to bring more chairs. "Sit down, sit down. What brings you three to Unified Jerusalem?" His manner and his crooked smile, Barak thought, as he spoke with relish the new journalistic term, verged on the imperial. The old Yiddish byword fitted Dayan: *He has a new skin.*

"It's Yael's birthday," said Luria. "We're celebrating. Where else? Fink's Bar."

Dayan patted her hand. "Yael, live to a hundred twenty!"

"Thank you, Minister."

"I hear you're becoming a Los Angeles millionaire, and you run around with all the film stars."

She laughed. "That's nonsense. I've come home to stay, Uncle Moshe." She touched the bandaged patch on Kishote's temple. "So as to take care of my crazy husband and my boy."

Dayan abruptly dropped his joshing tone. "Kishote, we were just talking about that piece in today's *Jerusalem Post*. It's stupid, ignore it! Your advance to El Arish was brilliant."

"Well, you're generous, Minister. I took heavy losses, and got trapped when the Jeradi Pass closed up. All that's true enough. And then Gorodish's breakthrough to me was very bloody."

"All beside the point." Moshe Dayan's head shake forbade contradiction. "When the Egyptians in Sinai heard our armor had reached El Arish that first afternoon, they were shattered. That shock started their entire line crumbling." He turned to Barak, and caught him in a yawn. Dayan frowned. "Zev, was the fall of El Arish played up in America?"

Barak dug a knuckle into his eyes. "The air strike was the big story, Minister, once it got out."

Benny Luria showed white teeth in a proud smile. "Yes, we managed to keep it quiet at first. Part of the deception."

Dayan waved a finger, and the bartender sprang to take drink orders. "My attack on Lod and Ramle in 1948 was like your dash, Kishote. Improvised. Costly. Ben Gurion even called it a prank. But it came on the first day the truce ended, and the enemy's morale was broken by that quick jolt. It spread panic and confusion, and they never recovered. Your feat was outstanding. . . . Zev, maybe you should go to bed." Barak was yawning again.

"Sorry, Minister. I'm fine. Long plane trip, long meetings," said Barak.

"I promised to take Zev to the Wall," said Pasternak. "That's why I'm keeping my driver up."

"The Wall? Count me in," said Luria. "I haven't been there yet."

"Me, either," said Yael.

Pasternak shot her a cold look. "No American beauties. Strict curfew and blackout in the Old City, and tough patrols."

"I'll take you there, Yael," said Dayan, sizing her up with amused appetite, "maybe tomorrow." The square neck of her linen suit stood away from her bosom, showing cleft and a flash of pink lace.

"That would be lovely, Uncle Moshe." Yael's pert tone was just short of impudence; a handsome woman aware of her allure and unafraid of power.

This is a strange business in which I hardly fit, thought Barak through a haze of weariness. Yet very Israeli! Elbow to elbow, Yael's husband and Yael's old lover; at Pasternak's other elbow, Yael's brother Benny, still detesting Sam for that early liaison; and Moshe Dayan lording it over them all. Everybody in Fink's Bar was covertly glancing at this table of stars: the Defense Minister, the controversial Don Kishote, the rumored Mossad head, the air strike commander, and a glossy American lady. Also himself, a vague obscure general, a military attaché or something.

Dayan's round black-patched face took on a business look. "Were you in America, Yael, when Abba Eban spoke in the Security Council?"

"No, I got on the first plane I could when the war started. My friends in California telephoned me about it, though. He was tremendous. Big headlines."

Barak knew this was not what Dayan wanted to hear. Eban was being sent to New York again, this time to address the General Assembly. Kosygin was coming there to head the Soviet delegation, and Dayan wanted to accompany Eban as Kosygin's opposite number. But the Foreign Minister was balking at that, as Barak could well understand. Even if Eban did speak, and however well he spoke, the famed general with the eye patch would utterly eclipse him. All eyes in the assembly hall, and all the TV cameras, would be on Moshe Dayan.

"Well, I heard good things about his speech, too, and I read it. Highly rhetorical. Of course his delivery makes a difference," said Dayan. "Still, I wonder how a Cambridge don, which is what he sounds like, can stand up to Chairman Kosygin."

"Maybe that's good," said Yael. "Keeps up the underdog image, which isn't easy, Uncle Moshe, after your terrific victory."

Barak and Pasternak exchanged a quick glance, mere eye flickers. This same simple argument, among others, had been pressed at the inner cabinet meeting. Eshkol had been silent, and the decision was still open.

"A good point, Yael." Dayan shrugged. "We'll see. Anyway, the General Assembly has no power, it's a debating society, so maybe a good debater is all that's wanted."

Yael retorted, characteristically pushing her luck, "Well, all the same, a General Assembly resolution created Israel."

"That's a silly thing to say, and don't ever say it again!" Dayan's tone turned freezing. "*We* created Israel."

She took the rebuke with an affected little smile at the others, but she was shaken. Sam Pasternak resented the way Dayan snubbed Yael — he was a giant, she was a woman — and wondered why her husband, sitting pale and mute, didn't come to her defense. Yossi Nitzan was not himself; the wound, perhaps, or else the newspaper attack. It was Zev Barak who spoke up. "Minister, an assembly resolution that goes against us by two-thirds will be a very bad turn of events." Dayan made a dismissive hand wave. "With your permission, sir, I'll go with Sam now to the Wall, while I can keep my eyes open."

"By all means, Zev," said Dayan, turning much pleasanter. "And listen, what you've been doing over in Washington has been outstanding. You're worth two brigades in the field."

"You exaggerate, Minister, but thank you."

Pasternak, Luria, and Barak stood up. "Oh, go ahead, go ahead, Yossi," Yael exclaimed. "I can see you're dying to go with them. I'll make my own way back to Tel Aviv."

"No problem," said Dayan, "I'll take you."

The four officers left. "Have a glass of wine with me, Yael, and we'll go," Dayan said. They had both been drinking Tempo.

"Thanks, I'd love it," she said with a relieved saucy grin.

"So. You're really giving up golden Los Angeles? Why?"

"Because you've won the Jews a great secure homeland at last, Uncle Moshe, and I want to live in it."

That struck the right note between them. His smile was both fatherly and admiring. He ordered the wine. "At any rate,

Yael, California has agreed with you. I can remember you running around the moshav, a dirty-faced little girl. You're a beautiful lady."

"You're too kind. I missed home every single day I was there. And in the end my son couldn't stand it."

She answered his questions about her dress business, which she intended to put up for sale, until the wine came. "Well," she said, fingering her glass, "no point toasting you, Uncle Moshe. You're the toast of the world."

Dayan raised his glass. "Here's to your Don Kishote. Take care of him, Yael. He has a future."

Soldiers on leave filled the crooked narrow street outside Fink's Bar, walking with girls or with each other, a young crowd making a lot of merry noise. Barak knew what it was to be merry after a war, with the death of friends eating at the heart. He loved these green-clad youngsters, felt their sadness for the fallen, shared their joy at being alive with the fighting over — for now. This time he had missed it all. Zeh mah she'yaish!

"Where's your driver?" he asked Pasternak.

"Outside Goldenberg's."

Benny said to Kishote, "Quite a commendation you got from Dayan."

"He was too rough with Yael," Pasternak said.

"Ha! Yael can take care of herself," said Kishote, "with Moshe Dayan or with anybody."

"She was being too smart with him," said Luria. "That's my sister for you."

"Why too smart? She's right," snapped Pasternak. The four senior officers were walking along, unheeded by the jocund soldiers. "Dayan at the General Assembly would be Samson among the Philistines. They'd itch to kill him with votes."

"And Eban?" inquired Luria.

Kishote said, "The lamb that chased the wolves."

The aviator laughed. "Not bad."

"He's a masterly speaker," said Barak. "Eshkol will send him without Dayan. That's my guess."

Pasternak said, "Mine too. There's my car. Strange, Goldenberg's is still lit up."

"People are celebrating," said Luria, "even the kosher ones."

Late diners were coming out and Don Kishote saw Shayna among them; unmistakably Shayna, though dressed very brightly in lacy blue satin, her hair piled up on her head beauty-parlor style. Without thinking he darted toward her and grasped her hand. "Shayna!" The Canadian emerged behind her with a gray-headed man and a very stout woman. Both men wore big fedora hats.

Shayna's mouth fell open. "By your life, Yossi! Don't spring at me like that, like a leopard or something!" She peered at him, her eyes round and troubled. "Are you all right? Are you healing up well? Yossi, you're so pale."

"Hello, there, Colonel," said the Canadian. "Mama, Papa, here's one of the great war heroes, Don Kishote. I showed you the newspaper piece about him. Colonel Nitzan, meet my parents from Toronto, Mr. and Mrs. Rubinstein."

The old people smiled and stared. The father held out his hand and said with a Yiddish accent, "Arthur Rubinstein, but I don't play piano." He chuckled at his own standard jest. "Well, the celebrated Don Kishote! I didn't expect to meet you, sir."

A few yards away, the officers were getting into Pasternak's car. Luria called, "Kishote! *Zuz!* [Move!]"

"Shayna, we'll be at the taxi stand," said the Canadian. He took each of his parents by an arm and walked off.

"What is this?" Yossi asked.

"What is what? Good night, Yossi." She did not move.

"Are you engaged? Are you getting married? What?"

"They came here to meet me and my mother."

"It's serious, then."

"Not your concern. I'm going to Canada next month."

"Shayna, for good?"

"For a visit. Think I'd leave Israel? How is Aryeh?"

"Great. He misses Aunt Shayna."

"Where's Yael?"

"In Fink's Bar with Moshe Dayan."

"I almost believe you."

"That's where she is, hamoodah." Pasternak was leaning out of the car window and gesturing at him. "She grew up on his moshav, you know."

"And she's really come back to stay?"

"So she says."

"Be happy, Kishote." She hesitated, lunged to kiss his mouth, and scampered off into the crowd and down the hill.

"Sha'ar Mandelbaum, Shimon," Pasternak said, when Kishote got into the car. The Mandelbaum Gate was the heavily barricaded checkpoint where, for nineteen years, diplomats and special visitors had been passing between Israel and Jordan-ruled Palestine.

"B'seder, Sha'ar Mandelbaum," said the young driver with a knowing grin at him.

"Zev, by my life, isn't this a joy, Jerusalem all lit up again? The blackout was something!" said Pasternak. "Shells bursting all over the sky. Searchlights, fires, tracers. We were back in 1948. Six days though, instead of seven months, and no water trucks."

"And a different outcome," said Luria.

"When my plane came in tonight," said Barak, "the sun was just setting, and already Tel Aviv was ablaze like a Luna Park."

" *'Truly the light is sweet.'* " Pasternak quoted Scripture. "After a blackout, you know it."

Winding through familiar brightly lit streets, the car all at once plunged into darkness pierced only by its headlights. Pasternak said over his shoulder, "Here we go. Unified Jerusalem."

Barak strained his eyes into the gloom. "But where's the Mandelbaum Gate?"

"What Mandelbaum Gate?"

"It's gone?"

"Not a trace. Jerusalem is one city. Gone."

"And the blockhouses, the pillboxes, the barricades?"

"Gone! Gone or going, all across Jerusalem." Pasternak handed pistols to them. "Take these. Just a precaution."

The driver weaved expertly through shuttered empty dark streets until the headlights struck the Old City walls. He braked. "Which way, sir?" he asked Pasternak. "Sha'ar Jaffa? Sha'ar Zion?"

"Sha'ar Jaffa."

Passing through the high ancient archway of the Jaffa Gate, which since 1948 had been all walled up and visible only across the gulf of no-man's-land, Zev Barak at last felt to his bones the sense of a won war.

*   *   *

Just inside the arch a blinding glare through the windshield and a harsh loudspeaker *"Halt!"* greets the car. A helmeted soldier with an Uzi walks into the blue glare. "Credentials," he says to the driver.

"These are senior officers, two generals and —"

"Credentials!" Rougher tone.

Pasternak leans across the driver and passes the soldier an identification card, saying, "We're going to the Wall."

The soldier straightens and salutes. "Let me talk to my platoon commander, sir."

Soon a bearded lieutenant appears in the glare and gives back the card with a salute. "We'll escort you, General."

"Why? We're armed."

"Strict curfew on, sir."

"Very well."

A jeep mounting a machine gun and a searchlight leads their car through stone alleys and low arches. The searchlight beam catches a line of bulldozers blocking the descent to the Western Wall. The lieutenant returns and leans on the window. "It'll have to be on foot from here, sir."

"No problem."

A corporal walks ahead of them, Uzi in his right hand, flashlight in his left, through narrow black streets between old Arab houses. The Old City is eerily silent. For a long time they do not speak, each of the four men sunk in his own thoughts.

Don Kishote is haunted by the glimpse of Shayna Matisdorf, hurrying away down the Jaffa Road sidewalk in a blue satin dress, perhaps his last sight of her ever; for who can say she will return from Canada, once she tastes the good life of North America? Pasternak carries with him the picture of Yael in Fink's Bar, elegant as a movie queen, her bosom and her underwear slightly showing, ignoring him and playing up to Moshe Dayan. And Zev Barak, almost hallucinating with fatigue, gets incongruous flashes of Queenie in the Growlery, Queenie out in the dark amid the flashing fireflies, the lilacs, and the roses . . .

Only Benny Luria's thoughts are professional and triumphant. Benny reflects with soul-deep pride that they are walking to the Western Wall now because the air force won the war in three hours, or if the truth were known, in the seven minutes of his squadron's first strike. Such at any rate is his bird's-eye view of the Six-Day War, and such it will always be.

Barak breaks the silence, gesturing at the shut-up Arab houses. "These people are a tragedy."

"Why?" inquires Benny.

"Because their way of life is ended."

"I don't follow you. They must accept that we've returned to stay, that's all," says the aviator. "After that we can live in peace together, and they can enjoy all the benefits of being Israelis. Where else will Arabs ever live the way they can here?"

"You dream," said Pasternak.

"I do not. The Arabs have lost. It's irreversible," says the aviator. "With the Arabs in the Land we'll sooner or later get along. Against the outside Arab countries we can hold out forever."

"The Arabs have not lost," speaks up Kishote. "We've only come through the Jeradi Pass."

Their footsteps echo as they go tramping down worn old stone steps. After a while Barak says, "If he understands that much, Sam, let's groom him for Ramatkhal."

"By all means."

"Sam, I'm serious."

"You think I'm not?"

"God forbid," says Yossi. "Me, Ramatkhal? What for? So for four years the *Jerusalem Post* can call me *pisher*?"

"Don Kishote as Israel's Chief of Staff," says Pasternak. "It fits. It figures."

"Now you dream," says Benny Luria. "An outsider like Yossi? Just because he got a pat on the back tonight from Dayan? Forget it."

"It can happen," says Barak.

"There's the Wall," says the lieutenant.

The flashlight beam shines high on the giant Herodian stones behind many bulldozers, parked in a long alley piled with rubble. Two soldiers are patrolling the alley, and at one end beyond the bulldozers there is an armed jeep. In fitful moonlight through scudding clouds the Wall appears almost deserted, except for a cluster of bearded black-clad pietists swaying in prayer. Far from them one plump little man in shirt sleeves and a big fedora hat leans his forehead on the stones.

"What's happening here, Sam?" Barak gestures at the bulldozers.

"Clearing a plaza so the Wall can breathe, and Jews can come to worship by the thousands, not a few at a time."

"We'll hear about this in the UN."

"It'll be done before the UN can say anything."

The shirt-sleeved man walks away from the Wall with bent head, climbs into the jeep and takes off the hat. White wings of hair and a bald pate catch the moonlight.

"By God, the Old Man," says Pasternak in a hushed tone.

The jeep disappears in the gloom. *A generation goes, a generation comes,* Barak thinks. Two weeks ago people were clamoring for B.G.'s return as Prime Minister. Tonight he is a fading figure of the past, lost in Moshe Dayan's penumbra. "I've known him all my life," he says, "and only once before have I seen him wearing such a hat, at the funeral of Chaim Weizmann."

None of the others speak, and after a moment Barak says, "I'm going up on the Temple Mount."

The lieutenant says, "Sir —"

"It's all right, Lieutenant. I remember the way well. I should have gotten there during the war, but with one thing and another I didn't. I won't be long."

Something in his voice causes Pasternak to gesture at the lieutenant. Barak climbs the old stairway to the top. The two mosques loom before his eyes, close and huge. Only a few Israeli soldiers pace the broad empty plaza, and a cool breeze brings the scent of freshly cut grass. Well, here he is, here where the priests of the two destroyed Temples served the Lord God for a thousand years, and here where the Dome of the Rock stands, as it has stood for thirteen hundred years, over the fabled place where Abraham offered up Isaac. *Har Ha'bayit b'yadenu?* Or does Don Kishote have it right, and have we just come through the Jeradi Pass? So Zev Barak, born Wolfgang Berkowitz, wonders as he walks out at last on the holy ground which it was his fate not to win.

Historical Notes

The tale is told. The curtain is down.

In writing a novel of Israel, one can be historically accurate to only a limited extent. The fog of battle, after forty-five years, still hangs over the scene. Serious Arab sources translated into English are as yet few. By comparison the Israeli material is copious, especially in Hebrew, which I speak and read. However, the events are too recent and too raw to be treated in cool perspective by participants, Arab or Israeli, or even by historians. The history narrated by *The Hope* has been the product of painstaking comparison of sources, weighing of possibilities, and interviews with persons involved in events, who often differ widely about "what really happened."

Artistic license is defined by Webster's Ninth as "deviation from fact . . . by an artist or writer for the sake of the effect gained." In historical fiction, invented characters often occupy offices or posts that were filled, at the time of the story, by actual persons to whom they bear no resemblance whatever. This happens in *The Hope,* but I trust Israelis so supplanted will judge that I have wielded responsibly the license of the novelist. Except for personages recognizable to most Israelis who know their history — David Ben Gurion, Yigal Yadin, Yigal Allon, Moshe Dayan, and so on, who always appear under their right names — I avow that there are no portraits of actual living persons in the story, and any guesswork about the "real" identity of imaginary characters is mere gossipy nonsense.

To Israelis the War of Independence, the Suez war, and the Six-Day War were each epics in themselves; but to bring to life Israel's struggle to survive, I found that the three wars had to merge in one swift tale of no outsize length. The artistic imperative was to compress, simplify, clarify, and hardest of all, to omit. Israeli readers will be far more aware of this, of course, than the general public for fiction.

In Talmudic learning, two phrases keep recurring: *shanuy b'makhloket,* "still in controversy," and *tsorikh iyyun,* "needing further study." Most major events in *The Hope* fall under one or the other heading. A few specific notes follow, for those readers who are interested to separate fact from fancy in *The Hope.*

PART ONE: INDEPENDENCE

The Latrun battles, the "Burma Road," and the story of Colonel David "Mickey" Marcus are all matters of history, but the supplanting of real persons by fictitious figures starts right here.

Colonel Shamir's number two was not the imaginary Sam Pasternak, but Colonel Chaim Herzog, who became a general, then a popular military historian, then Israel's envoy to the UN; and he has recently completed two distinguished terms as President of Israel. The raffish phantom Pasternak bears not the slightest resemblance, of course, to the illustrious Chaim Herzog. Pasternak enters the story at the start purely to animate the plot.

The narrative of the Burma Road is much simplified in this version. Herzog, Shamir, and the Harel Brigade commander, Amos Horev, were the main movers in creating the road which relieved and saved Jerusalem. The newspaper stories filed by the thrilled foreign correspondents who rode with the convoy are paraphrased. The death of Marcus and the transport of his body to America, escorted by Moshe Dayan, for burial with military honors at West Point all happened. The chartering of a horse-carrying airplane was a fact.

The *Altalena* episode is preserved in angry amber of Israeli controversy. Having searched the existing records, I have given a spare account, as clear and simple as I could make it. An Israeli consultant warned, "The *Altalena* is a minefield. Why not leave it out?" But nothing is more characteristic of Israeli life and politics than the *Altalena* affair; it shows the other side of the coin in this unique little nation's troubled if heroic beginnings.

Moshe Dayan's dash through Lod and Ramle and the episode of the Terrible Tiger happened as I tell it, though of course fictional characters ride in the Tiger.

The Roman road in the Negev, and its use by the commando battalion in General Allon's thrust to El Arish, are factual. As the War of Independence was winding down, Ezer Weizman, now the President of

Israel, and other pilots did shoot down five Royal Air Force fighter planes that intruded into Israeli airspace from Egypt. The incident brought a war threat from the British government, as described.

PART TWO: SUEZ

The farcical love scenes in Paris play in counterpoint to the political farce of the Suez war "scenario" cooked up there by the ministers. Those preposterous diplomatic doings really happened; that is the only reason for believing them. The account in the novel closely follows the available records.

The battle at Mitla Pass is an outstanding matter "still in controversy." This version has been dramatized from comparison of several sources. The heroic jeep ride of Kan-Dror to draw enemy fire is a true story.

Landing craft were actually brought overland from Haifa to Eilat, for resupplying Yaffe's brigade in its march on Sharm el Sheikh. Structures along the railroad had to be demolished, but the incident of the Russian dairyman is fictional.

The race between Raful Eitan and Avraham Yoffe to reach Sharm el Sheikh was in fact how the Suez war ended for the Israelis.

A footnote: The changing operational code names of the British and French landings — OMELETTE, MUSKETEER, TELESCOPE — are the real ones that were used. First to last, this doomed "scenario" was haunted by an aspect of low comedy.

PART THREE: MISSIONS TO AMERICA

The Idi Amin episode is apocryphal. He actually received parachute training in Israel, and as Uganda's dictator proudly wore the silver emblem. For obvious reasons, official Israeli sources shrug off the story that his jump was faked. I trust the reader finds the story entertaining and conceivably true, if of no historical value.

The protracted struggle of Israel to obtain battle tanks, to match the masses of Soviet tanks supplied to Arab armies, is historical truth. President John Kennedy's assurances to Golda Meir, as quoted word for word in the novel, are a matter of record; and the death of President Kennedy did come at a crucial moment of the Rabin mission to Washington.

PART FOUR: SIX DAYS

The War for the Water occurred as described.

The narration of the Six-Day War is based on the best military and political records, and is offered as reliable. Dwight Eisenhower's verbal message to Lyndon Johnson is factual. The MOKADE air strike, the armored dash to El Arish, the march into the Old City of Jerusalem, and the capture of the Golan Heights occurred as the book tells them. The debate in the United Nations, on which the political outcome of the war turned, is described with the cliffhanging drama that truly invested it at the time.

To sum up: whatever fictional liberties have been taken in weaving the phantoms of my invention through real events, *The Hope* is presented to my readers as an honest account of Israel's early history, as true and responsible as research could make it. As to whether the tale itself pleases, only they can judge.

THE OTHER FELLOW

One final word. In the dispassionate jargon of military planning and exercises, the enemy is usually color-coded Red, Orange, or Blue, at random. As Supreme Commander of Allied Forces in the West in World War II, General Eisenhower was wont to refer to the enemy with the neutral phrase, "the other fellow." In *The Hope* the other fellow is, of course, the Arab world.

The artistic aim of this tale is to plunge the reader into Israeli life in its early exciting years. The other fellow is but dimly discerned through a dense fog of mutual hostility and misperception, thickened by the dust and smoke of wars, terrorist raids, and cruel harm inflicted on both sides. Like my father before me I have been a lifelong Zionist, yet I pledge to my readers that there is no attempt in *The Hope* to caricature, distort, or defame the other fellow. On the contrary, though I have taken broad liberties in improvising conversations and speeches of Israeli leaders, it has been my care to ensure that *there is no word attributed to an Arab leader which is not directly quoted from the historical record, or the journalism of the time*.

Moreover, I have felt that learning what I could about the other fellow was part of the undertaking. I despaired of studying Arabic, which I understand is a rich and brilliant language; but I have made it a point to read the entire Koran carefully, in the English translation recommended by scholars of Islam, as well as later Islamic literature. I have studied Arabic history, ancient and modern. I have learned much, in particular, from the writings of Naguib Mahfouz, the great Egyptian Nobel laureate. I have had many searching talks with experts — Israeli, American, and Arab — and I believe I understand the historical underpinnings of the Arab-Jewish conflict. In a word, they amount to the resurgence of two nationalisms at almost the same moment of history.

In this conflict I think I see sprouting seeds of Hope. But even to say that much is to go beyond a novelist's task, and I leave the matter so, *"shanuy b'makhloket."* This I will add, and with it close these historical notes: reconciliation in the Middle East can come if and only if Zahal, the Israel Defense Force, remains strong and stands guard through the long night of hostility, until the dawn of God's peace. May it come speedily and in our days.

Herman Wouk

1987–1993